THE *FOOL'S GOLD* TRILOGY:

Sorcery Rising
Wild Magic
The Rose of the World

JUDE FISHER

THE ROSE OF THE WORLD

Book Three of *Fool's Gold*

DAW BOOKS, INC.
DONALD A. WOLLHEIM, FOUNDER
375 Hudson Street, New York, NY 10014
ELIZABETH R. WOLLHEIM
SHEILA E. GILBERT
PUBLISHERS
http://www.dawbooks.com

First Hardcover Printing, February 2005
1 2 3 4 5 6 7 8 9 10

DAW TRADEMARK REGISTERED
U.S. PAT. OFF. AND FOREIGN COUNTRIES
—MARCA REGISTRADA
HECHO EN U.S.A.

PRINTED IN THE U.S.A.

Acknowledgments

For their help and encouragement on this long and turbulent voyage, thanks are due to Emma, for brilliant feedback; to Ron and Danny, for seeing it through; to Betsy and Debra; and to everyone who wrote in urging me to get Katla and Saro together . . .

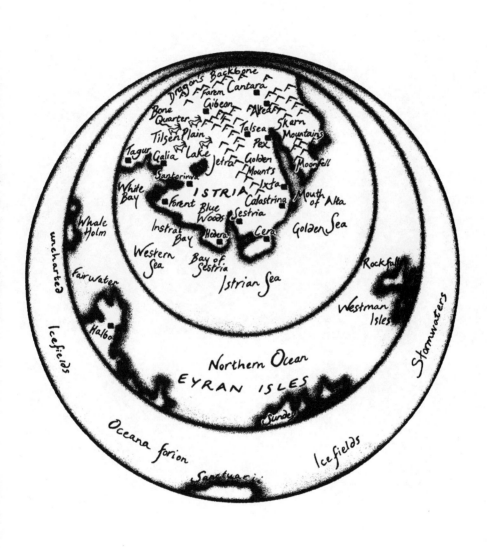

W HAT has gone before . . .

The world of Elda has three deities: the Woman, the Man, and the Beast. Their magic has long been lost, though legends abound. Some say the god Sur is held captive beneath the crust of the world, awaiting his recall. The goddess Falla and her great cat have not been seen for centuries; but it does not stop the people of the southern continent— the Istrians—from turning their worship into a fanatical religion.

Despite tensions, the people of Elda gather every year on the volcanic waste known as the Moonfell Plain, there to arrange marriages and trade alliances. This year is a special occasion, for the King of Eyra, Ravn Asharson, has come to choose himself a bride. All are outraged when he chooses not a well-born Eyran woman nor a noble Istrian beauty swathed in her veiling robes; but an unknown nomad woman whose merest glance fires men with desperate lust.

For Katla Aransen, daughter of the Rockfall clan, swordmaker, tomboy; and climber, it is the first visit to the Allfair: the first, and almost the last. From the Moonfell Plain there rises a great rock, called by the southerners Falla's Rock and by the northerners Sur's Castle, for their respective deities. Katla does not realize when she scales the Rock it is a sacred place—all she sees is a perfect climb—but by committing sacrilege she manages to set the spark for a mighty conflagration. Both

Eyra and Istria claim the Rock as their own, and Katla is caught in the middle of a furious debacle.

Even her family cannot save her, it seems, from the fires to which the Istrians are determined to consign her. Her dour and obsessive father, Aran Aranson, is distracted by dreams of gold, having bought what purports to be a treasure map. Nor can her brothers Halli and Fent, or her cousin Erno Hamson, who loves her dearly.

For Saro Vingo, too, it is his first visit to the Allfair. He is here with his family to trade horses and see his brother Tanto affianced to the Lord of Cantara's daughter, Selen. Selen's father is Lord Tycho Issian, a man of cruel lusts and fanatical beliefs. He must sell his daughter to clear his debts; but when the deal falls through, Tanto, as handsome on the exterior as he is corrupt and cruel within, is determined to have Selen by any means. But as he rapes her, she stabs him and flees, only to be found and rescued by Erno Hamson, who had been engaged in helping Katla escape her pursuers. Now, Katla is left to face them alone.

In the end it is young Saro Vingo who saves Katla. He saw her on the first day of the Fair and was enthralled by her; with the aid of a precious stone which has taken on terrifying magical powers, he wades into the fires to free her.

A great conflict erupts as the Rockfall clan escape the Fair with their injured kinswoman, and Ravn Asharson flees with his beautiful new bride to his ship for the long voyage north to Halbo.

Unbeknownst to all, including herself, this extraordinary creature, known only as the Rosa Eldi, is the lost goddess Falla, abducted by a mage hundreds of years ago. Rahe, a great king and sorcerer, defeated her brother Sirio (known to the northerners as Sur) and imprisoned him beneath the Red Peak. Then, he stole Falla away to his secret kingdom—Sanctuary, an island of ice at the top of the world—and there extracted all her magic and her memory, using it to gain power over all the world and make her his bodyslave. Finally, Rahe's apprentice Virelai—a strange, tall, pale man raised by Rahe since he was a child—unwittingly abducted the Rosa Eldi and brought her back to the world.

The Rosa Eldi, Rose of the World, will feel her memory and her magic returning, fragment by fragment: but still she remains in the power of men. In Ravn's kingdom, she will find herself the subject of intense scrutiny and suspicion. Ravn needs a child to secure his succession, but the Rosa Eldi is not mortal and cannot conceive his child, no matter how hard she tries.

When Selen Issian, having been rescued by Erno Hamson and a band of mercenaries under the tender care of Mam and now traveling as Leta Gullwing, arrives at the northern court heavily pregnant with the unwanted child of the man who raped her, it seems the new Queen of Eyra's wishes have been answered.

In Istria, Selen's father Tycho Issian, accompanied now by the sorcerer Virelai and a black cat, fans the flames of fundamentalism in the south, whipping up hatred and blood lust against the old enemy. However, his true motive is not religious, but profane in the extreme. At the Allfair, he glimpsed the Rosa Eldi, and was engulfed by desire for her. Now he will not rest until he can take her for himself. He will launch a holy war against the north to quench this lust, and burn a thousand nomads and heretics to assuage his torment.

Forces gather in both realms as the shadow of war creeps ever nearer. But Aran Aranson, safe at home at Rockfall, his daughter miraculously recovered from her wounds, has no thought for the coming conflict. All his thought is bent on adventure: a voyage into arctic waters to seek for the legendary island of Sanctuary, where his map tells him there is untold treasure for the taking.

Katla sails with the charismatic Tam Fox, leader of the mummers, to Halbo and there steal away the north's best shipmaker, Morten Danson, to fashion a fine icebreaker to sail into the treacherous waters of the far north.

The ship is built, the crew selected. All the able-bodied men in the area will accompany Aran Aranson, leaving the women of Rockfall unprotected. It is not long before raiders from the southern continent sail into Rockfall waters. News of the theft of Morten Danson has reached the warmongers of Istria. If they can abduct the finest shipmaker in Eyra, they can fashion a fleet with which they can carry the war to the Northern Isles. And taking a few comely Eyran women prisoner to sell in the slave markets of Istria can only add to their profits.

As fate would surely decree, Aran Aranson's voyage is disastrous—

struck by storm, by ill omen, and mutiny. Aran, his murderous younger son Fent, and the last remaining member of the crew, Urse One Ear, will find themselves adrift in the weird and hostile landscape of an island, which may be the famed isle of Sanctuary, somewhere between the world of men and the world of legend.

Prologue

WHERE am I?

Who am I?

Neither question gave up a simple answer, though the "where" might be easier to determine than the "who." Stars wheeled overhead in a clear night sky. Out of all that silver-speckled blackness the constellation known as Sirio's Ship, with its three aligned stars forming a single straight mast, appeared immediately to the eye. Orienting himself by this familiar pattern, he saw where the Fulmar flew ahead, north toward the Navigator's Star, the brightest light in the sky. Turning, he located the Stallion and the Twins, showing between high silhouetted peaks, and to the west of them the complicated patterns of the Weaving Woman and the Archer. A sliver of new moon lay between the paws of the Great Cat; soon it would drop and the stars would turn and dawn would reveal the particularities of his location.

He already had a suspicion of where he found himself. He had navigated too many ocean crossings; studied the heavens for too many years ever to be completely lost in this world of Elda.

And thus he knew himself to be somewhere in the depths of the southern continent. Even if the unusual configuration of the stars had not offered that evidence, there were other signifiers available. Volcanic sand crunched beneath his feet, which were bare. The air was dry and smelled of sulfur. It whispered against his skin, soft as a woman's caress. Frowning, he dropped a hand. Why was he naked? Naked and in an Istrian desert, somewhere below tall volcanic mountains?

He searched his memory, which yielded tiny, precious details:

Dread and fear; fury and hopelessness. Freezing saltwater which burned the throat and nose, and a terrible crushing, a searing pain in the chest, which spread through his entire body like wildfire through sere grass. From nowhere, or from everywhere, came a voice which rumbled through all that choking darkness, reverberating through the bones of his chest and skull so that it was almost as if the voice were his own, an internal command made massively manifest. Then, a sensation of great velocity, a roaring, tumbling, rushing through different elements—water, earth, air—or maybe it was himself flowing, merging with his surroundings in some bizarre metaphysical union.

The gap between "then" and "now" remained impossible to bridge. He felt hollowed out, scoured like a pot ready to be refilled. Bewildered and a little afraid, he shook his head, and the beads and bones woven into the long braids of his hair chinked lightly against the bare skin of his shoulders.

Then, putting the Navigator's Star behind him, he began to walk toward his destiny.

Captives

"**D**O you believe in magic, Tilo?"

"Sergeant, to you."

"Do you believe in magic, *Sergeant?*" This last was uttered with sarcastic emphasis. He and Tilo Gaston had grown up in the same rat-run of Forent's alleys, behind the shipyards where the whores and the destitute lived and where the air owned a permanent miasma of urine, salt, and tar. Yet even though they'd signed up for the militia on the same day, the dark man had managed to bag himself a rank Gesto could only dream of. He found it hard to believe merit had had anything to do with it.

Tilo Gaston ran a hand through his hair and stared at the figure in front of him, which was swaying awkwardly to the rhythm of the pack-horse he was tied onto. They had placed a bag over the pale man's head because Isto had insisted that a sorcerer could sear you dead from the inside out with his gaze—but Isto had never been the brightest coin in the bunch. There had been little resistance from the lanky albino creature, who seemed more like a dying eel than a magicker. Clammy and languid, he had said not a word since his capture, let alone tried to lay on them curses or enchantments. The other one, though—the lad—he was a different matter. Eyes like a man three times his age, a man who had seen far too much. You could believe a fair bit about a boy like that. But magic?

He shrugged. "Lot of strange things in the world. I've seen flowers bloom in the Bone Quarter and chickens with two heads. I've seen fish fall out of a clear sky and a stone bleed. I've stood on ground that shook beneath my feet and heard voices where there could be none. Unnatural phenomena, that's what they are."

Gesto tried to look interested and failed. He hated it when Tilo played the sage. It was just another way of reminding his old friend of the gap that had opened up between them. You wouldn't think that bearing a rank would make such a difference, but somehow it did; you got the pay, the choice of billet, and the best women, too. But why it encouraged Tilo to think it endowed you with a more valid experience of the world, he had no idea. He wished he had never bothered to ask his question.

If Tilo were aware of his comrade's irritation, he gave no sign of it. Unfazed, he continued, "I've seen traveling players disappear in a cloud of green smoke, only to pop up right behind you out of nowhere, and I once saw a Footloose woman produce a whole swathe of silk flags from out of her cunny; but that's illusion, that is: tricks and mirrors. But whatever it was you saw the boy do with that necklace thing the captain's got wrapped so careful in his saddlebag, I can't believe it was magic. Some sort of new weapon, I'd guess, or maybe just a shiny gewgaw that gave Toro's horse a fright so it tossed him off and broke his silly neck."

Gesto bristled. Besides himself, three men in the troop—seasoned soldiers too brutalized to have any imagination left to them—had sworn they had seen the boy blast Toro off his horse, and he had been right there when it happened! He might have been in pain from where that damned big cat had raked his leg, but there had been nothing wrong with his eyes, for Falla's sake! And he had seen the body. There hadn't been a mark on it, the only sign of Toro's precipitous demise being an expression of astonishment and upturned, shocked, white eyes.

"Well, I saw what I saw," he declared mulishly, and let his horse drop back in order to end the conversation.

His leg throbbed dully in the heat of the day, and his throat was parched. They had been riding steadily since dawn and it was now past lunchtime, but the captain showed no sign of stopping. Sand swirled up around them and got into the most unbelievable nooks and crannies. Trust the Goddess, he thought, in a moment of sheer heresy, to design a man to have so many awkward places in which sand could embed it-

self and irritate you so. To take his mind off these discomforts, he turned
to survey the rest of the troop and saw where the boy rode in the company of Isto and Semanto halfway back down the line. Like the pale man,
the boy's head was also swathed, his hands bound to the cantle in front
of him. He sat his piebald pony with a complete indifference to its un-
coordinated gait, so that he was thrown around each time the pony
lurched. Shoulders slumped, feet limp; every line of his body carried the
same message: that he did not care whether he lived or died.

The nomad woman had been quite lively by comparison. First, there
had been a great deal of wailing and weeping about the death of some
child; and when Garmo had told her he'd give her something to really
complain about and Sammo and Heni had stripped her and held her
down while he forced himself on her, she'd howled and shrieked and
rained imprecations and blows upon him throughout the whole encounter, which really hadn't taken more than a minute, for all Garmo's
drunken boasts about his sexual prowess. The funny thing was, though,
that his prick had swollen up and then gone black and painful the next
day, so—while she was quite attractive in an outlandish way, with her
light, curled hair, her veilless face, and pale, brazen eyes, not to mention
those lush tits—no one else had much fancied trying their luck with her.

Garmo would probably have to spend his entire share of the reward
they'd receive for turning in these prisoners to Lord Tycho Issian on a
chirurgeon if he wanted to save his cock from falling off, and serve him
right. Gesto had better ideas as to what to do with his money. A side of
beef and a flagon of beer at the Bullock's Head, followed by a good Istrian whore—no, two, he amended quickly—at Jetra's famed House of
Silk. Then go see how much it would cost him to bribe his own way up
to sergeant. It'd be worth it just to see the look on Tilo's face when he
turned up wearing a red braid on his arm, too. *Self-satisfied bastard,* he
thought, just as the arrow took him in the neck.

THE stench belowdecks was becoming unbearable. Fat Breta had
thrown up again, so weakly that she had been unable to clear the skirts
of her dress. Her retching punctuated her weeping: it was a miserable

sound. Between the tears and the vomit, at this rate she'd be a shadow of her former self by the time they landed at an Istrian port, if they ever made it that far, thought Katla.

As if echoing her fear, the ship listed deeply to the right, wallowed, and then lurched hard to the left, throwing them all sideways, so that Fat Breta's wailings were drowned under the cries of the other prisoners. Soon, even that noise was subsumed by the creaks of the ship's timbers under the strain of the sea and an incompetent steersman. Surely the poorly crafted planking which was all that held them up above hundreds of feet of Northern Ocean, would burst and the vessel spring a leak at any moment. It was not a comforting thought. As the ship hit another trough and rolled like a dying pig, Katla felt the bile rise in her throat and swallowed it down again. To be sick was unthinkable. She was Katla Aransen, daughter of a line of Eyran rovers, born to a life on the ocean waves. She had the sea in her blood! She had first set foot on a longship at the age of three-and-a-half and been sailing all her life, and never once had she thrown up in the seventeen years that followed, storm or calm; it was a matter of pride.

Not that there was much pride left to any of them, save old Hesta Rolfsen. It was hard to think about her grandmother, that tough old matriarch, and her terrible, heroic death. For all her sharp tongue, beady eyes, and bawdy humor, Katla was more like the old beldame than she would have cared to admit. On their first night aboard this foreign tub, Katla's mother, Bera Rolfsen, had told them all of the matriarch's resolute ending in an attempt to put some backbone into those who wailed and prayed for death themselves:

" 'Here I sit and here I will stay. Rockfall is my home. I am too old to leave it.' Those were her words." Bera's face had been as stern as carved wood as she had looked from one to another amid this telling—from Katla's shocked face, white in the darkness of the hold except for the black bruise on her chin which had ended her fight with the raiders, to Kitten Soronsen's tear-reddened eyes and Magla Felinsen's hunched figure; from Forna Stensen, her straw-yellow hair a wild tangle, to Thin Hildi, staring down at her mismatched stockings all torn to bits. Kit Farsen had made a small sound like an injured rabbit, then mastered herself as Bera's gaze fell upon her. "She took her place in my husband's great dragon-chair. I tried to cajole her, but she would have none of it, and when I tried to take her from there by force, she gripped so fast to the chair's carved arms that I could not move her. I pleaded with her to come with me, but she said she was too old to see any more of this world of Elda, but that much experience still lay before the rest of us, and that if no one survived her, who then would be left to avenge her death?"

"Me." Katla's voice was low. "I will avenge her. And not just my brave grandmother either. I will take vengeance for every one of those who died: Hesta Rolfsen, Marin Edelsen, Tian Jensen, Otter Garsen, Signy and Sigrid Leesen, Finna Jonsen, Audny Filsen, and all. Even little Fili Kolson and his old dog, Breda. I will kill the men who did this—I swear it on my grandmother's bones."

That had stopped Kitten's tears. "And how will you do that?" she jeered. "With no weapon and your hands shackled? Will you strangle them between your thighs—or screw them to death when they test you for their brothels?"

"Kitten!" Bera's voice was sharp as chipped flint.

Katla gave Kitten Soronsen such a look that she quelled. One day, there would be a score to be settled. "Do not ask me how; just accept that I will."

And she had meant it.

Now, quite suddenly, three days after making that vow, she was crying for the first time since they had been captured. She had come aboard the vessel unconscious from the man they called Baranguet's well-placed fist; and when she had come to, hurting and furious, she had been charged with adrenaline and resolve. Slow-burning anger, coupled with utter disbelief, had carried her through the next two days. At any moment she expected to awake and find herself chilly from sleeping too long in the wind on top of the Hound's Tooth. But the discomfort of being chained up in this stinking hold was clearly no dream, and the reality of her grandmother's stiff-backed demise pressed in on her with ever greater impact. Tears fell, searing and unstoppable. They burned down her cheeks, off her chin, and dripped onto her leather tunic. Then her nose began to run. Sur's nuts! There was nothing she could do about it but sniff furiously. Like the others her hands were chained to great rusted links stapled into the tarred timbers of the hold's floor.

Being taken captive had been vile enough: the manhandling humiliating, the knowledge of defeat and loss of control shattering. But tears would help no one; besides, she would not let any of the others see her cry. And so she closed off that part of herself and concentrated on being alive and relatively unscathed, even if confined to this filthy, stinking space, trussed up like a chicken in the belly of a bodge-built Istrian bucket, and heading for a less than pleasant fate.

Katla was, for the most part, a girl who lived in the moment. She rarely looked back; she generally considered the future with anticipation—or with frustration that she had not yet reached it. The physical world and her relationship with it was everything, and so she was dealing with some of the more abstract aspects of her situation rather better than her companions. Even as Thin Hildi wept and Kitten Soronsen wailed and Magla Felinsen droned on about the way Istrian women were kept as slaves, Katla kept her horrors confined to her current circumstances.

She had never traveled in the hold of a ship before and she did not like it. She was used to being up in the elements, watching the surf skim off the waves and the clouds scud across the sky, the sunlight spangling the water and the sail belling out like washing on a line. She was used to standing lightly on the bucking timbers of an Eyran ship built out of the knowledge and love of generations of seagoers and shipmakers, allowing her body to find its own center, to move with the rhythm of the ocean, feeling the healthy tensions of wood and iron and water and, somewhere far below, the resonances of the rock of Elda, the veins of crystal and ores which spoke into her blood and bones. It was a mystical connection, one which gave her a deep faith of rightness in the world.

Down here, with her wrists chafed by iron which had bitten into the skins of generations of slaves, amid the stench and the noise, it seemed she had lost the trick of it.

So, unable to do anything else, she gave her thoughts to the infinite number of ways in which she might kill a man, both quickly and slowly. *Baranguet,* she thought murderously, *I will start with Baranguet. . . .*

2

The Wasteland

IN this arctic region, day differed little from night. The sun, when it heaved itself over the horizon, offered only a kind of milky twilight for a few brief hours before sliding leadenly back into darkness. Above this short-lived band of light, the sky shaded first to cobalt, then to violet and indigo, before becoming as black as a raven's wing, and in that blackness—at least to Aran Aranson's weary, snowblind eyes—the stars were simply too luminous to gaze upon for any length of time.

But even if he could not look upon it, he knew, as if there were a lodestone in his skull, that the Navigator's Star hung directly overhead, and by its position he knew that they were as far north as it was possible to go—and yet it seemed as though the world of ice went on forever. Perhaps, Aran mused as he plodded grimly along the narrow isthmus that had opened out before them, they were already dead and this place was a world-between-worlds reserved for those men of ill-luck with whom the god did not wish to share his table. For there could be no doubt that he was an exceedingly luckless man. Even before he had embarked on this doomed expedition, he had lost a son and a wife and estranged his daughter; and now he was master of nothing. Since Bera had announced their marriage dissolved, Rockfall would return to her family, as was the Eyran way; he had no home. His beautiful ship, the *Long Serpent,* lay crushed by the merciless ice of the Northern Ocean. The best part of his crew he had lost to storm and sea, to murder and mutiny; and then to the teeth and claws of a snow bear. Some men had preferred to take their chances with the elements rather than accompany him on what they saw as a fool's errand, and so he had left them behind with precious few supplies and little chance of survival. To his knowledge, the man who accompanied him, and the burden he carried, was all that was left of his glorious expedition.

He turned. The giant, Urse, with his ruined face and single ear, who had once been lieutenant to the lord of the mummers, marched stolidly behind him, his huge feet planted in his leader's wake, head down, shoulders bowed under the weight of the third survivor of the expedition. Fent Aranson was wrapped in every item of clothing they could spare, yet still his skin was the delicate blue of a robin's egg and the blood had long since stopped seeping from his severed hand, as if his heart had already given up the ghost.

Aran Aranson set his face into the wind once more and squinted against the glare. To his snow-hazed eyes it seemed there were spirits all around them in this eerie, silent place: wisps of spindrift twisting off the tops of the dunes and banks piled on either side of their passage, curling into the air like a host of lost souls. If anything, the lack of lamentation and wailing added to the impression he had of being in a transitionary zone. Maybe, he thought, as his feet continued their exhausted trudge, they were fated to wander this terrible, freezing nothingness for all time, never gaining on their goal, nor leaving the tempestuous world of men any farther behind them.

URSE One Ear placed his feet in the churned-up ruts made by Aran Aranson and wondered for the thousandth time whether he would ever place them on soft green grass, pebble beach, or forest floor again.

As a child, growing up in the treeless wastes of Norheim—all bare rock and low scrub, gray horizons and sea-thrashed shores—he had possessed a powerful curiosity to see more of the world, believing that his homeland must surely be the most godforsaken place in all of Elda. He had seen some startling sights in his life, but these soulless tracts were the grimmest by far. Even in the semidarkness, the gleam of the nev-erending snow hurt his eyes, and the intense cold made his teeth and scars ache and brought vividly to mind memories he would rather leave buried. Many had asked him about the cause of the loss of his ear and about the furrows which ravaged that face, almost closing his left eye and lifting one corner of his mouth to expose a snaggle of teeth, so that he had come to resemble a farm cat kicked in the head by a bad-tempered horse, but Urse had never cared to volunteer the information. Over the years, these fearsome markings had caused no little specula-tion. Some surmised that he had been in one ax-fight too many, or had come to grief in some tragic nautical accident. The truth was worse, and still gave him nightmares.

He had joined Tam Fox's mummers' troupe nearly twenty years ago when he was barely more than a lad. At that time, the troupe had owned a bear—a great black, shambling fellow from the forests of central Is-tria—which Tam Fox had rescued from hawkers on the docks of Halbo who were using it to generate themselves a nice little income by solicit-ing bets on how many dogs could take it down. To cover their risk, they would privately goad the beast for an hour before the bout, taunting it with meat, beating it off with sticks and cudgels until it was murderous. As a result, it had carried more scars than Urse did now—obvious ones, around the paws and muzzle—but more, far more, invisible to the eye. They were much of a size, Urse and the bear; in one of the old languages their names corresponded, so he had come to feel a common bond with the poor creature and had taken over its care for the mummers' troupe. Then, one day, he had moved awkwardly, or his shadow had fallen across it in some way which recalled to it a past torment, and it had turned upon him with such terrifying ferocity that he knew his life was over. It had his head engulfed in its noisome, furnacelike mouth and was bear-ing its jaws down upon him when Tam Fox had intervened, hurling him-self upon the bear and blowing constantly on a high-pitched whistle which Urse could hear only in the vibrations it made in the bones of the creature's great skull. With a roar, it had spat him out and pulled away, only to be speared by Min Codface and the contortionist, Bella—but not before it had raked the mummers' leader thoroughly with its wicked claws, and taken Urse's ear and half his face with it. It was a miracle that he had survived his injuries; a miracle, and Tam Fox's patience and near-magical skill with herbs and ointments.

He had told Aran Aranson that he wished to join his expedition to the island of gold because experience had taught him he was unlikely to engage the affections of a woman sufficiently for her to agree to be his wife without the lure of a good farm (which he could never afford without a large windfall), but the truth was that when the mummers' leader was lost with the wreck of the *Snowland Wolf,* some significant part of Urse One Ear had gone down to the seabed with him. Tam had seemed almost supernatural in his energies and grace. That a life such as his could be snuffed out in such an arbitrary fashion had made him lose faith in his own worth and survivability. It seemed a fitting bargain to offer himself up to the god to do with as he wished by taking a place on this madman's quest. Through one ordeal after another he had endured, but when they had finally encountered the snow bear in these nameless realms, he had been ready to surrender his life to it, deeming it a fitting end, since his life was already forfeit to a bear. By typically random chance, however, it had chosen Pol Garson over him, and then Aran's son Fent. That it had not taken him was perplexing; like Aran Aranson, he sensed they had crossed over into some mythical place where men paid the dues they had tallied up in life, and had resigned himself to wait for whatever judgment would fall. Now he was not sure whether to feel relief or to brace himself for the next onslaught.

So when the great bird skimmed suddenly above them, it seemed like a portent. Yet, in front of him, Aran Aranson continued his oblivious trudge. He had seen nothing.

"Albatross!" Urse cried, hollowing his hands around the word. Aran turned like a man in a dream, and Urse repeated the observation, pointing overhead.

He watched the bird circle them and frowned. Something about it seemed unnatural. He could not determine why he thought this, only that its presence made him uneasy. Something, perhaps, about the way it had appeared to hover over them so effortlessly before wheeling away again. What was it about the creatures of this ice world? The snow bear had seemed too intent upon them for mere hunger, its mean black eyes as flat as a shark's, dual-natured, as if driven by another's will.

He marked the bird's passage as it vanished beyond an ice cliff which rose like woodsmoke in the distance and then, there being nothing else in this white world to distract him, returned his regard to the monotonous placement of foot beyond foot.

MANY hours later they reached the ice cliff and prepared themselves for another endless white vista, but once they rounded its western shoulder another world lay before them: a landscape composed all of ice—but what remarkable ice it was! Walls and buttresses curved like vast ships rose out of a frozen sea. Great towers swept skyward, aquamarine at their base to ethereal green and translucent pink-white at their mist-wrapped summits. Battlements and terraces ringed these towers around, and into them were carved not only eyelets and arched windows, but fabulous beasts like those in the ancient tapestries of Halbo Castle—winged gryphons and prancing unicorns, grinning trolls and fearsome dragons, gigantic hounds and monstrous eagles; or perhaps their eyes were playing tricks upon them and the whole was no more than some ice madness, a snow blindness of the mind; an extravagant *fata morgana* induced by their avid desire for some mark of man on this endless wasteland.

Indeed, Aran Aranson began to rub his sore eyes with the back of one frozen hand, as if to dash the bizarre vision away. When he focused them again, it was to see a figure approaching, a figure which did not trudge as they did across the snow, nor churn up the ground as it went, but which seemed to skim the surface of the ice without touching it, and this observation convinced him finally that he had lost his mind.

3

Stones

In the midst of the mayhem that followed, someone ripped the bag from Saro's head.

"That's the Vingo boy!" he heard a man cry triumphantly, and then there came more noises of chaos: the shriek and grate of sword upon sword, the urgent scuffle of feet and hooves, the thud of arrows finding their mark and mingled cries of agony and battle fury.

When his eyes had adjusted to the sudden blast of light, Saro looked about him, disoriented by this strange turn of events. It seemed the troop who had overtaken the nomads and captured Virelai, Alisha, and himself had themselves been overtaken by other militia. All around, his captors were either locked in hand-to-hand combat with men wearing similar gear, or lay dead upon the ground, stuck with arrows. He saw, amid all this horror, Virelai darting awkwardly among the milling horses, bent almost double at the waist, his hands reaching blindly in front of him. In other circumstances he might have looked almost comical, but with the bag still securely bound over his head it seemed a miracle that he should avoid the flying hooves.

"Virelai!" he shouted, and at once regretted it.

The sorcerer stopped his weaving trail and stood stock-still, his bagged head swiveling wildly, trying to pinpoint the speaker's whereabouts. As the horse came at him, Saro saw Virelai's bound hands come up instinctively, and entirely ineffectively, to ward it off; then he was down on the ground and the great beast was trampling him in its own panic and fear. When the melee passed over him, Saro could see that the sorcerer had been left lying upon his back, as unmoving as a stone. The force of the blow had driven the bag off the pale man's head. His white hair streamed around him, except where it was trodden into the mire.

Saro slipped awkwardly off his mount, ran to where the sorcerer lay, and knelt beside him. Virelai's eyes were closed. Colorless lashes lay still upon colorless cheeks. His mouth was open, but no rasp of breath issued from it. Saro saw where a purple bruise and a mess of open flesh marred the white temple. But when he examined the area more closely, there appeared to be no blood though the wound was clearly deep and damaging. In fact, the opening appeared not a bright scarlet but a strangely livid gray. This detail disturbed Saro even more than if the wound had been gouting cascades of gore. He leaned over the body and laid his ear to Virelai's thin chest.

Nothing.

Panic rising, Saro got to his feet and started yelling. "Help! Here! This man's stopped breathing. Help!"

No one took the slightest notice. As time slowed around him like a bad dream, Saro saw where dwindling groups of men fought one another, while others lay dead or dying, their feet drumming weakly in their death throes. Usually inordinately sensitive to the woes of the world, Saro was surprised to find that he felt remarkably little about these violent demises. The soldiers who had taken them had been brutal and coarse. In order to apprehend Virelai and himself, they had murdered defenseless old men and women, and poor Falo, and just for Tycho Issian's reward money. They had raped Alisha and joked while they were about it. They had boasted of the atrocities they had carried out against other nomads—whom they referred to derogatorily as "the Footloose"—and those they had witnessed by other militiamen as though they were mere entertainments and the victims less than beasts. In one notable conversation he recalled, a pair of his captors had discussed with some glee a new device which had just been created by a young nobleman from the south, a hero now confined to a wheeled chair after his brave attempt to rescue an Istrian woman from northern barbarians at the Allfair. You could, it appeared, contain two dozen or more heretics and magickers in this great sphere of wrought iron and cook them slowly over a fire. It prolonged the agonies of the unbelievers and brought them to the Goddess more perfectly than the traditional stake-and-pyre method. The Lord of Cantara was especially pleased by this innovation; he had taken to charging a viewing fee from the public for such events to fund the war effort and it was proving most profitable. They planned to attend the next such burning on their return to Jetra, and looked forward to it with some relish.

Saro had retched and groaned inside the stifling confines of his bag, and had earned a clout across the shoulders for his troubles. Now, scanning the ravages of the battlefield, it appeared that those men were either dead or dying along with the rest of their troop. He grimaced. Less of their ilk on the face of Elda must surely be a blessing in itself.

A little distance away, Saro saw where the captain of the troop who had captured them lay moving feebly in a pool of his own blood, the handle of a knife sticking up out of his belly. Night's Harbinger, the fine stallion Saro had stolen from Jetra's stables to make his escape, lay nearby, his neck all hacked and gouged. At once, a red wash of anger raged inside him. No animal deserved such ill treatment, let alone such a beauty as this one had been. Flashes of the race the stallion had won at the Allfair came rushing back at him, the race Tanto, his brother, had forced him to ride in order to win enough money for the settlement to buy his marriage to the Lord of Cantara's daughter. Deprived of the daughter, now Tanto had wedded himself to the father, it seemed. Tycho Issian and Tanto Vingo: a truly unholy alliance! And yet their vile pairing had only just begun. Saro clenched and unclenched his fists like a man ready to take on the world.

What on Elda would they be capable of if either of them was to lay hands upon the death-stone?

The death-stone. Even the possibility of Virelai's death meant little in the face of this danger. He must find it, perhaps even use it to drive off the remaining militiamen, yet even through his ebbing anger the thought of wielding it again was repugnant. He remembered with horrid clarity the guard who had fallen lifeless at his feet at the Allfair and the soldier he had seared from his horse in defense of the nomads. The coruscating detonation of the stone he remembered like a physical entity: a pain at the back of the eyeball, a vibration down the sternum, a weakness in the legs. The dead haunted his sleep; he had little wish to add to their number. Yet he knew it was better that a handful of men died here than a multitude perish in some future time as a result of his misplaced moral fastidiousness.

Steeling himself against cowardice, Saro squared his jaw. He shut his eyes and *listened*.

Even when they were separated, it seemed he could not be entirely free of the stone's influence. The simple pendant he had been gifted with by the old moodstone seller had, with the touch of the White Woman—the Goddess, as he now knew her to be—become the most dangerous object in the world; just as Tycho and his brother appeared to be wedded in some fateful union, so, it seemed, he was paired with his own nemesis. His sense of relief when the death-stone had been taken from him by the soldiers had been short-lived, for although it no longer hung around his neck in its soft leather pouch, he had been able to *hear* it. It called to him by day and night, a thin keening which scraped at the bone on the inside of his scalp like nails on rock. No one else appeared to be aware of this vile sound. It was the stone's love song and lament for him alone, a babe wailing for its parent.

He closed off the other sounds around him, opened his eyes, and focused grimly. It took only a few seconds to locate the thin call, some way distant and to his left, moving slowly, backward, forward, sideways. The captain's horse was an impressive bay with a fine arched neck and powerful chest, and just now it was stepping nervously out of the path of a gray with its rider dangling half-dead from its back. As soon as his gaze alighted upon the leather saddlebags it still carried, the noise in his head increased, became a buzzing as of many flies.

Saro closed the space between himself and the horse in a few short strides. The bay eyed him suspiciously and skittered away, eyes rolling. Knowing what would follow the action but making it anyway, Saro caught at the flailing bridle and laid a hand firmly on the beast's neck. At once he was assailed by the horse's experience of its world. Blood. Salty and sweet and tangy. Freshly-shed blood, men's blood. Horses', too. Blood and churned earth, human shit. The reek of it clung to the roof of the mouth, making the tongue sticky and rough. The gelding wanted to flee, but could find no clear path in which the scent was not strong. Its skin crawled with apprehension; its heart beat wildly. Saro took his hand off the horse's slick skin and in seconds the terror faded. The bay snorted and threw its head up, but it stopped its neurotic dance and its breathing came more steadily.

The death-stone was in the nearside saddlebag. He unlatched the buckle and felt inside. As if working the stone's will rather than his own, his fingers closed around a wrapped package. He drew it out and peeled away the layers. There it was, in its nest of fabrics. Caged in silver wire, threaded on its leather thong, the moodstone looked like the trinket it once had been, the simple piece of jewelery he had thought to purchase as a gift for his mother. He closed his fingers over it convulsively and shuddered at the familiar dull vibration which traveled up his arm. But at least the noise had stilled. He breathed a deep sigh, somewhere between relief and resignation, and started to unwind the thong to replace the death-stone around his neck.

The next thing he knew, something sharp prodded him in the back.

"Thought you'd do a little looting, did you, laddie?"

A dagger point was digging into his chest, held by a slab-cheeked man whose eyes glinted balefully.

"Gissit here!" he insisted, gesturing with his chin at Saro's hand, which had at the interruption closed instinctively into a fist.

"You don't want it," Saro said desperately. "Truly, you don't."

"That's for me to decide," the big man said, scowling. "Open yer hand or lose it."

Saro's fingers unfurled like the petals of some lethal flower. The soldier stared at what he held there, and his scowl deepened.

"Bit of tat," he opined.

Saro smiled weakly. "It is. Yes. Just a moodstone. Not worth much . . ."

The dagger bit deeper. "Even so," the man snarled, "it's winner's takings. Some gormless bugger'll pay me a cantari or two for it. Gissit here!" He snatched at the boy's hand, but Saro's reflexes were too slow to prevent what happened next.

As the soldier's grip closed over the moodstone, three things occurred with such apparent simultaneity that it would have been impos-

sible to say which occurred first. The flesh of their two hands seemed to
fuse, the stone glowed silver-white like metal heated to liquid, and Saro
felt the man's soul flee his body in a bewildered rush of regret and utmost terror. As his grip faltered and failed, the soldier's eyes rolled up
into his sockets and he dropped to his knees, his mouth stretched wide
in a soundless rictus.

The moodstone, as gray and lifeless as the man it had killed, fell
silently to the ground. Saro watched it tumble the few feet into the mud
as if down the endless length of the most vertiginous cliff. He blinked:
once, twice; wondered whether he would ever find the will to pick it up
again. Then voices were shouting at him and rough hands spun him
around. Two men: one was fat and grizzled; the other scrawny and pim-
pled. Both were garbed in boiled leather and chain mail; both had bloody
swords.

"That's the one!" the skinny one said.

"What, him?" The fat one was disbelieving. "He's killed a hundred
men and has to be approached with caution?" He laughed. "That one
couldn't strangle a rabbit!"

"No, it is. It's Saro Vingo," Pimple declared hotly. "I seen him in Jetra
with his family and his brother—you know, Tanto, the one in the
wheeled chair."

Fat Man looked ruminative, then a little anxious. "Get him quick,
then," he said to his companion, taking a step back.

Pimple glared at him. "Lost the use of yer arms, have you?" He
turned his attention to Saro. "Put yer hands out," he said, brandishing
his sword. Saro offered them slowly, and as he did so, he covered the
moodstone as unobtrusively as he could with his left foot, then pressed
down, treading it carefully into the muck. If he could just distract their
attention for a moment or two . . .

Pimple lofted his blade and tucked it in under Saro's throat. Then he
undid his belt with his free hand, whipped it expertly around Saro's
wrists and pulled it tight. "Right," he said to the older man. "I'll have the
reward on this one, and you, you lazy git, can fuck right off."

Fat Man snarled. "I saw him first."

Pimple sneaked a look to left and right to see if anyone else had
spotted his prize, but no one appeared to be looking in their direction.

In one fast and fluid movement, he spun around. A powerfully driven and precisely-placed elbow caught Saro just below the jaw, while, with his forward lunge he landed the bloodied swordpoint deep in his companion's belly. The Fat Man's eyebrows shot up in sudden surprise, almost reaching his receding hairline. Then, with a deep sigh, he sank to his knees.

Pimple let his sword arm drop along with the man. When his victim had stilled, he twisted the hilt with a flourish and ripped the blade upward. At once a great festoon of guts tumbled out over the steel in a noisome, steaming heap to land with a wet slither and slap around the older man's feet. Fat Man looked down sorrowfully. "You kept saying it was about time I lost some weight."

Pimple wrinkled his nose at the horrible stench. "Faw! I said that hotpot at the Limping Cockerel was off," he opined, but the fat man had at last passed beyond any interest in his diet. The thin man placed his right foot over his fallen comrade's, put his weight on it, and levered his sword back out into the light. Then he cleaned the blade on the dead man's tunic with fastidious care before resheathing it at his hip.

At last he turned to deal with his prisoner.

The Kettle-girl

KATLA Aransen had little chance to work her murderous fantasies. When the weather got rougher, the Istrians chained their captives' feet as well as their hands and left the women to fend for themselves as best they could while they fought the elements aloft.

None of the crew appeared to be seasoned sailors, as was to be deduced from the desperate lurchings of the ship as great waves broadsided her, or from the shouts of panic as water crashed down and timbers splintered. Katla itched to be up on deck, trimming the sail and angling the bow into the pitch of the waves. She loved a storm, but only if she could see something of it. Down here, it was as dark as sin, and what had already been an oppressive prison now became a reeking pit, filled with a more noisome stench than she could ever have imagined could be created by a dozen women of good Eyran stock. Less, now. A dozen of them had been taken from Rockfall but only ten of them were left: Katla and her mother, Magla, Kitten, Hildi and Breta; Simi Fallsen, a big dark girl from the north of the island who'd had the misfortune to be visiting the steading at just the wrong time, her friend, Leni Stelsen and the cousins, Forna Stensen and Kit Farsen. The other two had died, either from the wounds they had taken or from sheer terror. And it would be a miracle if the others didn't follow.

They had no dignity, and little humanity, left to them. Some had lost all or most of their clothing as the raiders manhandled them down to the shore. Some had been raped, before Galo Bastido had stopped his men from further damaging his potentially valuable goods. Some ranted; others hunched silently, curled in on themselves, giving way to misery and death. They all sat or lay in their own filth. Many had been seasick and were now too weak, or too empty, even to vomit. It had been four days since they had had any food other than bread so hard Thin Hildi had broken a tooth on it, three since the Istrians had brought them fresh water. Katla suspected the raiders had miscalculated their supplies, or maybe they had meant only to capture the shipmaker, and the women had merely been a bonus cargo. They had been at sea for sixteen days, so she reckoned they were either lost or were heading farther down the Istrian coast than she had expected. She thought about what she knew of the southern continent, which was not much. The men of the north charted only their own waters—sketchy, diagrammatic scribbles with rough charcoal on cured lambskin, showing treacherous reefs, safe channels, and fast currents; where fish shoaled in spring; where ships had been wrecked; the best passage for Halbo's harbor; or the rich fishing waters around the Fair Isles. So she had never seen a map of the enemy's lands, not even of how to reach the Moonfell Plain where the annual Allfair was held. The route for that sailing was a piece of near-legendary nautical wisdom passed from father to son and uncle to nephew down the male line of Eyran families. And although she had traveled with her own family to the Allfair the previous year, she knew only that the Moonfell Plain stuck out into the Northern Ocean like a thumb of land, and that beyond its ashy volcanic wastes, mountains rose to the south and a great sweep of coastline curled away out of sight to the east and the Istrian mainland. Where this ramshackle vessel and its pirate crew might be headed, she had little idea, other than the mention of the word *Forent,* which appeared, from the context in which it had been used, to be a port city and the center of the south's incipient shipbuilding industry. She deduced from this that Forent must be their destination. They had certainly gone to a great deal of trouble to lay hands on Morten Danson. Now he would surely be pressed into service to make ships for the Istrian war against her people. If the vile little vessel they were on was the best the wrights of the Southern Empire could produce, it was no wonder they had been forced to sail all the way to Rockfall to find themselves a half-decent shipmaker.

And what of her own fate, and that of her companions? Weak as they were from sickness and lack of sustenance, death and disease could not be far away. They were hardly going to be an enticing sight by the time they made landfall—if they ever did. She looked around through the murk of the hold. Even the prettiest of them, Kitten Soronsen, looked about as alluring as a leprous beggar, with her glorious pale hair lying lank and dirty over her shit-stained shift and her face all red and swollen. Bera, already a gaunt woman, looked as thin as one of Old Ma Hallasen's cats; even Magla Felinsen, with her loud mouth and capacious bosom, was greatly reduced. Their captors were going to have some work to do to make them presentable enough to fetch more than a cantari or two, Katla thought with a certain grim satisfaction. They might go as slaves, but as whores—? Any man desperate enough to desire any of them would have to be as blind as a mole and possessed of no sense of smell—even their captors had stopped pawing at them.

Katla knew a little more about some of the seamier ways of the world than most of the other women on the ship. She knew, for instance, that in the port towns of the Northern Isles, whores did a brisk trade in the alleys and slophouses around the harbor, especially when ships made landfall after several days at sea, but she also knew that for the most part that trade was their own. It was a course some women chose to follow. In Eyra, the money such women earned they pocketed themselves and spent as much or as little of it as they chose. But from what she had heard about practices in the Southern Empire, they were more likely to be herded against their will into some cushioned den and kept there by threat and by violence to service the lecherous and depraved. You would have to be both desperate and indiscriminate, Katla considered, to subject yourself voluntarily to the attentions of most of the men who would seek to pay to tup a woman. She had seen a few inebriated and ill-favored sailors and shoremen in her short life, enough to know that offering herself to them for a few coins would never be her choice of profession. But to be forced into such servitude, compelled to carry out who knew what bizarre perversions in an enemy city's brothel . . . She wasn't a particularly squeamish or moral girl, but she knew she would rather die.

ERNO Hamson sat with his feet dangling over the barnacled stones of the old wall, staring blindly out to sea, trying hard to control his frustration and hoping some ship—any ship—might come by. Pale sunlight struck down through the water in the inner harbor to where half a dozen wrecked boats lay drowned on the seabed, evidence of the raiders' destruction. This exact spot used to be his favorite place in all of Elda, and he had sat here on a hundred previous occasions, but never in circumstances like those in which he now found himself. For a start, this time there was no Katla Aransen at his side, her crabline disappearing into the lazy green waters below them as they bunked off some chore up at the steading. Indeed, he had very little idea of where Katla might be, except that she was not here at Rockfall, where he had so fervently hoped to find her. Above and behind him, the black smoke which had engulfed the steading on the hillside had disappeared, blown away on a stiff north wind which drove high clouds fast across a chill blue sky. The bodies which had lain scattered and defiled about the homefield had been buried, and anything useful which could be salvaged from the remains of the hall had been purloined by the rest of the mercenary troop of which he had until the night before deemed himself, if somewhat reluctantly, a member.

There had appeared to be only three survivors of the raiders' attack on the steading. Two were foreign women who turned out to be whores the Istrians had brought with them from Forent, then discarded. The third was Ferra Bransen. They had found her shut in a fish shed down near the harbor, but for the first two days she had been incoherent with terror, and appeared convinced that Persoa, into whose care she had been given, was one of the raiders, for she cowered away from even his gentlest touch, and wailed if he looked at her. Traumatized as Ferra was, she still could remember nothing useful of the events which occurred, nor any detail of the raiders or their vessel; but it had not taken much speculation to leap to the conclusion that since the shipmaker, Morten

Danson, was no longer to be found on the island, he had been abducted for a second time, and was now bound for the Southern Empire.

Erno had wanted to follow them immediately, of course, and rescue Katla. The stones of the steading were still hot from the fire when they had arrived, and the corpses strewn around the homefield had not yet begun to stink, so the raiders' ship could not have sailed far. He felt sure that with a good wind, and their superior sailing skills, they could overtake them and save the prisoners they had taken. But Mam would hear nothing of his entreaties. "They are vicious marauders, and we do not know how many of them there are. Besides," she had added, showing him the gleaming points of her sharpened teeth, "if they're reduced to stealing Rockfall women, they must be stony broke, and my troop doesn't get itself into dangerous situations without we get well paid for it."

When he had started to shout at her, and call her an iron-whore and a coward, she had simply punched him very hard on the side of the head, thrown him over her shoulder, and deposited him in a pile of hay in the western barn.

He had been left with a lump on his temple the size of a hen's egg. It was difficult to believe that a woman (even one who looked like Mam) could deal him such a blow with her bare fist, but he suspected he could probably count himself lucky that she liked him sufficiently not to run him through with the sword he had accused her of being too gutless to wield and left him to die in his own blood. He doubted there were many men alive in the world who had insulted the mercenary leader; certainly, none alive and still in possession of all their parts.

Joz Bearhand had been the one to revive him with a cupful of cold water, half a chicken, and a flask of stallion's blood. The water Joz had dashed in his face, and when Erno had sat up spluttering and disorientated, the big man had poured a good measure of the bitter liquor down his throat and gifted him with the chicken and a piece of advice. "If you want to see Katla Aransen again, it would be best you do so in this life, and not in some freezing corner of Hel," he had opined sagely. "We're mercenaries, boy. We follow our leader and go wherever the money sends us."

And when Erno had countered that he was not a mercenary, nor would he ever be one, Joz had simply grinned his fearsome grin and thrown a small, well-stuffed pouch up into the darkness. When, on its way down, he had snatched it out of the air beside Erno's ear, it had made a most tantalizing chinking sound, as of several sturdy coins coming to rest.

Erno, caught between a sudden desperate hunger—for the aroma of the cooked bird was teasing his nostrils mercilessly—and sharp curiosity, found himself a moment later asking rather indistinctly, through a vast and juicy mouthful, "What's that for, then?"

But Joz had disappeared into the night, money and all.

Erno frowned. Then the food and wine claimed his attention before these questions took firm hold, and by the time he had wolfed down the rest of the chicken, finished off the flask of stallion's blood, and drowsed off into a restless sleep as a result, night had fallen on Rockfall.

The next morning, when he went to look for the mercenary troop, he found they had gone, leaving him boatless and alone. Now, here he sat, drumming his heels on the seawall, waiting to see if it was by some odd practical joke that they had disappeared, and whether they would come back for him. Failing that, he reasoned, he was going to have to trek the length of the island—on foot, unless he could find and catch one of the Rockfall ponies which had been let loose to run across the wide moorland—and plead for the loan of a ketch from one of the northern shore families, if any there were left alive.

"Thinking of becoming a fishy, are you? Going to swim your way to her?" This was delivered in a bellow, followed by an unnerving cackle.

Erno almost fell in the harbor from shock. He had heard no one approach, had thought himself the only living soul left in the area. He pushed himself to his feet, his hand already drawing his belt knife.

It was an incongruous sight which greeted him: a skinny, bent figure adorned in a half-dozen mismatched skirts, with a fraying blanket for a cloak and wild gray hair reaching almost to the ground. The top of its head was bound with knotted, colored cloths, making it entirely disproportionate to the tiny body above which it bobbed. The oddness did not end there either, for behind the figure trotted a small white goat led along by a long piece of string.

Bemused, he waited for this bizarre entourage to approach.

"Fish or fowl? Foul or fair? What can be done with a handsome little drake left out in the sun? Take it home and stroke its pretty feathers, make its tail into a soup," the figure wheezed.

Erno frowned, not sure what to say to any of this. No one knew what to say to Old Ma Hallasen. She was, and had always been, as mad as a bat. As a child he had crept up on her little bothy by the stream, usually with the other boys, and once, when feeling particularly brave, on his own. Ma Hallasen was a witch. She ate stillborn lambs and pigs' eyes and put spells on animals and women who crossed her. She didn't like children and would chase them with a stick. To a ten-year-old boy, she had seemed a figure straight out of a tale: a troll-woman, or a roving spirit hungry for the flesh of the living. He had been terrified of her. But with the wisdom of his twenty-six years, Erno could understand why an elderly woman living on her own with only her goats and cats for company might not wish to be pestered by local boys throwing pebbles and worse at her when she sat out in her tiny enclosure, bothering no one. He forced his face into a hesitant smile.

Old Ma Hallasen peered at him from under her strange turban and returned a massive, gap-toothed grin. "Ah, my little pigeon, flown home have you, to find the coop all broken down and charry? Never mind, my pretty bird. Come back with Asta and me and we'll make you comfy." She laid a clawlike hand on his arm and gave him a grotesque wink. "Ah, little Erni, little Erno."

Erno took an involuntary step backward and found nothing beneath his heel but air. For a second he rocked precariously on the edge of the seawall, then the crone grabbed him with shocking strength and wrestled him to the ground. The goat nosed at him uncertainly, then started to chew his hair.

"Water is for fishies," she reprimanded him severely, shaking a bony finger at him. "What use are you to me or the Kettle-girl if you drowns like a ratty-beast?"

The Kettle-girl. In one of the ancient dialects, the word for *kettle* was *katla*. He stared at the old woman kneeling over him, and felt a new kind of fear. Perhaps she wasn't as mad as she made out; perhaps, as was reputed, she had the Sight. How else could she possibly know his attachment to Katla Aransen?

He pulled himself out from under the old woman and heaved himself upright, noticing as he did so the state of her attire. Some hems were stained, with mud, and blood and other unidentifiable fluids; two of the odd pieces of fabric were charred and holed. Understanding came to him, alongside a bitter fury. "You stole these clothes!" he shouted at her suddenly. "You took them from the dead women at the steading."

Old Ma Hallasen leaped away with disturbing vigor for one so old. A great waft of smells accompanied this action, among them a strong smell of smoke. "So what if I did? They wasn't no use to them up there!" Her beady black eyes flashed angrily. "They was long past caring."

Not really mad at all, Erno decided. He took her by the arm and was alarmed to find that sticklike appendage as tough and corded as a tree root. "What do you know about what happened here?" he demanded, shaking her a little harder than he'd meant to. "Where was the Master of Rockfall? Where were all the men? Why was no one here to defend the women?"

The old woman screwed her face up and wrenched herself away from him. For a moment he thought she was going to burst into tears, then she pursed her mouth and with tremendous venom expelled a great wad of saliva and mucus onto the stones of the mole where it spattered with a thick, wet slap. "Under the sea with Sur himself; or bound by ice in the roots of Hel, that's where."

Erno rubbed his face in frustration. "Please tell me," he pleaded. "Tell me what has happened here."

The crone gave him a lopsided stare. Then she gathered her goat up under her arm and without another word turned back the way she had come.

Erno followed her, feeling like a fool. What must they look like? he thought suddenly: Old Ma Hallasen bent almost double by age and the weight of the beast she carried, and him tagging along behind as if led by the very string on which she had led her pet.

He knew his way to the old woman's dwelling place, of course. The pathways of Rockfall were as familiar to him as the veins which tracked across the tops of his hands. It was a rundown little place, a turf-covered hummock shrouded by hawthorns and gnarled oaks by the side of Sheepsfoot Stream which came bubbling down out of the heathland at the foot of the cliffs to make a swampy mire out of what might otherwise have been a pretty upland meadow. No one else wanted it, or her. No one knew how old she was: it seemed she had always been on Rockfall, and so the ancient hovel at Sheepsfoot Bog seemed the perfect place for her. Like her, it had been around for as long as anyone could remember; no one could remember to whom it had once belonged. From the outside the place looked as dismal a home as any he could imagine, even with its little pen of multicolored goats and the thin striped cat stretched out on the roof, eyeing him inimically. The hovel rose like a burial mound out of the scabby earth, its door a flayed sealskin stretched across a frame of willowwood. Leather ties held it closed against the weather. There were no windows. A chair fashioned from the stern end of an old rowing boat had been propped in the sun on the south side of the mound, and a large stuffed sack lay atop it with a deep indentation in its center, where the old woman habitually sat. Behind the house, a pair of beehives buzzed with activity.

Why had she brought him here? Erno's heart thumped uncomfortably as he abruptly lost sixteen of his hard-acquired years and became again a curious, frightened boy, peering from the cover of the hawthorn hedge at the witch's hall, hoping and at the same time terrified that she would appear.

As if reading his thoughts, Ma Hallasen dropped the goat, which immediately kicked up its heels, skipped over the makeshift fence, string and all, and ran to join its fellows. Then she turned to face him, her seamed old face alive with glee. She was enjoying his discomfort, Erno realized: she played up to her role.

Then she grabbed him by the hand with those cold, knobbly fingers, undid the mangy leather door thongs, and led him into the mound.

The interior of the house made Erno's jaw drop. From the outside, it appeared less than the size of a fishing boat; but the inside was huge, stretching back into shadows beyond the unsteady light cast by candles ranged around the walls. Someone (surely not the old crone herself?) appeared to have hollowed a great cavern into the hill. Huge timbers, smoothed by age and use, supported the roof, and the floor had been dug deep into the ground to lend the room sufficient height for a tall man like Erno to stand upright without danger of thumping his head. Elaborately worked hangings flared out of the candle light, colors more rich

and varied than Erno had ever seen, for the dyes of the Northern Isles
tended toward the simpler shades of nature—browns and greens and
soft heathery purples and blues; such rare essences which gave these vibrant hues could be afforded only by the wealthiest lords. There was a
large wooden settle spread with furs and heaped high with cushions embroidered sumptuously in reds and golds, a carved table with dragon
claws curled in fabulous detail around balled feet, thick sheepskins on
the floor; a fire roaring away in a decorated iron grate, with an ingen-
ious flue which led who knew where.

When he turned to ask the old woman a dozen questions, he found
them snatched away. She had removed the turban and frayed blanket
and was now in the process of taking off her many skirts. Now Erno felt
real anxiety. Had she brought him here to couple with him? The very
idea was horrifying. He was about to push past her and duck out through
the door, treasures or no treasures, when she blocked his way. She had
stepped out of the last of the stolen rags, and now came at him in a simple plain black shift. Grabbing his arm, she hauled him with her deeper
into the dwelling place.

Beyond the front room lay another, and if the first had made his jaw
drop, this second chamber stole his breath away.

Along one wall, shelves were piled high with scrolls of vellum sealed
with wax and tied with ribbon. Flasks made from some translucent substance lined another shelf. Erno could not help but reach out and pick
one up. It was hard and cool, entirely smooth, and of a wonderful crimson hue. He held it up to the nearest candle, marveling at how the light
played through the object, sending flickering rays of red dancing across
the room. Awed, he replaced it. The old woman laughed. "Haven't you
ever seen a bottle before, Erno?" Her voice had dropped a note and mel-
lowed. "A young rover like you—en't you ever seen glass?"

He shook his head wordlessly and continued into the chamber. Another shelf revealed a pile of long yellow bones, and a skull with a single
oval hole in the forehead, but where the eye sockets should have been in
any ordinary skull, there was nothing but smooth, polished ivory. Erno
shivered and made the sign of Sur's anchor. The hair prickled up and
down his spine. This was a place no living man should enter of his own
free will. The Old Ones might claim his soul . . .

"Don't be afraid, Erno Hamson," said the mad old woman, sounding rather less mad now. "Come with me."

She took him by the hand and he followed her bonelessly.

At the farthest end of the chamber, a mighty sword hung on the wall. Its pommel was of a sheeny, lambent yellow metal which looked as if it might be warm to the touch and ended in the perfectly-formed head of a fox. The guard was intricately inlaid with horn and ivory and bone. The blade was long—Erno knew instinctively that if he were to lift it from the wall and stand it before him, its pommel would stand level with the center of his breastbone—half as long again as his own weapon. It was broad at the hilt and tapered to a fine point, and its entire length was pattern-welded to such a degree that the colors of the iron twisted and curled around and about like fabulous serpents chasing one another through a fog. If he narrowed his eyes, they came almost into focus, then were lost again, as if their forms were a trick of the light, or a rippling out of time. The tang was so elegantly crafted that it brought tears to his eyes: Katla Aransen would have striven all her life to make a sword like this. It had been forged by a master swordmaker and wielded by a hero from some lost age. His hands itched to hold it.

"Take it," the old woman said, but Erno found he could not move. Old Ma Hallasen tsked impatiently. "A blade like that could take a dozen pirates' heads in a single blow," she said gleefully, standing up on her tiptoes and reaching up to where the weapon hung on the wall. The sword was about as big as she was, Erno reckoned, but the crone removed it from its brackets with no apparent effort and seemed to stand as straight and tall as he was once she had it in her hands. When he took it from her grasp, he almost dropped it, surprised by its weight.

"Tee hee, tee hee!" Ma Hallasen cackled, back in character once more.

"I don't understand," he said at last, his fingers moving wonderingly over the pommel. "Where did these things come from? Who are you? Why are you giving me this?"

The crone regarded him with her head on one side, as if she were assessing whether he was worthy of the truth. Then she said, "This sword was forged by Sur's own hand and now belongs to my son. I believe you know him, though he's as old as your great-grandfather would be now."

Erno laughed at the old buzzard's hyperbole. "My great-grandfather has been in the ground these past forty years, but when he breathed his last he had reached the good age of six and eighty!"

Ma Hallasen gave him a delighted open-mouthed grin. It was not a pretty sight. "Ha! You do not believe me, nor have you guessed, then. Ponder on it, my handsome pigeon. The clue is in the sword." And with that she beckoned him to follow once again.

He went puzzledly, staring at the great sword in his hand, but unless he was being extremely stupid, it did not appear to offer any obvious answer. His armbones buzzed from holding it; but whether this was because of its great weight or for something intrinsic in the weapon itself, he could not tell. He concentrated on the feeling for a few seconds, but that only made his head buzz, too. At last he laid the great blade against the wall and looked around, his head clearer now than it had been while he had the weapon in his hand. They were back in the front chamber, and Old Ma Hallasen was opening a wooden chest Erno had not noticed before, and removing from it a large object wrapped in a piece of gorgeously colorful silk. For a moment, Erno's heart stopped dead in his chest and hung there like a cold stone. Scarlet-and-orange flames licked the hems of the cloth: it looked identical to the gift he had bought for Katla Aransen at the Allfair, the shawl for which he had paid all his savings over to a nomad woman. But then he saw there were birds woven into the upper part of the fabric and that, although similar, it was not the same weaving at all. A great and inexplicable sadness came over him. Katla had had the shawl with her the last time he had seen her, on the strand of the Moonfell Plain, before he had done her bidding and left her behind to face her pursuers.

Ma Hallasen whisked away the silk covering. Beneath it stood a globe of polished stone. Kneeling on the floor with greater fluidity than a woman of her advanced age should have, she gestured for Erno to sit on the opposite side of the table from her. She placed one hand on either side of the crystal and peered intently into it. Then she looked up into his eyes. A spectrum of light chased across the sere old skin and hollow planes of her face. She looked otherworldly.

"Think of her, the Kettle-girl," she urged. "I see your heart. It burns as brightly as if it were beating outside your shirt." She lowered her voice conspiratorially, though there was no one but the goats and cats to hear. "And I heard you weep for her up in the homefield as you and the sharp-toothed one walked among the bodies there."

He gasped. "I did not see you there," he said accusingly, as if by some magic she might have been one of the crows he had disturbed, which had fixed him with eyes just as beady, before flapping guilelessly off into the trees.

"People see me only when I wish them to," she said impatiently. "Now think of the Kettle-girl and put your hands on the crystal."

Erno did as he was told. He thought of Katla in the forge, beating out a sword, her face fierce with concentration and sheened with sweat, the red lights from the flames shining on her arm muscles and making a nimbus of her hair. And then suddenly, there she was. Her hair was shorter and her face was thin and there was a huge bruise on her jaw; and she was in some dark place. Other women whom he recognized curved around her into the distorted plane of the crystal. Their hands and feet were clasped by iron shackles.

"She's alive!" he cried, lifting his face to the gaze of the old woman. Immense relief flooded over him, followed immediately by a terrible despair. How would he find her? How could he even leave the island, let alone make his way to Istria?

"Look in the stone again, pretty pigeon."

When he did so, he saw a ship being rowed into Rockfall's harbor. With its sail down in the still air, it took him a few moments to realize what he was looking at. Then a great surge of hope welled up in him. Even with her back to him, he knew Mam's bulk and power. Besides which, it was impossible to mistake the identity of her oar partner, for a great ripple of colored images swirled across his back. Paired with Mam on the oar was her lover and assassin: Persoa, the tattooed man. It was the mercenary ship. They had come back for him!

Without a second thought, he leaped up from the table and strode toward the door.

"A gift spurned is an enemy gained." The old woman's voice was deep and resonant. It stopped him dead in his tracks. For a moment in the tricky light of the howe, it looked as though her hair was a great cloud of gold, that her features were larger, younger, more commanding. She looked less like mad Old Ma Hallasen than— He pushed the thought away; it was ridiculous.

By the time she had pushed herself upright from the table and slowly retrieved the sword from where he had propped it, he had successfully dispelled the disturbing image which had visited him. He laid hands upon the great weapon ruefully. "I am sorry, old woman," he said. "I did not mean to spurn your gift, if gift it is."

"More loan than gift," she croaked, an ancient crone once more, bowed down by the weight of her years and the aching of her old joints. "And you have enemies enough if you follow the course you are set on without adding me to their number." Still she did not let go of the sword. Erno found himself gripping it awkwardly, not sure whether to wrest it from her or wait for her to relinquish it to him. His arms began to shake with the strain of its great weight; but in that fitful light it seemed that hers remained steady as rock. She stared him in the eye. "This sword must find its way back to its maker," she said cryptically, and then cackled as his arms dropped suddenly when she let his hands take the full weight of the weapon. "Or else all will fail."

Then she hobbled into the darkness at the back of the chamber and merged into the gloom as if walking into a past time where he could not follow.

Blinking against the shock of the daylight outside, and bemused by his strange encounter and even stranger surmisings, Erno Hamson shouldered the great weapon and turned his footsteps down the path toward the harbor, feeling as if some distinct but undeserved doom had settled itself upon him. Quite how he would answer questions about the provenance of the sword, he did not know. By the time he had made his way to the sea wall, where the mercenaries were waiting, his mind was still an unhelpful blank. So he said nothing at all, though they all stared at him and the sword curiously, and when Joz Bearhand ran his hands appreciatively over the golden hilt and pommel, mumbled something about "an heirloom," which was as close to the truth as he could manage without opening himself to more difficult discussions. That night, as they set sail for the southern continent in pursuit of the raiders' ship, he slept with the weapon beside him, wrapped in his cloak, and dreamed about casting it into the ocean before the fate the old woman had spoken of could possibly attach itself to him, but in the morning it was still safely wrapped and he found he could not part with it. Besides, as Mam pointed out with her usual pragmatism, if the money which Margan Rolfson had pressed upon them for the rescue of their dearly beloved sister Bera and her daughter Katla, and the few silvers they had collected around the island from the other prisoners' relatives, ran out before they could accomplish the task, they could always sell the thing.

Erno did not respond by saying that selling the sword would be impossible, and Mam did not add that Margan had taken her aside and made her swear to put the women out of their misery by whatever means afforded to her if they had been too cruelly misused by their captors or others by the time the troop reached them.

And so each held to the secret things they knew as the ship sailed south.

5

The Master

ARAN Aranson had heard how sailors lost in arctic regions became prone to hallucination, their eyes and minds mazed by cold, by exhaustion, and by the neverending vistas of ice and air and ocean all melding together into a mutable, undependable landscape. They saw icebergs floating above the surface of the water like massive hovering palaces, fabulous castles towering hundreds of feet into the sky. Some saw the outline of their home islands situated in a new and impossible geography; others their wives or daughters limned by strange polar lights. Many of these men lost their wits entirely and were to be found muttering into their ale in seaport inns, wrapped about by this other, more miraculous world, a world they preferred not to relinquish. Unseeing, their eyes might skim past you to peer unnervingly over your left shoulder, their seamed old faces might break into a smile of welcome; but if you turned to look for the newcomer who had generated this ecstatic welcome, most likely there would be no one there.

Staring at the apparition now floating toward him, Aran felt himself in danger of imminent danger of joining their mad ranks.

To his snow-hazed eyes, the figure looked to be a woman arrayed in robes which rippled and flowed like a sea, and, like a sea, her long hair undulated in silver-gold waves around her bright face. Electricity crackled in the air between the two of them, igniting suddenly into streams of pale fire. Aran felt it play about his skull, felt an eerie tingling lift the hair on his head, then down his neck and spine. His eyes, when he closed them, replayed crazed images in harsh zigzagging configurations so that he could find no respite from them.

To Urse's eyes, the figure was male: an old, old man with a bitter cast of expression and a thousand wrinkles dragging down his features into a myriad of tiny sagging folds which bespoke not only advanced age, but also a vast and uncontainable disappointment with the world.

Fent Aranson said and saw nothing; but in the moment in which the apparition materialized, he twisted once on his bearer's back and gave voice to a small, inchoate cry.

The blue fire surrounding the figure crackled and darted, then abruptly dispersed out into the night air, leaving behind only the faintest luminescence. Then the apparition stilled and it sank slowly to the ground.

"Welcome," it said, and to Aran the word was redolent of summer fields and ripe grain, of harvest time and willing women; of warmth and comfort and the nostalgia of his lost youth. To Urse One Ear, however, it was the utterance of a trickster, a quavery voice striving for reassurance. "Welcome to the hidden stronghold at the tip of the world. Welcome to Sanctuary."

Aran Aranson felt his knees give way. He sank to the ground as if the last of his strength had failed him now that his objective was attained. It was Urse who demanded, "What sort of man are you that you appear to us in this bizarre manner, rather than striding out on your own two feet?"

At this, Aran called to the giant, "What are you saying?" And even as he asked this, the image came clearly to his mind of the woman he had glimpsed at the Allfair the last summer, the one sitting quietly behind the mapmaker's stall, with a sheet of shining hair and those hypnotic sea-green eyes, full of come-hither promise. Blood rushed to several chilled and forgotten parts of his anatomy. His pulse quickened. Embarrassed in case his discomfiture should suddenly show itself in no uncertain fashion, he turned away from the apparition to confront Urse One Ear, his face contorted. "How can you be so unmannerly to such a gracious lady?"

Urse laughed, showing his snaggle teeth. "Lady? This is no lady. The ice must have blinded you. It is a venerable old man who seems to be carrying a world of trouble on his shoulders." He frowned. "But even if your eyes were mistaken, surely your ears can tell the difference between the cracked and reedy voice of a graybeard and a lady's soft tones?"

Aran felt the lust which had infused his veins turning to blind fury. He took a step toward the giant, his hands balled. "Put down my son and put up your fists, Urse One Ear; and I shall even up your features for your insulting behavior!"

"No!"

This word of command flew through the air between them to hang like an invisible shield, and to Aran Aranson it was a mellifluous pleading which could not help but melt his anger, while to Urse it was an order he had no choice but to obey.

As unmoving as the frozen landscape around them, the two men stood facing each other, while the third lay slumped and insensate. The Master hovered around this tableau, scratching his beard. Both men were supposed to be visited by the same image—that of the most alluring of women: the Rosa Eldi, Rose of the World, whose gaze could fell a man with desire and bind him to her will. He shook his head. Was it his age, or the long sleep he had endured which was diminishing his powers so? With both men rendered temporarily inert as stone, the Master canceled the flying glamour and came down to the ground with a thud, his knees buckling with the sudden impact. Even such simple magics were becoming problematic. Something in the potion Virelai had administered must have drastically weakened his abilities that it took such effort to maintain a miserably basic deception. What if the effects were progressive? What if his capabilities should deteriorate further? He shuddered. He should never have filled the damned cat with his spellcraft; but how could he ever have guessed that his inept apprentice should have the gall and the wit to carry out such an audacious plan? He cursed again his lack of foresight and judgment, that he had created his own downfall. Had he bothered to scry his own future just once, he might have averted the disaster which had befallen him, would never have had to resort to such convoluted means of regaining what should never in the first place have been lost.

The Master shook his head, and his gray, unkempt locks tumbled about his shoulders in just the fashion Urse One Ear had so truly perceived. He walked between the two still figures and peered up into the big man's mangled face. Even bowed beneath the weight of the boy, this monster towered over him.

He was no beauty, and probably never would have been even had the grim accident which had befallen him never taken the ear and made such a hash of his cheek and jaw. The Master smiled with satisfaction. The Giant, without a doubt.

He turned his attention to the man called Aran Aranson. This man looked like one of the heroes of old, Rahe thought, with his sharp cheekbones and sunken, fanatical eyes; with his tangled black hair, his gray-shot beard and jutting chin; his single great eyebrow running in a furious dark line across a forehead as dark as seasoned oak. Even the salt-stained sealskins and ratty furs could not disguise his athletic build; and even the ravages of the journey which had brought him from the relative comforts of his island farm to this fabled land—through the worst of the world's elemental forces, through weeks of poor fare and bad sleep, through exhaustion, fear, and despair—could not extinguish the fire that burned within him: a fire fueled by ambition, a craving for wild experience, for things and places unseen by other men. Rahe could smell it on him like a glamour. He sniffed. A vague scent of musk and cinnamon came to him, though it was so cold that even the stink of a rotting beast or a frightened man's sweat left little telltale trace.

With a sure hand he plundered the warmth beneath Aran's sealskin jerkin. Between the skin—warm, hairy, the heartbeat a slow, sure pulsing thud—and the linen tunic the Eyran wore beneath the outer layers, Rahe found what he was seeking. Sealed in a soft leather pouch tied closed with a knotted thong was a roll of parchment, creased and flaking from overuse. With fingers trembling as much from fury as anticipation, Rahe unrolled this artifact, clutching it between fingerpads gone white from applied pressure as any effect of the cold.

It was elegantly done, this so-called map, he had to admit. At first glance it looked authentic—accurate and carefully drawn by someone who knew the contours of the coastlines familiar to the seafaring men of the Northern Isles—and had been expertly antiqued by a touch of the

Aging Spell he had himself stowed in Bëte, having no immediate use for it himself. That was the musk—he would recognize that wretched creature's odor anywhere. The spice smell he put down to the maker's own signature: rot-sweet and musty.

He traced the swathe of white space in the northernmost quarter of the map with the invented word *isenfelt* scrawled across it in his faithless apprentice's best calligraphy hand. "Icefields" indeed—or rather "ice" plus an old word for "pastures," but in a tongue so ancient no such concept could possibly have existed—for in those days there had been no kingdom of ice in this world, no floes and bergs, no uncrossable ocean. Those failures of climate had come much later to Elda, when the care of the world had been neglected, allowing it to fall into the disrepair which had allowed him to create this hidden island, indicated by the traitor's hand beneath the heart of a gorgeously-drawn windrose in the far righthand corner, a word beginning "Sanct"—

The Master's lip curled. Virelai. The little runt! The ignominy of the situation was unbearable: the greatest mage in the world of Elda laid low by one of his own spells which had been stolen and applied by his lowly and despised apprentice.

He clutched the map tighter, felt the greed and uncertainty eat into him. Visions of yellow metal, of glinting ores flashed behind the orbits of his eyes. Gold! Ah, yes. He had glimpsed it before, but now he saw clearly. Gold: that was the draw. Sanctuary's fabled treasure halls. Virelai had promised the adventurers gold to sail through unknown horrors to Sanctuary. He could imagine the scene at the Allfair, all the greedy shipowners crowding around—or, no—Virelai would have to have seen them one by one, have to have made each man feel special, singled out for glory. Entrusted with a secret mission, which no other must know about for fear of them beating him to the prize. *All you need to do is remove the old man, help yourselves to his treasures, a simple task.* Remove the old man.

The Master laughed, and the sound ricocheted off the ice to echo crazily around them, the sound of a thousand madmen enjoying a fine jest. *Poor Virelai,* he thought, for the first time feeling a tinge of pity, *he must have believed the whole story about the geas and the demons, or he would surely have killed me himself!* It was a fine jest indeed, a jest he had himself made possible and engendered. And so Virelai, in fear for his worthless, nonexistent life, had created—and rather well—these fake maps and promised wealth beyond measure to the men who would take on flood and storm, ice and terror, in return for murdering a weak and weaponless old man and stealing his gold!

The only gold in all of Sanctuary was buried deep in the tunnels on the stronghold: tiny outcroppings of the stuff, glittering away in the seams of rock exposed in those dark corridors, a stuff as worthless as Virelai's putrid soul—iron pyrites: fool's gold; and here before him the very fool who had survived every pitfall thrown in his way for the privilege of helping himself to a heap of sham ore.

When first he had deduced the magic of the maps, it had made him furious and vengeful. Now the Master laughed with every breath of air in his lungs, a massive, wholehearted laugh that shattered icicles a thousand feet away and felled seabirds drifting on thermals high above the cliffs. Men were such stupid, faithless creatures. Show them a glimpse of easy wealth and they would bargain body and soul, wife and child and lifelong comrades to its lure. His own dreams had been greater by far, and his achievements dwarfed their petty imaginations as a snow bear dwarfs an ant.

He thought of his snow bear now as he examined the third member of this ragtag expedition. It had been one of his better simulacra, he thought, though he had never meant it to take the boy's hand. Madman though he was, the lad would surely require two to do the job he had in mind for him. That was the trouble with the already-living. They still carried some spark of self-will with them that might show itself at some inopportune moment, triggered by some long-buried natural instinct. It really was most inconvenient that the bear had reacted in such a way. He pondered on this for a few moments, lifting the boy's sealskin hood away from his flaming red hair, perusing the ice-pale skin and delicate features beneath, peeling the stained and frozen wrappings from the cauterized stump. Near death, but still a flame of life burned brightly at his core. The remarkable thing about these poor, frail beings was that they were unable to perceive the futility of their tiny existences; they struggled to survive in even the most unpromising circumstances. They endured—what? thirty, forty, sixty years, if they were lucky enough not to succumb to sickness or bad weather, lack of food, or violence. They barely had time to scratch the surface of the world before being taken back into it to nourish the next round of living things. And yet still they clung to that tiny, useless scrap of life force, as if their existences were in some unfathomable way significant, meaningful, valuable.

The Master shook his head. He had come such a long way from his own origins that it was hard to empathize with the destiny of such as these.

The Madman, the Giant, and the Fool.

He lifted his spell of stillness and watched as the Giant and the Fool stepped puzzledly back from one another. Then he shed his glamour and allowed the one to see him as in truth he was—as the other had already perceived him—as a man aged beyond all realms of possibility, with iron-gray hair which flowed in tangles over his shoulders and down his back, a beard stained with all manner of fluids and foodstuffs, dressed in a long blue robe with a ragged hem, and a pair of tapestried slippers through the toe of one of which protruded a horny nail as yellow as a ram's eye.

"Come with me," he said, cocking a finger at them, and the warmth of his tone belied the magical command which he embedded in the words. Even as he spoke, they found their feet shuffling toward him, and all other thoughts fleeing their heads. "Come into my home and warm your bones, for it is as cold as sin out here. Come with me into Sanctuary and you shall eat your fill of the juiciest meats and the sweetest pastries, and drink mulled wine and strong ales."

And so Aran Aranson, erstwhile Master of Rockfall, his sole surviving son Fent Aranson, and Urse One Ear of Tam Fox's mumming troupe followed the strange figure who had appeared before them in the midst of the arctic wilderness through a surreal garden of ice, replete with sculpted statues and towering white pillars, elegant curving stairways and frozen lakes, into the confines of the stronghold of ice at the top of the world known in legend as Sanctuary.

6

The Heir to the Northern Isles

"**S**UCH eyes: did you ever see such eyes?"

The King of Eyra peered wonderingly into the crib, then turned to regard his lady wife as she sat on the edge of their bed after her evening bath, one slim white shoulder slipping seductively out of her gleaming ermine-trimmed robe.

"I swear they are purple. Such a color I have never seen in any child of our line; though the line of the brow is surely kingly. And he watches me so steadily, so boldly: he is surely a warrior born. He is a marvel, my love, a marvel! And so are you."

Ravn Asharson's own flint-gray eyes were alight with fervor, but it was a fervor born of pride as a parent, rather than out of desire for her. Once more, the Rosa Eldi felt a little cold shiver inside her. Ravn's intense involvement with the child drew his attention away from her, and thus she felt less loved. The Queen of the Northern Isles shifted her position an iota and the robe dropped lower, revealing the curve of one glorious breast to remind him of his priorities.

"He is certainly a very lusty and noisy babe."

She could barely stifle the edge that came into her voice. The baby seemed to command Ravn Asharson's adoration more than she did even when she exerted her will upon him. She never should have withdrawn the blanket of sorcery in which she had wrapped the King of Eyra all these long months. It had started as an experiment designed to test the extent of his love for her, and for a while nothing had seemed to change. He remained obsessed, his eyes seeking her when he could not be near her, his hands upon her whenever he was. But once the child was born, everything was different. If she had thought the behavior Ravn had displayed toward her before the birth was love, seeing the way he was with the child had made her reassess her whole world. Perhaps it was the way his expression changed when he looked upon little Ulf; as if someone had lit a sconce behind his eyes so that the hard planes of his face softened and affection shone out of him. Seeing him like that caused her physical pain: pain of loss, pain of abandonment. Power, which had seemed to be flooding back to her, now ebbed away.

And yet the child owned not the least part of her or of Ravn in its making; not even in one finger of its tightly-curled fist.

Mastering her rising panic, as she was slowly learning to do, she added more smoothly, "Truly, he is a fine heir to your throne, my love, a child of whom you can be truly proud."

Still he did not look up, but reached into the cot and stroked little Wulf's face with a finger far gentler than any he had laid on her. For a moment she felt a terrible despair. She—who could divert rivers with a thought, could call life from the frost-bound earth, heal a dying animal—could yet not win this battle for a mortal man's attention over a mewling child.

Something ignited in her then. Before she knew it, she had uttered his name in a tone of command he was powerless to ignore.

"Ravn!"

At once, his head came up and swiveled in her direction and she cast him a glance lustrous with sorcery from beneath her thick black lashes. She watched the swift dilation of his pupils, making his already dark gaze blackly intense. Holding that gaze so that all his thoughts of the babe fled away, she patted the pelt-covered bed beside her, and when he joined her there—walking like a man in a dream—she covered his mouth with her own. From that moment on, he was defenseless. She owned him body and soul, and with each movement of her body, reminded him of this both liminally and subliminally. She knew he would dream of her even as he slipped from her, desire slaked and flesh exhausted; she bound him to her that tightly. Such exertions of magic made her feel both more and less than she was: a powerful sorceress but also a woman who could barely command the attention of her own husband.

As it was, even without the child, she saw less and less of Ravn, for he was often bound up with councils and stratagems, summoned by his clamoring lords and chieftains to sit endlessly around chart-strewn tables, discussing war. What did she care for such matters? It did not touch her heart, brought no threat, except this dull loss of her husband's presence. She could sense the great expanse of the Northern Ocean which separated this rocky outpost from the distant shores of Istria. The beginnings of it could be glimpsed below the stout castle, beyond the harbor's sentinel towers and the sorcerous traps which lay beneath the dark sea there. When she reached out to it with her mind, all she felt was a vast and limitless void, for little moved upon its treacherous waters. No army could cross that ocean without her knowing it: yet she hugged that knowledge to herself and waited for the time to share it with her love.

She had other concerns to absorb her time. Maintaining the veils of illusion around the child and its nurse required her effort by day and night, more so now that the seither had gone. Festrin One Eye had vanished as mysteriously as she had come, and none had seen her leave. After the safe birth of the babe and the formal acceptance of the court of the little red squalling thing as the heir to the Northern Isles, the seither had woven yet another set of mazing spells around the king, his skeptical old mother, the Lady Auda, and all his scheming enemies. She had even tried to stifle the natural mother's memory of her ties to the creature, first with a decoction of herbs designed to soothe away the distress of traumatic events; and when that did not work, with a strong enchantment.

She had left the Rosa Eldi to maze the eyes of her beloved. There was, as she pointed out, no one better equipped to address *that* problem.

But after the seither had gone, her influence had waned, and only a seven-night later, the Rosa Eldi had heard two ladies of the court discussing her relationship with the child in less than favorable terms.

"You never see her cradle it," one said.

"Poor little thing," acceded the other—a towheaded woman with the massive figure which suggested she had brought a longship crew into the world in her time. She shot a swift glance across the flame-lit room at the subject of their conversation, apparently fully engaged with filling her husband's wine cup. "No maternal instinct, that one."

Her companion had nodded, thinking her position out of the pale queen's view, but the Rosa Eldi had a fine awareness of her surroundings. She could see and hear with as great an acuity as any feline. She knew the first speaker as Erol Bardson's daughter, the one Ravn had spurned at the Gathering on the Moonfell Plain. She was a sharp-featured girl, sharp-tongued, too.

"I have heard of mothers who cannot love their offspring," the older woman went on. "Particularly if the birth was hard."

"But she spawned the child in moments!" the other spat triumphantly. She lowered her voice, "Or so they say. . . ."

The pause had drawn itself out into greater significance than any words could offer. Then the matronly woman said, "Queen Auda does not believe the child is hers, you know."

"You'd better not let the nomad woman hear you call her that, nor the king either," her friend said hastily. Then, intrigued: "So, whose can it be, then?"

The other shrugged.

"The nurse is a pretty thing," the Erolsen girl mused, "and very foreign-looking, too. And they do say Ravn would not choose himself an Eyran bride at the Allfair because he had had his fill of northern women."

"Like yourself, you mean, my dear."

She gave the matron a keen look, her dark eyes like pebbles. "You are well aware of why he would not take me," she said angrily, a flush starting on her cheek.

The large woman smiled knowingly, then patted her on the hand. "Of course, my dear: your father. Of course. But now you say it, I wouldn't be surprised. He always had a prodigious appetite for female flesh, our Ravn. How long could such a wan creature like our new queen think to contain the lusts of the Stallion of the North?"

"There is no substance to her. Hold her up to the light and I reckon you could see right through her," the girl said spitefully.

"Perhaps she is just a glamour, a spirit sent by the south to suck the very soul from our king, rendering him as helpless as that poor babe. And then they will sail upon us and put us all to the sword. So Auda says, and that woman has seen much of war and sorcery."

This exchange confirmed for the Rosa Eldi that not only had the seither's enchantments lost their force, and that the Lady Auda was proving as hostile as ever before, but also that the suspicion with which she was regarded had spread far and wide through her new home. And it planted another, more poisonous, seed in her mind, too.

That mere gossipmongers should conjecture about the provenance of the child was distressing enough, but that they should make such ignorant judgments of her nature was insupportable.

Cradling her sleeping husband as he lay exhausted upon her breast, she cast her mind back to all she could remember.

First, and for a very long time, there had been nothing but a void in her memory, an absence of self. Such, perhaps, had been necessary for survival when she had lived as a slave, trapped in the chamber of the mage in his ice castle, then in the hands of his strange apprentice, who had sold her body over and over again, to tens, maybe hundreds, of men, during their travels. But even that time had surely been easier to bear than this, with its disturbing dreams and bewildering emotions.

Before she had departed, Festrin had tried to help with the dreams the Rosa Eldi suffered, those sudden flashes of bizarre places and folk and snatches of narrative, as of distant song, which made daily and nightly incursions into her skull. In the day the seither had dosed the queen with worm-root and in the evenings with sun's-eye, and for a while the dreams had receded into some deep, lost part of her so that, to the eye of others, it seemed that she dozed; though the Rosa Eldi could never remember a time when she had truly been in any state which could be called sleep. These stolen moments of oblivion she could pass off as tiredness caused by the greedy demands of the child, and no one questioned her. But the worm-root left her dry in the mouth and with strange pains in her limbs, and the sun's-eye made her feel leaden and barely alive, and so eventually she had had to stay Festrin's hand and try to deal with the dreams as best she could.

Once or twice she had felt some force enter her to meld with the shreds of a dream so that she was gripped by the sudden belief that she might rise from where she sat, apparently meek and quiet, and grow until she towered over Halbo's great stronghold, and stepping over its fortified, crenellated walls, bearing all their scars of old battles and the lichens of a thousand years, as if they were no more than a child's toy, stride—vast and unassailable—out of this chilly kingdom, with its foolish king and wailing heir, its rough lords and chattering courtiers, its rocky promontories and wet, gray skies—out through the wide ocean, across another continent filled with annoying, insectlike folk running here and there on their unfathomable errands, their heads stuffed with their tiny, idiotic concerns, to a place where bright sun shone on pantiled roofs and predatory birds with massive outstretched wings glided on hot air currents high above golden towers, where another being—equally vast and unknowable, complex and powerful—awaited her return.

She found herself drifting to this place in her mind now. When she closed her eyes, she could almost feel the heat of the sun on her skin—a warmth not felt in these harsh climes; smell some heavy fragrance, as of flowers far more generous in size and scent than any that grew this far north in the world. It was an ancient place: history permeated the golden stone of the buildings around her, investing every brick in every wall, every plank in every door, every trodden paviour in the road with significance born of great events; and, more than any of these things, it felt like home. But somehow it withheld itself from her, it kept its secrets. And something in her recognized that wherever this golden place might be—if it even existed as anything other than a dream—it must be a long way away from Eyra, and so she might never visit it. And that caused her such sorrow it was almost a physical pain.

The baby's meaty wail burst into the night air and continued at full bore until the chamber seemed stuffed with noise. The sound broke into her reverie. It was so disorientating that for a moment she thought it must have broken from her own lips. Gone from sleep to wakefulness in a second, Ravn sat bolt upright, alert as a mother cat.

"Something ails him!" he cried, clutching his wife by the arm so hard that she felt each of his fingertips as a separate pressure. "He is unwell."

Distracted from her idyll, the Rosa Eldi pulled away from him. "It is nothing. He is hungry," she said, then added sharply, "again."

Rising from the bed, she went to the inner door of the bedchamber, opened it quietly, and signaled to the woman seated beyond.

This figure rose at once to her command and moved silently into the royal bedchamber, her eyes averted.

She was short and sleekly dark, the girl known as Leta Gullwing, a slave rescued from the Istrians by merchants, was the tale Festrin had put around, who had lost the child she was bearing to stillbirth, leaving her with milk to spare. The queen had taken pity on the poor child, it was said, had become quite fond of her—another stranger in a strange land—and had made her the baby's wet nurse. It was just close enough to the truth to seem plausible.

SHE was a pretty thing, Ravn thought assessingly, with her black hair and doe eyes and that soft and rounded body. In an earlier life he would surely have bedded her by now and discovered for himself all the fragrant, secret curves he suspected lay beneath the demure robe she wore, though in the presence of his wife—so lithe and svelte, so long-limbed and graceful—she seemed just a little coarse and graceless. Not that that would ever have put him off in those lusty days of yore. When you inhabit an island kingdom possessed of limited bloodstocks, it is necessary to lower your standards from time to time. Besides, he had often found it invigorating to punctuate rich fare with plain. This foreign girl intrigued him more than he would have cared to admit. Perhaps it was her genuine care for their baby which stirred him so. He watched her now as she took the child from his cot and encircled him in her arms, then with a practiced hand slipped one of her lush breasts—its aureola so dark against her olive skin that in the half-light it looked almost black—from beneath the folds of her shift and presented it to the child's howling mouth. At once, two things happened. The baby's wail dissipated to a loud sucking noise, and Ravn experienced a pleasant flutter of sensation in his lower abdomen. A moment later, his cock was as stiff as a stick.

Embarrassed, the King of the Northern Isles clutched the bed linen close to suppress the offending item, but if his wife noticed his discomfiture, she made no sign of it. Regretfully, he drew his eyes away from the sight of the southern girl nursing his heir and concentrated his gaze on the long, elegant curve of the Rosa Eldi's back and the sheaf of silver-gold hair cascading down to the faint rise in the ermine-trimmed robe which denoted her slim buttocks, and was surprised to discern in himself a faint disappointment, an infinitesimal lessening of his desire for his wife.

Ravn was not a man made for fidelity. He had never been faithful to one woman for so long. Indeed, he thought, turning this thought over slowly in his head, he had never before been faithful to any woman. A sudden flare of resentment billowed up inside him. He was the king, for Sur's sake, and known affectionately by many of his subjects as the Stallion of the North. Why should he not continue to have his choice of bedmates, wife or no wife? If he wanted to tup the nursemaid, why should he not do so, now that he had done his duty and sired an heir? His forebears had certainly taken their pleasures where they pleased. Why, it was even rumored that Erol Bardson was somewhat closer to him in relationship than mere cousin . . . His grandfather had strewn bastards all over the Northern Isles, and he had been hailed for his remarkable potency rather than lambasted for a fickle nature. He was about to open his mouth to speak some of what was on his mind when the Rose of the World turned to face him.

Her eyes—as green as malachite and fringed with lashes of lustrous black, a wonder in themselves, considering the silvery gold of the hair on her head, and entire lack elsewhere—were lambent in her perfect face. Her gaze was so piercing that it was as if she could shine those bright orbits into the depths of his skull and illuminate every dark crevice therein. He felt distinctly uncomfortable, then hot with shame. Then the heat intensified. All at once the unworthy thoughts fled away from him—moths annihilated in the flame of his wife's regard—and his erection surged out from under him. He watched her mesmeric gaze drop and her lips curve into the most beatific smile.

"Ah," she said, and her voice was as low and reassuring as the tide lapping at a gentle shore. "I see I have a wife's duty to attend to."

She took three steps towards the bed, reached out, and cupped the King's balls with one smooth, cool hand. Ravn's cock—as if suddenly touched by lightning—leaped and bobbed at her touch. Then she looked back over her shoulder to where Leta Gullwing, oblivious to the sexual theater taking place only steps away from her, gave suck to the child. "Take the boy away," the Rosa Eldi said softly.

"I will take your son into my room, madam," Leta said quietly.

Then she opened the door to the adjoining chamber and slipped through it into the candle-lit darkness beyond.

Only the most subtle of observers might have noticed the very slight emphasis she had placed on two of those words.

YOUR son, she thought bitterly, closing the door behind her softly. *Your son, indeed.*

She turned to regard the baby lying swaddled in his sheepskin wrap upon his cot and Ulf gazed back at her soundlessly out of the soft white cloud of wool, a tiny dribble of milk bubbling from the side of his mouth.

How has it come to this, Leta Gullwing thought, *that I have given away my son, the only thing I seem to have in all the world that I could call my own, to be the heir to a strange king in a strange land, claimed by a woman whose expression changes not one whit when she regards him, while every whimper he makes tears my heart? And I cannot even remember how any of this sad tale came to pass.*

She rubbed her hand across her face in a gesture both of exhaustion and resignation. It had happened, and now she was caught inextricably in the web, like a fly whose futile struggle had ended. She could not flee alone, and she could not abandon her son; she had nothing she could trade for passage from this island, and there was nowhere, anyway, she could think to flee to.

When dark despair swept over her, as it did so often, little Ulf was her only consolation. Leaning over the cot now, she reached a hand out to touch the tiny boy, and quick as a flash he grabbed two of her fingers in a tight grip and carried them to his mouth, where he stuffed them between his bony little gums and sucked on them noisily, fixing her all the while with those disturbing purple eyes as if daring her to withdraw them. *Where on Elda had those eyes come from?* she wondered, as she always did. They certainly did not come from his mother, for her own eyes were the smooth deep brown of polished wood. But just who the child's father was remained a mystery to her. She could remember so little of her life before she came to this place, it was almost as if she had had no life. But the baby was very tangible evidence of some other existence, and her own looks and limited understanding of the guttural Eyran tongue clearly indicated she was not from the Northern Isles. Sometimes when she dreamed, she dreamed of a place in which the harsh light gave every shadow a sharply defined edge, where the air was hot and dry, where the buildings were made from a different stone to the uncompromising gray of the granite of these islands, where women floated past like apparitions, draped in diaphonous robes. Sometimes she dreamed of a dark-skinned man with a jutting black beard whose eyes sparked fire at her. Sometimes she dreamed that the thongs of a whip curled around her back, leaving behind painful welts and intense fury and she would wake with her heart hammering and her fists clenched.

After these dreams, two words would stay with her: two pretty, foreign-sounding words for which she knew no meaning at all. They slipped sideways in her head, sliding back down into her unconscious mind like silver fish in a black sea. The harder she pursued them, the deeper they dived.

Sudden silence from the cot; then a release of pressure. Ulf had fallen asleep at last. Leta withdrew her wet fingers and wiped them quickly on her shift, where they left little gleaming trails, like a snail's path. Undressing swiftly, she climbed into her own small bed, pulled the coarse blanket up over her hunched shoulders and tried to ignore the rising sounds of passion from the next room.

When she felt most alone, as she did now, she liked to imagine herself lying in the arms of a man who would cherish her against all the ills of the world. If she closed her eyes and concentrated, she could feel the hard muscles of his upper arm bunched beneath the nape of her neck, his warm breath on her cheek, his protective hand splayed across her hip. Between them, their baby slept contentedly, his brow as smooth and untroubled as a seawashed stone. *Nothing can touch you. Nothing can harm you. No one can take your child from you,* he would promise, over and over, until she fell asleep.

Drifting into the doze that presaged slumber, she grasped her pillow tightly. "Ravn," she whispered. "Oh, Ravn."

7

Katla

THE day before *The Rose of Cera* made landfall, two of the raiders staggered down into the hold with a barrel of saltwater which they set down with such a thud that a large portion of its contents sloshed over the side, drenching Thin Hildi from top to toe so that she began shrieking hysterically until the third—a man with a bundle of rags under his arm, and whose face seemed set in a permanent sneer—struck her so hard across the face with his free hand that her head snapped back on her neck like a broken daffodil.

One of the barrel carriers addressed something to the rags bearer in the hissing southern tongue, his face screwed up in obvious disapproval. Then he said slowly and with great emphasis in the Old Tongue so that all the women could hear and understand him: "Bastido said not to mark the merchandise."

"This?" The sneering man grabbed Hildi by the hair and wrenched her face into view. "Merchandise?" His face twisted into a mocking grimace. "Who in all of Falla's green and pleasant world would pay for *this?*"

Thin Hildi had never been what one might call a pretty girl, that much was true. She had earned her nickname easily enough at home in Rockfall even before being subjected to the privations of this voyage, but now, Katla thought, her shackled hands bunching into powerless fists,

Hildi's skinniness was pronounced—her face as peaky and gaunt as an old spinster's, her shoulder blades, jerking wretchedly with her racking sobs, like plucked chicken wings. It was indeed hard to see how she would command any price on a slave block. Fury swept through Katla yet again at the indignity of their situation.

"Leave her alone, you bastard!" she shouted in Eyran, dragging uselessly at her chains. The words were blasting through the close air of the hold before there was any chance for her to consider the wisdom of this outburst, but that was Katla through and through. A few seconds later, and after brief consideration, she reiterated—this time in the carefully enunciated common language: "Take your hands off her, you son of a whore!"

The sneering man pushed Thin Hildi away from him with the utmost contempt and stared at the filthy little creature who had had the temerity to insult him—*him*, Gasto Costan, free man of Forent Town, upholder of Falla's justice, envy of his neighbors for his fine villa (or rather, his brother's fine villa until, well he didn't like to recall the unpleasant circumstances of his good fortune . . .). No one insulted Gasto Costan and lived to tell the tale.

The man who had hit Thin Hildi had a slight cast to one eye, Katla noted, which in addition to his generally unprepossessing appearance made him look both shifty and lecherous. Even his fellows seemed to regard him with distaste. She watched one of them shoot the sneering man an unfriendly glance before turning on his heel and heading back up the steps to cleaner air abovedecks. The other, a gigantic man with a flattened nose which bespoke too many bare-knuckle fights, looked on uncomprehending. But Katla had a pretty good idea of what was coming next.

The sneer turned into an unpleasant grin. Then the man called Gasto Costan started to pick his away among the dumbstruck women toward her. "Give me the key, Agen," he called back to the big man. "I have plans for this one."

Reaching Katla, he squatted and looked her up and down with his head on one side, just like a vulture deciding which morsel of living flesh to prise out of its prey first. Katla glared at him with a pugnacious look in her eye, a look which promised violence and murder if only her wrists were unchained—a look which turned to outrage as he shot out a hand to fumble at her tunic. He managed to get one of her small breasts in a painful grasp, then she battered at his hands with the shackles, her whole body galvanized by repulsion. But all he did was laugh loudly, and shout back to the other raider, "Hurry up with that key, idiot!"

The giant obviously held a lesser rank than the sneering man, for after hesitating, he did as he was told and began to shamble across the hold, past the sprawling form of Thin Hildi, stepping awkwardly over shackled legs and piles of filth. There was a pair of rusty iron keys at his belt on a simple split loop, but it seemed to take him forever to extract them from this contraption and give them into the impatient hands of his superior. The first was no fit, but the second released Katla's shackles into the staple of iron embedded in the deck. Gasto Costan hauled her upright and held her at arm's length.

"With a bit of a wash, she'll be halfway decent," he declared, leering at Katla's bruised and grubby form. He asked, almost confidingly, "How would you like to worship the Goddess with me, little firehead? With hair that color I bet you'll make a fine initiate into Falla's mysteries."

Katla frowned. She had no exact understanding of his words, but she could have a pretty good guess at the context. With supreme effort she gathered what tiny amount of saliva she could summon from her dry throat and when he leaned in as if to kiss her, spat it with horrible accuracy right into the middle of his sneer. It was hard not to feel true satisfaction at his horror-struck reaction, even though she knew she had hardly improved her chances to avoid whatever vile fate he had in mind for her.

"Get away from my daughter, you pig!"

Bera Rolfsen strained at her shackles so that the chains came taut and bit into what little flesh remained on her limbs.

Now all the women joined in, yelling in their native tongue so that the hold was stuffed with a raucous hubbub. All except for Kitten Soronsen, who sat with her hands and feet pressed neatly together, watching silently as Katla Aransen got what she had long deserved.

If anything, the noise served to ignite Gasto Costan's anger further. Grabbing Katla with greater strength than she would have ascribed to such a puny-looking man, he thrust her hard at the other raider. Katla lurched forward, then lost her balance to the chains that still held her feet in place, and fell face forward against the giant, her shackled hands pinned against his massive chest. There, she found herself half-smothered in his sweaty embrace and for a few crucial seconds could not breathe, all her senses engulfed by his rank stench. A moment later her feet came free from the shackles and she was tucked unceremoniously under the giant's arm and heading at some speed through the hold.

"Dunk her in there!" the sneering man ordered, and the next minute, the world turned upside down. Plunged headfirst into the barrel, Katla opened her mouth wide to roar her protest, and found herself inhaling water which burned her eyes and throat and forced itself down her gullet. When she came back upright, hauled out by Casto Agen with her wrist-chains clanking, all she could do was cough and choke and retch for a very long time. Then, her feet once more safely on the deck, Katla shook herself like a dog, covering everyone in a five-yard radius in a sheen of freezing liquid.

Gasto Costan ran his hand disgustedly down his wet tunic, took out his knife, and advanced upon Katla with a gleam in his eyes.

"You mustn't damage the merchandise!" Bera cried in panic. It was all she could think of.

"I have no intention of carving up the little trollop," Gasto sneered. "I am merely going to clean her up and then consecrate her." With a flick of his knife he made to cut away Katla's tunic; but at the best of times it was a sturdy thing, albeit of stained and battered leather. Now, soaked with seawater, it was as tough as old boots and no pathetic little Istrian-made knife was going to make much impression on it. Frustrated by these attempts, he tried to haul the jerkin off her; but when he grabbed the hem and started to hoist it up past her waist, all he got for his pains was the vicious jab of a knee in a foolishly unprotected area.

"Little bitch! Hold her fast!" he shrieked at Agen, and slowly the giant lumbered forward. Katla took one look at the size of the man, reckoned her chances of taking him down at around nil, and transferred her attentions to Gasto Costan. With a speed he could never have foreseen, she leaped at him, her arms going up then down as fast as a striking snake; a moment later she was behind him, and he was between her and the giant with a set of chains locked tight across his throat and his little knife now transferred to one of his attacker's fists. From behind his left ear, Katla's grin shone out, all white and ferocious amid streaked skin and dark, shiny-wet hair. She looked like a water sprite—not one of the kind ones who would sometimes take pity on a drowning man and carry him gently to shore, but one of those which dragged a swimmer down into the murky depths, tangled his feet among the weeds of the seabed, and mercilessly ate him alive till he stopped struggling.

"You," she said to the giant in the Old Tongue, looking him in the eye on him to impress her will upon him. It gave her a crick in the neck. "Give the keys to that woman there." She nodded toward her mother.

She had to repeat this request three times, as well as jabbing the little knife hard into her captive's neck—enough to draw a very pleasing runnel of blood and a terrified yelp—before Casto Agen sufficiently grasped what he was supposed to do. The bunch of keys were back hanging from the other man's belt; the giant had to go down on his knee to extract them from the hook there. After a lot of undignified fiddling he stood up, looking somewhat at a loss, while Gasto Costan hissed curses at him in their nasty southern language. Then off he went across the hold to Katla's mother, like a half-trained and rather slow-witted dog.

A moment later, there came a thunder of feet and a barrage of shouting, and several raiders came pelting down into the hold. Casto Agen stopped a foot away from Bera Rolfsen with his hand extended, palm out, in the act of handing her the keys, as if someone had just turned him to stone. Then he turned slowly to survey the newcomers.

Baranguet was in the lead of the group. He had his favorite whip in one hand and a long, curved sword in the other. He did not look as if he would be much concerned at the possibility of damaging the merchandise, but behind him came a short, wide man—Galo Bastido, also at full tilt. It took a moment for Baranguet's eyes to become accustomed to the dingy light. Then he came to a sudden halt and gazed into the obscurity of the hold at the women, who instead of appearing beaten and listless now seemed to be alert and engaged by something he could not quite fathom. Having no chance to check his pace, Bastido cannoned into the back of his deputy.

Katla dug the blade of the little knife deeper into the already sore-

looking wound on Gasto Costan's neck till he cried out and drew attention to his plight. Distracted by this noise, Baranguet and Bastido stared
and stared at the bizarre scenario thus presented to them, and therefore
did not notice the giant slowly complete his mission by handing over his
clutch of keys to the Mistress of Rockfall. Bera's fingers closed carefully
around them, muffling all sound. Then she took a silent step backward
and subsided to the deck once more, into the shadows of the crossbeam.

Out of the corner of her eye, Katla saw this curious exchange. Her
grin widened. Now *this* was becoming interesting! In her imagination,
all sorts of possibilities played themselves out in glorious detail. All of
them came to a delightful conclusion with the hanging of both captain
and lieutenant from the yardarm of the ship while she, Katla Aransen,
heroine of the isles, steered them safely home to Rockfall.

Galo Bastido started to swear. That much was clear, even if the words
were not. He shoved Baranguet forward with a gesture which obviously
meant: *you deal with her.* The whipman, matching her feral grin with
his own, advanced, cutlass angled toward her.

"Another step," Katla declared loudly in the Old Tongue, "and I'll
skewer your shipmate!"

Baranguet laughed. Insolently, as if to test her resolve—she was,
after all, just a girl, and what girl would cold-bloodedly harm a man just
to prove a point?—he took a huge step forward. Katla jabbed the knife
deep into Gasto Costan's neck, making the man squeal in pain and
panic.

"For Falla's sake!" he shrieked at Baranguet, when the pressure of the
blade lessened, "she's a crazy girl, a little witch! Don't provoke her, or
she'll send me to the fires!"

"Where you sent your pretty wife?" Baranguet asked unpleasantly.
"Just because she fucked your little brother, who was smarter and richer
than you?"

"Shut up! Shut up! How dare you speak of that sacrilegious pair! You
know nothing of the sorrow it caused me to get my courage up enough
to do my duty and go to the Sisters—"

"Your duty," sneered the whipman. "I heard you went to the burning,
then moved into your brother's house a day later and hired yourself a
brace of whores."

"I didn't, I didn't!" cried Gasto Costan, horrified by the truth in all this. He squirmed desperately in Katla's steady grasp, but his efforts resulted only in a tightening of the chain across his throat so that his eyes now bulged with more than outrage.

"Unlock your chains, Mother," Katla called softly in Eyran across the hold. "Unlock them, and then pass the keys to Kitten."

Bera looked unsure of the wisdom of this. "Surely it would be better to wait until they leave us, and then to free ourselves silently and secretly?" she began.

"If we are left locked and unarmed in this hold, we will be in no better position to escape than when they first brought us to the ship," Katla reminded her. "We need their weapons, and we need the hatch open."

"Be quiet!" Bastido shouted. He shoved Baranguet out of the way and came at her. In the blink of an eye, Katla had twisted her wrist and tightened the chain. Now the sneering man could not breathe, or even cry out, but still Bastido came on.

Katla waved the little knife at him. It was, she thought, pathetically small and blunt, but she reckoned she could still put an eye out with it if push came to shove.

"Back off!" she yelled. "Or he dies."

Bastido laughed. "Do you think I care whether he lives—" and at this Gasto Costan began to writhe and weep, "—or dies? He's a vile little runt with all the morals of a rabid fox and the fighting skills of a twelve-year-old girl!"

"At twelve," Katla mused, "I won the Westman Isles wrestling contest for the first time."

Galo Bastido cocked his head on one side and fixed her with his small beady eyes. "You really are a very annoying creature," he declared. For a moment, it looked as if he was considering his options; then fast as a biting dog he darted forward and stuck his hapless crewman through the guts with his cutlass. Gasto Costan sagged in Katla's arms. Blood and fluid spread swiftly across his gaping tunic, followed by a sudden slippery outpouring of viscous tubing.

Katla gazed down at this horrible sight. "That's sort of spoiled my plan."

"One less man to pay," the captain quipped cheerfully, and advanced on her.

She stepped quickly backward, dragging her dying captive with her, then quickly extricated her chains from the groaning man and let him drop as a useful obstacle between her and the captain. Behind her, she could hear the click of a tumbler turning in a lock and chains clanking as her mother removed her shackles. She watched as Bastido's eyes tracked the sound and widened in disbelief. Then he let off a barrage of abuse at the huge man who stood uselessly by watching the women.

At last, Casto Agen came to life. Bending, he grabbed Kitten Soronsen by the wrist and hauled her to her feet. Kitten, of course, took one look at her attacker and swooned. The keys fell noisily to the floor.

In the midst of all this, with the captain's attention fatally distracted, Katla Aransen made her move. Scurrying in under the big man's reach while he was caught up with the fainting girl, she retrieved both the keys and the sword from the scabbard hanging from his hip, and danced away, tucking the little knife into her belt. Then her fingers deftly worked the keys into place like a close-hand magician about to faze his audience with a dodgy trick.

Neither of them appeared to fit. "Sur's arse!" Katla swore furiously.

Galo Bastido was coming after her again. *No time for messing around with this blasted lock,* Katla thought. She waited a few seconds until he was within range, then whipped up the sword. An inch closer and she would have had him; as it was, she nicked his cheekbone. The keys went flying. They arced through the air and came down again as neatly as if by design, in Casto Agen's hands.

Blood jetted out of the wound. Bastido said something clearly obscene in his own language, then smeared a hand across his face, leaving a grotesque trail down cheek and neck. His eyes glittered murderously through the spattered gore.

Damn, she thought, but there was no time for regret. She whirled the sword around her head.

He came at her too fast for caution, his cutlass raised for a barbarous downward chop. She felt the air part beside her ear and darted backward. A quick glance ascertained her surroundings and she leaped behind a big timber support. A bare second later, Bastido's weapon splintered the pillar, sending frayed chunks of oak spinning out into the dark air of the hold. Katla appeared around the other side of the post and jabbed her sword at his waist. But the captain was fast and well-trained; the cutlass came down on her blade with a great clang, the force of his blow setting her armbones ajangle and sending tremors down into her fingers.

Katla ducked and weaved. She was a head taller than her opponent; lighter and quicker, too, but he was built like a prize bull, bursting with year upon year of hard-trained muscle. She parried another bone shocker from him, then spun away on her toes and swept her own blade around low. Bastido took a step back, but it was not quite far enough. The edge of Katla's purloined weapon sheared across the big muscle of his thigh, making her opponent roar with surprise and pain. *Damn,* Katla thought; *another inch and I'd have had his leg off.* This judgment brought suddenly to mind a conversation with Tor Leeson about the good edge on one of her swords—

Take a man's leg off nicely, I'd say . . .

That womanizing bruiser, she thought fondly, though she had never been very fond of him in the life. He had had no gentle way with either swords or words, but he had died trying to save her from the burning. An Istrian blade in the back, they'd said. Fury filled her anew. Istrians were her enemies—and this man who faced her now more than any. He had murdered her friends and kin, burned her own grandmother in her family home. A nicked leg was barely a down payment on the blood debt he owed her.

Snarling like a mad dog, Katla ran at him, arms locked, sword extended. Galo Bastido threw his blade up to ward her off, but he had underestimated her pace and determination. The cutlass sheared off the Istrian sword with a shower of fiery sparks which lit the faces of both combatants for a few brief seconds. Then the cutlass described an elegant arc, gleaming silver like a leaping salmon, and spun uselessly out of the raider's hands.

Something moved in her peripheral vision, but Katla forced herself to ignore it and concentrate on her opponent. As Bastido staggered backward, she went after him, sword raised to deliver a killing stroke.

The next thing she knew she was falling backward and her arms felt as though they were being dragged out of their sockets. She stumbled, lost her footing, went down hard onto the deck, catching a cross-timber painfully in the small of her back. Something—somebody—had hold of her sword. She jerked her head sideways and saw that the thongs of a many-tongued whip had knotted themselves inextricably around the blade. She hauled fiercely, shearing through two of the thongs, but the man on the other end of it—Baranguet, of course—was not letting go.

"Hel's teeth," Katla groaned. She looked back. The raiders' captain was coming at her now, empty-handed but furious, his face a gory mask. She could see the whites all around his eyes. He was definitely going to kill her if she stayed where she was. She went momentarily limp; as she had hoped, Baranguet yanked hard on the whip. As he did so, she released the sword and flipped herself to her feet. She heard the whipman go down with a curse; heard the sword skitter across the deck. Then she ran at Bastido.

Her lowered head took him hard under the ribs in a time-honored Eyran wrestling gambit. She heard the wind rush out of his lungs. A moment later, she was astraddle him, her knees pinning his shoulders to the floor. She had outpointed Simi's brother, Gill Fallson, with a maneuver very similar to this, and he was built like a bull, as was this man. It was all in the speed; she could hardly match him for power or weight; but big men never expected a girl of Katla's size to put them down. She watched the raider chief's face twist into a grimace of frustration when he found he could not move his arms; then she grabbed the little knife she had taken from the sneering man and plunged it to the hilt into his eye.

"That's for Gramma Rolfsen!"

Bull-like, Galo Bastido began to roar. He writhed in agony. Appalled that he had not simply and quietly died, Katla leaped backward off him as if scalded. Slowly, deliberately, the captain levered himself to his feet, the hilt of the knife protruding obscenely. He fixed Katla with his one good eye blinking desperately and staggered two paces toward her, hands reaching like those of a sleepwalker. Katla took two steps back, hit a crossbeam and stumbled. A blast of pain shot through up her leg. "Sur's bollocks!"

Twisted ankle. Very painful, but not fatal as long as she didn't let it slow her down, for Galo Bastido was still advancing, lurching with all the horrible obstinacy of an afterwalker. Gritting her teeth against the agony, Katla pushed herself upright and skittered sideways.

A moment later, having come round in a panicky semicircle, there was nowhere left to run. The back of Katla's head made audible contact with one of the starboard ribs, and when she reached back with a questing hand, all she found was splintering wood sticky with caulking tar. She faced the raiders' leader, her eyeteeth showing in a feral grin. She was quick, she was tough, and she was very angry, she reminded herself. "Come on, then, you bastard," she taunted him, putting up her hard little fists. "Let's see what you've got left."

Galo Bastido snarled. He made a vile gurgling noise that might have been a curse, a threat, or a last breath. Then he took a huge, staggering step toward her, pitched forward like a hewn tree, and fell facedown between her spread feet. The hilt of the little knife hit the deck first with the unforgettable sound of metal forcibly striking bone and gristle. Katla grimaced. The raiders' captain lay still, but Katla had already seen a man who should have been well dead return to life. She waited another few seconds, and when he was still unmoving, booted him hard in the head with her good foot. He didn't stir at all.

"Got you."

A shocked silence floated out across the hold as if everyone was holding their breath; then Fat Breta started to scream and scream. Curses, shouts, howls of pain and fury rent the air. Women shrieked and men bellowed. Katla grabbed up the fallen cutlass from behind the still corpse of Galo Bastido and stared wildly about, trying to decide on her next course of action. She scanned the hold and its mass of bodies for sight of her mother, but in the midst of all the chaos it was hard to make out one filthy, half-starved Eyran woman from another.

There came a sharp crack, then a shout, followed by another and another. Little by little the noise and movement seemed to subside, all except the incongruous keening noise of a trapped seagull, or a tortured cat. One moment, all was chaos, the next a space was clearing in the middle of the hold and people were breaking off whatever they had been doing to watch something.

Baranguet had Simi Fallsen by the hair and his pet whip—now disentangled from the sword Katla had stolen from the giant—in his hand. Three women lay in front of him, red welts on their bare arms. Of these, in the gloom, Katla could recognize only Kit Farsen, whose face was turned up pleadingly, tears washing cleaner tracks down her grime-ingrained cheeks. The keening sound went on and on, then stopped abruptly as the whipman wrapped his fist one more turn around Simi's lank brown locks and yanked hard. Simi was a big woman—taller than the whipman by several inches, and even wider across hip and shoulder, but his hard muscles showed in corded swells down both arms as he bore her down until her throat bowed backward. A moment later there was a resounding crack, and Simi slumped to the deck at his feet, her head skewed at an unnatural angle.

"By the Lord," Bera Rolfsen was heard to say.

Thin Hildi made the protective warding sign of Feya's cradle.

Kit Farsen began to howl.

Baranguet laughed. "That one was very ugly," he announced to those assembled in the Old Tongue, his eyes alight with unholy glee. "And very noisy, too." He paused. "She must be descended from—what are those great, ugly beasts you northern people believe in? That dwell in dark places, in caves and under bridges?" He looked around. No one said a word. Ferociously, he kicked Kit Farsen hard on the arm. She shrieked and backed away from him, but he came after her. "What do you call these creatures?" he persisted. He caught up to her, whip raised.

At once, Kit's wail subsided into gulped sobs. "Tr—tr—" She took a deep breath, then wailed again as the whip cut through the gloomy air with a whistling sound and landed with a crack, catching her across the face. Blood spurted out of the cut. Tears sprang from her eyes. "Tr—tr—"

Kit had always stammered when she was nervous. The boys had taunted her for it when she could not repeat her lessons, until Katla had punched them till they promised not to do it anymore. Everyone was forever picking on little Kit Farsen.

"Trolls!" The word blasted out across the hold. "But there's not a troll in all of Eyra are as ugly as you. Your mother must have been a yeka and your father a warthog."

His attention distracted from the shuddering creature at his feet, Baranguet turned to fix his basilisk gaze upon Katla Aransen.

Katla stared back at him, fierce with fury. There was no weapon in grabbing distance and nowhere to run. She stuck her chin out and waited. Why was she always fighting others' battles for them? Halli would have warned her to keep quiet and seek an advantage, rather than rushing thoughtlessly into the breach. But she never seemed to learn. It was not even that she was friendly with little Kit Farsen, who was far too much a milksop to sustain Katla's boisterous company for very long, and she had hardly known Simi Fallsen; but no one deserved to die so needlessly, nor be hurt for the entertainment of a sadistic brute. "You are a coward and a murderer," she growled. "May you burn in the fires of that bitch-goddess you call Falla."

She put her fists up. It was, she had to admit, a pathetic gesture, but maybe if she could catch the tongues of the whip as it came at her, she could drag Baranguet off balance and that might at least give her a chance to run for a blade . . .

A few paces away from Katla, Baranguet cocked his head on one side and looked her up and down, clearly unimpressed. "Not much loss to us if you follow the ugly one. I can't see you fetching much, anyway," he grinned unpleasantly. "Where I come from, we like a girl with some flesh on her, not some skinny little fox's runt." He raised his whip.

Katla ran at him, but it was an unequal and very swift contest. A moment later the many-tongued whip lashed out and though she caught two of the flails with one hand, the rest wrapped themselves tightly around her neck. Baranguet began to pull, and they tightened again. As she sank to her knees, gasping for breath, Katla heard her mother's roar of protest, then the sound of a fist connecting with flesh and bone.

A blizzard of black snowflakes filled her vision. Then everything went fuzzy and dark and she heard and saw nothing more.

8

Alisha

IT was dawn when Alisha Skylark raised her head from the cold mud in which she lay, a chilly, gray dawn in which the sun made its presence known only by a bloody tinge to the easternmost clouds, as if it had little wish to examine the sights offered by the grim world below.

She was alive. She hurt, but she was alive.

For a few seconds a sharp buzz of elation revived her enough to look slowly from side to side, taking in her surroundings. Then harsh reality overtook optimism. The dead lay all around, oozing out the last of their reluctant fluids into the cheerless air. Dead horses, dead men. All scattered across the ground as if some gigantic hand had reached down out of the sky, scooped them up, mashed them for a moment in its fist, then thrown them down again at random. *As if the gods were playing knucklebones with lives,* she thought. *We mean nothing to them, nothing at all.*

The Wandering folk believed that some measure of goodness was innate to everything, that every life had its own unique place in the world, that every person was a tiny, colorful stitch in Elda's great tapestry; that the Three watched over all and together determined how such threads should be woven to make the most of every gift and skill, every act and outcome. But Alisha owed only half of her parentage to the gentle nomads. The other half came from a soldier who had raped her mother in the mountains where they had been ambushed. There had been rather too many times in her life when she thought she owed rather more than half her inherited traits to the latter than to the former. The nomadic people met every challenge with hope and cheer, believed the best of everyone they met, took each day as it came, and gave little thought to the future. To Alisha's mind, this made them impractical folk, vulnerable to the greedy, the exploitative and the violent; it meant they shored up nothing for the next day, had no thought at all of the days after that, and became everyone's victim. She found herself a strange anomaly among these happy-go-lucky folk, constantly anxious, constantly looking for some control over her circumstances. It was a fruitless attitude, but it had meant that when her mother—the healer Fezack Starsinger, who had led the caravan for as many years as Alisha could remember—had died, the other members had at once looked to her to take the old woman's place and lead them safely on their great journeys across the southern continent. How could they, who had no concept of responsibility, understand just how heavily this had weighed on her? Their expectation that all would be well she would have found daunting at the best of times; with persecution, hostility, and distrust around even the safest-seeming corner in this intolerant, fanatical empire, the burden she found herself carrying was terrifying, absurd. Moving into her mother's old wagon, with its symbolic stars-and-moon door and its shelves full of healer's potions and scryer's crystals, had made her anxious. Worse, she had felt like an impostor, a charlatan claiming gifts and a history not her own. When she looked in a glass, all she saw were the peculiarly light eyes and wiry red-brown hair of a woman who fitted into no clear social niche anywhere in this world. She hardly even seemed related to her own son, for Falo was the mirror image of his nomad father with his sharp, neat features, his dark skin and black eyes, his laughing carefree belief that if he fell, the world would catch him. If anything, his close fit with the Wanderers enhanced her own sense of alienation, excluded her further from their warm, tight mesh. And now even that link was severed. For Falo—beautiful, lively, gifted little Falo, who had barely seen out eight winters in the world—was gone from her, chopped down like sere grass by the careless backhand sword stroke of an Istrian soldier. The rest of her sadly depleted band had soon followed.

And she—Alisha Skylark, daughter of the most powerful scryer of all the Wandering folk—had not even been able to see the faintest echo of this huge and cataclysmic event coming toward them, despite all the hours she had spent poring over her mother's great crystal.

So much for responsibility; so much for anxiety; so much for control. So much for magic . . .

It would, Alisha admitted to herself now, in the midst of yet more carnage, be easy just to lie down and die and sever that last tenuous link with Elda. Indeed, for a long time she laid her head back down on the damp, churned earth and wept hot tears into it at the memory of her son's terrible death—undeserved, unwished-for, untimely. She cried until no more tears would come and she felt entirely emptied out of all emotion, all individuality. Then she waited for oblivion to take her, but all that happened was that time passed and the sun rose higher, and vultures began descending from the skies and trees and settling on the battlefield. But as they set about their grisly feeding, Alisha found she could no longer wish herself into oblivion. It was impossible to close her ears to the sounds around her—the shrieking and ripping and tearing, the challenges of one carrion bird to another, the aggressive bluster of wings; so much greedy life among the dead.

Before she even knew what she had done, she was on her feet and yelling at the vultures, waving her arms, cursing in fury, and they were lifting in a great flurry of discontent and flying off to settle in their roosts to wait their chance to return for more delicacies once this annoyingly alive madwoman was herself dead. *We can outwait you,* their avid, beady eyes promised. *We will still be here when all other living things have passed into the fires.*

Alisha Skylark, returned in some measure to herself by this inimical challenge to her humanity, drew her eyes from the vultures, and instead began to stare around at the battlefield. Even with their now-empty orbs gazing sightlessly into the hot air, she would have recognized many of those lying there, their uniforms soaked and stiffened by their bodily fluids, their limbs all contorted in their death throes. She should, she considered, feel some satisfaction that the men who had dealt out barbaric deaths to her loved ones and then defiled her had themselves met with such a violent and ignominious fate. But she just felt hollowed out, barely even human.

She began to wander randomly about the place, examining each corpse she passed with a dispassionate eye. Some of the cadavers were those of men she did not recognize, men who wore a different uniform from those who had annihilated her caravan, and this puzzled her, until she scanned the scene with a more focused and curious intent, and realized that young Saro Vingo was not among the dead. From his absence she deduced the men had come for him, no doubt spurred on to their atrocious deeds by the likelihood of some generous bounty. She began to pace about now, searching for a sign to corroborate her theory. There were bodies all around—fifteen? Twenty? More? She could not bear to count; even if most of them were enemies, it was such a waste of life.

Her eyes scanned the scene, around and around, so that one detail blurred with another—a hand twisted, palm up, as if to implore mercy; a face with one eye shut and the other missing as if making an obscene wink at death; a man wearing odd boots; a horse's teeth, yellow and attenuated, stained with blood. And then suddenly, a sharp stab of recognition.

Virelai, Virelai!

The strange, pale man with whom she had shared so many intimate embraces, with whom she had at one time thought she might spend the rest of her life, lay maybe thirty paces away from where she stood near a tangle of carved-up men and beasts. His body was contorted so that one arm was bent beneath him while the other was splayed out, and his knees were drawn up tight to his chest as if to ward off further attack.

Oh, Virelai . . .

Alisha's heart began to hammer against her ribs. Each breath she drew transferred little shock waves of pain through her entire body, a reminder—though she hardly needed it—that the essence of being alive was to be vulnerable to hurt. Some dried substance had matted in the long white hair near the nape of his neck, and a wound gaped at his temple, an awful pale, bled-out gray. His head was twisted away from her, but she could still see how his eyes were screwed tightly closed, though his mouth was stretched wide in a savage grimace. A blow to the side of the head appeared to have brought about the sorcerer's demise, a blow of disproportionate force, judging by the size of the wound, for it was hardly as if Virelai had ever been much of a physical threat to any man, let alone any armed soldier. That he should meet his death by such simple brutality, when he had been so superstitiously terrified of the demons his master's curse would unleash upon him seemed pathetically ironic. And that he should be able to die at all, given his true nature, was further proof of the arbitrary nature of the universe.

Suddenly, Alisha found her well of tears had not entirely run dry.

Overcome by this new and unexpected grief, she let the tears fall as they would. For a while she watched them drop, one after another, onto the ground between her feet. At first, they made a small puddle there, then began to seep away into the earth. She blinked and blinked, but they would not stop.

After an unknowable amount of time, she found that her bleary vision was fixed on something glinting obscurely in the dirt. She bent down, glad to have something to distract her from her misery, even if it was only a pebble washed clean by her tears.

But it wasn't just a pebble. With growing certainty, Alisha reached out to the object. She brushed the remaining mud away from its surface, then jerked her fingers back as if bitten.

The object gleamed at her, pearly and malevolent, full of light.

It was the death-stone.

She had known it from the first moment she had glimpsed it; had known it in her bones, rather than in her head. Her fingers still buzzed and burned from the split-second's contact. Unconsciously, she brought her hand up to her mouth, pressed the pads of her fingers against lips which moved in sudden, silent prayer to a goddess she had been ready moments earlier to renounce. Then, knowing that she was making an irrevocable decision, she reached down and grabbed up the pendant. It swung from its dirt-crusted leather thong, its opalescence absorbing every iota of light there was to be had from the dull day and giving it back to the world threefold. Alisha gazed at it, mesmerized as much by its deadly beauty as by the slow pendulum of its arcing movement from the nadir of the string. This was the stone which had been touched by Falla herself, inanimate crystal charged with Elda's own power to create an object which could suck the life out of any breathing creature with the merest touch.

She frowned. Then why had she herself not expired when she had wiped it clean?

Not caring whether she lived or died, but possessed by a reckless curiosity, she let the stone swing lightly against the skin of her other palm.

Nothing. Or rather, nothing but a gentle warmth like a ray of sunlight. She shut her eyes and focused on the sensation, letting it grow and take shape, letting it infuse her skin, then the muscles and bones of that hand, then radiate up into her arm and shoulder, her neck, the cavern of her skull. Mindlessly, the fingers of her free hand closed tightly over the moodstone. She felt it throb against her palm like a second heart. It was oddly soothing, as if she were surrendering her life to the stone, giving over all responsibility and decision to it. Volitionlessly, she began to move.

From somewhere distant to her actions, she was aware of kneeling by the sorcerer's corpse, of laying hands on that disturbingly chalky flesh; then there was darkness and confusion. Chaos consumed her. Voices sounded in her head.

Out of me . . . get out of me . . .

Let me go . . .

I did not ask for this . . .

The Goddess, the Goddess . . .

What is happening?

Who is calling me? Who are you?

No—

I cannot help it. It is not me.

Who then?

She— Aaaaahhh—!

Convulsively, Alisha Skylark flung the death-stone away from her and sat in the mud, breathing hard. She was too afraid to open her eyes. Then a hand touched her face, and someone spoke her name. . . .

SARO Vingo had plumbed the depths of human despair on a number of occasions, but never more so than now as he bumped his way through the scrubby wasteland bordering the Eternal City of Jetra, bound hand and foot and slung facedown over a soldier's pack animal. Considering the apocalyptic nature of what he had previously experienced, the smell of a sweating horse and the hot-and-cold waves of nausea caused by its incessant swaying should have registered as mere nuisance, but Saro had never felt so dreadful in all his life. Trying to take his mind off his current predicament, as scalding bile rose in his throat yet again, he recalled the self-disgust he had felt when he knew himself responsible for the deaths of innocent men at the Allfair; when being forced to take care of his loathsome brother after Tanto had been returned so unexpectedly and undeservedly to consciousness; when the full extent of the gift of empathy old Hiron the moodstone-seller had bestowed upon him had been revealed in all its awful glory; when he had been visited by the appalling vision of Tycho Issian's ambitions; and when, on a smaller but far more personal and poignant level, such death and destruction had been brought home to him by the sight of Falo, Alisha's son, lying lifeless and mutilated, his hacked-off arm still clutching his grandmother's stick. And all because of him and Virelai and the greed of a band of militiamen. But now those very soldiers and his sole surviving friends were lying dead and he himself had been captured yet again by soldiers who had ambushed his initial captors. All for money. All for power.

At least they won't get the death-stone, he thought savagely.

And they won't have Virelai.

He tried to push the image of that macabre, caved-in skull away into some recess of his mind, but it kept coming back to him in ever-increasing detail. He now recalled how the skin had been puckered all around the point of impact, how the interior of the wound, a great crater of a thing, had looked so pale and lifeless, as if every drop of his blood had to be absorbed by the thankless earth. How the white of bone had showed through the dead, gray flesh.

Saro was still thinking about the odd chalky nature of the flesh revealed by his friend's wound as they reached the shores of the great lake and began to traverse the narrow causeway which led to its towering rose-red walls of carved sandstone. He was gripped by images of death as they passed beneath the chilly shadow of the city's arched southern gate, where the stone had been leached away by the elements like flesh eaten into by some leprous plague; he was wrapped around by thoughts of mortality when they rode through dank passages fringed with black weed and noxious scale gleaming at the lapping waterline, through tunnels in which the horses' hooves echoed as loudly as the clang of weapons. As they turned a tight corner, one of the soldiers began to swear at another for bringing them in via the Misery—or this was what it sounded like to Saro's distressed ears, though the man's voice reverberated off the low ceiling and narrow walls like a blaring horn.

"That's what he said to do," the first man protested.

"Who? The Lord of Cantara paid us to bring him to Jetra, to his state room. Not down here. No one told me anything about this." He sounded thoroughly aggrieved.

"Not him, the master's new friend," the first soldier returned belligerently. "Caught me as we were leaving . . ."

Saro's heart stopped. His ears strained to hear the rest, and he could tell from the sudden quiet of the rest of the troop that others were listening, too.

"Stop talking in riddles, Tosco!"

The other man sighed melodramatically. Then he reached into his pouch and brought out a small roll of parchment, opened it with a maladroit fumble and read slowly. " 'The old cells' something, something—I can't quite read it, but look, see here: 'the Miseria.' Says so quite clearly."

"No one in his right mind comes down here. It's full of ghasts and demons . . ."

"Who said anything about him being in his right mind?"

Saro didn't catch the next bit of the exchange because at that moment the nag he had been bundled onto like so much baggage rammed itself into the wall so hard that he had to put a hand out to prevent his skull from being mashed. At once he was assailed by a terrible stench—if he had thought the smell of a sweating horse was bad, then this was infinitely worse—a sickly aroma of blood and vomit and shit all combined with a sharp and lasting afterscent of terror and pain. As the impact of the smell passed off, there came a new assault on his senses. Dark shapes all around, flickering torchlight, shouts and screams, disembodied at first, then closer and closer until they seemed to be inside his own head. They *were* inside his own head, he realized suddenly—and he was being dragged, toes scuffing against the slippery and uneven cobbles, by two huge men, their heads swathed by masks, their boots sloshing through unnamable substances streaming along the gutters on either side of the passageway. Everything hurt. The socket of his left arm raged with fire, and then he remembered how they had hung him by one wrist from a chain suspended from the ceiling and beaten him with sticks and chains, with their hands and their boots till he swung and spun wildly across the gore-streaked chamber. And he remembered how they had laughed when several of his teeth had sprayed out of his mouth and skittered across the stone floor, how they had reviled him and beaten him harder when he had pissed himself and one of them had caught some of that weak and bloody stream on his tunic.

And then the devil had come, that softly-spoken man with the sharp features, the expressive brown eyes; how he had commanded the men in a rebuking tone to take him down and stop their torture; the blessed relief as his weight came off his ruined arm, the welcome cold stillness of the stone floor. He remembered being taken into a room with a carpet, a chair, an ornately carved desk; how the brown-eyed man had offered him wine which had burned his ravaged gums; and how he had begun to talk and talk and talk as if he could never stop—ridiculous, inconsequential nonsense about his childhood and Ravenna's hair and the man had listened patiently with his fingers steepled and his head nodding, nodding his encouragement, and only later, much later, had he spoken about his wife's brother's secret temple; how the slaughter-goats had danced and shrieked; how they had prayed and drunk a saltwater toast to the old god. And then the softly-spoken man had pressed him for more detail, and more detail he had given him: more and more and more, like a wellhead unstoppered.

The next thing he knew, he was in his cell, unable to get comfortable: not because of the ever-flaming hurt to his shoulder and arm, but from some irritation beneath his right haunch. Further investigation had for long minutes seemed too exhausting, but the annoyance plagued him beyond endurance and at last he had been forced to address it. Reaching down, he had eased his hip away from the plank of his cell's hard bed and found—not a stone or a knot in the wood, but one of his own molars embedded in his flesh, where he had dropped down onto it from the chain. And then he had begun to cry and cry, ashamed for his weakness, for his broken body, for betraying his entire family to the Goddess's wicked priests and thus condemning them to the fires. He was weeping still as they dragged him down the long, stinking passageway to the death he knew awaited him—out in the city's arena at the pyres where he would surely find his wife, her brother, his children, his friends and neighbors all bound to their stakes before being consigned to Falla's flames.

This time, the nausea was unstoppable. Vomit burst out of Saro's mouth and down the flank of the horse, spattered onto the decaying stonework, where his stomach's acids would surely react with the excoriating air and bring yet more rot to this damned and evil place, replete with its tortured ghosts and traumatized memories, with the violence and fanaticism which had made Jetra the great rotten heart of the Southern Empire, its foul reality belied by the grace and serenity of its towering minarets, its crenellated walls, its age-old carvings.

They turned another dark corner, then rough hands grabbed Saro and, swearing at the mess he had made, threw him down onto the floor. He hit the polished stone hard and threw out a hand to save his head.

Death and stink. A man being gutted while another sat watching, taking notes.

Saro groaned in agony and rolled away, fetching up beside a wall rank with dripping water. The wall told him other stories: a woman raped by guards when she brought bread and ham for her imprisoned husband; a Footloose man bleeding slowly to death from a stab wound to the groin; terrified nomad children listening to the screams of their loved ones in the cells beyond; a thousand untimely, undeserved deaths.

Silently, Saro Vingo began to cry. He was crying still when a familiar voice hailed him.

"The wanderer returns!"

Saro's head came up with a snap. Even though he knew what to expect, the reality was still a shock. His brother, Tanto Vingo, loomed over him, as repulsively bloated and moonlike as he remembered; but dressed now in the most tasteless opulence that Jetra's ostentatious tailors could provide. His tunic—a confection of rose-and-purple watered silk, worn over contrasting hose in luminescent green—was wrapped around with great swags of leather and worked metal, though it could hardly be called "belted," since there was nothing to distinguish the region above from that below the cinctures. A boned collar in lurid, striated purple stood straight up from his shoulders like the angry threat-display of some vast frilled lizard. Massive rings of silver studded with jewels weighed down every finger, and a great amethyst caged in silver drew down the lobe of Tanto's left ear so that the jewel swung pendulously just above his shoulder. His bald head shone with sweat although he had obviously expended no effort in getting here, a fact attested to by the presence of two richly-dressed servants with dark circles staining their otherwise immaculate silk livery who must have carried his wheeled chair to this dank and steamy place.

The soldiers who had risked their lives bringing him here waited on the shadows, watching silently.

When Tanto smiled at him in a horrible parody of welcome, Saro noted with a certain satisfaction that his brother had lost yet another tooth from those rotting gums since the last time he had seen him. He stared down at the slimy floor again, since doing so was infinitely preferable to looking at that mocking, predatory grin.

Annoyed that his captive was not being suitably appreciative of his new finery and status; or rising to the bait, Tanto shot out a hand and grabbed Saro by the chin, wrenching his head upright. At the sight of Saro's tear-streaked face, he leered delightedly. "Weeping for your lost freedom, eh, brother? Or for fear of what may now befall you?"

Saro held his gaze determinedly, jaws clamped rigid, and said nothing, although fleeting glimpses of Tanto's recent vile excesses flickered in rapid succession through his head.

Tanto quirked an eyebrow. "Not speaking to me? How rude. To leave without even a farewell, too. Not very brotherly, brother. Our poor father was so beside himself at the thought of his youngest son disgracing our family—such cowardice and ingratitude, to desert from the glorious position in the army that Lord Tycho bestowed upon you and flee from the castle in the middle of the night, like the sneak thief you are—" he wagged a finger chidingly in Saro's face, "—having stolen his finest horse, the one he had promised to the Lord of Forent, who is, by the way also much displeased—that he renounced all his standing, and has pledged himself to the cause, joining the army as a rankless man."

Poor Father, Saro thought, his heart sinking, seeing clearly how Tanto had manipulated the situation. "And our uncle?" he asked quietly.

Tanto waved a dismissive hand. "Dead."

"Dead?" Saro experienced a shock of surprise, then of grief. The man who might be his true father was gone from the world. He was truly, terribly alone.

Tanto's grin widened. "You can't trust Jetran cuisine," he said softly. "All those herbs and spices. A cook has to be very careful when checking his ingredients. Nomad herb sellers are always seeking to find new ways to undermine the regime . . ."

His father exiled; Uncle Fabel poisoned. And clearly he was to be the next of the Vingo clan to be expunged.

"So you see, my dear Saro," Tanto said, bending his head so close that Saro was treated to a noxious whiff of decay, "now you must bow to me as head of this family; for not only are the family estates all mine, but the Lord of Cantara has discovered ancient statutes and entitlements in the Great Library here and has declared me Lord of Altea, with a stipend from the Treasury.

"So you may now address me not as 'brother' but as 'my lord.' "

He waited expectantly, but Saro continued to stare at him with stony loathing, refusing to be drawn.

Blood suffused Tanto's cheeks. "My lord," he prompted.

Reaching down beside the wheeled chair, he unclipped one of several devices arrayed there and came up again with a wicked-looking switch. He examined this item with fond care, weighed it in his hand, then began to beat its ornate head rhythmically upon the other palm.

"My lord," he prompted yet again, his black eyes glinting.

It was, he reasoned in that split-second of madness, a test of the extent of his brother's new-found power; whether he would act on his violent impulses here, in the clear view not only of his paid servants (who were, it was true, hardly likely to raise any objection if they were at all well acquainted with Tanto's temper) but also of the soldiers who had been paid so handsomely by Tycho Issian to bring him to this place.

"You murderous bastard!"

The accompanying gobbet of spittle struck Tanto's face with a satisfying smack, rolled slowly down the cheek, and dropped wetly into the corner of the frilled collar, staining the silk there an angry red, and coming to rest inextricably against the rolls of white flesh which had once been his brother's neck.

The blow which followed this rather sad act of defiance came as a surprise only in the amount of force which the supposed invalid had managed to put behind it. The switch cracked across Saro's face, broke his nose and shattered the bone beneath his right orbit. Half a knuckle-length farther and he'd have lost the eye. When he cried out, gristle and bone moved disconcertingly. Blood spurted.

Tanto wiped the gory end of the switch deliberately on the nearest servant's sleeve, leaving thick red stripes across the pale-blue silk, then returned the weapon to its place in the rack at his side. Leaning back in his chair, he indicated his brother with the merest tilt of his chin. "Strip him," he ordered the soldiers, then sat back in his wheeled chair with his legs out and his arms crossed like a lordling waiting impatiently for the entertainments to begin.

"VIRELAI?" She blinked and refocused, blinked again, stared hard. Familiar pale blue eyes framed by curtains of white hair stared back at her, pupils as small as pinpricks through a sunlit sky into the infinite darkness of space beyond.

"It is me, yes."

"But how—? You were . . ."

"Dead?"

"I thought so, yes; you were . . ." Alisha sought for a description which would not shock; failed to find anything that was not an entire lie, and gave up all attempts at diplomacy. "You were—you appeared . . . gone from the world . . . your limbs were stiff, your skin chalky-gray."

She watched his face as he absorbed this. Shock engulfed him, blind and terrible. Then his gaze skittered from her face to the hand lying curled in her lap, still clutching the moodstone. His head shot up and he searched her eyes urgently.

"Yes," she said, though he had asked no question aloud. "I touched you with it. I think I did."

Virelai took hold of her hand and peeled her fingers away from the pendant, which despite its recent work had returned to its normal dull color, as apparently innocuous as a sleeping mouse. He stared down at the mysterious object, his brow wrinkled, deep lines of repulsion gouging a course from his nose to the corners of his downturned mouth. She had never seen his face so alive before, so expressive. She had once thought him the most serene man in the world, but he had undergone many changes since those lost days. A few minutes later, and without a word, he pressed her fingers firmly around the object once more and sat back, his eyes troubled. They had changed color, she noted with curiosity. From the distant pallor of a fifthmoon sky, they were now the moody gray of a mountain storm. As distraction, she busied herself with tucking the pendant away inside her belt pouch, and when she looked up again, it was to see one of his hands unconsciously rising to spread itself across the place above his heart.

"I understand this no more than you do," she said at last. "I saw Saro Vingo use this very stone to take lives . . . ever since the Goddess empowered it. At the Allfair, and then down by . . . the river."

Tears sprang again to her eyes and she swallowed a sob loudly. It took a while before she was able to compose herself sufficiently to speak again, but the sorcerer said nothing and made no attempt to console her, seeming locked in his own thoughts. After what felt a long pause, she continued:

"There are . . . legends about moodstones that can revive the dying. In the olden days, when the magic was strong in the world. But I have never heard of a stone which could revive—"

"—the dead?" Virelai finished grimly.

The word hung uncomfortably between them until it could no longer be ignored.

She nodded unhappily. "It is a killing stone. It brings death, not life. How can a death-stone do what this has done to you?"

Virelai looked away from her, saying nothing. He took his hand from his chest, flexed the fingers, and sat staring at it as though it were the most remarkable thing in the world. Which, perhaps, it was.

In what seemed to her a conciliatory gesture, Alisha took it between her own. It was cool—Virelai's skin was always cool, dry and smooth as polished wood—but it was not as cool as it had been when they had lain together on those long, hot afternoons in her wagon, and holding him had been such a pleasure when she herself was sticky with sweat. She turned it over, examined it more closely, then looked up, eyes wide. "It's—"

"New?" he supplied. He flexed it again, stared unhappily at the unfamiliar elasticity of the skin, the bright color, the healthy texture. Then he bent and scrabbled at the hem of his robe, turning his ankle this way and that. "This was the worst leg," he said, almost to himself. Compulsively, he ran a palm over the shin, then around the back of the calf. "There was a hole coming here," he added on a note of rising panic. "Where's the hole gone? The skin was flaking away there . . ."

Leaning forward suddenly, Alisha pushed the hair aside from the temple which had sustained the terrible wound. The skin was smooth and unpuckered. Confused, her hands transferred themselves to the other side of his head, ruffled his hair until it stood out like a haystack, then sat back on her heels, making a complex, hieratic sign in the air. "It is a miracle," she breathed. "The work of the Goddess herself. She who is all-powerful, all-forgiving. She who is Love. Her power flows through the world again, praise be, praise be."

Virelai frowned. "The Rosa Eldi? Why would she help me? I never did anything but hold her captive and abuse her. I sold her to all those men . . ."

"Love knows no bounds."

"I cannot believe that!" Virelai cried, sounding suddenly as willful as a child. "I do not believe the stone did this. I cannot believe it. It must have been that the sun warmed me. I was just stunned. A horse had kicked me, I remember that. I felt the shape, the size of its very hoof. It must have just knocked me out for a bit. I—I drifted for a while, and I came round when you called my name. Yes, that must be the way of it. I was dozing, and in shock . . ."

"You know very well that is not the truth," Alisha said angrily. "You know it, but you won't admit it." She pushed herself to her feet in one swift, furious motion. "But there's something I can do to make you believe."

She turned and began to march away from him across the battlefield, stepping over the outstretched limbs of corpses, skirting pools of blood, arrow-stuck horses.

"Where are you going?" Virelai called after her, but she did not answer. "What are you doing?" Then, with growing dread, he watched as she went down on her knees beside a hulking dark shape, then cowered back as shocking white light blazed suddenly, brighter than any sun. "No!" he shrieked. "No, don't!"

Then he began to run, as far and as fast as he could away from the unnatural thing that Alisha Skylark was doing, stumbling and crying out as he went, tears streaming down his face and his heart thundering. He did not stop until the sun went in and hid the terrible strangeness of the world from his sight, until the moon came up, and he was more lost than he had ever been.

9

Foreign Shores

SHE dreamed of being on the ocean at the height of a storm, an elating dream of high seas and crashing waves, of windborne foam which skimmed off the tops of the churning breakers and stung the skin. Landbirds called distantly in the air above her, their cries evocative of a cat's mewing, or a baby's wail. Air and water, water and air. It was like a dream of flying, only colder and wetter. In fact, she considered, half in and half out of this voyaging mirage, it really wasn't very pleasant at all. What had started as a sensation of freedom and speed became, with increased focus on detail, a dream of constriction and discomfort.

Two seconds later, Katla Aransen came fully awake and found herself tied to a mast in the teeth of a gale. In the space of maybe three seconds she observed four things. Firstly, and somewhat significantly, there were rocks looming large and far too close. Waves were booming broadside against the hull so that the ship's timbers creaked with all the gusto they could muster. The crew were scattered around the deck in varying degrees of uselessness, looked terrified out of their wits. And lastly, and rather worryingly, the foremast was gone, leaving a splinter of rotten wood and a flapping tail of canvas slapping the planks wetly like a dying eel.

"Sur's nuts!" she cursed. It was all very well to have survived killing the ship's captain and attempting a bid for freedom, but to die like this—bound up (yet again, she thought with rising annoyance) with a length of thick, hairy rope around her arms and waist to the only other mast still in operation, subjected to the sight of a load of landlubber incompetents making an exceedingly poor job of steering this leaky old barrel, was ignominy indeed.

She turned her head and watched with fascinated horror as a huge wave surged in over the stern and the tillerman abandoned his post with a shriek and ran down the ship with his hands in the air, as if surrendering to some watery foe.

"Hel's teeth!" She turned back in consternation, seeing those big black rocks getting much too close for comfort, and started yelling with all the volume her constricted lungs could manage, "Hey! You—someone—for god's sake—steer this bloody thing!"

Her words fell into a momentary lapse in the storm's concentration and several heads turned to see who might be shouting at them in some high-pitched foreign tongue.

Katla strained against her bonds, cursing and swearing and spitting like a trapped feral cat. If she was trying to attract attention to her conscious state, she succeeded. Seconds later, Baranguet appeared beside her, whip in hand—as if that were of any use in the current circumstances other than dissuading the cowardly from jumping overboard and taking their chances with the sea. His oily black head came up to her shoulder, but he still contrived to leer up at her as if at this precise moment he held every scrap of power over her future in this world. She hated that.

"Let me loose!" she demanded in the Old Tongue, glaring at him.

The whipman laughed. "And why should I do that, little hellion?"

"Because someone needs to steer the damn ship."

Baranguet's sneer of a laugh turned by comic degrees into an expression of panic as he darted a glance past his captive's shoulder and took in the absence at the stern, their wavering course and free-flying rudder.

He uttered a long, loud and probably obscene expletive in Istrian which Katla at once committed to memory for future use in the southern continent, if they ever made it that far. Then he fled down the deck and started laying about a man in a striped tunic with the many-thonged whip, its snaking lashes making contact with audible cracks on the cowering crewman's hunched back. On and on Baranguet whipped the tillerman, but all that happened was that the deserter hunched lower and lower until at last he collapsed on the deck with a spreading red stain all down his back.

"Oh, very constructive," Katla muttered, rolling her eyes. She tossed her head to get the wet hair out of her eyes and appraised the rapidly approaching coastline with dismay.

Baranguet gave the now-unconscious tillerman a final kick, then glared around at the rest of his hopeless crew. Clearly, Katla thought, they had either lied through their teeth to take their place on board, or the man who had engaged them had got his priorities all wrong. Fighters they might have been; sailors they were not. No one seemed ready to take responsibility for the rudder. Those the whipman shouted at scuttled off to some other self-appointed task and tried to look suitably busy. She watched one man trying to coil a line until he had produced a single indivisible knot out of it; two others began to bail enthusiastically with a half-barrel itself so leaky that as much water as they scooped up spilled through its rotten staves and redeposited itself whence it had come. Another man did something with the sail above her so that one corner of it drooped drastically, then the wind grabbed hold of it and snatched the line out of his hands. The sail billowed, then emptied itself of air. The ship, entirely at the mercy of the elements now, slewed dangerously. Meanwhile, the rope, heavy with seawater and full of momentum, whipped across the deck and clouted a tall man in a prissy uniform tunic so hard across the shoulders that he staggered and fell against another man with cropped gray hair and both forearms notched with deliberate-looking scars, knocking him flat. This man hurled the other off him, then leaped to his feet and began to pummel him with a pair of meaty fists until Baranguet intervened with a shriek of fury and his whip.

In other circumstances, Katla thought, such a display of clownish incompetence might have had her laughing till she cried; but if she tilted her head just a little to the right, she was alarmed to be able to make out individual birds' nests and plants clinging to the cliff faces looming ever closer on the steerboard side of the ship. She started praying.

As if in answer to this endeavor, the huge key keeper strode swiftly across the deck, caught up the flailing line, secured it with an expert twist, and then made for the stern, where he caught hold of the wildly swinging rudder and began to wrestle it into submission. The ship, as if sensing someone was at last in charge, relinquished its willful suicide bid and became as submissive as a whipped dog.

Too late.

For a moment the *Rose of Cera* floundered uncertainly, then wind filled her sails and she lurched sideways. There was a terrible, grating din, then a screaming wrench of cracking timbers. Katla, thrown hard against her bonds so that both feet came off the deck, had a clear, brief view of the sea to her right—a boil of surf over reef rocks, slews of weed and foam—then the ship juddered back the other way and came to a shuddering halt at an awkward, drunken angle, bow down and shoulder into the waves. From disturbingly close by there came the sound of fraying rope, then a sort of unraveling snap and the next thing she knew, Katla had been thrown painfully clear of the mast and had fetched up with the larboard gunwale wedged into her solar plexus, staring down into a mess of rock and water and wood all swirling together in some unholy brew. For several seconds she could not draw breath; when she did, it was with a painful wheeze that bespoke bruised and battered ribs, and possibly a crack or two. But she was free. Even so, it took her a few moments to recover her composure sufficiently to look around and take in the situation.

Things were not looking good for the crew of the *Rose of Cera.* Two men were flailing in the ocean to the seaward side of the vessel, thrashing the water ineffectually with their hands and screaming for aid, but no one else was taking any notice. Another man was lying jammed up against the forward mastfish, clutching his thigh. A splintered spar stuck out of it, and blood was gouting. *That's three down,* Katla thought with satisfaction. Of Baranguet, there was no sign at all. But these small triumphs were immediately displaced by the sight of water erupting through the decking near the bow.

They were holed below the waterline.

"Mother!" Katla cried in horror, and levered herself upright. Then she set off for the hatch at an awkward, limping run.

There, she stared wildly down into chaos. Amid a dark welter of floating cargo and churning foam, the women were shrieking and tearing at their chains. The water was already up to their waists. For some—for Thin Hildi and Kit Farsen, who were short and weak—it would be minutes before the inflow reached their chins . . . For a moment, Katla's mind became empty with panic, then she remembered that it had been the giant whom she had last seen with the keys to their shackles. Legs shaking with pain and nervous energy, she limped toward the stern. No one tried to stop her; indeed, there seemed to be very few men left on board, as far as she could see. Could they have been knocked overboard by the force of the strike? she wondered feverishly, dodging beneath the remnants of the third sail. It seemed too good to be true; as long as the giant hadn't gone down with them . . .

But there was Casto Agen, sitting rigidly in the stern with the rudder gripped in a deathlock, as if he could not comprehend what had happened and thought if he only held the tiller tightly, he might still steer the ship to safe waters when this small crisis had passed. He stared at Katla blankly when she fetched up in front of him.

"The keys!" she shouted, then realized she'd yelled at him in Eyran. "Give me the keys!" she repeated, this time in the Old Tongue; but still he didn't make any move, either to help or to hinder.

Huffing in frustration, Katla dived for the big man's belt. Casto Agen jumped to his feet and tried to back away from her, as if he were being attacked by some mad and infuriating insect, but there was nowhere for him to go. She had her hands wrapped around the ring of iron hanging from his left hip, but after a lot of twisting and cursing could find no way of freeing it, so she hauled at his belt, dragging him bodily after her like a recalcitrant bull. Either her adrenalized strength was terrifying or the giant came willingly, but at last they reached the hatch, where Katla turned and mimed the opening of a lock, then pointed urgently down into the hold. "Down there, the women. We must set them free."

Now the big man nodded slowly. As they clambered down the ladder, Katla's feet met water far sooner than she had expected. She gazed into the gloom at the fluttering white hands, the terrified faces. "Katla!" cried one; and "Save me, save me!"

Away to the bow end, a great tide gurgled and billowed. The hole to the hull must be substantial, Katla realized with a chill. They would all go down, shackled and free alike, if she didn't act immediately. She turned an anguished face up to the big Istrian. "Help me," she begged. "Unlock their chains."

Casto Agen glanced briefly, once, above him and seeing no vengeful officer there, nodded once and pressed past Katla, jumping down into the chaos with a great splash which sent a wake writhing through the entire hold, drenching many of the women as it passed. Katla dived in, paddled swiftly into the midst of the hold and there trod water.

"Katla!" her mother called, and there was Bera Rolfsen, bearing up Thin Hildi as best she could, so that the little girl's face was just clear of the ever-rising water. Beside her, Kitten Soronsen's hair floated around her like a great golden collar. Her mouth and eyes were stretched wide in panic.

Casto Agen waded up to her and handed her the keys without a word. She grabbed them out of his hand before he could change his mind. "Lift them up for me," she shouted. "Keep them out of the water."

The big man nodded silently and took hold of Bera Rolfsen and Thin Hildi in a bear's grip. Thin Hildi grimaced and waved her arms around in panic, calling on Feya, Sur, and the goblin-queen of Hall Spring, of whom Katla had never heard. But then, Hildi always had been a bit strange in the head, she thought as she dived.

Underwater, it was hard to see through the miasma of swirling filth. Even before the raiders had resurrected this tub for its current mission, the accumulated grime must have lain everywhere in the hold: a combination of flaking rotten timber, years of disuse, and the traces of ancient cargoes, many of which—judging by the vile crustings she had had far too long to examine in the gloom of this voyage—had been human in origin. The Istrians had built an empire on slavery, on the exploitation of the hill peoples of the southern mountains, the Wandering folk, and any other poor bastards who could not defend themselves against its might and wealth. Katla cursed them all silently as she fought the burning in her lungs and eyes and sought to locate the lock which held Thin Hildi's shackles. Groping blindly, her fingers closed on it at last. It took a few infuriating seconds to fit key to lock, then there was a satisfying release of pressure and the bolt fell away.

Casto Agen ushered the freed women up the ladder to safety, then waded back and stood before a dripping Katla awaiting instruction. It was like having a well-trained, but rather slow-witted sheepdog at your command. She indicated Fat Breta and watched as he made his way across to her, then dived again.

The inherently complacent laziness of Istrian slavers meant that they bothered to make only one type of key and lock to secure their captives—such a simple affair that one key fit all the shackles. With the water rising moment by moment, it was just as well. Katla released the women one by one by one, though with a glint of the eye pinpointing her position, she deliberately left Kitten Soronsen to last.

By the time she surfaced beside Kitten, the water was up to her chin and she glared at Katla in outraged reproach. Tears were dripping from the corners of her eyes and slipping silently into the tide, which was just adding to the problem, as far as Katla could see. It was unfair, but she could not help grinning. "Now then, Kitten—" she started; but "Get me out of here, fox-bitch!" seethed the blonde girl furiously.

"You ought to be more polite than that, considering the situation," Katla said softly, treading water. "I might just leave you here. Who'd know?" She regarded her with narrow eyes. "Or care?"

Kitten Soronsen's mouth became a long, hard line against which the water lapped gently. Katla regarded her with her head on one side and waited. When the tide began to ripple into her nostrils, the blonde girl yelped and thrashed, which made things worse. Katla sighed. "I don't like you, Kitten, and I never have. You're a bully, a malicious gossip, and a sharp-tongued witch. But I might have a hard time living with the knowledge that I left you here to drown." Katla thought about this for a long moment, during which Kitten Soronsen rained the worst imprecations she could think of down on her head. "You know," said Katla at last, with the words "heathen troll-whore" ringing in her ears, "others might judge me harshly, but I think I could probably learn to live with myself . . ."

As she turned to swim away, she heard the outraged gulp of air Kitten took in for a final farewell tirade and knew that however much she wished to, she couldn't do it. Katla had never regarded herself as someone with a conscience, or a charitable heart; but to leave Kitten to drown just meant that the Istrians would have taken yet another Rockfall life. With a sigh, she made a last dive with the key in her hand, and released Kitten from her shackles.

She received no word of thanks; nor did she expect one. Indeed, as they swam toward the bright square of sky marking their exit into the outside world, Kitten's flailing foot caught Katla sharply on the side of the head. It might not have been entirely deliberate, but Katla knew she had made herself yet another enemy.

OUT on deck, blinking in the too-bright light, it was clear their troubles were not over. The women huddled together, looking sodden and large-eyed: elation at being released from their shackles below deck had soon ebbed away at the full realization of their current plight. The shore—marked by rearing cliffs and surf spraying off the jagged reef—was only a hundred yards away, but the *Rose of Cera* would never make it across that short distance, even if she wasn't wedged tight on the rock which had holed her. Water was gushing like a geyser now near her bow and the tilt of the deck promised an imminent demise.

There was no sign of any of the raiders, other than the big man, Casto Agen, who stood beyond the group of Eyrans, looking bemused. And the shipmaker, Morten Danson, was gone, too. As were the ship's skiffs.

Katla groaned.

"What now?" demanded Kitten Soronsen, clearly spoiling for a fight.

Swimming seemed their only option, but even if they managed to cross the expanse of choppy sea between ship and land in their weakened state, they would surely be dashed to pieces on the reef . . .

Kitten followed Katla's gaze toward the violent interaction of waves and rocks that constituted the shore, then back again. "You can't be serious."

Katla shrugged. "It looks like sink or swim to me." She left Kitten staring aghast at the unwelcoming coastline, then staggered across the rocking deck to where her mother stood with her arm around a sobbing Thin Hildi.

"There's no one left," Bera said, her face a study in dour resignation. "They took the ship's boats and rowed away."

"So much for the rest of their precious cargo," Katla said bitterly.

"I think they were more concerned for their precious lives," her mother returned. "And who can blame them?"

Katla scanned the vessel for anything they could create some sort of makeshift craft from, but she knew even as she did so that it was pointless. Even if they lashed a raft together from the decking and lines, the *Rose of Cera* wouldn't last that long.

"I'm afraid we're going to have to swim for it," she said miserably, trying to keep her voice down.

"Swim?" shrieked Thin Hildi, who already appeared as limp and sodden as a drowned rat.

And now they all started crying out in consternation and turning horrified faces to Katla. Kitten Soronsen strode into the midst of the gathering, her hair plastered down her back, her eyes flashing. "These women have already been through too much, Katla Aransen. How can you possibly expect them to swim through that?" She pointed dramatically in the direction of the reef. "They're too weak. They'll drown."

"Well, stay here and drown, then!" Katla cried furiously. She limped over to the gunwale and stared down. Even to seaward, the water looked dark and troubled, ready to swallow them all; landward looked far worse.

Kitten turned to the wailing women. "I shall stay here and await rescue," she declared. "There are bound to be other vessels coming past. One of them will surely stop to take us aboard. Feya would surely not abandon her own; no, nor Sur either."

"Neither Feya nor Sur gave much thought to us when we tried to defend our own at Rockfall," Bera Rolfsen said grimly. "And as for other vessels sailing by!" She laughed. "The southerners are hardly well known for their seamanship, or indeed their mercy, and we are too far from home to hope for an Eyran ship." She clenched her jaw. "It seems my daughter has the right of it and we shall have to gain our salvation by our own actions. I cannot say I much care for the idea of swimming to shore, but I do not see that we have any alternative."

"No!" Magla Felinsen, usually one of the more robust of the Rockfall women, collapsed in a heap and began to sob wildly. "I c . . . caaaan't . . . I can't swim!"

Bera and Katla exchanged stricken glances.

Kitten knelt by Magla's side and looked up at them accusingly. "You see," she said triumphantly. "It's just not possible. Magla will die if you make her swim—"

At this, Magla gave out a banshee howl that had Casto Agen making the superstitious sign of Falla's eye and glancing fearfully around.

Two camps were forming, for some of the other women went to sit down beside Kitten and Magla. They hugged their knees and glared obstinately at the Mistress of Rockfall—a woman renowned for her temper and her despotism—and her daughter, who was, they all knew, a wild hoyden, never happier than when involved in some dangerous and foolhardy venture and who had, for the Lord's sake, slept with a mummer . . .

Unaware of their silent judgment of her, Katla sighed. Then she lurched down the tilting deck to where the second mast's sail lay flapping in the ever-increasing offshore wind and with swift fingers detached two of the lines. These she then bound together with a sturdy double fisherman's knot, then whipped the full length of rope into a coil, one end of which she passed around her waist and tied securely. Trembling with intent, she returned to the group of women; most of whom now sat passively waiting for some miracle to occur.

"I'm going to try it," she announced. She attached the other end of the rope to a cleat, then beckoned to her mother. "If I don't make it, you can haul my corpse back in, or cut the rope and let the fishes have me. If I do, you can make the crossing with the rope to hold onto. Even Magla—" she glared at the red-faced woman slumped on the deck, "—should be able to manage that."

Bera nodded, though her face was ashen.

Then she addressed the big raider. "Can you swim?" she asked.

He stared at her, frowning. She mimed her question, pointing to the land. He looked appalled, shook his head. "Ah, well," Katla muttered. "Looks like I'm on my own."

She made one more survey of the awful prospect ahead of her, heart thumping as if trying to escape the challenge by breaking free of her chest, then, before she could change her mind, she kicked off her boots, stepped up onto the steerboard gunwale, and leaped off.

Before she had even had time to register the chill of the air which whistled past her, the sea had her deep in its embrace, and it wasn't letting go. It was shockingly, cruelly, murderously cold. It made the marrow in her bones ache, her teeth chatter uncontrollably, her flesh go numb. *Winter,* she thought. *It's even winter in Istria.* She hadn't given much thought to that. *Better start swimming.*

She struck out in the direction in which she remembered seeing the shore, but for a long time the waves were too high to see over. Then at last one picked her up and carried her to its crest. What she saw made her heart sink. The line of rocks guarding the beach beyond looked unbroken, impregnable, the surf that dashed against this jagged barricade a uniform wall of angry white water. Then the wave she was on bore her down into a trough and she saw no more. On she swam, head down, arms fighting the sea's resistance.

It was Halli who had taught her to swim when she was four years old. They were in White Stone Cove—she remembered the event now with awful clarity despite, perhaps even because of, her current circumstances—by chucking her bodily off the rocks there and laughing as she rose to the surface bubbling like a farm cat and thrashing the water with all her might. "Like this," he had shown her, safe upon the shore, spreading his arms in graceful arcs. "And kick your feet." Then he had dived in, as graceful as a cormorant, and come up beside her as she went down for the second time. Two days later, she had been swimming as lithely as a seal. But that had been summer—an Eyran summer, yes; but still summer—and in a sheltered bay. She might, she considered, have the technique and the will for the task in hand, but did she have the fortitude?

When the next big wave carried her up into the briny air, the shore was, however, far closer than she had expected. Panicking in case the next series of waves would throw her headfirst and unprepared into the rocks, she pulled taut the rope which attached her to the *Rose of Cera* and rested briefly, treading water, her lungs and muscles burning. Curiously, she felt quite warm now, warm and rather sleepy. At this realization, she blinked furiously, recognizing the dangerous early stages of body chill, and started swimming again. Details sprang into focus. The tidewrack lining the beach was very dark, almost black. Bladderwrack, most likely. It was all pebbles, pebbles and driftwood, rounded and smoothed by the rolling ocean. In contrast, the reef and cliffs which backed the beach were slanted and sharp, a glinting dark gray with great rows of sharks' fins. *Slate*, she thought miserably. *Worst type of rock to get wrecked on; cut you to ribbons as soon as look at you.*

But even as despair set in, her head and fingers started to tingle. Something drew her, diagonally, to the left. Too tired to resist—or even question—the instinct, and too weak to maintain a steady breaststroke, Katla found herself paddling like a dog now. The tingling became an insistent buzz which traveled down her spine and radiated up into her skull. Exhausted, Katla gulped a mouthful of seawater, choked and sank, thrashing. A moment later she was somehow *above* herself, looking down on a sorry scrap of battered flesh at the mercy of the elements, its dark hair plastered flat to its scalp, its pale limbs flailing pathetically. She felt sorry for it; then nothing at all. The land was more interesting, from this new perspective. Powerful and vibrant, humming with energies, it had endured for thousands upon thousands of years; would go on for thousands more, giving to and taking back from the sea in an eternal exchange of matter, each element nurturing the other. Millennia ago the cliffs had been a part of the great ocean, rocks from the northern wastes ground down to dust and held in suspension in the heart of the sea, to be laid down in minute layers, one upon another and another and another, compressed by the movements of vast plates of rock floating around the molten center of Elda, crushed into solidity and shoved up into rucks and outcrops. Alternately sharpened and smoothed by the erosive powers of air and water, they were ever mutable, ever-changing, their forms part of the constant chaotic relationship between weather and world. And Katla, too, felt herself inherent in this neverending stew of life, a tiny crystal of light and spirit held in trust between air, earth, and water; a quickened atom of being who owed her existence to them all, and would at some not-too-distant point in time return her constituents to them. For now, though, they let her be; more, they offered her their essential natures, their configurations, and their secrets till she was brimming with them, and at last, weighed down by this new freight of knowledge, she fell back into her body again, now all cold and forlorn, stranded halfway between the land and a sinking ship.

But the knowledge was still with her. Fueled by the generosity of Elda, Katla struck out once more with renewed strength and purpose. There was, she now knew, a small gap in the reef, a gap floored with sand

and fringed with kelp. Two more big waves picked her up and drove her forward and she let them take her where they would. Then, with the buzzing suffusing her entire body, she dived through the crashing rim of surf, down below the chaos into serene green depths, like a seal, like a seal. A few seconds later she had glided in between the dark fangs of rock on either side of the gap and was lying panting on the pebbled shore, waves lapping at her feet.

From the ship they saw a tiny figure skipping out a complex and compulsive victory dance, then waving madly at them.

"She's a marvel," Bera Rolfsen cried, breathing for what seemed the first time in an age.

"Katla! Katla!" the women shouted. "Well done, Katla!"

But Kitten Soronsen sat and glared. "I don't know why you're all celebrating. We're here and she's there. Who's to say the draw of the tide won't break our bodies on the rocks? Who's to say the rope won't break? Or that we won't die of cold before we're halfway there?"

At her words, several of the women quieted, suddenly sobered.

"I'm not risking it," Kitten finished. "You lot can do as you please; but I'd rather trust to the Lady Feya and the Lord Sur than to any plan of Katla Aransen's."

"Well," said Bera coldly, "you can stay here alone and go down with the ship. And be it on your own head, empty as it is." She pointedly turned her attention away from the blonde girl as if dismissing her from her thoughts, and shaded her eyes to watch Katla shinning up a rock to attach the rope around a rocky spike there. Even though it was now held up at either end, the middle of the rope dipped into the sea; yet it was still the best lifeline available to them. "Come on," she said briskly to Kit Farsen, "you go first. You're shivering. No point in getting any colder waiting around here."

At the older woman's bidding, Kit Farsen got to her feet a trifle unsteadily—she'd never been one to think much for herself—and allowed the Mistress of Rockfall to lead her to the steerboard gunwale. There, she quailed.

"You have to jump in," Bera pointed out. "There's no other way. Just grab the rope when you bob up again."

Bera made it sound perfectly straightforward, but Kit balked. The next thing she felt was a firm hand on her back, and then she was in the sea. "Feya save me!" she wailed, before a wave crashed over her. A moment later she bobbed back up, disoriented and spluttering, her eyes staring wildly. Galvanized by her predicament, she kicked herself around in a circle, spotted the line hanging overhead, and grabbed hold as if it were the only thing between salvation and chilly death; which, of course, it was. Then, without any further need for instruction, she hauled herself along it, hand over hand, through the churning waves, until she was through the surf, between the arms of the reef and safely on firm ground.

Amazed and filled with new hope, the women cheered; all but Kitten Soronsen, who had always hated to be proved wrong.

Then they followed, one by one by one: Thin Hildi, Fat Breta (who looked as if she surely must drown until she finally slumped ashore like a beached walrus), Forna Stensen, and the rest. Eventually there were only Bera, Kitten, and the big Istrian left on deck.

Casto Agen made no move to save himself, so Bera took off her shoes and stepped to the gunwale. "Coming?" she asked Kitten Soronsen.

But Kitten, eyes glinting with unshed tears, stuck her chin in the air and stared off into the wide gray sky.

With a shrug and a last glance at the statuelike raider, Bera Rolfsen stepped off into thin air.

She thought the cold would stop her heart; nothing had prepared her for the shock of it. She could not breathe, could not see for what seemed whole minutes. Then her head was up above the killing waves and she was sucking air into her lungs as if she could never get enough of it. Then she laid hold of the rope and dragged herself along it as fast as her frozen muscles would allow. Waves washed over her, pulling her down, but she never let go. "Thirty-eight, thirty-nine," went the mantra in her head. "Forty, forty-one . . ." One for each bone-chilling haul. When she reached fifty-two, she found herself among the breakers and boiling surf; at fifty-five, her trailing feet stubbed against sand; at fifty-seven, her knees struck the ground, and then she stopped counting.

Immediately, Katla was at her side, chafing her arms and legs. "Get up, Mother," she said urgently. "Get up and start walking, or you'll die of the cold."

Bera sat upright. There, in front of her, spread out across the stony strand were the other survivors, all marching doggedly about like the remnants of some particularly doomed and tattered army, rubbing their thighs and stamping their feet for all they were worth.

She looked back toward the *Rose of Cera*. From here the imminence of its demise was clear. It was nose-down, its stern sticking out of the water at a highly unnatural angle. There was no sign of Kitten Soronsen or of the big raider. Frowning, Bera shifted her gaze. About midway between ship and shore was a great splashing shape. The Istrian, it seemed, had decided to take his chances with the sea.

But as the titanic splashing which marked Casto Agen's progress approached the shore, it soon became apparent that the Istrian had not left Kitten to the fate she deserved. For there she was, clinging to his back, her face a perfect mask of fury. She couldn't say she was happy to see Kitten Soronsen again, but Katla could not help but grin at the thought of the indelicate treatment she had endured in the course of this unwished-for rescue.

As soon as the raider cleared the surf, Kitten launched herself off his back and hared up the beach, meeting no one's eye. Veering away from them all, she hurled herself down into the sand on the other side of the tideline and gave all her attention over to wringing out her hair and rags.

Katla turned to her mother, eyebrows raised, but it was Bera who spoke first. "Leave her be. There is already enough bad blood between you. Feya knows our situation won't be helped by adding to it."

Then, before Katla could protest that she had had no intention whatsoever of baiting Kitten further, Bera marched over to the big Istrian and said loudly and formally in the Old Tongue: "Thank you. It was good of you to grant my request." She bobbed her head at him in a particularly old-fashioned gesture, and then turned back to meet the questioning gaze of her daughter.

"You asked him to bring Kitten Soronsen?" Katla was aghast.

Bera shrugged. "I could hardly leave her to drown."

"It might have proved better for all of us if you had," Katla muttered indistinctly.

They spent a miserable night on the beach, which rendered up no shelter, food, or water. Katla had been all for exploring their new surroundings but her mother had been adamant. "We stick together, those few of us who are left," she declared. "When the sun comes up, then we shall decide what to do."

Katla couldn't sleep. She could feel the cliffs pulling at her, just as she had felt Sur's Castle calling her to climb when she first reached the Moonfell Plain. The rock in this southern continent tugged at her in ways she could not fully fathom, as if it were speaking to her in a foreign language of which she knew but a few words. But there was something urgent in its attraction, something elemental and strange. All night she seethed and fretted. And it was damned cold, too. Disliking most of her companions too much to put aside her pride and bed down with them for the warmth, she had made herself a hollow place in the sand, lined it with the dryest of the bladderwrack and lain there, assailed by its rank and salty smell, watching the stars roll overhead, trying to ignore her various hurts and discomforts. If she looked north, back over the ocean, she could see the Navigator's Star shining bright and constant, and she thought about her father and her twin and wondered where on Elda they might be now. Were they faring any better? She could not imagine they were any warmer, wherever they were; if indeed they were still alive. Which was but small consolation.

Smoke and Mirrors

THE old man turned and surveyed his visitors with satisfaction. The two who were conscious were staring about them in open-mouthed awe, as was only right and proper. Even if he said so himself, the Great Hall was a glorious achievement. His stronghold was probably the most magnificent building in all of Elda. Or rather, in all of *known* Elda, he corrected himself, remembering the extravagance of the basilica he had commissioned in his former capital, with its gilded mosaics and marble-inlaid floor, its fabulous carvings and gleaming golden dome. It had taken over a century as men measured time to complete the task of the vast mosaic alone, so intricate and finely worked was it. A sudden pang went through the Master then. *Just think,* came an unbidden voice, *you could have had all that and the Lady, too, if you'd been more careful. You wouldn't have had to flee to this gods-forsaken corner of the world and make do with shadows and turnips . . .*

"Now, then," he said, firmly pushing the annoying voice back into the darkness where it belonged, "let me take the boy and see what I can do for him." Then he lifted Fent Aranson from the shoulders of the giant as if he were no heavier than a reed, turned on his threadbare heel, and vanished suddenly and silently into the deep shadows beyond the Great Hall, leaving the two men gawping after him.

It was some time before Aran Aranson came back to himself sufficiently to take in the full import of where they were. He stared about his surroundings in wonderment. No man of his generation—and perhaps no man in history—had ever stood where he now stood: in the very heart of famed Sanctuary.

The hall was dominated by arched windows filled with some mysterious transparent substance which appeared to let the light in and keep the cold air beyond them out. These made the room seem chillier still, for the light that issued from them was so bright it seemed almost as tangible as the icy interior it illuminated. What saved the chamber from unrelieved austerity was a collection of hides of the most massive snow bears that could ever have stalked these arctic wastes, which were scattered here and there across the hard-packed floor, and a vast tapestry hanging above the hearth at the far end. Everything else was of ice—the tables, the chairs, the settles, even the lamps—great globes on stands which emitted an eerily pale and unnecessary light. He watched Urse walk like a man in a dream across the floor to the hearth and stretch his hands before its leaping fire. In another context, it might have seemed a comfortingly mundane gesture: a man in a cold place trying to warm himself. Except that the flames were green and blue and violet: every color alien to any natural fire.

"Urse!" he said loudly and cringed as his voice echoed noisily across the hall and fled away into the vaulted ceilings high above. Gazing up fearfully, he was alarmed to note that his call had disturbed a horde of tiny translucent creatures which had set to flitting and diving madly about in the deep blue shadows, their movements visible as a momentary flicker and shimmer amid the gloom.

"What are they?" breathed the giant, a look of apparent puzzlement creasing his ruined face. It was hard to read the big man's facial expressions when half of them were either missing or vastly distorted, but his brows were knit and he could not stop pulling at his single remaining ear, a tic the erstwhile Master of Rockfall had previously noticed Urse resort to in times of confusion and discomfiture.

Aran shrugged. "I thought they might be bats . . ."

The giant shook his head. "They're like no bats I ever saw." He looked down at the fire again, then shook his head sadly. "This is a terrible place, Aran. We have come to a terrible place."

His companion gave no answer but crossed instead to one of the great windows and stared outside, as if in the hope of refuting Urse's statement. In one direction, all he could see were vistas of endless ice, in the other a vast and sculpted parkland of snow with a mirror-flat lake gleaming in its center. Nothing moved on that sheeny expanse, though here and there it seemed that the corpses of ducks and oddly-shaped swans floated upon still waters. A pair of graciously proportioned balustrades flanked a sweep of stairs which ran from the stronghold out toward the lake, and on these were also strewn a number of strange objects—what looked much like half a sheep appeared to have been draped along the bottom step, and a number of smaller and even less identifiable creatures lay scattered across the frosted lawn.

Frowning, he turned back to his companion.

"It's not what I imagined," Aran said quietly. Who knew what the old man might hear in this unnatural place?

Urse cracked what might have been a rueful smile. "You mean, where's the gold?"

"Ssshh." Aran moved softly to the doorway and peered out into the maze of corridors. But of the Master and Fent there was no sign. It had been hard to consign the boy to the mage's care, but somehow when the old man had taken him, he had found himself unable to object, unable even to move his feet to follow, and then it seemed he had simply forgotten to be concerned—that, or the old man had made some spell over him. For Aran Aranson had no doubt that Sanctuary was a place made by and filled with sorcery.

His hand crept down to the dagger which hung at his belt, and he unhitched the blade and brought it up into view, running a thumb along its edge. Keen it was, and of good Eyran iron, forged by his own daughter in the Rockfall smithy. But could even the finest blade be keen enough to cut the throat of a sorcerer? His heart quelled at the very thought, now that he was here and the deed imminent. Shaking, he sheathed the blade, and ran a hand across his face.

Despite the arctic setting, sweat was pouring down his cheeks and neck. Embarrassed, he rubbed it away. At his collar, his fingers ran across the thong of leather he wore around his neck, then moved down to the pouch which hung from it. There, they fluttered like moths at a flame. Without a moment's conscious thought, Aran reached in and touched the curl of parchment which nested inside. As if it were indeed a flame, it gave out a tremendous heat: comforting, reassuring, compelling. He pulled out the map and gazed at it. At once, clarity returned, a warm glow of confidence and certainty. He turned to the big man.

"When the mage returns my son to me, then we will kill him."

Urse One Ear regarded his captain mildly. "It would be a shame to kill an old man."

"We came here for his gold; I will not leave this place without it."

"If you kill the old man, you may never leave. Besides, he does not look like a rich man to me, a man who has a lot of gold. Not with those ragged clothes and holed shoes."

"Pretense and deception. We will make him tell us where it is," Aran declared mulishly. "And then we will kill him."

"Tell me how will we leave this place—with or without the gold—when we have no ship to bear us? Shall we fly like eagles bearing carrion, or like bumblebees laden with pollen?"

But Aran Aranson was immune to the big man's jibes. "When he returns, I will make him tell me where the gold is. And then he will reveal to us where he keeps the ship on which he traveled here."

"A ship?"

The Master had reappeared in the doorway, his footsteps soundless on the ice. Behind him, Fent Aranson followed like a sleepwalker, eyes unfocused, his long face with its fringe of auburn beard showing no hint of expression. The old man smiled, cunning as a fox.

"A ship, you say?" Then he laughed, a huge sound which set the pale creatures in the shadows to wheeling and flapping again. "Ah, the naïveté of men. Charming, so charming." He caught Fent by the arm and propelled him forward. "Go to your father, my boy," he whispered, and as if set in motion by the turn of a key, Fent marched across the floor of the Great Hall with leaden legs and came to a halt in front of Aran Aranson. There, he issued no word of greeting; indeed, gave no sign of recognition of either of the men who stood watching him, their eyes as round as plates.

"As you can see," the Master said. "I have restored him, as well as I can, for now, at least."

Aran tore his gaze away from his miraculously restored son and stared at the mage in consternation. Had the old man heard him planning his death? Surely he must have, for he was smiling still, and it was not a smile to gladden the heart.

"May I see that?" the Master asked, inclining his head toward the parchment in Aran's hand.

Aran looked down guiltily, then back at the sorcerer, his panic rising.

The old man reached out a hand, flexed his fingers, and as if magically summoned, Aran Aranson found himself crossing the room, his hand outstretched before him, the map lying curled, exposed, and naked on his palm. He wanted to clutch the parchment into a ball, to hide it beneath his clothing, to make it disappear. But his hand remained strangely unwilling to do his bidding, as if it now belonged to another master than the man to whom it was attached. Two strides away from the mage he halted, then watched in appalled wonder as the map rose into the air and floated into the grasp of the old man. Immediately, despair set in. He was lost; all was lost. It had all been such a waste, the entire enterprise—the kidnap of the shipmaker, the building of the *Long Serpent,* the selection of its crew, the disastrous voyage and the treacherous trek across the ice—all seemed no more than a sequence of follies, follies which had whipped up a maelstrom of madness and taken the lives of many good men. For the sake of sheer greed, he had lost what he held dear: his family, his steading, his reputation. He was a broken man. For the first time in his life, Aran Aranson felt the most profound shame. He hung his head and wept.

For his part, the Master took no notice of this display of emotion. He did not even bother to look at the map a second time, but merely held it to his nose and sniffed the parchment as if its scent brought him comfort. "Ah," he sighed. "Squid ink mixed with cat's urine. Bëte, ah Bëte, my dear, I shall have you back yet."

Then he tore the precious chart into tiny pieces and, uttering a single word of power over them, dissolved the fragments into thin air.

"Now," he declared in a voice which permitted no objection, "come with me."

They followed the Master out of the Great Hall—the Giant, the Madman, and the Fool—their feet obedient only to his word. He led them down corridors embedded with precious stones and seamed with pyrites which glittered its tawdry seductive gold and they saw nothing of it, for he wished it not; he led them up stairways carved into the ice, up and up and up until their breath filled the air with clouds of steam and their lungs protested. But no sound did they utter, for it was not his will that they should.

At last they surmounted the one hundred and sixty-eighth step, and there an intricately carved door stood closed before them. On the Master's word of command, the door swung open without a creak. And now they could not help but cry out, for the light hurt their eyes, so bright it was, so radiant and many-colored.

"Behold the world!"

One spell had lifted, but it seemed another had fallen over them. At first, they had no idea of what they were looking at; it was too strange, too unexpected, too hard to fathom. Then, one by one, they were able to descry a huge oval bowl set upon a plinth of ice, bathed in ever-changing light. Above it, the center of the roof lay open to the gray arctic skies, and this was where much of the light was sourced. But all around, amid a spiderweb of chains and levers and pulleys were crystals great and small, a few thinned by some unimaginable force to slivers as long as a man's arm, yet only as thick as his smallest finger; others whole and polished to facets so that fractured light from them rebounded from the ice, the other crystals, the surface of the bowl, the men's faces. Aran Aranson stepped boldly up to the plinth, and Urse followed, dragging the oddly-languid Fent in his wake. There, they gazed into the bowl, and were mightily confused by the vista offered therein. It appeared to be a swath of dark ocean, jammed with frazil ice which was intermittently lifted and let fall by invisible rollers, so that the entire surface rose and fell, undulating like some great sleeping beast. In the far left of the scene, a broken ship lay on its side, wedged amid the ice. It was not the *Long Serpent,* which had gone to its demise beneath just such dark waves of ice, but a similar vessel; even so, a chill of memory and recognition ran through their bones at the very sight of it. The Master let them dwell on that sorry image for a few more seconds, then he laid hold of a lever, adjusted the angle of a large crystal, and the scene veered crazily, racing through colors like seasons flowing one into another and out the other side; and then suddenly where there had been frozen sea, now there was another landscape entirely—an expanse of ochre stretching as far as could be seen. This, too, seemed full of waves, for it was striated with long curving lines, great crescents and arcs, elegant as birds' wings. Aran frowned. He had never seen anything like it.

Smiling, the Master turned another handle and the focus shifted, closing fast, diving vertiginously from crow's view to ant's. "It's sand . . ." breathed Urse One Ear, amazed. "Fields of sand."

Just like a sea, Aran thought, remembering travelers' tales of such, tales dismissed as fable, of thousands of miles of wasteland so parched that a man lost there would die in a single day under the pitiless eye of the sun, if he had not luck or aid.

Fent Aranson simply stared at this inimical place unblinking and said not a word.

"They call it the Bone Quarter now," the old man mused. "Though I remember when it was a fair land of tall reeds and gentle rivers frequented by ibis and doves."

Aran and Urse could make nothing of this statement. Instead, they watched, amazed, as he turned the levers again and brought another vista crashing into view. A black volcano ascended into glowering red clouds, indeed, was making those very clouds, belching out gouts of cinder and glowing ash as if it would burn up the whole world. None of them had ever seen such a thing in their lives. They had heard the word *fire-mountain* from the tales that the old folk told on winter nights, for this was how Elda had come into being according to one legend of the north: a great sea of fire had covered all the surface of the world, islands and continents had formed from the shooting cinders as they cooled; the First Men—their most distant ancestors—had been ejected in spurts and falls out of the flaming depths. But it was hard to give credit to such tales, for an equal and opposite myth about the birth of Elda had it that Umla, the Great Mother—who was, according to varying versions, either a vast milch-cow or a huge cat—had given birth to a single offspring which she called Elda and which at first seemed no more than a formless lump until the Great Mother had licked it into shape, thus making the mountain ridges and the islands, the rivers and the seas, and had poured herself into the heart of the new world, and from that inner being had poured forth all the birds and animals, the men and the women so that Elda would have them to love and care for.

There did not seem much love involved in the creation of the scene before their eyes; indeed, it appeared a place inimical to all life: for what creature could breathe air filled with burning fragments and charged with noxious gases? What bird could fly through flaming clouds? What beast could forage for nourishment on its burning, barren slopes? To Aran Aranson it seemed the antithesis of life, this mountain of fire. It seemed the location where the world would draw to a terrible close, rather than the source whence life had come.

"Where is this place?" he asked the mage fearfully.

The Master, without taking his eyes from the hellish scene before them said nothing for many long moments. Then he swung the levers once more and plunged the bowl of light into vivid turmoil. "That place is known as the Red Peak," he said softly. "And one of you will be going there as your task."

"Task?" said Aran sharply. "What task?"

The old man smiled, though there was no warmth in it. "You did not think I had brought you to my Sanctuary out of the goodness of my heart?"

Urse and Aran exchanged stricken glances. "We thought . . . we . . ." the big man started, before stuttering to a halt.

"We thought you had taken pity on our plight," Aran Aranson finished for him.

The mage's smile widened, revealing long yellow teeth amid the copious beard. "Pity," he mused. "Ah, I have almost forgotten the meaning of the word. " 'Pity stayed his hand.' Is that not what one of the old myths tells us? When the hero strikes down the beast and sees the fear in the creature's eyes and recognizes that it has a soul which matches his own and cannot bring himself to make the killing stroke?"

Aran frowned. He knew the tale—what child did not? For Sur had spared the life of the great dragon known as the Long Serpent, and it had finally repaid his compassion with treachery, rising up out of the waters of the Northern Ocean a year later to overturn his ship and kill his crew. It was a tale passed down from generation to generation and, like the story of King Fent and the Trolls of the Black Mountain, it had a maxim at its heart: deal with your problems today, for they will only get larger if left.

"It was not pity that brought you here," the mage told him, "but greed, as well you know," and his eyes were flinty. "But your greed shall be rewarded with treasures beyond any you imagine, if only you will pay my price."

And before the men could say a word, the Master stepped up to Urse One Ear and passed his hand across Urse's forehead. The giant swayed where he stood. Then the mage muttered a string of sounds which Aran Aranson could make no sense of—except for the word *bet* which was repeated over and over; and this word he remembered he had heard the old man utter before, though he knew not what it meant. He watched Urse's face contort itself as if he were suddenly terrified, but when the mage tapped him lightly on the temples, his eyes were as clear and unafraid as they had always been, and he seemed quite unchanged.

"You have your task, my Giant," the Master said in a satisfied tone.

In response, Urse nodded slowly. "I have my task," he said, and his voice was not his own, but leaden and inflectionless.

Aran stared at his shipmate in horror, then at the old man. "What have you done to him?" he cried accusingly.

"Done?" The Master laughed. "I have given him purpose where there was none before. It is my gift to him: the greatest gift any man can receive. The Giant now has a reason to live, and to die. He should be grateful to me, for he will become a legend in his own right."

The Master turned to Aran Aranson. "And now it is your turn."

The dark man backed away from him, his gray eyes sparking with fear. "Do not touch me or expect me to accept this gift!" Aran backed toward the door. "I will take my chance with the arctic wilds and leave this place empty-handed rather than take any task of yours!"

The door behind him swung closed with a soft thud, and when he turned to grab at the handle, he found there was none—nor, indeed, any door.

The Master smiled and wiped his brow. "This magic is an exhausting thing sometimes," he said. "Let me show you something in the glass before we proceed further. I would not wish to damage you through lack of care or strength." And he led an unresisting Aran Aranson back to the bowl of light and twisted the levers once more.

Clouds and landscape sped past below them. Buildings of stone loomed up and veered away, hillsides dotted with cattle, a hundred half-made ships bobbed in a shallow anchorage. Aran glimpsed women running from soldiers bearing flaming torches, a town square packed with an avid crowd; men marching across rough terrain. He saw carts full of weaponry trailing one another along paved southern roadways, he saw a monstrous creature rising up out of a stormy ocean and then disappearing from view so fast that he was not able to ask for a closer view; then more sea, waves breaking on jagged reefs, a swirl of gulls over the bays and headlands of a familiar coastline. There was a sudden blurring as the Master swung the crystals swiftly, and then suddenly there was Halbo, the sentinel pillars rising grimly from a choppy sea and a towering castle of granite shining pink and gray in a setting sun.

"Ah," breathed the mage, "now we shall have her."

He adjusted the viewing crystals minutely until the scene hovered like a bird's eye view of Eyra's capital. People were milling about the town below the castle's walls, laying in stores it seemed, for dozens of carts were progressing to the gates laden high with provisions, while on the hill on the landward side other carts were coming out empty. Down at the docks there was a ferment of activity. Men scurried here and there, unloading cargoes from barges, piling up shipments on the quayside and then transferring them to the waiting carts, mending sails, coiling lines, stacking weaponry. Hundreds of ships were arrayed in the harbor beyond, riding safe at anchor, jostling one another like a flock of seabirds sheltering from a storm.

"War," breathed the mage. "A time of violence and great opportunity."

Now he brought the vista in closer. On top of the castle lay a garden which had remained green, even in the midst of winter. And in the midst of that green was a pale fire—a woman in white, her silver-blonde hair spilling down her back like a waterfall. When she turned, he felt his heart still and then break into a swift and ragged rhythm. In her arms she held a child, a small black-headed thing wrapped in a scarlet shawl, mouth stretched in a soundless howl. Behind her stood a man—King Ravn Asharson—his long black hair blowing in the wind, a fond smile etched on his handsome face as he took the child from his nomad-wife's arms and rocked it to apparent silence.

"What?" cried the Master. "That cannot be. It is most unnatural, uncanny, impossible . . ."

A cloud fell between them and the woman, allowing Aran to drag his eyes from the scene.

"Surely it is the most natural thing in the world," he said, staring at the mage.

"Indeed," said the Master shortly, "it is not."

He reached abruptly across the space between them and grasped Aran by the forehead, his long bony fingers spanning the flesh between hairline and brow.

Wrenching himself away, Aran cried out. "No! I will do her no harm. Not for you, or any other—"

The Master steadied himself against the bowl. "Believe me," he said vehemently, "you will do as you are bidden, or you will die here, the most painful death I can devise, and I know many ways to make a man suffer."

"Nothing you can do to me can be worse than what I have already done to myself."

The Master raised an eyebrow. This one would need to have his spirit broken before he would be the useful tool he required. With apparent nonchalance he waved a hand.

"Have it your way, for now. Let me show you a little of what I can do, and maybe then you will change your mind about resisting me." Then he turned to the silent, volitionless creature which was Fent Aranson. "You will go to the Red Peak," he told him, enunciating each word with great care. "You will travel south through all of Istria with my protection upon you until you come to the Dragon's Backbone. Then you must find the mountain of fire. Within it lies my enemy." He closed his eyes. "He has been there for a very long time. More than three hundred years, and I feel his strength returning. If he breaks free, nothing can save me. You are the key."

Fent's eyes focused for the first time, and settled on the mage's face. He smiled: a beatific smile as of one blessed with a divine secret.

"I am the Madman," he said. "I am the key."

"You are bound to my service. I have a great task for you."

"Bound to service . . . a great task . . ."

"Repeat after me," the Master said, holding his gaze intently. "The Madman must find the Warrior."

Fent's eyes gleamed with an inner light. "The Madman must find the Warrior," he repeated.

"And kill him."

"And kill him."

"Now give me your injured arm."

Slowly, Fent raised his truncated limb and extended its charred stump toward the mage. The Master regarded the ruined arm sorrowfully. "I am sorry that my snow bear had to take your hand, but the one I shall give you now will be stronger by far." Taking the burned end in his own grip, he summoned all his strength and uttered three words of command. At once, the air filled with buzzing. Down from the eaves came a swarm of translucent creatures: not bats, it seemed, nor any other recognizable beast. Bigger than bees they were, and smaller than birds. Beyond that, it was impossible to make out any detail, since they moved so swiftly and so constantly around the site of the injury. Like spiders, they wove a glistening web: but no gossamer was this, for what they spun appeared to be strands of a substance that gleamed like silver or moonlight on water.

A fierce light filled the icy tower room, a light which was neither white nor blue but some painful aspect between these two and Aran had to shield his eyes from the glare. As the buzzing grew louder, he held his head, trying to shut out the noise. Turning, he found Urse One Ear already hunkered down on the floor, whimpering like a tortured animal. The silence, when it fell, seemed deafening, as if all the sound in the world had been sucked into a sudden void. Vivid red afterimages chased each other across Aran Aranson's eyes. Even with the wicked light fled away, it took him several seconds to focus.

A dark figure stood before him. He knew in the logical part of his mind that it must be his son: his youngest boy, twin to Katla, who had gone bad in so many ways yet remained always Fent; at the same time, it clearly was not. He squeezed his eyes shut, to allow the image to dispel, as if this new apparition was itself an aftereffect of the mage's spell, some chancy trick of the light. But when he opened them again, the figure was still there, as unnerving as ever. He quailed before it, suddenly afraid.

The Master walked in a circle around the boy, admiring his handiwork. "Well, well," he said at last. "It seems I have outdone myself. The old powers are not lost after all!"

Looming behind Aran Aranson, Urse One Ear got slowly to his feet, looking disoriented and confused. At last, his eyes came to rest on Fent Aranson—or whatever Fent Aranson had become—and then it seemed he could not drag them away. Mesmerized, he stared and stared. When the figure moved toward him, he cried out and turned to run. Out of nowhere, the door reappeared, opened itself, and allowed him egress. His receding footsteps echoed away down the winding stairs.

The Master laughed long and hard. Then he placed a comforting hand on Aran's shoulder. "Do not worry. He knows the path he must follow now. I have conveyed to him his task, and now you must learn to accept yours."

Aran stared at him wildly, the whites showing all around his dark pupils. "What have you done to him?"

In response, the Master smiled. "Do not concern yourself with that, my friend; for he is more now than he was, and what father would not wish such for his son? Now you and I will make a voyage of discovery, for there is something you need to see before all your ties to the petty things of this world are broken and you will give yourself wholeheartedly to the deed you must do for me."

Kitten's Revenge

DAY dawned a cold and streaky red. "Sailor's warning," Katla thought. "Unfortunately, a day too late."

Her bones creaked. If she breathed in hard, her ribs burned. Her right leg felt like a lump of wood, except when she tried to flex some life into it. Sharp pain shot up into her thigh, making her wince.

"Sur's teeth, what a mess I'm in." And that wasn't even taking into consideration the throbbing of her head every time she moved it, or the shudders of heat and chill that kept running through her.

No one else was awake; and she had no wish to disturb them, for now. She had a plan—of sorts.

Farther down the beach the rope lay like a sleeping serpent, stretched out where she'd left it to dry. From her assessment of the cliffs, they reached to the height of maybe seventy or eighty feet. She hoped there would be enough rope for the task, given that most of it was unavailable to them, attached as it was to the ship. She located the knot which held the two lines she had used to make the single length together and picked it up. The rope was still damp, but not sodden, the knots shrunken and clinging from use and it took her ten sweaty minutes to part the two ropes. Sighing with relief, Katla coiled the freed rope as she walked landward, the crunching pebbles digging painfully into her bare soles.

At first close examination the cliff proved flaky and undependable, the sort of stuff that would come away in your hand or crumble underfoot at just the wrong moment. She shivered. Even falling onto sand from halfway up would mean serious damage. She didn't usually allow herself such dangerous conjectures; but she wasn't even sure she could trust her abilities in the state she was in, let alone the rock.

She walked eastward, scanning the cliffs as she went, looking for a possible route to the top. It looked dreadful stuff: compacted shale, more like piecrust than rock. In places, it had tumbled down in little avalanches of earth and stone, but the ravines left by these falls looked even more dangerous than the sheer faces which flanked them. Soon, she reached the end of the bay. There was no way around the headland from the beach. The rock plunged black and vertical into rough water. Sighing, Katla walked away, the rope weighing her down till her joints moaned and creaked. Moving west again, she came upon a vein of quartz she had missed on her first cursory inspection. It was perhaps a foot across, narrowing as it rose to the summit. Harder than the surrounding rock, it stood proud against the shale like a rib, curving away from the eye into the light. Katla put a hand to it and was almost blown off her feet by the blast of energy it gave back to her. At once, she felt invaded. Voices seemed to jabber at her, many of them, all talking at the same time; or maybe it was just one voice speaking in different tongues, creating a great clamor of sound from which she could take nothing intelligible. She took her hand away and the noise vanished. Experimentally, she touched the shale and got nothing back but a background hum, low level, easy to ignore. But the shale wouldn't do, even for her, let alone the rest of the women, most of whom had never even climbed a tree, let alone a cliff. Even so, she walked to the other end of the bay, knowing as she did so it was wasted effort, that the rock had made its best option known to her. Wearily, Katla retraced her steps to the quartz vein and uncoiled the rope. Tying one end around her waist, she scanned for holds, then stepped up onto the shining rib.

Again the voices came, such a racket she could hardly think what to do next. Gritting her teeth, she shut them out, shooed them into that quiet place in the back of her skull where she deposited her fears when she climbed. She moved up, swapped feet in an incut, tested the hold above her head and finding it was a huge, secure jug of a thing she could get her fingers sunk in, she swung up on it, ran her feet up to meet it, then pushed down on a straight arm, and with her right hand wedged in a crack in the shale, levered herself upright and onto the big hold. In no time at all, it seemed, she was thirty feet up the cliff. *Better not fall now,* came a small voice in her head, one Katla recognized as belonging to what small sense of self-preservation she owned. The other voices were right alongside it, groaning away like scolding relatives.

"Oh, shut up!" she told them all, then realized she had spoken out loud. *Must be going a bit mad,* she thought. A shudder passed through her, then another. Her knees felt weak. *Not good. Not good at all.*

Determined now—and trying to ignore the thought that she probably couldn't reverse the route now even if she wanted to—Katla pushed herself onward and upward, hands and feet in bare contact with the rock delivering little jolts of energy up through her spine. These, in conjunction with the benevolence of the rock's configuration, seemed to conspire to offer her the power and grace she needed to dance her way up the rest of the route. Near the summit, she glanced back over her shoulder, relieved to see there was still a tail of rope on the ground. Shifting her gaze, she took in the wreck of the *Rose of Cera,* now a roosting place for a whole host of gulls. *Nature is greedy,* she thought suddenly. *It will take everything back to itself in the end.*

That thought seemed to rob her of the last of her strength.

At the top, she rolled over the edge and lay there for a moment, weak and panting with the sweat pouring off her and her limbs trembling uncontrollably. *It wasn't even that hard,* came the little voice again. *You're not well. Not well at all.*

Go away, she told it fiercely. *I'm fine. I have to be.*

She pushed herself to her feet and looked around for a useful anchor point. Not much to choose from: a couple of stunted bushes and some worried-looking sheep. She opted for the bushes, found a boulder hidden among them and made a fairly safe belay, though whether or not it would hold Fat Breta remained to be seen. . . .

Garnering her strength, she ran along the edge till she came in line with the women and began shouting. For some reason, they were milling around in various states of confusion, some of them still struggling upright, some staring vacantly out to sea. They turned their faces up to the sound of her voice like flowerheads turning to the sun. She waved, indicated the rope, ran back toward it. When she returned to her anchor point, she glanced down again, and was surprised to find them all following swiftly along the beach. She'd been expecting delay and protest, from Kitten Soronsen at least, but by some strange overnight change of character, the blonde girl was leading the charge up the strand and the rest of the women were with her. In the midst of the group her mother was waving frantically, first at Katla, then at the sea.

Katla frowned, then shrugged and watched as Thin Hildi beat Kitten to the end of the rope and tied herself on with such alacrity Katla feared for her safety. *Two granny knots, and she'll be off the end of that,* she thought. But Hildi was already climbing before she'd had a chance to take the rope in tight. Casting all else from her mind, Katla gave herself over to the task of belaying the girl, who was moving up the cliff like a rat up a haystack. *She's a natural,* Katla thought with amazement, for Thin Hildi had never seemed much use for anything other than gossip, turnip peeling, and sewing neat seams. Using her back as a brake, she took the rope in, breathing hard to keep up with Hildi's frantic upward progress, until the girl's head popped into view, her cheeks bright red with exertion and her eyes bulging. When the cliff edge came within reach, she launched herself at it, rolled over the top and lay there winded like a beached seal. Then: "Men . . . in boats!" she wheezed as Katla fiddled at the inexpert knots she'd tied around her waist. "Come back . . . to look for us."

Alarmed, Katla looked out to sea. "Oh, no," she groaned. She leaped to her feet and threw the rope down again, watched Bera push Kitten Soronsen back and tie Fat Breta into the end and the girl start scrabbling hopelessly up the route. This time, Katla had to haul with all her strength. As she did so, the details of her glance out across the shining waves came back in fits and starts: three skiffs, stuffed with men. Istrians. Raiders. Too far away to count or identify them. Out beyond the wreck. Rowing around it, not fast.

Two more enormous heaves and Breta was safely up. Katla untied her and let the rope down again.

They don't know we're here, she realized with sudden delight.

*They're still checking the ship. With any luck, they'll think we've
drowned.*

By now the boats had circled the wreck and one was heading west.
She grinned to herself; but then she saw the giant, Casto Agen, striding
down to the shore and wading into the shallows. Puzzled, she watched
as he breasted the breakers, then seemed to search for something. A moment later he appeared to find whatever he had been looking for. It was
the rest of the rope which was still attached to the ship. Her heart sank.
She watched him grab it up and start to haul himself toward the wreck,
hand over hand and without a word, it seemed, for the raiders remained
oblivious to him.

Then it dawned on her. The big man was mute.

But he certainly wasn't invisible. She watched as one of the raiders
stood up in his skiff so that it rocked wildly, and pointed in the direction
of the ship. The next thing she saw was the boat changing course.

"Climb quicker!" Katla yelled down to the girl on the rope.

It was, of course, Kitten Soronsen, and she stared up at Katla with
fierce loathing.

"I'm climbing as fast as I can!" she screeched, then, under her breath,
muttered, "Bitch."

Katla wasn't listening. She was watching with horrified fascination as
the boat's crew hauled the giant raider into the skiff, then started in
toward the shore with a great splashing of oars. The others followed suit.
Katla looked down at the beach again. There were still four women
down there, including her mother, and she knew that no matter how
fast they climbed they'd not all make it to the top before the men
reached them.

"Get the rope undone!" she shouted.

Kitten threw the end at her harder than was strictly necessary.

"Mother!" Katla yelled, throwing the rope down. "You next!"

Without pause, Bera Rolfsen calmly tied Magla Felinsen on. With her
muscles burning and the sweat running into her eyes, Katla cursed her
mother's selflessness, the raiders' persistence, and Magla's ineptitude in
equal and obscene measure. "God's tits, Magla," she declared, dragging
the girl over the edge at last, "you weigh more than our prize ewe!"

She pushed the trembling girl to a place of safety, then set about the knot around her waist. But the weight of Magla Felinsen combined with her own vicious hauling had tightened them impossibly. Katla stamped her heels with rage and frustration. "No knife!" she muttered furiously, madly, to herself. "Where's my sodding knife when I need it?"

Kitten Soronsen approached now. "I have a knife," she said softly. "I took it from the big Istrian when he brought me through the sea."

"Thank Sur," Katla breathed. She held her hand out expectantly, but Kitten looked away.

"I'll remind you now of how you left me till last in the hold," she said. "And of your insults, too." She took the knife from the rag she wore as a belt and let the sun play across its blade.

It was a small piece, and cheaply made with a great deal of ornament around its handle, too small to make a weapon, too large to peel an apple. *Typical piece of Istrian tat,* Katla thought inconsequentially, even as she yearned toward it.

"A sharp-tongued witch, am I?" mused the blonde girl, running her finger up and down the blade.

"My mother's down there," Katla said through gritted teeth.

"I know. She was pretty rude to me, too." Kitten tilted the metal so that its sheeny surface reflected her face.

The first boat was making its way through the breakers now, threading a passage between the horns of the reef where Katla had swum through, as directed by the giant in its bow. Time was running out. While Kitten was engaged by her own image in the knife, Katla made her move. But as soon as she put her weight on her injured ankle, it buckled under her and she fell back gasping.

Kitten stood over her, her shadow blocking out the sun. "I never liked your mother," she said silkily. "She has a nasty temper. But perhaps hard labor in an Istrian brothel will temper her spirit."

Growling like a bear, Katla launched herself at Kitten Soronsen, who stepped neatly out of reach, tipped up her palm over the edge of the cliff, and let the little blade slide off into clear air. Katla watched it tip end over end, twinkling silver, until it hit the ground eighty feet below.

Tears rose to her eyes. With a trembling hand, she rubbed them away.

"I'll kill you for that, Kitten Soronsen," she declared. And she meant it.

"You'll have to catch me first." And with that, Kitten took to her heels and pelted away into the Istrian countryside, scattering the watchful sheep.

Magla, Hildi, and Breta watched her go, their eyes wide with shock. Katla stared at the diminishing figure as if the power of her regard might wither her to ashes. Her head throbbed and her limbs ached and she was so tired she could barely speak, let alone move, but somehow she hauled herself over to Magla and began to apply her fingers to the knots again. There was nothing else to do. By sheer force of will (and her teeth) she got the first loosened, then the next; but the third was stubborn. By the time she'd searched out a suitably sharp piece of slate and sawed through it, it was too late. Baranguet and his men had her mother, Kit Farsen, Forna Stensen, and Leni Stelsen pinioned facedown on the strand.

"ARE you all right, Katla? You're as pale as milk."

Katla blinked and stared, blinked and stared again. Thin Hildi's face swam into view. Then a hand came at her, laid a cool palm across her forehead.

"By Feya, you're burning up!"

"I'm fine," Katla replied abruptly, though she felt terrible. She pushed Thin Hildi's hand away and stared out to sea. Two of the raiders' boats were rowing eastward, laden with their captives and the rescued giant; of the third there was no sign. She couldn't think clearly, couldn't think at all. The options came to her slowly, as if her thoughts were veiled from her. They could make a run for it across the clifftops and out into the Istrian countryside beyond; they could stay here and fester and wait for an Eyran vessel to pass by, which she dismissed immediately. Or they could go back down the rope, back to the beach, and try to make their way along the strand and around the headland to the east, which the raiders would hardly expect. And get cut off by the tide, or starve to death.

"What are we going to do?" wailed Magla.

"Shut up," said Katla, more fiercely than she'd intended.

Not east: the raiders were heading that way. West or south, then. Kitten had gone south. Katla never wanted to see Kitten Soronsen again, unless it was with her foot on her neck and a good blade in her hand. Using Magla's shoulder as a crutch, she levered herself to her feet, noting the shooting pains in her limbs as she did so.

"Follow me," she croaked.

Under other circumstances—in other words, not inflicted with shaky limbs, a fever, and a throbbing head; and not on the run from a band of cutthroat slavers—she would have found this part of the Istrian continent lovely. It was rugged and yet picturesque, combining some of the rough beauty of Eyra with the softer lines of good arable country. Secret dells and steeply wooded hills gave out onto wide fields dotted with sheep and prosperous-looking farmsteads. Under other circumstances, that is, on her own and unencumbered by three hopeless creatures who followed her like sheep, bleating, "Where are we going?" "How are we going to get home?" and "I'm so cold I may die!", Katla would have thoroughly enjoyed the prospect of sneaking into one of those farmsteads, liberating a decent pony or two, and trotting off through the countryside to see what sort of mischief she might get into. But the likelihood of stealing four horses and sneaking away with three women who had likely never sat an ancient, stumpy little island pony, let alone a fine-bred Istrian beast with a full set of teeth and a mind of its own, seemed an absolute impossibility. But what choice did they have? Before they had even covered half a mile, she was so exhausted, she could drop.

"I'm hungry," complained Fat Breta.

"You're always hungry," returned Thin Hildi spitefully.

"I'm frozen half to death," added Magla, shivering. "And we need to eat." She said this in the most accusatory tone, as if their situation was all Katla's fault.

Katla wiped a hand across her face. Her cheeks were burning; she felt light-headed. The idea of food nauseated her, but she knew Magla was right. That they all expected her to provide for them made her suddenly indignant. "What do you want me to do—run down a sheep and strangle it with my bare hands? Rip it to pieces so we can eat it raw?"

They had the grace to look abashed at that, sheepish even. Katla found herself grinning lunatically at the poor pun, and it was at this point that she knew she really was unwell. A moment later she was sitting on the ground with her head between her knees. Everything inside her skull was spinning. She opened her eyes. Everything out there was spinning, too. Then she fell over on her side and lay like one dead.

"What's wrong with her?" said Magla peevishly.

"She's sick," Hildi replied in a low voice. She sounded scared. "Very sick."

Fat Breta started to cry. "What'll we do? What'll we do?"

There was a long moment's silence.

"We could carry her," Breta sniffed.

"*You* can carry her," Magla returned unfairly. "I'm certainly not going to."

Fat Breta wept louder.

"We could leave her—" Magla started, eyes aglow with daring at the idea. "We could leave her here and make our way along the coast to a port of some sort . . ." There she stopped, imagination having failed her.

Thin Hildi snorted derisively. "And then what? Ask a kindly Istrian sea captain to sail us home? We're at war, Magla Felinsen. Eyra is at war with Istria and here we are—four Eyran girls lost in enemy territory with no money, no weapons, and no word of their language between us."

They all fell silent after that, considering their fate, while at their feet Katla writhed and sweated in her feverish sleep. Silent that is until, some time later, Magla heard voices.

"What was that?"

They crowded into the hollow of the trees as if by doing so they might become part of the bark, but Katla Aransen's tawny tunic made a great, bright pool of color against the grassy floor and they could not move her. Thin Hildi bobbed her head up and gazed fearfully in the direction of the voices. It seemed that minutes went by as she stared and stared, then: "Men," she whispered hoarsely. She sat back down, even paler in the face than she had been before. "A lot of them, all wearing blue cloaks and helmets with great crests, leading their horses."

"They don't sound much like the men who stole us away," Magla said doubtfully.

Fat Breta's face brightened. "Perhaps they'll help us go home." Her stomach rumbled fiercely at the very thought.

Hildi laughed. "I do not think so, Breta," she said more kindly than the big girl perhaps deserved. Then her expression became solemn. "Though they look rather more reputable than the men who brought us here."

Now Magla took a turn at spying on the approaching men.

When she sat down, her eyes were thoughtful. "These men don't look at all like slavers," she said softly. "They must surely be soldiers. Officials, by their appearance. And they are very well turned out, very finely arrayed indeed . . ."

No one pointed out to her that on first sight she had thought the raiders rather fine in their outlandish garb, with their long silver earrings and oiled black hair.

She caught Hildi by the arm. "We should give ourselves up to them," she said fervently. "I am sure they will give us better treatment than the brigands who sacked Rockfall. And Feya knows we will not survive for long out here without food or shelter."

And before either Thin Hildi or Fat Breta could utter any word of protest that maybe such was not the best idea, Magla Felinsen was on her feet hailing the Istrian militiamen.

12

In the Desert

VIRELAI ran until his lungs were full of dust. Then he ran some more. He ran till his eyeballs felt seared by the sun; then the sun went down and still he stumbled on. He had no idea of where he was, and cared less, as long as he was far away from Alisha Skylark and the stone she had laid upon him. He had traversed an area of desert, then one of thorny scrubland, been deadended in a dry gulch and had to climb out, half-blind, in twilight, with every muscle he owned trembling in panic at the likely consequences of a fall onto the spiky rocks below. He had crossed a river, without meaning to, for soft sand had gradually become soft mud which had tried to suck him down and down, so that in plunging forward to be free of it, he had abruptly found himself in water up to his knees, and was out the other side before he'd barely had time to notice the change in elements.

Now, with all light gone from the sky and his heart hammering in sudden fear, he could go no farther. As soon as he came to a halt, every part of his poor body shrieked for attention. Everything hurt. And hurt in a way he was not used to: insistent, inescapable aches and pains, rends and tears and distress. His leg muscles felt burned and stiff, and there was a dull throbbing in the bones of his shin. His chest was as tight as if someone had bound it mercilessly with ropes; he could hear the air wheezing in and out of it with every breath he took. He could *feel* the air inside him, scouring out his lungs, in a way he had never felt it before. And as soon as he registered one complaint, another surplanted it. He had a thorn in the big toe of his right foot, a gouge from a sharp stone in the sole of his left; some vile desert plant had applied tiny mouthlike suckers in a long row across his calves; his thighs felt as though they had gone to wood, they were so hard and stiff, but a wood that had been set afire in some dry forest blaze. Insect bites stung and itched, and sweat—a substance he had never produced before in all his life, let alone in such quantity and pungency of odor—had run freely, then dried and chafed between his legs and under his arms.

And through it all, his head was plagued by a question he dared not examine, let alone answer.

Whatever was it that Alisha Skylark had done to him? And how had she dared to take such a decision upon herself? Given the stone's properties, she might as easily have destroyed him, blasted him off the face of Elda like those other poor souls, with their eyes seared white in its killing light and their bodies as limp and empty of life as a child's straw doll. As it was, even death might be preferable, for his body—more alive than it had ever been in his entire existence—was proving to be much more of a torment to him than a blessing.

If this is what it means to be alive and fully human, Virelai thought, *then I will settle for my old half-life back again, whatever its peculiar limitations.*

He sat down heavily upon the sandy ground and put his head in his hands. This availed him nothing more than a grim pulsing in the veins at his temples and a new ache at the back of his neck, so he applied himself to locating and extracting the thorn which had lodged itself rather firmly in his right big toe. This endeavor, requiring much concentration and the problematic coordination of a thumb and forefinger trembling with exhaustion, took so much time that a faint blush of light tinged the eastern skyline by the time it was successfully completed. But the relief of the pain was immense, blissful, washing over him like a warm wave.

"Extraordinary," he muttered. Even his voice sounded different to him, emerging as a full-blooded croak rather than his usual dry-leaf whisper.

His new body was telling him things, urgent things. He was thirsty, he realized. Hungry, too. How long was it since he had taken any sustenance?

The militiamen who had taken them captive in the far south had given him some brackish water out of a poorly-tanned skin and a hunk of un-leavened bread—when? About two hours before they had been ambushed. But how long had he lain on the battlefield, unconscious, oblivious to the violence and murder that had gone on all around him? He shook his head. It was impossible to know.

Now, too late, he remembered the stream he had run through without the slightest thought for drinking from it, which was stupid, from any living being's perspective, though maybe less so from his own. He had required very little maintenance in his prior form, though he had not realized it at the time. He had eaten when others ate and had drunk when others drank, and barely tasted the food or the liquids he took down, and his excreta—such as they were—had been minimal. He had never thought about the mechanisms involved before now: they had seemed remote, inconsequential, uninteresting. Now the basics of human life were revealed for the glorious tyrannies they were: he must eat, and drink, if he was to live.

Wearily, he pushed himself to his feet and looked behind him. His progress to this point was marked by vague indentations and scuff marks in the sandy soil, marks which stretched away across dunes and through the sparse brush, marks which were highlighted along their lefthand edges by the rosy light of the rising sun.

He had no destination, so turning back on himself seemed less of a chore than it might have done to any other traveler in this wilderness. Indeed, he reasoned, any direction might prove as useful, or as perilous, to him as any other. The stream he had waded through could not be far away. The hem of his robe was still damp from the crossing. Finding in himself a new resolve that might loosely be considered as a will to live—a resolve which seemed an integral part of this unfamiliar new existence—he squared his shoulders and forced his complaining muscles to retrace his steps.

AT the northern bank of the stream he had crossed in the small hours of that day, Virelai came upon an area of churned ground and a heap of discarded belongings he had missed in the darkness. The marks in the mud were fresh, giving slightly under the hand rather than baked hard as stone, and showed a mass of hoofprints and the impressions of a number of large boots. It seemed the militiamen who had attacked the troop which had held them prisoner had passed this way, and not too long ago. This surmise was borne out by the presence of a scrap of fabric which lay off to one side at the foot of a thorn bush. It was faded and striped in pinks and greens, and he recognized it at once. It was a much-loved weaving Alisha had made as a youngster under the tutelage of one of the older women in the nomad band, and although it was inexpert in its bled dyes and wobbly edges, she had kept it as a liner in the base of her old wooden chest until Falo had taken a liking to it, as small children will. Thereafter, it had gone everywhere with him, usually trailing from his mouth, softened and moistened by his constant chewing during the time when his teeth came in. Once Falo had passed through that stage of his childhood, he had demanded the cloth be draped over his bed at night. Without it, he would not sleep.

Looking at the fabric now, forlornly draped over a boulder in the middle of this inhuman place, brought a sudden and unwonted lump to Virelai's throat. The last time he had seen the cloth had been in Alisha and Falo's wagon on that fateful day when the soldiers had come for them. Falo's last day on Elda.

Sadly, he walked over to it and picked it up. Beneath it lay no boulder, but Alisha Skylark's seeing-stone.

The massive crystal lay dully in the dirt, its polished surfaces dusty and ungiving. The soldiers had obviously jettisoned it like any other rubbish. It was heavy and slowing them down and they could see no use for it, so they had thrown it down here, along with the cloth it was wrapped in.

Virelai looked at the stone with his head on one side, as wary as a bird viewing a snake. He had been raised among stones such as this, for the Master had a large collection of crystals and he knew their power. The crystal he had stolen from Sanctuary had shared a similar provenance to Alisha's stone, which had been unearthed from among the hot rocks of the Dragon's Backbone, where the Golden Mountains met the volcanic peaks of the south. Discovered in Alisha's grandmother's time, it had been passed down to that wise old seer, Fezack Starsinger, and thence to Alisha herself. And although Alisha had contested that the stone had lost much of its ability with the death of her mother, Virelai was not so sure this was the truth of the matter.

The proximity of the crystal made his new skin crawl. It vibrated. It sang. He knew he would never be able to leave it where it lay without at least touching it. Even so, the exigencies of his thirst drove him harder. With one eye on the crystal, in case it were somehow to burrow into the ground or meld itself with its surroundings, he backed down to the water's edge and scooped handful after handful into his grateful mouth and throat. Among the detritus the soldiers had left behind, miraculously, he found a discarded waterskin, punctured in one corner, but perfectly serviceable if carried upside-down. This he filled. There was, unfortunately, no food. He pushed away all thoughts of hunger, since there was little he could do to ameliorate those pangs.

He could put off his interrogation of the crystal no longer. Propping the waterskin against the thorn bush, he hunkered down on his heels and laid his hands on the stone. At first, all he registered was that the seeing-stone was wonderfully cool, even though the sun had risen high above them and was as hot as a bread oven. It fit his spread hands like a boon. Unthinking, he caressed it, running his fingertips lightly over its surface, allowing his palms to make firm but gentle contact. Nothing happened. It felt like the piece of dead rock that it was—lumpen, chilly, burdensome. Even Alisha had hated it, he recalled.

As if responding to this memory, the stone came abruptly to life. It buzzed, sending tiny tremors up his arms. Then, humming like a hive of bees, it appropriated him, invading his sight, his sensations, his skull, until colored lights swirled in the depths of his head and his eyes were filled with visions.

He saw: fifty or sixty men and women burning in a great round contraption formed of complicated bars of white-hot metal which held them all prisoner amid the flames, but allowed the crowd of onlookers a clear view of their torments. On a dais behind the crowd sat the bloated creature he knew to be Tanto Vingo, dressed in rich purple, with a crown of bright flowers wreathed around the bald dome of his head and two scantily-clad women twined about his legs. Beside him, a wooden frame had been erected. And upon this frame was stretched a naked figure, its wrists and ankles bleeding from the spiked wire which confined them. Its eyelids had been sewn grotesquely open, but even so, he knew Saro Vingo's face as well as if it had been his own. In the background, elegant rose-red walls and turrets rose into a vivid sky streaked with purple and red, and ragged streamers of thick black smoke . . .

Virelai blinked and stared, horrified by these vile images.

It is impossible, he thought, his mind racing wildly. *It cannot be.* He thought hard. They had been captured by the second brigade of soldiers only two days ago—unless he had lain unconscious for longer than he thought. And they had been far, far from Jetra when the ambush had come. Then he remembered something old Fezack Starsinger had said.

It sees all manner of things, she had told him when he had first joined the troupe, *my scrying-stone. It is of the finest crystals from far down in the earth, closer to her magic than the others, you see. If it favors you, it can show not only events in our world now, but also those taking place in the past, and in the future. Things which may come to pass; warnings, portents, and signs, it offers them all to me. It is the earth magic speaking, my boy, showing us what we need to see, to guide our actions and our thoughts. Elda looks after her own, my dear. Even as she takes us back into her bosom, she looks after her own.*

I am seeing the future, he thought dully. *A terrible, terrible future.* He felt no emotional attachment to the burning people in the ball of fire, although no one should die so horribly under the eyes of a monster. But to see Saro so treated, and by his own brother, was more than he could bear. Of all those left living in the world, he counted only Saro as a friend. The intensity of his outrage took him greatly by surprise. He felt it as a physical presence in his chest and in his head, a swelling of heat hard against bone and muscle.

A mad thought came to him. He would save Saro! He would journey to Jetra and find him, release him from his vile bondage, and spirit him away to safer regions.

But even as the thought came to him, despair overwhelmed it. How could he, Virelai, failed apprentice mage, enigma, and trickster, achieve such a grand aim? He was lost in a desert, brought back from the dead:

an unnatural thing in an inimical place. He had no power, no plan, no map of the future.

But perhaps the crystal knew better. He laid hands on the stone again and brought the image of Saro clearly to mind, concentrating every scrap of willpower he could muster.

Unhelpfully, however, instead of Jetran vistas the crystal now offered him desert light and billowing ash-clouds. A blurred view of towering rock. Streams of fiery red snaking out of fissures, coursing between boulders, cooling into steaming ribbons and heaps.

What place is this? thought Virelai fearfully. As if in answer, the crystal drew back its focus so that he now saw the scene from afar—a sharp red peak gouting black smoke and yellow fumes into the sky, a great swath of boulder-strewn sand stretching below it. Two tiny, separate, silhouetted figures could be discerned to east and west in the far distance, making their way—not toward the viewer, but crazily, suicidally, toward the ash-spewing mountain. One was some huge creature, for it walked on all fours. The other appeared human, its head encircled by a tawny nimbus of hair; but whether this was its natural hue, or whether it took its color from the fiery air, it was impossible to tell. The first figure stopped, turned, appeared to sniff the air; and then Virelai saw and knew it.

Bëte. The Beast; as large as life and healed from whatever wounds it had taken in that rout by the river.

He shivered. Something odd and unsettling was afoot here, and he had no understanding of it at all.

Virelai closed his eyes and touched his forehead to the stone in weariness. At once, he jerked back as if burned. With terrible clarity, Alisha Skylark came riding into view upon a black horse. He shrank back, aghast.

He knew that horse. He had seen it lying stone-dead on the same battlefield where he had himself been raised.

A trickle of sweat ran into his eye and he blinked it away desperately, wanting, but not wanting, to see what the crystal now showed him. The view came closer. He saw Alisha's jutting chin, the rosettes of white sweat which had crusted on her forearms and face, and on the flanks of the black stallion; and he saw its mad eyes, dull as a dead fish's. The crystal stayed with this view of horse and rider for many minutes, as if unwilling to relinquish contact with its former owner. Virelai saw them crest a dune, saw Alisha shade her eyes, then urge the stallion down the other side with barely a pause. They galloped across a dry riverbed without bothering to examine it for any sign of water; they passed a great spotted lizard which reared up on the rock on which it sat, spreading the frill around its neck in alarm. Neither horse nor rider appeared to notice the beast. Even with her fingers knotted in the stallion's mane, Alisha's right hand was clenched in a fierce fist. Inside that fist, he knew, was the death-stone.

He could bear to watch their inexorable progress no longer. Appalled by Alisha's lunatic determination, by the continued, unnatural existence of Night's Harbinger, he pulled his hands away from the stone, tied it into the spill of cloth, and retrieved his waterskin.

If anything, the sightings of Bëte and of the nomad woman confirmed his resolve. He could never go south. There lay potential horrors even worse than those he had foreseen in the Eternal City. Dragging the heavy crystal behind him, Virelai started northward again.

Among the Houris

"WHA— Get off! Get off me!"

Katla Aransen came awake in a fury, her fists striking out to right and left. One made solid contact with something which gave beneath the blow and a voice cried out sharply in a foreign tongue.

She sat up and stared about her. She was surrounded by what appeared to be a swarm of gigantic butterflies—fluttering figures swathed in colored robes—all of which now seemed to be keeping a wary distance.

Disoriented and confused, she wondered suddenly if she had ingested something which was making her hallucinate.

The fluttering things were closing in again. "Go away!" she shouted, and winced as her loud voice echoed off the stone.

The creatures gathered in a knot.

Katla felt as though she had stepped into a dream. Someone else's dream, and not a pleasant one, at that. She decided to search for an immediate escape. Looking around, she found she was in a large, tall-ceilinged stone room, an unusual thing in itself for a girl raised in a turf-roofed steading. On the opposite side of the chamber a fire crackled in a soot-stained hearth. To her right ran a long wall with a huge, iron-bound wooden door set into the middle of it. A pair of narrow arched windows gave a distant view of cloud and pale gray sky. In the center of the chamber a large metal container belched clouds of aromatic steam into the air.

None of it made sense. Where was she, and how had she got here?

She recalled climbing the shale cliff, Kitten Soronsen's treachery, watching her mother fall prisoner to the raiders. She remembered feeling very, very ill and worrying how Hildi, Breta, and Magla could possibly fend for themselves if she slept. Beyond that, she could remember nothing at all.

She looked down. Her situation got worse. Her clothes—rags, really—were tumbled in a heap beside the couch on which she sat.

All of them.

She could not remember the last time she had been naked in anyone else's view. Then she could. Keel Island. Tam Fox. *But even then,* she thought, pushing the pain of that rich and sensual memory away, *I still had a sock left to me . . .*

Grabbing her clothes to her, she leaped to her feet and made for the door.

"And where do you think you are going?"

A familiar voice. Katla came to an abrupt halt as one of the voluminously-robed figures moved between her and the door. Whoever it was, they knew the Eyran tongue, though no Eyran woman worth her salt would ever be found wearing a bizarre draping of turquoise silk which left only the lips and the hands visible. The lips were painted, too: a bright and sparkling damson-red. They looked like—well, the effect was oddly obscene. Even so, Katla found herself staring at that mouth as though it might hold the key to the whole conundrum. Its chiseled lines, the swell of the lower lip; the way it curved into a contemptuous smile. Though men might admire such a mouth, it seemed to Katla cruelly set, and she knew it only too well. . . .

Suddenly it felt as if her entire rib cage was filling up with bile.

"Kitten Soronsen!" she snarled. "I might have known you'd survive. And looking just like an Istrian whore!"

"I hardly think you're in a position to claim the moral high ground, standing there all naked and filthy, a woman who opened her legs to a *mummer!*" Kitten sneered.

Katla's hands became hard claws. She flew at the other girl with loathing, ripping and rending the flimsy silk as if she wished it were Kitten's own flesh. Soon the turquoise robe was no more than a ruined mess tangling around Kitten's feet. Tripping in its silken folds, Kitten went down, shrieking with rage and Katla fell upon her, consumed by thoughts of how glorious it would be to bury her fingers in flesh, in hair, in eye—

At this, the robed women intervened, pulling Katla away and clucking fiercely in their unintelligible southern language. No butterflies, these. Even in the depths of her blood lust, Katla was surprised that these seemingly fragile creatures should be possessed of such a powerful grip. But Gramma Rolfsen had always warned her never to judge a horse by its color, a man by his hair, or a woman by the cut of her dress, and Katla learned yet again how appearances could deceive. She struggled hard, but the fever was still in her and before long her arms and legs felt like lengths of wet rope: against the determination of the Istrian women she could do nothing at all.

A taller figure, all in black, came forward. "Cover yourself!" she barked at Kitten Soronsen, throwing a dark robe at her. "Your body is gift of Goddess, not to parade wantonly in such manner!"

The blonde girl bowed meekly. There was something very wrong about this—something wrong, too, about Kitten Soronsen's palely naked body. Katla could not think what it was, but it niggled at her. She craned her neck for a better view, but then the harridan strode forward to interpose herself between the two of them. Taller and wider than Katla, she seemed almost to block out the light. She inclined her head and regarded her captive minutely. Katla could feel the weight of the woman's gaze upon her even through the veil she wore, raking up and down, taking in every detail, every bruise, every flaw. It was an unpleasant experience. She felt like one of her father's prize mares being sized up at Sundey Market. *Any minute now,* she thought, *the creature will start feeling up my legs and commenting on the shape of my fetlocks . . .*

Indeed, the dark-robed woman started to bark out commands to the other women, commands which set them scurrying here and there about the chamber, gathering items, preparing for a task. Katla did not like to think what that task might be. Now the woman leaned in closer.

Her lips, revealed through the unflattering slit in the veil, were pale, unpainted, shapeless, and ugly. Two thick black hairs sprouted from a mole beside her mouth.

"You northern women like demons," this creature spat, her words heavily accented. "You have no manners, no restraint. You should be ashamed. How your men can love you, when you so rough and nasty?"

Katla laughed. "And how much do you think your men love you when they wrap you up in these awful robes and shut you away like prisoners?"

The black-robed woman pursed her lips. "We choose to wear Goddess's robes. It a matter of respect." She gestured to two of the other women and together they advanced upon Katla.

Katla put up her fists. Tremors of fever ran through her so that she shivered where she stood. "Come any closer, and you'll learn the meaning of 'rough and nasty,' " she promised.

"Do not be afraid of her," Kitten Soronsen called out. "She's too ill to do you harm. See how she trembles and shakes."

As if cheered by this, the women advanced again. With deceptive speed, the black-robed woman dodged Katla's flying fists, ducked beneath her elbow, and caught one of her arms painfully behind her back.

Katla yelped. *I must be getting slow,* she thought miserably, as her arm was forced yet higher. *But, damn me, I don't feel well.*

Even as she thought this, her knees buckled though, with the tall woman holding her up, she could not fall. The others came now, sensing her weakness, caught her feet, lifted her off the ground. The next thing she knew, there was an immense splash and she was engulfed.

Lashing out desperately, Katla erupted from the perfumed bath with liquid gushing from her hair, her ears, her mouth. The women stepped back, alarmed, but Kitten stepped forward, clutching a wicked-looking long-handled brush in one hand and a strong-smelling yellow bar in the other.

"Hold her down and I'll do the honors," she announced, and a cruel smile curved those chiseled lips.

Katla stopped thrashing, she was so appalled. "When exactly was it that you turned traitor, Kitten Soronsen? When the Istrians caught you, or when you slipped from your mother's womb?"

Kitten shrugged. "I decided to make the best of a bad situation." She winked at Katla. "I think I might quite like it here. But I can't imagine you will."

Katla glared at her. "And what about the others?"

"They're downstairs with the lesser houris, being scrubbed down and prepared for the slave blocks," Kitten said coolly, soaping up the bristles of the brush.

The blood rose in Katla's head till all she could hear was a buzzing in her ears like a hiveful of bees. She wanted to leap from the bath, stark naked, and stop Kitten Soronsen's cruel little mouth with that vast bar of soap; she wanted to pummel her to pleading submission; she wanted—

But the women's grip tightened as though the intent that trembled through Katla's muscles spoke directly to them, and she could do nothing at all.

Kitten laughed and the candlelight played off her sparkling lips. Inconsequentially, Katla marveled that a captive northern woman like any of the rest of them should have had such luxuries as paints and perfumes lavished upon her. Just what *had* Kitten Soronsen said or done to have won such favorable treatment? It was very disturbing. In her befuddled state she couldn't see the logic in any of it at all. And why were they treating her to a bath, too? A swift dunking along with the rest of her compatriots would surely suffice for a trip to the slave blocks. . . .

Then Kitten set about Katla so ferociously with the bristle brush and soap that Katla had no further opportunity for logical thought, and for a long time in that room there were no further words of Eyran uttered which did not consist entirely of profanity and threat.

KATLA had never been so clean in her life. It was not a natural state of affairs and she did not like it at all. Life on Rockfall—or at least a life spent running, climbing, riding, fishing, gathering ragworm and bilberries, and generally grubbing around—did not much feature scented baths and the liberal use of washcloths. Skin which had never been fully exposed to the air since Katla had learned to crawl fast enough to escape the attentions of her mother and grandmother now glowed uneasily in the candlelight. She had never felt more naked in her life. It was as if all her protective camouflage had been stripped away; no prize mare now, she felt like a sheared sheep staked out for the wolves.

By the time they finally pulled her out of the steaming tub, she was too exhausted to fight anymore, though she took childish pleasure in having splashed as many of them as she could with the scummy water. Then they held her down and dried her with soft towels and two women rubbed some strong-smelling oil into her skin with strong fingers which gouged her muscles and left her aching and wrung out. And all the time they kept on muttering away in their sibilant tongue.

"They say you not look after yourself," the tall woman in black told her at last. "They say your skin like plucked chicken. Not soft. Not smooth. More like boy's, all rough and hard. No man want bed with such woman!"

"Bed?" said Katla suspiciously. "What do you mean, *bed?*"

But the woman turned away without answering and gestured to her helpers. A few seconds later, the sharp scent of lemons wafted through the air, and something sweeter, too. After a lot of milling about, a low table bearing a small stove and a sturdy pot appeared.

Katla frowned. What were they at now? It seemed odd that they should stop in the middle of their ministrations to brew up a drink, but these southerners were strange folk.

One of the women began to dip strips of white cloth into the mixture with a pair of tongs. Then she lifted it out of the pan and advanced upon Katla.

"Lie back and don't fight," the leader of the women advised her, "and it will hurt less."

Every muscle in Katla's body tensed as tight as a spring. What on Elda could anyone do to hurt her with a little strip of wet cloth? A moment later, two of them had her on her back and the woman had applied the hot cloth to her groin. Katla was outraged. How much cleaner did they require her to be for whatever bizarre ends they had in mind? This was appalling, absurd treatment; and far past humiliation. Fingers dug into her skin, smoothing and pressing into intimate areas no Eyran woman would ever have had the gall to touch, and the next thing she knew, someone had ripped the offending cloth away and her groin was on fire.

"Aaaaaarrrgh!"

Shock gave her monstrous strength. The tight-sprung muscles now fueled with adrenalized fury, Katla threw off her captors and charged across the room, bellowing like an enraged bull. She stood with her back to the wall, a woolen tapestry harsh against her skin, her breath coming in great heaves. When the women did not immediately advance upon her, she chanced a look down at the wounded region. A wide band of red, hairless flesh glowed where there should have been a nest of orange curls. Now she realized why it was that the glimpse she had been afforded of Kitten Soronsen's long, pale body had disturbed her so.

"Feya's tits!" she shrieked. "What perverse and filthy practice is this?"

The black-robed woman put her hands on her hips. "It is your people who filthy and perverse are," she declared. "Covering Falla's gift with dirty old hair like some smelly bear. There should be nothing between a man and a woman when they come together to worship the Goddess."

That was a phrase she'd heard before, and she had a fair idea of what it meant. Suspicion hardened into certainty. "Your precious goddess can rot in Hel," Katla snarled. And she made a dash for the door.

Hauling it open, she flew out into the corridor, and collided with a richly-dressed man of middle height, with sharply-carved features and raven-black hair held back by a silver circlet. The two of them went down in a tangle of limbs, but desperation made Katla the quicker to her feet. She turned to run down the passageway, but the dark man lunged out and caught her by the ankle. She hit the ground so hard that all the air rushed from her lungs, and all she could do was to curl into a ball, choking for breath.

The man sprang to his feet, grabbed her by the wrists, dragged her upright, and held her at arm's length. He looked her up and down, then turned to the black-robed woman. "Whatever have you been doing to her, Peta? She looks as appetizing as a scalded cat!"

"My lord!" the woman in black exclaimed, hurrying out into the hallway with her head bowed. "We had not finished preparing her. It is unseemly that you should look upon her sinful body in this forbidden state." In her hands she carried a piece of shimmering fabric which she draped hastily over Katla's angular form.

Far from hiding her body from the newcomer's gaze, the robe was sheer and clinging. If this was "seemly," then these southerners had some very strange ideas about propriety. When she looked up, the richly-dressed man was regarding her with a half-smile which suggested both amusement and faint disgust. He pushed Katla back toward Peta, who took her by the wrist, her sharp nails digging unnecessarily hard into Katla's skin.

"I have seen quite enough," he said shortly in Istrian, wiping his hands on his velvet tunic, "to know that this one won't do. You should know by now that my tastes do not run to scrawny little northern hellcats. I have had my doubts about your ability to run this harem for a while now, and brawls and naked women escaping down corridors just won't do."

Katla stared at the lord while he addressed the black-robed woman, her mind working rather more slowly than she would have wished. She had no idea what he was saying, but he did not seem overly impressed by her, which was a relief; for she recognized his face, from somewhere, and the sight of him made her feel even more anxious than current circumstances seemed to demand. Her temples throbbed and she was engulfed by a wave of nausea. When she closed her eyes, images swam up at her, haunting and disorienting—memories of the Allfair, brief, hallucinatory glimpses of a journey, men in blue cloaks, trees flashing past, flames, faces, tall buildings and lit sconces, Hildi's weeping face, the Rosa Eldi coiled like a serpent around the Eyran king, Istrian lords striding and shouting . . .

Her eyes flew open. "Rui Finco," she croaked before she could help herself, and was rewarded by a look of utmost surprise on the dark man's face.

The Lord of Forent recovered himself swiftly. He inclined his head. "Indeed," he acknowledged in the Old Tongue. "I am flattered that you should know me, for I am quite sure I do not know you. Perhaps you might like to share your name with me so that I am not at such a disadvantage."

Katla bit her lip and cursed her slow wits. What could she say? If she gave her name, he would surely remember who she was and her current indignities would fade to nothing by comparison with the likely punishment that would ensue. Speak too loudly, or give a false name and Kitten Soronsen would score the ultimate revenge upon her.

Katla Aransen was a tough girl and a pragmatist, rarely given to histrionics. She did not flirt, she did not dissemble, she did not play games. But with nowhere to run or to hide, and with no weapon at hand, it was the only ruse she could think of.

"My lord," she said softly in the Old Tongue. "Forgive me . . . I feel most unwell." She clutched her hand against her forehead to keep the flimsy veil in place and crumpled to the floor.

She hit the ground harder than she had planned; so much for all those pratfalls learned in the mummers' troupe. She'd be bruised from knee to hip from this, but so much the better for verisimilitude.

Even so, she could feel the lord's gaze on her, as sharp as a knife.

"She's neither pretty nor healthy," the Lord of Forent chided his harem keeper. "Why is she up here and not downstairs being readied for the marketplace?"

"My lord . . ." Peta hesitated. "I thought . . . I thought her unusual coloring might appeal to you . . . You have no red-haired women here. I think once she is properly presented, it may be worth your trouble. She is . . . shall we say, spirited?"

Rui Finco laughed. "I shall take your word for that." He peered past her shoulder to the women crowded by the door. "Jana, Pala, you shall have the honor of my company tonight."

Two of the women detached themselves from the group and ran to his side. He flung an arm around one and gave the other a lingering kiss through the slit in her veil. Then he leaned in close to the black-robed woman.

"You have three days to make her ready for me. If you fail me in this, Peta," he said, his voice dropping to a dangerous growl which made the hairs on Katla's neck rise, even though she could not make out the strange Istrian words, "you will join the Eyran on the slave blocks. You've run my harem for too long; maybe a fresh hand will do them good."

Then he hoisted the smaller of the two houris over his shoulder, slapped the other on her capacious rump, and stalked off down the corridor.

There were several moments of anxious silence, then the houris ventured out to gather around Katla and Peta, clucking like hens. They lifted Katla with more care than she had expected, carried her back into the chamber, and set her down on the couch. She heard the door swing to with a soft thud. This time the bolt was shot home.

"Well now, madam," Peta said softly, laying her lips close to Katla's ear, "you may fool the Lord of Forent, but you not fool me. Now my future depend on you. Do not think you bring me down and survive. I will see you dead first."

Then she hit Katla so hard in the gut that the air rushed out of her. Even as she retched and choked, Katla marveled at the woman's power: Peta had struck her with the flat of the hand, not with a fist which would leave a lasting bruise. Years had refined a technique like that, years of bullying and brutality.

THAT night they depilated all her body hair; there was nothing she could do about it. Six of them held her down while Peta applied and then ripped away the sugared-lemon cloths with a ferocity which left Katla in no doubt as to her dislike for her captive. By the end of this torment, Katla had a fairly good idea of what was in store for her, for the black-robed woman took immense pleasure in telling her at length in her broken Old Tongue: she would be oiled and perfumed and prettied-up and presented to the Lord of Forent as his sexual plaything. She was to satisfy his every demand without complaint and with a smile on her face or, as Peta put it, waving a wicked-looking little curved dagger under her nose, "I will cut off your women's parts and send you to the Sisters. Then you will wish you had done as I bade you, for there will never be pleasure for you in the world again." Katla had no idea who the Sisters might be, and she had no wish to find out, wished still less to have anyone tamper further with her person. Whatever Rui Finco might say about sending the two of them to the blocks (an infinitely more attractive proposition), in these quarters, at this time, Peta's word was law.

After they had degraded her as much as was required by their weird customs, they sat her up and poured some vile-smelling concoction down her throat which stung and burned, and made her sleep till past noon the next day.

When she awoke, it was with a clear head and no fever. She felt weak and thirsty, but, even so, better than she would have felt after a night on stallion's blood. She looked around. She was in a different room, and two other women—one in a blue robe, the other in lilac—sat guard in cane-woven chairs by the door, their hands busy with some sort of intricate tatting. Their fingers moved with deft purpose; and Katla remembered how Gramma Rolfsen had been proficient at the same art, sitting by the central fire in the steading's hall, her handsome, lined old face intent on the patterned strip which was growing moment by moment in her hands. At this memory, and the flood of thoughts which followed it, Katla's jaw clenched. Her grandmother was dead, her mother taken prisoner, her father was Sur knew where in the arctic seas; she had only herself to rely on and here she was, trapped in an excruciating double bind. If she were true to her nature and fought her captors tooth and claw, she risked her life or mutilation. If she complied and saved her neck (and parts), she would have to submit to the very man who had sent her to be burned.

Simple rebellion would not do. She would have to bide her time, feign compliance, wait for an opportunity. She sighed. Bera and Hesta had between them tried for years to train her to patience, but it seemed after all that life was going to be her most effective teacher.

As soon as she sat up, the two women put down their tatting and got swiftly to their feet, alert to her every move. Clearly, they had been trained well. The woman called Peta ruled her harem with a certain degree of menace. That in itself might prove useful.

"Hello," said Katla. She forced a smile.

The two women appeared to exchange a glance, for their veiled heads turned minutely to one another. Then the one in the lilac robe approached the bed.

"You feel better?" she asked. Her voice was mellifluous, her lips painted a lush rose-pink. A tiny silver star had been affixed to the runnel above her mouth. It glittered in the pale light.

Katla nodded. "What's your name?" she asked.

"Mela," the woman replied. "I called Mela. What your name?"

That gave Katla pause. If she lied, they had only to ask Kitten Soronsen. But it still seemed foolish to part with the information lightly. In response, therefore she smiled and frowned, as if she had misheard the question. Then she said, "What is that thing you wear above your lip?" She touched her finger to the corresponding spot on her own face.

The woman put her hand over her mouth and as she did so, Katla could see that the top of her hand had been painted with a myriad of fine reddish-brown lines which radiated out from the wrist and curled in undulating patterns to the base of each finger. Her nails were short and exquisitely shaped and painted with some rosy color. If the hand was anything to go by, the rest of her must be sleek and polished to perfection. If this was how they presented their houris for his lordship's pleasure, they were certainly going to have their work cut out dealing with her!

The two women gabbled something at once another in the southern tongue, then laughed.

"It means . . ." Mela started, then hesitated, giggling. "I suck well."

Katla wasn't entirely sure she'd heard this right, but she had a nasty feeling that she had. "Oh." It was hard to think of anything else to say on *that* subject which would not elicit details she had no wish to know. She tried again. "Have you always lived here?"

Mela shook her head. "My family from Hedera Port. Mother die of plague; father too poor to keep me. Sell me at market."

Katla looked horrified, but Mela waved her hands at her as if banishing such an unpleasant expression. "And where you come from?" she asked. "You speak funny, very harsh noise, very loud."

"I'm from the north. From Eyra—"

"Eyra!" the second woman cried. "They say so, but we not believe them. We at war. You enemy!"

"I know," said Katla. "Raiders came to my island and raped and killed many of my people. Then they set fire to our home. My grandmother died in the fire, but my mother and I and some others they stole away to sell as slaves."

The two women exclaimed in shock. "That terrible," said the one in blue. "You not choose to be here, then?"

Katla laughed bitterly. "Hardly. Why would any woman choose to be a whore?"

"That not what we called," the one in blue said primly. "We houris. Courtesans. We very good at what we do. We proud of it."

"You are?" Katla was astonished. "But you're slaves, slaves used for sex."

Mela shrugged. "It not so bad. Better here than most places. Better than being sold to horrid old husband, use you when he want, give you no money. Here get paid and well treated. Not have to pray too much. Only bed one man most of time, and handsome one, too."

"Mela!" the second woman exclaimed, then carried on in Istrian.

Again, the hand came up over the girl's mouth. "Agia says I should not say such things about our master, but is true. He not only handsome but very . . ." she paused, searching for a phrase, "nice in bed. Like women lot."

Katla sensed Mela would have embroidered upon this description given the least provocation. She changed the subject swiftly. "If he likes women so much, why does he cover you up?" Katla indicated the voluminous robes both women wore.

The woman in blue tilted her head. Katla could tell she was being regarded carefully. Instead of answering, she said at last, "Why you dress like man?"

"It's practical," Katla said shortly. "I mean, you can hardly climb a rock or run very fast in one of these things, can you?" She plucked despairingly at the gauzy thing they had draped over her. The veil lay crumpled on the floor by the bed where she had no doubt cast it off in her restless sleep.

Mela now retrieved the veil and held it out to Katla, who took it but did not put it on.

"That not what women do," the woman called Agia said primly. "Women sacred. They help men perform worship. We too precious to behave like . . . urchins, running around, touching the earth and suchlike. Such behavior is dirty, bad. That why we at war."

"What?" Katla thought she must have misheard. "We're at war because your people disapprove of how my people behave?"

The woman in blue nodded rapidly. "Your women, they have lost the Way. Your men not treat them right, not treat with respect, not honor the Goddess."

"My people worship no goddess," Katla said. "Our god is called Sur.

He is lord of the wind and the sea, of rock and wild places and the creatures of the deep." She thought about this even as she uttered it. The Eyrans paid their respects to the Storm Lord with occasional prayer (mainly at time of need), with their anchor pendants and their superstitions, with the odd muttered phrase, but the old rituals had fallen by the wayside. It was rare indeed that anyone slaughtered animals in his name, or cast sacrifices into the sea. The last time she remembered a serious rite being observed had been Tam Fox's blessing on board the *Snowland Wolf* to handfast her brother Halli and her best friend, Jenna. Even then, she had been surprised by the rather old-fashioned solemnity of the occasion which had seemed to hark—in its primitive hair-cutting and weaving, the incantation and supplication made—from another age, when the gods were closer to men. But if Sur had heard the prayers offered up or accepted the binding Tam Fox had cast into his waters, it did not seem that he had any wish to keep the bargain made for the honor paid him, for a monster had risen from the deep and wrecked their ship, and all those bright lives had been lost forever in his ocean. *So much for gods,* she thought. *I'll have none of them.* "But our religion is not so . . . restrictive as yours."

"Restrictive?"

"You seem to have a lot of rules, and to enforce them with punishment and pain. Burning, and the like." Her mouth felt dry even as she said this. She flexed, unthinking, the hand the flames of the pyre had withered.

"It is men who make rules," the older woman said. "We worship the Lady Falla in our own way, with our mouths and our hands, and when the time right, with our bodies and souls."

"Agia is correct," Mela said. "Men make rules, write them down, send people to the fires who not follow observances. I not think, in my heart, the Lady likes to have people fed to her fires. She goddess of life, not death."

"Mela!" Agia took the lilac-robed girl by the shoulders. After gabbling at her in rapid Istrian, she turned to Katla. "Do not take notice of what she says; her people had nomad roots. She get in much trouble if you repeat what she say."

"From the Lord of Forent?"

Agia put her hand to her mouth. "Not so much my lord, he less strict than others. But Peta will beat her. And if the lord's friend hear about it, then big trouble. He worship the Goddess with a fierce love, send many, many people to the fires."

"And who is his friend?" Katla asked, curious.

Agia dropped her voice to a whisper. "My lord of Cantara," she said. "Tycho Issian."

A shudder passed through Katla Aransen. She remembered the ranting tirade of a thin, dark man with eyes full of thwarted passion; the cowardly, bleeding boy who had condemned her with his lies; a terrified girl running through the night air. Selen Issian, daughter of Tycho Issian. Ah, yes, that was a name she remembered too well.

"And he is here, in this castle?"

Agia glanced swiftly back over her shoulder as if he might at any moment appear. "He due to arrive any day."

That was worse news than any she had so far received.

"The other women say," Mela crowded in close, "that he is mad with lust for the northern queen—"

"Shh!" Agia was scandalized. "You get us all burned!"

But Mela would not be stopped. "You know it is true, Agia. Remember what the wizard did to Balia and Raqla, how he made them like her, all green eyes and yellow hair and thin as post. And that why we go to war with your people—to fetch her back for him. That why you here, too," she finished triumphantly.

"What do you mean?"

"He preach, all over country, make people angry, fill them with hate. Tell them how your people barbarian, treat women bad, keep them from the Way of the Goddess. So we must . . ." she paused, seeking the right word in the less familiar Old Tongue, "we must . . . liberate you all. He say Eyran women be brought south, to free you from bad ways, from your evil men, make you like us. Obey men." This last was said with an edge of venom which had not been present in the girl's previous observations. Katla marked it well.

So it was not her so-called sacrilege alone which had sparked this war. That much was something of a comfort, if comfort there was to be gained from the situation. "It seems to me," she said after a while, "that you are the ones who need liberating."

Agia's hands flew up to her mouth. "You mad!" she declared. "I want no more of this. I fetch Peta. You not say such things when she here."

Katla watched her unbolt the door and her heart leaped with sudden hope; only to fall again at the sound of a key turning securely in the lock on the other side. She sighed. No chance of escape, then, at least not at the moment. She might as well sow some mischief instead.

Leaning in closer to Mela, Katla said firmly, "I think your people have it all wrong about the northern ways. We are not barbarians. Indeed, my people consider some of your customs as primitive—I mean, these— what do you call them again?" She touched the girl's lilac robe.

"Sabatka," Mela said.

"Sabatka. Well, it's very pretty, but really it's just designed to hide you from other men's eyes, isn't it? It's all about ownership—horses teth- ered in stables, pigs in pens, oxen yoked to a cart, and you women wrapped up in silk and hidden away from the sight of others. Your men are afraid that if they give you any freedom, you may take it and walk away from them! And who knows what might happen then? You might question what they do, you might have opinions, you might take power of your own. So what do they do? They shroud you in these hideous things, lock you away, treat you like toys for their pleasure, and tell you it's the Goddess's will; and you let them do it!"

Mela had gone very still, as if she was trying hard to concentrate on Katla's unfamiliar pronunciation of the Old Tongue. But she did not protest or cry out in horror. Rather, from the pensive line of her mouth and the inclination of her head, she seemed to be giving careful consid- eration to these seditious words.

Katla gave her some moments for it all to sink in, then ploughed on. "No man has ever told me what to do, and no man ever shall. I choose my own path, and fight for it when I have to. I can tell you more, if you would like."

It was an offer which would send her to the fires if she had misjudged her audience.

She had not.

Mela caught her by the hand and squeezed it tight. Her painted mouth curved into a delighted smile. Then with one clever, painted nail she removed the tiny silver star from above her top lip.

"Well, that's a start!" Katla muttered cheerfully. And then she began to tell Mela about a woman's lot in the Northern Isles: how as children they were educated alongside the boys; how they often chose their own husbands, and could renounce them if the marriage went awry; how they ran the farms when their husbands were away and held sway over their own households, even when the men came home; how they could earn their own money, and inherit estates; how some of them traveled and fought and had no man at all, but lived by their wits and their skills. Like nomads, even. But even as she framed these concepts for the Istrian woman, something gnawed at her. Life was not entirely equitable for the women of Eyra. They worked hard and they died young. Men still had more freedom and more power, and there were as many instances of injustices and oppression as there were different people in the islands. But at least there were laws which enshrined a woman's rights as well as any man's, and no one burned anyone else. But there was still much room for improvement.

Even so, her conviction seemed to have won the Istrian girl over, for by the time Aglia returned with Peta and her women, Mela's eyes were shining so brightly, Katla could see them gleaming through her veil.

14

Treachery

AUDA, the king's mother, sat in her carved chair at the corner of the hearth in Halbo Castle's Great Hall and regarded her son and daughter-by-law with the ancient, hooded eyes of a raven assessing its next meal. This impression was heightened by her dress and demeanor. Huddled in the shadows in the thick black widow's weeds she steadfastly refused to give up (even though her husband had been dead for four years, and she had not loved him for the best part of twenty-four), with her beady eyes reflecting the light of the fire and her arthritic fingers wrapped like claws around the handle of her stick, she looked very much like the carrion bird for which her family was named. At fifty-five, Auda was not an old woman by Eyran standards, where a rigorous climate, a culture of toughness, and a refusal to mollycoddle could result (if famine or disease did not intervene) in a very ripe old age. Eyra had more than its fair share of old crones, and it seemed as if Auda were driving herself toward such status with a grim will, as her once-fine appearance, generosity, and gentle spirit were daily transforming into bitterness, frustration, and malevolence.

It had not always been so.

At fifteen, she had been a celebrated beauty, exotic in a region known for its pale blondes and striking auburn-haired girls, with her lustrous black hair, her hazel eyes, and regal bearing. Every lord and chieftain in the Northern Isles in that time had striven to win her hand. Contests had been held by her father, feats of bravery and skill and downright idiocy—horse fights and sword fights, wrestling and archery, seal catching and cow tipping, tree chopping and spear casting. Ashar Stenson, prince of Halbo, had been the victor in every event in which he participated. Handsome he was, with his flowing yellow hair and plaited beard, his weather-tanned skin and his sharp blue eyes, his great stature and well-muscled limbs. The scars of a hundred duels and battles crisscrossed his forearms and puckered his chest in a fascinating web which told of fates run their course and lives cut short, and the famous luck of the royal house. She loved him at first sight. At thirty-three he was confident and attractive, a man who had outlived one wife already (dead in childbirth, and the babe, for shame, as well) and had a well-earned reputation for his lusty pursuit of the ladies of the court—a man, in short—in comparison to the scores of callow boys who came to ply their suit. But even so, Auda had turned him down, much to the chagrin of her father and uncles, who plainly saw the political advantage to be had in marrying their charge to the heir to the throne. Whether she had done so out of willfulness or arrogance, none could determine. None but Auda herself.

The truth of it was that she had been awash in an unfamiliar sea of desire. It frightened the wits out of her. She had never stood to win so much—nor yet to lose it. And so she withheld herself. This merely provoked Ashar to pursue her harder. He wooed her with furs and amber and silver, with fabulous weavings from the southern continent, with bards sent to sing her praises and with declarations of devotion. He had her brought to Halbo and showed her the castle that would be hers should she accept his troth. Still she would not take him. He tried to force her one night. She bit his cheek, leaving a mark which never fully healed, and fled the city. How could he resist such a hellcat? He sent armed men after her entourage and had her brought, raging, back to Halbo; where instead of paying a seither to marry them whether she would or no, he stripped to the waist and had four men beat him close to senseless in front of her for his temerity, until she cried out in horror and agreed to wed him.

There was blood on the sheets after their first night together; his (from the lashing) and hers from the virgin wound. She believed, in some ancient, pagan, instinctive way, that this melding of their essence—like the binding of a seither's enchantment—would keep them together forever, but she was wrong.

For three weeks after the wedding she was in bliss. By the end of the first month, he lost interest in her, and continued his lascivious affairs with every other woman under the northern sun, thus confirming her fears: that he was a man driven by the need to hunt and to conquer, a shallow man who preferred novelty and illicit liaisons to spending his nights in the conjugal bed. He swived her maybe two dozen times in the first year of their marriage, then never again. Unsurprisingly, she did not fall pregnant, a matter of political inconvenience and great bitterness to them both, though after that first year, he could not bring himself to touch her even for the sake of begetting an heir. Bastards abounded; most died in blood feuds brought about by the political maneuverings of one clan or another. And then, twenty-four years ago, the inconceivable had happened. Ashar Stenson—by then known as the Gray Wolf or the Shadow Wolf, for his cunning exploits in battle as well as for the mane of silvered hair he wore to his waist—fell in love, for the first and only time in his life. With an Istrian woman, the wife of his greatest enemy, the Lord of Forent.

With the irony that suggested the gods regarded those folk whose prayers they were offered with the utmost contempt, preferring to twist their fates into painful knots rather than to grant favors, the Lady of Forent duly conceived, from the single encounter the King of Eyra had managed to visit upon her.

The result—a baby boy smuggled into the northern court, claimed and raised as Auda's own at the violent behest of her griefstricken, guiltridden, passion-maddened husband, against all sense and propriety and against the prophecy of a seither she had once loved like a mother—was the man who now reigned as King of Eyra: Ravn Asharson, Stallion of the North. She had nurtured him as her own all these years and had never spoken of his origins, out of fear of her own fate if her part in this treachery to the nation were to be known as much as out of any sense of loyalty or love. The bitterness this situation had engendered had eaten her from the inside out as surely as any canker. Now, she looked upon the man who was thought by all to be her son, and the nomad bitch he had taken as his wife, and felt the bile rise in her throat.

She had done all she could to raise Ravn in the Eyran way, to instill in him the true northern values of courage and honesty, honor and shrewdness; but in the end he had been true to his tainted roots. Traveling to the southern continent just like his father, he had gone and brought a foreign whore back to his bed. Like every weak man, he had been led by the demands of his insistent cock instead of choosing himself a good northern bride who would respect her heritage, her position, and her husband's mother. Worse—for she could have found some secret way to be rid of a mere bed-partner—he had taken the whore to wife and apparently got upon her a son, an heir to whom the Eyran throne, and all the weight of the Northern Isles' proud history, would pass in time.

It was insupportable. From the pride and love she had learned to feel for this handsome boy she had raised as her own, her softer sentiments had hardened and turned increasingly—day by bitter day—to fury, resentment, and loathing. Like Sur's raven, she hoarded these treasures. Like the raven, she carried vengeance and death in her heart.

At the outset of this sorry affair she had cried down woes on Ravn for the shame of taking a nomad whore for his bride; she had predicted doom and disaster, for himself, for his family, and for the whole country. And when none of her words would sway his will (or what was left of it once that pale sorcereress had sapped him with her lascivious appetites) she had dwelled with steadfast purpose on her desire to see the Rosa Eldi put off as infertile, or preferably dead. When the woman did not fall pregnant, she thought all her prayers to Feya had been answered; to ensure matters stayed that way she had brought the seither here. But that ancient being had betrayed her, and turned instead to do the bidding of the whore. Somehow (and Auda could feel the poison of magic at work in it, could feel it in the hair on the back of her neck, which rose like a dog's every time the child was nearby) the seither had helped the Rosa Eldi, the Whore of the World, to conceive and give birth to a boy Ravn now cherished as his heir. This single act made the woman's position unassailable. Except to basest treachery.

There they were, the little family group, lit by the warm colors of the fire: the Stallion, the Whore, and the Child. And just behind them sat the wet nurse, who was never far away.

Auda regarded the girl from the safety of her secluded seat. She was very pretty, in a doe-eyed, foreign sort of way. No one appeared to know a damned thing about her, except that her name was Leta Gullwing and she had come in by ship from the south, which should have been all Auda required to loathe her entirely. But something about the girl, something sorrowful and yet determined, something damaged yet optimistic, reminded her of her own younger self. She saw, with the shrewd observation born of years of watching from the shadows, how the girl watched Ravn with sly, stolen glances; how she seemed to melt when he held his ill-begotten child, with its huge, ugly head and its unearthly violet eyes, how her cheeks pinked if he addressed her, how she looked quickly away as if she might betray herself. Auda recognized obsessional devotion when she saw it. It was how she had looked at Ravn's father, longingly, confusedly, when he had no care for her. And, like his father, Ravn was oblivious to her attentions.

Fool, she thought to herself. *All men are fools.* It was time for a woman to show her mettle. Left to himself and the Whore, Ravn would destroy Eyra and all it stood for. Already the royal line was tainted. She had given him every chance to redeem his poisoned heritage, but he had failed her and his people. Now was the time to act. Wrapping her shawl closer about her, she slipped from her seat and left the hall unnoticed by all but the hound which lay outside the side door, who sniffed at her hand uncertainly, not sure whether it would earn for its attentions a scrap or a cuffed head. In the end, it won neither. The Lady Auda swept past it as if it were not there. Her mind was on higher matters entirely.

In her chambers, her servant awaited her. The girl had changed the rushes on the floor and stoked up her fire, but still the room smelled musty and damp. *I shall have finer quarters soon,* she thought, crossing to her sewing table. There, she withdrew two threads of fine wool from a tray of assorted skeins laid out for the tapestry work she did in order to limber up her stiff joints, and with awkward fingers tied a series of knots into each piece. Then she wound them into tight bundles, extracted a small leather pouch which chinked when lifted, and beckoned the girl close.

"Take the red one and this pouch give them to the master of the dungeons," she said softly. "Make sure no one else sees you. I don't care how you manage it . . ." She paused. The girl was attractive, in a robust Eastern Islander way and had a certain lusty reputation. It was always useful in Halbo Castle to have a pretty servant at hand who had the ability to come by information in exchange for a favor or two. "Promise him a kiss or . . . something . . . when he does what is asked of him. And when he has read the red string, show him that you have the blue. But on no account let him take it or unravel it. That one must be passed unread to the one it is meant for. Accompany the dungeon master down to the cells. When he unlocks the requisite door, give the blue thread to the man inside that cell."

The girl nodded, then frowned. "And then what?"

Auda smiled. "And then you let him take his . . . kiss . . . and you have completed your task, and shall be rewarded as you deserve."

"There is a pretty gown in the market just like the queen's," the girl said covetously. "I would very much like it. Though it is . . . rather expensive."

Auda inclined her head. The idea of Ana bursting out of diaphanous white silk cut for a spear-thin woman was quite ridiculous. "Of course, my dear, I am sure it will suit you well," she said graciously. "Run along now, and mind no one sees you."

ANA thought about that dress all the way to the Sentinel Tower and down into the dungeons: it helped to keep her mind off what might be lurking in those dark corridors full of echoing footsteps and dripping water. The sconce guttered as she walked, casting strange shadows onto the ancient stone walls, illuminating spiderwebs strung out across the ceilings and the fat occupants which squatted patiently at each locus awaiting its next repast. Narrow stairways wound down and down and down, the steps slick with wear and seepage—of water, or something worse—and the stench got so bad by the third flight that she had to pinch her nostrils closed with her free hand.

Bram will love me in it, she thought. *He won't be able to keep his hands off me.* There was a dance coming up on Fifthnight, just over a week away. She had thought she'd have to wear her green dress, the one with the embroidered bodice, but it seemed so old-fashioned and frumpy in comparison with the new fashions inspired by the queen. Pale colors, floating fabrics, and mother-of-pearl trim had replaced bright, sturdy velvets and wool in the wardrobes of all the ladies of the court, whether the new style suited them or not. It did mean you had to dash between fire-warmed rooms down chilly castle corridors if you didn't want to freeze your tits off, but it was well worth it for all the attention you got from the guards, or the chieftains and their retinues gathering in Halbo for the muster to war. *That chieftain from Black Isle,* she thought, skirting a particularly noxious puddle, *he has a bold eye.* The memory of his flirtatious glance as she served in the Great Hall made her shiver. Perhaps she was setting her sights too low with Bram. Wearing a dress like the one she'd seen in the market, with its low-cut bodice, its fine sleeves, and shimmering skirt, she might catch more than a mere sergeant in the King's Guard: a clan chief, perhaps; even a lord.

Thoughts of the coming war did not concern Ana. She was a girl who lived from day to day and didn't like to spend much time thinking if she could help it. She knew that Bram would sail south to Istria to fight, the handsome chief from Black Isle, too. Whether or not they would return was in the hands of the god. But there would always be other attractive men around while they were gone, even if they did not come back. What was a real shame was never having a chance to entertain the king himself, for it was said by many he didn't confine his charms to noblewomen but had been generously evenhanded in his affections—before he'd gone away to the Allfair, at least. She'd arrived at court only the week before he sailed and had been far too overwhelmed to have set her sights that high in such a short time. Then he'd come back with the peculiar, pale woman from the South, and had had eyes for no other woman ever since. Which seemed a waste. *The Rose of the World—a strange name that, for such a fragile creature. She was more like a snowdrop than a voluptuous rose, so fragile it looked as if you could snap her in two between your fingers, just like that!* Ana couldn't understand what the attraction could be to a man like Ravn Asharson. She hardly seemed a fitting bed-partner for the Stallion of the North. *He needs a proper mare!* She giggled to herself and nearly tripped down the next stair, steadying herself against the dank wall.

She rounded the final curving stairway to the dungeon keeper's chamber without further mishap. No one saw her and there seemed to be no guards on this level at all: unsurprising really, since most of their charges had been released into the care of the Earl of Stormway and were learning the ropes ready to be drafted onto ships bound for the southern continent when such became necessary. At the door to Flinn Ogson's chamber she smoothed her hair, tugged her bodice lower, and knocked loudly. There was a moment's pause in which she heard the clink of a flask and goblet and the sound of them being hastily tidied away. She stifled a laugh. Did he really think everyone was ignorant of his habits?

The door opened a hand's width and the dungeon master peered out, looking irritated at the interruption. His eyes were bloodshot. His breath almost knocked her down. "What d'you want?" he slurred, apparently addressing her cleavage.

"Well, that depends." Ana bobbed a curtsy to show him even more, then handed him the red string and watched as he turned a shoulder to her and unraveled it with clumsy fingers. Sometimes she wished she'd been more diligent at learning her knots, but it always seemed a lot easier to tell people things than have to go to so much trouble.

The man looked at her again in an assessing way. He leered at her. "Well then," he said, "best get the dull bit over with. Then we can have some fun." He took the sconce from her and beckoned her to follow.

Down into the bowels of the dungeons she followed his broad leatherclad back. At the bottom it was hard to breathe, as if every poisonous smell from the entire castle had been dropped into this well of lost souls. Ana hoped very much that whatever favor the man expected to claim it would at least be in the relative comfort of his own chambers than in one of these filthy cells. It was a good job she'd worn her old homespun. She fixed her thoughts on the pretty white dress again, and let her fingers play over the first knots on the coiled blue thread. A meeting. Interesting. Surreptitiously, she removed the thread from her pouch and unrolled a bit more of it. Something about a man . . . something, something . . . a woman . . . She raised an eyebrow. Perhaps the old woman wasn't quite as dry a stick as she made out. Perhaps she was arranging a liaison with a condemned man! The idea thrilled her. It was quite romantic, really, if you thought about it; or it would be if it were a beautiful young girl, rather than the old bag, offering some poor criminal his last taste of love . . . She smiled, even as she picked her way through the rat droppings and pools of other, unnamable substances in Flinn's wake to the last cell of all. The dungeon keeper took a vast ring of keys off his belt and unlocked this last door, then pushed her ahead of him. Ana shivered. Perhaps *she* was being offered to the prisoner! She hadn't been prepared for that possibility. Quickly, she thrust the blue string at him and watched as he perused it. *He must have been rich once,* she thought idly. *That robe had cost a fortune just for the marten fur. Pity it was ruined now. Though perhaps with a good wash . . .*

Then the man stared at her, his eyes gleaming. She looked swiftly away, embarrassed despite herself. When she glanced back, it was to see his fingers running back and forth along the thread as if he were not quite sure of its import. Then he tucked it into his robe and stood up, wiping his hands on his thighs. He held one out to her.

"Thank you," he said, and she was struck by his educated tones. *A nobleman, then. Hard to tell in this light, and with that straggly beard.*

She stared at his hand, and took a step away. "Don't mention it," she said. "Sir."

"Come on, then," Ogson said brusquely. "Both of you."

He led them back up the winding stairs to his chamber and ushered them in ahead of him. He made a great show of relocking the door (couldn't have the girl thinking she'd be away from here with just a kiss) and stashing the keys back on his belt, then turned to the girl. She was staring at the prisoner with a puzzled expression on her face.

Then: "Oh!" she exclaimed. "You're Erol Bardson, the king's cousin. The trait—"

Flinn Ogson grabbed her by the hand before she could be even more indiscreet and pulled her toward his bedchamber. "Wait for me," he called back over his shoulder to the prisoner.

"Oh, I'll wait," said Erol Bardson. "I've waited three months, I'm sure I can manage another ten minutes."

The dungeon keeper turned back. "It'll take longer than that," he said, affronted.

"I doubt it." The lord took charge of the dungeon master's chair, put his filthy boots up on the table, and rocked backward. Beneath the table he could just make out a flask and goblet. As Flinn Ogson disappeared into the other room with his hand on the serving girl's commodious rump, he rescued the inexpertly hidden items and helped himself.

"NO one saw you?" Auda's mouth pursed suspiciously.

"No one."

"And the bodies?"

"Down the garderobe and in the embrace of the wide Northern Ocean." He'd done the dungeon keeper first, then taken his time with the girl who, thinking it would save her life, had been quite willing, at first. His lips curled at the memory. "Feeding the Nemesis by now," he joked.

"Ssh!" Auda made a sign against ill omen. "There is altogether too much sorcery in this world without invoking more. Perhaps we shall have a chance to cleanse it, you and I, once this deed is done. Restore the kingdom to its pure northern roots."

Erol Bardson raised a grime-encrusted eyebrow at the king's mother. "You will forgive me, lady," he said softly, "if I see a certain irony in the situation. Seeking aid from our mortal enemies seems a rum way to restore the Eyran line. Not—" he forestalled her sharp retort with a hand gesture, "—that I am complaining. I am more than happy to take your commission, and the throne also in time, if you will have me."

Auda shifted uncomfortably. "Perhaps as regent," she said stiffly. "We must see how the knucklebones fall."

She beckoned him out onto the balcony, a solid granite affair topped with spiky iron railings. Three iron ravens adorned the most prominent spikes. Finely worked they were, each feather delineated with infinite care. Then one of them bobbed its head, uttered a low caw, and flew to Auda's outstretched hand.

"Ah, Memory," she said softly. "You were always the boldest."

She turned to the Earl of Broadfell.

"Memory lives up to his name. Send him to me when you need secret passage into the city and I shall see to it that you . . . and your allies . . . are admitted."

She handed the raven to him and it cocked its head and fixed him with the beady gaze of one contemplating the exquisite juiciness of the eyeball it saw within easy striking distance of its beak.

Erol held the bird away from him in distaste.

Torments and Miracles

TANTO Vingo stared out of his window into the courtyard and drank in the perfect view—ancient time-eroded cobbles; elegant terra-cotta pots filled with bright blooms, spills of vine and bougainvillea against soft orange-pink stonework; an elegant marble fountain fashioned centuries ago by Firo, the greatest sculptor of his age; and thirty naked nomad women being lashed into submission by a handful of his most trusted guards.

His new chambers in Jetra's ancient fortress were very fine, he had to admit. Circesian rugs carpeted the beautifully tiled floors, the walls were blanketed with fabulous tapestries and chased silver goblets lay strewn across the vast oak table among the remains of an exquisite banquet. The kitchen staff had excelled themselves this time. They had prepared roast swan stuffed with goose, chicken, quail, and hummingbirds; two suckling piglets filled with grapes; a haunch of venison; lamb fetuses in a rich gravy of rendered cats' hearts; two savory beef and mushroom pies; a huge confection of cream and fruit and liqueur-soaked cake; breads and pastries; and rice spiced with safflower. It was more than enough to feed a dozen hungry lords, but he had eaten it all himself, alone but for a pair of slave girls who brought him a spittoon whenever he required it or wheeled his great chair to the privy so that he could empty his guts to make room for more.

He belched out of the window again and was satisfied to note that two of the women were begging for mercy now and were ready to worship the Goddess with the captain and his men. He would have them all raped and then burned anyway, though they did not know that this prior trial would prove to be a mere entertainment. His new flame contraption had undergone another amendment; it would be useful to test it in private before making the spectacle a public event to which he might invite his beloved brother.

Forty minutes later, all the women had been raped, the guards' energy and enthusiasm was spent, and he was bored again. He signaled the serving girls to wheel him back to the table and there picked distractedly at the remnants, even though he had no appetite for the food, none at all.

The chamber had once been the receiving room of the lords of this province: Hesto and Greving Dystra, once loyal, respected members of Istria's Ruling Council, now sadly reduced to a pathetic, stinking, weakened state by a bloody flux which had mysteriously come upon them the previous week. He was quite surprised they were still alive. Their frames, already old and frail, had been wasted almost to nothing by near-constant vomiting and diarrhea. There was nothing left to them now but skin and bone and deep-burning spirit. He planned to destroy the last of that this very afternoon.

It was intoxicating to have the run of the Eternal City. With the Dystras sadly incapacitated and the Lords Prionan, Sestran, and Fortran having sped north to Cera and Forent to make good the northern defenses and oversee the construction of the new fleet, now that Rui Finco's men had brought them the northern shipmaker they so desperately needed, Jetra lay in the hands of Tycho Issian. And since the Lord of Cantara was much taken up with his own plans for an attack on the Eyran capital, he had appointed Tanto his deputy in all things. *What I could have done,* Tanto thought with genuine regret, *if I had still been in possession of all my bodily parts, my strength, my health, my looks!*

His first act upon finding himself effective ruler of this domain had been to order all the castle's mirrors covered. The first girl who had been summoned to tend him had shown her disgust at his condition with a curl of the lip. He had tied her to the bed and as she lay back expecting the usual treatment under such circumstances, he had cut those lips from her with his sharpest knife; then her cunt-lips for good measure.

Then he had ordered a physician to sear the wounds, an act which he had also enjoyed, and had ordered her cast into his brother's cell, making sure she knew who it was she was to be sequestered with. It was a filthy place, the Miseria, and filthier now that he had ordered the guards never to clean it. The whore's wounds had become infected in no time at all. Chained hand and foot to the seeping wall down there, Saro had watched her die and could do nothing to alleviate her suffering. Tanto had watched him weep and realized with glee there was no end to the torments he could inflict upon his brother, and no one to stop him either.

THE Lord of Cantara was far too busy to concern himself with reports concerning Tanto Vingo's many depravities, most of which he would in any case have dismissed as either highly exaggerated or stemming from the overly squeamish sensibilities of observers. No, Tycho Issian's mind was bent to the exclusion of all other matters on devising a way to take back the Rosa Eldi, a woman for whom he had agreed upon a bride-price and who had been unfairly and inconceivably snatched away from him at the previous summer's Allfair. Still he burned for her. His mind and body gave him no surcease from desire. If he slept—which was rare, and brief—his slumber was filled with troubled dreams, and he awoke in a state of uncomfortable tumescence; awake, her naked image hovered provocatively before his eyes even as he preached in the Great Hall, the market squares, and the campo, paraded his troops, or addressed a room full of advisers. If he stumbled in his speech, entranced by a flash of her pale, rose-tipped breasts or his vision became glazed at a glimpse of her luminously hairless pudenda, no one had the temerity to remark upon it, to his face.

Behind his back, however, rumor had it that the Lord of Cantara was entirely off his head.

This impression was enhanced both by his physical appearance—disheveled, unkempt, his black eyes blazing, pupils dilated like bottomless pits; and by the "advisers" he had gathered about himself. A more ragtag collection of hucksters and ne'er-do-wells you could never imagine. The few respectable men among them were traders with some knowledge of the layout of the northern capital, a group of veterans of the last campaign against the Northern Isles and a handful of disciples genuinely moved by his impassioned pleas to the populace to rise up and bring Falla's word to the barbaric north. But the rest represented the worst elements in Istria. In the grip of his mania, Tycho Issian appeared to have lost all sense of perspective and propriety, for he surrounded himself with sellswords (who'd fought for both sides and cared not a damn why, so long as they were paid), mountebanks, and shysters; old men with a score to settle; young men out to make a killing; those driven by anger, by greed, and an eye for a business opportunity. In short, the sort of folk always to be found fanning the flames of conflict.

The most recent addition to this tribe was Plutario, a man who had been brought to Tycho Issian's chambers secretly one night since he had been overheard claiming that he was able to render folk invisible (under precisely the right conjunction of stars, which had so far never quite seemed to align themselves correctly). It was an irony remarked upon only in private by those well out of the southern lord's earshot, that in a land in which even growing the wrong herbs would currently get you burned as a magic maker, Tycho Issian would openly take such a man into his employ.

On the basis of the knowledge and surmise provided by this motley band, Tycho had drawn up maps, charts, and diagrams of the city and its castle, as well as planning a fair division of its women and its spoils. However, no one as yet had a plan for getting past the harbor defenses. It was well known that Halbo had never been sacked from the sea in all its long history. Attacking from landward meant sailing through the treacherous and well-fortified Sharking Straits, then making a hazardous trek southward over a formidable mountain range. The man who proposed this course was a yeka trader. He had, he said, a thousand or more of the beasts which were born to this sort of work. They had originated in the lands beyond the Dragon's Backbone and had traversed the Golden Mountains and the Skarn. They could haul wagons and each carry half a dozen armed men, which would be more than enough for a shock raid on the capital, storming the castle, and disabling the guards in the Sentinel Towers to allow a fleet to sail in and finish the job.

Tycho was so excited by this prospect that he fairly danced with the man—until someone pointed out the logistics of transporting a herd of such vast beasts by sea. Given the addition of soldiers, crew, oar slaves, equipment, weaponry, and supplies—let alone the captives they would take from Halbo—they would require a fleet of a thousand ships. Currently, they had precisely thirty.

At the point of this realization, Tycho Issian bellowed for everyone to leave.

All except Plutario, whom he beckoned to stay.

"I need you," he reiterated, "to veil our ships with a secret mist, one which human eyes cannot penetrate. That way we can steal into their harbor unseen and storm the castle. Then I can steal the Lady away, and be gone."

Plutario looked surprised. He was not a man who had yet learned to guard his expressions, but fortunately the Lord of Cantara was still in need of the abilities others claimed for him. "Forgive me, my lord," he started, in his soft Gilan accent. He looked nervous. Small beads of perspiration burst out across his forehead. With his unusually pale complexion and fat-softened features, he looked like a cheese sweating in the sun. He licked his lips, started again. "I was under the impression—and this may be entirely my error, lord, for my understanding of the affairs of great men like yourself is sadly lacking—that you . . . that you wished to sack the northern city, to bring the Way of Falla to its people . . . To kill the heretic enemy and liberate the ill-used women . . ." He paused, seeing his master's eyes narrow dangerously. "As well as the Lady, of course . . ." His voice trailed away to nothing. He knew himself to be in a perilous situation, and not just for raising this delicate point. He had not volunteered himself for this service but had been tricked into the castle and delivered to Tycho Issian by a man he had once thought a friend, who had sought to further his own dubious ends by providing the Lord of Cantara with an imaginative gift. Thus misrepresented, Plutario Falco found himself fatally compromised, for in truth he was no sorcerer but only a mere conjurer, a man who entertained at banquets with his neat sleight-of-hand trickery. He was an entertainer, a prestidigitator; a player of games. But, unfortunately, he had no genuine magical ability whatsoever. If he had, he would have used his skill to render himself invisible one minute after meeting this madman, escaped the city, and fled for his distant island home as fast as his feet—or a magic carpet—could carry him.

"The Lady is the key," Tycho said sharply. "Without her, the rest means nothing. If we take the Rose of the World and kill her consort, the north will fall to us. I know it."

Plutario silently cursed his stupid mouth. "Of course, my lord, of course. What know I of such matters? I am only a simple . . ." he struggled for a useful description; failed ". . . man," he finished lamely.

"Indeed," the Lord of Cantara said distractedly. "Indeed." He paced the chamber, hands clasped behind his back. "Armies and herds of yeka and a thousand ships will avail us nothing. All I need is a little magic." He swiveled on his heel, fixed the cringing conjurer with a gleaming eye. "Surely that's not too much to ask?"

"No, my lord. Let me consult the alignments in my star charts again to determine the optimum hour for such a venture . . ."

Tycho Issian fixed him with a look so venomous that Plutario felt his knees go to water. After a pause which was pregnant with malice, the Lord of Cantara said quietly, "We shall expect a full demonstration of your skills tomorrow night, alignment or no alignment. Or I shall give you into the hands of Tanto Vingo for use in one of his experiments. From the look of you, you should burn long and slow, like tallow."

ALISHA'S crystal had proved to be worth its burdensome weight. As if it had decided to adopt its new protector, it showed Virelai to a recent kill by desert cats—some large, unidentifiable rodent left mauled and half-eaten among the rocks beneath a stand of flame trees—and allowed him to channel a fire through its quartz heart with which to cook the thing. He had never been so ravenous. Or rather, he corrected his thought, he had never been ravenous at all. It was a delicious sensation, tearing into the seared flesh with his stomach rumbling away in anticipation of the feast, feeling the meat juices bursting on his tongue, dribbling out of his mouth. No sooner had he finished his meal than he remembered Al-isha's and the nomads' refusal to eat the flesh of any other creature and felt abruptly ashamed. But he told himself that he had not caused the death of the creature he ate, and without it might be near death himself, and by such persuasions soothed his qualms, though the memory of the delicious taste of the meat, so different to the wasted, sorcerous things the Master had magicked into existence to sustain them on Sanctuary, revisited him tauntingly for hours and days to come.

The seeing-stone also showed him to an old well in which a battered leather bucket hung from a tattered rope and the water tasted fresh and sweet. It offered him landmarks he might guide himself by, and as the sun began to dip into a blood-red sky, it led him within sight of the Eter-nal City.

Here, the crystal became stubborn, refusing to allow any glimpse of what might await him inside those rosy sandstone walls. Instead, it of-fered the deeply unsettling view of Rahe, Lord of Sanctuary, leaving his arctic stronghold with a dark man in a small vessel. Virelai watched this bizarre tableau with an icy hand around his heart. In his head he could hear the terns wailing their mournful cries, the distant roar of unseen waves. He remembered his own escape from the ice realm and the cir-cumstances in which he had left his erstwhile guardian. He recalled Rahe's towering rages and his awesome powers, and in his head a single phrase repeated itself, over and over, a mantra, a warning, a harbinger of doom:

The Master is returning to the world . . .

He was coming back to Elda. He was coming to find his erring ap-prentice and exact his revenge, with some strange man in tow who looked tough enough to twist Virelai's head right off his shoulders.

Virelai took trembling hands off the crystal and tried to think. *What if it is not true-sight? Just a possible future, something that may never happen.* It was a tempting evasion, but he knew, from the buzzing in his bones caused by the contact with the stone, that such was not the case.

His immediate instinct was to flee south, to disappear into the desert, to make for the hills where he had been born, and hope to escape his fate. But that way lay Alisha and the death-stone and whatever horrors she awoke with it. He did not think he was strong enough in his mind to witness the raising of the dead. Although he might use the stone against the old man . . . But even as he considered this, he knew he could never do it. In the presence of the mage, he would become again the terrified child he used to be. And if the stone came to the Master's hands, he would surely be obliterated.

But if he ran away now, fled to save his own skin, what would become of Saro Vingo?

He rolled the seeing-stone into the spill of cloth, confined it with a viciously tight knot, and kept on walking north.

The priests were calling the eleventh observance as he approached the city, their wailing song floating through the still air like a charm upon the land. It was a prayer designed to soothe the faithful, a plea for the Goddess's mercy and blessing as they went to their beds, but now that Virelai knew the identity of the One to whom it was dedicated, it gave him no comfort at all. He entered the orchards which bordered the southern edge of the city, but at this season the trees were empty of fruit, their leaves dropped to form a thick carpet which rustled as he walked. The last time he had come this way had been with the Beast, huge as a mountain cat, its eyes lambent in the darkness, and he had been sorely afraid of it. He had used the voice of command to compel Saro to accompany him south and at the time had felt no compunction at doing so. Now, his conscience struck him hard. Had he left the boy to his own devices and forsaken his own wild stratagems, Falo and the other nomads would most likely have made it to the safety of the mountains, Alisha would not be running mad with the death-stone, and Saro would be wherever he was headed on a black stallion charged with natural energy, rather than the creature out of nightmare which last he had seen galloping south with empty, soulless eyes. He had no plan for how he would find Saro, let alone save him and flee the city; but rather than allow despair and cowardice to set in before he had even made an attempt, he pushed his doubts and fears away with a force of will he had never owned before.

There were no guards on the walls, and the postern gate, miraculously, was open. Virelai slipped unseen into the city he had sworn never to set foot in again. He had no idea where they might have taken his friend, but he found himself treading carefully up the back stairs toward the quarters Tycho Issian had occupied when he was last in Jetra. They were empty and in disarray. Virelai's spirits leaped. Perhaps the Lord of Cantara had left the Eternal City; perhaps he had taken Saro with him, north to Forent maybe, where Rui Finco would be overseeing their war plans.

In which case the vision the crystal had shown him was false after all. A tremendous sensation of relief came over him even though it would mean a long hard journey on foot and a postponed crisis rather than an immediate one. At least he would not have to see his friend tortured.

He had no sooner thought this than a terrible cry rang out, echoing down the corridors. His heart jumped erratically. The cry came again, shrill and piercing; the cry of a wounded animal?

He flattened himself against the ancient stone wall and was disturbed to feel it vibrate beneath his palms and back. When the scream came again, he knew, with some part of himself to which he had never previously had access, exactly where it had come from.

Suddenly, volitionlessly, he found his feet carrying him toward the sound. Down two flights of stairs they took him, around a corner, past a suite of rooms in which the Vingo clan had resided during the council meeting. These, too, lay empty and abandoned, the furniture overturned, the finer artifacts gone from within, as if ransacked by some marauding host. Had enemies come this far south? He shook his head as if answering an unseen question: that was surely impossible in the short span of time which had elapsed. A riot, then, an uprising of the people? But he had seen how the populace had responded to Tycho Issian's orations in market square and city hall, wildly applauding his words and cheering his every sentiment. Perhaps the Lord of Cantara had staged a coup, and cast the established lords out of Jetra? Virelai was not a worldly man, in any sense of the word. He did not understand politics, had no experience of war, civil or otherwise; the chaos he encountered as he traversed the castle was unsettling. What was clear was that something strange and threatening had taken place in this city since the last time he had been here, when all had been elegance, order, and perfection.

The cry came again, more of a moan now. It was followed by loud voices, then a slamming door and the sounds of footsteps hurrying down the corridors in the opposite direction to where he stood with his heart hammering. Virelai waited, then pushed himself around the corner. There were three doors ahead of him. The first he tried was locked, the brass handle cold. The second opened onto an empty chamber stacked with sheet-draped furniture. The third door showed a strip of light along its bottom edge, and the sound of soft keening emanated from it. Bending down, Virelai looked cautiously through the keyhole but could see nothing. Nothing, that is, except a large room with tables covered in scrolls and parchments, many of which appeared disarranged. A dozen candles burned raggedly from sconces around the walls: their guttering flames and the erratic play of light they generated were all that moved. Virelai frowned. Then he dropped to his knees and peered through the gap beneath the door.

An eye stared back at him.

It was a pale eye, gray-green of iris, the white shot through with a crazing of red. It did not belong to Saro Vingo. For a moment, Virelai thought himself to be looking at the glazed orb of a dead man; then the eye blinked. He scrambled to his feet, prepared to run away, but instead his hand wrapped itself around the brass handle and he found himself stepping into the room.

The man was lying on the floor with his head twisted sideways and his legs splayed out. His face was bruised and puffy and there was blood in his hair and spattered around him. One of his arms lay at an unnatural angle to his body. At the sight of Virelai, he had become silent; now the air between them filled with expectancy, but the sorcerer did not know what to say. After a few seconds he ventured, "Are you all right?" which was idiotic but at least showed he meant no harm.

The eye blinked furiously. "Hardly."

"Can you move?"

The body began an awful shuffling motion and eventually levered itself onto one side, the broken arm flopping uselessly. More effort followed, and eventually the figure sat up, revealing itself as a man in his middle years with a balding head and a lot of pink flesh. One eye was closed, the lid swollen purple; the other stared at Virelai, now kneeling at his side, and then at the wrapped crystal, with suspicion.

"Who are you?" the man asked.

"No one, really," said Virelai, unwilling to offer his identity up too easily. "I was looking for a friend of mine. Who are you?"

"My name is Plutario Falco. Some called me 'the Magnificent.' " He laughed, coughed, and spat out a tooth, which he regarded mournfully. "Not very magnificent now. Not that I ever was, really. It was all just tricks, you see. My Lord of Cantara set me a task, which I failed miserably. You can see the results of his fury for yourself. They'll hand me over to the Tormentor tomorrow."

"The Tormentor?"

The man gave Virelai a broken smile, then tossed the tooth onto the floor. "Where have you been these last weeks?" he asked. "Not in Jetra, that's for certain. Tanto Vingo, the cripple from Altea, Tycho's right-hand man who seems to have the run of the whole city, now that all the other nobles have gone north and the Dystras are on their deathbeds. He's known as the Tormentor now for all the torture and burnings that are his special pleasures."

Virelai shuddered. Tanto Vingo. He remembered the sluglike, white-faced boy with his burning-coal eyes full of calculation and pent fury, so different from the mild, open regard of his younger sibling, being wheeled about the castle in a great wicker throne. He recalled, too, the tales of the slaves, overheard in whispered conversations, tales of cruelty and temper; he remembered how Bëte, with the instinctive understanding of an animal, had avoided him assiduously.

"And what of his brother, Saro Vingo?" he asked with dawning dread.

Plutario grimaced. "Down in the Miseria," he said. "Poor lad. Dragged him in out of the desert, I'd heard, where he'd been stupid enough to run away and join a nomad band rather than fight for his country. But when Tycho Issian's got hold of the exchequer and there's a bounty on your head, there's not too much chance for escape. They say they'll punish him for desertion and that there's no love lost between the brothers. I daresay I'll be making the lad's acquaintance for a brief while before we both succumb to Tanto's pleasure." He shifted his weight, wincing at the pain that shot up his arm. "You don't have a knife, or something sharp, do you?" he asked a moment later.

The sorcerer shook his head.

"Pity. Be better to do away with myself quickly and quietly before they give me over to that monster."

Virelai looked appalled. "You can't take your own life. Surely nothing

can be so bad that it would drive you to do that . . ." The words trailed
away, for even as he said it he knew it wasn't true. Suddenly he was
brought back to a time in Sanctuary's ice tower when Rahe had shown
him the world that lay beyond, how the mage had shown him man's cruelty to man all over Elda—the rapes, the burnings, beatings, and torture. Whole villages overrun by soldiers, slaves whipped under a merciless
sun, a man stretched on a flaming rack. Nomads being stoned by angry
mobs, cast into huge pyres. Men nailed to great wooden frames and left
to die in agony. And it came to him with a sudden, terrible comprehension that the sights the Master had afforded him on that fateful day had
been not a simple view of the depredations which were taking place at
that time, but a window into the future, this future. The old man had
tried to warn him, but he had ignored the mage's words and had followed a course of action which had set off a sequence of events leading
to the very horrors the world was now facing.

*Sanctuary I named this place, and sanctuary it is. You should thank
me for bringing you here and saving you from all that greed and horror . . . It all decays and falls away, boy: life, love, magic. There's nothing worth saving in the end . . .*

Virelai felt a buzzing in his head, a rising sensation in his chest. The
man was saying something, but the words were just a blur. "No," he
said, then: "No!" He reached out blindly, caught Plutario by the shoulder. "NO."

He had no idea whom he was addressing: it might have been himself.
It might have been a rejection of the Master's nihilism, or of this broken
man's despair. It might have been a challenge to the entropy of all
things, an outraged demand of the Goddess, in whom it all began. White
light filled his mind; white noise, too. There were two voices, locked in
a spiral of sound; then silence.

Virelai opened his eyes. The man, Plutario Falco, was sitting staring
at him with something approaching terror in his face. Where the bruise
had closed his left eye, the skin was as pink and glowing as a newborn's.
He backed away from the sorcerer, pushing off the floor with his hands.
Both hands. With a shock, Virelai realized the broken arm was whole
again, the bones knit, the shoulder joint relocated.

"Wh—who are you?" Plutario stammered. He flexed his fingers in bewilderment. "You've healed me. It's a miracle. I can't believe it. Is it magic? True magic? By the Lady, I never believed it existed, I thought it all was chicanery, tricks and sleight-of-hand, a bit of clever flimflam like my own. But this—" He raised an amazed smile to his savior. There was a gap where the knocked-out tooth was missing; the molar lay still upon the floor, bloody at the root.

Not a complete miracle, then, Virelai thought inconsequentially. But what else could it be called, and how had it been accomplished? His mind sought wildly for explanation: failed. After a while, tears began to roll down his cheeks, another new experience.

"Don't weep, man!" Plutario cried, hauling him to his feet. "You're free and I'm whole. We can escape this place and never look back!"

"I cannot leave without Saro," Virelai said dully.

"Give him up, man. He's as good as dead, that one. My life is yours. Let me repay you in fine style. I'll tell you how—I have friends down on the Tilsen River and they have a boat. If we leave here now, tonight, we can pay a ferryman to take us to them. Have you ever been to Gila? It is a wonderful place, my homeland—wine, women, and song from dawn to dusk and no priests or fanatics to spoil the fun. I can't think why I ever left." He paused, considering his words, then grinned. "Well, for what reason does anyone ever come to the Eternal City, eh, my friend? Money! there is always money to be made in the Eternal City, especially in my trade—or there was before they started persecuting magic makers and gearing up for this mad war. Come with me to Gila and live like a prince and you'll soon forget about this whole sorry business."

"I can't do that. I must rescue Saro. Where is the Miseria?"

Plutario shook his head sadly. "You're mad. No one goes into the Miseria except as a guard or a prisoner, and of the latter none get out alive unless they're on the way to their own execution."

Virelai looked desperate.

"Well, my friend, I must be on my way," Plutario said at last. "I'll be glad to leave this place. The Eternal City has been nothing but a nightmare for me ever since that jackass Barzaco told the Lord of Cantara I could do magic for him."

"What sort of magic?"

"Oh, he wanted me to make his ships invisible or something, so he could sneak into Halbo and rescue the Rosa Eldi woman. Something nonsensical, and would he listen to me when I said it was all just tricks, that sort of thing? He would not. My idea of making people invisible involves curtains and trapdoors and a lot of blue smoke. He's a crazy man, that one. Believes in the whole shebang."

Virelai grabbed him by the shoulders. "I have an idea. And yes, your life is forfeit to me, and I have an idea of how you may redeem the debt . . ."

The Miseria

"I LIKE this not at all."

"It was never a matter of liking."

"If they catch us, we are dead men."

"Not an hour ago you were prepared to take your own life, so you are already in profit by an hour."

"An hour does not profit me much."

"There is much that can be done in an hour. The future course of the world may change in less."

"I'm just a trickster, a charlatan, a mountebank—what care I for the future course of the world?"

In the gloom of the corridor, Virelai turned his pale eyes on Plutario Falco and looked him up and down. The uniform was as detailed as he could remember it—a blue tunic and breeches worked with silver braid, tall black boots, a gleaming silver helm. There were no fat men in the Jetran Guard, and so the conjurer was a shadow of his former self, a shadow which glowed slightly around the edges, which might seem to the casual eye no more than a trick of the light, rather than the evidence of the rather poor glamour he had employed. He was reserving what little remained of his sorcery for what came next. He had been surprised his small skills had worked as well as they had, without the cat or any other aid, yet remembering how quickly the illusions he had used to make could evaporate, there was no time to spare.

"Your life is forfeit to me. You said it yourself. I shall release you from your debt as soon as we have the Vingo boy safe."

Plutario shook his head wearily. "I do not know why I allowed you to talk me into this. Surely you have mazed my mind as well as my body."

Down they went into increasing darkness, their footsteps ringing on the stone. It seemed remarkable that no one came out to see who made such a racket, but what was left of the soldiery of Jetra had clearly been assigned to other duties, or, knowing the entrances to the Miseria so well secured, did not bother to guard them as well as they might, especially now that chaos reigned in the Eternal City. The stench became stronger the farther down they went, until Plutario held his hand over his nose and mouth. It was not the honest smell of human sweat and waste—or rather, it was not simply that—but a more disturbing aroma altogether. The scent of cooked meat mingled with an iron tang, until the air itself felt thick and fatty, as if it might leave a residue on your face and hands, might slick the nostrils as you inhaled, and coat the lungs with an impermeable grease. Even breathing it made Virelai feel complicit in whatever vile acts had been perpetrated here.

"Faugh!" exclaimed the conjurer at last. "I thought they confined their burnings to the Grand Campo and the Merchants's Square."

Virelai felt the disgust rise in him, as acrid as bile.

"Come on," he said shortly, quickening his pace.

The sound of voices brought them to a halt on the next level down, then laughter and the chink of glassware. Sweetsmoke and incense drifted along the corridor outside the guardroom, hazing the air. Virelai pressed his companion back against the wall and studied the men inside intently. A moment later he removed Plutario's helm and, muttering softly, rubbed his palm across the other man's face. Then he stood back, examined his handiwork, and added a scar to the conjurer's left cheek. A belligerent man stared back at him, bold and bloodshot of eye, with a jutting jaw and a vein-reddened nose.

He had never tried to transform himself. Without a mirror it would be difficult, since he was used to viewing the changes he essayed as he made them and adjusting those features that did not match the template.

The houris he had worked on for Tycho's pleasure, with their wide hips and dark skin and hair had been of a different species to the Rosa Eldi, and effecting a transformation which would last for an hour or more had been challenging. With luck, he would need to hold these disguises for a short time only. With a sigh he closed his eyes and concentrated on the man facing the door, dealing out the cards. Then with the guard's face focused clearly in his mind's eye, he touched his own features. The prickle of the sorcery took him aback. It was less painful than unsettling, as if the skin were crawling over his bones, unanchored from muscle, cartilage, and ligament. The buzzing that accompanied it sounded like a wasp nest in his skull; the vibrations traveled through his skeleton and earthed themselves in the flagstones beneath his feet. When he touched his face again, he knew it was not his own. The chin was shorter and more compact, the jaw broader, his vision more widely spaced.

Beckoning his companion, he laid a swift spell of concentration on the men inside the guardroom so that they studied their cards intently for a few seconds as they passed the door. Then the murmur of their voices rose again.

Plutario, who had little idea of what had just transpired, tapped Virelai on the shoulder as soon as they were out of earshot. "Now what?" he asked plaintively. His face ached and prickled; he felt uncomfortable in his own skin, but even so, he wanted to save it and be out of here as quickly as possible.

"We go down to the cells."

"And then what?"

Virelai turned and watched with satisfaction as Plutario almost fell down in shock.

"By Falla, what you done to yourself?"

Virelai gave him an uncharacteristically wolfish grin, revealing three silver-capped teeth, a detail he was particularly proud to have captured. "You may also ask, what have I done to you?" he jibed. "But do not get too attached to your new handsome appearance, for I fear it will not last, and, because of that, we cannot delay."

They took the remaining stairs down into the Miseria at a run, then halted as two guards came into view.

"You took your sweet time relieving us, Manso!" the first one growled. "I'm off duty till noon tomorrow and every damned minute out of this place is precious to me."

Virelai shrugged. "Keys?" was all he said by way of response, as low and guttural a sound as he could make it.

"Still nursing your sore head, are you?" He turned to the other guard. "Bet us he could drink a flagon of Circesian Amber in the time it took Bosco to take a piss. And he did it, all right. Hellish stuff, that. Serves you right!" he thumped Virelai on the shoulder and handed over a huge bunch of rusted keys. "Here you go. Not that you'll need them. These bastards aren't going anywhere till tomorrow's burning."

They picked up the cloaks which were hanging over their chairbacks.

"You two're goin' to be chilly!" said the other guard, noting their lack of outerwear. "It's as cold as Falla's tits down here."

Virelai cursed himself silently: the men in the guardroom had a fire to keep them warm and had discarded their cloaks; he hadn't thought to include them in the illusion. "Bosco was sick on them," he said quickly.

"Filthy fucker!" said the first man delightedly. "Here, take ours. Where I'm going, I don't need a cloak; nor any other togs either."

"I do!" the other guard protested. "It's bloody nippy on dawn watch."

His companion cuffed him round the head. "Come on, Lady Lavender, let's get your poor delicate bones up to the fireside, let these two buggers get on with it."

Virelai watched them till they disappeared into the gloom, then waited until the clump of their boots echoed away to nothing. Then he went from cell to cell, keys in hand.

The sights he saw made his heart pound in his chest. In the first cell, two women lay in a heap against the wall like broken dolls, their limbs dislocated, their finger ends dark with dried blood. One of them had no eyes; the other a blackened hole where her lips and tongue had once been. Neither of them made a sound. They might be dead. He hoped they were. In the next two cells a number of naked men were chained to the walls. Some were stuck through with metal spikes, the skin so reddened and puckered where the cruel shafts penetrated the flesh that it was clear they had been driven in and left like that for days, maybe even weeks, a trial of the prisoners' will to live, a test of their mortality. One

man had succumbed to death. Flies buzzed around his head, landed in
the pits of his eyes. The stench of him followed the pair as they walked
the corridor. Now Virelai learned to glimpse quickly and move on. Behind him, Plutario heaved his guts up so that the sharp smell of vomit
joined with all the other aromas of human misery.

In the last cell of all, he found a corpse which had rotted down to the
bone, and a ragged, bloodstained figure.

"Saro!"

The head came up slowly.

"What do you want?"

"It's me, Virelai."

"Manso, I know you love to taunt me, but I have little wit left to field
your jibes tonight."

Impatiently, Virelai shook his head. "No, it isn't Manso, I just wear
his appearance, for a little while. We have to get you out of here. Can you
walk?"

The figure laughed like a rusty gate. Then with a hand made clublike
by swaddling bandages it pushed aside the filthy, tattered cloth which
covered it.

"Oh, my heaven . . ."

Behind him, Plutario fell to his knees, retching.

"My brother likes to take a little piece of me every day. He believes
each part of me he takes makes him stronger."

Virelai clutched the bars of the cell. He rested his forehead against
the cold iron, felt hot tears threatening, and blinked hard. The crystal
had shown him many horrors, but it had not shown him this. He wiped
his hand across his eyes and tried to pay attention to the keys, sorting
through them one by one.

"You won't find it there," Saro said. "Tanto keeps it with him at all
times. No one else is allowed to enter this cell. He comes every day, twice
a day—I thought it was him when I heard voices." He coughed into the
bandages, a racking sound which made him double up. When he recovered, he smiled wanly, head on one side. "Is it really you, Virelai? I was
sure you were dead on the battlefield. I saw you fall. Or am I going mad
down here? I often think I am. I see all sorts of strange visions."

"It is me. I was unconscious, then Alisha . . . helped me."

"Is she still alive? Is she with you?"

Virelai shook his head. There was no way to talk about what she had done, what she was going to do. "She took the stallion and headed south."

"Night's Harbinger?" Saro sounded amazed.

"We don't have time for all this charming small talk," Plutario said crossly. "If we can't open the damned cell, we'll have to leave him and get ourselves out of here before someone finds us and invites us to board in one of these delightful chambers. We tried and failed, and it's really unfortunate and I'm very sorry for your friend, but look at the state of him! Even if you were able to get him out of here, what could he do? And since you can't get him out, there's nothing more to be done. I came with you as you asked of me, now let me go."

Virelai sighed. It was hard to deny the logic in any of what the con-juror said, hardhearted though he was. "Go, then," he said at last. "Thank you for coming with me. I hope you make it to the ferry."

"And what about this?" The conjurer gestured to his face and torso.

"It'll wear off in a little while."

"Shame. It's in better shape than my own body. Never mind. See you in Gila sometime, I hope." Then he leaned past Virelai and waved to Saro. "Sorry, my friend. I used to do a good trick with locks and keys, but my criminal past is far behind me now. Fare well." He paused. "Or something."

Then he wrapped the borrowed cloak about his shoulders and left.

Virelai stared despondently at the lock. He stared at it so long that his vision blurred. Bright streaks of light scored the inside of his eyelids. He shut his eyes tight, and the light coalesced, made a shape. When he opened them again, the shape was in front of him, clear and precise. He laughed.

The keys buzzed in his hand. He chose one and inserted it into the great lock on the cell door, said the words which brought illusion to re-ality and let the magic flow down the bones of his arm. With a clunk, the door flew open and a moment later he was at Saro's side.

"Virelai, that was extraordinary. You're a real sorcerer! But you said you had no magic . . ."

"I understand it no better than you do," Virelai said, shaking his head. "Something in me has changed, and yet at the same time something much greater than me has changed. Maybe it's that the Goddess has returned, the Rosa Eldi is in Elda once more . . . Perhaps it is her doing. I don't know, I just don't know. Illusion was all I could manage before, and that only with Bëte's help. But upstairs, I healed Plutario, mended a broken arm—"

"Can you heal me?" Saro's eyes were wide. "It's rather more than a broken arm, though." With his teeth, he unwrapped the bandage from his left hand, held what lay within out for Virelai's inspection. All the fingers and the thumb were gone, leaving blackened, tar-seared stumps. "He doesn't want me to bleed to death. That would be no fun for him at all. Though I have prayed and prayed for such a release . . ."

"I don't know," Virelai said truthfully. "I don't know whether I can bring back what is there no longer." He remembered the tooth lying on the floor of the chamber, the gap that remained in the conjurer's mouth. "I can try."

He took one of Saro's maimed hands between his own and stared at the mess that cruelty, iron, fire, and infection had left there. *After all,* he told himself, *when I healed Plutario, I thought only of his arm and head. I gave no thought to the lost tooth.* He closed his eyes and remembered his friend's hand, tan and warm, with its strong thumb, its long, square-tipped fingers, its bitten nails. He thought of that hand, grooming Night's Harbinger, holding a cookpot, clutching the death-stone. Through the blinding light of the artifact as Saro brandished it in his defense, he saw the bones of the fingers that were missing, dark shadows amidst the glow, like ghosts of themselves.

The now-familiar beehive of noise filled his skull. Instead of fearing it, this time he sought it out, welcomed it, allowed it to suffuse him. There was a color associated with the sound, a brightness not white, but a pale, clear gold. He found that if he did not resist it, it felt warm and mellow, coursing through his bones and veins like a great burst of energy. It was life, he realized with a sudden shock of understanding. Life, pure and simple, and he was channeling it into the man whose hand he held. Whose fingers closed around his . . .

He opened his eyes. Between his palms lay Saro's new hand, perfect in every detail. He looked down. Saro had feet again, pale, bony feet with toes and ankles and small tufts of hair on the knuckle joints, instead of swollen, burned, pus-filled stumps. As if to test the extent of the wonder, Saro wriggled his toes. Together they watched this small motion word-lessly, as parents might marvel over the movements of their new child.

"This is more than mere sorcery, Virelai. By the Lady, it's a miracle—"

They were both so enraptured that neither of them heard the ap-proach of feet, the grate of the cell door . . .

"You!"

A rough hand caught the pale man by the shoulder and wrenched him backward so that he fell at the speaker's feet.

It was Tanto Vingo, standing upright and with no wheeled chair in sight, his face puce with fury. Without further preamble, he kicked the sorcerer hard under the ribs so that the air rushed out of his lungs. "What in Falla's name are you doing in this cell? Don't I pay you well enough to keep out of here?" He kicked him again, so that Virelai grunted with pain. "Well, don't you listen to my orders, you sniveling bastard? Which one are you?" He hauled on the uniform tunic, turning him face up. "Ah, Manso. You don't look well, Manso, I must say. A little pale around the gills. Worried I may lock you up in here with my beloved brother and throw away the key?" He leered at the fallen man, then frowned. "But I have the key. How did you open this door? Is there a du-plicate no one told me about? By Falla, I'll have Bandino's head for this if there is—"

"It was not Manso's fault," Saro said swiftly. "I picked the lock."

"I'd like to have seen that! Ha—we could display you in the market square and charge good money for such a trick. See the fingerless crip-ple pick a lock with his teeth. Though you won't have those for much longer—"

So saying, Tanto threw Virelai hard against the ground and turned to regard his brother. Saro watched in satisfaction as the vicious sneer be-came an open-mouthed gawp, as Tanto's balled hands fell loosely to his sides.

Tanto blinked once, twice, again. "How—?"

Saro stood up. Beneath his bare feet the stone of the cell felt warm and the faintest vibration ran through it up into his legs and torso. He felt wonderful. He felt stronger and more alive than he had ever felt in his entire life. He laughed and watched as Tanto quailed away from him. "Surprised, brother? Thought you'd whittle me away bit by bit until there was nothing left but a bloody, beating heart?" He waved his new hands in front of Tanto's horrified face. "Be sure your crimes will find you out. It seems the Goddess did not wish for me to be reduced in such a way." Sidestepping his brother, he took Virelai by the arm with a powerful grip and levered him upright. "Now my friend and I are going to leave this place and you are going to sit quietly in this cell and ponder your fate. Give me the key, Tanto, and I will not harm you. The guards will release you later, unless of course—" he grinned, "—the key mysteriously disappears with us."

"No! You cannot leave me in this foul, rat-infested place. With that—" Tanto gave the skeleton of the whore he had left to die in Saro's cell such a violent kick that bits of rib cage and pelvis shot across the floor, skittering to a halt where the iron bars stopped their pellmell progress. Then he started to wail. The outraged, incoherent, unstoppable bellow of a tantrum-gripped toddler boiled into the close air of the tiny chamber.

Taking careful aim, Saro punched his brother hard on the jaw. The blow fell with cracking, satisfying precision, and as his fist connected, Saro was graced with a memory of such perfect clarity it was as if he were transported from this place of torture to a glorious sunny day beside Katla Aransen's knife stall at the Allfair the previous summer, a day before the entire world had run mad. He could see Katla's surprised face, her hawk's-wing eyebrows arching, her sea-gray eyes alight with startled amusement. In just such a way had he hammered his brother down to stop him calling the guards, but then it had been to save Katla's skin rather than his own. He had been thinking about the Eyran girl a lot in the grim darkness of the cells, as if her feisty spirit and that corona of fiery hair were a beacon in his soul's night. Somewhere out there, beyond the tiny, stinking cell which his whole world had shrunk to she was still alive: it was a thought which kept him alive even when he prayed to die.

Tanto crumpled to a heap on the filth-laden flagstones. His jeweled collar sprang apart at the impact, showering the floor with gemstones which glittered in the muck. He lay there with only his chest moving beneath the vast tent of his belly-stuffed robe.

"Give me a piece of rag so I may bind his mouth," Saro said. "I don't know how long he'll be unconscious, or how long it will take us to find the lakeside passage that leads out of here."

Virelai obliged cheerfully. It was remarkable to see his friend restored to such health and vigor that he was able to pick himself up on feet he had just reacquired and with a new fist lay his brother out cold. It might not exactly be the way of peace the nomads spoke of, but it gave him faith in the future. It gave him faith in himself. *The magic is in me,* he thought over and over as he tore a strip from the filthiest part of the bandage that had swathed Saro's mutilated hand. *I have become a sorcerer who can heal the sick and wounded. What more may I do with such a miraculous power?*

"Virelai?"

"Sorry, I was thinking." He gave the cloth over to Saro and watched as he bound it tightly around his brother's bloated face.

"Hope he chokes on it," Saro said uncharacteristically.

"We could . . . kill him," Virelai offered suddenly. "It would be the best thing for the world."

"I cannot," Saro said simply. "I know I should, but he is still my brother."

"He is no brother to me." Even as he said this, Virelai wondered if he could kill a man, even this loathsome creature. It would certainly be an easier job while his victim was unconscious, but he could not quite imagine how he might rid Tanto Vingo of his life, could not fully picture his hands around that fat, slick neck, squeezing and squeezing.

"No," Saro said, and in his voice there was a lifetime of despair. "I could never ask you, of all people, to do this. Whatever magic you have in you, Virelai, it is a positive force, life-generating, not life-destroying. Do not sully your gift with Tanto's death. Let us instead escape this terrible place and find Alisha, wherever she may be. I owe her Falo's life, and those of her friends. It is because of me that they died, and I must repay that debt. Somehow."

Virelai looked away. There was a lump in his throat that made it impossible to speak. He knew he could not go south, but he could think of nothing to say. So he watched mutely as Saro brought the iron door clanging shut and locked it with the key Tanto had carried.

"Is there nothing we can do for the poor creatures in the other cells?" Saro asked, pocketing the key.

Virelai shook his head, suddenly weary. "Only release them from their torments forever."

Saro looked agonized. "It would be kindest, I know, but even that would not be right. Can you open their doors and remove their chains, so they may at least die free?"

It was a small thing, but it would take the last of Virelai's strength. Most of the prisoners were in no condition to benefit from the gesture, but he did what Saro asked. Some shuffled to the open doors and stared at the two men outside—a young man in shining health but filthy rags and an odd-looking Jetran guard whose face seemed to shimmer and shift if they looked too long. Most remained cowering in their cells, nursing limbs long-numb from the manacles which had confined them, glowering distrustfully at these newcomers, for who knew what fiendish new trick the Tormentor had in store for them with this odd turn of events?

Along dark, slimy tunnels they made their way, down and ever down. Once they took a wrong turn and were suddenly overwhelmed by a sweet-sour stench. Virelai steadied himself against the wall, then pulled his hand back in dismay to find it covered in a thick, black grease which clung obstinately to his fingers. It was hard to rub off, even on the rough serge of the uniform tunic, where it left vile, sticky streaks.

"By heaven, what is this foul stuff?" he said into the air, not even expecting a response.

Saro turned, his eyes gleaming in the chancy light. "Do not ask," he said grimly. "You would not like the answer."

They rounded the next corner and came suddenly on a high-vaulted chamber and a dead end where the ground dropped sharply away into some great, wide well. Narrow stairs led down to some kind of observation platform. Driven by some compulsive curiosity he could not explain, Saro walked down onto it and stared over the edge. As his eyes adjusted to the gloom, he made out the remains of some huge metal contraption which appeared to have burned through at a crucial point and collapsed inward upon itself so that it looked like some vast dead spider. Below this, lay a mound of ashes, and shards of bones piled up in heaps. Scattered teeth gleamed in the char like pearls.

Saro, horrified, let out a moan. He had seen this place before. His brother had enjoyed imparting the knowledge of it to him. With his maimed hands and feet, he had been able to do nothing to ward off Tanto's touch through which the vision had invaded him. It was the pit in which Tanto—the Tormentor—had earned his name, carrying out one obscene experiment after another into the burning capacity of his inventions. Hundreds, maybe even thousands, of nomads and other innocents had died here, consumed in agony by flames, showered by droplets of molten metal.

Saro firmed his jaw.

"I was wrong," he said suddenly. He turned and caught Virelai by the arm, shook him to emphasize every word. "I'm sorry. I was wrong, terribly wrong. We must stop this horror."

Virelai opened his mouth to protest. He was tired, so tired. But Saro, buoyed up by his newborn strength and vitality, was already vanishing so far into the gloom so that he had to run to catch him up.

By the time they returned to the cells, there was mayhem. Some of the prisoners who could walk were milling aimlessly about; others were lying at full length on the ground with their arms stretched through the bars of Tanto's cell, trying to grab up whatever gems they could reach. Some were trying to carry the broken women up the stairs.

"Quickly—"

"Stay there," Saro said, his voice trembling. "Just stay there and don't watch me."

Stepping over the jewel thieves, Saro unlocked the iron door, pushed through it and went to kneel at his brother's side. "Goddess forgive me," Saro prayed. He had never truly believed in her presence till today; she had given him life, and now here he was about to take another's. There was, perhaps, a strange symmetry to the deed; but the thought did not comfort him much. Then, before he could change his mind, he clamped his hands over Tanto's nose and mouth and pressed down hard.

At once, images began to flood through him; images of horror and debauchery, of petty cruelties and great sins, until his skull was filled to overflowing with them and he had to scream and scream to let them out into the world whence his brother had enacted them. The body beneath him now became rigid, then thrashed as wildly as an unbroken horse.

Tanto's eyes flew open. Bright and black with malice and fury, they fixed on his younger sibling—the pathetic weakling brother he had always despised. Anger turned soon to terror as it became clear that Saro would not relent. Terrible groaning sounds began to come from the Tormentor, emerging urgent but muffled by the bandages and his brother's determined grasp. Saro shut his eyes, kept them clamped hard shut, and held on grimly, warding off the sights Tanto offered him—the rapes, the wickednesses, the murders, the tortures, the burnings and rackings and amputations; all the wanton hurts he had inflicted on cats and dogs and horses and men and women and slaves and so many others who had done him no wrong.

Even in this invalid, bloated state, Tanto was remarkably strong. His struggles seemed to last for an eternity. In the long, long time it took for his brother's life to ebb away, Saro felt something break deep within him, and knew the act was changing him forever. Even in death, it seemed, Tanto had achieved another victory.

"Enough!"

The voice was harsh with fury. Saro fell sobbing upon his brother's still form, exhausted in both flesh and soul. Disconnected words babbled from his lips, a cacophony of nonsense. Then rough hands grabbed his shoulders, dragged him away from the corpse, and set him on his feet, while others pinioned his arms behind his back and secured his wrists with thick rope.

"By the Goddess, what have you done?" Tycho Issian, the Lord of Cantara, strode past his guards into the gloomy cell and looked down at the figure on the floor, its eyes gazing glassily into the darkness. He made a superstitious sign and prodded the corpse with his foot, then prodded harder when the first attempt elicited no response. Waves of blubber shuddered down the length of Tanto's trunk, but the eyes maintained their bloodshot, congealing stare in a face gone purple with blood and panic.

"This sneaking mountebank warned us as much—" Tycho hefted into view the still-bleeding head of poor Plutario, his eyes rolled upward, his visage his own once more, "—when we chanced upon him trying to escape our mercy. We could hardly believe what he told us, yet now we see it for ourselves. To kill your own brother is a most heinous crime—"

But Saro was not even looking at the man who berated him so, or at the bloody prize he carried. The babbling had trickled to a whispering halt and his shocked gaze was fixed on something else entirely.

Bemused that neither his outrage, nor the shocking trophy, was holding the young murderer's attention, Tycho turned to ascertain the source of Saro's fascination.

Out in the passage between the cells a most incongruous sight met his bewildered eyes. There, between two of his trusted militia stood the man they had just taken prisoner—the guard who had so treacherously allowed this foul deed to take place—with his uniform half-ripped from him and his features, lit by the torch one of the soldiers carried, in an apparent state of flux. Even as he stared, he saw how it wavered between one paler, more aquiline form and the swarthy visage disturbingly similar to that of the man who held a dagger at his throat. It was almost as if one face floated beneath the second, first one gaining precedence, then the other.

The glamour was beginning to fail. Virelai would have known as much from the despairing look in Saro's eyes, even if it were not for the queasy sensation he was experiencing, or the fact that if he stared down the length of his nose he could see a shimmering blur which came momentarily into focus white and fine, then switched back to a nose which was dark and fleshy, complete with hair-sprouting mole.

The men, who had not till now looked closely at their prisoner, having taken him swiftly in the heat of action, now began to make warding signs and back away in fear.

"Manso . . ." a sergeant breathed, staring between the two. "Which of you is Manso?"

"I am, you twat!" the second man shouted. "What in Falla's fires are you talking about, Gesto? You just took fifteen sodding cantari off me ten minutes ago upstairs!"

Virelai hung his head, too tired and miserable to contest what was soon to be a hopelessly lost battle. His sorcery was failing him, he had failed his friend, and now they would both die horribly.

The next thing he knew, his head was being forced roughly upward. Tycho Issian's mad eyes stared and stared. Virelai quailed away, but the southern lord was intent and held him still, grasping his chin in a viselike hand. Where before there had been fury and disgust in the man's face, now there was a strange avidity, a desperate greed which seemed to consume him from within. His eyes burned with it as with a terrible lust.

"Virelai . . ." he breathed. Then: "Virelai?" he asked sharply.

"Yes," said Virelai mournfully. "It is indeed Virelai."

Tycho Issian grinned—an awful, manic expression which made his mouth stretch so wide that the sorcerer thought for one benighted moment the lord would savage him with those wicked white teeth that gleamed at him now in the gloom.

"Virelai . . ." This time the name was almost a caress, Tycho spoke it so softly. "Your sorcery has improved immeasurably since last I saw you. And without that damned cat, as well. Those Forent Castle girls . . . ah . . ." He sighed. "Whatever spell of seeming you used on them may have changed their appearances considerably, but they never looked at all like the one they were designed to. Yet just now I saw you with my own eyes and believed you to be Manso, to the bone—until the illusion wore off."

For the face he looked upon was no longer that of the lumpen guard's captain but unmistakably that of the pale man, the one who had once tried to sell him the Rosa Eldi, the one who had lost her and bungled all attempts to regain her before the northern king had snatched her away; the one who had given tin the appearance of silver for weeks on end— enough that he had been able to trade a fortune out of it—but had never yet managed to make one human being look exactly like another. He took in those fine, pale features, the almost colorless eyes with their flat black pupils, dilated now so the iris showed as no more than a thin corona, the sharply boned nose, the angular planes of the cheeks and jaw, the finely delineated lips and the long, pale, braided hair and he laughed, a huge, echoing sound in the small space of the dungeons. It was a disconcerting sound to hear in the Miseria. The mad, the maimed, and the half-dead in cells up and down the corridors that bled away from the central chambers woke from whatever pain-filled reverie they had drifted into and (where they had the arms to do so) hugged themselves anxiously, wondering what would follow such a bizarre and inappropriate noise.

"Ah, Virelai!" the Lord of Cantara exclaimed, drawing the sorcerer into a deep and unwelcome embrace, "What wonders shall we achieve together now?"

Repulsed by this unwanted intimacy, Virelai drew back. "I c–cannot work magic for you, lord!" he stuttered.

"Cannot, or will not?" The tone was menacing.

Virelai's whole body quivered with fear. He could not quite believe he had said what he had said; surely, he had not meant to say it at all, would take it back in a heartbeat . . .

Again the southern lord laughed, but this time the sound was sepulchral. "Bring the lad here," he called back over his shoulder.

Two of the guards dragged a resistant Saro out of the cell. As he passed, Saro's gaze swept across Virelai's face. The look in his eyes was pleading, intense. Minutely, he shook his head, but whether it was an involuntary jerk or a meaningful signal was impossible to tell.

"Take this idiot boy away, strip him, and nail him to the crossframe in the Campo," Tycho ordered. "He shall witness the performance of his brother's last invention. I believe we have two hundred Footloose and heretics who will fuel a good blaze. That would surely be the most fitting tribute to Tanto's genius." He paused, then added with silky ease, "And make sure you sew his eyelids wide open so he does not miss any detail of their punishment. It will be good for his soul, to see so many who sully Falla's name chastised by her cleansing fires, so that he may travel to the Goddess in a state of grace when I despatch him to the Lady myself."

"No!" Virelai was agonized. Here, in prospect, was the vision the crystal had shown him, the insight into evil which had prompted him to make this fateful journey to try to save his friend. He fell to his knees and grasped Tycho's rich velvet robe in both hands. "Do not do this, my lord!" he cried. "I have seen a vision of this terrible scene, and it brings no honor to your lordship's name!"

"How touching, Virelai," the southern lord declared with a grim smile. "But it will not avail you to concern yourself with his fate, or with my good name, for as soon as the Vingo boy is dead, I am going to strip the hide from you, strip by tiny strip until you relent or die."

Virelai had never been a brave man. Even when the sensations of his body had been diminished, he had still feared the concept of pain. With horrible clarity he remembered the flight he and Tycho Issian had made from the burning tent at the Allfair, how Tycho had laid about him indiscriminately with his sharp little knife, stabbing and cutting his way to freedom. He remembered the beatings and the humiliations he had suffered at the other's hands. He knew he would carry out to the letter exactly what he threatened, and enjoy every second of it. Now, following the awakening of his being, the reinvigoration of his flesh, by whatever Alisha had done to him with the death-stone, he knew that his experience of pain would be even more excruciating that anything he had previously endured. He knew, too, that Tycho Issian was a cruel and vengeful man, that to assist him in his endeavors was to ally himself to evil. But how could he let his friend die, and in such vile circumstances? He bowed his head, torn apart by this terrible dilemma, remembering Alisha Skylark's words to him in the desert south of this city: *You have a great choice to make, Virelai, and upon it will rest all there is that is worth saving in the world . . .* But how could he know which choice to make? He knew so little, and all he did turned out badly.

Rosa of the World, Falla, hear me, he prayed silently. *Forgive me the many sins I have committed against you, and help me to do the right thing now.*

Then he raised his head and fixed his eyes unwavering on Tycho's black gaze. "Saro has already endured too much," he said softly. "And if he is harmed in any way, I will die before I work the smallest act of magic for you, lord." Even as the words trembled from his lips, he felt a great peace descending on him, a deep calm like a blessing. Surely, he had made the right choice. But as swiftly as the calm had entered him, his certitude ebbed away, leaving him feeling emptied out and despairing.

The Lord of Cantara's eyebrows twitched, then shot skyward. He was not often surprised by the way men behaved, for he always expected the worst of them, and was thus rarely disappointed. He shrugged and beckoned to the guards. "Take the Vingo boy to the finest suite of rooms in the castle and make him comfortable there," he declared, and watched as they tried unsuccessfully to mask their surprise. "Tell the steward he is to be accorded every honor and hospitality, and to fetch him a chirurgeon without delay, but he is not to leave the rooms except under guard.

No one is to do him the least harm; and if any man among you speaks a word of what has occurred here, I will have his tongue, his eyes, and his bollocks removed, roasted, and fed to his children. Are you clear about that?" The men all nodded swiftly. "And take that . . . abomination . . ." he gestured to the bloated corpse of Tanto Vingo, "—down to the burning pit and do away with it with pitch and flame. If any ask you where he may be, tell them I have sent him to be with his uncle." He smiled thinly. Then he turned to Virelai. "We have a bargain. Mind you do not renege on it, for I hold your comrade in trust, and I think you know what I am capable of if you displease me in any way."

Virelai nodded mutely, and knew himself a damned man.

Dreams

THE seithers, who are the oldest folk on Elda, maintain that the
Three—the Man, the Woman, and the Beast—speak often to the people of
the world in their dreams; only then do they have time to pay attention
to what they are being told—without the distraction of illness and child-
care, husbandry and household management, lawsuits, social engage-
ments, penury, and feuding to come between their conscious minds and
matters of greater importance. Those whose dwellings have foundations
on crystal-bearing rock are known to have the strongest dreams, for the
deities of Elda have always channeled their energies in this way, but even
those on the sea may be touched by the gods, for water is a good con-
ductor of dreams. However, there are those in the world who, through
obsession or obstinacy, close themselves to the messages they are sent
and, waking from a restless sleep, willfully continue to pursue the path
they have chosen, even though it may mean their death, or worse. . . .

IN a strange ship propelled by unseen spirits and guided by an ancient
man whose beard streams behind him in what is no natural wind, Aran
Aranson dreams of his home in Rockfall, of his wife—young as she had
been when first he wooed her—running down the strand to meet him

at the harbor with her red hair loose to her waist and her keen eyes searching the standing crew of the approaching ship, and in his sleep he smiles. . . .

URSE One Ear lies curled into a ball in the lee of a great tree and shivers, for night has fallen swiftly in the southern continent and the air is chill. But he carries some protection from the one who set him this task and so he will not die as others might in this inimical place from lack of shelter, food, or water. He has tracked a great animal by day and by night since being transported to this place; now as he dreams, he sees its huge spoor stretching away into infinity, five-toed footprints in earth, in rock, in air. It is all he thinks about awake, all he dreams of when he sleeps. There is nothing else left to him, or so it seems. . . .

FENT Aranson—or whatever he has become since the Master of Sanctuary had his sorcerous way with him—does not sleep, at least in no fashion a man might recognize as natural. Instead, eyes unblinking, he walks and climbs and slithers down scree slopes; walks and climbs and carries on his journey down through the Skarn Mountains and into the Golden Range, heading south, ever south, brooking no obstacle and taking no rest. But all the while there are thoughts running through his head, bright flashes and scraps of life which may be memories or visions or even dreams, and he sees little of the terrain he covers, mile upon mile upon mile. . . .

IN the slave chambers in Forent Castle, Bera Rolfsen turns restlessly in her sleep and dreams of her husband. In her dream they are standing hand in hand watching the ice-breaking ship burning on the shore of Whale Strand. Her eldest son waves to her beyond the flames; they both wave back. Then he walks through the fire to their side and the three of them walk together back up the well-trodden path to the hall at Rock-fall, a hall as pristine as the day it was built. Gramma Rolfsen sits rocking in her chair in the sun with the twins, identical at three, tumbling at her feet in the dirt. . . .

IN a more lavishly appointed chamber three floors above, Kitten Soron-sen runs a hand down her smooth flank and dreams the touch is that of a handsome foreign lord, but in the next room Katla Aransen's dreams are of violence and escape. She is running, running, running, down endless dark corridors in which all the doors are locked. She knows, for she has tried them all. Behind her, she hears pounding footsteps of soldiers and knows that if they catch her they will rape her, each and every one. She has no weapon, or she would turn and fight them, to the death. Rounding a corner, the breath sharp in her chest, she sees a distant light and a figure silhouetted within it; a tall figure bearing a flaming sword. The light makes a fire of this warrior's hair and she knows, suddenly and painfully and with the perfect logic of the dreamer, who the figure is and what he represents. Without faltering, she runs to him. The flaming sword takes her through the heart, as she had known it would, with a bright, rupturing heat. The fall into oblivion is the most blissful sensation she has ever experienced. . . .

ON board the mercenary ship Erno Hamson embraces the bundle in which the greatsword is wrapped and dreams he holds Katla Aransen in his arms. She is thinner than he remembers, and harder muscled, too, and when she turns to smile at him, he sees his death shining in her eyes. . . .

IN his suite of rooms in the heart of the Eternal City, Saro Vingo twists and roars, his hands locked forever around his brother's throat. Those wide black eyes gaze up at him unblinkingly, as trusting as a dog's. "Beloved brother," the corpse whispers, "how can you do this to me?" Despair erases all the reasons he thought he had; and suddenly he finds it is his own face staring back up at him, accusing and quite dead. . . .

VIRELAI, in his former life, had never been accustomed to dreaming. When he slept, it was without disturbance or delight. But now he shivers in his sleep. Looking down from far above, he sees himself, a tiny white worm of a thing, a dark shadow falling over him, about to be devoured. . . .

TYCHO Issian, on the other hand, burning with desire in his silk sheets, dreams the same dream of rapture over and again, a pair of long pale legs scissoring open to admit him into the heart of a rose. . . .

IN far Eyra, the Rosa Eldi (who never truly sleeps, but lies as still as she may in the great royal bed so as not to disturb her beloved husband) listens with her preternatural hearing to the small sounds of Halbo Town—the soft breathing of its inhabitants, the whimper of its dogs, the footfalls of its cats, the crackle of hearth fires burning down to the embers, the scratch and rustle of rat and pigeon in a thousand rafters; the coupling of sailors and whores in the alleys by the docks, the wind through the lines on the ships of Eyra's fleet, anchored safely in the harbor, the susurrus of the sea; and, far below the wind-ruffled surface, the relentless stirrings of the Nemesis. She lies there, cocooned by these local sounds and recalls the distant voices which have touched her consciousness that day, the voices beyond the sharp, snide conversations in the Great Hall, the rumble of the men in the war room, planning and counting, talking up a storm. She brings to mind the prayers that have been offered up to the god Sur during that long day—sometimes aloud, sometimes whispered secretly, or not uttered at all—from shepherds at watch on bare island hillsides, fishermen caught in a blow in the midst of the Northern Ocean, from men about to draw steel upon each other in the pursuit of an honor feud, now replayed in dream. Little do any of these folk realize they have had an audience for their prayers—which they consider more as superstitious gestures to ward off evil or to attract good luck than as a dialogue with a deity they believe long-vanished from the world—nor who that listener is.

Stranger still, then, to eavesdrop upon the prayers that have drifted up to this enemy capital from the far southern continent, prayers made to a goddess she does not yet recognize herself to be, though one in particular has resounded ever since, repeating itself over and over like a mantra, a mournful plea from a lost soul, a voice which made her bones shiver and her neck prickle. For that voice had named her both as Rose of the World—a name which she knows to belong to her—and Falla; which until that moment, she did not know as her own. Taken by surprise by the personal impact that voice had made on her, she had answered that lone prayer—moreover, and without meaning to, had answered it aloud, her voice echoing out in her chambers so that those present stared and touched their foreheads knowingly. *Save him!* she had cried; *save him, even though to do so may be to destroy all I hold dear. . . .*

Even now she does not know why she answered so.

Now she lies, twined in a miasma of other people's hopes and dreams and feels her own identity coming back to her, slowly, vaguely, a dark, dawning shape, just out of reach as through a fog. . . .

18

Treason

HE had stretched the map with some difficulty across his favorite Gilan oak desk and held it down at each rough corner with a weighty silver goblet. Absentmindedly, Rui Finco now filled one of these with wine from the flask he cradled, picked it up, and drained it off. At once, the unruly map coiled up like a live thing, curling in on itself with a snapping sound as if to protect its secrets. He swore as he flattened it out again. It was not an Istrian map—that much was obvious from the crude lettering and scratched-out errors—for any southern scribe worth his salt would have looked with shame on such an abominable piece of work and consigned it to the fires. Moreover, it had been fashioned out of some strange material which looked and he suspected, if he were to get close enough to discern it, smelled, of badly-cured goatskin. A few stray hairs on the back of the thing attested to its barbaric provenance. Prodding it back into position with distaste etched in every line of his aristocratic face, the Lord of Forent perused it again.

Still it refused to yield up anything he did not already know, and rather less in some areas than he did. The southern continent, for example, was quite the wrong shape, extending far beyond the Dragon's Backbone where any fool knew the world ended. To add insult to injury, Forent had been misspelled as Firent, Cera marked with a cross but no name, and Jetra titled Ieldra in the old form, as if the mapmaker refused to admit Istrian sovereignty over the old country. Yet it was not the Istrian section of the map which interested him but the upper quartile, where the Northern Isles had been delineated in finer detail than one would have expected from such an inept hand. There lay the Westman Isles, complete with their fantastically fractured coastlines, their jagged headlands and reefs; farther east were the smaller islands of Sundey and Far Sey, then—across a wide expanse of ocean marked with spouting whales, shoaling areas, and seal breeding grounds, came the mainland of Eyra. This had been minutely detailed in calligraphy so small and untidy as to be practically illegible. Rui sighed and squinted and reapplied himself to the area around the northern capital, searching for a weakness.

Out in the seas beyond the city the Deeps, the Flow, the Troll's Teeth, and the Suckingstone told one story. Inland, Longmarsh, Middlemarsh, and Nethermarsh, Precipice Heights, Killing Tor, Black Ridge, and Snowfell told another. He glanced at a place farther up the coast enticingly called the Needle's Eye, which appeared to mark a narrow channel between what might be high cliffs. Could one land a ship, or ships, beyond such a point and march an army overground from there to take Halbo from its less well guarded northern side? But inland from the Needle's Eye he found, after much eye-watering concentration, only Black Bog, Dead Man's Marsh, and Swallowing Sands.

You had to say that for the Eyrans: they didn't waste time with classical references and metaphor when referring to their geographical features. He had no doubt that each of these features would turn out exactly as promised by their names.

After another fifteen minutes of fruitless inspection, he straightened up. His back ached. He rubbed the base of his spine and cursed the chill which had this season settled on the northern coast of Istria. Forent winters were usually mild—albeit misty and damp, which also got into the joints—but for some reason this year was the worst he could remember. And he wasn't getting any younger. There would hardly be any point in conquering the North at this rate. If an Istrian winter could afflict him so, how would he fare in Eyra?

When we take Halbo, he thought, *I'll have every damn rug, tapestry, and brazier in Forent shipped north. That might warm up that drafty stone heap of a castle. And a couple of well-built Eyran women to warm the bed, too.* How will I style myself? he mused. Lord of the Northern Isles had a good ring to it. But he preferred the sound of King Rui. The family resemblance between him and the Stallion might serve him well in that respect; though how the northerners were likely to react to discovery that their young lord (swiftly and stealthily disposed of in the heat of battle) was less than the pure-blooded Eyran prince his lineage-fixated subjects believed him to be was hard to judge. Presumably, they would feel cheated when they found out that their precious royal blood-line was so thoroughly tainted, and with the blood of the old enemy, too. But he'd always found that money spoke louder than dissenters, and he believed in paying for both loyalty and enforcement. One way or another, he'd make it work. It would be a costly affair, but once he had the Eyran fleet and its captains at his command, the seaways would be his. He would open up all the old trade routes—the Ravenway, the Whale's Path, and the Dragonsway—and the bountiful benefits thus generated would soon quell any doubts. Amber, furs, sealskins, and ivory from the islands along the Whale's Path; wine and fruit and spices and silk from the lands at the end of the Dragonsway; and from the Ravenway to the Far West—well, who knew what wonders were to be brought out of that region when that legendary route was navigated once more? Treasures of lost civilizations to be plundered at will from crumbled temples, abandoned palaces, and collapsed tombs, jewelery of solid lapis and silver, the original sardonyx statues of Falla and her cat of which all of Istria's representations of the Goddess were rumored to be mere copies, and gold—rich, pure gold. That elusive yellow metal which men spoke of in hushed voices and saw only in tiny fragments of ancient artifacts reputed to have come out of the Far West millennia ago. It was rumored there was a full-sized scepter in Halbo made entirely of the stuff, which weighed so much no man could hold it for more than a few minutes before his muscles began to shake. Fished out of the moldering wreck of a bizarrely-styled vessel off the treacherous Troll's Teeth by foolhardy divers, the scepter was believed to be Eyra's greatest treasure.

King, then, he thought again, imagining the huge golden scepter lying in his lap across his robes of state. He could almost feel the weight and heft of it . . .

A loud knock at the outer door broke this pleasant reverie.

"What is it?" he yelled.

The door opened tentatively and his personal guard, Plano, stuck his head around it. "A visitor, my lor—" he started, only to be elbowed rudely out of the way by the Lord of Ixta.

"What the hell do you want, Varyx?" Rui said sharply.

Varyx meandered over to the desk and glanced idly at the map stretched over it. "More use to the poor bloody goat than to us, that thing!" he noted cheerfully.

Rui Finco glared at him. "If you've nothing more constructive than that to offer, you'd best leave now."

"Oh, I have something far more useful, something you'll thank me for . . . in very tangible ways."

Rui looked at his old friend askance. Varyx was a fool—an entertaining one, and very rich—but a fool nonetheless. He laughed. "I've girls aplenty, the best part of Jetra's wine cellar now residing in my own, and Eyra's greatest shipmaker laboring night and day to create the finest fleet ever to set sail from Istria. What more could complete my pleasure?"

Without being invited, Varyx took a leisurely seat on one of the couches and swung his feet up onto one of the gorgeously-patterned tapestry cushions the Lord of Forent's mother had embroidered with her own hands. Irritated, Rui Finco took three strides across the room and liberated the cushion from this indignity. "So, come on, Varyx, what is so important that you feel compelled to interrupt my day?"

Varyx looked sly. "Promise me first that if you are pleased with what I bring you, you will reward me suitably."

"Suitably?"

"My pick of your Eyran girls, for a start. We can talk about the rest after we achieve our goal."

Rui Finco raised an elegant eyebrow. "Ah. You've heard about the girls, then."

"Who hasn't? Little northern fighting cats, they say."

"What else do they say?"

Varyx rolled his eyes ceilingward and thought about this. "Pale skin," he said appreciatively, "freckles, even, in the most unexpected places. Gold hair—or red—lean and well-muscled, very wild and spirited. And can't speak a word of Istrian."

"I promise you they can curse like troopers in the Old Tongue. And some of them would break you in two." He paused. "And enjoy it."

Varyx grinned. "Lovely. Can't wait."

"Whatever you have will need to be special indeed to warrant such a prize."

"Oh, it is." He rubbed his hands together, as if warming them before applying them to an expanse of the pale skin he could see in his mind's eye. "My pick, you promise?"

With a sigh, the Lord of Forent nodded. "Out with it, then."

Exhibiting considerably more energy than was his wont, the Lord of Ixta leaped to his feet and bounded to the door. "Bring in the visitor, Plano."

The door guard, sword drawn and looking thoroughly mistrustful, ushered in a hooded figure. A large black bird perched on its shoulder.

"Oh, do put the sword away, man," Varyx said testily. "If he was an assassin, he'd have spitted me by now."

Plano looked to his master. Rui Finco waved him away, though Varyx's logic irked him. What professional assassin would risk death to kill the rather stupid and ineffectual Lord of Ixta when the far more powerful and dangerous Lord of Forent was close at hand? He braced himself, hands on hips, ready to draw both concealed daggers if need be, and watched the hooded man with hooded eyes. The bird stared back at him, unblinking.

"Who are you?"

With a flourish the figure threw back his cowl and the raven danced neatly sideways, then readjusted its position. Rui Finco frowned. The newcomer was a man with a fine-boned face and dark chestnut hair. His gray eyes and pale skin made him a northerner, and this was confirmed when he spoke. "Welcome beg I, lord mine," he said in execrable Istrian.

"Use the Old Tongue, man!" Rui snapped.

The man bowed. "I thank you for your indulgence, my lord. I have come to offer you my services."

"Another one," Rui Finco groaned. "I've had them all here, seeking money and advancement—chancers, opportunists, and double-dealers. Which are you?"

"A goodly mixture of all three," the Eyran returned without missing a beat. "Allow me to introduce myself before you dismiss me out of hand. My name is Erol Bardson, Earl of Broadfell, and . . . cousin to King Ravn Asharson." He paused then winked conspiratorially in a manner which caused the Lord of Forent to wince. "Though it's possible that our relationship may be somewhat closer. The Gray Wolf spread his seed liberally, they say."

An inward tremor of dismay roiled in Rui's belly. Another one, indeed. Was the man aware of his own unsavory connection with the tainted royal line? Likely not, he decided. No change of expression marred his handsome face. Instead, he said smoothly, "A defector, then, with information to offer?"

Bardson inclined his head.

"And in exchange for this . . . information you want—what? Money? Men?" He fixed the self-proclaimed earl with a gimlet stare. "Or our support in taking the northern throne for you?"

The Earl of Broadfell looked taken aback. Then he shrugged. "Actually, the king's mother has her beady eyes set on that. However, if she were to be swept up in the horror which descends when her capital is sacked—mayhem, fire, sword, terror, panic, and flight, friend turning against friend in the heat of battle—you know the chaos that is likely to ensue in such a situation—then, although it would be a terrible tragedy to lose both figureheads of the Eyran state in a single day, it would of course be my solemn duty to step forward to take the crown, as the nearest blood relative."

At this, the raven bobbed its head mightily and let out a raucous cry. Both men frowned.

"I take your point," Rui Finco said tersely, after a moment's pause. "But the northern throne is a considerable prize. What 'service' are you offering that I can't lay hands on elsewhere?"

"I can help you to get one ship, maybe two, past the Sentinel Towers and into Halbo's inner harbor, and lead a small number of men thence by secret ways into the castle."

Now he had all of the Lord of Forent's attention. "You can? And how might that be accomplished?"

Erol Bardson laughed. "I am not such a fool as you take me for. If I were to tell you that now, I doubt I'd be needing any other quarters for the night than a hole in the ground or a sack in the sea!"

Rui Finco's lips quirked. "True enough. But why should I believe you to be who you say you are and not some scurvy trickster?"

The man bent his head for a moment and rummaged in a leather pouch hanging from his belt. "I brought you this," he said, offering a small linen-wrapped object. "The Lady Auda retrieved it. She thought you might like to take it back—"

Rui Finco peeled back the linen. Inside, just as he had expected, was a small marquetry box. With knowing fingers he triggered the secret mechanism and watched as the concealed drawer shot out. Within lay a large ring sized to fit a man and worked in the form of a wolf biting its own tail. The Gray Wolf's own ring. The last time he had seen it was in his booth at the Allfair the previous year when he had shown it to Ravn Asharson as a sign of his own secret knowledge. The Stallion had swiped it and run for his ship; to have laid hands on it, this man or his accomplice must surely had have close access to the king.

He took out the piece and held it in his palm. It was cold and weighty, solid silver. As if the connection of the metal with his skin released some kind of spell, he was suddenly thrown back twenty-odd years, to the day when they had brought his mother back from her abduction to the North. It was only the second time he had seen her face, for in Eyra she had abandoned the traditional sabatka, along with her religion, her family, and all her morals. For a long time, all he had been able to do was stare once more upon that peculiarly naked visage, with its huge black eyes and proud nose, feeling at once repulsed and fascinated, and more abandoned than when she had first been stolen away. For there, on a chain around her neck, she had openly worn this very ring, marked out like the concubine she was as the chattel of the barbarian king. She was no longer big with child by then, for like a cuckoo in the nest, the baby Ravn had been installed in the nursery at Halbo and claimed as the royal pair's own. Rui felt his heart contract. Now, he could remember the stench of the fires in which his father had burned his mother for her adultery, a spectacle which the old man had made him watch. It was not a sight—or a smell—he could ever forget.

He replaced the ring inside the box, closed the drawer again, and examined the other man's face. Guileless blue eyes met his gaze; either Erol Bardson was a consummate actor, or he did not know the significance of the object the box contained. In which case this was perhaps more of a message from the old woman herself. It must have been bitter indeed, after all those barren years of marriage, to be forced to adopt another woman's offspring as her own, and that of a foreign woman to boot. And Bardson had mentioned that the Lady Auda wanted the throne for herself. Two vipers in the northern court, each puffed up with their own venomous ambitions, could prove a very useful aid to his cause.

"Excellent!" he proclaimed, shaking off the old horrors. "Plano, take our visitor down to the steward and tell him he is to give the Earl of Broadfell the Safflower Room and to send up hot food and good wine, the Jetran stuff, not the cheap rubbish. And something for his bird." He watched Bardson bow and smile and retreat with the guard, then he turned to the Lord of Ixta and there was a gleam in his eye. "Well now, Varyx, this is becoming very interesting indeed. Shall we go and find you a girl, then?"

FORENT Castle was one of the oldest fortresses in Istria. Its foundations had been laid in the time of Emperor Seram and the fabric of the castle had sprung up thereafter in a remarkably piecemeal fashion, depending on whether its lord had won or lost funds in the many civil commotions and full-scale wars which had followed. Rui maintained his private quarters in the oldest part of the castle—the foursquare granite keep hewn into the bones of the cliff above the city and the sea. Here, the walls were so thick that not a sound permeated from one room to the next, which was just how he liked it. Despite the famed decadence and frivolities of Forent Town, its lord preferred to keep himself to himself, although others were rarely accorded the same privilege. For Rui Finco's licentious great-grandfather, Taghi Finco, had seen to the construction of a number of secret entrances and egresses from the chambers he had occupied, and a maze of concealed tunnels excavated within the thickness of the walls at great expense and the cost of no few lives. From his quarters, therefore, Rui could traverse, unseen, many levels of his castle, appearing and disappearing at will. And where Taghi Finco had made use of these hidden ways purely to indulge his hedonistic vices—visiting dozens of illicit courtesans while publicly maintaining a stable, fruitful, and exemplary marriage—his descendant had other uses for them.

The current Lord of Forent had gained for himself a reputation for shrewdness bordering on the supernatural, an uncanny knack of knowing others' business and second-guessing their moves, and a particularly unpleasant intuition about the darker corners of their lives. He had, at one time or another, invited every significant lord, politician, and merchant in the empire to enjoy the hospitality for which Forent was rightly famed. While they made free with his liberal servings of rich food and fine wines, with the unparalleled collection of beauties and experts in his seraglio—and his rather less well-known collection of very pretty boys for those with a taste for the truly forbidden—he had watched and made more than mental notes of all they said and did while within the bounds of his castle. Thus he knew the sexual proclivities of all his potential rivals, their financial standing, the state of their marriages, friendships, and political alliances, and their dearest ambitions. It was amazing what a man would tell a whore in the deep of the night.

Rui had learned the art of catnapping early in life (and much else besides). After discovering the secret passages, he had made himself a child's fortune extorting pouches of cantari from his father's many visitors. He was never too overt in his knowledge, never ostentatious or obvious but became the master of the subtle hint, the double-edged word, and the penetrating stare. Even the most thick-skinned of his marks found themselves donating to his funds rather than endure that knowing gaze, and the implication that he might let slip an indiscretion to his father or their peers.

What none knew was how as a boy of ten and nearly a man by the standards of the day, Rui Finco had been a witness to one of the great acts of treason ever enacted in modern times, or how, instead of raising the guard and calling down death and destruction on the bold intruder, he had watched in a state of rising perturbation as the man who looked remarkably similar to his own father—supposedly miles away up the coast engaged in desperate battle with Eyra's invading force—had entered his mother's private chambers and there cast off the glamour which held the imprimatur of the Lord of Forent to reveal himself as the Gray Wolf himself, King Ashar Stenson, Lord of the Northern Isles: Istria's worst and bloodiest enemy. Instead of shrieking for help—or casting herself through the open window onto the jagged rocks two hundred feet below in order to preserve her honor, if not her life, as one predecessor had done under similar, if less sorcerous circumstances—the Lady of Forent had gasped in shock and dropped her whisper-soft sabatka in a crimson pool around her ankles so that she stood naked before the intruder, naked that is except for her delicate body jewelry—the glinting silver chain which encircled her waist and looped down from the ring at her navel; the tiny rings in each rosy nipple—which marked out her nomad origins, about which none but her husband had known. Galvanized by this unexpected welcome, Ashar Stenson had thrown off the great gray wolfskin by which he was so famously known, and unbuckled his armor piece by piece swiftly with deft fingers so that the metal-studded leather fell to the floor in a heap until he was down to no more than a woolen undershirt and linen breeches: revealing himself to be a huge man, wild with hair and muscle. Only then had she flown at him with fingers like talons, but instead of clawing at his eyes, she had dragged those last garments from him, a ravening creature, and at last they had fallen upon one another like starving dogs.

He had not been able to tear his gaze from their extravagant coupling, had not been able to make a sound for fear of drawing their attention to his presence; he had stood there for an hour or more with his legs trembling and his eye pressed so hard against the rocky spyhole that its corrugations had left a bruise, until their sweaty appetites were finally slaked. Then the great northern lord had called in the sorcerer who had made this foray possible, wrapped the Lady of Forent tenderly in his wolfskin, and laid her across his shoulder while the nomad muttered over his crystals and transformed the pair into a traveling man and his baggage so that they might leave the castle unrecognized. And then Rui had known he was forever lost, for he was fatally implicated in his mother's fall from grace, complicit in her treacherous lust, knowing himself tainted by her blood. He had never spoken of what he had seen, but he remained forever haunted by the ghost of that passion. It had made spying from these secret passages an addiction he had never been able to overcome.

So, sometimes he merely played voyeur as others panted and writhed; sometimes he pleasured himself silently, then slipped into the chamber when the guest was gone to complete his enjoyment with the nicely warmed-up houri left tangled in the sheets. And sometimes he just liked to watch the women when they did not know they were being watched.

Lately, he had spent many enjoyable hours spying on his newest visitors—the ladies from Eyra. He knew all their names now; knew, too, their voices, their forms, and to some extent their natures, though as yet he had bedded none of them. In the flesh, they had been something of a disappointment, for their paleness held less allure for him than he had expected. Dark women, women who looked like his mother—olive-skinned and supple—were what he preferred rather than women who were as tall and pale and stringy as most of these newcomers. He supposed he should try one or two of them just to get used to the idea of it before finding himself surrounded by them in Eyra's capital, but the concept did not greatly appeal. Last night he had had the women in the slave quarters brought up to the chambers occupied by his better houris and watched the reunion of the nine women Bastido's men had captured from Rockfall. It had been a most touching event. There had been tears and embraces, and a lot of jabbering in their guttural northern tongue. Then, just as they were rejoicing at being together again, he had had them separated once more. They had been a lot quieter and more pensive since then, especially the fiery redhead he had set Peta the task of grooming for him. In truth, he found little appeal in her scrawny limbs and boyish frame, though she was the most interesting in other ways. No. He was bored with Peta and her overbearing methods, so setting her an impossible task would prove to be an entertaining way of removing her from the harem. She'd fetch a decent enough price on the slave blocks alongside the rest. An experienced whoremistress was quite a rare commodity. Agia would make an eminently acceptable replacement.

"So, Varyx," he said now, turning to his friend, "how would you like to proceed—have them all in at once so you can make immediate comparison, or draw it out and see them one by one?"

Varyx smirked and a dribble of red wine ran down his chin. He wiped

it away absentmindedly with the back of the hand not clutching the vast
goblet of Jetra's finest and reclined a little farther onto the couch. "Oh,
one by one, Rui, most certainly. And then all together. Best of both
worlds, y'know?"

Rui gestured to the slaveboy who stood by with the wineflask. "Go
fetch Peta," he said, taking the flask from the lad's hands. "Tell her to
bring the women up to my dressing chamber. We shall have them in one
at a time."

The boy—one of Rui's many bastards—flashed a grin and left the
room with alacrity, hoping very much that he'd be allowed to stay.

BY the time Peta and Agia ushered the first veiled figure into her lord's
receiving chamber, Lord Varyx was patently plastered. His face was
flushed, his eyes were bloodshot, and he seemed to be having difficulty
focusing. Peta found that she was inordinately irritated by this. She had
spent the last several hours overseeing a frantic preparation of the
women—having them bathed and oiled, shorn and painted, then draped
in very proper sabatkas. She knew that her master preferred to see his
houris in sheer robes which barely hid a detail; but she also recognized
the power of the tantalizing glimpse. The northerners had been sullen
but for the most part quiescent during this demeaning process. The
least disobedience had resulted in a whipping with a wet cloth, which
stung the skin but left no lasting mark. That had quelled all but the
most rebellious and uncooperative of them, and she had a strategy
firmly in place for keeping that one compliant. . . .

Peta enjoyed her life as the mistress of Rui's seraglio. She had a loom
of her own, pleasant quarters, and more power than she could ever have
imagined when she was a backstreet slave in the Eternal City. Since that
grim time she had been bartered and traded all the way from Jetra to
Gibeon, from Gibeon to Cantara, from Cantara to Cera; and at last from
Cera to Forent, picking up new tricks and tales of others' misfortunes all
the way. Rui Finco was a relatively indulgent master; in comparison
with many other women in her situation she had few complaints. And
life as a common servant would be hard indeed now that she was past

her prime. She had no intention of allowing a skinny little northern bitch to ruin the prospects of her comfortable old age in Forent Castle.

"Make your obeisance and tell the lords your name," Peta chided in the Old Tongue, pushing the first girl firmly in the back.

Forna Stensen bobbed her greeting and mumbled out her name.

"Your hands, girl," Peta whispered crossly, and Forna held out her hands to be admired, palms first then backs, so that the candlelight glittered on the strange colored lacquer they had applied to her fingernails. Then she curled her right hand as she had been shown, left hand cupped below it, and as gracefully as she could manage, moved it up and down. When performed by a properly trained Istrian houri such a gesture was deliciously suggestive, but Forna looked more as if she were milking a cow.

Varyx guffawed. "By the Lady, she'd pull your cock right off!"

Rui sighed. "Don't bother with the trimmings, Peta. We're not at the marketplace . . . yet. Let's see what she's made like."

Peta inclined her head. "Show the lords your pretty feet, my child," she urged Forna, and Forna Stensen stuck one pink appendage out from under the hem of her demure robe and waved it about in a lumpen sort of way.

"Not my type," the Lord of Ixta exclaimed, sitting back. He waved languidly. "Next!"

Rui Finco raised an eyebrow. For all his bravado and his reputation, Varyx was something of a traditionalist, it seemed. For some reason, he found this rather amusing; and yet he had to admit that there was a certain simplicity to it. Besides, if he followed tradition to the letter, Varyx would never see much more than her hands and feet anyway, since even whores tended to keep their capacious robes on when worshiping the Goddess. It seemed ridiculous to him not to appreciate a woman's entire form, but many would regard him as perverse for even framing such a thought, let alone acting upon it.

Agia conducted Forna outside, then returned first with a fat girl, then a thin girl, neither of which met with approval, then a large and clumsy one who trod on the hem of her robe as she came through the door and went sprawling in such a manner the men could see more than they wished of what lay beneath the concealing robes. After her came one with warts on her fingers which Peta had in the time available to her been able to do nothing about, and she was immediately sent packing. Next came Leni Stelsen. Neatly put together and graceful in her movements, she matched the Istrian ideal far more closely than her predecessors. Varyx was intrigued. He ran a bold hand over her foot, even venturing so far as to lift the hem of her robe an inch until Peta tsked and drew the girl away.

"Not bad," he said with a leer.

The Lord of Forent fixed his seraglio keeper's disapproving mouth with a hard stare. "Keep that one outside, Peta," he said smoothly. "We may recall her later," and watched as she bundled Leni away.

Now a taller girl swept in behind Agia. She wore, Rui Finco noted with some annoyance, a finer robe than the other women, one which clung to her curves and moulded itself against her legs. Whichever one she was—and he had his suspicions—she must have gained Peta's favor in the short time she had been in the castle, which in itself was no mean feat. He beckoned her over and she came with a swaying gait, throwing out each hip in a graceful arc, her painted toes pointed, her hands pressed with apparent modesty to her crotch, which merely served to draw attention to that area. Reaching the couches where the two lords reclined, she bowed deeply and the way she caught in the fabric of the sabatka gave them both a clear outline of her not insubstantial breasts.

When she straightened up, the men were treated to the sight of an exquisite pair of lips, finely delineated and colored in glistening pink and silver. A small silver star twinkled in the middle of the philtrum; seeing the lords mesmerized by this detail, the tall girl formed her mouth into the coyest of pouts then shot the very tip of her tongue out into view to touch the star and back again quick as a snake, leaving a bubble of saliva on her gleaming lower lip. Varyx spilled his wine in his haste to inspect her more closely.

"Now this one is rare," he proclaimed, breathing heavily. He reached out and touched a swell in the fabric and sighed contentedly as Kitten's soft hand closed around his probing finger. "Rare, indeed."

The Lord of Forent leaned forward. He knew exactly which of the women this one was, and having seen her naked was not driven by curiosity to see her undressed, but her blatant sexuality intrigued him. "Have her disrobe," he said to his harem keeper.

"Really, Rui, I'm quite happy to touch her through the cloth—"

"Have her disrobe!" he repeated sharply.

"My lord!" Peta was scandalized. "This is slave market behavior, not to be indulged in by honorable men . . ."

This was too much for Varyx. He grabbed Rui Finco by the arm, almost weeping with delight. "She thinks we are honorable men, my friend! How extraordinary. How wonderful! How long has it been since we were honorable, Rui? Thirteen? Fourteen?"

The Lord of Forent prised the other man's wet fingers from his velvet sleeve, noting with irritation how the nap had been marked. "Really, Peta. Anyone would think you ran a chapter of Falla's Sisters rather than a whorehouse."

"Seraglio," Peta corrected him sharply. "My lord."

"Although money may not be exchanged at the time, my dear, my guests pay for your girls' services in many other ways, believe me."

Peta's head remained stubbornly still. He could tell that instead of regarding the floor with due deference she was staring at him with her little gimlet eyes glittering away behind that veil.

With a sigh Rui Finco levered himself to his feet. "Whatever is the point of keeping a bitch and having to bark oneself?" he declared into the close air of the chamber. Behind him, Varyx sniggered drunkenly, a sound which came to an abrupt halt as the Lord of Forent whisked the shimmering robe from the northern girl, revealing Kitten Soronsen in all her statuesque glory.

"Oh . . ." Varyx was beside himself, almost literally. His body might have been sprawled on the day-bed, but his eyes and mind were elsewhere entirely. "I'll have this one, Rui, truly I will."

But his friend was not listening to him. "What are you called?" he asked, head on one side like an acquisitive robin regarding a worm.

Kitten bobbed her head. "Kitten Soronsen, my lord." She gazed up at Rui Finco through her lashes. It was a frank look, not the blushing, deferential glance he was used to. Interesting.

"Kitten, as in 'little cat?' "

Kitten smiled, revealing the tips of sharp, pearl-white teeth. "Yes, my lord."

"I wonder if I could make you purr."

That drew a blush. "I am sure you could, my lord."

"Well, perhaps I shall. But I have a task for you first."

"Yesh . . ." Varyx was on his feet now and wobbling unsteadily toward them. "A very . . . pleasant tashk indeed."

Turning swiftly, Rui extended one hand, fingers splayed, and pushed Varyx firmly back onto the couch. The Lord of Ixta landed in a heap with his legs in the air and a most perplexed expression on his face. "Now then, Rui . . . fair'sh fair. It'sh my choice. You shaid sho . . ."

"Oh, you shall have your choice, my friend. It's just that this one is not part of the deal." He turned back to Kitten Soronsen, knelt, and retrieved the crimson sabatka. This he held out to her graciously. "Put on your robe, my dear. Now, tell me: do you know a man called Erol Bardson?"

Kitten's eyes grew round. "He is King Ravn's cousin."

Rui grinned. "Excellent. So that much is true, at least." He looked past her to the mistress of his seraglio. "Is she schooled, Peta?"

The woman laughed. "I would hardly call any of these northern women 'schooled,' my lord. They came to me as rough as dogs and I have had little chance to teach them our ways. But she is the best of a poor bunch."

"Do you want to be rich, Kitten? Rich and pampered and treated like an empress?"

Her eyes grew rounder. Then she nodded quickly.

"You shall spend your first night in my service in the company of this Erol Bardson, and you shall make him as comfortable as he wishes to be. Do you understand what I mean by this?"

Again, Kitten nodded.

Rui caught her by the elbow and guided her to one side, his voice no louder than a whisper. "You will ask him why he is here and whether someone is paying him. You will ask him what he knows of Halbo City and its famed Sentinel Towers, which you have heard are impossible to pass from the sea. Then tomorrow you shall tell me all he says. You are an Eyran. He will talk to you more freely than any of my other women. And if you perform this service well for me and glean such knowledge as you can, I will reward you richly and keep you here in Forent Castle rather than sending you to the slave blocks to become the property of some filthy old merchant. Do you agree?"

Kitten flashed him her most winning smile. "Oh, yes, my lord, I do."

"Excellent. Agia?"

"My lord?"

"Have Plano conduct this lady to the quarters of the Earl of Broadfell and explain that it is my wish he makes the most of Forent's famed hospitality."

"Yes, my lord."

Peta said nothing, which in itself conveyed her displeasure. She watched Agia guide Kitten away with her hands on her hips, a most belligerent stance.

"So, Peta, we have two ladies left for Varyx to choose from, I believe?"

"There are two left." This was not what she had expected at all. Varyx should have seen Kitten Soronsen and the whole charade should have been over; instead they were left with the hellcat and her difficult mother. She wondered if she might get away with bringing Leni Stelsen out again instead of the fox-haired brat, but any hope of this was immediately dashed.

"I'm looking forward to seeing whether you have succeeded in taming the little redhead," Rui said with a cruel smile. "I'm sure you won't have forgotten our bargain, Peta."

"Indeed not, my lord," Peta returned through gritted teeth.

Agia made to move through the door to fetch Katla, but Peta waved her aside. "I'll get her," she hissed.

As soon as the door was unlocked, Katla was on her feet. With Plano gone, now was as good a time as any to make a run for it, if she had the chance; but Peta blocked the doorway with her robust frame. "You see this?" the seraglio keeper asked softly. She inched a wicked-looking little blade out of her sleeve so that it gleamed for a moment in her palm.

"Mmm," said Katla, trying to sound uninterested, though the sight of the weapon riveted her.

"Embarrass me any way—take one wrong step or say one wrong word—and this lady—" she indicated the dark-robed Bera Rolfsen standing behind them "—feel its kiss from here—" a sharp-taloned nail touched her right ear, "—to here." The nail drew itself across her throat to the other ear. "I make myself clear?"

Katla glared at her through the annoying veil.

"She your mother, I believe," Peta added silkily. "At least, that what Agia told me when you were reunited yesterday." She leaned in closer to Katla. "We have no secrets here in this seraglio, so I also cut her if you tell any more your dangerous nonsense to my girls about how free are Eyran women, you hear?"

Katla's eyes narrowed. One quick foot inside the other woman's instep and she knew she could have Peta on her back and the knife in her hand. Her fingers itched and buzzed as if she could feel the blade nestled in her palm already.

The door opened and all immediate chance of escape evaporated. "Is there a problem, Peta?" Rui Finco asked smoothly. "You see, my lord of Ixta is becoming rather . . . tired and emotional and would like to make his choice." He smiled. "Before he passes out."

He ushered both Katla and Bera ahead of him into the receiving room, where Varyx was slumped on the couch, snoring gently. The Lord of Forent smiled. He had watered his own wine while adding a tasteless but very potent rye spirit to Varyx's, never having had the least intention of allowing him to spoil his prize merchandise. Nevertheless, he took the precaution of crossing the room and shaking the man by the shoulder. To no avail: the Lord of Ixta blew and whistled, then curled himself around his friend's arm, murmuring obscenities. Rui removed himself with a curse, then turned to face the women.

"Now then," he said to Katla in the Old Tongue, very quietly and very firmly. "Remove your robe."

Katla stared hard at him through the sheer veil. "Go fuck yourself," she replied grimly. In Eyran.

Rui Finco had no need to understand the northern tongue to know her meaning. Neither did Peta. While the Lord of Forent grinned from ear to ear, Bera Rolfsen yelped involuntarily as a sharp blade jabbed into her back.

"Sur's knackers!" Katla swore. She bent, grabbed a handful of the stupid silky robe, and ripped it upward in a single angry sweep. It tangled around her head. She fought clear of it, then threw it to the ground and stamped on it so that the little silver bells draped around her shaved, perfumed, oiled, and painted ankles tinkled sweetly. Arms folded, she stood naked and trembling in fury before the man who had sentenced her to burning.

The Lord of Forent laughed. "Such a little firebrand!"

He walked around her, taking in the view.

"Much better, Peta, I'll give you that. Nice skin, now that you can see what was under all that grime. Unusual hair color, very striking. The braiding is pretty, and the henna work, too. Whose hand is that?"

"Mela's," the seraglio keeper responded gruffly. Mela had for some inexplicable reason volunteered for this painstaking and intricate task on the most awkward of their charges, yet it seemed from the delicacy of the twined flowers she had inked the length of the hellcat's spine that the Eyran girl had meekly allowed her to carry out her duties without a struggle. The two women must have struck up quite a friendship, despite their different backgrounds and circumstances. She didn't like it at all; it fit no behavior pattern she understood. Something was wrong here.

"Stringy little creature, though, isn't she? Not much meat on her." He squeezed Katla's bicep and she jerked herself away in disgust. "Strong, though: muscles built for stamina." He ran a finger lightly down her back, then cupped her right buttock in his palm. "Bet she could ride a man all night and gallop him like a prize mare."

With a shriek of outrage she could not hold back, Katla whirled as fast as a dervish, grabbed the Lord of Forent by the hair, and brought her knee up hard so that his jaw connected with the bone with a resounding crack and his eyes rolled upwards. A moment later, Rui Finco was sprawled flat out unconscious on the floor of the receiving room. His pretty silver circlet came to rest with a clatter by the couch.

A moment's uneasy silence rolled across the chamber. Then it was shattered by the sound of swearing in two very different languages. When Katla spun around, it was to see her mother being borne to the floor by the much heavier mistress of Forent's harem, knife in hand. Blood spattered both women's clothing. Peta's arm went up for a killing stroke. Like lightning, Katla grabbed up the wine flask and brought it down on her head with a thud. The last of Jetra's finest gushed out over the mouth of the vessel and, soft as leather, the silver flask caved in on itself. Peta lurched to her feet. Red liquid trickled down her sabatka, pooled on the floor at her feet. Behind the veil, she growled. Then she came at Katla with the knife.

An immense, roiling anger filled Katla Aransen. This . . . woman . . . had betrayed her kind, had run her harem like a prisonmaster, had procured women from the slave market for her lord's perverse pleasures, had trained and ruled them with fear and brutality. Had made a favorite of that little traitor, Kitten Soronsen. Had wounded her mother—Sur knew how badly. And, Katla reminded herself grimly, had subjected her to the worst indignities of her short life.

She backed up, dodged sideways, and slipped under Peta's knife arm, catching her wrist as she went, but the silk of the sabatka slipped in her grip, so that suddenly Peta was facing her and the wicked-looking blade was descending toward her face. Ducking away, Katla thrust out a swift foot and hooked it around her opponent's ankle, then crashed her body into the harem mistress's and tried to lever her over. It was like trying to flip a boulder. Peta stood firm and gradually bore down upon Katla Aransen instead. Katla caught hold of the billowing fabric of the woman's robe and wrapped it around the knife. The blade sheared through the fabric soft as a whisper and was in her face again a second later.

You've met your match now, came a traitorous voice in her head. *She's much stronger than you, and she's armed. What chance do you have? She'll drive you down and rip you to shreds! So much for your vaunted wrestling prowess, Katla Aransen, so much for your pride! This is how you will die, shaved and painted and naked and defenseless under the knife of an Istrian whoremistress. Will they make songs about such a heroic end? I think not. Better to have gone to the fires at the Allfair last year than like this, in shame and ignominy. . . .*

Desperate now, Katla tore at the sabatka, hauling it upward to fend off the blade and confound her attacker. It was a flimsy shield. Ribbons of fabric spun to the ground and Peta kept coming at her, roaring now, low and guttural, frustrated and full of blood lust. Katla backed away, until a low table caught her in the crook of the knees so that she lost her balance and went crashing down in a limb-flailing somersault onto the other side of it, landing painfully on her back, the wind knocked out of her. She did not let go of the robe. It came with her in a swath of ripping silk, a great tent of a thing rent with so many tears that the candlelight shone through it like holes in the night sky as it fell down upon her.

Someone howled like an animal on the light side of the sabatka. It was her mother's voice. Katla knew it even through its wild distortion. With superhuman effort she caught her breath, thrust the destroyed robe away from her, rolled, and came to her feet and the most extraordinary sight. A big, fat, naked figure was staggering around the room with a shrieking Bera Rolfsen astride its back, her veil bandaged firmly over its eyes so that it lashed out blindly with the little knife. Weird shadows leaped and rocked around the candlelit chamber in almost comical imitation of this bizarre scene, but when Peta and her rider swung around to face Katla in their careering progress, things became odder again.

Peta—whoremistress of Forent Castle, keeper of the seraglio, tyrant of Rui Finco's houris—was no mistress at all, but something else entirely. Her shaved pubis gleamed in the dancing light; and so did her little bobbing penis.

Katla stared and stared—could not help herself.

Peta was a man.

Or was she? For while other parts were absent, or so small as to be invisible, other parts were vastly, flabbily in evidence. Above a swag of white belly, two vast tits swung and bounced.

This unusual information embedded itself in Katla's skull, stopping her still in her tracks for several valuable seconds. Then the reality of the situation invaded her again and like a dog casting away a rat, she threw off her fascination and hurled herself into the fray.

Even Peta was no match for two Rockfall hoydens. Down she went in a heap with Bera and Katla on top of her, and suddenly the knife was— as she had known it would somehow be—in Katla's own hand. Istrian blade or no, it sang to her greedily. All she had to do now was to plunge it down hard and it would be over. Katla felt the blood lust calling her, felt the contact with the metal buzzing through her veins and into her bones, making her hot and light-headed and wanton; yet something in her resisted the call. It might have been the terror in Peta's black eyes; or an unconscious acknowledgment of their shared predicament. Or it might have been the sound of the door of the reception room swinging wide open to admit a contingent of armed guards with Plano at their head.

But it was the Lord of Forent—looking somewhat dazed—who caught Katla by the wrist and twisted mercilessly till the blade came away into his own palm.

"Well," he said, stepping back and staring down at the extraordinary tangle, "I see you have been keeping something from me, Peta, all these years."

The guards were all muttering now. Some gawped openly—at the Rockfall women—for they were the first of these fallen creatures they had seen—then at the whoremistress and her unfamiliar configuration. A couple of them began to laugh; others made superstitious gestures and felt their own genitals contract in mute sympathy. Eunuchs were not unheard of in Istria, but they were figures out of another age of the world, and another place. In Gila and the Spice Islands it had been commonplace to geld the men who guarded the houris—but never here, in civilized Forent.

"Get them up and make them decent!" Rui Finco roared at Plano. "And you—" he indicated the guards, "—one word of this beyond these walls and I may revive an old custom." He cupped his balls, stared at them meaningfully. "I hope you understand me well."

The men paled and nodded swiftly.

Then the Lord of Forent turned back to survey his captives. "You have disappointed me, Peta," he said softly. He laid a hand upon the seraglio keeper's shoulder, but the other made a swift movement. Peta's eyes widened; then his knees buckled. Blood gushed onto the floor.

"As for you—" he stared at Katla, who dragged her eyes unwillingly from the reddened knife in his hand to meet his gaze defiantly, "—did you really imagine I'd ever invite you into my bed? You're fit only for coupling with a wolf. What man in his right mind would pay to poke such a scrawny, rabid bitch? It might be kinder to slit your throat here and now and have done with it. But I have a better idea." He paused, then addressed Plano again. "Take these two to slave master Figro. Tell him I am sorry to send him such poor pickings, but if he gets me a reasonable price for them, I'll see he gets the rest of the Eyran girls to sell, and that should make up for the effort."

He watched as Bera and Katla were bundled in cloaks and hauled away, then he crossed the chamber, retrieved his circlet, and donned it swiftly, then drew back the tapestry which was hung over the entrance to the passageway down to the Safflower Room, and disappeared into the wall.

Erno

Eᴿɴᴏ Hamson kicked his heels morosely against the side of the ship. It was full dark now and he had been watching the constellations shifting through the sky for longer than he could bear. When Persoa swarmed silently up over the gunwale he almost throttled him with his bare hands, his impatience was so great.

"Well? Do you know where she is?"

The hillman flashed Erno a grin, his white teeth and the sheen of his eyes all that was visible of him in the night. There was a soft scuffling sound as the hillman undid the bundle of clothes he had carried above the waves and dressed himself again. When he came into the circle of the lantern where Mam sat waiting on the deck, there was blood in his hair, where the sea had not washed it away. At once, she was on her feet, her hands questing over him, all incongruous concern.

"Are you hurt? Tell me you're not hurt!"

As if a badly injured man could possibly swim from that distant rocky shore and board a ship with nary a complaint.

Persoa lifted Mam's vast mitts to his face and kissed them several times, on the palms, the fingers, the wrists. "Do not worry. It is not my blood, my dove," he said gently.

"Then whose is it?" Erno demanded, his voice shrill with irritation.

The hillman sat down on the sacking beside the lantern, his limbs coiling under him with fluid grace. He was, Mam said, one of the finest assassins in the world even though Doc and Dogo disagreed, since they'd managed to take him captive after he'd spitted poor Knobber that night in the back alleys of Forent. Mam was a bit soft where Persoa was concerned; there was history between them, and they were making more of it day by day.

"After I swam to shore, I made my way inland and then back down the valley into the village in the next bay," Persoa replied, his southern accent making the words soft and sibilant. "In the back room of an inn called The Turkeycock, I found one of the raiders. We played three hands of cards, and I contrived to lose atrociously. Having fleeced me, he was good enough to buy me a flagon of the local brew and we got talking about women, as you do." Mam gave him a narrow-eyed look, but the hillman smiled slyly. "He had a low opinion of northern women, I am sorry to say, my dove. He finds them coarse and ugly. I asked him how he formed this opinion and he told me at no little length."

Erno leaned forward eagerly and the lamplight behind him made a silver-gold halo of his hair. "Tell us at short length, for Sur's sake," he said. "Is Katla still alive? Have you seen her?"

Persoa held up his hands as if to ward off the northman's words. In the flickering light, his hands were delicate, as elegant as a woman's. You could see why Dogo made fun of him. Even if it was behind his back.

"Patience, my friend. They say it is a virtue, but although mercenaries are not known as virtuous folk, it is still a useful tool in our chosen trade."

"I never chose to be a sellsword," Erno huffed. "I'm only with you to find Katla Aransen, so tell me—is she still alive?"

Persoa looked around at his companions—at Dogo and Doc snoring off a cask of ale in the stern, their arms around the two Istrian whores they had rescued from the island; at Joz Bearhand's still figure at watch; at Mam picking at those fearsomely pointed teeth, and finally at the light-eyed Eyran lad whose heart was burning up inside him—and shrugged.

"They took a dozen or so women from the island. He did not know their names, but he was most graphic in the way he described them, and one in particular. It seems she was a firebrand, and not just from the color of her hair. Apparently, she instigated a riot during which their captain met an unfortunate end—"

Mam laughed. "That's our Katla. Good girl, she is: a proper scrapper. I always said she should join the company: she'd make a fine sellsword, and that's the god's truth."

"Then the ship came upon heavy weather, or some other ill luck—he was somewhat hazy about the details—and they were forced to abandon it before it foundered—"

Erno clutched at the hillman's wet shirt. "Please tell me she didn't drown. Not Katla, surely? I could not bear for her to drown, chained in a slave ship—"

Persoa shook his head. "She did not drown, my friend." There was a gleam in his eye. He would not speed his narrative, for he enjoyed a good story and this one was particularly entertaining. "Though for a long time the raiders thought she had. The last he saw of her she was tied to the mast, and in the panic as they abandoned the vessel, no one thought to unchain her, or any of the women below decks—"

"Bastards!" Erno exploded, beside himself with rage and anxiety.

Mam patted him absently on the knee. "Hush, lad, I suspect this tale has a better ending than you may think."

Persoa dropped her a lazy wink. "The raider laughed about this, said they were not such a valuable cargo that his men were willing to risk their own necks by going down into the flooded hold while the ship was sinking so fast, but that bad coins get washed up where you least expect them. He and the survivors returned to the wreck the next day to salvage what they could, for there are Istrian chirurgeons who will pay decent money for a foreign woman's corpse; but they were astonished to find that the women had somehow managed to get clear of the ship and swim to the mainland. They recaptured some of the women on the strand there; but the last time he saw the flame-haired one, she'd scaled the cliff and was headed away into the Istrian countryside with a pretty blonde girl, a fat girl, a thin girl, and a girl with a face like the back end of a horse—"

Erno snorted, a clear picture in his mind. "That'll be Kitten Soronsen, Thin Hildi, Fat Breta, and Magla Felinsen." He shook his head despondently. "Katla could be anywhere by now."

"How now, Erno? A moment ago you feared Katla Aransen drowned, and now Persoa tells us she got away. Let the man tell his tale and you may find you have less cause for despair than you think," came a gruff voice out of the darkness. Joz Bearhand, while maintaining his careful watch at the steerboard gunwale, had been listening to the hillman's narrative with absolute concentration.

"This is not the end of it," Persoa said softly, his voice falling a note so that the hairs prickled on the back of Erno's neck. "After I had followed the man around the corner of the inn to take a piss, we fell into talk with another of his company who'd apparently forayed as far up the coast from Forent. It seems the talk of the town is of how the Lord of Forent has a number of Eyran women in his keep. They were not happy to have lost their booty to his lordship, I can tell you."

"That'll be the others," Erno said morosely. "The ones who got taken on the beach. Not Katla."

"Think again, my friend. They say one of them has hair the color of Falla's fires—"

Erno looked up, startled. "Katla, a prisoner at Forent Castle?" He leaped to his feet. "We must set sail at once!"

Mam laughed. "If you think six of us are going to storm Rui Finco's keep, you'd better think again, my lad."

Persoa took one of her hands between his own. "How much did the Rockfall folk pay us to bring back their women?" he asked guilelessly.

The mercenary leader regarded him with sudden suspicion. "Why?"

"How much?"

Mam cast a hard look at Erno, then leaned across and whispered something in the hillman's ear and he sat back, grinning delightedly. "Easy!" He gabbled away at the mercenary leader in his outlandish tongue for a time, during which she nodded and laughed and made assessing faces. Then she jumped to her feet. "Weigh the anchor!" she cried. She clapped Persoa on the back. "Set a course up the coast for Forent!"

It was a clear night: and with an eldianna at the helm sensing the underlying rocks and the movement of the currents, they'd be safe from shipwreck. There was, however, considerable rebellious muttering from Doc and Dogo when they were dragged from their sodden sleep and told to man the lines, though Mam would not tell them precisely why they were required to do so at such an ungodly hour. Nor would she tell Erno what was going on either. The boy was a hothead, and a potential liability, especially now that he was in possession of a powerful sword. And that silver-blonde hair would be hard to disguise, but she suspected she'd have a hard time persuading him to be left behind on the ship while they went to take care of business.

Stymied by the mercenary leader at every turn, Erno gave up and went after the hillman.

"What's the plan?" he demanded, but Persoa just tapped his nose enigmatically. "It is best you do not know till the time presents itself," he returned unhelpfully, and would say nothing else until Erno asked him again about the blood. "Ah." He put his hand up to his close-shorn hair, felt the sticky patch at the back and, bringing his fingers away, examined them closely before wiping them on his tunic. Persoa smiled, and for the first time since he had known him, Erno suddenly saw the assassin in the hillman, steely and dangerous behind that finely-drawn face and gleaming brown eyes.

"After what they did at Rockfall, how could I suffer such men to live?" He spread his hands. "I cut their throats in the alley. The first I was forced to kill quickly; but the other I killed slowly so that he would feel every second of his death and have time to ponder the reason for it, which I told him, softly, as I did the deed. He could not scream of course. If you cut in a certain way, the blood spurts, but they can make no sound. Baranguet's boasts will not sit well with my lady Falla. She does not smile upon those who rape and murder defenseless women. I know she will set her great cat upon him as he enters her fires and that it will rend his soul from him and swallow it down like a rat!"

He spat hard and deliberately on the deck beside Erno's feet, then bent over the gunwale, scooped up a handful of seawater, and rinsed away the last traces of blood.

FORENT Town was alive with activity. They found it hard to get lodgings, for what decent rooms there were for hire had been commandeered by order of the Ruling Council to provide billets for the troops and crews which had been mustered here, and the workmen who labored under Morten Danson's eye to create the fleet which would storm the north. Eventually, they found themselves down by the dockside where hundreds of makeshift shelters had been erected out of old canvas and sailcloth. The whole place stank of mildew and ale and piss. They would have had better conditions on board their own vessel except that, as Mam pointed out, if the Lord of Forent were to recognize the ship they'd nicked from him the last time they'd been down this way, he'd have them all drawn and quartered and not bother with the hanging at all.

As it was, only Persoa had the luxury of being able to walk the streets undisguised, for to be an Eyran in this town—even an Eyran sellsword—was liable to land you at the least in unnecessary fights, and at worst spitted by an overzealous patriot looking to earn a bounty. Feeling as if he still stuck out like a fox in a hencoop, even after the hillman's best ministrations, Erno readjusted his hat and squinted ahead of him out of the eye which didn't bear a patch (which Persoa had made him wear, saying that a pair of blue eyes would mark him out as a foreigner at once; but the patch would draw an observer's notice before they had a chance to look at the other eye). His hair had been hastily dyed ("Not again!" he had protested. The squid ink smelled foul as they dunked his head and still did—he moved through a fishy miasma all his own; in crowded places people quite subconsciously moved away from him) and he had exchanged his homespun Eyran tunic for a richer southern version nabbed by Persoa from a market stall. Mam—whose weird braids, sharpened teeth, and belligerent demeanor were impossible to disguise—had gone the whole hog in a vast black sabatka, while Joz Bearhand had, after much grumbling, been made to shave off his beard, rub dirt into the pale skin thus revealed, and dress as a rich Gilan merchant; Dogo and Doc meanwhile made a remarkably convincing chirurgeon and his apothecary in shabby black robes and square hats. Sur only knew where the hillman had laid hands on these costumes, but there appeared to be no sign of blood on them.

The only weapons Mam would allow them were small and concealed in their clothing, though Erno happened to know Mam had a full-length sword strapped to one thigh under the Istrian robe; she walked with a curiously stiff gait. The red sword he had reluctantly left wrapped in sacking in their ship, which lay demasted, beached, and camouflaged three coves east of here.

Erno watched, nonplussed, as Mam reached into her voluminous robe and came out with three leather pouches of coins which she quickly distributed to Joz, Persoa, and Doc with the instruction to use them only if absolutely necessary, and they stashed the money away hurriedly before it attracted attention. "What about me?" Erno demanded, thrusting out his hand.

From behind the thick veil Mam gave a hollow laugh. "You just stick with Persoa and do what he tells you."

And before he could remonstrate with her, she fell into step behind the giant figure of Joz Bearhand and disappeared into the crowd.

"Come along, my friend," the hillman said, taking Erno by the shoulder. "We go this way."

"Where? And why the money?"

But all he got for answer was one of the eldianna's enigmatic grins.

Erno followed Persoa into the maze of backstreets away from the harbor. Despite the pretense of being a hardened Istrian freebooter, it was hard not to gaze in bumpkin wonder at every vista that presented itself. Forent was the largest Istrian town he had ever visited, and its style of architecture was quite different to the rough-hewn simplicity of Halbo or the low, turfed dwellings of the Westman Islands. Here, the houses were tall and crammed together so they seemed to loom into the sky. They had many windows, all paned with glass, shutters, intricate iron balconies, turrets, and tall chimneys which belched smoke into the thick morning air. Gutters ran down the sides of the paved streets and stank to high heaven. And over them all towered the massive granite walls surrounding the castle and the great keep itself.

Erno had thought they would be heading directly for this impressive building, but Persoa veered off suddenly to the right.

"I thought you said she was being held prisoner in the castle!" Erno protested loudly.

Persoa frowned. "Keep your voice down," he hissed.

He turned down another alley, past a bakehouse whose lush scents reminded Erno about his growling belly, past a winery and a coster-monger's, past a tavern where two barrel-chested men were wrestling kegs down a ramp into the cellars, past a potter's and the shop of a ceramic artist whose own work was all in tans and terra-cottas, but whose display boasted a fine selection of expensive Jetran blueware in order to hedge his bets and ensure he could equip the tables of even Forent's most houseproud nobility; past a lacemaker and a glassblower and an outfitter's offering a tailoring service. The next alley took them past leatherworkers turning out piles of jerkins and boots and greaves and vambraces, all seemingly cut to a single size and pattern. Cutting right, they found motley squads of soldiers queueing all the way down a street which resounded with the fall of hammer on anvil. Through the gaps in this crowd Erno could spy thousands of swords and spears stacked against the walls and two men in official uniforms doling them out. He stared and stared as the implications of this mass production struck home.

Persoa turned to find his companion transfixed and had to double back. "Not that way, my friend," he said, drawing the Eyran away before they were noticed. "Not unless you want to enlist as an Empire man."

"It really is war, then," Erno said unhappily. "I never really believed it would happen." He paused, thinking. "But how will they carry the fight to the north? They have no ships—" He stopped suddenly. Larger events had abruptly come into focus.

The hillman grimaced. "Now you know why Rockfall was raided," he said softly. "It was not just for the women, however remarkable they may be."

Erno clenched his jaw. "I should be in Halbo to defend my people." There was a wild look in his eye. "Except that . . . the only person I really care about is here in Forent, and without her there is nothing in the world worth saving."

Persoa patted him on the shoulder. "Then stop gawping at the sights like a farm boy and follow me." His grip tightened so that for a moment Erno felt the tips of the hillman's steely fingers through the sturdy cloth of his cloak. "And do exactly what I say. We must not draw attention to ourselves until the time is right; and then you must do exactly what I say. Do you understand me?"

Erno had no idea what the eldianna meant by this, but he nodded impatiently. "Yes, yes, all right—now let's find Katla!"

Down more alleys they went at such a pace that Erno had soon lost his bearings. And then, quite without warning, the warren of packed streets debouched into sunlit space and they found themselves standing in Forent's central market square.

It was packed with people. Or rather, as Erno corrected himself instantly, it was packed with men. All sorts of men, rich and poor, soldiers and merchants, beggars and farmers, laborers and journeymen. Many appeared to be looking rather than buying, and the majority of them were gathered in a huge knot in the far lefthand corner of the market, with those at the back of the crowd desperately craning for a view.

Erno was taller than most Istrian men by half a head, but even he could not see what it was that was drawing the attention of the crowd so. Matters became no clearer the nearer they got, for the throng became more closely knit with every step they took. Erno trod on someone's foot and was elbowed hard in the ribs as another man jostled past him, and a moment later all forward momentum ceased. Persoa tapped the man in front on him on the shoulder and they spoke rapidly for a while in Istrian, before the man pulled away and himself tried to push farther into the crowd.

Erno had picked up more than a word or two of this foreign language in his time. He grabbed Persoa by the arm. "The women!" he cried, his eyes wide with fear. Without thought, in a sudden access of panic, he used his native tongue. "They're selling the Rockfall women!"

"For Elda's sake, shut up!" the hillman hissed. He dragged Erno off to one side, apologizing all the way to those he stepped upon or banged into. For a small man, he had extraordinary strength: there was little Erno could do to free himself without turning it into a fight.

And all the way, he heard the voices:

"—so white their skin—"

"—I never saw hair like it—"

"—she must be Falla's own—"

"—I don't much fancy the fat one—"

"—ah, but think of the novelty value—"

"—take a heathen to your bed—"

"—said to be as wild as beasts—"

"—bite and claw and beg you to give her more—"

and one, deeper and disapproving, "It is not Falla's way to show off the flesh of women thus. It is an abomination—"

At the edge of the crowd, Persoa hauled Erno into a less frequented side street. "Now then," he said, and Erno, feeling a sharp prick at his waist, found that the assassin had drawn a small dagger upon him. He stared at it, aghast, then transferred his gaze to the eldianna's furious face.

"Wha—?" he started, only to have the blade jabbed against his gut.

"You," said Persoa, "are going to wait for me here. You are not to move one step from this doorway—" he indicated a faded wooden door beneath a signboard offering fortune-telling and crystal-reading. With each enunciation, the daggerpoint prodded harder. "I will return in a short while. No matter what happens, you will wait here. Understand?"

"But why?" Erno was infuriated in his turn. A shadow of suspicion clouded his mind. "You're going to take the money and make a run for it!" he cried angrily, grabbing the assassin's knife hand. "What care you about Katla Aransen, or any of them? You're just a rootless, faithless sellsword!"

Persoa unpeeled Erno's fingers from his arm as if they belonged to a small child. "Erno Hamson, I am neither rootless nor faithless. I honor my people, who belong to the hills; and my faith is in Elda and its deities. Finna asked me to carry out this task, and for her I would do anything. It is only because I know she cares for you that I do not stick you where you stand and leave you to expire in a pool of your own blood. Now stay here: you are both too conspicuous and too headstrong to do what must be done. I will bring your woman back to you if it is humanly possible. Now, hear me again. Stay here and await my return!" When Erno opened his mouth to protest, he added, "And do not delay me further, or all will anyway be lost!"

Erno hung his head. He felt tears pricking at his eyelids and found that he was profoundly ashamed, but whether it was for the insult he had given the eldianna or for the apparent powerlessness of his situation, he could not tell. When he raised his head, the hillman had vanished, melting into the crowd with unnerving stealth.

Erno waited. For perhaps ten seconds. Then he began to barge his way forward along the edge of the crowd, causing many to turn in anger at his rough treatment; but when they saw his size, and the strange eye-patch he wore, most of them stepped aside. In a tiny gap thus generated he suddenly glimpsed what held them so rapt. On a raised dais at the front of the square stood a group of guardsmen in castle uniforms, several figures in all-encompassing black robes, and five near-naked women with their hands and feet chained. Katla Aransen was the third in line.

Her hair flamed in the sunshine and Erno's heart felt as if it, too, had ignited.

Now the Eyran began to shove in earnest, ploughing a course through even the most resistant; until he tried to push aside a big man in a roughspun tunic, a man almost as wide as he was tall; when he turned, he stood eye to eye with the northerner. "Sod off!" the man roared. "You get here late, you stand at the back, and tough luck to you!"

Erno took one look at that bellicose face and realized that no manner of polite negotiation was going to persuade the man to step aside. With all the reckless power of the truly desperate, he drew one fist back then exploded it into the other's gut. For a moment, it looked perilously as if his obstacle had been unmoved by this experience, then the man clutched his midriff, staggered, twisted, and collapsed like a felled tree. Erno was past him and pressing quickly forward as people turned to stare in amazement and dawning horror as the big man's fall brought down one after another in his vicinity. As those closest tried to avoid being crushed, they collided with others, and suddenly one onlooker after another was stumbling and falling against their neighbors. Shock waves spread out from this epicenter until a great swath of the audience had gone down in a flail of limbs. Erno sidestepped a tumbling man and abruptly found himself in clear space with an unimpeded view of the dais. Suddenly instead of ogling the women, everyone seemed to be looking at him—those still standing in the crowd, the guards, the slave master, the auctioneer; the Rockfallers. With a shiver, he felt Katla's keen eyes upon him, watched as they narrowed and her kestrel-wing brows drew together in a frown.

He mustered his best Istrian and yelled into the momentary silence, "A hundred cantari for the redhead!"

Katla looked thunderstruck, then appalled, but whether this was at the ignominy of being bid for at all, or whether it was because the bidder looked so disreputable, who could say?

For a few seconds Erno's brave (nay, foolhardy, since all he bore with him about ten cantari) offer fell into an eye of calm; then the storm broke all around him. "A hundred and ten!" yelled a man in a rich crimson surcoat to his right.

"Twenty!" This from a dark-skinned merchant.

"Twenty-five!"

"A hundred and twenty-eight!"

"One hundred and thirty!" The man in crimson again.

"One hundred and fifty!" cried Erno.

There was a lull. People looked from one to another in disbelief. One hundred cantari was a fortune, the cost of a townhouse on the outskirts of Forent City, or a pair of trading ships; but one hundred and fifty was surely madness for one woman, however unusual her coloring.

"She's not even pretty," said a man just behind Erno's left shoulder.

"Too skinny for my taste," replied his neighbor. "Besides, I came to bid for a body-slave, not sign my entire fortune away! Fifty cantari was my limit, and that was pushing it."

"Er, one hundred and fifty," called the auctioneer, trying to recover his equanimity. He stared at Erno with suspicion. "I have a bid of one hundred and fifty cantari for the girl with the hair of fire from the gentleman with the eyepatch—"

There was a small commotion on the other side of the crowd and some raised voices.

"Any advance on one hundred and fifty?" This came out as more of a plea than a brisk summation of business, but no one responded. The auctioneer stared wildly around. He knew his traders; he knew what a man with one hundred and fifty cantari to squander would look like, and the tall man in the slouch hat and eyepatch was not it. There was something awry here, for the last one he had sold had also had red hair, albeit streaked with some gray, and she had gone to a man he knew well, a seneschal from Cantara, for the sensible sum of thirty-eight cantari.

"One hundred and fifty-five," came a sharp voice. It was the man in crimson again.

"One hundred and sixty!" returned Erno immediately.

"One hundred and fifty-five, I have one hundred and fifty-five," called the auctioneer, avoiding the dubious bidder's eye.

"One hundred and sixty!" bellowed Erno.

"For one hundred and fifty-five cantari to the gentleman in red," declared the auctioneer, and the slavemaster helped the successful bidder onto the dais. He was a man of middling age and girth, richly turned out, but otherwise nondescript of appearance, who barely gave his purchase a second look as he passed her to make his payment to the clerk.

"That's outrageous!" Erno screamed. "You heard me outbid him!" He turned to those around him. "You all heard me!"

But they would not look at him. He did not fit in here and they felt uncomfortable, with his appearance, with his sudden disruption to what had been a very pleasantly forbidden experience—the chance to look upon some foreign women in the flesh, to remark upon their oddly pale skin and hair, the turn of their limbs, and the suggestive curves of their breasts—by some strange alchemy his expensive bid had made them all feel cheap.

Where was the greatsword when he needed it? Erno cursed his stupidity in leaving it behind, cursed Mam for refusing him a weapon of any sort. He gathered himself to make a final surge for the dais, but a familiar and furious voice sounded in his ear. "Stop making an exhibition of yourself, Erno Hamson. There is nothing more you can do. Turn away now and walk back to the doorway where I told you to wait and we will work out how we may salvage the situation."

Erno looked around, quite willing to take out his frustration on the assassin, but Joz Bearhand was already thirty feet away, winding a sinuous course through the crowd. He turned and stared once more at the dais, but if in that one sharp look Katla Aransen had recognized him, she would not acknowledge him now. Instead she was observing her mother being draped in a midnight-blue sabatka and led away by two men in livery. Her face looked drawn and pale, as if all the fight had gone out of her. When the guard came with the keys to unlock her shackles, she waited quietly with her wrists held out, then meekly allowed them to throw one of the enveloping robes over her.

Erno watched in disbelief. The Katla he had known—the bubbling, fizzing kettle-girl—would have hurled herself recklessly into the crowd rather than suffer such humiliation, would have stolen a dagger from an onlooker and fought her way to freedom.

He opened his mouth to call out to her, to reassure her of imminent rescue, but as he did so he found that his throat had developed a hard, choking lump, and a moment later tears were welling behind the tight eyepatch and then cascading down his cheek.

With his head held low, he turned and made his way back through the crowd, which parted, relieved to see him go so that they might return their attention to the fascinating sights on the dais.

20

Adrift

THE Master rubbed his hands and muttered plaintively, but it was no good. The little boat was becalmed. The continuous use of the magic required to propel the vessel all the way from Sanctuary through icy seas and heavy weather had left him exhausted and out of sorts. He needed to rest, to build his reserves. But how could he trust his passenger not to tip him overboard if he slept?

He glanced at Aran Aranson now and the Rockfaller glared back, beetle-browed, suspicious even through the miasma of the holding spell.

To make matters worse, after the sun had gone down, it had become ferociously cold and he had no idea where they were. Not knowing this had been all very well while his magic held true, for by sorcerous instruction the ship had known where it was going, but now that the spell had faded, it was dead in the water. As would be both its occupants unless he managed some kind of miracle.

Relaxing the holding spell on his prisoner was his only choice. It would enable him to gather enough strength to warm himself and the man could at least row them some of the distance and that would keep *him* warm. Slowly and carefully he lifted a corner of the spell and with his mind felt the man's consciousness stir, like a cat beneath the hand.

Row us onward to Halbo, he commanded, using the Voice.

Aran Aranson blinked.

Halbo, the Master reiterated. *Pick up the oars.*

The Rockfaller twitched. Then, like a man in a dream, he took an oar in each hand and slid them into place. Seeing the neat fit of oarhandle through rowlock, Rahe could not help but congratulate himself both on his powers of observation and his magecraft. He leaned forward and tapped Aran on the knee almost fondly. "I was the world's greatest sorcerer once, you know," he said proudly, but the man was not even looking at him, let alone responding with suitable awe, but had begun to scull with a slow sure pace. Rahe lifted the holding spell a little more and watched the man's expression change, become less befuddled, more his own. He began again. "What is your name?" he asked, to make sure Aran was listening.

"Aran Aranson," Aran replied expressionlessly.

"Good, good. Well, Aran Aranson, you are in the midst of the Northern Ocean with the man who was once the most powerful mage in all of Elda. I still am, though time has taken its toll, as it does upon us all. And when I had *her* with me— Well, she was the most immense *resource.* You cannot imagine. Taking magic from her was like dipping your cup into an endless well of sweet water in the middle of a desert. It was extraordinary, enchanting. And she was so innocent. She knew so little, you see. And of course I made sure she knew less and less as time passed; she had such power, such power. It could have been most dangerous, to all of us."

"She?" Aran echoed dully.

"The Goddess, my friend, the Rose of the World, the Rosa Eldi. The heart and soul of this mournful, multitudinous world. The wellspring of magic and love, and who knows what else? Too much power is a perilous thing, and women are unpredictable creatures. I deemed it better for the world that I keep her in a safe place." He smiled smugly.

A crease appeared in Aran's forehead as if he were remembering something difficult, then his eyebrows drew themselves into a single forbidding line, and on he rowed without cease. With each stroke of the oar a mantra began to sound in his head: *Rockfall, Bera, Katla. Rockfall, Bera, Katla.*

The Master settled himself into the bow of the vessel and drew his fur robe closer. It was good to tell someone after so many years. How many had it been since he had sundered the Rose from her roots and brought her to his secret place? Two hundred? Three hundred? He had, in truth, lost count. And all that time there had been no one to tell, no one to boast to. No one but the boy. And he could hardly have told *him* the tale. . . .

On he talked, on and on; and on Aran rowed, though the wind was cruel on his skin and there was ice in the air.

Aran let the words wash over him: meaningless, mad words which touched him not. Instead he read the stars, the sea, the path of the moon.

Rockfall, Bera, Katla. Rockfall, Bera, Katla.

As if the vessel responded to the power of this silent chant that flowed through the rowing man, it veered subtly westward and after a while caught a little wind. The boat picked up its pace. The slack sails filled and bellied and they sailed on, the oars soon merely a useful adjunct to the power of the night air. If Rahe noticed the change of speed or direction, he made no mention of either but continued to talk on and on. Individual sounds fell into Aran's mind, becoming jumbled with his own internal word scheme, so that now, as he rowed, the rhythm extended itself into something far more surreal:

Rockfall, white legs, Bera, Red Peak, Katla, earth power . . .
Rockfall, pale skin, Bera, gold cave, Katla, the cat . . .
Rockfall, hot cunt, Bera, reborn, Katla, Dark One . . .

When the old man finally fell silent and dozed, Aran watched him and wondered whether that sliver of light below the eyelids meant the old man was still capable of observing him, for who knew how a wizard slept, or if he slept at all?

Rockfall, Bera, Katla.

An idea was skimming toward him through the fog in his mind. Like a ghostly tattered vessel, it parted the mists and sailed into clear view. He sat up straighter.

Rockfall, Bera, Katla.

Might he not tip the old man over the gunwale and have done with him? He could manage the craft alone, and alone would probably make better speed. He shipped the oars and inched forward on his seat, and still the old man did not move. But when he tried to stand, he found an invisible barrier between them. Down he sat once more. He stared out to sea, gathering his scattered thoughts, trying to recall how he had come to be here. He sat like this for an hour or more as the good wind pushed the vessel before it, salvaging odd fragments of memory—a sail whipping wildly in storm winds; a cloud of buzzing flies; white bones against silvered wood; a ship going down in the black water between plates of white ice; angry men's faces; a snow bear with blood around its maw—and he shivered.

He had a sense that momentous things had happened, and that he was in some way responsible for them, but what they were, or why they had come about remained elusive. He set his jaw. All that mattered now was the future.

After a while a small island came into view. Aran stared at it, his memory jarred. The Navigator's Star was at his back; the Leopard was rising to his right and the Dragon to his left. It was Whale Holm. He took up the oars again and carried on rowing: one more day at such speed would bring them not to Halbo, but to his home, his wife, and his daughter.

IT was late morning before the mage roused from his stupor. He came awake not like a man refreshed by a good night's sleep, but more like a man surfacing from deep water, slowly and painfully, his eyes blinking against the light.

A gull skimmed overhead, its wail mournful. Aran smiled. He was in home waters now. In the small hours of the night he had navigated the vessel between Sundey and the Cullin Sey: it would not be long before he saw the stacks and cliffs of the Westman Isles. He could feel the draw of the land in his bones.

"What makes you so happy?" the Master asked suspiciously. He looked around at the ice-free water, the dancing, foam-topped waves. Then he closed his eyes and laid a palm against the vessel's bare strakes. A moment later, his eyes snapped open. "You have altered our course!" he accused. He leaped to his feet, too quickly, surely, for a man aged more than three centuries?

Aran gave him a straight look. In another world, his temper had been known to make men quail, but the old man was another matter. "I have," he admitted. He indicated a shadow on the far western horizon. "That is Rockfall, my home. We should reach it before sundown."

The Master glared at him. How could he admit that the holding spell had failed? Offering weakness to such a one as sat opposite him was tantamount to handing him a weapon. Even though he was the most powerful mage in the world (which was probably not claiming much, given his current state) and the other a mere treasure hunter, in truth they were just two men alone on an ocean in a small, unstable craft. It would not take a great deal for the other to unship him. Besides, would it be such a disaster if the man was to see what was left of his home? Rahe had seen the devastation through the crystals in his viewing chamber. The shock of that discovery would likely break this obstinate man's will, make him more malleable and less taxing to deal with. After all, he must reserve his powers for a time of real need. Which would surely come anon. He could not imagine that the King of the Northern Isles would give up his prize without a fight. At last he gave Aran Aranson a sly smile. "Well, then, we shall make a brief visit to your home, and see what hospitality awaits us there."

ROCKFALL did not look ready to offer them much of a welcome, it seemed to Aran Aranson as their small craft rounded the Hound's Tooth. There were no fishing boats bobbing at their moorings, no folk going about their business in the harbor, no smoke rising from the home fires which were usually kept burning all through the winter in these remote isles. He frowned, shaded his eyes.

Behind him, Rahe gave a secret smile. He reckoned they could be gone from here within an hour or two, at the very most by daybreak. He could picture the scene. He, magnanimous in his sympathy, would lead an unresisting Aran Aranson by the arm down the hill from his ruined steading. The erstwhile Master of Rockfall would be pale, nerveless, numb in body and spirit. To an onlooker it would seem an odd reversal: a frail old man guiding a powerful, virile man as tenderly as he might a lost child. He imagined this so clearly, it brought a tear to his eye.

Aran could no longer bear the tension. He grabbed up unnecessary oars, even though the craft was gliding with magic-filled sails, and started to row with frantic haste.

"Calm yourself, dear boy," the mage urged gently. "Save your strength."

But now a figure came into view, and another. For a moment it was hard to make much sense of them, but as the vessel came in sight of the harbor wall they resolved into a tall old woman leading a goat on a string.

"Old Ma," Aran breathed. A smile wreathed his face, sudden light breaking through thundercloud. All was well. If an elderly creature like Ma Hallasen could survive a hard winter with the men gone, someone must have looked after her and her beasts.

He shipped the oars, stood up, and waved his arms. The craft rocked perilously. "Tell my wife I have returned!" he cried as soon as they were within hailing range.

Even as he voiced the words, he knew something to be amiss. Something about Bera, about the way they had parted. Probably an argument. He dismissed this hazy anxiety. He and Bera were always exchanging hard words about something or other. She was that sort of woman, never satisfied to do what she was told, to see his point of view. Her contrariness had always attracted him; it was one of the things he most loved about her, even as it infuriated him to the point of madness. And their daughter was the same, if not worse. His smile broadened. His beloved Katla, most headstrong of daughters. Soon they would be trading words again and she would show him the latest object she had forged, a new pattern weld, a refinement of a classic design.

And old Gramma Rolfsen, too, maker of the best yellowcakes in Eyra, owner of the sharpest tongue and the pithiest wisdom.

Suddenly he was ravenous. Saliva flooded his mouth. His belly grumbled. When had he last eaten? Try as he might, he could not recall. A feast! They would break into the best of the winter stores and show the old man what true Rockfall hospitality meant. Bera was not always the most welcoming of hosts, he knew, especially to unbidden guests, or those rumored to have magical powers. Guiltily, he remembered how she had tried to turn away the seither, and the whole sequence of bizarre events that had set in motion. Strangely though, even though the days and nights surrounding visit of the mummers came clearly into focus, the logical end of the sequence eluded him—something to do with a voyage, something . . . wonderful . . .

But the old woman made no move to rouse the hall. She just stood there on the broad stone mole watching him. The goat watched, too, its golden-slotted eyes unblinking. Then her gaze moved to his companion and he watched her expression change.

He did not know Old Ma Hallasen well; no one did, really. She was mad, that much was acknowledged, and acquaintance was best left at that, if you valued your own sanity. But even so, he felt he could read her face as if he had known her intimately. There was anger there—fear, too—but most of all a deep, deep loathing.

In eerie silence, the craft glided up to the seawall. There, it halted as if of its own accord. It did not nose into the stone with the old familiar grating sound he was so used to, from returning as a boy from fishing expeditions in a tiny skiff, to captaining his first sailed boat, to bringing a longship in to moor for the first time. There was no bustle with lines and cleats, no yells and joyful whoops; not even the barking of dear old Ferg, come to greet his master home. Aran Aranson shivered. He set his foot on the incut stairs, noting even as he did so that they had been left to grow slimy with green weed. No one had used this mooring for many a week, months, more? All at once he felt like a character in an old folk tale: the boy who fell asleep in a fairy ring and slept for a hundred years. Waking, he had found himself in another world to the one he had left, and all the people he had loved long dead and gone. His heart broken, he had gone back to the fairies, as they had known he would do, and given up to them his life and soul, for he had no more use for them.

The old woman's shadow fell over him. She had drawn herself up to her full height and seemed impossibly tall. Behind the silhouette of her bony form, the sky was red as blood.

"Aran Aranson," she said, and her voice was low and powerful, a long way from the reedy babble he remembered. "You are a luckless man. Seeking treasure, you sailed away; but greater treasure you left behind. Seeking fool's gold you have lost true gold. Chasing after an impossible dream, you have forged your own doom. Thus it ever was with men." Her words reverberated in the air between them, and as she shifted her burning gaze to the man behind him, the Rockfaller felt dread settle in his chest, as cold as iron.

"And you, Rahe Mage," the madwoman went on, "are no better, for all your genius. Tricks and flimflam, colored dust thrown into the air to maze the eye, to mask the ugly greed and lust that lies behind the clever hand."

"I thought you were dead."

"You hoped I was dead."

Aran stared at the vagrant woman, then at the sorcerer. All they had in common was their apparent age, and a sort of extravagant shabbiness that suggested a faded grandeur. There was some mystery here which was beyond strange, but it would have to wait. With Rahe's attention fixed on the old woman, the holding spell evaporated and Aran Aranson ran up the slippery steps in two bounds, pushed past Ma Hallasen, jumped over her goat, and dashed along the harbor, his boots echoing on the cobbles.

Rahe and Old Ma watched him go. There was some shadow of sympathy on the woman's face, but the Master was impassive.

"I saw the smoke in my crystals," he said at last. "I take it they're all dead?"

"Dead or taken, and no thanks to you."

"Me?" Rahe turned injured eyes upon her. "I can't see how any of this is my fault."

Ma Hallasen sighed. "Your sort never can. What do you think is likely to happen when you go and disturb the natural order of the world? Human nature is neither benevolent nor peaceable, left to itself." And when Rahe maintained his air of wounded innocence, she put her hands on her hips and thrust her chin at him. "What I am saying, *husband,* is

that if you will go and steal the soul of the world and use her magic and
her body—"

"I—"

"Do not even think to deny it, for I know *exactly* why you had to have
her, you with your failing powers both as a sorcerer *and* as a man. You
are all the same, puffed up with ego and vanity and ready to sacrifice anything to make yourselves feel powerful again. So you set me adrift on the
ocean, and off you go and steal the Rosa Eldi to make her your whore!
And what happens? This!" She gestured behind her with a fierce sweep of
the hand. "Rapine and murder and disgrace. On a small scale, or a large,
it is all the same in the end. Remove the checks and balances which
maintain Elda's equilibrium and chaos ensues. It doesn't take very long
for humankind to drift back into their old ways; they make tribes, they
fight one another, steal each other's land, and set about doing it over and
over again until there's no one left to fight. Then they split into factions
and it all starts again. And we women are picked up, used, bred from, and
cast aside as we get old. It's the same in every world.

"Yet Elda has a goddess, the Rose of the World, a woman with some
real power to make things better, and what happens? A man—a sorcerer,
supposedly wise and powerful in his own right and doing very nicely
with a lovely kingdom of his own, and an exceptional wife—gets all carried away at the sight of a pretty—oh, all right, an *exquisite*—face, kills
her husband, knocks her over the head, and carries her off to his stronghold, abandoning his poor old wife along the way. At least you cast me
off for a goddess, and not some brainless little chit. I suppose that's some
small consolation—"

Rahe said something indistinct.

"What? Don't mumble!"

"I didn't kill him," he enunciated sharply.

Old Ma Hallasen, intrigued now, sat down on the edge of the mole,
her feet dangling, and gathered the goatling to her, so that it settled into
the crook of her arm and began to gnaw contentedly at her sleeve. He
noticed that she wore multicolored, many-holed leggings beneath the
eccentric layers of skirts, and a pair of slippers patched together out of
a dozen bits of old tapestry. Rahe tucked his own ragged shoes beneath

his robe. It was uncomfortable to see Ilyina again; they had always been too much alike.

"So what did you do to him?"

"I buried him under a mountain."

She whistled, then gave a great cackle. "Your skills must have improved after you tupped the poor girl! Under a mountain, eh? That's impressive."

"Not just any mountain. The Red Peak."

"You buried the Warrior inside the Great Volcano? Then why is he not dead?"

Rahe shook his head. "I don't know. He should be. I thought he was. Nothing can survive the heat of that thing. It's the very furnace of Elda down there. But he's not."

The old woman's eyes went big and round in mock horror. "If he's not dead, he'll be trying to escape his prison. And when he does, then he'll be wanting his wife back, and your guts for bootstraps! Oh, dear me, I wouldn't be in your breeches, husband, not when Sirio comes looking for you."

The old man grimaced. Then he shrugged. "Well, I have that in hand. Though I wish now I hadn't put his damned sword in the boat with you. It would have been fitting to give the boy that mighty weapon to deal death to the Warrior—"

Now Ilyina threw back her head and gave a full-throated laugh. "And I thought the fine sword was a gift you'd left me for our son—I even named the boy for it! But no, you filled that ridiculous ship with all those trinkets and treasures to make it look to any who found me like some ancient ship burial, rather than plain murder!"

"Our son?" Rahe looked thunderstruck.

"Husband, there was not just one life at stake when you gave me the sleeping potion and sent me off into the mercy of the ocean's embrace, but two. When I awoke, months later, it seemed I had crossed more seas than any alive now know to exist and my belly was as large as a whale's!"

"But—" Rahe stammered. He frowned. "I hardly touched you in all those months after I first glimpsed the Goddess—"

"Well, someone molested me in my sleep, then!" the old woman declared huffily. "And that someone had your wild red hair, for the lad inherited it from his father, not from me!"

Rahe grimaced. "I was never very good with children, anyway."

"It didn't stop you sowing your seed far and wide, though, did it? All those damaged children, with one eye, or overly long bones, or second sight, or strange powers, or cursed longevity—"

"They didn't all have one eye," Rahe retorted defensively, forgetting he had always denied the illicit forays of which she now accused him. "Festrin did, yes; and Colm Red-hand; but some of them were very handsome."

Old Ma's eyes grew misty. "Ah, he was that, our Tam."

"Tam?"

"Tam Fox: as fine a hero as ever strode Elda. In his time he's killed dragons, scaled mountains, swum seas, crossed deserts, found untold treasures, defended the weak, and fed the starving—and then what does he do? Instead of taking power into his hands, he gives it all up to become a mummer. Comes to me one day with the sword wrapped up and asks me to keep it for him, saying: 'Mam, I am renouncing the ways of men. I shall travel the world making mock of their violence and folly, for Sirio knows that force of arms has availed me nothing.' " She laughed. "He rather took against the Rose of Elda after I told him the tale of how you cast me off for her. His troupe made quite hilarious sport of her at the last Winterfest here, long gold hair of straw, great big tits, and all—"

"She doesn't . . ." Rahe's voice trailed off as another thought struck him. "Then he knows I am his father?" He looked suddenly aghast. "Why did he not come to seek me out in all these years—these centuries?"

Ilyina regarded him with a sardonic eye. "He was not overly eager to make your acquaintance. In fact, it is as well he put aside his warrior ways and entrusted his sword to me, for were he here now, I believe his anger would likely overcome his scruples and he might well demand satisfaction of you on behalf of his dear old mam."

"Where is he, then?" Now Rahe was seriously alarmed. It was one thing to know his enemy was trapped inside a volcano and many thousand miles distant; but it was quite another to have spawned such a dangerously disgruntled son, and one who seemed to have eluded his omniscience.

The old woman gave him a horrible yellow-toothed grin and tapped the side of her nose. "They thought he was dead, but I have seen him in my crystal—"

This explanation was interrupted by a terrible, keening cry.

Aran Aranson had discovered the fruits of his own folly.

THE scrap of red fabric caught in the roots of the old hawthorn at Feya's Cross almost stopped him in his tracks, for it was the same bright color of the handfasting robe that Katla had worn at the Gathering. Then logic caught up with his racing fears and reminded him the dress had long been lost. He had just quelled his beating heart when he rounded a corner and came upon a moldering heap on the side of the path. Long yellow bones protruding through a dry mat of gray hair curled in on themselves to form a starkly elegant shape. An intricate arrangement of claws and pawbones hid the end of a familiar muzzle.

Ferg.

His heart pulsed so hard it felt as if it would break out of his ribs. Their beloved old hound had lain down here to die; and no one had bothered to bury his carcass. Now he knew something was terribly wrong.

It took him three minutes to sprint up the steep hillside, through the old plantation, across the sheep pasture, over the drystone wall, and into the homefield.

At first he did not notice the hastily-raised mounds, the stacks of broken and discarded weapons, the strewn rags or scattered bones, for his gaze was riveted by the sight of the great hall of Rockfall itself, the steading he had renovated with his own hands, the home where he had loved his hard-won woman and where they had raised a family and guided the affairs of their retainers and allies, now unrecognizable. Proud and austere it stood, brooding and ruined, a blackened relief against a backdrop of pink-lit, snow-covered mountains: an eloquent reproach, an untimely reminder of his madness.

The ground felt suddenly unstable beneath his feet. Legs buckling, he came crashing to his knees. The shock of contact with the rock of his home unhinged something in his mind—whether it was the careful guards which he had himself placed on his thoughts, or the cloaking spell in which Rahe had wrapped his memories—and at last it all came flooding back to him: the Allfair, the map, the dream of gold, the loss of his son Halli on the return voyage from the raid on the Halbo shipyard, the making of the *Long Serpent,* the estrangement from his wife, the bad blood with which they had parted, the desperate expedition through the arctic seas and all its consequent disasters; and the realization that in taking every able-bodied man out of the island on a mad, obsessive whim, he had left his home and his family—all he truly cared about in this world—at the mercy of every unprincipled, bloodthirsty raider who could sail a boat or wield a weapon.

Now the details leaped out at him: the spent arrows, the fire-licked stones, the tumbled walls, the charred and collapsed turf roof. All these told the same inescapable story—of assault, resistance, a heroic stand . . . a tragic failure. Before him lay a mound bearing a knotted string which swung pendulously in the evening's light onshore breeze. He did not have to move far to read the tale of those knots: "Here lies Hesta Rolf-sen, giver of wisdom, brave of heart, dead of fire."

He gave out an unearthly cry. It started as a low, guttural grunt of agony, rose in pitch to an agonized bellow, then broke the bounds of all humanity to become the howl of a broken animal.

Afterwalkers

A CONTINENT away, another had breached the boundaries of humanity.

Alisha Skylark, astride a great black stallion, led a ragged army deep into the dead lands of the Bone Quarter. It did not matter to them that the sun beat down like a hammer on an anvil, that the sparse oases had run dry, that the scouring desert winds blew their freight of sand into dunes before them, revealing in their wake the rocky bones of Elda or the skeletons of the long deceased. It did not matter that wide-winged vultures circled curiously overhead or that monsters erupted out of the ground and fled before them; they were all beyond life here. But for the woman who had raised them, it was a different matter.

Since she had brought Virelai back to himself with the power of the death-stone and wakened Night's Harbinger in the midst of that scavengers' feast, Alisha had reanimated soul after soul on her journey into the badlands. She had begun with her son, Falo.

It had been easy enough to retrace her steps back to the site of the vicious ambush by the Jetran bountymen, for it was as if something ineffable drew her south through the night and the day, something which obviated the need for navigation or a lodestone: and there by the river's edge on that wide apron of soft grass beneath the trees she had found his corpse where she had seen him fall. These past weeks, in the heat and the damp of the glade, Falo's body had not fared well. His skin was soft and mottled and swollen with the eggs of flies and carrion birds had taken his eyes; his severed arm lay at a distance from the rest of his pathetic remains, its blackened fingers still curled around the wooden knobkerry with which he had attempted to defend her.

Driven beyond reason by grief, madness, and the possession of the eldistan, she had knelt beside his noisome corpse and pressed the stone upon his forehead with a prayer to the life-force of the world, and in a blinding white light through which she could see only the black shadows of his bones knitting themselves together into some semblance of order up he had got—stiffly, mutely, but inexorably. He was still one-armed and blind, but the stone had gifted him with some kind of new skin that harbored neither maggots nor decay. He recognized her. Of that she was sure, for he turned his head toward her when she spoke his name, inclining one gray ear delicately in her direction as if straining to catch the far tones of her voice, but it seemed that he would not speak, nor do anything unless she willed it. Then she had raised the rest of her erstwhile companions. One by one, the nomads had clambered to their feet—the two old men, followed by Elida and her sisters. Set in their new ashy skins, their decorative piercings twinkled and rang; stones and beads rattled in their braids; feathers and scraps of colored fabric swung jauntily as they moved.

From a distance they looked lively and energized. But up close an observer would have shied away from the emptiness of the dark eye sockets, the grimacing jaws, the clutching hands.

Driven by the one who had woken them, they walked without tiring, without food or sustenance, by the light of the moon or the pulverizing heat of the day. But when Alisha took her attention from them, they came to a halt in mid-stride and stood like puppets hung from a peg waiting for the puppetmaster to animate them again. Often, caught up in a prolonged daydream in which her mind slid sideways into blessed nothingness, stupefied by the sun and the swaying gait of the stallion, she would forget to drive them and turn to find them strung out one by one in the sands behind her in various stages of puzzlement and oblivion. Then she would have to shoo them back into line, impress her will upon them, send them ahead so she could keep an eye on them.

South and farther south they went, into lands long abandoned to the desert. They passed wells whose leather buckets had crumbled away to join the dust of the well-bed a hundred feet below and Alisha brushed a little precious liquid from her last waterskin across her parched and blistered lips and clutched the saving eldistan tighter to her chest. They passed the tumbled-down walls of ancient dwellings outcropping like natural features from the dunes; they trudged through the demarcations of enclosures, stables, barns, grainhouses, all now awash in sand. They walked unknowing above the remnants of gorgeous mosaic pavements, bathhouses, and arenas, through shards of pottery, the shattered bone remains of livestock and domestic pets, over once-cobbled streets and gardens, between the stumps of trees mummified by the blazing air. They passed fallen statues with their features eroded into blind and pitted planes and once, carved out of the soft rock of a great red sandstone cliff, a primitive depiction of the Goddess herself, age upon ages old, no more than a collection of squat spheres, a head, a full-breasted torso, and a vast belly, the vestigial legs open wide across a dark chasm as if the figure were giving birth to the entire world. Alisha scanned that eyeless, pitiless, rose-red face and felt the death-stone pulse in her hand. The power inherent in the likeness lifted the hairs on her spine.

22

The Pursuit

BERA Rolfsen had been dispatched to the stronghold at Cantara, Fat Breta to some town in the Blue Woods, Thin Hildi and Leni Stelsen had been purchased by a merchant bound for Cera; Magla Felinsen by a brothelkeeper in Gibeon (which made her weep and wail fit to wake Sur himself, full fifty fathoms below the Northern Ocean); Kit Farsen and Forna Stensen had been taken by a man from Ixta who had made a sudden fortune selling ropes and rigging for the new fleet. Of Kitten Soronsen there had been no sign at all. Clearly, the Lord of Forent had taken a liking to her, but Katla Aransen did not envy her that dubious honor one bit.

Neither was her own fate clear.

After the bitter humiliation of the slave blocks, Katla had been bundled into the back of a closed wagon with eight other women, all Istrian. Some of them might also have been on the slave blocks alongside her; in their uniform dark robes, it was hard to tell. For the first hour of the journey, she listened to them talking softly in their soft lilting voices, and after a while, worn out by the events of the past days and soothed by the sound of the women and the rhythmic swaying of the wagon she put her head down and tried to sleep, there being nothing else she could do. She had never felt so tired, so defeated, so bereft of ideas.

Sleep came slowly. When it finally stole over her, it brought her a dream.

She was wandering through the streets of an unfamiliar city. Its walls were all of warm colors—ochre and pink and terra-cotta—and wells of dark shadow fell slanting between the houses. Cats lay in these shadows avoiding the sunlight; creatures not much like the sturdy farm cats of home, with their shaggy coats and tufted paws and ears, but sleek and tawny with long tails and faces as precise as ax-heads, more like foxes than cats. They twined around her legs, and around those of her companion. She turned to smile at him and found that she could not see his face, for the hard light made it too luminous to focus upon. He took her hand in his own and drew her close to him, and she felt the contact as a buzzing of energy which ran up her arm and into her chest and skull. There, it met the surge of power which rose through the soles of her feet and filled her legs and torso with endless possibility and delight.

When she awoke, it was with such a sense of loss and regret that she felt sick with it. In the dark, the other women were either sleeping or talking quietly, a sussurus of foreign sound. The tears, when they came, threatened never to stop.

After a while, a hand touched her suddenly on the knee, patted gently, and withdrew.

"You all right?" asked a concerned voice in the Old Tongue.

Katla stifled a sob and pulled herself together, a little shocked that the woman had spoken. She nodded rapidly, hoping to avoid any further inquiry.

"Tell me," the woman who had touched her leaned forward, "are you the one they speak of, the firehead from the north?"

Katla was not feeling much of a firehead at the moment, but, "From Eyra," she agreed at last, "yes."

"Ay-ra." The woman spoke it thoughtfully, weighing each syllable. "You have caused quite a stir in my Lord of Forent's castle."

"I have?" Maybe that blow to his parts had done more damage than she'd thought.

"With all your talk about your way of life, the way the women of Ayra live. Is it true, that you do what you please, that you have your own money, and marry as you will? Or not marry at all?"

And before Katla could reply, another figure leaned forward. "We hear you tell *men* what to do!"

That made Katla laugh. "Well, maybe not quite that." She thought for a moment, and then she told them what she had told Mela and the other women in the castle. While she spoke, the first woman translated with surprising speed from the Old Tongue into Istrian. They asked her question after question. How did one divorce a man? Was it really as easy as announcing it before witnesses? Wouldn't such a disgraced man's family catch her and have her burned? How did northern women spend their days? Were they allowed to teach and be taught? What if a woman didn't want babies, was she shunned away? And, very quietly and shyly: what if a woman preferred other women?

Katla answered them all, surprised by the liveliness of their curiosity, the sharpness of their intelligence. She chided herself for her own thoughtless use, and abuse, of what they saw as such freedoms; she chided herself for thinking of them as less than herself, because they wore their veils and thus seemed to have no individuality, because they let the men of the Empire treat them as they did, because they seemed so submissive, complicit in their captivity.

Suddenly, they were all talking at once. Night fell, but the wagon rolled on. They came to a halt and still the women talked. A man banged angrily on the side of the wagon and yelled at them through the slats. In response, one of the women ripped off her veil and stuck her tongue out in his direction. The other women laughed raucously. Then one by one, they all followed suit, some uneasily, others with defiance.

Katla slowly took off her own veil. There was a moment's silence, then a plump little dark woman pointed at her and giggled.

The woman who had tapped Katla on the knee laughed and translated. "She says you look like a bread stick taken out of the oven too soon!"

But as they approached their destination, all the women quietly donned their robes once more.

"IF you had done as you were told, we'd have saved them all!"

"If you'd told me your plan, maybe I'd have trusted you!"

"If I'd told you the plan, you'd have coshed me over the head and taken all the money to save Katla Aransen!"

They had been raging at one another like this for hours, Mam and Erno. In the end, they had failed to rescue any of the women. Erno's ill-considered bid for his sweetheart had inflated the price of all the other Eyran women beyond what they could afford; since they were all divided throughout the crowd, it had not even been possible to pool their resources and save one or two. In the end, they'd had to call it a bad day and slip away to lick their wounds and consider their next move.

"I don't understand why you will not let me go after her alone!"

Mam sighed. "It's for your own good. How far do you think you will get, alone in a foreign country? You don't even know where she is!"

Erno thrust out his chin. "I'll find out. I'll buy the information—someone must know!"

"With what?"

"With a fair share of the money you've conned out of her uncle!"

The mercenary leader shook her head. "You'll not get a silver until we've had a proper chance to think this through."

"You don't care a damn about any of them. You're just going to divvy up the spoils and sell your swords to the next poor sucker who happens by!"

It was a long night, during which it transpired that no one knew or had been able to find out exactly where the merchant who had bought Katla was from, or where he was going.

Infuriated, Erno leaped to his feet from where the hillman had knocked him down the last time he had erupted. "If you won't give me any money, then I'll bloody well beat the information out of someone!"

Joz Bearhand placed himself silently in front of the only exit, massive arms crossed. "Sit down and cool off," he warned Erno. "Getting yourself killed isn't going to help anyone."

There was nothing he could do but simmer furiously and wait for Mam's seemingly interminable decision. Doc and Dogo were for giving up the entire business, pocketing the fee they'd so far received, and finding themselves a better-paying job; the others argued that they'd accepted a commission and were therefore honor-bound, which made Dogo laugh so hard he almost wet himself, then promptly did when Mam thumped him in the crotch. Eventually, after Mam and the hillman had a short conversation which it seemed was not going to be made privy to anyone else, the mercenary leader declared that the group would travel south to Cantara. It was, after all, Margan Rolfson who had put up the largest sum for the safe return of his sister Bera; in typically pragmatic fashion, Mam had deemed the rest would have to fare as best they might. Protest as he might, Erno had no choice but to go with them.

THEY left Forent in the middle of the night, on horses liberated from a livery yard on the edge of town. The fox-handled sword was slung across Mam's back. She knew if she let Erno carry it, he was more than likely to decide to go it alone, to gallop into the nearest market, sell the princely weapon for whatever he could get for it, draw far too much attention to himself in the process, and get them all tracked down and killed. Besides which, it was a handsome piece and she'd taken quite a fancy to it. Mam was not a woman much given to vanity, but somehow it fit her hands in a way that made her feel she might be the fastest, most dangerous fighter on the face of Elda. She knew all this because on the night when she and Persoa had collected their belongings from the ship, unable to resist its seductive spell, she had unwrapped it and practiced long, graceful swings and lunges, short and deadly stabs, by the light of the moon. The look on the eldianna's face had been most gratifying. He had looked completely petrified.

They made good time, stopping only to water the horses and steal food. Twice, they came off the main road south to avoid other travelers. The first was a well-armed baggage train; then as the sun hit the zenith, they spotted a large band of men heading north. From the undergrowth, with the animals hobbled well back from the thoroughfare, Joz and Persoa spent almost twenty minutes watching them pass. Neither of them remarked on this to the other; there was no need. It was Erno who asked the obvious question.

"Soldiers?"

Joz nodded. "Aye. Over a thousand of them."

Erno frowned. "Why so many? Are they come to reinforce the coastal towns?"

Mam looked pityingly at him. "They'll sail against Eyra before the next full moon, mark my words. Crazy bastards."

"But—"

"All they needed from Morten Danson was his expertise," Doc explained. "Once they have templates from him for the vessels, they can turn them out at speed. They have quite a remarkable operation in the Forent dockyards—teams of men set to fashioning the same piece of ship again and again; one team for the keel, one for the mast, one for the crossbeams, one for the strakes, another for the mastfish, and so on. The construction is carried out in dry dock with laborers hammering together the component parts under a foreman's supervision, then the body of each ship passes on to the next crew who raise the mast and set the rigging. Very efficient process, very quick."

"You sound as if you admire them!" Erno was shocked.

Doc shrugged. "Such functionality has its own attraction."

Joz shook his head. "Even with the best design in the world, I wouldn't reckon much to Istrian workmanship, let alone seamanship! Even if they do make it across the Northern Ocean they'll never take Halbo: the harbor defenses are too well fortified. And what's the point of harrying farther afield? That's not the Istrian way. The whole thing's a wild-goose chase."

Mam laughed. "Aye, and the Rosa Eldi's the goose."

"I prefer my birds with a bit more meat on 'em," chortled Dogo. "Nice bit of breast, eh Erno? Oh, I forgot, your girl doesn't have much in the way of breasts—"

This remark was followed by a shout and a crash and Erno and the little man disappeared with a flurry of fists and kicks into a bramble thicket, during which the hillman stole a kiss from Mam and ran a hand appreciatively down her rump. They grinned at one another. They had a wild-goose chase of their own to pursue: it was what they enjoyed best.

ON the third day, Persoa slipped from his horse to interrogate the road. He knelt on the ground, fanned the dust off the bare rock beneath, and pressed his palms to it. Then he got to his feet, brushed his hands on his breeches, and informed them that the wagons bearing Katla Aransen had passed this way less than an hour ago. A bright light of hope burst in Erno's skull. Then he frowned.

"How can you know that?"

The eldianna gave him a wry smile. "The road speaks to me," he said enigmatically. "And so does the stone."

"What stone?"

Mam shook her head at him. "Something to do with Knobber's moodstone," she said with a grimace. "Don't ask me. Some weird hill magic."

This confused Erno greatly. He had never met Knobber, and knew him only to have once been a member of the mercenary team; but he knew what moodstones were—he remembered a stall selling them at the Allfair the previous year. But when he asked Persoa to tell him more, the eldianna looked dazed and uncomfortable, as if in pain, and changed the subject.

They kicked their horses into a gallop and gave chase. After twenty minutes of hard riding they caught sight of a caravan of wagons far ahead. Erno's heart leaped into his mouth. Was Katla in one of those wagons? His palms began to sweat. Nothing would stop him rescuing her this time. Nothing . . .

As they began their descent into the steep little valley, the sun slipped behind a cloud and a chill fell across the landscape. A moment later when the cloud had passed, sunlight caught something bright on the top of the hill which the wagon train had crested and then a myriad of bright reflections blazed out. Erno shaded his eyes. The hilltop was bristling with shield-bearing soldiers.

"Falla's tits!" Mam swore.

There was no question of continuing their route past official militiamen. Forced to abandon the main road south, they found themselves on backwoods trails, following tracks through unfrequented scrubland and rocky wilderness. Settlements were few and far between, food and water hard to come by. One of the horses broke a leg in a marmot burrow, but at least they ate well that night. The next day another went lame and had to be abandoned. Dogo doubled up with Doc on his nag, and Persoa ran lightly and apparently tirelessly ahead of the group, but they could not keep up the pace necessary to head off the merchant's wagons before he reached the safety of Jetra's rose-red walls.

Not even his first sight of what was reputed to be the oldest city in all of Elda—the tranquil blue of the lake, the elegance of the soaring towers, or the brightly tiled minarets—could alleviate Erno's gloom. He glared from under his hood at the ferryman who took them across the lake to the hidden eastern gate so hard that the poor man shook as he took Mam's coin; he glowered at the doves roosting under its sandstone eaves. He cared not a whit for the ancient carvings or the fabled statues Persoa pointed out. When they passed beneath the rank entrance into the poor quarter, his nose did not even wrinkle at the stench unleashed by the free-flowing sewers there. He paid scant attention to the few uniformed guards left to keep order in the streets and less to the extravagant fashions of the city's denizens. He paid no mind at all to Mam's instruction to keep his mouth shut, his ears open, and his weaponry out of sight. When they split up to quarter the area and make their enquiries, he stalked about impatiently in the hillman's wake, catching him by the elbow whenever he fell to making pleasantries in order to hurry him along. His grasp of Istrian was good enough to understand the unhelpful answers given by the hawkers and servants Persoa queried; but not so fluent that he could form his own questions. His blood was beginning to boil.

By sunset they seemed to have discovered nothing of use. There was no slave market in Jetra, for there was no one, it seemed, left in the city to buy slaves: all the lords and landed men had been called north to answer the muster. A strange lassitude hung over what was usually a bustling hive of commerce, and those still in Jetra were scraping whatever living they could off each other. The lords of the city—Greving and Hesto Dystra—had passed into endless night, carried off by a flux, leaving the governance of the place in the hands of a lesser noble. Many of the winter inhabitants of Jetra had dispersed to their rural retreats to hoard supplies and avoid the tax collectors. And there were no Wandering folk to be seen anywhere—usually the best source of information since they moved across the continent from town to town gathering news and gossip as a magpie gathers shiny objects: with little practical application for them, but with a certain gleeful fascination.

But when the streets had cleared of their daily traffic and the city fell quiet, Persoa tried his next line of inquiry—from the very fabric of the Eternal City. He ran his hands over walls and wells and statues. At once point he got facedown on the ground in the middle of an abandoned square and lay like a dead man. The failing light of the sun gleamed redly off Mam's sharpened fangs when Erno asked the inevitable question.

"Wait and see," was all she said.

At last, the eldianna came back to them. He looked thoughtful, which at least was better than despairing.

"Well?"

"He's here. Or at least his baggage is."

Mam nodded. "Good. Where?"

"Inside the castle, somewhere in the west wing."

The mercenary leader looked surprised. "I wouldn't have thought a mere merchant would be that well connected."

"Given what he paid for the girl, he's got to be rolling in it." This from Dogo.

"True enough."

Joz Bearhand coughed. "Actually, I heard something—" He took Mam by the elbow and drew her aside.

Erno strained to hear their conversation, but Persoa said quickly over the top of their hushed tones, "I should explain some of this to you. To alleviate your anxiety. The man who bought Katla came here. The moodstone tells me this, you see. I slipped it into the merchant's baggage." And when Erno stared at him, uncomprehending, added, "I can feel it. Through the rock, the walls, the ground. I feel it here," he touched his scalp. "And here," his hands, his ribs. "It is what an eldianna is. My people have a—what would you call it?—a connection with the world, an affinity with rock and crystal, and especially with these stones they call the Goddess's Tears. Each one resonates quite differently." He smiled.

"So she's definitely here?" Erno persisted, his attention caught.

The eldianna opened his mouth to respond, but at once his pleasant features contorted, his face becoming abruptly a mask of agony.

"What is it?" Erno asked, alarmed. He caught Persoa by the arm, and drew back at once as if burned. Where he had touched the hillman, his palm and fingers tingled uncomfortably. "Are you ill, hurt?"

Persoa steadied himself against the wall, his breath coming in short bursts. A few seconds later it was as if the spasm had passed and he was himself again. "By the Lady, a death-stone," he muttered wildly, and in the wan light his face looked sallow.

"A what?"

Persoa blinked. He rubbed his hand tiredly across his face. He looked tired. He did not want to open this subject, but Erno's intent expression made it clear he would be unable to avoid an explanation. He took a deep breath. "For some time I have felt an occasional disruption of the world's energies. It's been getting worse the farther south we come. Down in the desert lands near my home someone is using a death-stone—and when they do—" He paused, sucked in his breath. "I feel my soul withering inside me."

Erno remembered the shadow which had fallen across the hillman's face on the road from Forent, his dazed expression, the time he had pulled up short as he ran ahead of them, clutching his side. He was intrigued.

"You mean you can feel something that's happening hundreds of miles from here? I don't understand."

"You've seen moodstones, yes?"

Erno nodded. "At the Allfair, being sold as jewelry and gifts, yes."

"Once, such stones were used for healing—channeling the spirit of the world through a person's body to cleanse and balance. That is why they change color when you hold them—to show the healer your disposition and the resonance of your body's energies. But over the years, as magic was lost from Elda, the healers were persecuted and made outcast, and the true purpose of the stones became degraded to the playthings the Istrians make of them today. But in the wrong hands . . ." he shivered. "Each crystal is a piece of Elda—taken from the veins which channel the Goddess's power through the rock of the world.

"They call me 'eldianna'—man of Elda—because I belong to the world. Among other attributes I have inherited the ability to feel this power. For me, it is like another sense, another way of seeing the world. I use it to navigate. My mother used moodstones to see into another's body and cure aches and pains in the joints; my grandfather used his stone to read the thoughts of another's mind and offer wise advice." He spread his hands. "For my people, such things are second nature. But in these paranoid days they would burn me for witchery if I spoke openly of these abilities. I do not touch moodstones anymore if I can help it. It is too dangerous. And this stone that I can sense is perilous indeed.

"It is said that if the Goddess breathes upon a moodstone, it gives the stone, and the one who wields it, the power over life or death. It can deal death to thousands or restore the dead to life; in the wrong hands it can even wield power over the Goddess herself. There is an old tale told by the hill people. They say that hundreds of years ago Falla made such a death-stone for healing a wise king whose health was failing him because his people came to her and begged her to do so. But this king was also a crafty sorcerer. Fully restored to himself, he stole the stone from the Goddess and used its power to imprison her brother, the god, and to steal away Falla and her familiar, the great cat Bast—"

Mam appeared suddenly to slide an arm around Persoa's waist. "You hill people and your stories!" Then she grinned at Erno. "Tomorrow, we rescue your lady-love, but tonight I think a couple of jars in the Eternal Swan in order."

Erno began to protest, but Dogo grabbed his arm and began skipping maniacally down the alley with him. "Let's water down your ardor with a flagon or ten of Jetra's finest, eh? Keep your hood on, your head down, and shut up!"

THERE was a mixed clientele in the Eternal Swan that night, and not a militiaman to be seen. "Gone north," the innkeeper explained. "To join the muster." He regarded Joz suspiciously, taking in his scarred forearms and meaty hands.

"Aye," said Joz sagely. "This is our last stop before we do the same." He nodded vaguely in the direction of his companions, sitting in the darker part of the room.

"Good man!" The innkeeper thumped the last two flagons down and waved Joz's proffered cantari away. "You go and carry the good fight to those bastards! And bring a couple of those Eyran girls back for me, eh?" He gave Joz a sly wink, then went to serve another customer.

Erno spent the evening watering down his beer, rather than his ardor. He made one flagon last the best part of two hours, and when Dogo teased him for it, went to the bar for the next round. The rest were just too drunk to stop him; as long as someone was fetching the drinks, it didn't seem to matter.

"Water," he said in careful Istrian.

"Water?" The innkeeper laughed. "I guess you want a clear head for your long journey tomorrow."

Erno caught the words *journey* and *tomorrow* and had to fill in the rest for himself. "Yes," he agreed quickly.

"Where you from?" the man asked.

Erno thought hard. "Ah, Ixta," he muttered.

"Ixta! My wife's from there. Nice place, if a bit lively at the moment." He grinned at Erno's blank expression. "Some of you north-coasters find the Jetran accent a bit hard to understand," he said, in the Old Tongue.

"Indeed." Gratitude washed over the northerner. "Tell me," he said quickly, leaning forward. "They say a merchant brought an Eyran girl in here today, took her into the castle . . ."

The innkeeper nodded. "Thinks to ingratiate himself with Tycho Issian, he does. Seems the Lord of Cantara's got a bit of a problem." He leaned forward conspiratorially. "One of the houris told a friend of mine—" he winked, "—that the current caretaker of our fair city has a permanent hard-on. Obsessed with pale-skinned, fair-haired women, he is. Can't get enough of them. Quite literally . . ."

Something in Erno quivered in outrage. And then he became very still.

Tycho Issian. He recognized that name. The innkeeper's gossipy voice receded into the background as he concentrated. *Tycho Issian. Issian.* Suddenly, the name was a sun burning away the fog the seither had set around his memory. *Selen Issian.* Selen Issian poking a charred chicken with a stick as it roasted over a fire on the beach. Selen Issian furiously hurling a sabatka into the flames. Selen Issian wading after him into the ocean. Selen Issian choking up seawater in the bottom of a skiff—

"Wasn't he the one had a daughter called Selen?" he interrupted sharply.

"Terrible business," said the innkeeper. "Abducted by Eyran brigands at last year's Allfair. Her father was stricken with grief, went round the country preaching fire and brimstone. It's him we have to thank for this war, Goddess bless him."

Erno carried four flagons of free ale back to the others, a scheme hardening in his mind.

"Going for a piss," he said indistinctly and left in a hurry.

Dogo guffawed. "He holds less drink than a five-year-old!"

"How would you know?"

Dogo laid his head on Mam's arm and gazed up at her adorably. "I was that five-year-old!"

ERNO stealthily retrieved the greatsword from behind the door, slung it under his cloak, and ran through the darkened streets toward the castle.

23

Katla and Saro

"JUST as Falla's embrace is all-encompassing, enfolding all mankind within her bounteous, welcoming arms to soothe their troubled souls, so a man may be saved by a woman with whom he worships the Goddess in the sacred harmony of the sexual act. Just as the Goddess shakes free each unclean thought and deed from the sinners who come to her as she might shake loose the dead leaves from an autumn tree, leaves which will char away to dust in the heat of her holy fires, so may lying in the heat between a woman's legs purge away a man's sins.

"There are many positions in which a man may bestride a woman to gain the greatest ecstasy and thus join his soul to holy Falla's being.

"The first of these is the stork—"

"Stalk or stork?"

Saro dipped the quill into the inkpot and shook free the excess liquid. He was weary and the flicker of the candlelight hurt his eyes. He hardly slept anymore: when he did, nightmares visited him in the form of his dead brother, his face swollen and black, his eyes bulging. Staying awake was preferable, even though it made him slow and stupid. The inky letters were beginning to blur into one another. They had long since ceased to make any sense to him.

Tycho Issian stopped in his tracks, turned, and cast a scathing look at Saro. "Stork, boy, for goodness' sake. Stork." Leaning against the daybed in the middle of the room, he lifted one leg and demonstrated the position. "Virelai is a far more competent scribe than you, for all your long ancestry and fine schooling. But even a sorcerer cannot be in two places at once."

Saro sighed and scratched out the word. "Where is Virelai?" he asked, hoping to gain himself a short rest.

"Engaged on a project for me. In fact, he is remarkably tardy in discharging his duties." The Lord of Cantara straightened up and went to the door. "Go fetch the sorcerer," Saro heard him tell the guard in the corridor. "And the girl. Whatever state she is in. Tell him I will not take no for an answer. He should know better than to argue."

Another girl. Saro grimaced to himself. Despite all Virelai's best efforts none of them came out looking much like the Rosa Eldi. Istrian women were too rounded, too dark and lush for any illusion to hold for long, let alone one so demanding of its subject. Or perhaps, he thought, remembering how their likeness to the prison guards had faded, it was just that the pale man's magic was not strong enough. He wished it were otherwise. He had grown to despise the Eternal City, this castle, these chambers. But more than anything, he had grown to despise himself: for his weakness, his lack of grit, his failure. And it was hard to forgive Virelai for saving him, however good his motives.

To distract himself from these damaging thoughts, he reached over and picked up the glass paperweight holding down the sheaf of parchments on the desk. It weighed heavily in his hand, a pretty thing— blown glass in classic Jetran blue, with the image of a swan, its neck arched into an extravagantly submissive bow, set at its heart. Candlelight flickered in the depths of the orb, catching the eye, carrying the watcher into what seemed another world.

There came the sound of voices out in the corridor, then the Lord of Cantara reentered the chamber and threw himself down on the daybed—a man filled with too much energy and no outlet upon which to expend it. Saro noted with some repulsion that the lord's robe was tented out in a most obscene fashion. Clearly he had removed the bandages he wore for propriety. Behind him, the guard held the door open to admit Virelai and a figure swathed in a fine azure sabatka. The pale man's gaze swept over Saro, then away again at once, as if he were embarrassed. There was a spot of hectic color in both his cheeks, something Saro had never seen before. He seemed agitated, excited. His hands would not stop moving. They fluttered up to his face, then knotted themselves together, then flew apart like birds. He was trembling.

"I think I have achieved the task your lordship set for me at last," he said, and his voice was unsteady with some unreadable emotion.

The guard hovered at the door, intrigued.

Virelai took the swathed figure by the arm and brought her, unresisting, to stand before Tycho Issian.

"Behold, my lord!" he cried, and swept the shimmering robe away.

The Lord of Cantara sucked in his breath. "It cannot be . . ."

His dark eyes flooded black with desire, he pushed himself upright on the couch.

Saro watched the tableau before him with little interest. In these past weeks, he had seen too many naked women and transcribed too many lewd descriptions of what might be done to them to retain much sense of the erotic when confronted by these odd displays. From his position behind the woman all he could in any case see was a long sweep of silver-gold hair, almost brushing the backs of her knees, shapely calves, and a pair of elegant, long-boned feet with shell-pink nails. Then she turned around.

The body was perfect: slim, white, and glowing, with the most extraordinary breasts—round, uptilted, rose-tipped. His hands itched to cup them. The lines of the face were delicate, yet strong; alluring, yet ethereal, even if the expression was exquisitely blank. He scanned the etched lips, the aquiline nose, the arched brows with growing amazement at Virelai's skill. A pair of dark-fringed, sea-green eyes looked back at him dispassionately, the eyes of a victim resigned to whatever dreadful fate might await her.

Then those eyes flashed with a sudden, unmistakable shock of recognition.

Saro frowned. He had encountered the Rosa Eldi amid the killing fields of the Moonfell Plain; but this was not she. This was but a simulacrum, manufactured by a sorcerer in the confines of his hellish laboratory from whatever unpromising material today's merchant had brought in. There was no possibility that this creature could know him.

Unless, he thought gloomily, the man had traveled up from Altea with some poor servant girl from the Vingo home.

"Where are you from?" he asked suddenly, even though he knew it would displease Tycho Issian to have the girl speak and ruin the illusion.

"The island of Rockfall," the figure replied tersely, and a sudden hardness had come back into her. He watched her fists ball at her sides and a tremor run through her thin frame as if she would launch herself at him then and there and rip his heart out with her fingernails.

And then he knew her . . .

All at once, a great surge of adrenaline crashed back into him. He grinned stupidly, a man reprieved from his own death sentence. "Katla Aransen," he said softly, his voice almost a whisper. "Is it you in there? Are you truly alive?"

At this moment there was a commotion at the door, as if the guard there was scuffling with someone. A moment later, a tall man strode into the entrance. He glanced at the naked form standing on the rich Circesian rug and recoiled.

Virelai hurriedly bundled the woman into the encompassing sabatka and drew her away to the door. It would not do to show his handiwork too freely. The Lord of Cantara might not have him burned for witchcraft, but there were many others who would have no hesitation in sending him to a pyre.

The man stared at them, then shook his head as if collecting himself and came forward. "Lord Tycho Issian?" he said, addressing himself to Saro.

Saro, seated behind the great desk, stared at him, bewildered.

The Lord of Cantara unwound himself sinuously from the daybed, adjusted his robe and stood before the visitor, his face like thunder. "I am Tycho Issian. Who are you and what business do you have with me?"

"I have some information for you," the hooded man said.

The Lord of Cantara frowned harder. "Come and talk to me tomorrow," he said curtly. "I have other matters to attend to now."

"So I saw," Erno returned smoothly. "This information is about your daughter."

Tycho bridled. "My daughter?"

The guard, having retrieved his composure, stood awkwardly by the door. Tycho afforded him a single, scathing glance. "Get yourself gone,

Berio. Attend my orders." He waited until the man had closed the door, then asked smoothly, "How could you possibly know anything about my daughter?"

"I have seen her."

The Lord of Cantara sucked his breath in between his teeth. "Where?"

Erno smiled. "I have a proposition for you, my lord," he said and watched with dismay as Tycho Issian's attention wandered to the shrouded woman behind him. He looked impatient, distracted, utterly uninterested.

"I heard that your lordship may have taken delivery of a woman from the Northern Isles this day," Erno persisted loudly.

Those sharp black eyes swung back to focus on him. They were brimming with malice. "What of it?" he snapped.

"I would buy her from you."

"I will not sell her!" the Istrian lord said flatly.

"Not even for information as to your beloved daughter's whereabouts?"

Tycho Issian gazed at him with narrow eyes. "I will make a bargain with you," he said softly. "Tell me what you know and I will allow you to live."

This scenario was not playing itself out at all as Erno had expected. He felt suddenly foolish, out of his depth. He had thought to make a trade with a distraught and loving father, not a reptilian creature with all its thoughts bent on satisfying some immediate and perverse lust.

"Unhood yourself," the Lord of Cantara demanded. "Let me see who it is who dares to thrust himself past my guard and into my private quarters at such an hour."

Slowly, Erno drew back his hood.

Tycho took in the visitor's ill-dyed mane of hair, his light eyes, and strong jaw. "What is your name?"

Erno had prepared for this. "Alesto Karo," he said.

"Your parents had a fondness for sacred poetry, did they?" the Lord of Cantara spat venomously.

Erno nodded, disconcerted by the man's response. He had taken the name from one of the best known ancient Istrian ballads, a lay so popular it was recited even by the northern bards. Alesto—the mortal man plucked from Elda to pleasure the Goddess herself—who had sacrificed himself in her fires for her love. It had seemed quaintly appropriate at the time.

But Tycho Issian's face had become dark with blood, as if a storm were brewing inside him. A moment later it was unleashed. "You think to steal my goddess, do you?" he roared. "You come here offering lies and extortion in the presence of this vision! You slimy worm, you fetid toad, you filthy snake! Alesto the Lover, indeed. More like Alesto the Crawler! You are not fit to lick the soles of her feet—you . . . you . . . dungfly!"

Erno swung around to see to whom the madman could be referring, and saw only the draped figure by the door. Confusion set in; then with a horrible rush of intuition he could not explain, he knew her. "Katla!" he cried in Eyran, "is that you?"

There came a sharp intake of breath from the figure. Then it simply said, "Erno . . ."

His heart ignited. He whirled around only to find the Lord of Cantara advancing upon him murderously, the front of his robe thrust out by some giant erection. Now Erno saw the imminent danger Katla faced, and at the same time cared nothing for the peril he was in himself. In fact, he realized, he cared nothing for anything or anyone beyond Katla Aransen at this moment. If he could only save her, the rest of the world could burn.

He put his hands out in a placatory gesture.

"My lord, I have not finished with my bargaining—"

This drew Tycho up short. He stared at the man called Alesto suspiciously.

"I know that your lordship is engaged upon a holy war with the north," Erno said as quickly as his facility with the Old Tongue would allow him. "I have heard tell of a mighty weapon which would help you win this war. An artifact which has the power—they say—over life and death."

Both Virelai and Saro became deathly still; as if sensing their attention, Tycho listened.

"It is a moodstone, graced by the touch of the Goddess, to become what the hill people call a death-stone. It can heal the sick and raise the dead. It can strike men down in their tracks. Imagine what you could do with such an object, such a weapon. I know a man who could lead you to it, if you will only give me the girl—"

"No!"

It was a wail of inhuman despair. Behind the Lord of Cantara and the man who would trade all Elda for the sake of a single woman, there was a sudden blur of motion. Then with savage strength, Saro Vingo pushed the Istrian lord aside, his face a mask of hatred, and hurled himself at Erno Hamson. His arm came back and then descended as fast as a striking hawk, and the candles in the chamber lent whatever it was he held in his hand a wild blue light.

It all happened so quickly that Erno had no understanding of what had transpired. It was as if one of Sur's lightning bolts had struck him out of a clear sky. He swayed where he stood, blinking stupidly through a thick curtain of blood, trying to recall what it was he had been saying, and why, but all he could think of was sitting on the mole at Rockfall Harbor on a late autumn evening, fishing for crabs with a girl whose hair flared crimson in the dying sun, wanting to lean over and kiss her, but fearing that if he did so he would spoil the moment.

That perfect moment.

A slow, rapturous smile spread itself across his face. "Ah, Katla," he whispered, "Katla . . ." And then he crashed to the floor, his cloak billowing up and over his ruined head like the wings of a crow mantling over its kill.

For two—three—seconds no one moved. Then Katla Aransen leaped across the space between her and the fallen man and with a single practiced motion swept the exposed greatsword from the scabbard across the dead man's back. It was too big for her, and heavier than she had expected; but even so, the weapon sang in her hands, a fire which burned up her arms.

The Lord of Cantara had no hesitation in saving his own neck. He grabbed Saro Vingo and shoved him at the robed woman with all his might. Saro went stumbling, the bloodstained paperweight flying from his hand to shatter into a thousand bright blue shards against the far wall, and collapsed in a heap at Katla's feet. There, instead of hurling himself upright again or trying to escape, he knelt on the floor, breathing hard, his throat stretched out and vulnerable, his hands spread, willing her to deal him the death he deserved.

For a long moment they gazed at one another. Saro could feel the heat of her loathing scorching through the azure veil. He waited for the killing stroke to fall.

And Katla would gladly have dealt him the death he sought, were it not for the sudden appearance of the guard.

"Don't kill her!" shrieked Tycho Issian. "Just get the damned sword away from her—"

Berio looked at Katla, a bizarre apparition in azure silk. Istrian women knew nothing about swords—you could tell by the way she was holding it. He laughed. He had been interrupted by a shout just as he was in the pleasurable process of taking a dump, which was in itself annoying—but to be interrupted just to disarm some loopy whore was beyond a joke.

"Come on, love," he said reasonably, advancing on her with his own weapon in his hand. "Drop the sword."

His patronizing tone infuriated Katla, even if the foreign words were no more than a jumble of sound. With a howl of rage she ran at him and took his arm off neatly at the elbow, sword and all. It described a graceful arc, gouting an elegant fountain of blood through the air, and landed at Virelai's feet, spattering gore up the front of his robe. The sorcerer—already deathly sallow—paled further; and fainted.

More guards were coming: with the preternatural senses of a woman suddenly eager for survival, she could hear their footsteps on the stairs. She glared at the southern lord, at the boy kneeling on the floor, at the fallen sorcerer, the dying guard. Bending swiftly, she pulled back the cloak and kissed the dead man gently on the forehead.

"Erno Hamson: I will avenge you, I swear it."

Then she turned and ran, the greatsword tucked awkwardly under her arm.

SARO Vingo cast one wild look at Virelai's still form, then another at Tycho Issian, standing stunned as if by the sight of so much blood, so close to his own precious person, and fled after Katla Aransen.

He caught up with her in the stairwell, facing off a pair of uniformed guards, bemused by the sight of a silk-shrouded houri wielding a huge and gory sword. As it was, the greatsword was not an ideal weapon in such an enclosed space, but the guards seemed to be making up their minds to deal with the bizarre situation. The first one drew his own sword—a stubby, brutal-looking thing—and advanced up the stairs. Made nervous by the sudden appearance of Saro in her peripheral vision, Katla lunged forward with a swiftness the guard had little expected and stuck him with considerable precision through the neck. Cartilage creaked and parted. Blood fountained. Kicking his flailing body off the point of her blade into the path of his companion, she spun around, teeth bared at Saro like a beast at bay. Red-streaked and lethal, the greatsword hovered suddenly at his own throat.

"Tell me why I should not kill you!" she demanded fiercely.

"If you kill me, I cannot save the world."

"A large claim." Through the azure veil, eyes glittered balefully. "I have sworn to avenge my friend, who came to save me."

Saro looked anguished. "I had no choice. Oh—"

Tycho Issian had emerged from his chamber into the shadows at the end of the passage, a curved and wicked-looking blade in his hand.

"I don't suppose you've any more useful paperweights?" Katla asked scornfully. In the same breath, she kicked out at the second man, catching him on the kneecap so that he swore and lowered his guard. The angle was too narrow for the greatsword. Frustrated, Katla shoved past him like a charging bull and sprang down the remaining stairs. "All yours!" she called back over her shoulder.

Saro regarded the recovering guard nervously. What use was weapons training when you had no weapon? In desperation, he drew himself up and adopted his loathsome brother's haughtiest tone. "For Falla's sake man, get out of the way!"

Born to a life in service in that most orthodox of cities, the guard all but bowed and stepped aside politely. If the man had had a forelock, he'd most likely have tugged it.

Taking his opportunity, Saro dived after Katla, stopping only to retrieve the dead guard's sword.

The Eyran girl ran on to the end of the passage and down another flight of stairs, a blaze of azure against the dark sandstone walls. Down here on the second level of the castle where visiting nobility usually stayed, all was silent and dark, since no one had bothered to light the sconces. Neither had they stationed any guards on this floor, but pursuit was not far behind, and Saro had little more idea of the way out than the robed woman who ran grimly beside him. They passed door after door, but instead of checking for a possible escape route, Katla just kept running. At last, turning a tight corner, the greatsword caught in the billowing blue robe and tripped her headlong, then spun away from her with a clatter fit to wake the dead.

"Sur's bollocks!"

A moment later she was on her feet, seething with bad temper. She tore the veil from the rest of the sabatka with a vicious rip, revealing ragged hair of barely shoulder length, distinctly more red now than gold. Then she grabbed up the back hem of the robe and knotted it up at her waist, transforming it into a most outlandish garment indeed. Grinning triumphantly, she reached to retrieve the blade, only to find it in Saro's hands.

At once, she sprang at him, a bundle of coiled energy, Eyran obscenities pouring from her. Hatred seemed to crackle from her skin, her hair, her eyes: she looked wild, foreign, mad, possessed.

Saro backed away, terrified. The images coming at him from contact with the greatsword were bewildering, unspeakable. He held it out to her unsteadily, an offering to propitiate a primal force of nature.

"Here, take it. I only picked it up for you—"

Their eyes locked, and in that moment Saro acknowledged that the dream he had hugged to himself of the girl he had encountered at the Allfair was just that: a figment, a construction of his own feverish mind. The sight of the figure which had stood in defiant challenge on top of Falla's Rock, her hair a nimbus of fire, her naked limbs gleaming in the early morning sun, had all but stopped his heart. The memory of those sea-gray eyes and those arched kestrel-wing brows had visited him in his sleep night after night after night. He had, he admitted, harbored secret desires for her in life; then mourned her in what he had thought to be her death. Now, confronted with the unpredictable and elemental truth of her—more goddess than girl—he knew he had deceived himself if he had ever imagined they might be together.

She took the sword from him gravely, her fury ebbing as swiftly as it had risen. As her anger ebbed, so did Virelai's illusion, and she was Katla Aransen once more. But the delay had proved lethal. Within seconds, Tycho Issian came hurtling around the corner, knife at full stretch before him, followed by a contingent of guards.

Katla grabbed Saro by the arm and together they flew around the next bend in the corridor, only to be confronted by a dead end with a door set in it. A locked door. Katla wrenched at the handle, but the effort was futile. They turned and faced their pursuers, swords drawn.

"To die like this," Saro said through gritted teeth, "would be a good end." He was surprised to find he meant it.

Katla flashed him a feral grin. "Get ready to die, then, but don't forget to take as many of the bastards with you as you can!"

Seeing that the pair meant to make a serious fight of it, Tycho Issian allowed the guards to overtake him. It had not escaped his attention that the goddess he had been preparing to mount had somehow been transformed into a dreadful redheaded hoyden. His interest in keeping her alive wilted abruptly. "Kill them both!" he ordered and left the militiamen to do just that. He had seen enough blood in one day.

Despite the odds, this task was not to be easily achieved. The passage was too narrow for the Jetrans to come at them more than two abreast. Katla ran at the first pair, shrieking like a banshee. A spatter of hot blood hit Saro's face, making him blink in shocked stupefaction. He had no more time to register the mashing sweep of Katla's greatsword or the vile sight of brain through bone as the first guard toppled before the second man was upon him. With sheer gut instinct, he raised the purloined weapon and iron screamed on iron. The force of the parry numbed him so that he almost dropped the sword, but the killing stroke was deflected. Throwing out a wild hand for balance, his fingers brushed Katla Aransen's bare arm, transferring instantly to him a rage and confidence he knew was not his own. Whatever its source, it saved his life. With a skill and speed that should never have been possible for Captain Galo Bastido's worst pupil, he feinted left and brought the tip of his sword up under the guard's right arm, skewering him so hard through the ribs that the air came whistling out of his lungs and he slumped forward onto Saro.

The rush of the man's death stymied him so that he stood there for precious seconds under that weight, absorbing his agony and despair. It was Katla who kicked the dying man clear, but a moment later two other guards had taken his place and more crowded in behind them. Soon, it was hard to find sufficient space in which to wield the length of the greatsword. With a curse, Katla relinquished it to the flagstones and swiped up one of the fallen guards' short swords instead. This, she swept about with such ferocity that the men were forced to retreat a pace, then two, until they were backing into one another, losing their balance, cursing. When disarray turned to complete shambles, their sergeant barked something at them and they all pressed themselves back against the walls, leaving the ground clear between the officer and their quarry.

The sergeant lowered his crossbow at Katla, grinning. "Seems a shame to shoot you dead, lovely," he leered. "Perhaps we'll just wing ya and have some fun." Then he turned the weapon on Saro. "Not much use for you, though, son. None of my lads fancies arse much." He wound back the mechanism with slow deliberation.

Behind the sergeant, there was a movement in the shadows, and abruptly the point of a blade appeared through the front of his tunic, so that it rapidly changed color from fine Jetran blue to sodden red. As he toppled, his bulky shape was replaced by the lithe form of a hill man, withdrawing his elegant desert blade with economic grace. Behind him came a figure out of nightmare, its sharpened teeth gleaming in the darkness; then a small fat man, a tall gaunt one, and the looming figure of a giant.

"I think the odds are a bit fairer now, don't you?" Mam jeered. Hot wafts of beer breath filled the narrow space they shared.

The guards turned to defend themselves, but half of them were drunker even than the mercenaries, the rest barely awake, and one pissed himself in terror, even as two blades pierced him, front and back.

24

The Melting Pot

THE messenger from Forent arrived the next day. The missive he carried was both brief and to the point. An expeditionary force was ready to set sail and awaited only the presence of joint commander Tycho Issian, with or without his sorcerer. Despite the arrogant tone of what was in effect a summons, the Lord of Cantara sensed Rui Finco's glee, and his impatience. He had a plan, he was confident of success; they must strike swiftly.

Tycho Issian was not convinced. Still inflamed by his sight of the transformed woman the night before, he found himself in turmoil. He must capture the Rosa Eldi to keep his sanity, but in order to keep her, they would have to subdue the barbarians entirely. And what of this "death-stone" of which the intruder had spoken?

A mighty weapon . . . an artifact with power over both life and death.

He would have scoffed at the very idea, had not the Vingo boy leaped up and struck the man down before he could say more. For a mild-mannered lad, Saro had shown admirably murderous zeal, but whether he had been spurred to the deed to make the man silent, or because he had perceived his outland origins was likely to remain a mystery. It was a great shame he had made his escape. On the one hand, he would have been well employed on any foray into enemy territory; on the other, he might have cast more light on the matter of this killing-stone. Tycho felt his fingers itch at the very thought of wielding such ultimate force. He had never regarded himself as a power-hungry man. Fervent, yes, and pious. Between them, he and the boy's brother, Tanto Vingo, had brought hundreds of souls to stoke Falla's fires before the cripple had been so un-timely dispatched to join them.

But how many more might he be able to offer the Lady if he had do-minion over all of Elda? And how better to achieve such dominion than by laying his hands on a magical weapon?

Since Virelai and Saro appeared to have struck up an unusually close friendship, he had taken the precaution of having the sorcerer confined to the rack while he was still unconscious. With Saro gone and Virelai a natural coward, he was sure a judicious turn or two of the screws would render up further information about the stone.

"HE was obsessed, besotted."

"He spoke of nothing else."

"Do you remember his face when I told him she was still alive?" Mam turned to Dogo.

"Could've fried an egg on it!"

"Thought he was going to dive overboard and push the damned boat to Rockfall!"

Katla sat there, staring at her feet. She did not know what to say, how to respond. She felt numb, stupid. Instead of replying, she turned to stare at Saro Vingo, lying on his side at the back of the stable, trussed up like a goose for the oven, a clout in his mouth. His hands were clenching and unclenching though he was fast asleep; and runnels of sweat ran across his face even though it was a chilly night.

"We should just kill him and leave him here," she said at last. "He's just another filthy Istrian when all is said and done."

Persoa raised an eloquent eyebrow.

"Don't take offense, my honey-boy," Mam said softly. "Hill tribes is only technically Istrian." She leaned across to Katla. "Girlie, quiet down. I know you're upset about the lad. We all are. But at least this one should fetch us some hard cash, and Altea Town's not far from where they've taken your Ma. Providential, really. Sur must be smiling on us." And she treated the gathered company to her ghastly grin.

"AND you say there are no slaves in your country?"

"Nor any houris?"

"Well—" Bera Rolfsen hesitated. "We have no slaves, that is true. We have bondsmen and women, but we pay them for their work and afford them home and shelter for the duration of their lives, and often their own piece of land and livestock to tend. As for ladies such as you call 'houris,' well, we have a different word for them—"

"And what is this word, may I ask please, Be–ra?"

Bera could not help but smile beneath the enveloping black robe, despite the discomfort of the wagon and the rather dire circumstances in which she found herself. "Er, whores . . ."

"And your 'whores,' do they learn the sacred arts and worship the Goddess with the men who visit them?"

"Such an act is not generally regarded as sacred in my country," she said primly. "It's more of a business transaction."

"You mean, the men pay these women directly?" The speaker sounded puzzled.

"Of course. Do they not here?"

"Never!" The woman was shocked. "Women never touch money in *my* country. It is defiling." She paused, then whispered something to the woman beside her in Istrian. When the second woman responded, two or three others joined in the discussion. At last she said, "Hana here says there are men who take payment for what we do and do not donate all the money to the shrines as they say they do."

Bera laughed. "I'm sure they don't."

"But that is very wrong."

"In Eyra," Bera said firmly, "women choose with whom they share their bodies, and if they take payment for it, that is their own business. No one can force them without punishment. Women are regarded as equal to men under our law, even within marriage. We are educated alongside our brothers. We run our own homes, we have our own money, and we inherit property. And if a husband turns out to be a bad lot, his wife can declare herself divorced from him. I have done this myself."

This was astounding news. Then: "Your men must be very weak!"

"Not at all. They are big, strapping men, hard of muscle, strong of arm, fierce in war—"

"Weak of mind, is what I meant."

Bera laughed. "Well, they are but men, and they have their weaknesses, as all men do."

"And why did you 'divorce' your man?"

So Bera told them the sorry tale of Aran Aranson's obsession, his greed for treasure, his dream of gold, his love of adventure, and the romance of Sanctuary; how he had channeled all their resources—both financial and human—to the construction of his expedition ship. How their son had been lost at sea. How their island had been left undefended. How they had heroically held off their attackers for so long; how her daughter had taken the lives of many raiders; how her own mother had died a stoic death.

There was an awed silence at the end of all this. Then the woman told the same story, at what seemed even greater length, to the rest of those who spoke only Istrian; and soon they all had something to say.

The first woman tapped her chest. "Felena," she explained. "Felena Taro. My father gave me to his brother and his brother's friends when I was twelve. They returned frequently, and we ate better after they had gone. Then, when I was fifteen, he gave me to the Sisters. I dare say he took money for that, too," she said darkly. "Teria, over there, says she has worshiped Falla with more than three hundred men, so someone must be very rich for all her efforts. Finita has an idiot brother, who can barely make a sum or write two words, yet he has inherited all their family estates, while she was sent to the blocks. And Hana's father is a lord who lost all his fortune gambling and made her part of his last stake. She was then exchanged with another man for the price of two camels. Two camels!" Now her voice was shrill with outrage. "That is all they think we are worth. If they cannot raise a good bride-price for us, they will take whatever they can lay hands on, and care nothing for our welfare. In some parts of the country—in the Blue Woods and the Skarn

Mountains—baby girls are left out on the hillsides to die, to nourish the wolves and the foxes, they are worth so little." She paused. "Although there are some men who value their daughters more highly. Finita says the Lady of Cantara's poor daughter was stolen away by brigands at the Allfair last year, and that that is why her husband—Lord Tycho Issian— has launched this holy war against your people. He does so to bring her back; and to liberate your women from the barbarian practices of the North, to bring *you* back to the Goddess."

Bera snorted. "Barbarian practices, indeed! I think it is the women of Istria who need liberating, not those of the Northern Isles! Besides, this holy lord of yours is the one who tried to have my own daughter, Katla, burned at the Allfair when she brought news of what had really happened to his daughter Selen."

Now she had their attention. "And pray, lady, what happen to her?" begged another in broken Old Tongue.

"Why, it was not good northern men who took her! She was raped by the man who was to be her future husband, one Tanto Vingo—"

This elicited hisses and tongue clickings and a great deal of chatter and more questions asked and answered. Despite the complaints of their handlers, they were still full of fascinated conjecture and lively debate four days later, when the wagon drew into Cantara.

"WILL he never wake up?"

Rahe strode up and down the main cavern in a magnificent huff, every so often stopping to stare down at the prone body of Aran Aranson.

Ilyina smiled to herself. She knew her husband too well. He would be away from here in pursuit of the golden one as fast as he could, were his navigator awake and in any state to wield an oar. She was enjoying the subtle torture of delay she was inflicting on him. In the pretense of checking on the Eyran's health, she bent over his pallet and ran a hand across his forehead.

"How is it with you, Aran Aranson?" she said softly, while her fingers tied privy knots in his hair that would bind him to sleep for another week at least. She had a promise to extract from Rahe before she would allow him to leave, but he was not yet sufficiently worn down by frustration that he would agree to it. Another week or so should do it, she reckoned. He had never been a patient man, the Master, despite the longevity of their kind, nor did he seem to be improving with age.

MAKE no move till I have smelled you well.

The voice rumbled in his head, inescapable as death, and so he stood stock-still, barely daring to breathe. To be all but naked in this fearsome place was grim enough; but now to suffer the perilous attentions of this fanged creature seemed a trial too great after the many hard miles he had traveled.

I know your scent . . .

A tenebrous shape prowled about him. Lit by a hunter's moon, its vast muzzle quivered with curiosity and its vast amber eyes seemed to whirl in the darkness, as if the beast were sifting through all the scent-related information it had ever gleaned.

You smell like him, but you are not him, it said at last into his mind. *Which is as well. For if you had been him, I would have had to eat your head.*

There followed a brief pause, a lull before violence. Then there came another great rumbling which set his skull aquiver, made his heart beat fast and his legs tense for evasion, until he realized that the sound was not a growl which signaled murder, but the monster enjoying some private amusement.

In all his long life, he had not known that cats had a sense of humor.

It did not make him feel any easier about his new companion.

Invasion Fleet

RUI Finco gripped the gunwale and stared out into unrelieved grayness. Gray sky; row after row of gray waves, rolling relentlessly to a gray horizon. His expression was intent, his knuckles white. Not from fear of the unknown, for he had crossed this ocean before; not from seasickness, for he did not seem to suffer. No, his tension was caused by embarrassment at the scene which had played itself out on the quay the previous day, and from a certain fury at his own shortcomings.

He had, he had to admit, given too little thought to the practicalities of the voyage, too much to the wished-for outcome. He had visited the Forent shipyards only once in all the long weeks during which Morten Danson had been overseeing the construction of the invasion fleet, and that had been early in the process, when the ships were little more than curved, bare keels. He had nodded sagely, admiring the clean lines of the wood, the workmanship of the laborers, but his mind had been on other things. Dreams of grandeur and riches; dreams of power.

So when he had walked the length of the dock with the Eyran ship-maker yesterday in preparation for the embarkation, he had asked a very stupid question. "Where is my flagship?" he had demanded brusquely, his eyes flickering dismissively over the troop ships with their open rowing benches and stacked crates of weaponry.

"Why, here, my lord," Morten Danson had replied proudly. His extended hand indicated a longship fine of prow, proud of line, and entirely devoid of shelter or any sign of comfort.

"That?" He had stopped dead in his tracks, his mouth gaping. "Where are the cabins? Is there more of the vessel below the waterline that I cannot see?"

Twenty years ago, during the last war with the Northern Isles, he had crossed the sea in a vessel of solid, old-fashioned Istrian design, a three-decker galley with two hundred slaves chained to their oar benches in the deepest compartment and the outer parts of the second deck around the comfortably appointed sleeping quarters, chartroom, and well-stocked kitchen used by the nobles and their officers. Only the lowliest members of the crew spent their time above decks in the teeth of the weather.

But unfortunately such vessels were constructed solely for bombast and close-range bullying; as serious, ocean-going warships, they were useless. Unstable in any but a mild sea, unmaneuverable in all but the widest and deepest of channels, the majority of the fleet had foundered before even reaching their destination.

Which was why he had gone to the trouble of acquiring a master craftsman from the Northern Isles to design a fleet which would weather the heavy seas of the crossing. Beyond that, imagination had failed him. And so he had not considered such things as living quarters and other quotidian matters.

"I can't sail an ocean in that! Where will I sleep? How shall I have any privacy? Besides—" as the true implications struck him, "—I'll be soaked, frozen!"

Morten Danson turned a bemused face to him. "The ship is what it is, my lord—one of the finest examples of my craft I could create under the time constraints. This is how the men of my country travel, both king and commoner—" His eyes widened suddenly.

The Lord of Forent had turned to discover what had attracted the man's attention, and found a long snake of servants making their way down the cobbled streets from the castle bearing all manner of goods with them. In their vanguard, six stumbling slaves struggled with a vast four-poster bed, complete with swaying silk hangings and a mound of coverlets.

Behind the Istrian lord, a bark of laughter was unsuccessfully stifled. Rui Finco had whirled around, his face accusing. Morten Danson amended his expression swiftly. "The men of Eyra will sometimes—if the weather is particularly bad, or if a lady is brought aboard—erect a tent for shelter. But usually they prefer to sail light and to sleep in bags made from sealskin sewn into a walrus hide—"

"Seal? Walrus? We have no such creatures in the southern continent!"

The shipmaker looked thoughtful. "A sleeping roll made from bearskin or sheepskin would be warm, my lord." He paused. "If not particularly waterproof."

Rui Finco groaned. He waved the stumbling servants away. "Take it all back to the castle, you fools. What place is there for such luxuries on a ship like this? Imbeciles!"

He caught Morten Danson by the upper arm and his fingers tightened mercilessly. "One word of this to anyone and your head shall adorn my prow," he warned. "Now go and sort out a tent for myself and another for the Lord of Cantara. The men will have fend for themselves. And you'd better do the same for each of the other captains, or there'll probably be a mutiny."

Now, he turned back from the rolling waves and surveyed his rolling ship. The sail was full. It sped along the tops of the waves like a mountain goat. He had to give the shipmaker credit for that, at least. Beyond their creamy wake, the rest of the fleet trailed away into the vanishing point. For the first time since the intense embarrassment of that scene on the dock, Rui Finco felt his heart swell with pride. Here he was, master of his own fate, leading an invasion force by craft and stealth into Eyra to avenge his family's long-lost honor. He took in the leather tent in which he had smuggled on board his bundle of silk-and-wool covers, some wine, a lamp, and his stack of diagrams and charts and summoned a smile. He, at least, would be enjoying some measure of comfort on this voyage. Unlike the poor bastard amidships, heaving his guts up over the side. Grinning, now, he left the command of the vessel with his sea captain and sought a retreat beneath the leather shelter.

THE "poor bastard" was Virelai, who was finding the motion of the ship impossible to bear. It was strange, he thought, in a rare lucid moment between heavings, that he had not experienced this torture on his escape from Sanctuary in that tiny sloop, which had been even more at the mercy of the waves than was this great ship. He had already wished himself dead a hundred times since they had set sail the previous day. He, who had rarely experienced physical extremes of any kind in his short existence, was now subject to all-consuming nauseas, thumping headaches, and tooth-grinding stomach gripes. He had never felt so mortal, not even when subjected to Tycho Issian's attentions in Jetra's dungeons.

The Lord of Cantara had had him racked in his quest for the killing-stone the dead stranger had spoken of. Tycho had obviously had a low opinion of his courage and willpower, for after only two hours of torture, during which Virelai had let his mind unfetter itself as his body could not and produced for the entertainment of the southern lord snippets of the songs with which Alisha Skylark had sung little Falo to sleep, lists of herbs, and the names of every yeka and the nomad with whom the sorcerer had ever traveled—all of which was as close to telling his torturer the whereabouts of the death-stone as he dared—Tycho Issian had given up and released him from the bonds without doing him any further damage. Had the Lord of Cantara owned any subtlety, he might have deduced some warped logic in all these ramblings, but the man was so obsessed, so impatient, that he simply could not be bothered to give it any thought, and had decided that the sorcerer knew nothing, that the stranger had been raving, and that Saro had brained him out of sheer personal loathing.

Virelai, in the relative safety of his chamber that last night in the Eternal City, with his arms and legs regaining their sensation in the most painful manner possible after blessed numbness, had been surprised by his fortitude in not giving away what he knew. He had, over the days which followed, congratulated himself on his loyalty to Saro and to Alisha, for all her madness, on his integrity and his strength: never qualities he had considered that he owned. And then—just as he was getting used to seeing himself in this more flattering light—he had found himself in the middle of an ocean on this vile, pitching ship, throwing his newfound pride up over the side along with his lunch, his breakfast, and yesterday's dinner.

"I TELL you, it should be me who fetches her out, not you!"

The Lord of Cantara was puce in the face now, a color evident even in the unsteady light of the guttering candle. He had pushed his way into the Lord of Forent's private shelter without any query or acknowledgment and demanded to be the first to set foot on foreign soil.

When Rui Finco had explained, with considerable care and patience, that the first part of his plan required only himself and Erol Bardson, Tycho Issian had erupted.

"You mean to take her for yourself! I know it, I know it! You want to steal her and fuck her, right under my nose!"

Quieting him down without demolishing the makeshift tent had required determined effort, followed by a sharp, breath-stealing punch under the ribs. At this, the Lord of Cantara had subsided into all the lush bedding, where he had stared around, still wordless from lack of air, with growing suspicion, taking in the other man's fine clothing, the elegant silver circlet with which he held back his long dark hair, and the extravagant surroundings.

Finally, he accused, "If you do not mean to have her, then why all this luxury?"

It was a fair sneer, but Rui Finco was neither a fair nor patient man. "Look at you!" he returned. "This is a mission which requires stealth and secrecy, not hot blood and irrationality. Given one glimpse of the lady in question, you would surely be lost to carnal appetite, and then where would we be? Our heads must rule our hearts—and all other bodily aspects—or this whole venture will come to naught. Besides I have been to Halbo before and have some knowledge of its geography—"

He did not add that this single occasion had been twenty years before when taken prisoner by King Ashar Stenson himself, only to be released when—to avoid the fate of the other lord and their sons (that of being quartered and flung to the four winds by the Eyran king's infernal machine)—he had ignobly claimed to be a common seaman pressed into service with the Istrian navy, and set free on one of the few surviving ships to carry a message to the Southern Empire.

"—And I by one means or another extracted from the Lord of Broadfell certain intelligence on the subject of the secret ways into the northern capital. Further duplication of such labor and effort would be pointless indeed. Besides, I am not entirely sure you are pretty enough to persuade his lordship to divulge his hard-won information to you.

"But I promise I shall hand the Rose of the World into your care as soon as ever I can. I have no interest in her myself. None at all."

"You swear you will not lay a finger on her?"

"I swear."

"By all that is holy? By the Lady Falla herself."

"By Falla's fiery cunt, I swear it."

Tycho Issian regarded him furiously. "Take that back, blasphemer!"

Rui Finco raised an eyebrow. "The entire oath?"

Gritting his jaw, the Lord of Cantara flung himself upright and bundled his way out of the tent with such violence it seemed he would take the whole structure with him.

"GIVEN my antipathy for sorcerers, you may wonder why I insisted on your presence aboard this vessel."

Desperately nauseated, Virelai dared not open his mouth to answer the Lord of Forent for fear of what might spew out of it if he did. Instead, he bobbed an assent and tried hard to look as if he was interested in what the man had to say.

Rui Finco stuck his head swiftly out of the door flap, satisfied himself that the crew were otherwise occupied, then ducked back in and secured the fastening. He turned up the wick on the lamp. Instantly, it seemed, the air inside the tent became close and warm. Virelai's head swam.

"I gather from the Lord of Cantara's reports that your skills have improved considerably since our last encounter."

Virelai looked even more uncomfortable, if that were possible.

Rui Finco watched him closely, his black eyes narrow with calculation. "I have heard that you have perfected your ability to . . . change the nature of things . . . even people." Head on one side, he waited for the sorcerer's response.

Virelai gulped, wiped a hand across his clammy forehead. What had Alisha done to him with that thing? He had never felt so bad in all his life. The ship hit a larger swell, pitched, and rolled, sending him staggering forward. The Lord of Forent stopped his progress with an outstretched hand, pushing him down onto the makeshift bed.

"Put your head between your knees, man, and take some deep breaths," he said, almost kindly. Virelai did as he was told. When he felt able to, he sat back up again. Rui Finco handed him a goblet. "Drink that."

Virelai sniffed at it suspiciously, but it was only water. He drank it down, watching the Lord of Forent over its brim. Rui poured out another measure from the flask and his hand reached out for it instinctively, but the lord held it back from him.

"Change that into wine," he said.

Virelai stared at him. He didn't even want to *smell* wine in his current state, but he knew what happened if you refused this man anything he demanded. Summoning the most specific memory he could muster, he took the goblet from Rui Finco's hands, closed his eyes, and focused his thoughts away from his nausea. Turning water to wine was one thing, but turning it to vomit would never do.

King of the North

"**N**O one has seen Erol Bardson these several weeks, sire."

Ravn Asharson sighed heavily. If there was one subject which did he did not wish to reopen, it was this preoccupation the Earl of Stormway had with his unpleasant cousin and the elaborate conspiracy the man was supposed to be embroiled in.

"He's probably licking his wounds in his northern stronghold, keeping his head down, if he's any sense at all."

"He's not in Broadfell."

Ravn swiveled to regard his ancient retainer with a glimmer of curiosity. "How do you know this, Bran? Have you been there?"

Stormway mumbled something into his beard.

"What?"

"Spies, your highness."

"Spies?" Ravn sat bolt upright, amazed. "You have your own spies?"

"Actually, they're your spies, Ravn. Or your late father's, anyway. If you did but take a little more interest in affairs of state, or the chancellery, you would know such things."

Ravn Asharson rolled his eyes. In his head was an image of broken-down, grizzled men, survivors of the past regime, crawling arthritically through sodden undergrowth, failing to scale walls, listening at doors with half-deaf ears, misreporting what they thought they'd heard. He grinned broadly.

"And what do *my* spies tell you, then, Bran?"

"That he is not to be found in any of his usual haunts. That no one on the mainland has seen hide nor hair of him since he made his escape. That no ship returning from the Fair Isles or the Westman Isles has word of him. That even his ward has no idea where he is—"

"You would trust that little minx's word?" She was a sly one, Erol Bardson's niece with her pretty, foxy face and her limber body. He'd never taken her to bed, though he'd had more than half a mind to in earlier years, but even his underdeveloped political sense had warned him off such intimacy.

"We . . . questioned her, sire." Stormway looked carefully past Ravn's shoulder and would not meet his eye. The girl had been defiant, at first, then had wept and railed at her treatment, cursed the king, his witch-wife, troll-child, and all. They'd tried not to hurt her too much, though her will was strong. In the end, she'd passed out, and he hadn't had the heart to continue. "She knew nothing. But someone, in Halbo, someone with sufficient knowledge of the secret ways around the castle, and the funds to have the dungeon master disposed of, helped him escape. That says to me money, power, and a conspiracy, lord."

"And are you sure it was not the dungeon master himself who took Erol's bribe and made a run with him?"

"We found his remains this morning, sire. Washed up on one of the skerries up the coast. Carried there by the prevailing currents flowing west out of the harbor. From the state of him, he'd been in the water for weeks."

Ravn wrinkled his nose. Then he shrugged. "He wasn't much use, old Flinn. More wine-sack than soldier nowadays, is what I'd heard."

Stormway raised an eyebrow. There were times when his king took him by surprise. He might seem naive and callow, concerned only with tupping girls and having the sort of fun that came with unlimited access to the royal coffers and cellars, but every so often Ravn let slip an observation like this which made him believe there might be more to this young man than was immediately apparent.

"I know perfectly well who helped Bardson escape."

Bran sat down as if his knees had suddenly given way. "You do?"

"I do."

Stormway waited, but all Ravn did was to swill the golden liquid in his goblet and hold it up to the candlelight. "I like these glass things, Bran. You can see whether it's horse piss or decent ale you're drinking. Was it Cera donated them, or Jetra?"

The earl waved this away as the nonsense it was. "Well, who was it, then? I've spent weeks trying to discover this treachery, and you say you've known all along? Tell me, man, for Sur's sake!"

Ravn smiled. "When the time's right, Bran, I will." He paused, taking in evidence of his old retainer's growing temper. "The man's too cunning to have taken ship from Halbo. I don't suppose you've checked with the harbormaster's records at Fairwater on the night Erol escaped, seen if any boats left unexpectedly from there?"

The earl huffed, then shook his head.

"Well, what are you waiting for? Have one of your geriatric spies slung over a horse and send him off to find out. Now leave me to my beer and come back when you've something more interesting to talk about."

He watched Stormway stomp out of the door and sat back, considering. He had his own information network; and he had his own faculties, too. It had been a shame when little Ana had gone missing; and rather too much of a coincidence. An aged codger like Stormway was less likely to notice the disappearance of such a luscious little plum, but Ravn had had his eye on his bitter old mother's pretty maid for a while.

"I SWEAR that baby winked at me when the dressmaker was adjusting the bodice of my new gown yesterday."

"Don't be silly, Herga. It probably had something in its eye."

"But have you seen its eyes? They are passing strange. I've never seen a color quite like it on any other child. Heather-purple, violet even."

"Why, Herga, you are becoming most poetic in your old age."

"I have not yet turned thirty! Mind your tongue, Firi Edelsen. But surely you have noticed something about the creature—I hesitate to call it a baby."

The other woman became thoughtful. "Ah . . . he is most well grown for his age. A very strapping child. But then, you would expect that of the Stallion's babe. Yet none of mine were ever quite so alert at such an early stage, I think. His gaze does follow you most attentively."

"It is unnerving." She glanced nervously around. "But, you know, although 'tis treason to say it, I do believe it looks nothing like either its mother or its father!"

"Herga—"

"Shhh—keep your noise down, Firi, or you'll surely land the witch's curse upon us. But no, think about it: she so pale and willowy, her eyes as cold as sea ice; he so like his father—that great jaw and jutting chin. Yet the babe has a different shape to its nose, and no chin to speak of at all. And it is as big as a twelve-month child already, which is surely not natural." Her voice dropped to a whisper. "In some of the outer isles, I have heard, a woman who has difficulty conceiving may go up into the hills at full moon, trap herself a buck rabbit, open it up with a sharp knife, and fill it with whatever she may of her husband—bits of hair and nail clippings, and his seed, of course. And then," she put her hand to her mouth as if to mask what came next, which was not at all polite, "she must rub it against herself, down there, till she . . . you know . . ." She shifted uncomfortably, watching the repulsion on the other's face, a woman who would not know the difference between a buck and a doe, let alone how to catch or kill one, had probably seen rabbits only neatly skinned and dressed in Halbo Market and wouldn't dream of . . . well . . . "And then," she continued briskly, "she must wrap it up in swaddlings, take it home, and sing it to life all night while everyone else is asleep. And the next thing you know, her belly is all swelled up like a three-month pregnancy, and six months later there's a great big baby boy." Here, she paused for effect, enjoying the fact that Firi's eyes had gone round with anticipation. "Except it's no ordinary baby, for when the moon is full, it grows a coat of fur and runs off across the hills."

It was this last detail which made Firi burst into gales of laughter. "Are you telling me the queen's child will grow a white scut and long ears and go kicking up his heels when the moon next waxes large?"

Herga clicked her tongue angrily. "There's no need to take a folk tale quite so literally! But some kind of magic is at work here, mark my words. And the Rose of the World and that thing she calls her child are surely at the center of it."

THE Rose of the World had escaped the confines of the castle. She had also—for a few moments, at least—escaped the confines of the identity which had been thrust upon her.

Standing on the edge of a cliff above Halbo with the wind in her face and the winter sun crowning her with pale fire, she looked out upon her world and knew it for her own.

The sea spread itself below, stretching in apparently limitless abandon, a vast mirror to the sky. Soon, both would be hers for the taking, she could feel it in her bones. So, too, the gulls which planed overhead, their mournful cries drifting like lost souls through the frosty air, and the plants which survived in this precipitous place: the cushions of thrift, sea campion, tormentil, and lacefoot, the springy turf in which they grew, the thin, acid soil beneath, and the worms and centipedes and millipedes, the tiny colonies of life laboring away in that dark kingdom, hidden from the human eye. So, too, the very bedrock of this continent, with its pulsing heart of feldspar and mica, its veins and chambers of crystal and quartz; veins which flowed down through the cliff on which she stood, plunged far below the waters of the Northern Ocean and out into the lands beyond. Hers—all hers.

She was Falla; she was Feya; she was the Rosa Eldi.

But more than any of these, she was the Soul of the World.

A great calm had come over her as she acknowledged this fact, but the calm was short-lived. For a soul is but one aspect of any being, be it human or divine, and she was divided from those two who made her complete: the Man and the Beast. Without them, she drifted like an unmoored boat. She might have volition and some little power, but for the time being she was at the mercy of others, up here in this rocky little kingdom, a world away from the rest of herself. Yet despite the distance which separated them, she sensed that the other two were alive; she could feel them both just as a spider may sit at the center of the gossamer world it has woven and feel the brush of a butterfly's wing at the farthest extent of the web it has made.

They would come together. For a brief moment, a great strength flowed into her. They would reunite and the world would be made whole. *I will find you!* This wordless cry spiraled down through the core of her, through her legs, braced against the cutting wind, through the soles of her feet, pressed down into the granite on which she stood. She felt the message leave her like a sheet of flame, felt it course into the rock.

With her eyes closed, she followed its route, down through the quartz and into the rock strata below the ocean's choppy waves. Away it fled like a trail of wildfire, down into the heart of the world, and as it did so, a surge of power discharged itself in her, radiating through every bone in her slight frame to set her body singing with life.

The baby in her arms squirmed suddenly, and beat his little fists against her chest as if to quell this disquieting change; suddenly she was goddess no more, but a thin, weak woman standing on a clifftop with a squalling child (not her own) in her aching arms and a gaggle of complaining attendants all going on about their sore feet and the cold and the rough path and the early hour and how it just wasn't seemly behavior for a queen to be traipsing around in the wilds like this, without the least preparation, without a cloak and at such an ungodly hour, with the poor wee starving thing mewling at her empty breasts? No wonder her husband was with her less and less. The novelty had worn off, and not before time.

This last comment jolted the Rosa Eldi back into a rather less divine aspect.

"I can hear you!"

She turned to confront the moaners, and an unearthly hush fell. She had not spoken loudly, but she had used the Voice, and now they all stood there, trembling, unsure as to why they felt suddenly afraid and beset.

It was true, she realized. Ravn was away from her increasingly often with the wrights at the shipyard, with his weaponsmaster and his generals. And she, in turn, had been distracted by the child, which disturbed her in a way she could not define, and by the thousands of voices which whispered in her skull, calling on her in anguish and ecstasy, in conversation and in meditation. All snagged at her attention. And so the enchantment which bound her husband to her had loosened its ties. If she was not careful, she would lose him altogether.

A shiver ran through her at that thought. She must go back, now.

Walking toward the gathered retainers, she handed the child to the wet nurse and summoned what power she could harness.

"It is cold, I grant you. And probably best that we return to the castle. But is it not the most beautiful day?"

And when she said this, it was; they realized what she said was true. It *was* the most beautiful day, even though snow was falling, thick as rose petals shed from a sullen sky. And as this understanding reached them, so their aches melted away, their chilblains stopped throbbing, warm blood suffused even their extremities and the air seemed clearer and brighter, and the hardy winter blossoms and berries they passed on the winding track down to the city were arrayed in splendor. Every one of them was smiling and chattering as they made their way back into the castle's west gate.

All except for little Ulf, who turned his violet-black eyes on the woman who was responsible for this minor miracle and bellowed with all his might.

"WHAT ails you, my rose?"

Several nights later, Ravn Asharson, Stallion of the North, knelt beside his wife and brushed the silk curtain of her hair away from her brow, which was uncharacteristically wrinkled in concentration. He had never seen her look like this before; always she was serene, indifferent to the world and what took place in it. Even in the throes of passion she seemed strangely at peace, a creature sublimely at home in her element, gliding effortlessly through an ocean in which others would be wrecked and drowned. It occurred to him with a sudden revelatory start that at some time in the recent weeks a change had taken place in this woman he called his wife, and that he had not been privy to it.

She looked full at him then and he felt his heart contract and his blood beat hard, as it always did when he was in her thrall. *Those eyes,* he found himself thinking, for the thousandth time, *a man could lose himself forever in those eyes.*

"There are many men praying tonight, Ravn. I hear them sending their thoughts out into the world. They fill my head like bees, but their words are not honeyed."

He looked at her then, bemused. She did not often initiate conversation, but she did have a strange propensity to make statements such as these: large, oblique, bewildering. At first he had thought such pronouncements reflected her ineptitude with language, that she was grasping after concepts she could not adequately frame, and so he would nod and smile encouragingly, and change the subject to firmer ground. Sometimes her words seemed nonsensical, meaningless; then he wondered whether she was in her right mind. In the beginning it had not concerned him overmuch, for all it took to dispel any doubts as to the wisdom of his choice of wife was a single glance from her sea-green eyes, the touch of a single fingertip upon his cheek. Thereafter he would be lost to hot desire, and coherent thought would become an irrelevance, mere jetsam cast up on passion's tide.

But lately it had begun to concern him. A mad wife—it would not do. Raik Horsehair had had a mad wife. It was said they had chained her in a dungeon at the foot of the Sentinel Towers and left her there to rot. Some said she was there still—in spirit at least—weeping and wailing and making dire predictions for the future of the world. No one walked the lower levels of the Towers after dark; Eyrans were a superstitious people. Ravn had always prided himself on his pragmatism and hard-headedness where such things were concerned. But now he found old wives' tales and nonsense rhymes circling in his head like so many crows: "If the wife be mad, sons will be bad, if she be bad, she'll drive all mad"; "a lackwit wife makes for halfwit children"; and clearest of all: "madness runs in the blood."

It made him look harder at his son, and that was disturbing, too. When the child hurt himself, instead of crying as any normal babe would, seeking reassurance, releasing his pain, little Wulf would simply swell up until he was purple in the face and his eyes would bulge so that you thought he might choke. And then he would grab hold of whatever object lay closest to hand and beat, beat, beat it against whoever might be within range. And if no one was available to his rage, he would turn the weapon upon himself, thumping until bruises came. The first time he had done this, there had been a flurry of activity and much cosseting and attention; after that it had happened more frequently. This very afternoon he had thrown just such a silent tantrum, attacking Leta Gullwing in apparent fury with the silver spoon with which she had been trying to tempt him with solid food, but when his father had walked into the room, little Wulf had turned that riveting violet gaze upon him and then very calmly started to hit himself hard on the head with the spoon, raising welt after welt before Ravn himself had snatched the thing away in horror.

And yet the boy was hale and whole; and his. Seed of his body, heir to his throne, which made him quell whatever concerns he harbored. As he must now with his strange wife.

She laid her head upon his chest. Without those wondrous eyes upon him, he felt his mind clear. "Praying, my rose?"

"Praying for their souls, some of them; praying for victory, others. Their women pray, too, for their safe return."

Ravn frowned. *Praying for victory . . . for their safe return . . .* Did she truly hear the voices of others? It was surely impossible. Perhaps a vision, a dream had come to her. It was not unknown, though rarely spoken of in the Isles. Seithers might be visited by such prophetic voices; but an ordinary woman? He knew even as he framed the thought that the Rosa Eldi was in no way "ordinary." Questions crowded in on him. Could the enemy be planning their campaign so far ahead? Winter was a dangerous time for men not used to the changeable ways of the weather to put to sea, and the Istrians had never been known in all the annals of history to contemplate such a thing. They had no skills in the mastering of wind and tide, of navigating under fog or flood. Let alone of constructing vessels which would bear the brunt of the Northern Ocean at its least magnanimous. Though the climate had been unusually mild this year . . .

A sudden sharp thought jabbed at him. "Tell me, my dove, do they pray for fair seas?"

Her hand clutched his tunic convulsively.

"They do," she whispered. "They do."

To Steal a Rose

A TINY boat rocked on a dark sea. Inside it, two figures hunched over their oars while a third sat upright in the stern, his face hidden by a cowl. The prow was adorned with what appeared to be the figurehead of a raven.

Then the figurehead took flight and, skimming the moonlit waters, vanished into black night.

CHARTS had been spread over every available surface of the room. Three men pored over them by the guttering light of many candles. Two were old men with long gray beards and braided hair. One of these had only a single hand. He stabbed at the chart before him with a leather-wrapped stump.

"I say they'll sail probably head up the eastern coast, and try to find a way down through the Sharking Straits to land here, at Black Strand."

Egg Forstson looked gloomy. "A shame Ness allowed the fortifications to fall into wrack and ruin." He tugged his beard. "Remind me why it is you think they're coming?"

Stormway and his king exchanged a glance over the Earl of Shepsey's bowed head. Then Ravn said quickly, to steer the old man away from this difficult subject, "Actually, Egg, I've addressed the matter of the Shark-ing Straits."

The old retainer's head shot up again. "You have?"

"I've brought it back under Crown rule."

"But the last I heard, it was overrun with brigands. Pirates and cor-sairs, using it as a base for their nefarious activities."

Ravn laughed. "Careful what you say, old man. That's my navy you're talking about."

"Navy?" The Earl of Shepsey's voice rose by an octave.

"Where else have all those ships at Fairwater come from? Did you think I'd doubled my fleet in the blink of an eye, and with no master shipbuilder at hand?"

"But they're completely untrustworthy, sire. They'll turn and run at the first sign of trouble."

Ravn shrugged. "That remains to be seen. So," he reapplied himself to the charts, "if the Istrians do make it into the straits, they should lose a goodly number before they figure out a trap's been set." He chuckled. "We left the ruins to stand, Egg, rather than rebuild. Could afford nei-ther the time nor the manpower required to overhaul the towers, so rather than waste either, we decided to turn dereliction to advantage. Their intelligence may have told them the fortifications are run down, and that the straits are unguarded. But I've sent a hundred good men north with ballistas and pitch. If ships try to make a passage between the towers, they'll burn half their fleet before they know what's hit them. And the other half—" He grinned. "We'll know about them before they get a chance to cross Blackfell. Ness has his ravens and two fast ships. So if exposure doesn't get them as they cross the hags, then I will, com-ing up here, across Sursmere—" he pointed out the track on another map, then swept his finger around in an arc, "—while Stormway takes his troops to circle around them from Trollsfoot."

Ravn stood back and swept his hair out of his eyes. Beneath that dark mane, his face was flushed, his eyes shining. He had not, Egg thought, looked so . . . well . . . *himself* in months.

Egg Forstson, irritated at not having been consulted about any of these plans, thrust out his jaw pugnaciously. "And if they come straight for Halbo?"

Even Stormway laughed at that ridiculous notion. Everyone knew the city was impregnable.

AS the little boat bumped softly into the rocks below the Sentinel Towers, the sound of its landing muffled by the cork buffers slung from its gunwales, it started to snow. It came lightly at first, tiny flakes which melted on contact with skin or sea, then in great, soft swathes. The two rowers shipped their oars and the three of them sat there silently, waiting. Water slapped the hull. More water trickled down the rock beneath the tower, its hulking mass looming higher than any headland. Tiny lights showed at intervals up its great length, some flickering, others stationary.

Virelai gazed upward, feeling cold dread envelop him like a mist. It wasn't just the passage from the great ship to this freezing cliff which assailed him so, he was sure, but something else, something unnatural. The tower itself? Certainly it looked too tall and adamantine to have been raised by mortal hands. Perhaps the old tales were true and giants *had* dwelled in this land before the men of Eyra. A larger wave came and the boat rocked unsteadily, and then Virelai knew that whatever horrors the tower might contain, he had rather a thousand times meet them than be at the mercy of the black water and whatever lurked beneath it.

A new light appeared through the haze of the blizzard, closer than any of the lights in the towers. It wavered and bobbed with the rhythm that suggested it was being carried by someone walking toward them. All three of them watched it coming, fascinated, though the sorcerer noticed that both his companions had pulled their cloaks back the better to reach their swords. It did not fill him with confidence. What use were swords in a little boat like this? One poorly judged move and they'd be in the sea, and all a good heavy blade would do was to carry you down to a watery grave like a well-flung anchor.

There was a whirring sound and something brushed the back of his head, then his cheek as he turned—too quickly—in his panic. Now the skiff rocked with a vengeance, making Rui Finco curse him in urgent, horrid whispers. Virelai had no doubt he meant what he threatened. He blinked away tears, and as he blinked them away, the darkness in front of him coalesced into the shape of a bird: the northman's raven, returned to his shoulder. Moonlight licked palely off the eye that regarded him askance. Then the white light turned to flame, and the sorcerer looked back to find a dark figure on the rocks above them, a small lantern held aloft. It was a woman, he was surprised to note. An old woman, the lamplight illuminating a nest of crow's feet round her dark eyes and a sag of jowls which suggested an embittered nature.

"Well, get up here where I can see you, then," Auda said softly, and her voice was not welcoming.

Virelai went first, scuttling sideways like a crab and clutching onto weed, crag, limpets, anything, he was so desperate to be out of the boat. Erol Bardson followed with a single athletic bound, his raven extending its wings for balance. Last came the Lord of Forent.

Auda held the lantern to his face, then drew sharply back, her face a mask of repulsion. "You," she hissed. "I should have known it would be you who took the traitor's bait. You look just like her, damn you. Promise me now that you'll say nothing of his provenance. Just kill him quick and quiet if you must. Promise me that or you'll regret it."

Rui smiled, but not with his eyes. "Why," he said lightly in the Eyran he had so carefully practiced these many slow weeks. "You must be the Lady Auda. I fear my mother did you a grave wrong. Is the cuckoo in his nest?"

"He's with his lords in the maproom at the top of the castle's west tower."

"And the lady?"

Auda gave him a narrow look. "You'd spit her, too?"

It was one way of putting it, he supposed. He nodded. "Ah, yes, we'll take her as well."

She shook her head. "In her chambers. Erol knows where." She thought for a moment. "And you can slit the throat of that troll-child while you're at it," she added viciously. She looked to the bird, and without a word spoken it flew from Erol Bardson's shoulder to her own. Then she turned away and the arc of golden light went with her so that they were left feeling their way with nervous feet and hands along freezing rock now slick with new snow, while the sucking sea gushed and churned below them. "I hope you've got reinforcements," she said over her shoulder. "It'll take more than a turncoat, a renegade lord, and a sickly boy to take Halbo."

THE Rose of Elda felt them approaching before they even entered the keep. She felt the sorcery that took place in the chambers at the foot of the Sentinel Tower and it made her shiver. *Rahay* . . . Something of the old man's had penetrated her domain. His signature was in the magic, she knew it too well. There was something beyond the trace of that spellcraft, though, something more familiar and yet entirely alien. *Bëte?* She sent the inquiry questing out through the castle walls, but no response came back. Not the cat, then . . . She steadied herself against the pillars of the bed.

"My lady?" Leta Gullwing watched the Queen of the Northern Isles curiously, but with little liking, as she swayed where she stood, her eyes closed and that perfect face just a little pinched, as if in pain or concentration. "Are you well?"

Now she could hear their voices with that preternatural sense of hers, sharper than a cat's, sharper than a bat's. She heard, too, the voices of the guards as they stood down and let the men pass without challenge. She knew they were not who they seemed, though she could not blame the soldiers for their error. Illusion was a simple magic, obvious to the initiated, but to a soldier it might as well be as powerful as the sorcery which bound a goddess into slavery. She clenched her fists.

"I am quite well," she said softly, though her mind was racing. What to do? Raise a hue and cry and bring violence crashing about them all? It was the third of the men that made her keep her counsel, the one from whom sorcery leaked like water from a sieve. The closer he came, the more powerful was her sense of him: afraid but compelled, and more dangerous than either of his companions could know. They were coming for her. Of that she was sure. "Take little Ulf into the nursery," she said aloud. "Go in there with him and close the door, be quiet as mice. Do not come out no matter what you may see or hear. Do you understand me?"

She used the Voice. Blank-eyed, the girl gathered up the child, who swiveled in her arms and fixed his supposed mother with a dark and venemous stare. Then Leta opened the door to the nursery and took him away.

The Rosa Eldi let out a sigh, but whether it was of relief or fear, or a determined centering of all her power, it would have been impossible for any observer to know.

Moments later, the door to her chamber opened and two men entered.

TYCHO gripped the stempost of the ship and gazed into the blizzard as if by the very power of his will he could burn light into the scene he so desperately wished to view. Damn Rui Finco for leaving him behind. The man was a libertine, a sensualist, a sinner of the first order. How could he possibly be trusted to keep his hands off such a rose? He pushed the thought away irritably before too disturbing an image could form. Even though each breath he exhaled clouded visibly before him, he found that he had begun to sweat, a runnel of salty liquid running down his temple into the corner of his eye. It stung like hell. Furiously, he wiped it away. His tunic was sticking to him, too. He had not washed properly in the best part of a month. When he raised an arm to catch hold of a line as the ship pitched forward on a roller, the pit stank like an old dog.

Disgusted, he staggered back to his flapping canvas shelter, grabbing a pail of seawater on the way, and despite the freezing air stripped naked and scrubbed his skin till it was red and raw. He could not present himself to the Rose in this foul state; he must purify himself. Easier said than done. Glancing down, he found his erection standing out from his belly, stiff and ruby-tight. Where other men complained of their balls withering in the cold and their pricks entirely vanishing from sight, still he was afflicted as he had been since first laying eyes on the Rosa Eldi.

Again the thought insinuated itself. *How can Rui fail to be affected? He left me behind because he thought I would lose my head, but I have been dealing with this desire for the better part of a year, and he has no experience of her seductive gift, no expectation, no defenses. It will knock him flat.*

The image came, no matter how hard he tried to block it: the Rose of the World spread-eagled on a fur-strewn bed beneath the taut, pumping buttocks of the Lord of Forent.

No!

The force of his denial made the word echo out around the ship so that men stopped what they were doing and stared at the candlelit tent, wherein the Lord of Cantara was clearly silhouetted in all his priapic glory. Already amazed by the falling snow—for some their first experience of this strange northern phenomenon, they stared. Then they shook their heads and carried on their tasks—bailing, mainly, the timber had not had sufficient time to soak and swell its seams full shut—and muttered to each other.

"Nutter," declared one of the Farem slaves to his oar partner, who nodded in agreement.

"Pulling his daisy again," observed the man behind sagely.

"Got to be mad to be bollock-naked in this weather," said a north-coaster, shaking his head. "Though you have to admire his resilience. Mine's the size of a walnut."

"An acorn, more like!"

Tycho heard them laughing and clenched his jaw. He took a new length of clean linen and began the laborious job of binding himself flat. The piece he had removed reeked. Having to piss over the side in a high wind was a messy business at the best of times. He resolved to curb his appetite for the woman until they were safely back on Istrian soil. It would be too sordid to consummate their passion here, amid all this filth and discomfort, and with only a thin sheet of fabric between them and the prying eyes and ears of the bawdy crew. He had survived these many months; he could surely last another two weeks.

Or could he? The thought of the barbarian king rutting with her, constantly, productively, planting his filthy seed in her was more than he could bear. The urge to claim her, to scour Ravn's memory and his presence from her was achingly hot. Stallion of the North! Even the monicker was an insult, a slur upon her, and all women. That such a savage had stolen a vision and made her his mare was revolting, beyond words.

Now it was Ravn Asharson's face which sprang up before him. Young and handsome and chiseled, with a triumphant, laughing light in his eye. The whelp! Loathing rose in him like bile.

How dare Rui deny him his due revenge! He had purchased the woman fair and square. Or if not purchased, exactly, he had certainly agreed on a deal for her, only to lose her to a barbarian's whim. It was insupportable that he should not sever the thief's head from his strutting, lustful body. Instead here he was, bobbing uselessly on the waves with the rest of the fleet, waiting, waiting, waiting.

"You'll get your chance, believe me, Tycho," Rui had assured him as the skiff was lowered. "When we take the Rose, Bardson will raise the alarm at the due time and they'll pursue us out of the harbor and slam right into your tender embrace. It'll be a slaughter. We'll grapple their ships and fire them, then you can kill as many of the heretical bastards as you want."

It was not enough; nothing could ever be enough, and the waiting was just too hard.

He fell to his knees in anguish. "Falla, hear my plea. Give me my enemy so I may exact retribution from him. Grant me the grace to put out those eyes which have feasted on her naked form; let me rip out at the root the sacrilegious member which has dared to penetrate her mysteries." He buried his head in his hands. "Oh, Falla, look kindly on your chief advocate and defender. Deliver my love to me and I shall be your slave for the rest of my life."

The candles guttered. Then it was as if a soft breeze caressed his face. Deep inside his skull he thought he caught the whisper of a reply. It told him what to do and moments later he strode out onto the deck, half-dressed and radiant with knowledge.

THE first of the two men wore her husband's face; but she could see his own beneath, as if floating beneath a scummy pool. He was not dissimilar to Ravn, she thought, with his high cheekbones, his angularity, and dark eyes; yet there was no beard beneath the illusion, and he was older by far, his cheeks etched by years of dissatisfaction, dissolution, and cynicism. Here was a man who believed in nothing, loved nothing, cherished nothing; was nothing, for all his confidence and his daring, and not worth her husband's shadow.

She looked through him to the second intruder.

Waves of terror emanated off this man, interfering with the fine trickery he had woven to hide himself from view. He had, she saw at once, tried to throw a glamour in front of any onlooker, so that their gaze would slide harmlessly away from him to alight on some other thing. The shimmer which surrounded him was annoying, hard to focus on. She could feel the essence of him more than see his true appearance, but what she felt evoked something nameless in her—a kind of painful yearning.

The first man strode forward, and she transferred her scrutiny to him. His gaze was lambent, the pupils as wide and black as an owl's. She felt his desire like a heat and smiled, her coral mouth twisting upward contemptuously.

"You are not my husband," she said softly and watched the dismay settle over the blur of his features. She put out her hand, fingers splayed, and time itself slowed, the man halting in mid-stride, his accomplice shimmering at his shoulder.

It was hard to think. There was a distant background hum of folk calling out in desperation to her—people starving, dying, their land dying with them, far away, far away; then other voices came leaping out at her from the sea much closer at hand—men invoking her name in curse, in prayer, or in casual, careless reference. One, more intense than all the rest, snagged her attention. She felt his vitriol, his murderous spirit questing out, seeking justification, divine reinforcement.

I know you, she thought. The signature of his mind was unmistakable, vile. *I remember you.* He had come for her, driven a thousand miles and more by the depths of his obsession. *All this way,* she marveled. A mortal woman might have been flattered by such devotion; but even at her weakest and most disempowered, the Rose of the World had never been mortal.

Thoughts crowded in on her.

They have come from the south.

They lie in wait. For Ravn . . .

They will mutilate his beautiful body.

They will kill him.

But then they will sail south.

Across the whole wide ocean . . . home . . .

She lifted her hand and time came flooding back. She felt the disruption to the natural world she had caused by even this tiny holding back of the inexorable. *There are so many disruptions out there,* she thought distractedly. *Yet all will be chaos if I make the wrong choice.*

It was an impossible decision. The woman in her warred with the goddess for fleeting, eternal moments.

A TINY boat rocked on a dark sea. Inside were two figures. Sailing out of the west, the moonlight limned them in ice, picking out the haggard face of one and the eager craftiness of his older companion. The haggard one was rowing, but the vessel seemed to skim the waves faster than any man-powered boat should move, and despite the light wind—which elsewhere blew from an entirely different direction—the vessel's sail was full and taut. The blizzard swirled around and above them, but kept its distance.

Hollow-eyed and hollow-souled, the other was easier to control now. Something had gone out of him at Rockfall; he was a defeated man, a shadow of himself. He had, as the old women of Eyra would say, "had the stuffing knocked out of him." What was it Ilyina had called him? A luckless man. That was it. A man whom Fate had marked out for special attention, sorting through the tangled threads of his dreams with her wicked fingers, allowing him the privilege of choosing which colored string he would pull—gold, for greed? blue, for ambition? red, for passion?—and see what part of the careful tapestry of his life would unravel fastest.

His current walking death should surely prove a perfect foil to the Rosa Eldi's peculiar persuasiveness. His grief for the predicament of his wife and daughter and his own part in leaving them defenseless rendered him a perfect, empty vessel for the Master's use. Rahay had the necessary spell ready to return the goddess to her prior compliance. Now all he had to do was to slip into Halbo in the guises he had prepared for them and let the Fool do his work. . . .

The Rose of Elda

THE Rose of the World felt the weight of his gaze on her once more, like the brush of a dirty rag. So she reached out and touched him, letting loose the full force of her seductive power, and watched as he was buffeted by it, as by a great wind.

For a long moment, all volition fell away from him. He could not remember what he was here to do, even who he truly was, for in those mesmeric sea-green eyes all he saw reflected was the image of Ravn Asharson, King of the North. When she touched his arm, his whole skin felt inflamed with passion. He wanted nothing now other than to shed not only his clothing, but that sheath of skin as well, to meld himself with her astonishing presence as wholly as he could. He found he was trembling from top to toe.

Again, the Rose of Elda smiled. The glamour was too strong for such a weak man to withstand. She called some of its power back into herself and waited for the intruder to make clear his purpose.

Rui Finco shook his head, blinked. He felt as though he had just wakened from the most blissful dream. He dreamed he had stood before the Goddess, that she had smiled upon him and taken him into her fires. Never a religious man, the ecstasy he experienced in the wake of this vision stunned him. *Perhaps Tycho Issian is right*, he thought. *Perhaps we are here on a sacred mission.* His own reason for leading the invasion force north had been entirely venal; now he felt abruptly ashamed.

This precious lady must be rescued from the barbarians and returned to the land of faith and righteousness: that was the key. It was all that mattered.

"Take me, then," the Rose of the World said simply. "Now." She turned to pick up from the bed the hooded, ermine-lined cloak her husband had given her to keep the Eyran winter out of her bones, and felt hot tears burning her eyes: and that in itself was some kind of miracle. *I do not understand*, she thought desperately. *I am the Goddess, so this parting should not touch me, but leaving this mortal man makes my heart feel as if it will break. Yet the people of my world cry out for me. They need the Three to be together once more, so their lives may be cradled in our care. Who can I turn to for aid and direction? It seems there is no one to listen to* my *prayers.*

She had never felt so alone.

As if sensing the turmoil in the room beyond, Ulf twisted suddenly in Leta Gullwing's arms, evading her muffling hand. A monstrous bellow of outrage emanated from behind the paneled door to the nursery.

The shimmering man moved before anyone else had time to react. He wrenched open the door, revealing the occupants to his companion. His gaze distracted from the mazing power of the Rosa Eldi, Rui Finco smiled delightedly. "Ah, the son and heir," he breathed. He walked past Virelai into the hidden room. Still lustful from the nomad woman's magic, his eyes roved appreciatively across the girl in whose arms the howling child writhed. "And his *very* lovely nurse. It seems your ladyship will have company on our voyage back to the motherland," he declared cheerfully over his shoulder.

Leta stared at him, uncomprehending.

"I need no company," the Rosa Eldi said from behind him, but the man was not listening.

The Lord of Forent reached out now and traced the line of the girl's cheek. Her dark skin was velvet-soft and she was coloring now, embarrassed by his unambiguous attention. "You have the appearance of an Istrian," he said softly. "How well you would look in my seraglio. Where are you from?"

"My l–lord," she stuttered. "You know me. I am Leta Gullwing . . ."

"A pretty name for a pretty girl. I look forward to better making your acquaintance, though I cannot offer you the most luxurious of bedchambers on my ship."

"Your ship, my king?"

Rui blinked. Of course, he still wore Ravn Asharson's likeness. No wonder the girl was so uncomfortable—the King of the Northern Isles making a frank sexual advance to her right in front of his wife! He laughed. "No matter. You will know soon enough."

He stared with some distaste at the bawling baby in her arms and for just a moment Ulf stopped crying and scrutinized him in return. Then he reached up to tug at the beard he so loved to play with, and his fingers slipped right through the illusion. There was a moment when little Ulf glared in fury at this deception, then he set to howling with a vengeance. The noise rang out around the chamber, echoed off the stonework, the pillars, and the beams.

The heir to the northern throne had certainly inherited a powerful set of lungs. And if he continued to wail so, it would surely attract unwanted attention.

Rui glared at Virelai. "Make it be quiet!"

Virelai looked alarmed. "It's a baby. What do I know about babies?"

Little Ulf was reaching tantrum-pitch now, his chubby face livid.

The Lord of Forent reached for his dagger. "Then I will have to shut it up myself—"

"No!" Leta Gullwing wrapped herself around the child, muffling its cries in her bosom.

"Lucky boy," Rui grinned as the baby subsided at long last into choking sobs. "You can show me how you do that later. But now we must leave. Bring what you need for the child's comfort." He watched as she frowned in consternation, then gathered bedclothes, linens, and a well-chewed wooden teething ring into already full arms. "But why, sire . . . ?" she started to ask.

The shimmering man hastened across the royal chamber, opened the outer door, and consulted a figure standing outside.

"Hurry, my lord," he called back.

It was as if the proximity of the magic which created the shimmer had also somehow disguised the man's voice from her. Now that he was at a distance, it came into abrupt focus. The Rose of the World knew that voice well. Betrayal vied for a moment with a terrible upswelling of joy.

"Come along, now, Leta," she said distractedly, overwhelmed by these unfamiliar emotions. "All shall be well, all manner of things shall be well . . ."

DOWN dark corridors they walked at a determined pace: a goddess, a mother with babe in arms, a sorcerer, a usurper, and a traitor. They passed knots of folk in court dress, who bowed; they passed retainers and servants and others who did not appear to see them at all.

Virelai felt light-headed. He thought it was probably the use of so much magic, which was working far better than he had ever expected. Rui Finco still looked a perfect match for Ravn Asharson, a remarkable achievement given the state of terror he had been in at the Allfair when he had last set eyes on the man. And Erol Bardson—well, all he had done there was make him dark and change the cast of his face. He could not help but congratulate himself when they passed two richly-arrayed women on the stairs and they carried on chattering without surcease. Yet when they had passed around the corner he found himself frowning. He had not cast an invisibility glamour, so why was it they had not been seen? The faces of others they passed went suddenly blank. People stopped moving. It was most bizarre. *Perhaps*, he thought with a desperate need to rationalize, *I am doing it without even realizing in my wish to be out of here as fast and as safely as possible. That must be the reason.*

But he knew it wasn't.

Even if he had not known her to be the Goddess, he would have recognized that the Rose of the World was a different woman to the one he had brought to the Allfair last year; that woman had been all temptation and compliance, a creature who could be manipulated and gained from, whose power was easily tapped off and stolen. A woman who had no idea of who she was. The woman with them now was another matter. He could feel the power emanating from her in waves. It was diffuse and golden, unchanneled, benevolent; now he knew her for who and what she was, he felt terror and awe grip him whenever he looked at her. And so he made every effort *not* to look at her.

They were about to cross the courtyard outside the west gate when there came a cry of warning. Men with torches appeared suddenly along the castle walls. A great flurry of activity was occurring in their wake: orders were shouted, though the words were carried on winds above their heads, and so they ran, Rui Finco, hauling the pale woman with him, the others keeping pace—through the courtyard, along the wall, between the trees dotting the snow-covered sward leading down from the castle toward the harbor. As they cleared the last of the great oaks, a contingent of armed soldiers came up from the Sentinel Towers to meet them.

Rui broke out into a sweat. He drew his sword, but the man at the front of the group merely saluted. "We've come to escort the queen and the prince to safety my lord, as you ordered. Been looking everywhere for them, but it seems you found them first."

The Lord of Forent stared at him, trying to concentrate on the cadence of the Eyran language. "Ah . . . yes." He paused. "I'll come with you."

The soldier looked anxious. "Won't you be leading the men to battle, sire?"

Something had gone badly wrong. Rui Finco assimilated what little information there was available to him and tried not to panic. He nodded furiously. "Of course, man, of course. But I must make sure my wife and child are safe first of all. Future of the kingdom, and all . . . You . . . ah . . . muster the troops . . . all of them . . . up in the—" he searched for the correct vocabulary ". . . the . . . ah . . . courtyard there." He waved vaguely back up the slope toward the open ground they had crossed some minutes before.

Now the man looked thoroughly alarmed. "Me, sire? I'm just a sergeant. They won't follow me."

"You're a general now," Rui declared, clapping the man on the shoulder. He raised his voice. "You hear me?" he addressed the rest of the contingent. "This good soldier—" he broke off, looked the bewildered man in the eye, "—what's your name?" he hissed.

"Guthrun, sire," the man said slowly, "Guthrun Hart. Navigator on the *Sur's Raven*, sire, you remember?"

Rui winked. "Got you there!" He grinned, Ravn Asharson's grin in perfect replica. Then he shouted aloud once more, "Guthrun Hart is your general now: I've promoted him. Do what he says and pass the word!"

"Up in the West Square, my lord?" Guthrun sounded dubious. "Not on the quays?"

"I need to address the troops," Rui returned. "Put some . . . backbone into them."

Guthrun absorbed this. Then, "Aye, sire," he said at last and gave his king the open-handed salute used by generals. It felt strange to do so, but also kind of satisfying. Bela would never believe it. "Perhaps if I were to take a token from your highness?" he suggested suddenly. "So that there's no question—"

Now Rui Finco was irritated. "Oh, for Falla's sake, man—"

"Falla?"

Shit. He winked. "Your ears must be deceiving you, Guthrun. Here," he fiddled at his sword belt. "Give me your . . . weapon, and take mine."

A massive smile wreathed the soldier's face. "Yes, sir!"

A moment later Rui found himself carrying a worn but serviceable Eyran sword, while Guthrun examined his new weapon. It was not as richly worked as he had hoped. There was no pattern welding, no silver on it at all. And it felt a bit light: not much heft. All in all, it was rather disappointing. Still, he considered, Ravn was a fighting man with a reputation for fast footwork, and this was probably not his finest sword.

And so he raised it aloft and led the soldiers away from where any invading force were most likely to land.

OUT of sight, they started to run now, their feet crunching in the new snow, but as they emerged into a cobbled alley with a view down the hill between the ramshackle dwellings and warehouses, the Lord of Forent skidded to a halt.

The Istrian fleet, which he had left anchored well out of sight around the headland, with clear orders to await his signal for ambush, was invisible no longer. Just beyond the mouth of the harbor a flotilla of ships was limned in silver by a fickle moon, with one vessel well ahead of the rest.

Rui Finco groaned. "That bloody hothead Tycho Issian—"

Erol Bardson paled, his ambitious dreams burning away like morning mist. "They'll raise the chainwall and trap them. It'll be a massacre." When he turned to the Lord of Forent, the whites showed all around his eyes. "We should flee inland," he said suddenly. "Take horses to Broadfell and bribe a shipman to take us off down the east coast."

"Cross a hundred miles of hard country in a blizzard with the Queen of Eyra and a bawling child?" Rui Finco grimaced. Then he turned to the sorcerer. "Can you transform her?" He indicated the Rosa Eldi, whose lambent eyes were fixed on the dark waters of the harbor below them.

Virelai shook his head vigorously. "N–no, lord," he stammered. "I am exhausted."

"We should slit her throat, as the old woman suggested. The babe, too," Bardson said viciously. "It has to be done at some point anyway."

At this, the Rose of Elda turned her compelling gaze upon him and the Earl of Broadfell snarled like a cornered wolf and made the sign of Sur's anchor; which had no effect on her at all, for all she did was to smile at him, a smile of immense compassion and understanding.

"Don't use your spells on me, you witch! Where I come from, we would place a sealskin bag over your head and stone you to death." He backed away from her.

She stepped forward and reached out to him. But instead of succumbing to the gentle suggestion she tried to lay upon him, Erol Bardson lashed out furiously. His fist connected with an inexorable snap on the hinge of that exquisite jaw. For a moment she swayed where she stood; then those mesmeric green eyes rolled back in her skull and the Queen of the Northern Isles—part woman; part goddess—crumpled till she lay, white skin, white robe, and white fur, upon the white, white snow.

Rui Finco was aghast. "In Falla's name, what have you done?" He stared at the Eyran traitor. "You've killed her! By the Lady, you've killed our only bargaining piece!" He turned and grabbed Virelai by the arm. "You—get down there and bring her back to us. I need her alive!"

The sorcerer quailed. "I— she's . . . She—"

"She's what? Dead? Well, at least make her seem alive. She's no good to us like this. Do whatever you have to do!" The Lord of Forent hauled him by the collar and slung him down roughly beside the prone body.

She's the Goddess. She cannot die . . .

Virelai felt the words he had been about to blurt out hammering around his head. The freezing slush soaked through the knees of his breeches, but he didn't feel it at all. His fingers quested out toward her, faltered. It would be the first time he'd touched her since the Moonfell Plain, and he had known so little about her then. He was ashamed, frightened. Even unconscious, she terrified him now that he knew her true nature; and if he were to touch her, surely she would know his? A man who had sold her the length and breadth of the Istrian coast; who had harbored unclean desires for her himself, desires which had remained unfulfilled only because he had not been capable; who had agreed to sell her to the man who had launched a false war to steal her back. Surely, given the untapped and hidden power he sensed inside that frail exterior, she would rip his soul apart?

Trembling, he reached out and brushed her neck. A voice sounded in his head, as if from a very great distance: and what it said shocked him. He jerked back, as if burned, and scrambled to his feet so quickly his head spun.

"She— I—" He rubbed his face with hands that no longer felt like his own. "She's . . . alive, my lord. She'll come round, given time." He averted his eyes, both from the Istrian lord and from the woman on the ground.

Rui Finco glared at him, then decided further argument would gain him nothing. He turned to the Earl of Broadfell. "Carry her," he ordered brusquely, and when the man demurred, he drew a dagger and made his determination clear. "We've got to get her onto a ship and away from here!"

TYCHO Issian strode up and down the vessel, sword in hand, shrieking orders and imprecations. The rowers rowed hard, expecting to be spitted at any moment. You only had to take one look at the man to know he had gone completely off his head. He hadn't even stopped to take down the sail, so here they were in darkest night, picked out as clear as day with thirty square yards of undyed white canvas flapping about above them, as large a target as any archer could ever ask for. But why Cera and Prionan and the others had so witlessly followed him into this peril, who could say? Everyone knew that the harbor at Halbo had some sort of special defense system—some said magic, others that it was some kind of mechanical device. They waited for some disaster to befall, cringing as they came in under the towering black cliffs.

As they sailed in abreast of the Sentinel Towers, some of the rowers from the hill tribes of Farem began to get agitated. They cast down their oars and dragged at their shackles, jabbering incomprehensibly in their native tongue and pointing at the water. Tycho took the lash from the whipman and whipped them himself. Torn between their terror of the mad lord and of the unknown magic lurking around them, they buckled to the immediate threat to their flesh and took up their oars again. Their souls were lost, no matter what they did now.

RAVN Asharson, King of the Northern Isles, stared out of the maproom window in disbelief. "They have lost their minds," he croaked.

Stormway was at his shoulder at once. He screwed up his eyes. All he could see out there through the swirling snow were white sails, which made no sense at all. White sails? No northerner worth Sur's good salt would carry white sails, yet the ships were undoubtedly Eyran in appearance, low in the water, with curving stemposts and the sleek lines of predators. The moon lit them so that they looked like some spectral force, sailing out of history, their oars manned by afterwalkers from ancient battles. At the sight of them, his stump itched and with the superstitious instincts of his ancestors he found himself making the sign of the anchor to ward off ill luck and evil spirits, until Ravn saw him doing it and laughed.

"Do you think they're ghosts, old man, come back to haunt you? Maybe they've come to bring you back your hand!"

"More like to take the other," Egg Forstson said sourly, girding on his sword belt. "It seems Istria has made good at last on its long promise to carry a holy war to the north."

"They shall carry their 'holy war' to the seabed, damn them! When the first ship comes in range, give the signal to the towers to winch up the chainwall," Ravn told his grizzled lieutenant.

Egg paused.

"What?" said his king sharply. "There's no time to waste, man. Get to it!"

"The chains may not work, sire."

"They've been maintained with absolute care: I know—I've inspected the mechanisms myself."

The Earl of Shepsey grimaced. "They were designed to stop bigger vessels than these, lord. The sort of ships the Istrians have always built. But from what I can see, the ships coming in are more like our own fleet in design, shallow-drafted. I'm not sure they won't sail right over the chain."

Stern-faced, the king digested this unwelcome piece of information.

"The Nemesis then, lord?" Stormway asked reluctantly.

Ravn stared at his old adviser as if he were mad. It was well known the creature was quite mythical. "Damn. Just raise the chains anyway, Egg, and take the archers with you, pitch and brands. I'll not trust to luck. Stormway, with me—we'll take the boats out and meet them head on!"

Down through the castle they hurtled, two old retainers and their king, raising the alarm at every turn. Men came stumbling out of bed-chambers in various states of disarray, with goblets in their hands, naked with swords. Voices were raised in confusion and urgency. Torches were lit against the heavy darkness of the night. The hollow echo of booted feet rang in every stairwell. Women screamed. Servants to fetch chain mail and weaponry, to rouse any who still slept, to convey wives and children to the safe places in the keep, or out into the town to carry or-ders to the forces gathered in the inns, the barracks, the stables, the warehouses and fish sheds. From stillness and calm, suddenly all of Halbo was a chaos of activity.

Down in the courtyard below the keep, Ravn Asharson came upon a great crowd of men milling restlessly about, with one young man run-ning around in front of them trying not very successfully to keep order.

"Guthrun?"

His ship's navigator spun around. For some reason he seemed puzzled by the sight of his monarch. "Sire?"

"What are you doing?"

"What you ordered, my lord. I've gathered them all here, but it's been hard to get them to obey. They all want to get down to the quays—"

Ravn frowned. "Where's Hogny?"

A huge yellow-bearded man stepped out of the ranks, his face puce with irritation. "Here, sire. This young whippersnapper seems to think that you put him in charge—"

Ravn rolled his eyes. There had been talk of madness in the Hart clan, but now was not a good time for it to emerge. "For the god's sake, man, what were you thinking?"

The big man became mulish. "He says you gave him your sword as a token of the command."

Ravn laughed, patted his hip. "Trollbiter is exactly where it ought to be, at my side. Let's see this mighty weapon, then, Guthrun."

The young man looked as though he might burst into tears. He swept the sword in question out in front of him, as if offering it back to its rightful owner. Where there had—he could have sworn—been a decent workaday Eyran blade, there now lay across his palms a wicked-looking curved sword of clear southern origin.

Ravn took it from him, plainly angry now, too angry and confused, too, to notice the blur of the edges, or the waning buzz of hasty magic the metal still bore. "I haven't got time for this nonsense. Take him away," he said to one of the other guards. "Lock him in one of the fish sheds till this is over. He's obviously lost his wits." Then he raised his voice so all could hear.

"Men of Eyra: this enemy force has the gall to enter our home waters with brazen white sails, so confident are they of their success. They come to storm our capital, to raid our city, put our defenders to the sword, and carry off our women! We have fought this enemy for three hundred years and they have driven us farther north with every successive attack. Now they dare to come against us in the heart of our homeland, as if they begrudge us even this and would drive us into the arctic seas.

"They call us barbarians, but it is not we who cry heresy and burn those who disagree with our madness. They call this a holy war, yet they send against us slaves, mercenaries, and pressed men! They call us savages, but without copying our ships they would barely have made it out of their own ports! And if their own women are willing and hot-blooded, what do they want with ours? I know that every good Eyran man has twice the brains and the brawn of any feeble southerner—"

At this a cheer rose.

"—so let us meet these lily-livered, ranting wife-stealers with hearts of iron and fire. Many of you will have lost fathers and grandfathers in the last war—now is the time for revenge. Let us go forth and do deeds they will sing of in the days to come! Let us carry the fight out to our enemy and show these Istrian bastards what good Eyran men are made of!"

Swords aloft, calling on the name of their gods, their ancestors, and their loved ones, the defenders of Halbo ran down to the docks and began to launch every ship moored in the harbor, every vessel laid up in dry dock, and every skiff and ketch and tub besides.

The Battle of Halbo

FOR worshipers of the fire goddess Falla, there can surely be no worse fate than death by drowning. To be swallowed by an antithetical element is terrible enough. The men of Istria believe their souls must be ferried through the Lady's fires if they are to enter her paradise and gain the rewards for which they have striven all their mortal days, but to be lost to the realm of the enemy's sea god is tantamount to everlasting damnation. In addition, the southerners' hatred of water is so pronounced that few Istrians learn to swim. Even those who can stand little chance of life in water of temperatures barely above freezing—let alone with the chaos of battle all around them. Certainly, the commanders of the invading force had given little consideration to such matters. Their mission was sacred; the Goddess would certainly smile on their endeavors.

For the men of Halbo, the city's very survival was at stake. Decisions taken in haste might mean the difference between the sacking of their town and ultimate victory. Yet the timing of the raising of a chainwall was a delicate matter. The choice facing the defenders was whether to prevent all invaders from entering home waters—by balking their progress, forcing them either to sail away disappointed (an optimistic wish) or to wait outside the wall, effectively laying siege to the city by letting no ship in or out, or of splitting the invasion force by allowing the first ships in the line easy access, before cutting them off from their fellows.

For reasons of expediency as well as out of bloodlust, the Eyrans opted for the latter stratagem.

The first ship, sailing some distance ahead of the rest, passed by the Sentinel Towers unscathed. Seeing the flagship's success, a number of other vessels followed swiftly in her wake before the winches took the strain. Slowly, the chainwall was raised, stretching half a mile across the dark harbor just below the surface of the sea to the winding rooms hollowed out in the feet of the two towers. The twelfth ship to thus gain access suffered a lucky escape, only her steerboard grating on those vast links of iron, said to have been forged in the ancient days with a mixture of blood and seithers' charms. Rudderless now, the *Pride of Hedera* stumbled in behind the rest. The next vessels in the line were less fortunate.

With a groan of protesting timbers and the shrieks of men both shackled and unshackled, the *Southern Wayfarer* and the *Sestria* were violently upended as the chainwall caught and pivoted them skyward.

Death by drowning is said by some to be a peaceful way to leave the world; but to those men flung without warning into the chilly waters of Halbo's harbor, the black sea closing over their heads so that even the moonlight was blotted out, with—in the case of the rowers—iron shackles binding them to links set into the splintered deck, the fate which took them was far from pleasant. Arms thrashing in vain, legs pumping, lungs filling with scouring brine, body growing more numb and heavy and saturated by the second, down they went, and down they stayed.

Now came the fire the souls of those thus lost might have welcomed: fire on the heads of arrows shot from the arrow-slits of the Sentinel Towers; fiery balls of pitch cast from ballistas atop the defenses, the undyed sails a perfect target amid the darkness of water and air. *The Cockerel* caught alight and blazed like a torch; but it was less of a blessing than the southerners had wished for. Now men who had sent nomads and magic makers, adulterous women and heretic men to bubble and crisp in the cleansing pyres of the Goddess learned the reality of that hot embrace. Those who were able to jump overboard found abruptly that they welcomed the proximity of the freezing waters; but the slaves were consigned to burn where they were chained, screaming in agony.

The Lord of Cantara stood at the prow of *Falla's Mystery* and stared fixedly through the smoke and snow, oblivious to all but his own obsession. Behind him, all was destruction and death; before him, the citadel in which lay the woman he adored. Grimly, he willed the ships onward.

But now there were other vessels moving in the gloom: shadowy hulks with no masts or stemposts raised; small skiffs and fishing boats; smacks and ketches and dinghies, coming toward them full of armed men, fighting men.

Tycho Issian was not a fighting man, by nature or by inclination, though he wore a sword as a symbol of his role as joint commander of the invasion. As the edge of the rising sun pierced the cloud layer on the eastern horizon, it presaged the advent of the first Eyran ship and limned the defenders in bloody crimson. Thus haloed, these huge, shaggy men looked suddenly more terrifying than any nightmare conjuration. Tycho wrapped his fists around the unfamiliar pommel of his weapon and clenched his jaw.

I will avenge your dishonor, my rose, he swore silently.

He turned to his men. "Kill them!" he roared. "In the name of the Goddess, kill them all!"

Then he ran back down the ship and took cover behind the huge Galian mercenaries he had personally picked as his bodyguard, and battle commenced.

FROM their vantage point on the rocks below the east of the towers, it was impossible to tell which way the battle was going. Judged on numbers alone, it seemed that the Istrians must hold sway, for the chainwall had indeed failed to prevent access to the shallow-draughted ships, and now the harbor was crammed with invading vessels. But the Eyrans fought grimly and with a skill, determination, and discipline which their opponents could not match. Men in tiny boats wove a daring passage in and out of the longships, hurling spears and other missiles at the enemy, sometimes flaming torches, sometimes themselves. They fought, Rui thought, almost admiringly, like wolves; but wolves with a plan. To be in the midst of that onslaught would be daunting indeed. He wondered how Tycho Issian was coping with the responsibilities of his role—if he were, in fact, still alive.

He waited and he cursed the southern lord who had put them all in peril, and still the Rose of Elda lay like one dead.

The dead, for their part, washed in against the rocks, battered and bloody and weed covered; some horribly wounded, stuck through with spars and wood shards, spears, or arrows; hacked and mutilated, their heads and limbs cloven, others merely pale and drowned; or black and burned. Istrian and Eyran alike, reduced to wreckage and tidewrack. Flotsam came bobbing in to join the dead with each successive wave— smashed kegs, broken strakes, and splintered oars; fragments of charred sail and mast; discarded fishing nets, floats, crabpots, and buoys cut loose from commandeered vessels.

In all this time, the Rose of the World made no move, nor sighed, nor spoke, but as she lay unconscious, glistening tears rolled unchecked down that smooth white face.

Behind her, the servingwoman fed the royal child, which seemed to care not one whit for all the drama which surrounded it, nor for the cold, as long as it had a tit to suck and warm milk dribbling down its chin. Lucky brat, Rui thought, scanning the melee with a sinking heart.

It was some time before the Lord of Forent spotted an opportunity; and the chill which gripped him like an ague may have played a part in addling his wits. "Bring the boat in," he told Bardson wearily. "We'll have to take our chances."

THE ship which had led the attack now fell back among its fellows, Ravn saw with contempt. So much for leading by example, he thought, as his father had always taught him. "Go after it!" he counseled his steersman.

"There's a number of vessels between us and her, sire," the man returned. "It won't be easy."

It wasn't. For an hour they battled their way between both enemy and allied ships. Burned-out hulks hindered their progress, and other Istrian vessels intervened, sometimes with deliberate aggression, more often because they found themselves unable to maneuver out of the way.

There was smoke everywhere: from the southern ships they had fired; from the missiles hurled back by the Istrians. He had killed Sur knew how many of the enemy; he had lost count. Blood ran down his arms, down his sword. He fought back to back with one man, then another when the first was cut down; a third after that. But still the southerners kept coming, ship after ship after ship. All new, he noticed, all of familiar design.

Damn Morten Danson. If he ever laid hands on the man, he'd hang and quarter him personally for this treachery.

He was tired. They were all tired, but they were not just fighting for themselves or for their families, but for the Eyran way of life; an Eyran future. If Halbo fell, Istria would take this, their last stronghold, and make it their own. The men would be put to the sword, the women raped and sown with Istrian seed, a new generation of children who would know nothing of their proud heritage and whose Eyran mothers would be shrouded in cloth and stashed away for sex. The idea of his wife being subjected to such ignominy lent him renewed power and an enemy's head was suddenly cleaved from his shoulders with such force it flew clean off and landed with a splash in the gore-tinged surf.

The sun climbed in a crimson-streaked sky and he remembered abruptly his mother's words of doom:

Blood will come from the south and mar the snows of Eyra; white skin will gape and run red. Sorcery has risen, wild magic all around. Fire will fall on Halbo. Hearts will wither, many die. . . .

Perhaps this was the end of everything, then: his doom. If so, he would seek out the Istrian leader and take him down to Sur's Howe with him—by whatever means he could.

AS the tall cliffs of Eyra's mainland loomed ahead of them, the Master gave out an almighty roar of frustration, rousing Aran Aranson from his stupor.

"What?" he asked blearily. "What do you see?"

When the old man said nothing, Aran swiveled in his seat. Black smoke streaked a sky made bloody by the risen sun. Plumes of it; towers of it. No mere bonfires, these: no whale rendering or festivity had created such a smog. Halbo City must be afire. He turned back, aghast.

"Are they here?" he cried. "The enemy?"

At last the mage fixed him with his fearsome stare. "Your enemy, not mine. All men are the same to me. The one I seek is here, but not as I left her, ah no. We may already be too late—"

The luckless man frowned. Dulled by magic, by pain, and by grief, he shook his head, took a firmer grip on the oars, and recommenced his chore, while the old man ranted and raged.

THE din rang all around them—the ring of iron on iron, shouts of fury and fear, the crackle of fire, the cries of the dying. The noise of the wailing child was entirely drowned by the cacophony around it, which was the sole satisfaction Rui Finco could derive from the situation. One moment, *Falla's Mystery* had been in clear view, drawing away from the fighting vessels as if to flee the battle, the next, a burning ship had drifted between them and their destination and smoke engulfed everything. Pieces of falling timber and flaming sail rained down around them, forcing them to abandon a direct course.

When they cleared the immediate danger, the Lord of Forent stood up precariously in the stern and waved his hands to dispel the smoke. "This is chaos," he declared through gritted teeth. "Chaos."

A larger than average wave lapped in over the low gunwale and sloshed around in the bilges. They had, he noted bitterly, nothing to bail with. He teetered and sat down quickly before he lost his balance and made a more intimate acquaintance with the ocean. From dry ground it had all seemed so simple: the flagship in plain view and a mere two hundred yards away; all they had to do was to cross that small expanse to safety. But that small expanse might as well have been a raging sea.

"We could row beyond the harbor into open water and wait out the battle," Erol Bardson shouted above the noise.

Rui Finco scanned the unwelcoming sea beyond the towers and shivered. Waves stretched away to the far, tilting horizon, gray and chill and topped by long windblown ridges of breaking surf. Never had the Northern

Ocean seemed so inimical. The difference between traversing any part of it in a finely crafted longship and this flimsy little tub had never been so apparent. "If we hit any waves larger than the last, we'll be lost for sure. Just keep rowing, damn you!"

With the sea leaking in and the cold in his bones, the Lord of Forent wished with a passion they had not left the shore; wished he had given the Earl of Broadfell's original plan—to flee inland on some solid nags—more serious consideration. Anything was better than this.

Lady Falla, get us safe aboard an Istrian ship and I will worship you for the rest of my life. I will give up the women and the wine and become your priest. Just deliver me from this hell!

It was an unspoken prayer; but as if he had offered it up with due pomp, ceremony, and bloody sacrifice, it brought a miraculous response. Ahead of them, the smoke cleared suddenly; and there was *Falla's Mystery*, looking remarkably intact, apart from some charring near the stern.

"Give me your oar, you fool!" Rui Finco pushed the ineffectual sorcerer out of the way, took his place on the cross bench, and put his back into the rowing as if the ship ahead of them was a mirage which might vanish in seconds. Moments later, wood groaned against wood, followed by muted exclamations of amazement and delight. Eager hands reached down, and the Lord of Forent and Erol Bardson lifted up the shrouded figure of the unconscious queen, and watched as she was passed wonderingly into the vessel. The serving girl got to her feet with the babe cradled firmly in her arms, and stood ready to be transferred next, but Rui Finco pushed past her and launched himself over the gunwale of the rocking ship, his legs waving in the air like an overturned beetle until at last he tumbled thankfully onto the deck. After that, there was such a rush to bring the other passengers aboard that the longship listed dangerously and the captain yelled for discipline and came to find out what all the fuss was about. But when he saw what had been fished out of the ocean he swore in amazement, and went to fetch his commander.

"My lord—"

"Not now, Haro."

"We've taken aboard some survivors. I think you'll want to see them for yourself, sir."

Tycho Issian was annoyed to be so distracted. The battle was going well: another of the Eyran vessels had just succumbed to fire, its crew leaping overboard as flames consumed the last of the rigging and brought the sail tattering among them. He watched the *Leaping Pig* bear down on the men in the water, battering them with oars, with spars and spears and anything that came to hand.

"Kill him, yesss—excellent!" The Eyran went down, his skull split apart, one hand stretched beseechingly to the sky. A man to his right shrieked as a spear pierced him where he trod water. At last Tycho turned to the captain. "Did you see that? Right through the guts. We shall slaughter them all before this day is out, blasted heathens! So much for the power of this Sur they call upon; so much for their pagan beliefs. We shall scour the north clean and—"

Something behind the man's shoulder distracted him from this diatribe. He frowned and stared. There was a woman on his ship, a woman with her arms wrapped around a wailing bundle. She looked a lot like . . . she was—

"Selen!"

The woman looked confused, fearful. She turned this way and that, disoriented by the sudden noise, the press of men, a half-familiar voice. Someone took the baby from her and wrapped a cloak around her, and now she looked even more bewildered than she had before.

Tycho broke the spell. He strode down the ship, pushing men roughly out of his way. "My daughter," he croaked. "It is my daughter Selen."

Rui Finco wiped bilgewater off his breeches and interposed himself between them swiftly, before the man could press home this insane claim. "Her name is Leta Gullwing, and I claim her as my booty!"

The Lord of Cantara's gaze swiveled reluctantly away from the riveting sight of his lost daughter, returned to him suddenly amid bloodshed and horror in this foreign place, and his eyes bulged in shock.

"You!" The single word emerged as a howl of outrage. Saliva bubbled on Tycho Issian's lower lip. The walnut hue of his face deepened and flowered dark red; sweat burst out on his forehead.

Rui Finco frowned. Clearly it had not been the best idea he had ever had to leave the Lord of Cantara in charge of the fleet, for the stress of such responsibility had sent him mad. "There, now, my friend," he said soothingly and stepped forward. "Calm yourself." He put out a hand to give the man a reassuring pat on the shoulder; and was suddenly privy to a searing sensation and the sight of that hand flying far from the arm to which it had all its natural life been attached, gore spouting furiously. Like a man in a dream, he watched the obscene item land with a splash in the waters of Halbo harbor and vanish from sight. Then he stared at the gushing stump where his hand had been. Only then did the pain and realization come crashing in.

"You have gone mad! I am the Lord of Forent—"

But even this did not have the desired effect. Instead of returning to his senses and falling at once to his knees in shame, Tycho Issian leaped away, flourishing his stained sword and shrieking, "I have him! I have him! Take him, put him in chains. Shackle him to the mast!"

Two of the big Galians came forward immediately, grabbed the prisoner under the arms, and dragged him away. Blood jetted from his wound, marking his passage with a foul trail of crimson.

Leta Gullwing, who had in another life been Selen Issian, watched this tableau play itself out before her in horror. Then she ran at the man who had once been her father and rained down blows upon him. "You monster! You vile, bloody monster! What have you done? You have maimed him! Do you not know the King of the Northern Isles when you see him? And yet you treat him like a common criminal, no worse—a wild beast. I spit upon you, your goddess, and your war—"

And she did. The gobbet landed with surprising force upon Tycho Issian's cheek, slid slowly down it like a slug.

The Lord of Cantara wiped his hand across his face in disgust, then wiped his hand on the fresh clothing he had donned to greet the Rose of the World. Things were not going at all to plan. He regarded the woman he had thought to be his daughter with repulsion. This creature, with her flashing eyes and filthy mouth was not the doe-eyed girl who had been stolen away at the Allfair. This was a harpy, a termagant, a thing of the gutter, no doubt defiled by all and sundry, and welcoming each newcomer with open legs. She was vile; she was not his child, seed of his loins, pride of his house. He would have her put over the side, but he had other matters to attend to—

"Out of my way, harlot!"

He shoved her hard and she went down in a sprawl, and then he was past her and his way was clear. His enemy, the King of Eyra, was his, a captive, securely chained to the central mast. Elation rose in him. None could deny him his right now. The time for reckoning had come.

The man looked half dead already, which was distressing; he had lost a lot of blood.

As if reading his thoughts, the ship's chirurgeon stepped forward. "Let me cauterize his wound, lord," he suggested. "He'll be of no value to us dead."

"Value?"

"As ransom, my lord. Now that you hold prisoner the King of the Northern Isles and his wife, they will surely surrender—"

Wife? Tycho Issian frowned. "Wife?" he said aloud and the chirurgeon nodded and indicated the crowd of men astern who were gathered there, staring down at something with utter fascination. Reluctantly, they parted at his barked order to reveal a pale form, apparently asleep. The woman's hair had escaped the confines of its ermine hood to fall in long, picturesque tresses around a perfect face. Even with her mesmeric green eyes closed, her presence was still spellbinding. The crew moved aside reluctantly from where they had stood gazing in wonder upon such a startling sight: a woman wrapped in seemingly peaceful sleep amid carnage and nightmare, rosebud mouth slightly parted and curved in a provocative bow of a smile. All that marred her beauty was a livid patch at the angle of the jaw. This, then, was the woman who had started the conflict, the one the barbarian king had chosen over their own, their Swan. Seeing her lying there in all her vulnerable glory, none of them could blame the man. She was, truly, the Rose of the World.

Tycho Issian stumbled forward, fell to his knees. His heart clenched like the muscle it was, a hard, jolting contraction which rippled through his chest. He thought he might die, but to die so, gazing upon that face, was to die in bliss.

"My lady," he whispered.

Her eyes came open, and now his heart turned over and fell away like a dove struck by a hawk.

THE Rosa Eldi blinked. She had been in another place, a place which was dark and full of memories. Not her memories, exactly, but familiar all the same. Voices spoke to her, *were* her. In this ineffable place they existed together, the Three who were One, and More. Now she knew that she was not alone after all. Which was as well, for the state of Elda was parlous already and would be worse. But help, in a raw and primal form, was at hand. She turned her gaze upon the man who stared at her, knowing what must be done. Blood must sometimes be shed, to save a world.

"I know you," she said. "I have felt your prayers."

Her voice thrummed through him like the great vibration of a purring cat; or the distant eruption of a mountain of fire.

"I am your servant."

His eyes bored into her, rapt, unresisting. She could burn him, break him, use him as she would. Her smile widened. "Your name?"

"Tycho Issian, my lady. I am the Lord of Cantara."

"And where would Cantara lie?"

"To the farthest south of Istria, bordering the desertlands, my lady."

The wide green eyes flared briefly. "And can you see the Red Peak from there, my lord of Cantara?"

"On a clear day, my lady, one may spy its vapors from the towers of my castle and sniff a hint of sulfur on the air."

Now she sat upright, smoothing down the great fur hood so that it fell away from her luxuriant golden hair to reveal bare white shoulders and listened with satisfaction as he inhaled sharply at the sight of her. "Excellent. And shall you take me there, Tycho Issian, to your towered castle in the desertlands?"

His name upon her lips was the most powerful spell of all.

"I shall. Oh, I shall. But first, my rose, I must avenge your honor." He held his hand out to her and she took it and stood. Fire ran up his arm, took burning root in his heart. He guided her to the figure bound to the mast and watched as she viewed the man with complete dispassion.

"Behold this so-called king," he declared. "Revealed as the wretch he truly is."

At this, Ravn Asharson's head came up slowly. His vision was glazed, his mouth agape in agony. At last, he managed to focus on the fact that two figures were standing before him. One he could not see properly, for its bright visage hurt his eyes. So he turned his attention to the other, began to frame words. "It is me . . . you fool. Wearing the sorcerer's illusion still . . ." He tried to swivel his head to search for the pale man, but they had bound him too well.

The Lord of Cantara regarded him with loathing. "You disgust me! Have you no shame, no honor?"

For a moment, it seemed the man's face flickered and blurred and seemed to subtly change; then he was Ravn Asharson again. Dark eyes fixed themselves mournfully on the woman at Tycho Issian's side.

"Ask her," he groaned. "She knows the truth."

The Lord of Cantara turned to the Rosa Eldi. "Is this the man who stole you away?"

"Ah yes," she breathed. "That is him, the thief."

"Please," whispered Rui Finco, the blood loss making him close to fainting. "Look at me. You saw through the magic, you said it—tell him, for Falla's sake—"

With a bellow of rage, Tycho Issian rushed at him. "How dare you look at her so?" Gouging fingers buried themselves in the bound man's face. There was a squelching sound, a terrible cry, then clear liquid spurted.

"By Falla, how well can you see now?" Tycho Issian howled. He held out two vile objects, making a triumphant circuit around the maimed figure, oblivious to the disgust of his crew, who backed away as if to distance themselves from this sacrilegious act. It was not so many generations since the Istrians had had a ruler of their own, an emperor, a man of royal blood, ordained by the gods. To see a man of rank thus treated went against every notion of chivalry their ancestors had owned and passed down to them. The Goddess would surely strike down the man who did such deeds in her name.

But Tycho Issian was beside himself now, almost dancing with glee. "Can you see the error of your ways?" he taunted, waving the gory eyeballs in front of the blinded man. "No? Have you nothing more to say; no apology to make to this rose you have so foully plucked?" He looked down at the revolting things he held in his hands, then tossed them out into the sea.

"I . . . am . . . not . . . the . . . King of . . . Eyra . . ." the figure panted, tears of blood streaking his once-handsome face.

"No," hissed his enemy. "You are a worm, a rutting worm who has dared to defile my rose."

"My lord," the chirurgeon intervened. "Enough—"

"Enough?"

"He is dying, my lord. Let him leave this world with some grace—"

This last suggestion was cut brutally short. Tycho Issian stabbed the impertinent doctor once through the throat, kicked his jerking body aside, and buried his tainted blade in the torso of the chained man, ripping downward with all his might. With a hot gush, the man's intestines flooded out onto the deck, rope after glistening rope of them, and then the mad lord cast his sword aside and gripped them with his own hands, hauling, cursing, his feet slipping in all the blood and viscera.

A woman started to wail in the background; rain began to fall. Pale light shafted down through the ragged clouds to illuminate what was left of the Lord of Forent as the sorcerer's illusion failed at last. But without his eyes and with his face covered in a sheet of blood, not even his own mother would have been able to tell the difference between Rui Finco, and her other son, Ravn Asharson, now standing on the foredeck of *Sur's Raven*, gazing in horror at the apparition twenty yards ahead of him.

He had just given the order to his helmsman to ram the enemy flagship when the waters erupted beneath them, and, after three hundred years of confinement in the seithers' bonds which chained it to the seabed beneath the towers, the Nemesis finally arose. . . .

RAHE fell back into the stern of the vessel, exhausted and grimacing. He clutched his withered ribs and rolled from side to side, wheezing.

Aran Aranson shipped his oars and regarded the old man with some alarm. Was he dying? He looked as if he was suffering some kind of excruciating attack. Aran did not understand what had been happening around him: one moment they had been sailing blithely across the ocean, skimming the waves so that his oarstrokes seemed a mere adjunct to the magical propulsion emanating from the man he had learned to call "Rahay," or "the Master"; then the smoke-filled haze above the cliffs of Halbo had come into view and the old man had started cursing and swearing and beating the boat with his bare fists, apparently furious. Some time after this excess of temper had finally subsided, Rahe had closed his eyes and begun a lot of muttering in a language Aran could not follow at all, a muttering which was sometimes accompanied by arm-waving and stamping feet and sometimes rose in volume to a bellow which made him clamp his hands over his ears.

Now the old man opened his eyes and grinned maniacally at the one he had dubbed "the Fool," his paroxysms of laughter giving way at last to a series of guffaws and an expression of utter craftiness.

"What?" asked Aran bitterly. "What is so funny?" He was irritated that the old man was not dying; that he was enjoying himself quite so much seemed an affront, to him and the world in general. Somewhere under that pall of smoke, the men of Halbo were dying, the women, too, most like.

"She has no idea how to control it!" the Master chuckled. "She thinks it is her friend, her pet—but she has loosed a monster!"

"What monster?"

"The Nemesis! Oh, folk have made up all sorts of stories about the thing that is reputed to lurk beneath the waters of Halbo's harbor, but they don't know the half of it." He paused, suddenly delighted. "The half of it—of, I am so witty, ha ha!"

Aran Aranson knotted his fingers in his hair. It was as much as he could do not to belt the old man. "Half of *what?*"

Rahe cocked his head. He looked, Aran thought, with that mane of white hair and those cold, pale eyes, like Old Ma Hallasen's goat. Then he remembered that Old Ma was in truth Old Ma no longer, and that was not a comforting thought either. "Ah, I forget how little you know, my Fool. When the world was made, the gods gave it a threefold protector: the Warrior, the Woman, and the Beast. When they are together, they are more than the sum of their parts—the Three who are More—but separated, they are less than their singularities; I managed to break them farther apart still so that they could do me no harm. As a man may split an acorn with an ax-blow, so I split the Woman and the Warrior from themselves, body from soul, anima from animus; and the most brutish aspect of the Beast I banished here, chained with spells in Halbo's sea.

"The cat now wanders the desertlands, disconsolate, but its bestial self is rampaging monstrously free among Halbo's invaders and defenders. Oh, the carnage it must be causing! I cannot wait to see the chaos."

Aran frowned. This was all too metaphysical for him. Never a particularly superstitious man, he had no liking for such abstract and fanciful meanderings. "I have heard the myths of the beast of Halbo, trapped in a great cage of iron locked by seither's spells, but I had always thought such stories to be symbolic of the harbor's chainwall," he said slowly. "But now you are telling me that the creature actually exists?"

"Ah yes," the mage said cheerfully. "And it has spawned offspring, too, for its appetites are mighty, albeit with lesser beasts which can slip through the bars of its cage."

Painful memories of his son Halli's death at sea assailed Aran now. They had said that wreck was caused by a sea monster; though that had been far away from the mainland. He shut the thought away, for it burned like gall. "Then who may have the power to loose such a beast?" he asked, bemused. "Who is this 'she' of whom you speak?"

Rahe looked at him as if he were half-witted; then remembered he was only a mortal, and one without a hint of magic in his blood. "The Rosa Eldi, my boy. She who was once the goddess of this world."

Aran's brows drew together in a single black line across his forehead. The Rose of the World. The woman their king had taken to wife at the ill-fated Allfair last year. But she was a nomad, a mere Footloose woman . . . wasn't she? He remembered abruptly the glimpse of a green eye and a white hand on the coat of a black cat behind the mapmaker's stall, and the way his heart had been set racing as he left that place with the scrap of parchment promising treasure and adventure clutched so tightly to his chest. Then he remembered how Ravn Asharson had been so entranced by that strange, pale woman that he would give no mind to saving his daughter Katla from the fires of their enemy. If this was a goddess, the response she demanded from the men around her was little short of tawdry. Who could love or respect such a being?

He made the sign of Sur's anchor, in case he prompted that god to strike him down at once for even entertaining the possibility of there being a rival deity.

"And she has set this monster free?" he said, his voice full of disbelief.

"It seems she has tried, indeed, for her magic is in the air. But she is not strong enough yet, and so I have given her a little help." He dropped Aran Aranson a conspiratorial wink.

The Rockfall man digested this slowly. Then: "Why would you do that?" he asked.

"A little chaos can only help our cause, my boy."

FREEZING, blood-tinged water cascaded over them all. In the stern, Virelai screamed and clung to the gunwale as if his life depended on it, which was indeed the case. Selen Issian, her previous life slipping back to her in unpleasant little starts and flashes of memory, curled herself protectively about the only thing that still mattered in her world, and sought for the will to survive this new ordeal. Her father, Tycho Issian, wrapped one arm around the Rosa Eldi—who was, it seemed, too stunned by the sight of the terrible thing she had raised from the deep to object to this manhandling—and the other around the mast, crushing them both against the body of the dead man. Meanwhile, the captain of the vessel, Haro Orbia, caught hold of the massive mastfish and molded himself around it, muttering prayers to the Lady of Fire.

Others were neither so fortunate nor so galvanized by terror.

Two of the big Galian mercenaries, who had been gawping at the monster with expressions of the utmost horror and the slow-wittedness of their inbred lineage, tumbled like mannequins dropped by a bored child and fell, shrieking, over the side and into the sea. Erol Bardson, riveted for long seconds by the sight of the royal ship bearing down upon them with his king and chief enemy at its prow, failed to recognize this new danger until it was upon him. As the deck tilted violently, he grasped desperately at a length of chain which hurtled past but only succeeded in diverting its passage so that it whacked into his face, rendering him half-insensible. By the time he had regained his senses sufficiently to review his situation, it was far too late. One moment he had left the deck and was airborne and everything was dreamlike, slow, surreal; the next, he was staring into what appeared to be a vast dark cave half full of water, weed, and unidentifiably-chewed dead things, a cave fringed with scimitar-like shards of pale bone, and time sped up horribly so that he did not even have the opportunity to wonder what would happen to his pretty ward Finna, his wife, or his home, before the sword-sharp teeth of the Nemesis pierced him in a dozen places, back and front, and his life was extinguished.

If there had been tumult and confusion before, now there was pandemonium. Centuries-old enmity was forgotten in the face of common threat. Vessels beyond the immediate range of the monster turned tail and fled for the safety of the quays, or for the open sea. Those in its path slewed and stalled as men abandoned their posts and dived overboard. Some climbed the mast for a better view and hung gibbering from the yardarm, transfixed by the sight of this thing which was neither whale nor shark nor anything they had ever encountered in this world before, even in the worst of their night terrors.

The flukes of the beast's great tail thrashed the water and broke apart two skiffs which had desperately rowed away from its snapping jaws. Broken men and splintered wood shot into the air and then vanished beneath the bloody, frothing spume of its wake. When it rounded on one of the Istrian ships, many of the crew jumped overboard on the lee side, while their braver comrades smashed oars and spears against the monster's giant slablike head. All this achieved was to add new wounds to the myriad scars etched across the beast's blunt muzzle, scars gained from eons of battering itself against the spellbound bars of its cage; and to enrage it further. Rising out of the water, the Nemesis balanced precariously on its vast tail and hind fins to tower sixty feet in the air over the terrified crew, blotting out the sky and all light and hope; then it crashed down with murderous intent into the center of the *Southern Wayfarer*. The beautifully crafted vessel, made from whippy green unseasoned oak that would flex and curve with the running seas and high rollers of the Northern Ocean, could offer no resistance to such a direct onslaught. With a dreadful groan, the timbers broke and scattered, while the keel, the chained rowers, and two dozen men of Istria, were carried down into the dark waters beneath the creature's bulk.

After that, the Nemesis did not rise again; and none knew its movements. Was it lurking, gathering its energies for another frenzied attack; had it been fatally injured by the wreckage of the *Southern Wayfarer,* or was it grazing the seabed far below them, feasting on the sumptuous pickings scattered across reefs and outcrops, tangled in the kelp beds, washed into sea caves and grottoes?

The northern king's flagship had been carried away from its quarry in the backwash from the monster's dive. It smashed against the *Maid of Ixta* and sent her rocking and reeling into her sister ship, the *Lady of Cera,* which rolled dangerously, losing several members of her crew to the brine; then with dextrous handling from the steersman, the *Sur's Raven* ploughed through a patch of blessedly open water and came to rest alongside the old *Troll of Narth,* whose blackwood strakes had seen worse battles than this in its hundred-and-thirty-year history.

Ravn Asharson, still trembling from shock and adrenaline, gazed with a breaking heart upon the devastation in his harbor. He took in the foundered and sinking ships, the strewn timbers, and dead men of two continents. Beside him, Stormway leaned on his sword, breathing heavily. The leather wrapping had come unfurled from his stump. New blood dripped from it.

"Not so mythical, as you see, sire."

Ravn gave him a hard stare, then yelled with all his might, "Men of Eyra, back to the quays!" The lust for battle had gone out of him, as it seemed to have from the other participants in this conflict, for everywhere men were sheathing their weapons, shaking their heads, binding up comrades' wounds.

The order was picked up and passed along to other friendly vessels until there was a general movement toward the port.

Those Istrians not drowning or dying, or engaged with trying to right their own ships watched them go with little regret. It had been a madman's mission to bait the barbarian king in his own home; some resolved to pay more attention to the intuition of their brethren from the Farem Hills in years to come.

Of the southern nobles who had sailed north with the invasion force, the Dukes of Cera and Calastrina had been killed in the initial engagement; the Lords of Santorinvo, Tagur, and Gibeon had lost their lives in

the course of the battle which ensued; the Duke of Sestria had been upended into the bay when the beast first erupted to life and no one had
seen him resurface or hung around to save him if he did. Varyx, Lord of
Ixta, lay wounded and raving on the foredeck of his vessel. No one knew
what fate had overtaken Rui Finco, the Lord of Forent, last seen on the
damaged flagship, *Falla's Mystery*. None, that is, except Tycho Issian,
Lord of Cantara; who stared over the top of the bowed head of the
woman he had come all this way to rescue at a certain silver circlet holding back the long dark hair of the ruined man chained to the mast and
knew with a sudden awful certainty that the King of the Eyrans was not,
after all, the man he had in his mindless fury blinded and disemboweled.
Swiftly, he slipped the circlet from Rui Finco's ruined head and into his
tunic. He did not think anyone else had yet stumbled to the same conclusion, and it would not be helpful if they did.

Then he stared back into the chaos of the harbor.

A proud fleet had left Forent the best part of a month before. Now,
only a ramshackle collection of battered, burned, and broken vessels remained. But he had his prize; and the northerners had retreated.

When all was said and done, it was the most glorious victory.

30

Aftermath

FALLA'S Mystery and the remnant of the Istrian fleet fled for home across the Northern Ocean, and with great good luck—for them—the weather held fair. In weeks to come, men would talk about the unseasonable calms that stilled those normally turbulent waters, and the stiff northerly wind which followed, filling the sails by day and by night, and many would give up their thanks to the Goddess, who had clearly intervened with the elements of the world on their behalf. Even so, the *Sea Lord* and the *White Lion* never made it home to any port in Istria, and none knew what had befallen them: whether they had foundered due to damage taken in the battle for Halbo, from construction defects which had not been apparent on the voyage out, or poor seamanship; none could say. There were later rumors of mutiny and a slave uprising, and some said ships similar to the two missing vessels had been sighted in the south of the continent, as far away as Gila and even Circesia, with new names and a motley crew, but by then greater events had overtaken all and no one had time to be concerned about the whereabouts of a handful of rich men and their officers.

The *Maid of Ixta* limped into Cera with a poorly repaired mast and half her crew. Varyx was still alive, but only because of the swift action of his chirurgeon in severing the arm that would otherwise have festered and killed him.

Many of the surviving vessels had found themselves masterless; of these, a number fell beneath the command of mercenary soldiers engaged by the Lord of Forent, and these men, seeing an opportunity, went harrying along the coast of the Eyran mainland. From Longfell and Langey they stole fifty-five women and girls; from Sharpnose and Blackness a further thirty-eight, for their husbands and sons had been called to Ravn Asharson's muster in Halbo, and many of them now lay dead at the bottom of the sea, or wounded in the makeshift infirmaries set up in the fish sheds and warehouses on that city's quays.

The *Man of Oak*, under the command of a black-coaster called Peto Iron Arm, raided along the shores of Berthey and brought away the wives and daughters of Longmarsh, Hawkridge, and Haddocks Chair; but not without a fight, for they were tough women and resourceful, and had no wish to be traded in the Istrian slave markets and made whores to their enemies. Many of Peto Iron Arm's crew came away from these violent sackings with broken bones, stab wounds, and bruised faces; and not all of them survived their injuries.

The *Golden Lady of Skarn* met with worse fate; for she was wrecked on the treacherous reefs off Oxfirth, and there the old men, women, and children came out into the shallows and instead of rescuing the survivors, battered them to death with whatever farm implements had come to hand when the wrecking call went out.

Of those vessels still afloat, eleven of the invasion fleet were unable to make their way out of Halbo's harbor as a result of broken rudders and burned masts, or because in the heat of battle their crew had smashed through their shackles with stolen swords and deserted. But Ravn Asharson, having discovered his wife and child gone, was in no mood for clemency.

When a search of the castle and grounds rendered no clue to the Rosa Eldi's whereabouts, he questioned servants, retainers, and courtiers—all to no avail. In the end, he went to seek advice from his mother, the Lady Auda, as to where his wife had hidden with little Wulf for the duration of the battle, for she had an information network concerning the comings and goings of all in the castle and its vicinity which was second to none.

But when he rapped on the door of her chamber there was a moment's pregnant silence within as if the occupants had stopped whatever they were doing and held their breath. Then the door creaked open a hand's width and Lilja Mersen, his mother's ancient bodyservant, stuck her nose through the gap.

When she saw who was knocking for admittance, she shut it again with a clang. Ravn stood there, mystified. It was true that he and his mother had not been on the best of terms these past months, but she had never shunned his company, however aggrieved she had been by his choice of wife. Besides, he was king! He rapped again, more loudly.

This time it was Auda herself who came to the door.

"What do you want?"

It was not a friendly greeting. Ravn frowned. "Let me in, Mother, and I will tell you."

The door inched open, but still the old woman blocked his way. "You may tell me here."

Ravn looked over his shoulder to where a knot of courtiers were advancing along the corridor, their gossip suspended as they watched in fascination the king being denied entrance to his mother's chamber. Determined now, he stuck a leg through the opening, pressed the door wider despite Auda's resistance, forced himself inside, and shut it again before the courtiers could snoop.

There was a scuffle of activity within the room and Lilja stood with her skirts spread to hide something on the bed. Ravn looked away, irritated. Let the old woman have her secrets, then: he had no time for such nonsense.

"Don't bleed on my carpet."

He looked down and found that, indeed, blood was still dripping from a number of wounds on his arms and chest; he had not even noticed until now, such had been the concern for his family. He stepped onto the flagstones, noticing that the old woman made no move to attend to his injuries.

"Where is my wife?"

Auda snorted. "You have mislaid her? How careless."

Ravn glared at her. "Don't play with me, Mother. You always know everything."

"Gone, my son, and good riddance, say I!"

"Gone?"

Now the old woman cackled with unbridled glee. "You really didn't know? Gone with the southern lords on their ships; taken the babe and the nurse with her, too, and sailed for Istria, whence she came. That's how much she cares for you, my boy, but I can see that even though the witch is far away by now, you are still caught in her thrall!"

Ravn felt dizzy, then sick; and not from blood loss.

"When?" he croaked. "How long?"

The old woman shrugged. "If I know anything, she will have been on the first ship to flee, no doubt with its poor captain under her spell."

The King of Eyra found many emotions battling within him; anger came foremost. He raised his hand as if to strike the old woman, but she matched it with a defiant face as if to will him to do it, and his rage subsided as swiftly as it had stirred, leaving him feeling empty and bereft. Then he turned on his heel, flung open the door so hard that the ironwork rang against the stones of the wall, and ran down the corridors bellowing for Stormway and Shepsey to attend him immediately.

The old king Ashar Stenson, the Gray Wolf, had been possessed of such towering rages that men had fled the country rather than bring him bad news; in his time he had killed messengers, roasted heralds, spitted emissaries, and beheaded envoys. His captains and generals had learned to temper even the most evil tidings with carefully worded optimism and fair omens. His son, nevertheless, had always been a boy of a sunny disposition, given to easy laughter, casual banter, and disarming charm. Yet, when it took the best part of a week to clear the wreckage from Halbo's harbor before the remnants of the northern fleet could begin its pursuit, Ravn Asharson displayed worse temper than even his legendary father had shown. News of abductions of women along the southern coast and from the outlying islands only served to heat it further.

The three hundred and seventeen Istrians who had been stranded in Halbo when the rest of their fleet sailed all perished by summary execution by hanging or, when the gibbets were full and no more trees could be spared to make more, simple stabbing—lords, officers, or slaves, it made no difference: if they spoke no Eyran, Ravn had them killed with no recourse to the Were Law which had for centuries been invoked on behalf of all prisoners of war.

"They came to steal my wife and your women," he declared. "This is not an act of war, but one of common thievery and thus shall they be punished."

One evening while the king was pacing up and down the quays watching the ships being outfitted for the foray south, an old man and his companion, who seemed vaguely familiar, accosted him. Ravn was impatient, listless, uninterested in anything other than the pursuit. When the old man announced himself as a powerful mage who would offer his services to help the king regain the Rose of the World, he gave a sharp bark of a laugh and told him to be gone before he found a gibbet with some hanging space left. The old man raised an eyebrow, then split the giant hawser stone of the harbor mole in two. When the incinerated dust settled, it found Ravn Asharson stopped in his tracks, stroking his beard consideringly.

ONLY Aran Aranson was privy to the fact that when the king had left the scene, the hawser stone was back in place, apparently untouched, though the air around it smelled strange. And only Aran Aranson was privy to the effort even this trick had cost the Master, since he was the one who had to carry the old man up into the castle to their temporary quarters that night, the mage being too weak to make his own way. Privately, Aran was becoming less than impressed by the old man's vaunted powers. Raising the monster seemed to have drained him so thoroughly that he fell asleep and snored through the hubbub which followed and, rather significantly, the departure of this "goddess" he had come to reclaim.

WORD carried fast in Eyra: by runner, raven, or rowing boat. There was now talk of a great sorcerer who would join their effort, who might even be Sur himself come back to them in their time of need. Their victory over the old enemy was surely guaranteed. When the muster began in earnest, there was no shortage of men to fill the ships; for many of those involved in the fight for Halbo had survived the battle and swum to shore; or had rowed themselves expertly out of the way of the worst dangers. Many more had lost wives, daughters, wards, nieces, and cousins in the raids by the southerners on their coastal towns.

Three hundred years of bad blood simmered to the surface. Not one man aboard the Eyran fleet was untainted by desire for revenge, the craving to regain family honor, to make a name which would resound for centuries to come, to scour the world of his enemy.

For three hundred years the men of Istria had warred with the men of Eyra. It was more than a pattern, it was a birthright, a belief system, a law of nature. It ran in the blood and the bones and the brains. And surely there was nothing in the world which could challenge or dispel such an ingrained, unquestioned, fundamental ideology, a way of life and death in which every man was complicit. It would be like trying to change the path of a tempest or a raging torrent; like standing in the way of a charging bull or an eruption of lava; like casting chaff into a storm. . . .

31

Traveling South

THEY traveled by night to avoiding attracting attention; by day they slept under hedgerows, behind rocks, and in copses while one or other of the mercenary band stood watch. Slung over a mule with his hands tied and a gag in his mouth, Saro Vingo felt like the poor cargo he was in the eyes of this tough troop of men and women: produce which would be traded for the best price when they reached his home town. The ignominy shamed him; but worst of all was Katla Aransen's refusal to accept his apology for the death of her friend.

When he had tried to explain it was his only recourse to prevent Erno from revealing more information about the death-stone which would enable the Lord of Cantara to scour his enemies from the face of the earth, Katla had fixed him with a look of unremitting skepticism and then gagged him with her own ungentle hands. "Do you think I am such a fool that I will stand by and listen to such nonsense?" she had sneered. "If you were truly concerned that Tycho Issian was such a threat to the world, why then did you not strike *him* dead with your little ball of glass, rather than my brave cousin, who risked himself to save my life?"

Saro had no answer to that, for Katla or for himself. He felt stupid, lethal, irredeemably responsible. Haunted as he was by a more personal sin, he had allowed himself to be overwhelmed by such self-disgust that he had not even thought beyond that first rush of panic, had not thought he could take such an active part in changing the course of grand events. He deserved Katla's scorn. More, he deserved to die.

He tried to sink into oblivion, to let the sway of the mule stay his thoughts; he tried to will himself to cease existing, for surely death would be a better prospect that to be presented to his mother like this—a craven captive bearing unbearable tidings: the death of her favorite, her beloved son Tanto, at his own tainted hands and the death of Fabel, his true father, at Tanto's. But no matter how much he hated himself, he survived. He ate what food he was given, drank water, continued to breathe; when he slept, the nightmares came. But despite it all, it seemed that the Goddess must have some requirement of him, that she was so stubborn in keeping his shade on this side of her fires.

One night the hillman came over to where their prisoner was tied and took the gag from Saro's mouth.

"Katla has just told me exactly why it was that you killed her kinsman," he said softly.

Saro hung his head. "I am worse than a fool," he tried to say, but his mouth and throat were parched.

Persoa untied Saro's bindings, then took the stopper from his waterskin and held it out to the lad. "Drink as much as you wish," he offered kindly, "there's more where that came from."

Saro swigged until his belly felt fit to burst. Then he looked about. "Not around here," he said, frowning. All that could be seen in any direction were thorn bushes silvered by moonlight, dry sand, and gritty soil. The half-dead landscape was rendered more lifeless still by night's harsh monotones.

The hillman smiled. "It's farther underground than it would usually run, but I can divine it. Like this." He squatted, laid the palm of one hand flat upon the ground, and cocked his head consideringly. Then he came upright again, grinning, his teeth startlingly white in the darkness of his face. "Over there," he said, gesturing south and east, "maybe half a mile; there is a spring running below the limestone."

Saro regarded him askance. "How can you know that?"

"I am eldianna," the hillman explained, and watched as Saro's eyes became round with surprise.

"I thought they existed only in the old tales," he said. "The legends of the south."

Persoa shrugged. "It is an ancient skill, that is true." He lifted his head for a moment as if listening to something far away, then came and sat down close to Saro, his long legs folded neatly. "I understand why you killed poor Erno," he said at last. "To stop him speaking of a great and dangerous mystery."

"I should have killed the Lord of Cantara," Saro said, his jaw clenched with shame. "But I panicked."

"You killed him to stop him speaking of a death-stone."

Saro nodded. "Katla thinks me mad. She will not listen to me."

Persoa took one of the lad's hands and pressed it between his own and Saro felt a jolt of energy fly up his arm, followed by a suffusion of heat and a strong sense of well-being. The touch of the hillman, instead of filling him with the usual torrent of intrusive images and unpleasant insights, offered him the vision of a still pond, clear and calm, an oasis in a troubled world. "I do not think you mad," the eldianna said, "for my people know of the existence of death-stones and what they may do. Tell me what you know and I promise I will listen to every word and then trade you my own knowledge."

And so, with the cool night breeze whispering through the thorns, Saro Vingo told the hillman all he knew—of the moodstone which had come to him in such violent circumstances at the Allfair; of the unwanted gift of empathy which had accompanied it; how the thing had come to lethal life in his hands when the pale woman had touched it and how he had killed without thought by wielding the stone; how he had discovered the real identity of the pale woman from the nomads with whom he traveled; how one of those nomads had taken the stone when it had fallen in the skirmish and used it on his friend, the sorcerer Virelai, who was now such a changed man. Then he told him how the Lord of Cantara was so wrapped by lustful obsession that sought to take the Goddess as his own; how he had engineered a holy war to steal her back from the north, which was ironic in the extreme, given that the man had no knowledge of her true nature; and then, with his eyes averted and his voice hoarse with horror, he told the eldianna of the terrible vision which had overtaken him in Jetra's Star Chamber when the lord had clutched his shoulder—of Tycho Issian wielding the murderous rays of the death-stone against a milling, screaming horde; and how he knew that this devastation was but a beginning, for the man was deadly and mad, and would suffer no living thing to survive it if stood in his way.

Through all this, the hillman said not a word. His dark eyes scanned Saro's face earnestly and with such an expression of acceptance and understanding that by the end of his account, Saro could not help but sob like a child forgiven an all-consuming misdemeanor.

"Not all such visions are true-sight, my friend; some show the worst possible future. But I understand why you did what you did."

"When Erno offered to tell him where it might be found, all I could think was to shut him up—"

"And so you bashed his head in with a paperweight."

Katla Aransen materialized between the stunted trees as if detaching herself seamlessly from one of their gnarled branches.

"Katla, Katla," the eldianna said admonishingly. "You are too rigid, too judgmental. You should acquire some tolerance."

"Tolerance! Tolerance is what allows our enemies to murder our own and get away with it. Tolerance lets them take our land and enslave our women." She thrust out a belligerent jaw. "You say I should be tolerant, but the Empire has no understanding of tolerance—it burns those who disagree with its stupid religion or any who don't fit in with its laws or its society. Cold iron is all that Istrians understand, and that I can provide them with."

Her sword was halfway out of its sheath. Saro cringed.

Instead of leaping to his feet to ward off whatever unpredictable violence might flare up, Persoa offered Katla his angular, lopsided grin. Then he reached out and touched her arm, gesturing for her to sit down. Remarkably, she released the sword's hilt and sat, though she watched them both with suspicious eyes.

"I know what you are thinking," Persoa said easily. "That in truth we are both Istrians, Saro Vingo and myself, both tainted by centuries of bloody warfare with your people and by the worship of a deity very different from your own. You think we may be in league, no?"

Katla shrugged. She looked sullen, a girl bored by a school lesson. "I don't know what to think."

The hillman inclined his head. "That is always a good place to start."

"What I do know is that he killed my cousin, for no good reason."

"I am sorry—" Saro started, but Persoa waved a hand to curtail the apology.

"What is a 'good' reason to kill, Katla Aransen?"

Katla laughed. "You, a paid assassin, ask me this?"

The hillman grimaced. "I am good at killing, that is true; but I am not proud of that skill. Maybe my long proximity to death has made me more aware of the cost of taking a life. Tell me, Katla, how many have you killed?"

"Twelve men," Katla said proudly and without hesitation. She'd kept count. "If you include the guard whose arm I took off in the lord's chamber. Can't imagine he survived that."

"Twelve men. And what have you learned from those deaths?"

"That a dead enemy does not rise. And the more of them you kill, the fewer of them there are to do you or your family harm."

Persoa's mouth pursed, but he made no retort. Instead, he turned to Saro. "And you, Saro Vingo. How many deaths are there to your name?"

Saro paled. Tears sprang to his eyes. He bowed his head, ashamed that the bold northern girl should see him so affected. "Six men," he said quietly. "Including my own brother."

Katla's eyebrows shot up. She remembered his braggart brother mauling her knives at her stall. "Well, that's no great loss," she snorted. "Still, six men, that's not bad for a milksop like you. What did you use, poison?"

Saro's head came up sharply. Eyes which glittered silver in the moonlight fixed her with a fierce, if damp, stare. "One you saw me kill with iron; one, I will not speak of; four died from the power of the death-stone I told you about, three of those as I tried to save you from the pyres."

"What?"

"They got in the way. I thrust the stone at them, unthinking. I had no idea it would kill them. All I could think was that they were going to burn you unless I could reach you first."

Katla looked away now, not knowing how to respond to this new information, which ran so contrary to her own memory of events. Besides, how could you kill anyone by touching them with a little stone? Sharp iron was another matter. How she itched to be away from all this, in her own forge, doing what she knew best.

Persoa stared intently at the lad. "You risked your soul," he said.

"And how many have you killed?" Saro asked bitterly.

"One hundred and ninety-three men, and four women."

"So how's your soul, then?"

"I have killed for many reasons: in self-defense, in hatred, and out of compassion," the hillman admitted. "But mainly I have killed for money, for the skill I have in taking a life swiftly. I dedicate each death to Elda. The Lady must weigh my soul when I walk through her fires. I think it is feather-light by now and I am not proud of that.

"But you are two young people whose souls are not yet beyond re-demption." Persoa glanced at Saro and then at Katla; both looked thor-oughly unconvinced. He rubbed a hand across his face. "I am no orator or bard," he said at last. "And people are happier to listen to a song of war than a song of peace, but I ask you to hear me out.

"For centuries your people have fought one another, northman against southerner, each time heaping aggravation upon aggravation. But in all that time, their weapons have been crude and limited in effect. Now a new element has entered Elda, and it is growing in strength day by day; for a death-stone draws its power not only from the hand which wields it, but also from the life-force it takes, or that which it drags back. Someone has been wielding it often of late; soon its power will be devastating. Already, the balance of the world is out of kilter, for hate far outweighs compassion as its people prepare to go to war again. If the Lord of Cantara lays hands upon this stone and uses it as a weapon, the destruction will be unimag-inable, and soon there will be nothing left on Elda but hatred and despair.

"So I ask you, Katla Aransen not to add to the burden of hatred which drags us all down into darkness. Saro did not kill your kinsman for no reason. He did it in an excess of terror, not for himself, but for the world, and though his aim may have been displaced, his intention was not. Katla, forgive him for this death."

Several seconds of silence stretched awkwardly between them. Then, instead of answering the hillman's plea, the Eyran girl looked squarely at Saro. "Did you really try to save me at the Allfair? I thought you were plowing your way through the mob to kill me."

There was an expression on her face which Saro had not seen before. Even so, he held her searching gaze steadily.

"I tried to reach you, but I failed. The men I killed got in my way. Saving you was my only thought. I did not mean to kill them." He paused, his face a mask of anguish. "I thought you were dead, all this time—"

"You risked your life for me."

It was a simple statement of fact. Saro nodded, suddenly out of words.

Katla gazed away over his head and seemed to mull this over for a long time. No one said anything. At last, she sighed.

"Erno's death is not mine to forgive, but his own. You should ask forgiveness of him, not me," she said stiffly. Then she braced her hands on her knees and rose, joints cracking. It looked as though she might say something more, but then she shook her head and strode away into the darkness, wrapped in thought.

Saro watched her go, his eyes full of misery. The hillman patted him on the arm. "She is proud and her people have been harshly treated by the south. They cradle their vengeance, the Eyrans, with as much care as they would cradle an infant. Give her time, my friend. She will come round."

But of that, Saro was not so sure.

THE farther south they rode, the drier and hotter the land became. Rocky streambeds were exposed for the first time in centuries, and the reeds and bullrushes which normally lined their lush banks were sere and brown. No birds sang. The only life they saw were lizards skittering from under the horses' hooves into the lee of boulders, a striped sidewinder which wove swiftly away into the roots of a dead tree, and occasionally the shadow of a vulture fell over them as its owner circled overhead on a fruitless search for carrion.

This, Saro could see with his own eyes, for the hillman had prevailed on Mam to let him ride the mule, rather than be slung across it, and Katla, rolling her eyes, had not demurred.

"Don't even think about trying to escape," the mercenary leader leered. "You won't get far. That beast can hardly be bothered to walk, let alone gallop, and if I have to break a sweat retrieving you, I can promise you'll regret it." And she flashed her sharpened teeth at him just enough to underscore the threat.

There was, Saro thought gloomily, nowhere to run to, even if he had a decent mount. All that could be seen for miles around was scrubland and thorns and a pitiless blue sky.

TWO days later they crossed a ridge and came down into the plains which had once provided the grain which fed all of Istria. No more. Land that had once been sown with wheat and corn offered ranks of lifeless stubble, between which the topsoil had become so light and desiccated that it had blown elsewhere, leaving a skim of sand over bedrock. They passed parched irrigation ditches and empty ponds, orchards of orange and pomegranate trees now reduced to leafless twigs herded together by drystone walls.

Even with all the men called to war and no one left to tend the crops, the change seemed drastic to Saro, whose homeland this was. There had been dry years before, years when they dug deep wells and passed leather buckets from hand to hand to keep their fruit trees alive; years when scouring winds blew great channels between the crops and no rain fell between Fifthmoon and Harvest Moon, but he had never seen anything like this.

If the plains of Istria were reduced to desert, how much worse would it be farther south, near his home in Altea? Panic gripped his heart. With his uncle dead, his father with the army, and no sons to care for her, how would his mother fare? The mercenaries might receive precious little for the return of the heir to the Altean estates; precious little, or nothing at all.

In the hills north of Pex, they stopped for the night and Mam sent Persoa and Doc down into the town for news and whatever provisions they could find. Their food was all but gone. Even their water supply, despite the supernatural divining powers of the eldianna, was running low. Their stomachs rumbled and complained, though they would not die just yet. But the horses were rib-thin and exhausted.

Mam poked desultorily at the stew she and Joz had made of what little was left in their stores—a piece of dried mutton so scrawny and tough that Katla suggested they would be better off adding one of her boots instead, two withered onions, a handful of meal, one of oats, some dried apricots, and a twist of thyme. It made for thin pickings. Eventually, Dogo went hunting around for anything else he could find and came back with an empty meal sack. This he upended over the bubbling pot, then stared in curiously at what had fallen out.

"Serves you right, you little buggers!" he grinned.

Katla peered over his shoulder and made a face.

Mam, deadpan, kept stirring.

"Just a bit more meat," she said, feeling the prisoner's eyes on her.

But when the poor gruel was ladled out, two fat white maggots floated on the surface of Saro's portion. He looked at them lying there, feeling his guts lurching. At least they weren't moving. Or were they?

He put the bowl aside.

This seemed to give Katla Aransen yet another cause to despise him, for she picked up the spurned bowl and maintaining eye contact all the while, drained off the lot without hesitation.

THE moon was up before Persoa and Doc returned. Their grave faces and empty hands told more of a story than any words.

Doc peered into the cookpot and helped himself to a portion of the stew and the hillman followed suit. Mam watched with narrow eyes and made no attempt to coax anything out of them until they'd finished eating.

At last, the big man said, "War's started, then."

Mam raised an eyebrow.

"Big fleet of Eyran-designed ships left Forent Harbor just before full moon—"

Katla Aransen swore vilely and stabbed the little knife she had been cleaning into the ground repeatedly. "Bastard. Bastard, bastard, bastard." Had Morten Danson being lying there, he would now be punctured many times over, his lifeblood leaking away into the hardpan.

"After that, the information gets a bit shaky," Doc admitted. "Some say they never made it, others that there was some big battle at Halbo, and one old trailman I spoke to said he'd heard something about a monster rising up out of the waters and swamping the fleet."

At this point, Katla stopped stabbing her dagger into the dirt and glanced up. "What sort of monster?"

Doc shrugged. "Who knows? Sounds unlikely, doesn't it?"

The Eyran girl looked away from him, then buried the knife in the ground so viciously that it snapped off at the hilt.

"Break a blade, fate is made," intoned Joz Bearhand softly.

Katla stared at the shards, eyes glittering. She blinked rapidly, then cast the useless hilt away into the bushes.

"Fate? I care nothing for fate. I don't believe in gods or goddesses or magic or curses or prophecy or death-stones or any of that nonsense— whatever any of you say," she said grimly, glaring around at all of them, as if daring anyone to contradict her. "I believe that if we act, we make things happen; and if we don't act, things happen to us. I'm fed up with having things happen to me. I'll make my own fate. I'll make my own decisions and my own mistakes, and if I bring down ruin on my own head, well, at least it'll be my own fault. I won't boast that I've made the best decisions in my time, or that I haven't hurt others when making them, but I'll stand my ground and take the consequences, come what may. I'll eat dirt if I have to."

"Aye to that," Mam averred heartily, breaking the awkward silence that fell. "But I fear we'll all be eating dirt if we hang around here any longer." She stood up and wiped her hands on her tunic in a businesslike fashion. "Let's get going," she said. "Altea's what—two, three days south?"

Saro nodded.

"Let's hope your ma's got some provisions laid in, then, eh?"

THERE were no workers in the orchards around Altea, and the trees appeared withered and fruitless. As they rounded a bend at the top of a steep hill, they came upon the stinking carcasses of two white oxen lying by the side of the road, their stomachs flyblown below starved and ribby flanks. On the lee of the hill the cart the beasts had been drawing lay abandoned on its side. A pathetic tumble of possessions spilled out of it into the dust of the road—some Jetran pottery, broken by the fall; bundles of fabric; parts of a loom; an old wicker chair, its pretty fretwork polished and gleaming from the rub of years.

Saro wailed and jumped down off the mule. He knelt amid all this sorry jetsam and pulled the chair free of the tangle, then leaned his head on it and sobbed.

Joz dismounted and came to stand beside him.

"What is it, lad?"

Saro turned a miserable face to the big man. "These are my mother's things. This is the chair she nursed us on, me and my brother; this is the chair she sat in, day and night, by the side of Tanto's bed when he was ill and looked as if he would die. And then in the end I killed him after all. Oh, Mother, how can you ever forgive me, if you are even still alive?"

His voice trailed off to a whisper. Joz, ever a man of great heart, laid a hand on the lad's shoulder, but this just served to make Saro sob louder. The rest of the group watched this outpouring of grief uncomfortably, all except for Persoa, who slipped silently from his horse, crossed quickly to the wreckage, and gently drew the young Istrian to his feet.

"Your brother was an evil man," he said. "And he was responsible in part for what has happened here."

Saro looked at him through red eyes, mystified.

"Many forces have acted upon this region," the hillman said, "that it should be leached so dry. The climate has been changing ever since the Goddess came back to the world, for wherever she is, there is beneficence, and she is a long way from here. Water is her element, and I can feel it running, drawn to her as a lodestone is drawn to the north. And I suspect that the death-stone, too, has taken its toll. But those we spoke to in the town of Pex had other things to say about the starvation the folk of the south have endured these past months.

"During his time in Jetra your brother held sway, and he was a tyrant in many ways beyond the most obvious. Not only did he make a name for himself for the torture and burning of thousands of innocents; he also demanded that every town render up to him vast amounts of food and wine. Those who did not at once comply with his orders found themselves accused of sorcery and burned with the nomads that were rounded up." He sighed and shook his head. "I was amazed that the soldiery of the Eternal City should be complicit in such ill-doing, but when I questioned further, I was told that every scurvy villain prepared to take Jetra's coin signed up to do Tanto Vingo's bidding while the rest went off to war, and were paid most handsomely for it . . . and not only in cantari.

"He has bled the country dry, even as far as his own estates. I think you have done the people of Elda a very great service in removing such a wicked soul."

Saro hung his head, taking all this in. When he lifted it again, his eyes were clearer, though still troubled. "And what of my mother?"

Persoa looked over Saro's shoulder to Mam. Their eyes locked for a moment, then the mercenary leader said with forced cheer, "She probably gave these things away, lad. To someone worse off than herself."

Saro shook his head. "No. She would never had given her chair away, not to anyone."

"Looters?" Dogo suggested gleefully.

Saro fixed him with a hard stare. "If there have been looters at work, then things are dire indeed."

No one else had anything to say. Saro got back on the mule with a pale, strained face and they rode the track to the Vingo estate in silence.

The villa was deserted. Expecting the worst, with lurid images of death and decay imprinted in his mind, Saro breathed a sigh of—if not relief, then something close to it. Even so, to see the place he had been raised abandoned and bereft of life was a desolate experience. Out in the courtyard, his mother's flowerbeds, over which she had lavished such care even in the hottest season, were crusted with cracked soil and withered plants. The well was dry and even its leather bucket was gone, leaving just a frayed tangle of bleached rope swinging in the breeze. The storehouse had been ransacked and empty flour sacks and cheesemolds lay strewn across the floor.

The mercenary troop fanned out to quarter the area more effectively, searching for any signs of life or food, leaving Saro to wander the villa on his own—but whether this was a gesture made out of compassion or awkwardness, he did not know. He went from room to room, feeling like a ghost haunting its lost home. Everywhere there was broken furniture, shards of crockery, empty bottles. Drapes, clothes, and linen lay trampled on the floor, dirtied by many feet. It looked nothing like home anymore.

Someone had lit a fire in the chamber he had shared with his brother when they were children. The remains of one of their beds, smashed into firewood, lay in the ashes, along with a scatter of charred bones which looked to have belonged to a small animal of some sort.

He pushed at them with his boot, and the pile collapsed with a sigh, black dust billowing out into the room. Something skittered out from under the second bed and ran frantically across the room, mewling.

It was a kitten.

Saro stared at it, amazed. Brindled and big-eyed, it ran into a corner and stared back, terrified but defiant.

Picking up a bed sheet, Saro approached carefully. All the lank fur on the kitten's neck stood on end and it hissed and spat at him, and then when he engulfed it in the linen, sank its claws and teeth through the fabric into his hand, but Saro held on grimly as the tiny creature's terror and fury flowed through him. Then, for the first time since old Hiron Sea-Haar had gifted him with this unwanted empathy, and with no conscious thought for what he was doing, he turned the tide of the sensations which buffeted at him and allowed a wave of calm and gentleness to flow back in the opposite direction, and after a while the kitten stopped biting and lay compliant in his hands.

IT was maybe two hours later when Dogo and Joz Bearhand returned to the villa with a bagful of scavengings and found him dozing on the front steps in the last of the day's sunlight with the creature curled up asleep in his arms.

"Aha!" said the little man, grinning from ear to ear. "I see you've found us some supper!"

Saro's eyes snapped open. The kitten, its nap disturbed, burrowed its head further into the crook of his elbow. "It's not for eating," he said fiercely.

"Not for eating?" Dogo looked amazed. "All things are for eating. I've had many a tasty cat stew in my time. Boil it up with a bit of rosemary, the meat comes right off the bone lovely. Tastes just like chicken."

Saro got to his feet, tucking the little beast so firmly under his arm that it meeped anxiously. "No one's stewing this kitten," he declared. "You'll have to kill me to take it."

Joz grinned. "No worries, laddie." He held out the bag. "We've enough here to keep us going for a couple of days. No one's going to eat your cat."

Dogo leered evilly. "Not till the third day, anyway."

They had found a root cellar in one of the outbuildings in which a fallen roof had defeated the looters. After much backbreaking excavation, it had rendered up a number of rather desiccated vegetables, a sack of rice which the mice hadn't got at, and some moldy cheeses, which looked a good deal more palatable once the rinds were removed. Doc had found some nettles and burdock growing around what was left of the lake, and some bales of dry hay in one of the barns, so at least the horses could be fed. But it was Mam and Katla who had made the best find. As the sun dipped below the jagged horizon of the mountains, they led a skinny, stumbling cow into the courtyard and proceeded to butcher it on the spot.

"It was on its last legs. I doubt it would have lived another day," Mam said matter-of-factly as she cleaned off her dagger.

In the end, they threw everything they could fit into the old iron cauldron from the kitchens and cooked it all up together, while Joz hung strips of meat over the fire to smoke. While Mam and Dogo cooked, Katla crouched beside Saro and examined the kitten curiously. She put a finger out and the kitten sniffed it, then began to lick it vigorously, wrapping its tiny paws around her hand and digging its claws in for purchase. Without a word, Katla pulled back her hand, got up, and walked away.

Saro watched her go, feeling unaccountably sad.

"It's a gift from the Goddess," Persoa said softly from behind him. "The little cat. It's her gift to you."

"Perhaps I'm her gift to it," Saro replied.

The hillman smiled. "If such a tiny creature can survive amid such desolation, then so shall we all."

Saro raised an eyebrow. "Not much hope for the poor cow." He remembered what Alisha Skylark had said of the nomad way of life, about sharing the world with its creatures rather than eating them, and felt ashamed at the way his stomach rumbled at the gorgeous aromas emanating from the cauldron.

The hillman laughed. "No, that is true. But tomorrow it would have been dead and only the crows and the vultures would have benefited. Besides, it seems it is not only we humans who will eat well tonight."

Saro looked up and found Katla Aransen standing over him. In her hands she held a gleaming hunk of raw meat, and a sharp knife.

"Something for your kitten," she said shortly, and squatting down, she began to cut off tiny pieces for the beast, which sat bolt upright on Saro's lap, its gold eyes gleaming with firelight, not knowing whether to purr or growl or snatch at the food.

In the end it did all three at once.

An Unexpected Encounter

O N the next day as they crested a high ridge, Joz pointed out a plume of dust in the valley below them. "Soldiers on the march?" Mam asked, squinting. Her eyesight was not as sharp as it had once been, not that she was going to admit it to anyone.

Joz shook his head. "Wrong direction," he said tersely. "Whoever they are, they're heading south and west."

Persoa climbed higher up the ridge and stared out into the harsh landscape, shading his eyes. When he came back, he looked mildly surprised but would not say why. "Let us ride on," was all he would offer. "I do not think we are in any danger."

As they closed on the dust cloud, Saro's guts gave a tiny lurch—of fear, or anticipation? He did not know. But as the travelers ahead of them began to pull aside into a rocky defile to let them take precedence on the road, the dust cleared abruptly and he saw a number of great lumbering beasts pulling carts, shaggy-haired and long-horned. Yeka!

He turned excitedly to Mam. "They're Wanderers!" he declared with relief. "Nomad folk." So some of them had evaded his brother's devices after all.

Mam made a superstitious sign. "Just keep riding," she said.

But as they drew level with the group, Persoa made a complicated genuflection, called out something in the nomad folk's lilting tongue, and rode into the defile to speak with them. The men of the caravan had gathered at the front of the group as if to defend the rest. There were eight of them—five young men and three old men—all in billowing patchwork trousers belted with many-colored braids. The red dust of the road coated their skin and clothing, and what little hair they had, for each wore only a topknot confined with brass rings; silver dropped from their ears and jangled around their wrists. They were thin, but not starved-looking, and they watched the newcomers with wary caution, though none of them was armed. Behind the men, a number of women and children peered out from between the wagons with a mixture of suspicion and curiosity. Saro stared. Surely it could not be . . . she looked older, a woman, rather than the child he remembered. He blinked and stared again. It was—

"Guaya!"

A girl in the group with enormous eyes and silver rings in her nose and eyebrow stared back at him, at first uncomprehending, then alarmed. She slipped behind an old woman with feathers in her hair as if she could not bear to look at him, or for him to look upon her. One of the young men said something in the nomads' strange tongue.

"*Hvier-thi? Hvi konnuthu-thi Guaya?*"

"*Rajeesh, minna seri,*" Saro replied, much to everyone's surprise. "*Ig heti Saro Vingo, di Altea de la. Ig reconnina Guaya sala Allferi. Hen ferthi—*" here vocabulary failed him: he mimed a puppet dancing for them.

The men all laughed and nodded. "*Mannetria! Ah, mannetria,*" said the oldest of the men. He made an odd little bow. "*Ig heti Feron, periana Hiron. Guaya minna nestri es.*"

"What are you talking about?" Katla demanded crossly, riding up to join them. "Are you making some sort of bargain with them, trying to escape?"

Saro glanced over his shoulder at her. "The pretty girl by the second wagon—Guaya—is a friend of mine. I met her at the Allfair last year and was with her when her grandfather was killed in the rioting. The old man here is her uncle." He turned back to continue his conversation with the Wandering folk.

Katla stared into the group till she found the one he meant. The girl stared back, unabashed by the Eyran's interest. Katla was annoyed to note that she indeed merited the description Saro had applied to her, if not one even more fulsome, for she had an exotic, foreign beauty. "How do you know their language?" she asked sharply, interrupting his discussion. "I thought you were an Istrian, not a Footloose man."

Now Saro turned around to face her and his expression was grim. "I traveled with the nomads last year before the caravan I was with was set upon by militiamen from Jetra. They killed everyone but me, my companion Virelai, and a nomad woman called Alisha Skylark. It was a massacre; they didn't stand a chance. They don't fight, you see, these people you so rudely refer to as 'the Footloose.' They believe in living peacefully on Elda, leaving as little trace of themselves as they may, taking no life, be it man or animal."

Katla curled her lip. "Hasn't done them much good as far as I've heard," she said.

"*Alisha?*" said one of the other men suddenly, gripping Saro by the arm. "*Konnuthu-thi Alisha Skylark?*"

Saro started at the touch, abruptly assailed by a hail of images which left him reeling. As quickly as he was able, he peeled the man's fingers away. "*Donniari revenna,*" he explained softly, his head spinning. "*Eldistan Hironi . . .*"

That set them all talking excitedly, until Saro waved his hands exhaustedly. "Please," he said in the Old Tongue, "I can't understand you all at once."

One of the old men came forward now. He bowed, first to Persoa, then to Katla, and last to Saro, whom he addressed. "We know Alisha Skylark," he said haltingly. "We see her a moon ago, not alone, on horse. We ask her join with us, she say no, place to go, very important."

Saro's heart raced. "A black horse?"

The man nodded. "Very fine, very fine."

"And she traveled with others?"

The old man turned to his companions and they conferred for a while, quietly but intently. Then he said, "With son, Falo; and some others we not know so well. Or not . . . recognize."

"Falo? But Falo is dead. I saw—" He hesitated, the horrible image of that brave nine-year-old lying on the ground by the river where they had been ambushed, his arm hacked off, fingers still clutching his grand-mother Fezack's old knobkerry.

"Had lost an arm," the old man added helpfully. "The boy, only one arm."

Saro felt a chill run through him.

One of the women from the group called out something and the old man nodded. "She say he have no eyes either, but I not see that for myself."

Persoa turned to Saro, his face gaunt. "You saw the boy die?"

"I did not see him fall, but I saw his corpse," Saro said. His heart felt like a lump of lead hanging in the center of his chest. It thudded painfully against his ribs. "He was most certainly dead. No one could survive such a wound."

Persoa closed his eyes. "So, it is true, then, what I have felt. She has been using the eldistan to raise the dead."

The old man's face clouded and he said something rapidly to the rest of the group. The old women made signs to ward off evil. They muttered *"Ealadanna kalom, ealadanna kalom,"* over and over; then one of them pointed south and said, *"Suthra ferinni, montian fuegi."*

"Montian fuegi—the mountain of fire—the Red Peak?" Persoa asked, stricken.

They all nodded.

"And where are you going?" Persoa asked. "To join her?"

The old man shook his head vehemently. "Only the dead can survive in that place. We go to Cantara."

The hair rose on the back of Saro's neck. "Why would any nomad go to Cantara? Its lord is a monster. He has killed thousands of your people!"

One of the young men said something unintelligible, but Saro caught the words *Tycho Issian* and the gesture he made—a finger drawn across the throat—was universal, though uncharacteristic of the gentle wayfaring folk.

"His mother rule while he away. She good woman, good to us Lost People. Take in many, feed and care, very kind, very kind."

"Do you know," Saro asked anxiously, "anything about the folk who dwelled back there?" He gestured toward Altea. "There was a lady, Illustria Vingo, my mother."

But the old man shook his head. "People long gone."

So that was that, then.

"May we travel with you?" Persoa asked. "To Cantara?"

At once a great smile wreathed the old man's walnut-brown face. He nodded rapidly, shook the hillman vigorously by the hand. "Much honor," he said. *"Eldianna mina, si beni eldianni."*

WHEN they made camp for the night, Saro sought out Guaya. He sensed that misunderstanding and distrust lay between them and the way she had avoided his eye made him uncomfortable. He decided he would try to speak with her, if not to justify himself then at least to reestablish some form of friendly contact. After polite inquiries, he found her curled up in one of the wagons, restringing one of her puppet figures by candlelight. She looked up, alarmed, as he stuck his head in through the canvas door flap. "It's all right," he said softly. "I'll go away if you don't want to talk to me."

Guaya said nothing, but she put the mannequin to one side with exaggerated care and drew her knees up to her chin. Saro took this an invitation, or at least not a rebuttal, and climbed into the wagon to sit beside her. Silence fell. Guaya looked at her hands, then began to clean paint from under her fingernails in an absorbed fashion.

"You look well," Saro said desperately after a while.

She made a face.

"You also look older," he said, then put his hand to his mouth. "Sorry."

She frowned. "Times have been hard. There hasn't been much to eat." She looked up at him then and he saw that there were shadows under her eyes and beneath her cheekbones, and felt an idiot.

"I know." Another long silence fell between them, which Guaya seemed disinclined to break. Saro tried again. "I am glad your people traveled in a different caravan from Alisha's."

"Why?" she said, looking up at him accusingly. "Because you didn't want to see me?"

"No, no—because you have survived, whereas they . . ."

"It is a very terrible thing," she said at last.

Saro nodded.

Her eyes searched his face. "And you were there when they were attacked?"

He nodded again. "I killed one of the soldiers," he said defensively.

She snorted. "That does not recommend you to me. Taking yet another life by violent means hardly improves the world."

Saro hung his head, wishing acutely that he had not come here. He had known all along that she despised him, as she despised all his kind. He remembered her furious diatribe against the Istrians, how the Empire had killed her mother and her father; and her grandfather, too. And since it had been his own brother who had taken the old man's life, he couldn't blame her for hating him and all his people.

Guaya saw that he had taken what she had said to heart. "Anyway," she said in a lighter tone, "just how old do you think I am?"

Confused by this abrupt change in subject, Saro floundered. "Er, thirteen . . . fourteen?"

Guaya looked thunderstruck. Then she laughed, her whole face suddenly alive with humor. "Ha! I am eighteen: I will be nineteen in three moons. Do I really look such a child to you?"

Saro was shocked—by his own stupidity as much as anything else, for now that he looked at her, he realized it was her fragility that had misled him, that and his ignorance of how women looked, so used to seeing them wrapped in their enveloping robes was he. "No!" he said, more sharply than he'd meant to. "I don't, no. I just hadn't . . . really . . . thought about it much." And that just made it worse.

Now her lower lip protruded and a line appeared between her eyebrows. For a horrible moment he thought she might cry. Then he remembered that the nomads never wept tears, except for happiness. Or was that yet another myth?

"So you have given me no thought at all since the last time you saw me."

"No—I have thought about you often, truly I have." But usually, he admitted to himself, it was more that he thought about how ridiculous and patronizing he must have seemed in her eyes, the rich Istrian come to bribe her with blood price for the old man's death, as if a bag of cantari made everything all right again. Yet another proof, if proof were needed, of the Empire's empty morals and money-grubbing ways.

Her eyes shone. They were not black, as he had first thought them, though in the dim light of the wagon her pupils were huge, but a rich, deep brown, like the water in an autumn stream, or the coppery eyes of a toad. That last thought made him laugh.

Guaya was taken aback. "What? Why are you laughing?"

He could hardly tell her about the toad. "I . . . er . . . because I have forgotten my own age," he improvised quickly. "I cannot remember if I am twenty-two or twenty-three . . ." And even as he said it he knew it was true, and that he had forgotten his own birth day.

Guaya took his right hand firmly and laid it palm up on her lap where the glow of the candles infused it with a golden light. "I shall tell you." She bent over his hand and traced one of the lines there with a delicate finger. "Twenty-three," she said softly, a smile curving her lips. "And I see there is a great love in your life, though your ways have long been parted. But you are destined to be reunited, though the path is full of obstacles. See, here—" But when she looked up again, she found that Saro's expression had become momentarily slack with the impact of the touch, and she dropped his hand quickly.

Saro sat in a dream, bathed with warmth. Over and again he saw himself from the nomad girl's perspective, taller than he thought himself, more handsome, more charismatic by far. He saw himself protecting her during the fight which had left her grandfather dead, felt himself gripped by his own strong hands, felt safe in his own embrace. He saw the way he tried to staunch the old man's blood while the battle milled all about them, a vain attempt that appeared to Guaya both heroic and selfless. Images swirled, broke apart; coalesced. Now he saw himself seated rod-straight on a fine black stallion, a hero out of a lost age; then he felt the girl's terror hammering at his own chest as he disappeared from view between pounding hooves. Again the scene changed, and now he saw himself walking through the fair with his head up and his jaw jutting: a determined man with fire in his dark eyes. As Guaya, he felt himself quail, felt the way her heart leaped when she saw him, felt panic and confusion carry away the words she had meant to say and transform them to words of accusation and anger. The last image which visited him was the way he had once appeared to her in a dream, a dream full of sweet touches and singing skin. And although it was another's dream, he could not help the reaction his own body made to it.

Suddenly the contact was broken. All those snatched moments fled away.

"I forgot. I am sorry . . . I forgot—"

Guaya sounded distraught, but Saro was still too wrapped in sensation to respond in any useful way. Instead, he gazed at her, feeling a little drunk, a little giddy. He had, indeed, it seemed, received a gift on that fateful day when he had visited the moodstone seller's stall, despite all the horror that had followed. He turned this new idea over in his mind. After all that had happened to him, all that he had done, it seemed impossible that anyone should care for him.

"Guaya—" he whispered, but she would not look at him. He reached out and touched her cheek, and the skin was hot beneath his fingers. "Guaya," he repeated, and now she met his eye, her cheeks burning.

"I forgot," she said again. "I forgot you could see my thoughts." She ran a hand across her face as if she could erase them.

"I thought you hated me," Saro said softly.

"Hate you? I could never hate you, though it would be easier for me if I could."

"If you knew what else I had done—"

In response to this, she reached out and stopped his mouth with her hand. "No words," she said. "Not now." Then she leaned across and sealed his lips with her own.

Saro closed his eyes and let himself fall into her, and when she enfolded him he felt the embrace from inside and out: a most bizarre and intense sensation. Too intense. He pushed himself away and stared at Guaya, panting.

She blinked at him. "What? What is the matter?"

Saro shook his head. "I don't know. It isn't . . . it isn't right."

"There is no right here," she said softly. "There is only us, and love and comfort." She cupped his cheek in her hand, a gesture of infinite tenderness; then she drew him against her again, and he found that not only could he not resist, but that he did not wish to.

How they both became naked he did not know—it was all too fast and too confused, for as long as they touched, he was both the nomad girl and himself and it was hard to tell where one finished and the other began. Was it his hands who unlaced her thin dress, or her own? Was it her hands who found the ties that held his breeches up and unknotted them, or his? He didn't know—was beyond caring. In the end, it hardly mattered, for suddenly they were skin against skin. Then her legs were around him and he was inside her and they were both engulfed by a sea of beating blood and hot breath. For a few seconds he felt he was drowning and fought to separate himself, as if he feared he might lose himself forever in this hot tide. Then a reckless insouciance which he knew was not his own picked him up like a great wave and hurled him into the current and he had no choice but to give himself up to it and allow it to carry him away.

It was impossible to tell how long they rocked together, drifting in and out of one another's minds. He felt the penetration he made as a welcomed invasion; then was back in his own skin, feeling how the girl beneath him clenched and pulsed. He felt great waves of affection wash around him, through him, over him. There came a moment when sea became flame, greedy and insistent; and then a coruscating wildfire which devoured everything in its path. He felt himself burned up, all he had been and all he had done reduced to ashes and cinder so that he found himself in a howling wasteland, devoid of emotion, devoid of sensation. Little by little, he became aware of details: how the juddering candlelight illuminated a strip of brightly woven blanket; how the grain of the wool was rough against his knees; how one of Guaya's hands lay softly about his neck; how she looked up at him expectantly.

And suddenly he was back in himself again. And Guaya, though they still lay entwined, felt as separate to him as if they were two islands in an ocean.

He gazed at her, confused. Something of great magnitude had just taken place, something beyond their physical joining.

"Well?" Guaya lifted an eyebrow and one corner of her mouth quirked upward.

It was not the expression of an innocent, but of a knowing and powerful young woman.

Saro, out of his depth again, sought for the right words. "That was . . . wonderful, amazing."

Guaya clicked her tongue. "No, numbskull, not that." She paused. "Though it was very pleasant." She reached up and clamped her hands on either side of his face. "What am I thinking?"

Saro stared at her. "I don't know." He frowned, concentrating. It was true: he didn't. Suddenly it was as if a great shadow had lifted from him. "I don't know!" he cried joyously. He hugged her, and she was a mystery to him, a wonderful, unknowable mystery. "Guaya, what have you done?"

She rolled out from under him, sat up, and smoothed back her hair. "Taken back my gift."

That confused him. "Your gift?"

"You thought it was my grandfather who gave you the power to know others' minds, along with the stone. But it was not Hiron Sea-Haar who did it. It was me. I don't know why exactly—whether I meant it as a gift or a punishment." In the golden light of the candles her expression was earnest, determined. "You were so naive, you see. You knew so little. You looked at your brother and all you saw was a swaggering bully; you looked at your people and you merely saw ordinary folk. You never saw beyond the surface of things."

Saro considered this. "Whereas my brother was a monster in the making, and my people were arrogant and cruel?"

Guaya nodded.

"I killed him, you know, my brother Tanto." His eyes narrowed with misery. "I . . . I . . . choked him till he gave up his ghost."

Guaya laid a hand on his arm. "Even though we nomads do not believe in the taking of even the most evil life, I would say that that deed was truly a boon from you to all of Elda, though I know it has exacted a high price from you. But you will have no more bad dreams now, I promise." She paused. "Shall I tell you why else I gave you my gift?"

Rather than waiting for his assent, she reached down and picked up one of the puppets from the floor where it had fallen, knocked off the bed in their haste. Its strings lay tangled and knotted around its painted limbs so that it was hobbled and hamstrung.

"I saw how it was when you looked at me. All you saw was a

precocious little girl, so clever with her puppets and her old songs, so outspoken with her adult opinions, and I wanted you to know—" She bit her lip. "I wanted you to know me; and yourself. You are a good man— better than the rest, more sensitive, more intelligent. I thought you would take the gift as I meant it to be taken and use it for the good of others. I am sorry. It was a stupid and manipulative thing to do. I should never have done it. They do not call me the Puppeteer for nothing."

Saro gazed at her, appalled. He had just shared his body with this girl—this *woman*—but with every passing second she was becoming more strange to him. He did not know how to feel: angry, relieved, betrayed, or all three at once.

He took a deep breath. "Have you any idea what it's been like for me?"

Reluctantly, Guaya shook her head.

"Everything. I saw everything. A single accidental touch in a crowd and I would know a man's every thought—his guilts, his secrets, his hatreds, his loves; the last woman he slept with, the last meal he ate. I have felt men's souls run through my fingers like sand. I have known the things about them they would not tell their dearest friend, their brother, or their wife. I have been privy to dreams and nightmares and not known whether I would emerge from them as myself. I have felt men's spirits slip away, and every time it was as if I died with them." He began to shake. "When I . . . when I tightened my grip around my own brother's throat, I felt his terror and his loathing like . . . black bile in my veins, eating away at everything that was good in me. And still I choked and choked him and wished as he wished that I could die in his place." Now he stopped, overcome.

Guaya sat there mute, her hands pressed to her mouth. Tears stood in her eyes.

"So for all that you say I am a good man," Saro went on at last, "I know that I am not. The gift you gave me showed me the worst of all that I share with others. I am no better than they, for I have killed and lied and hurt as have they all. You cannot care for me. No one can. I am not worthy of it. I should never have embraced you, never have allowed you to embrace me. It was wrong. My heart lies elsewhere—"

"Stop, stop." Guaya's tears began to fall now. So much, Saro thought inconsequentially, for the myth that the Wandering folk wept only for joy. "That was a purer gift than my first and I will not have you spurn it. Love freely given should not be turned away or regretted. But my first gift was a terrible mistake and I have taken it back. No one should have to learn so much of human nature, I understand that now. There is a good reason why our innermost thoughts lie hidden, for no matter how well-intentioned we may be, there is always something bad—some darkness or selfishness or desire—that mars each thought and deed. The only way through life is to be able to ignore those taints, or how could we ever love or trust or hope?"

"I did not think. I meant to give you insight, not send you mad." She began to sob. "I wanted you to look at me and see me as a woman: but instead all I have done is to curse you and blight you forever."

Saro reached out quickly and took her hands between his own and it was immensely comforting to be able to make this simple gesture without fear of being deluged by another's being.

"Hush now," he said softly. "It is mended now. I forgive you." He paused, thinking, for in truth all was not yet mended by any means. "And the stone? Can you remove the curse from that, too?"

Guaya took her hands away from him, then shook her head. "Only the giver may take back the gift."

Saro stared at her, his heart falling. "Then I must seek out the Goddess." But first, he realized, he would have to find the stone itself. The thought made him shudder.

A charged silence fell in the wagon then, to be broken only by one of the candles guttering down into a hiss of molten wax. A moment later, the door flap rustled and a plaintive cry issued from the wagon's steps.

Saro laughed. "I believe we have a visitor."

At the sound of his voice, a small brindled head appeared in the canvas opening, followed by a lithe and brindled body. The kitten stopped suddenly, gave a yowl, then ran smartly across the wagon, jumped up onto the bed between the two naked humans, and then, as if some natural order had thus been restored to the world, set to grooming itself with purring complacency.

But seconds later, the kitten was followed by a second rather less serene or welcome visitor.

DRIVEN by a mixture of curiosity and pique, Katla Aransen had quartered the encampment like a dragonfly hunting for prey. There was something she needed to ask Saro Vingo, and it was most infuriating that he was not at hand to answer her at once. In the middle of a group of wagons she came upon Dogo, Doc, and Persoa sitting and drinking with a number of nomad men. Not in the mood to join them, she hung back and listened to their banter. Doc was teasing the little man mercilessly.

"You had it off with her in the back of one of the wagons?"

Dogo puffed out his chest. "Yes, she chose me. Walked right up to me, she did, tapped me on the chest, and crooked her finger at me to follow her."

"That's just a polite greeting among the Lost People," Persoa grinned.

For a moment, Dogo's face filled with consternation and doubt. "I didn't force her," he said quickly. "She had my breeches off before I could ask for a price."

Doc regarded his comrade solemnly. "And seconds after that it was all too late, I suppose?"

"Far too late." Slowly Dogo caught up with the implication. "Damn you, I wasn't that quick. She seemed to like it well enough anyway. She wanted to know my name."

"So she could boast of being pricked by the famous Dogbreath of Dalina?"

"She was most interested in my name, as it happens. Or I think she was. She said something I could not understand and then did this—" He looked to the hillman and repeated the girl's elaborate mime.

Persoa chuckled loudly. "She said that the breath of the dog is hot because it comes straight from the heart."

Dogo beamed.

"They think it a lucky thing. They believe that dogbreath cures babies of the croup."

"Aye," said Doc with a sardonic grin. "It knocks 'em dead."

"And she wouldn't take any money from me," Dogo finished with a bewildered shrug. "I tried to give her some, honest."

That made Doc guffaw. "Gave her plenty, eh, Dogs?"

Persoa smiled. "If they like you, they'll accept no payment. They say the act of love is a shared pleasure and a gift from one person to another, and money spoils the giving."

Dogo raised an eyebrow. Then he grinned from ear to ear. "My birth day, Winterfest, and Lady's Day have all come together, then!"

Katla frowned and moved away feeling uneasy. She wasn't sure why the little man's delight in this sudden prospect of bounty should unsettle her so, but it did. As she moved through the camp, one of the men stepped out of the shadows. He bobbed his head at her and flashed her a sharp, wicked glance, all white teeth and gleaming eyes. The rings and bones hanging from his ears rattled gaily as he moved, as did the pendants hanging against his darkly tanned bare chest.

"*Rajeesh, minna bellina.*"

Katla inclined her head, not sure what he meant.

"*Ig heti Ballaro. Ev thi?*"

That much she thought she understood. "Katla. Katla Aransen."

The nomad said her name several times over with different emphases on the syllables. In his rich foreign voice it sounded impossibly exotic and strange. Then he laughed and caught her by the elbow.

"*Genga at mir, minna bellina Katla. Ig vili konnuthu-thi sare i luni.*"

"What?" She had no idea what the words meant, but his gesture was unmistakable, as was the way he was now caressing her left breast. "Get off!" She extricated herself with a furious flourish and stood away from him, bristling like an angry cat.

The man shrugged and tilted his head. He made an expression which suggested both sorrow and disappointment, then touched the skin above his heart and pointed away into the wagons.

Katla set her jaw and stalked off into the gathering darkness in the opposite direction, feeling both faintly humiliated and at the same time oddly amused. From what little she had been able to make out in the fading light, the nomad had been young and handsome and the wine she had drunk was making her skin buzz so that the touch of him stayed with her, full of heat and promise. Abruptly she recalled another night such as this, one which had also involved too much wine and firelight a long way from home.

She groaned. More sensible by far to find her own sleeping pack and lie down away from all this unwonted conviviality. Giving up the idea of trying to find the Istrian, she turned to set a path back to where her horse was tethered, and almost tripped over a small dark shape, which skipped out from under her feet and began to trot ahead of her, purring hugely.

It was Saro's kitten.

"Out for a walk, are we?" Katla said, amused. "Well, let us walk together for a little way, then, eh?" Obviously the creature had remembered her scent on the meat. "Fickle little beast, aren't you?" she added after a while, as the cat gave no sign of abandoning her. "Why aren't you with your master?"

As if in response, the kitten ran up to one of the wagons and started rubbing its head against the wooden steps leading up to it. Then it looked back at her expectantly.

"What? You want to go in there?" Seeing the silhouetted shapes candlelit from within, Katla grinned. "I do not think these good folk need your company, little cat."

But the kitten was undeterred. On it went, clambering up the tall steps with remarkable gracelessness, and when it reached the door flap at the top, it stuck its head inside, followed by the rest of it, until there was just a tip of black fur left waving around on the outside.

Katla ran up the steps after it and grabbed the disappearing tail. Instead of giving its ground like a well-behaved animal, the kitten dug its claws into the floor of the wagon, yowled with fury, and dragged itself out of her grasp. Without any thought except annoyance at being thus bested, Katla dived after it.

It took a moment for her eyes to adjust to the dim light of the wagon's dusky interior, but when they did, she wished she had not followed the cat, had never seen the blasted thing, nor the entire nomad encampment. Inches away from her, Saro Vingo sat stark naked on the bed with the candlelight burnishing his sweat-sheened skin—*all* his skin: and beside him, her dark eyes brimming with laughter, her dark-tipped breasts rising and falling with merriment, was the nomad girl he had called Guaya. Between them both sat the kitten, looking most proud of its rude discovery.

Katla's mouth fell open.

This set the girl to laughing aloud. Katla glared at Guaya, just as she had at the nomad girl's cousin scant minutes before, then transferred her furious attention to Saro. The Istrian gazed back at her, startled, then grabbed at the bedclothes, which promptly slithered off onto the floor, leaving him even more exposed than he had been before. A new gust of delight shook the nomad girl, and all at once Saro found that for all his mortification he was laughing, too, for the situation was just too ridiculous for words.

Katla looked from one to another in rising fury, sensing they deliberately mocked her. Then she flung herself out of the wagon, jumped to the ground, and took off at a run. Having no wish for further awkward encounters, she dashed head down through the encampment, skirting the fire and the musicians without any response to their cheerful invitations to join them, until she found herself back where the horses were tethered and all was quiet. There, she grabbed her pack, a purloined cloak, and a flask of wine someone had carelessly left lying around and set off grimly into the scrubland. Finding a soft dune in the lee of some thorn bushes, she cast herself down with a hefty sigh.

Overhead, the Navigator's Star shone down impassively, the brightest point in a sky spangled with a thousand specks of light, the only constant thing, it seemed, in all the world.

"You're huffing and puffing like an old dog, Katla Aransen," came a voice out of nowhere. "Has someone stolen your bone?"

Katla sat bolt upright in shock and stared in the direction of the voice. A moment later moonlight shone on a silver-blonde head cresting the rise.

"What are you doing out here?"

"Same as you, it seems," Mam growled.

Katla drew her knees up to her chin as the mercenary leader came crashing down the dune in her huge boots, deluging her in an avalanche of sand. She came to a halt beside the Rockfaller, her sharpened teeth gleaming in the dusk.

"So," she cajoled, "why aren't you down there having it away with one of those pretty Footloose boys?"

Taken aback by the uncanny accuracy of Mam's aim, Katla went on the offensive. "Why aren't you?"

Mam shrugged. "One southerner at a time'll do me."

It was the most romantic thing Katla had ever heard her say. "Aren't you worried he'll be availing himself of their vaunted hospitality?" she asked, too sharply.

A stillness fell between them.

"Aye, well. It's what they're known for, the Footloose. Might as well be called Quim-loose or Cock-loose," she said with a bitter laugh.

Katla bit her lip, remembering the tableau which had met her eyes inside that candlelit wagon. "And men are faithless beasts," she said at last.

In the darkness, Mam raised an eyebrow. "Found the Vingo lad, did you?" she said after a while.

Katla stared at her, bridling. "I . . . I wasn't looking for him," she said defensively.

"But you found him."

"In the arms of a little nomad whore."

"Men's pricks are like divining rods. They twitch and rise at the slightest hint of a damp hole."

Katla choked on her wine.

"Besides," Mam went on, thumping her on the back. "Since when did you give a damn about where Saro Vingo was poking his rod?"

"I don't!" The denial came out as a splutter half of outrage, half of coughed-up wine. She turned away from the mercenary leader and spat heavily into the dirt. "Anyway, if you think Persoa's lying with a nomad woman, why don't you go down there and root him out?" she said nastily.

"What Persoa does is his own business. I do not own him and he does not own me."

"If I ever have a man, I shall never share him," Katla said fiercely.

This time both eyebrows shot up. "I thought you said you would never take a husband, Katla Aransen?"

The conversation was not going at all to Katla's liking.

"Who said anything about husbands?" she said crossly, shoving herself to her feet and grabbing up her belongings.

She stomped off into the night, found a spot between some boulders, wrapped herself in the cloak, and tried to use the last of the wine to dull her thoughts. But they were not to be stilled. Round and round they went, buzzing like a hive of bees, and by the time dawn light tinged the sky, she had slept not a wink.

33

Cantara

FOR twenty-three years Cantara, the southernmost inhabited town in Istria, had been the domain of Tycho Issian, a bone tossed by the Ruling Council into the path of a barking dog to keep it quiet. It was little loss to them. Other than the title which accompanied the prize, Cantara had had little to recommend it. Perched precariously on towering sandstone bluffs in the lee of the great mountains presided over by the Red Peak, the town had been poor, crumbling, and disease-ridden, the population a ragtag mix of those too poverty stricken or lethargic to have the wherewithal to up sticks and leave for a better life elsewhere. Mountebanks and ne'er-do-wells avoiding warrants on their heads from all over the Empire rubbed shoulders with escaped slaves and women who had been condemned to stoning for adultery, indecency, or merely for raising a protesting voice—women whose relatives had managed to smuggle them south beyond the eye of their accusers—and a mass of shanty dwellers with nomad or hill blood, eking out a hard living from the arid allotments bordering the desertlands.

To this Goddess-forsaken place Tycho Issian had come, and soon the folk of the region began to realize that the grim existences they had lived till now had been days of wine and roses compared to the time which was to follow. Before long, the gibbets lining the road from the north bore swollen, rotting fruit; it was said that when the wind blew from the south, you could smell Cantara's justice as far away as Gibeon and Pex.

The able-bodied gathered their scant belongings and headed for the hills; the slower either perished from famine, or were put to the labor of scratching out a citadel for their new lord from the very rock itself. Many perished from exhaustion and accident. Four hundred lives had been lost in the creation of Cantara's castle. The foundations were reputedly built not of rock and sand, but blood and hair and bone.

When the lord traveled north—which was blessedly often—the town breathed a collective sigh of relief and handed itself over to the more tender mercies of the lord's mother, the redoubtable Flavia. This lady had taken it upon herself to offer to succor to the needy, to take in refugees and wayfarers, and even to offer hospitality to nomads as they passed through the Issian lands.

Which was why, for want of any other option, the caravan had been heading for Cantara.

"Coroman Piedbird and Redita Fullmoon say the lady has emptied out her grainstores and cellars and bade her seneschals carry loaves and cheeses to the poor," Persoa explained as they rode. "As far away as Galia the Wandering folk honor her name; and from all over the Empire they have come now at the hardest of times when there is nowhere else to turn."

They passed no soldiers on the road, nor any other travelers. Everyone, it seemed, had already gone north, in preparation for battle. Two days brought them within sight of the town. At first glimpse it was an impressive sight. A turreted fortress spanned the breadth and depth of a great tongue of red rock which thrust itself out from the hills behind it and towered up into the pitiless blue sky. Below sprawled the town itself, a great ramshackle collection of dwellings carved into the myriad sandstone pillars which littered the plain, and hundreds of meaner buildings of baked mud and wood filling the gaps between the pillars and creeping up the side of the outcrop. The entire place was teeming with life; it was like riding into a termite mound.

Women, children, old folk, dogs, chickens, cats, geese, and goats crammed the streets and filled the air with their noise. No one seemed much surprised by the appearance of another group of travelers, even one so motley as to comprise both sell-swords and Footloose.

Saro stared about in amazement. Despite its proximity to Altea, he had never visited this southern town, nor wished to, while its lord was in residence. The Cantara of his imagination and his studies was a far different place from the Cantara he found before him. Far from being the miserable frontier town where only the desperate and defeated fetched up, this was a thriving hub. And something seemed very foreign about it, something he could not quite define. He stared about at all the activity, at the people hurrying here and there on errands, at the traders and their stalls, at the stacks of baked bread and rounds of cheese, the baskets of dried fruit and the panniers of grain, at the children playing catch-frog and where's-the-wolf, and then it came to him with a sudden shock that was almost physical.

The women went unveiled.

Saro was not the only member of their group to notice this. Mam caught Persoa's arm and said something in a quiet voice which made the hillman shake his head and look disconcerted. For her part, Katla stared frankly about with her mouth open. A small flame of hope beat suddenly in her chest.

No one challenged them as they rode into the castle's courtyard. Indeed, there seemed to be no guards in sight in this inner sanctum, only a great many women and a few old men. The old men looked up sharply from their tasks, as if caught in the performance of an illicit act. The majority of the women sat in concentric circles around the smaller group in the center. Some wore robes of fine silk and satin, others the plain black sabatka of the slave class. The eyes which turned to survey them were outlined with kohl so that their regard was bold, but their lips were pale and unpainted. Some of the women had let their hair fall loose about their faces, as if compensating for the missing veil, but others had defiantly braided their hair tightly across their heads, the better to be able to view the objects they held in their laps.

Books. Books and parchments, old and new. Tablets and styli and quills.

Mam frowned. "What is this?"

Beside her, the hillman grinned in sudden comprehension. "A class," he said softly. "The women of Cantara are learning to read and write."

Katla Aransen looked mightily unimpressed. Reading had never been her strong point. She knew enough knots to get by in a tavern or a market, and her mother and no one had ever managed to introduce her to the arcane art of writing.

Abruptly something caught her eye; at the same moment Saro Vingo gasped.

"Mother!" they exclaimed in one breath.

In the second row of women, a head turned sharply. Illustria Vingo locked eyes with her second son. Her hands flew up to her face like two white doves, pressing themselves over a mouth which could suddenly form no intelligible words.

And at the heart of the circle, a tumble of red hair streaked with gray flew wildly as Bera Rolfsen leaped to her feet.

The two women of the Rockfall clan regarded one another across the sea of faces, eyes wide with disbelief. Behind Bera, a tall, white-haired woman rose gracefully from the stool on which she had been seated, a small leatherbound volume in her hands.

"None enters this place bearing weapons," she declared in a voice which carried clearly through the dry desert air. "Speak your names and your business. If you come in good will, you are welcome to our hospitality; if not, I can assure you there are no riches here left to rob."

Mam strode to the front of the group. "Mercenaries, my lady. On our own business, and with no violence in mind, if we are left to ourselves. We come to ransom Saro Vingo to his family, or what is left of it."

"Ransom?"

"He is our prisoner, and his actions have cost us dearly."

Flavia of Cantara raised an eyebrow. Then she turned to the small, elegant dark-haired woman whose fingers were still pressed to her lips. She smiled. "What say you, my dear Illustria? What price is worth the release of such a son? Does not rumor have it that he took the life of his elder brother, a crime which usually bears the penalty of being sent to Falla's fires?"

The woman peered earnestly at the Lady of Cantara, blinking rapidly, apparently still in shock.

The tall woman turned back to Mam. "I do not believe in the buying and selling of human flesh," she said coolly. "Every soul belongs to itself and no other. And every soul must bear responsibility for its actions.

Saro Vingo, if you be he, step out and speak what truth you may about the matter of your brother's death."

Saro slithered from the mule more because his fingers lost their grip on the saddle than out of any direct volition. Once on the ground, he found that his trembling legs would not bear his weight. Sinking to the ground, he bowed his head: a supplicant before his judges.

In a low voice he said: "The rumors are true. I killed my brother, Tanto Vingo. In the dungeons of the Eternal City, where he had imprisoned me, I did this terrible thing. Had I left him to live, many thousands of innocents would have succumbed to his tortures, but I know that however good my intentions, in killing him, I have not only damned myself but also broken my mother's heart, for he was always her favorite—"

"Oh, Saro—" Illustria Vingo's voice rose in a wail.

Flavia Issian's basilisk gaze fell upon the wailing woman and her noise tailed away into stifled sobs. At last she turned back to Saro. "So," she said dispassionately, "you admit yourself a murderer?"

Saro stared at the ground. Then he lifted his eyes to the women, his jaw set decisively. "I fear it is not only my brother's death for which I am responsible. I killed a man called Erno Hamson to stop him speaking a dangerous truth. There was a soldier who attacked a troupe of nomads with whom I was traveling, and a Jetran guard who was trying to prevent my escape. And I caused the death of two men at the Allfair. I was trying to save Katla Aransen from the pyre to which they had unjustly consigned her for the attack upon your granddaughter, my lady, Selen Issian."

Flavia Issian's eyes narrowed. "I have heard strange rumors about my granddaughter Selen. Tell me what you know of that affair."

"Only that it was not the Eyrans who attacked her, but my own brother, frustrated that the marriage settlement that had been arranged between the two of them had fallen through."

"So you would add rape to the other crimes of which you would condemn your dead brother?"

Saro nodded mutely.

"And the girl, Katla Aransen." Flavia's sharp eyes roved over the lithe form of the Eyran in her borrowed leather armor, taking in her fierce expression, and the way her fist clenched around the hilt of her undrawn sword and drew a swift conclusion. "What was your interest in trying to save her? Mere justice, or something perhaps a little . . . more personal?"

Saro flushed. The old woman's eyes seemed to bore right through him as if she were indeed weighing the measure of his soul. "I . . . ah . . ." he started, then gathered himself and in a firm tone declared. "I loved her."

The crowd of women breathed as one, entranced by his words.

"You, the son of an Istrian noble, would admit to loving a barbarian woman to the extent of risking your own life?"

"Yes."

The women looked from Saro to Flavia, and then to Katla. For her part, the red-haired girl at the heart of all this appeared to be deep in thought, as if the old woman's inquisition and the boy's subsequent response had answered some question of her own.

Flavia's lips curved into an amused smile. "It appears," she said, and it seemed that she addressed the entire gathering, rather than Saro Vingo alone, "that the differences between our two peoples are less than others would have us think. An Empire boy may share his heart with a northern girl, just as northern women may share their experiences with Empire women, and turn about." She indicated the visitors. "And who would ever have expected to see nomads traveling with a female sell-sword of Eyran extraction, a Galian dwarf, a giant Northern Islander, and a Farem hillman?" Her black-eyed gaze passed assessingly from one to the next. "But is this not what the forbidden text of Aspian tells us?" She flourished the battered-looking volume in her hand. "That long ago we were all one and the same, a single race of folk who lived and loved in harmony? Before the balance of Elda was disrupted and men's greed and distrust rose to the surface and violence became the order of the day?"

The women began to murmur. Some looked down at the tablets on their laps, as if the scratches upon them echoed the same dangerously subversive ideas.

"Falla would not smile upon our so-called 'justice,' nor the blood sacrifices we make to gain her favor. The Lady is a gentle goddess, who wishes love and plenty for all her people."

Saro stared at the woman who made this pronouncement in amazement. Such sentiments would surely consign her to the fires of which she spoke, the fires her own son had fanned to blazing pyres.

"Nor would she condone this ridiculous war our men are fighting in her name. Liberating the women of the north—what nonsense!" Now she turned her attention back to Saro, her black eyes coming to rest on him in deep contemplation. "We have heard unpleasant rumors and reports of your deceased brother from far and wide, young man. From merchants and refugees, from those Wandering folk who have been lucky enough to elude persecution, and from the women my seneschal and his staff have been bringing here from all over the Empire. It has not been an easy time for your mother; she felt she had lost her beloved son long before your violent action took him from this world."

Saro looked from the Lady of Cantara to the woman to stood at her shoulder, eyes brimming with unshed tears. He could not remember the last time he had seen his mother unveiled. He felt his own eyes filling up in response. Staggering to his feet, he lurched toward her, and the crowd parted to ease his passage. Flavia Issian stood aside to allow Illustria Vingo to slip past her, and a moment later mother and son stood face to naked face.

After a while, Saro whispered, "Forgive me, Mother."

In response, Illustria gave him a crooked smile and tears began to spill down her cheeks. In a gesture of infinite tenderness, she raised her hands and cupped Saro's face between her palms.

"My son, my beloved son. I always knew, you know . . ."

"Knew what, Mother?"

"About Tanto. I knew his little cruelties. I knew his lies. I always knew what he was, what he might become. But I hid that knowledge from myself. I thought that if I loved him enough, he would become the better for it."

"Perhaps you loved him too much, Mother."

"And you not enough?"

Wordless, he nodded.

"I loved you so much I could not bear to show you how much."

"Because I was Fabel's child, not my father's?"

Illustria's eyes went round with shock. She clenched her hands over her heart. "How could you know this?"

Saro's mouth twisted in pain. "I have been shown many things I had no wish to know."

"And your fa—and Favio, does he know?"

Saro shook his head.

Illustria Vingo looked away. "It was hard to lose both of them in swift succession. Hard, indeed. I do not think I could bear to lose Favio as well. There is too much hurt here for recrimination, Saro. Can you forgive me for all these years of deception?"

Now Saro's tears fell, too. "Can you forgive me, Mother? Because I do not think I can forgive myself."

Mam watched this touching scene with a glint in her eye and the world's most cynical smile. Then she stepped up to the Lady of Cantara, hands on hips. "It is hard to come so far without some form of reward," she said. "My men and I have precious little to show for all our efforts. If you will not allow us to ransom the boy, we may have to come to some other arrangement." She scanned the crowd. "That lady there," she pointed to Bera Rolfsen. "How about we exchange like for like? Release her into our care and we will return her to the bosom of her family."

Flavia Issian laughed and turned to face the woman Mam indicated.

"Well, Bera Rolfsen," she said with a smile, "what say you? Shall I 'release' you from my employ and give you over to this rabble?"

Bera smiled back at the Lady of Cantara. Then she said to Mam, "I am no prisoner here. More than that, I have no wish to return to Rockfall. That part of my life is done. My steading is burned, my mother is dead, my husband gone away, and my errant daughter stands with you, looking like the hoyden she is. What is there in Eyra for me to return to?"

Mam saw a fat purse slipping swiftly away. "Your brother Margan charged me with finding you and bringing you safely home."

Bera snorted. "Margan! My dear, fat old brother merely thinks to marry me off to some rich trader and make himself a tidy profit into the bargain. Keep whatever he has given you and forget the rest, for my work now is here with Flavia and these women. I like being a teacher. It is more satisfying to bring understanding to those who crave it than to those who would rather be scaling rockfaces or wrestling with their brothers."

"Mother!" Katla was stung.

Bera Rolfsen cocked her head and regarded her daughter gravely. Then she burst out laughing. "Ah, Katla, you were ever easy to tease. But what I say is what I wish, for now; until we know which course this mad conflict will take. Flavia has been more than kind, and I would like to do what little I can to repay that kindness. Take a look around the folk gathered here, for you may see other familiar faces."

Katla gazed around the group of women and was surprised to see she had failed at first glimpse to see fair heads among all the dark. Over by the horse trough stood a somewhat thinner Magla Felinsen and Kit Farsen; sitting in a knot of Istrian women poring over a parchment, Forna Stensen, always the most attentive of her classmates; and grinning like a well-fed cat in the middle of the circle was Fat Breta, who now heaved herself to her feet and launched herself at Katla, wrapping her arms around the taller girl's torso.

"I never thought I'd see you again! I never thought I'd see any of my friends again."

Katla had never really thought of Fat Breta as a friend, had never considered that she had any friends at all—just her brothers; one of whom was drowned, and the other just as surely lost. Bemused, she hugged Fat Breta back, then carefully detached herself.

"But how did you get here?"

"The Lady sent out her seneschals to buy us back from the men who bought us at the slave market—Kit and Forna all the way from Ixta; me from Feria in the Blue Woods; and poor Magla . . ." she tailed off.

"Poor Magla, what?"

Breta lowered her voice. "From a whorehouse in Gibeon," she whispered.

Katla remembered Magla's cruel jibes about Tam Fox. It took some effort to compose herself, but she managed it at last.

"Have you come to take us back to Rockfall, Katla? I would like to see the sea again." She paused. "And though they've been very good to us here, I'd dearly love to get my teeth into a good shank of mutton."

Katla smiled. "I don't think so, Breta. Not yet, at any rate."

"So, daughter, will you stay here with us?"

"All I know is weaponcraft and how to be contrary," Katla returned. "I never was much good with books, or even knots."

"We are all learning different things from each other," Bera said softly. "We are sharing our skills. Some of what I have discovered is quite remarkable. It is a pity your father has vanished off into the blue yonder . . ." She colored prettily.

Katla caught her breath. "Mother! But I thought you had divorced him."

Bera came back to herself, set her jaw. "I have, yes, and there's an end to it." She paused. "You have not heard anything about the expedition, have you?" There was a note of yearning in her voice which did not pass her daughter undetected.

But all Katla could do was to shake her head.

THEY stayed in Cantara for a few days, resting and exchanging stories with the Eyrans and the women of the town, listening to the songs of the Wandering folk and watching their puppetry, their dancing, and their acrobatic feats. Katla learned to juggle, badly. Saro found he could carry a tune with the best of them. The two of them eyed one another nervously and could not find anything to say which would not make things more awkward between them. Guaya watched them, narrow-eyed, but with the sort of half-smile which might denote either regret or resignation. Bera fashioned herself a reed whistle for the first time in twenty-five years and joined in with the musicians. Dogo sought out the nomad woman who had bedded him for free and sampled her delights so noisily in the back of one of the wagons that he drew a crowd of curious children who, seeing him entering the wagon from afar, had thought him one of their number for his small stature. Mam got tipsy and tried to undress Persoa in the full view of the women of Cantara, who crowded around to stare at his strange tattoos, exclaiming and cooing. Some of the bolder ones even reached out to trace their fingers over the designs.

"What does this show?" asked one coyly, touching the black tail of a beast disappearing below the waistband of his breeches.

"It is the tail of the Lady's cat, Bast," he replied with all courtesy, and had to push Mam away when she offered to show them the rest.

"And this?"

An older woman with her hair braided in many plaits moved her fingers across a tattoo on his shoulder blade.

Persoa considered. It was hard, sometimes, to remember the designs that had been inked on his back. "Tell me what you think it is," he said softly. The woman squinted. "Look like sword, but on fire."

"That will be the flaming sword, then," Persoa said, trying not to smile.

"And this one, down here?" She prodded him in the small of the back.

"Coming out of the mountain of fire?" Persoa knew that one. He checked its progress regularly, could tell by the itching of his skin when the designs began to change. Sirio must have found a way to exit the volcano if this was where the figure was now.

But the woman frowned. "No, not coming out, going in." She leaned closer. "And his head all wreathed with flame."

Now Persoa looked alarmed. "Mam!" he said urgently. He caught her by the wrist. "Mam, take a look and tell me what you see."

Mam grinned indulgently, the firelight flickering off the alarming points of her teeth, and extricated herself from his grip. Then she spun him around, her strong hands spanning his narrow waist. Cross-eyed with qat and araque, she bent to examine the area where the woman had pointed. She came back up spluttering.

"That's a new one!"

"New?"

"Well, there was a tiny mark there when I looked last, but I thought it no more than a mole. But now it's as she says: it has hands and legs and hair like fire. And it's running toward the volcano, not away from it."

"A mirror!" Persoa cried to the gathered women. "Does anyone have a mirror?"

Two of the women went bustling off, giggling and chattering. They had seen too much magic by now, too many illusions and tricks from the nomads; this was clearly more of the same. They returned a few moments later with a fine piece of Galian silverware polished to a high sheen. It took the eldianna a little while to position himself so that he could see the new design. When he did, the muscle of his heart clenched so hard he thought he might faint.

"I must leave," he said in a low voice to the mercenary leader. "Tonight. I must leave tonight."

"Tonight?" Mam was aghast. "I haven't finished drinking yet."

"Well, then, I must leave without you."

Mam regarded him with a bleary eye. "Have it your own way," she said belligerently, and went to refill her goblet.

By the time she came back, the hillman had gone.

PERSOA had covered his tracks well. A mule was missing, but there were no hoofmarks in the dirt road beyond the south gate, nor to the west nor the east. There was too much traffic on the road north to tell one set of prints from another; but none had seen a man fitting the eldianna's description.

Mam went about grim-faced—partly on account of a thumping headache, mainly in self-recrimination. In the end, she set her pride to one side and went into the Footloose camp to find a scryer. She went first to Guaya, but the dark-eyed girl merely shook her head and professed no knowledge of the crystals. Mam didn't believe her, but allowed the girl to direct her to one of the old women. On the steps out of the wagon, she cannoned into Saro Vingo, looking a little green around the gills. An odd look passed between the two young people, then Saro darted off again. Mam looked sharply at Guaya.

"Something going on between you two?"

The girl regarded her askance, lips quirked, then bent her head. In her arms lay a tiny brindled kitten, which regarded Mam with bold black eyes, then promptly buried its head in the crook of Guaya's elbow and went to sleep.

The old woman Guaya took her to had only one eye, and that clouded with cataract. Mam opened her mouth to complain, but the crone cackled before she could get the first curse word out.

"Come to see if I can find your man, have you?"

Mam stared at her, dumbfounded.

The old nomad winked, then offered her open palm and wiggled dry brown fingers like a bird's claws under Mam's nose. The mercenary leader tsked, but finally dug around in her belt pouch and dropped a silver piece into the crone's hand. The woman bit it—a pointless gesture as far as Mam could tell, since she appeared to have no teeth left in those sunken old gums—then shuffled off into the depths of the wagon and returned with a shrouded object.

This she carried carefully down the steps and into the sunlit court-yard, spread a cloth on the ground, dusted the crystal with her sleeve, and made the first hand passes over the crystal. Within moments, she had attracted a number of spectators.

Mam frowned. She hadn't been expecting an audience. But she didn't appear to have much choice in the matter. With a sigh, she clumped down the steps and crouched beside the Footloose crone.

"What do you see?"

For a time the old woman said nothing, but the lights in the crystal spun, sending a spectrum of color out into the air. The colors played over Mam's blunt features, rendering them by turns softer and more feminine, then harsh and rugged.

At last the scryer spoke. *"Eldianni suthra ferinni, montian fuegi."*

"What?"

"South he goes, toward the Red Peak, the mountain of fire."

"What on Elda does he want to do that for?" Mam fumed. "He can't be. No one goes there. Look again."

The crone raised an eyebrow at the mercenary's peremptory tone, but did as she was bade. Caressing the crystal, she spoke softly to it as if ca-joling secrets from it, and gradually the colors inside the seeing-stone swirled and pulsed, the tones shifting to sea-grays and greens.

"A ship, I see," she murmured. "No, many ships. Tattered and torn." She narrowed her remaining eye, came in close to the crystal as if to get a better angle on the vista it presented. Then she recoiled with a shriek.

"What?" cried Mam. "What did you see?"

"Manni kalom. Ces Issiani ealdanna kalom. The Lord Tycho Issian." She spat into the dust. "That evil man, still alive, despite the good Goddess."

"And just where is my son?"

The voice was patrician, demanding. The crone looked up to find Flavia Issian, Lady of Cantara, at the edge of the circle, watching her with hooded eyes.

Two silver coins landed on the ground beside the old woman. The crone gazed at them in disbelief, as if they might somehow vanish again, then scooped them into her skirt's capacious pocket. "*Sjanni, minna koni.* He is at sea. On a ship."

"Where on a ship? Heading north for Eyra, or returning home?"

The scryer made a face. "The sea is the sea, my lady, it all look the same to me."

"Look closer. Has he a woman with him?"

With a sigh the crone reapplied herself to the crystal, passing her hands across its surface, twisting her head this way and that, muttering all the while. At last, she looked back up. "My poor old eye not good, my lady. Vision painful today." Another pair of coins landed in the dirt, but the old woman shook her head vigorously. "*Cantaro nethri, minna koni.* There is no need of more money, my lady. I mean what I say. My eye is clouded."

"Well, let me try, then," said Flavia Issian impatiently.

Puzzled looks were exchanged throughout the growing crowd, but they parted to allow the Lady of Cantara through. By the time she reached the old woman, the two coins in the dust had vanished. She made no sign of acknowledgment of this theft but instead knelt down on the spread cloth beside the scryer and studied the crystal intently.

"Rose quartz," she said softly. "Not bad; but not one of the finest I have seen." She brushed it with a finger, shivered. "Out of the black hills south of Farem?"

The old woman looked impressed. "*Havthi konnuthi, minna koni. Havthi seith.*"

"*Sa, sa, havtha seith. Jeg i Faremi brin.*"

"You were born in Farem?" Mam had learned just enough of the Footloose language to make some sense of this exchange.

Flavia Issian looked around the circle of fascinated listeners, her aquiline features serene. She had made a decision, and there was no going back on it. "Yes, you have heard correctly. I was indeed born in the Farem Hills. My father was a tribesman and my mother one of the Wandering folk. I am not proud of having hidden my heritage all these years. I will admit I was afraid to do so at the start, and it became more difficult to acknowledge as the years passed and my circumstances changed. I have been cowardly, I know. The lords of Istria have been cruel to my people, none more so than my adopted son, for all that I have tried to raise him as my own and in the true faith. Too well, I fear, did that lesson take hold." She sighed. "Better that I speak the truth late than never at all. Now let me see if I can tell where Tycho is, so we may all choose which path we should take."

Now she laid hands on the stone and bent all her concentration upon it, and the crystal responded with a burst of light.

The first thing she saw was an expanse of sand dunes stretching away to a horizon hazy with fumes, dark with the silhouette of distant hills. A shambling collection of folk trudged across this unforgiving landscape, led by a small figure on a vast black stallion. Annoyed by this irrelevance, she rubbed her palms across the sphere and watched as the scene dissipated and gave way to one of water and dark cloud. Twilight was falling somewhere far to the north of Cantara, twilight which enveloped the sails of a dozen ships. Behind them, Falla's Eye had risen, bright and unblinking. They sailed away from it, heading directly toward the scryer.

"They come south," she said, to no one in particular. "And their ships have seen battle." The marks of conflict were clearly observable: hacked strakes, charred sails, missing crew. Even she could see there were not sufficient men deployed aboard the lead vessel, for great swathes of open deck were apparent, which should have been swarming with busy seamen.

Something caught her eye. She tilted the stone a little, leaned in for a better look, and became very still. Her hands came away from the stone as if burned. She closed her eyes and her mouth worked silently. Bera, standing close to her, recognized the lovely prayer the Lady of Cantara had been teaching them in the past weeks, and frowned.

When Flavia raised her head again, tears stood in her eyes.

"Forgive me, my Lady. Forgive my son. He knows not what he does."

She scanned the watching faces. "We must go north," she said. "The Goddess is returning to Elda."

THE horses pawed the ground in an aggravated manner, for their riders were impatient to be gone and they knew it.

"Come on, Saro," Katla Aransen muttered under her breath.

"Where's he got to?"

Mam shaded her eyes and stared down into the harsh light striking the imposing sandstone battlements of Cantara's castle walls. Down below, all was hubbub and chaos. Yeka, horses, wagons, carts, and people milled around in the dust outside the gates, yet more streamed out of the town minute by minute. It was an extraordinary sight and an even more extraordinary occurrence. The women of Cantara, guided by that indomitable matriarch, Flavia Issian, had made a grand decision. They would set out on a great journey, north, to the coast, to where the Goddess would make landfall, even though they had no idea of what they would do when they got there, or of the hardships which might attend them on the way. Oddly, none of them cared. All their lives they had entrusted their fate to the will of others; the decisions they had made had amounted to choosing which sabatka to don of a morning, what color to paint their lips; for others no more than what to buy from the market that day, what to bake that evening. Many of them had never before left the confines of the town and had no conception of what such an undertaking might entail; others had been transported across the continent, but under the guardianship of men—to be sold, or wed, or used in ways over which they had no control. It was a mad, heady decision; it made them giddy with fear and noisy with laughter and chatter. It was like stepping off the edge of a cliff. Except that, if they fell, the Goddess would surely catch them. Wouldn't she?

Infected by their gaiety and recklessness, the Eyran women determined to travel with the women of Cantara. Some went out of curiosity, or newfound faith, or to cement bonds of friendships only recently acquired, some because the far south of Istria was too foreign and strange to their eyes, and the farther north they traveled, the closer to their lost homeland they would be.

Dogo, Doc, and Joz had decided to go north for another reason entirely. There was no money to be made in this, emptied-out waterskin of a region, and if their leader had decided to eschew money for the sake of love (or whatever she might call the strange attachment she had to the hillman) that was her lookout. Where there was war, there was opportunity. Every sell-sword knew that.

As for the nomads—well, who knew what prompted them to retrace their weary footsteps north? They were traveling folk, wanderers, foot-loose. They never stayed long in one place.

A sense of great change was in the air, but whether such change would bring disaster or miracle in its wake was impossible to tell. Be-sides, life could hardly be much worse for many of those packing up their belongings and setting off into the unknown.

For her part, Katla envied them their optimism and sense of purpose. Her own decision had been more complicated by far. Part of it involved the feeling that she was a lodestone drawn not to the Navigator's Star, but to the south, where a distant voice called her in her sleep. Partly, she had a hunger for adventure which could never be answered by retracing her steps; and, though she could not admit it, she could never have rid-den off with her mother and left so much unspoken between herself and Saro Vingo. The unquestioning hostility with which she had regarded him since the death of Erno Hamson had dissipated, to be replaced by something more nebulous and mutable. After coming upon him naked in the nomad girl's wagon, her dreams had been both rude and confus-ing: she had woken from them flustered and sweating and extremely bad-tempered. It made her uncomfortable in his presence; it made her want to hit him. But sometimes it made her want to do something else entirely. Katla was not a person who enjoyed such contradictions. A long ride south with only Mam and the Istrian for company would surely clear the air.

She watched a small figure detach itself from the melee down in the valley below and resolve itself gradually as Saro Vingo astride a tall bay gelding. As they breasted the hill, Saro's long dark hair and the gelding's tail streamed out behind them like war banners, and her heart ham-mered hard—once, twice, before settling back into its normal rhythm.

"Let's go," she said tightly to the mercenary leader. Wrenching her mount around with ungentle hands, she galloped off across the ridge.

34

The Rosa Eldi

As the gray cliffs of Istria's north coast came into view on the far horizon, Tycho Issian felt a rapture enter his soul. In a day—less—they would dock in Cera and he would commandeer the fallen lord's castle for his own pleasure. He would lead the Rose of the World into the most famed of all Istrian castles, with its marbled halls, fanned pillars, vaulted ceilings, and sumptuous hangings. He would lead her perfect feet along silken Circesian runners and glorious woolen carpets; he would take her hand and bring her to the chambers of the dead duke himself, where the spotted skins of Skarn lions overhung the exquisite furniture, where the walls were lined with beaten silver and stacks of lilies in Galian pots scented the air. If he closed his eyes, he could smell the sandalwood and safflower the slavegirls would strew in the hot bath in which he would immerse himself before claiming at last the most beautiful woman in the world.

He had been most punctilious on the voyage home, had barely laid eyes on his prize for fear he would be unable to master his passions and fall upon her, grunting like a hog. Which would never do. No. First he must have her shriven and purified, have the priests release her from the foul taint of the northman's touch. Have the bonds of that most barbaric marriage slaked away by blood sacrifice and have himself joined to her, flesh to flesh in place of that rutting, stinking stallion.

Clearly the Goddess smiled upon his venture, for their passage home had been swift and safe. There had been no sign of pursuit. He had had a lookout posted on the rakki and the stern throughout their voyage south, and neither had seen anything more threatening than a breaching whale. Could a war be won so quickly? It could, he breathed. It was a holy war, a true cause.

His Rose had been returned to him.

And soon he would unfurl those precious petals and plunge himself into the heart of that tight bud. His fists clenched at the effort it required not to tear off every scrap of his clothing, to rip down the shelter which veiled her presence from him, and hurl himself upon her here and now. Breathing heavily, he took himself off to the bow, where the bucking sea and lashing spray would cleanse his skin, and his thoughts.

SELEN Issian rinsed out her bloodied linen in the pail, rubbing till her knuckles were raw. Nothing would shift the stains: it was as if the salt in the water was setting the blood there like a dye. Trying to remove it was as futile as trying to erase the memory of her past. Hidden from her for so long by some trick of the mind, or by some foul sorcery, her entire history had returned to her in vivid flashes following the shock of Ravn's death. Yet again she cursed her lot. Better that she had died at Tanto Vingo's hands or, if not during that assault, in the waves when she had plunged into the sea after Erno Hamson.

The child, as if aware of her negative thoughts, fixed its violet eyes upon her and wailed: a malevolent, baleful presence.

She glared back at it, forcing a new hardheartedness. "Stop your noise," she said sharply, as the volume of its roar increased, though her breasts ached and she longed to pick him up. "Do not look to me to feed you. She has claimed you as her own, and she can have the care of you."

She wrung the cloths out with vicious hands, as if wringing the neck of one of the chickens she had never dared to kill when the Eyran had brought them to the beach.

"What good can come of a child born of such a deed?" she mourned. "You even look like him. You have his eyes."

The baby waved its fists at her and kicked its feet. It screwed its face up and let forth a howl of utmost rage.

The Rosa Eldi, lying with her eyes closed and her hands crossed on her chest, like a stone statue in the Halls of the Dead, stirred. She brushed the tips of her fingers across her face like a woman emerging from the depths of a dream and sat up slowly. Her sea-green eyes, not yet quite focused, swept over the screaming child, the strewn clothing, the pail of water. At last they came to rest upon the woman she knew as her body-servant, Leta Gullwing. Her gaze was infinitely sad, infinitely gentle. Selen looked aside, feeling the hatred she nursed so carefully slipping away.

"Will you not feed the child, Leta?" the Rose of the World asked.

"I have no milk."

It was no less than the truth. Her milk had dried up abruptly; and just as that flow had ceased, so her moon-blood had returned for the first time since the birth, returned with griping aches which made her tense and wretched.

"Ah." The first frown Selen had ever seen on the Rosa Eldi's face now creased her forehead. "I am sorry. I have been remiss. There have been too many other things to think about, too many requests for my aid."

It was Selen Issian's turn to frown. All the woman had done was to lie silent and motionless on the couch for the past few days. She had not risen, even to wash or to use the pail; she had eaten not a morsel. She had thought her sick or dying. Now it seemed she was deluded.

Anger made her blunt. "Why take my child if you cannot feed or care for him?"

A cloud passed over the Rosa Eldi's face and for a long time she spoke no word. Then, "For love," she said simply.

Selen stared at her, feeling the bile rise up.

"If you loved him so much, why not give him a child of your own, unless you feared to mar that perfect body, that pretty skin? If you loved him, how could you foist another man's baby upon him?"

The queen's eyes darkened, became misty. Her lower lip appeared to tremble for the briefest second, then firmed itself so swiftly Selen thought she might have been mistaken. Her voice was steady when she spoke again. "He needed a child. For his throne." Dully, she repeated the words she had heard so often. Still the ways of men seemed incomprehensible to her. Succession, inheritance, bloodlines—what mattered such things if there could be love and trust and comfort? "But I could not give him the baby he craved. There is no life in me. None at all." She looked down at her hands, clasped tightly in her lap. Even though her skin was ivory-pale, the knuckles showed whiter than the rest.

A barren woman, then. Nothing more than that. Still Selen was not satisfied. "So you and that woman . . . that *seither* . . . cut my child out of me and you took it as your own, presented it to him as his heir?"

The Rose of the World nodded slowly, but would not look up.

"And then you hazed my mind, took away my memories and all that made me who I was?"

Again, the barest of nods.

"A second theft, just as heinous as the first! What made you think you had the right to do such a thing? I had been poorly enough treated before ever I met you, but thought I had found some place of safety in the northern court; and yet when I came to you, you stole my child and my mind!" Selen Issian stormed on, and there was no stopping the torrent of her fury now. "And all for something you call 'love.' *You,* who have no idea what the word means! If you loved him, as you claim, why have you come unresisting to the Lord Tycho Issian, a terrible man: a cruel man, as I too well know, for he is my father! If you loved Ravn, as you claim, why have you not wept at the loss of him?"

And at this a single fat tear dropped onto the back of the Rosa Eldi's hands and slid off onto her silk underrobe, leaving a dark, wet mark like a wound.

Her face, when she lifted it, was ragged with emotion. She moved her mouth as if to form words, then threw her head back and that mouth became a maw, a sea cave into darkness. The wail that issued from it enveloped Selen with such force that she subsided with a thud onto the floor. So powerful was it that it shocked even the child to quietness.

It was a cry like the wail of death itself, and it spread swiftly across the entire ship.

Beyond the leather shelter, men stopped coiling ropes, bailing bilgewater, stowing gear, gutting fish. The lookout, a thin dark boy, balancing precariously on the rakki above the sail, abruptly lost his grip and came plummeting down to hit the deck with a crash and a cry of his own. Virelai, crouching unhappily among the wounded men, wrapped his arms about his head in a vain attempt to shut out the noise. At the helm, Tycho Issian, spun around with a curse half-formed on his lips and stared down the length of his ship, bewildered, his ears painful, an echo of the noise hurtling around the inside of his skull.

Seabirds in the vicinity veered sharply from their onshore course. And beneath the waves, where no normal sound travels, the basking sharks of the pelagic waters dived into colder, darker zones than was their wonted habitat, and found there shoals of pollock and mackerel, sardine and ling fleeing away into the regions frequented by deep-sea fish—the redfish and rabbitfish and halibut—which rarely crossed their paths.

The Rosa Eldi's sorrowful cry traveled on like a seismic wave.

North, it flew, whipping the sea to a frenzy in its path. By the time it reached the ships of the pursuing fleet, the waves it brought were almost sixty feet high.

In the leading vessel a man sat amidships in a gimballed chair he had fashioned for himself to reduce the worst effects of the passage. He wore a vast robe which repelled all weather; his wild hair and beard were trimmed, and in his hand he held an ivory staff. Rahe had decided to make a certain effort with his appearance in the eyes of the king, investing himself with might and nobility, which should at least dissuade Ravn from tipping him overboard if the going got rough and he failed to live up to expectations. But even he was not prepared for this.

As they closed with the southern fleet, he had been feeling his magic deserting him moment by moment. She was doing this to him. He knew it. She was draining his magic out of him, drawing it back to herself. He felt weaker with every day that passed; he was beginning to wish he had never left the safety of the place he had for good reason named Sanctuary.

As the unearthly cry flew over him, every hair on his ancient body rose at the sound of it, an instinctive reaction, like that of a wild dog suddenly alerted to the presence of a predator. And then the first of the giant rollers came sweeping down upon them and even as the ship mounted its steep bank he was engulfed; not by chill water, but by a terrible despair, and while he knew it not his own, still he could not withstand it, but opened his own mouth in turn and wailed with all his might, a wail that was echoed by that of Ravn Asharson and Aran Aranson and of every other mortal aboard, a sound which was then buried by the breaking of the first massive wave.

AS the last echoes of her scream died away, the Goddess emerged into the light. The sun, which till that moment had been blanketed by a heavy white layer of mist, now burned its way clear, striking incandescent rays down upon the ship and the surrounding sea. Blinded by this sudden brightness, men shielded their eyes and gazed upon the woman they thought of as the Queen of the Northern Isles.

But in that sudden brilliant sunshine she seemed more than any woman, more than a mere queen. In that sudden brilliant sunshine she stood tall and proud, and her long hair shone silver-white like a waterfall. So, too, did her pale skin shine, luminous and flawless. And every man among them longed to reach out and touch her, just to lay their fingers against her arm, to cup her face in a gentle palm, to pin back that fall of hair to the nape of her delicate neck, to kiss a fraction of that extraordinary skin. But none could look for long upon her, for her visage was too bright, too perfect, and the gaze which fell upon them from those sea-green eyes lanced them like quarrels shot from a bow. They had to look aside, and as they did so, each felt a hot wash of shame overcome them: shame not for looking upon this perfect woman, but shame for every cruel or wanton deed they had in this life performed. Shame for every man they had struck, whether in bar brawl or in war; shame for every woman they had wronged. She walked to the nearest man—a north-coast fisherman with the weatherbeaten skin and white crow's feet of a man who spent his time squinting into the sun—and placed the tips of her fingers on his brow. At once, he closed his eyes, his senses assailed. Images tumbled around his skull: the time he had hit his small sister, blackening her eye; how he had lied to his mother and the way her pale mouth, exposed by the unadorned slit in her plain blue sabatka, had pursed with disappointment, but she had said nothing for no Istrian woman was ever allowed to criticize any man; the baker he had struck in an alley after an argument about a game of stones; the knife he had stolen from a fellow crewmember; the whore he had used before making this voyage, the way she had moaned when he pushed her down on the bed; the coldness he had shown his wife when she dared to ask where he had been; the man he had killed in the battle for Halbo, stabbing him through the eye as he waved for help in the churning waters . . .

When she withdrew her hand, he fell to his knees, tears streaming down his face. She passed to the next man, a Jetran who had spent eight years in the Eternal City's militia, then a further six as a bountyman. The lightest touch of her fingers sent his eyes rolling back in his head.

Inside this man's mind she saw: the sister he had sold to a man from Galia who gave him a good horse and a pair of boots in return; the knees of a nomad girl forced apart, how he had thrown a rag over that defiant face to stop her looking at him; Footloose men slung, beaten, and bloodied, across a string of mules like so much baggage; stoking the fires in a chambered room filled with choking smoke and screaming people.

"Forgive me, Lady, forgive me!" he cried.

The Rose of the World found that she did not wish to grant such easy absolution. Inside her soul a vein of iron stood fast and cold. *Let them suffer,* she thought, *as those they have harmed have suffered. Let them feel torment and distress.*

This thought came to her with a small start of surprise, for all those who had sent their prayers to her had prayed to one who was gentle and forever merciful, one who would pardon and forgive their every wrongdoing. Was it her time back in this world which had hardened her so, or had they always been deceived as to the nature of this goddess they so blindly worshiped?

She left him moaning and moved on.

The third man had been a priest for a time, had called the observances and strewn the safflower in the fires. He had made new prayers for the worshipers from Ixta and Cera; he had blessed children in the name of Falla and presided over marriages. But when she laid her fingers on his brow, she saw no pacific benevolence there, but the rolling eyes of a ewe as the sacrificial knife bit into her bared throat; the way a booted foot kicked an unconscious Footloose man into the pyres; how he bound three nomads and their children to the stakes as the other men built up the stacks of wood and oil around them.

The next man she touched was a slave at his oar, a man captured in the southern hills. She saw: a girl-child put out on a moonlit mountainside to live or die, as pleased the old gods; a man brained with a rock, silver coins spilling from his hand; a weeping woman, a bawling child; an old tribesman trampled underfoot in a headlong escape.

On she went, touching a slave here, a crewman there.

She saw children neglected and abused; women consigned to no life but chores, to brothels, and hard service, to death in childbed or from exhaustion and despair. She saw all manner of animals sacrificed in the name of religion—to appease *her!* She saw men killing other men, raping women, enslaving tribesfolk; sending Wandering folk to the pyres to "cleanse" their souls.

And each man she touched knew for the first time the wrong he had done.

So this is Elda, she thought. *This is my world—a place in which greed and power and ill-intent brings suffering and death to the poor, the weak, and the oppressed. This is the world from which I was stolen, but it is a world I do not recognize or recall. Is it my memory which is at fault, I wonder, or have I been absent for so long that all the good in it has drained away?*

And then, at last, she came to Tycho Issian.

They stood there face-to-face, the Rose of the World and the Lord of Cantara, but he gazed upon her boldly with shameless eyes, eyes which burned with heat and lust, and this time it was she who turned away. This man she could not touch; there was something about him which terrified her still, Goddess or no. When he reached out to put his hands on her, she gave herself up to a dead faint and she crumpled at his feet.

WHEN the great waves and the howl of wind passed over them without taking their ships into the depths of the Northern Ocean, King Ravn Asharson sank to his knees and gave up his thanks to Sur.

"Surely he is watching us and willing on our pursuit," he cried triumphantly to Rahe, never noticing that the old man was white with exhaustion and terror, nor that his knobbly hands had acquired a new tremor.

The mage roused himself with an effort and looked Ravn squarely in the eye.

"Summon no gods," he said sternly. "Put your trust instead in the good oak of your ships, the strength of your men, and in my good offices, for powerful sorcery will stand you in better stead by far than calling on some unpredictable and wanton being."

"Of course, of course." Ravn nodded enthusiastically. "Now tell me, Lord Rahe, can you not make our ships go any faster? We must gain upon them and overtake them before they make landfall, or we shall have a hard time of it."

But the mage shook his weary head. "Have I not given you fair passage so far, young man?" he demanded, claiming good weather that had never been his to bestow. "There is only so much I can do for you without attracting unwanted attention."

Ravn narrowed his eyes. "What do you mean?"

Rahe extricated himself from the gimballed chair and leaned in close to the barbarian king. "The use of magic permeates far beyond its intended sphere, young man," he said softly. "Every time I use my powers on your behalf, it leaks down through the waves to the very sea floor. You cannot imagine what lurks down there, unseen except by those whom disaster takes. Monstrous creatures, many-limbed horrors with beaks and teeth; tentacled terrors as large as the greatest whale. If the magic touches them, they feel compelled to seek it out; and when they do, it is not done gently."

The King of Eyra regarded him skeptically, though he well remembered the eruption of the creature which had caused such havoc in his own harbor. He cared nothing for monsters. Monsters could be dispatched or evaded, but if the Istrians made safe landfall, he would lose his advantage and lose his best chance to reclaim his beloved wife and child. He felt the urge to take the old man by his scrawny chicken neck and force the magic out of him. But instead, taking a deep breath, he said with the diplomacy he had learned so hard these past months. "Very well, lord mage. Let us reserve the best of your abilities for the battle ahead." *And if you fail me then, I shall personally feed you to whatever monsters inhabit the Istrian home waters.*

Then he turned and walked away to speak with his steersman; if the mage would not help him, then he must indeed trust to good men and good oak.

Rahe, watching after him smiled in his turn, congratulating himself yet again on his own quick-wittedness and subtlety.

A sea battle would not suit his own plan well at all. No, let the Istrians make land and then he would have them all: Goddess and apprentice, beast and brother.

WHEN the Rose of the World came back to consciousness, she was no longer on a ship, that much was clear. Her eyes swept her surroundings with curiosity. She was in a chamber like none she had ever known, in this life at least. The walls shone silver as if by some magic men had managed to make a paint from metal and sheathe stone within it. Bright tapestries hung from carved wooden poles, replicating all manner of wonders. Tumbles of red-and-pink roses cascading over the forms of naked women, each breast another flower among so many, each aureola a swelling bud. Gryphons and unicorns battled one another; serpents and knights were bound in unholy congress; a many-legged creature rose up from a churning ocean to claim a pale ship. A fire blazed in a vast inglenooked hearth; sconces bore a hundred candles; pots of burning incense and bowls of safflower stood on every table. Across each massive piece of furniture—of which there were many—lay the hide of some poor dead beast. She looked upon each one and recognized them all: spotted cats and striped horses, minks and ermines and foxes. From the center of the polished stone floor the head of a snow bear stared back at her, its intelligent black eyes replaced by balls of silver which mirrored blankly the dancing candlelight. Its claws had been removed, but its ivory fangs gleamed in an eternal humorless grin.

"Poor beast," muttered the Rosa Eldi. "I hope you bit the one who killed you before he took your life and reduced your rich existence to this piece of moth-eaten, meaningless carpet."

She rose up on the bed on which she lay and found that, too, covered with skins of dead animals. The ermine-lined cloak Ravn had given her lay draped across the chair beside her. She regarded it sadly. How strange that she should never till now have regretted those tiny lost lives it represented, strange that some lost part of her had now returned to burn with a vengeful fire. "My creatures," she whispered. "You are all my creatures and each of you deserve the chance to live and die as you choose."

She thought about this for an unknowable time. While she thought, the candles burned lower, and some guttered and went out.

How was she to take back this world of hers without causing such death and suffering as she had witnessed in the minds of her subjects? But take it back she must; all around was evidence of cruelty and hurt, and if she did not act to save it, then she was complicit in that wickedness.

Then another thought occurred to her. If there was such evil in the world, where had it come from, if not from those who created Elda in the first place? And if that were the case, then did she have the right to interfere at all? The last time she had acted, it had been without thought, without weighing the consequences of her actions, and that day many men had died. She remembered, too, the boy at the Allfair, the boy with the eldistan. She had not meant to let her powers run rampant that day either, had not even known then who or what she was.

Such a choice: to wield her powers and cause possible devastation; or to sit idly by and watch the world pass into wrack and ruin? She needed her siblings, the Man and the Beast. Without them, she felt frail and fallible, certain to choose the wrong course and have all eternity to rue it.

She lay there all that long night, listening to the sounds of this new place, to the men and women coming and going, here within its walls, and far below, down in the parklands and the byways which surrounded the castle; she listened to Tycho Issian being laved and anointed by the slavegirls in his adjacent chamber; listened as, against all natural odds, he succumbed to sleep rather than to his ravening urges; and then she listened to the voices which crowded into her head.

Some were prayers and some were curses and some were pleas; but some were more direct and came to her with purpose and intent.

"We are coming!" they declared. "Our Lady, we are coming to you."

Cera

AT first light she rose from the bed, which she had stripped of its animal pelts, leaving just a crumpled covering of white wool, and crossed the chamber to the window. She pulled back the velvet drapes which shut out the sun and blinked as it flooded in like water through a breached dam.

Down below, far below, was a crowd of people. They were not milling around in the usual way of folk going about their daily tasks: none pushed carts or carried baskets or drew mules by their halters. They were not moving toward the market square to buy or sell goods; they were not lining up at the baker's for bread nor the vintner's for wine, nor did they seem to be on their way to labors elsewhere in the city. Instead, they had gathered at the foot of the tower in which she was held captive, or as close to the foot as the steep mound on which the castle was constructed would allow them to stand, and they were all gazing up, motionless and silent, their faces—where she could see them—rapt with hopeful expectation.

She, in turn, gazed back at them. The majority were women, many of whom wore the outlandish garb and silver piercings she had come to associate with the Wandering folk with whom she had spent so many months while traveling with Virelai. But most of the rest were veiled and she knew them to be Istrian.

Some of the men she recognized. There, a dozen or so folk away from the front to the far left, was the north-coast fisherman whom she had touched on the ship which had brought her here. And beside him was the erstwhile priest of Falla. They had shaved their heads and rubbed ashes into their pates: an ancient symbol of penance. Other men she did not know by name or face, but by type: there were nomads with braids and topknots and bright scarves, hillmen marked with the facial tattoos of their clans, slaves from the galleys which had followed in their flotilla.

And there were children: a hundred children and more, some holding their fathers' hands, some staring upward with their mouths open, some hiding their faces in their mothers' skirts.

She looked down upon them, bare-headed and bare-faced and after a while there floated up to her a murmur. As if possessed by a single compulsion, the Istrian women cast off their veils, their eyes seeking hers without the shielding fabric.

The Rosa Eldi smiled. And as if she greeted each of them personally, every man, woman, and child in the crowd smiled back.

So engrossed was she by this sight that she did not hear the chamber door behind her open nor her visitor enter. At that moment every shred of her awareness was poured outward and downward into the silent crowd, into the shining rope of their connection.

So when the visitor's hands encircled her waist, for a moment she did not know it. When his fingers tightened their hold and he began to draw her away from the window, she was—for a moment—confounded. Then she spun in his grasp and found herself gazing not into the smiling face of a well-wisher, but into the dead black eyes of the Lord of Cantara, and what she saw there was not love or hope but a lust which would let nothing stand against it.

At once, old memories rose up and she was lost, the goddess in her fled away through the fog of her fear, leaving her a vulnerable woman like any other vulnerable woman in the hands of an attacker. But still his hands were on her clothing, albeit her thin shift, and not her skin; so she was not privy to the full darkness of the mind which lurked behind those black eyes.

As if sensing her terror, Tycho Issian smiled. He had waited for this moment for the best (or worst) part of a year. He had been prey to wild desire, unruly obsession, desperate measures. Visions of her had driven him to distraction—to torture and murder and war. He had dreamed of the beauty he held now every day, every night, whether asleep or awake; he had pictured this very scene a thousand, thousand times, although the details had differed in large ways and in small. In some dreams, she had come to him willingly, her arms open, her eyes longing, her robes cast to the floor. In others she had cowered before him and he had forced himself upon her in a gratifying tide of fire.

He had never imagined what would happen once he had doused this fire, once he had ravished the object of his desires. And he did not think about it now, as he tore away the thin shift she wore, took it by its delicate embroidered yoke and ripped through seventy-four hours of painstaking work by the finest seamstresses in all of Eyra and watched it crumple to the ground.

The Rosa Eldi made no attempt to extricate herself from the tangling cloth but stood there as still as stone. The Lord of Cantara found himself looking down upon her ankles—pale, delicate, exquisitely sculpted. Then he dared to raise his eyes further. Sleek calves rose to knees of perfect symmetry, above which slim white thigh muscles rose in taut, defined relief. And above these . . .

Tycho Issian felt his own legs give way beneath him as if the cartilage and ligaments, the network of tendons and muscles which kept him standing had turned suddenly to chill water. His breath caught in his throat; his chest felt suddenly constricted. Musk enveloped him, exotic, undeniable. On a level now with that naked pudenda, he gazed and gazed with his heart in his mouth.

A pair of soft velvet petals, tinged with rose pink.

Smooth, fleshy petals, inviting him to press them apart.

White petals . . .

NOW that it came to the moment he had dreamed of, he found he could not lift his hands, could do nothing but stare and tremble and breathe noisily through his mouth like any randy hound.

And then she stepped out of the ruined shift and moved away from him, and he cried out in pain and fear and looked up and found that her sea-green eyes were bent upon him. And he whimpered. He could not help it, could not even stop his mouth with his knuckles.

That small sound girded her courage. Her chin came up. Her eyes flashed. The sun spilled across her skin, igniting it with a pale fire. Suddenly where before she had been all vulnerable, frail temptation, now she stood as straight as a spear and her beauty shone like armor. Where before she had been warm and soft and yielding, now she was as cold and terrifying as an unsheathed blade.

It was as if she taunted him with her nakedness. Tycho Issian blinked, looked away from her shining presence, and found he could clench his hands into hard fists.

"I know what you are doing," he said furiously, all the compressed, thwarted frustration of these several months now raw in his voice. "You are trying to face me down. And I will not have it!"

"Indeed, you will not."

He was not mistaken: she sounded amused. She was suppressing a laugh—he was sure of it—a laugh generated by his trussed-up erection, his pitiful devotion, his pathetic, subservient posture.

"How dare you! You, for whom I launched a fleet into the dread seas of the Northern Ocean. You, for whom I dared all, brought war—roused an entire nation, just for you. You, whom I have personally delivered from the hands of barbarians, whom I have saved from perversions and disgrace!"

"I did not need saving."

He risked a glance at her, but it helped him not at all. She stood there, more relaxed now, her weight shifted slightly onto one foot, one leg angled out so that he could glimpse a fraction more of the mystery which obsessed him so. And now he could not look away.

"How could you? How could you let that barbarian touch you? You let down your defenses for him, you let him invade your sacred body."

"I loved him. It was no invasion."

Tears burst out of Tycho Issian's eyes then, tears of rage and horror.

"Love? How could it be love? No one could love you the way that I love you. All he wanted was a child to secure his succession!"

She tilted her head to look at him curiously. "Ah, yes, the child."

"You gave him a child." His face was a mask of misery, horribly contorted as he struggled to stop the shaming tears.

"I gave him a child," she echoed. "Unfortunately, it was not my child to give."

"I saw you, with my own eyes, in the crystal. I saw you, all swollen and proud and bursting with it. I saw you standing there beside him, with your hands folded so primly and protectively on top of your great belly. I *saw* you!" he bellowed.

A tiny line appeared between the Rosa Eldi's fair brows.

"The child was not mine. It was your daughter's."

Silence fell between them, silence except for the ragged breathing of the man crouching on the floor like a beaten dog. Then: "My daughter's?" he echoed plaintively.

"Selen Issian. Whom I knew for a time as Leta Gullwing. She is with it now."

Now the Lord of Cantara was entirely perplexed. "How can that be? I gave it into the . . . care of the Duke of Cera's seneschal. To be . . . looked after."

The Rose of the World closed her eyes and now Tycho Issian found that he could both move and breathe. He got to his feet and stood there, swaying slightly, as if drunk, or faint.

Selen had a child? The thought of which brute northerner might have fathered it upon her was too foul to approach. Then another thought occurred to him. He groaned. "They are together? The . . . child . . . and my daughter?" He paused as the calamity of this struck him. "By the Lady, are they both dead, then?"

"Dead?"

"The seneschal . . . his orders . . . were to kill the child."

"This does not surprise me," she said slowly. "For I know you have killed many children. Many women, too; many men. What could one more death mean to you?" She paused. "Unless it were your own."

Now the Lord of Cantara went sickly pale.

"I do not know what you mean," he rasped. His brow wrinkled horribly. "How can you know these things? Are you a witch?"

"I see many things."

"You have seen my death?"

"How quickly the concern for your daughter and her son is eclipsed," the Goddess mused, "by the prospect of your own demise."

She stood there, her lips quirked in a cold smile. He felt a shudder run through him and he looked away, for if he stared longer, he felt sure he would see his death reflected in those jade eyes.

The Rosa Eldi watched the man tremble, watched the sweat bead his forehead and his gorge rise with the bile of terror. At last she said, "Your daughter is with her son. In the kitchens of this castle where she is even now giving him warmed milk to stop his crying. The seneschal had . . . a change of heart." And was even now standing with the crowd below the window, gazing upward, wishing for miracles. Like the others, he had been touched by a blessing in the night, had heard the voice of Falla and been assailed by the scent of musk and roses.

"Thank the Lady," he breathed, though he hardly dared believe it.

"I wish no thanks from you."

This puzzled him further. He blinked. Then: "Stay here," he ordered, unnecessarily.

He sped past the door guards, took the stairs three at a time; and arrived, disheveled and perspiring, at the kitchens in a faster time than even the most terrified slave could have achieved. Flinging open the double doors—doors designed to allow egress for the massive banquet trays for which Cera had, in the time of its dead duke, been famed throughout the empire—he burst in and stared wildly around. In shock at this unannounced interruption, someone dropped a cooking pot with a clang which reverberated off the stonework, and this was followed by a frenzy of activity as someone else was burned with hot soup, someone was trodden on, the hounds started baying, and a baby started to wail its head off.

Tycho Issian's head swiveled like a striking snake towards this latter noise. There, in the corner of the room, seated on a tall stool at the peeling table, was the woman he had once thought of as his daughter, brazenly bare-headed and cradling a brat with a bright red, roaring face.

"Selen!"

Everyone fell silent. A pair of the Duke of Cera's hunting hounds slunk through the doors to the yard, followed by the stableboy, who shouldn't have been in the kitchens at all, and two veiled dairy maids.

The kitchen staff backed away, trying to make themselves as inconspicuous as possible. All of them knew the Lord of Cantara's cruel reputation.

"She said you would be here. You have conspired against me, I see, and though I do not know how you have contrived this reunion, believe me when I say I shall find it out. And wearing no veil, you shameless trollop— That, too, will be remedied shortly," he raged. "Is that your child?"

Selen Issian stiffened as if she felt already the kiss of her father's lash. Intrigued by the sudden change in his mother's demeanor, Ulf stopped his wailing and turned to regard the shouting man with his unnerving violet eyes.

"It is." Selen's arms went tighter around the wriggling bundle.

Tycho crossed the room and gave his daughter a hard look. She held his gaze defiantly so that at last he was forced to stare down at the baby instead.

"It looks little like the usual run of Eyrans to me."

"Why should he look Eyran at all?"

He regarded her as if she were half-witted. "Why for his parentage, of course. And because the . . . queen . . . passed him off as her own."

Selen's jaw firmed. "She took him from me."

"Ravn is, I suppose, dark, so she may have got away with it, for a time." He cocked his head and scrutinized the bundle. Then he looked up sharply again. "Is it his child?"

Selen flushed. "No," she said, very quickly. "It is not. Though better it had been. This child was got upon me by Tanto Vingo when he ravished me in my tent at the Allfair last year."

That made her father's mouth drop open. "Tanto Vingo? Surely you are mistaken. The boy fought off a host of Eyran brigands, and took a terrible wound . . ."

"I am not mistaken. Not in the least. And it was I who stabbed Tanto Vingo, in my own defense. I hear it carried him near to death," she finished with some satisfaction.

"Death came to him," the Lord of Cantara said grimly. "But it was not from the wound he took." He leaned in closer.

The baby screwed its face up and howled again, louder than ever before. But rather than recoiling, Tycho Issian reached over and lifted him out of Selen's clasp and held him at arm's length, so that his feet kicked in midair.

At once, little Ulf stopped crying. He wriggled in his grandfather's arms and stared up at him. Then he reached out and grabbed at his lord's chain, the great ornament of office Tycho had donned this morning as he prepared to impress himself upon the Rose.

The Lord of Cantara grimaced. "He has a good eye for silver! And what a grip." He tried to prize the little creature's fingers off the chain, but Ulf was not letting go. "So, you would take it from me would you, little man? You think to inherit my title and my wealth, do you? You think to wheedle your way into my affections and steal what is not yours?" His voice rose in pitch. "I shall be lord of this whole empire before long. I cannot have grasping little bastards dogging my steps, trying to take what is mine. Not when my own son will soon be born."

"Your son?"

He raised mad eyes to Selen.

"I shall marry the Rose of the World and beget many sons upon her," he declared. "She shall carry one after another after another till I have made a ruler for every province in Istria, and they shall all answer to me, and me alone."

His daughter smiled thinly. "You had better think again," she said. "For the lady is as barren as the Bone Quarter. Why else do you think she stole my child?"

"You lie!"

And at this, Ulf opened his mouth and, turning in his grandfather's hands, vomited a copious, foul-smelling stream of milk onto Tycho's rich crimson robes.

"Aaaarggh!" The Lord of Cantara regarded the damage to his finery, horrified beyond words. Catching up the boy by an ankle, he swung him violently away from him, then let go with a flourish. Ulf flew through the air, his eyes wide with amazement at this new experience. A second later, he struck the nearest granite pillar headfirst.

Dazed silence swathed the room. Then Selen Issian fell from the stool and scrabbled across the tiles to Ulf's body. A pale pink translucent liquid had begun to leak out of the upmost ear and trickle down the side of the tiny skull.

Lord Tycho Issian stared down at the pair of them with an unreadable expression on his dark face. Then he turned and walked quickly from the room.

ON his way back up the stairs to the tower room, he glanced out of one of the arrow slits and was bemused to see that a large group of people had gathered at the foot of the castle. When he reached the next level, he swung into the first stateroom he came to, taking no notice of the occupants—Lord Varyx of Ixta and a group of women apparently tending to his wounds, which seemed well enough healed that he had been able to remove a good deal of their clothing with his one remaining arm—walked over to the window and looked down.

"What in Elda's name—?" he began.

There were hundreds of them. Women, children, merchants, farmers, soldiers, fishermen, slaves, Footloose. And not a modest sabatka veil to be seen. He leaned out, fuming. "Away with you!" he yelled. "You women, veil yourselves at once!"

The crowd lowered their gaze from the tower room to this new distraction, but finding it irrelevant to their purpose, moved their eyes back to the Rosa Eldi's window.

"Get away!" he bellowed again. "Away!"

But they were not even listening to him. He leaned out of the window and twisted around to see what it was they could be looking at, but saw only stone and sky. He frowned, then turned on his heel and strode out into the corridor.

"You, guards!"

The two soldiers playing dice at the end of the hallway looked up boredly. They were Cera castle guards; they had very little to do to earn their keep, and they liked it that way.

"Go disperse the crowd outside. Drive them away."

The soldiers exchanged a glance. "They're not doing any harm," the first one said belligerently. He had been winning rather handsomely and didn't trust Coro to redeem his debt if they didn't finish out the game. Besides, he had no idea who this loudmouthed noble was, and since the good Duke of Cera had lost his life in the storming of Halbo, no idea to whom he was supposed to report in his absence.

The Lord of Cantara came toward them with thunder in his face and the guards straightened up reluctantly. Reaching the end of the hallway at a run, he kicked over their table with more violence than seemed necessary so that dice, goblets, and tallystones skittered everywhere.

"I am Tycho Issian, Lord of Cantara, and leader of the Ruling Council, and now that your do-nothing duke is dead and gone, I am master of this castle and you will do my bidding NOW!"

They went to do his bidding with alacrity.

Tycho raced up the stairs to the tower room, suspicion itching in his head. She must have called for help, he thought. Somehow, she must have let them know that she was being held prisoner. But this made little sense, he thought. The people outside were Istrians, or nomads, and either cared little what should become of the Eyran queen, or owned loyalty to nothing and no one. So they must be curious, then. He smiled as this idea came to him. And why not? She was the most beautiful woman in the world. It was no wonder they should come to gaze on her.

Suddenly he regretted sending the guards to disperse the crowd. How much better it would be for his reputation and status if he were to display his prize to them all, show them the woman he had saved from the heathens.

On the next level he found another knot of guards and sent them to countermand his previous order. "Tell the people to wait there and I shall bring the Queen of the Northern Isles, the Rose of the World, out to them that they may feast their eyes upon this prize I have brought back from our great victory in the holy war against the old enemy."

By the time he burst into the tower room, he had imagined the crowd swelled to a thousand and more, imagined how they would cheer his name, how they would demand that the ancient title of emperor be bestowed upon him, the only man worthy of the name in three hundred years, how that demand would roll out across the continent, gathering weight and pace, till none could gainsay it.

The Rosa Eldi stood naked where he had left her.

"Well," he laughed, with forced jollity, deliberately pressing away the fear that she instilled in him. "We must clothe you and you must stay close to me: two steps behind, no more nor less, as is meet and proper for my finest chattel."

"Clothe? What need I of coverings?"

Tycho felt the blood come to his face. "All women must be covered. They are temptation incarnate. No man can be trusted not to act upon his impulses."

The Rosa Eldi gazed upon him. "Are you so weak that you cannot curb your desires?" And she smiled, her eyes full of knowledge, and power.

The Lord of Cantara stormed across the room to the ermine robe. "Allowing women free congress among men is the root of every evil and catastrophe!"

He threw the cloak at her. "Put this on while I find you a veil."

She stepped backward and the cloak fell to the floor.

She looked at its fur mournfully.

"Dead things," she said. "All around you is death."

Tycho frowned. "Just put it on."

But all she did was to stare at the cloak, then lift troubled eyes to him. "You killed the child."

Tycho shivered. "I did not mean to," he lied. He looked down to see whether it was a splash of blood that had betrayed him; but his hands were clean and the tunic was all of crimson velvet and if the baby's blood was on it, it did not show. The vomit, however, did. "Damn the bastard!" He tried to rub the milk stain away, but it was sticky and revolting on his hand.

He grabbed the lilies out of a nearby vase and strewed them on the floor, then upended the contents over his tunic and scraped fretfully at the fabric with the underside of one of the great-cat skins draped over the couch.

She watched him curiously, this man for whom appearances meant so much more than truth. When he brought her the sabatka from the adjoining chamber, she allowed him to hang it upon her, shrugging elegantly away from him, till there was silk between them and she need not fear his touch. The veil hid him from her, which was a blessing.

"THE nomads say the woman the Lord Issian has up in our poor duke's castle is the Lady Falla returned to us in our time of need."

"I thought she was the barbarian queen, captured during the raid."

"The folk I passed on their way here earlier seemed convinced of her divinity."

A laugh. "She has performed miracles for them, has she?"

"I know nothing of miracles. But they say she is wondrous fair."

"Worth a look then, miracles or no."

"MY child is sick, let me through."

"If your boy is ill, you should take him home and tend to him, not drag him out on this cold day."

"If the Lady touches him, he will be well."

"If the lady touches him, she'll catch whatever he ails from, more like!"

"It is the falling sickness he has, not the fever."

"Why should some pale whore have the power to cure the falling sickness?"

"Hush your mouth. She's no whore, she's Falla the Merciful. Everyone is saying so."

"My brother was at the Gathering when the northern king chose her above the Swan. She's a nomad whore, no more no less, and anyone who claims otherwise is a fool."

"Call me a fool then, Rivo Santero: I shall not see you on the blessed side of the Lady's fires."

"SHE touched me and I saw the wickedness of my life."

"Does that mean you'll be giving away all your worldly goods, then, Caro?"

"I have done so already. I am with the Wandering folk now."

"With the Footloose? Did you give your wits away also? They'll burn you, you idiot." A pause. "Anyway, who did you give your things to? Why did you not come and find me?"

"I have seen the wickedness of your life, too, friend."

"I like my wicked life, it suits me well."

"Let her touch you, and you'll see what I mean."

"There's a particularly wicked part of me I'd love her to touch."

"You are a profane man, Gero. There's no hope for you."

"WHERE'S your veil, Ferutia? Have you no modesty?"

"I shan't wear it anymore."

"If you do not put your veil on, I shall drag you home and lock you in the cellar until you're pleading to put the damn thing on again."

"None of the other girls are wearing theirs."

"Then they're likely to take a beating, too."

"If you lay one finger on me, Uncle, I shall join the Footloose."

"Then you'll be damned to the fires, and good riddance to you. I'll put the torch to the pyre myself."

"BY heaven, there's my wife!"

"How can you recognize her in this great crowd, man? Be sensible!"

"She's not wearing her sabatka. Her face is bare, the hussy! She told me she was going to the market with her sister—by the Lady, just wait till I get her home . . ."

"By Elda, you're right, it's Allicia, so it is!"

Silence. Then:

"How in Falla's name do you know what my wife looks like?"

"THERE she is!"

"Where?"

"See—at the gate."

"I can't see very well, there are too many people. Hold me up, Mica. Ah, yes, now I see. Ah—she's removed her veil. She is very lovely . . . oh . . . But who is that ugly man in the red robe beside her?"

"Shh. It's Tycho Issian, the Lord of Cantara."

"Aiee, let me down, before he lays eyes on me! He burned Celesta Moonrise's father and sister! We should leave now, while we can—"

"Hush now little Wren. We can't leave, the throng is too dense. Besides, I must see her. She will protect us, I know it."

"But if she cannot protect herself, how can she protect us?"

"Protect herself?"

"They say he took her prisoner and brought her south to ravish her."

"There is a pattern in all things, Wren. Only the Lady knows the pattern."

"Why has she been away so long? Does she not care about her people?"

"Sshh now, Wren, come down now and let's see if we can get a better view over there."

"STAY back!"

"Sergeant, move those people back!"

"Don't push!"

"I can't help it, everyone's moving forward—"

"Ah, no, the soldiers are pushing from the front . . ."

"Help me, my sister—!"

"I've lost my little boy. Kano, where are you? Aiee!"

"I'm falling . . ."

THE Rose of the World gazed out into the crowd in anguish. She turned to the man at her side. "Help them."

Tycho Issian stared at the chaos where the crowd were being crushed between the advance of the soldiery and the walls of the city. "What more can I do? They are a mob—they must be controlled."

"What you call control is murder."

"If the guards cannot hold them back, they'll storm the tower."

"Let them."

"Let them? Are you mad? Come, let me escort you back inside, to safety."

She turned her piercing gaze upon him, and he quailed even as his balls burned and throbbed. "Help them."

"You have taken off your veil!" he said angrily.

"It lay between me and my people."

He could make nothing of this. "I cannot help them," he said instead. "The soldiery will deal with them."

"If you will not help them, then I must."

Closing her eyes, she summoned deep awareness of her surroundings. The wall, the great city wall—if she could just make a hole in it through which the people might escape, it should suffice. But how? Living things were hers to command, not the hewn, dead stone of these fortifications. Beneath the stone of the courtyard and the walls beyond her thought ranged, down through the granite flags and the rubble of the old city they had used as foundations, down through the topsoil. She found roots and worms and centipedes; ancient seeds and pods, and a deep aquifer fed by three thin streams off the inland hills.

Lady Falla, save me!

Delicacy was crucial. She bent all her will on it, and the water moved to her intent, slipping gently between bedding planes, into air pockets in the hardcore, pressing up beneath the stones, taking every line of least resistance; but still there was not enough to serve her purpose.

Goddess, save my child!

More. She needed more. Her mind fled out across the floodplain, summoning back the river, draining irrigation ditches, emptying wells.

Help me, Lady!

She had never channeled such a mass; it was demanding, exhausting. To force her will upon it occupied her utterly, though the screams and prayers and invocations snatched at her attention. Up it came, the water, up and up beneath the flags, beneath the old walls. She let it wash against the foundations, helped it move some of the sand and grit away, loosening the structures.

Delicately she worked now, drawing up the water, undermining the stonework so that part of the wall began to tremble and bow—

"Come with me now!" Someone cupped her face, shaking her, skin to skin—

And suddenly her mind was invaded. Death, a terrible fear of death, gripped her, mazing all her thoughts. In panic, she stepped backward to sever that vile connection. For a moment she was free; then a hand gripped her bare arm beneath the sabatka. Somewhere, she stood in a howling black desert while some monster mauled at her naked body; somewhere else, a mass of water crashed out of her control.

She cried out and opened her eyes.

Tycho Issian's face swam before her in horrific detail. But over his shoulder the view was worse by far.

Far from creating an escape, she had created a disaster. Where the ancient wall—a wall which had been constructed in the time of the Emperor Tagus and withstood a thousand years of sieges, bombardments, and fire—had stood, now there was nothing but a roiling cloud of dust, gouts of violent water, and the screams of the dead and dying. Instead of making a small gap through which the people could escape, the water had demolished the entire length of the wall; the massive stonework, instead of falling outward into empty space, had toppled inward, crushing very folk she had been trying to save. Water—released from her gentle, guiding spirit—now gushed and roared gleefully, busting up through the flagstones, hurling masonry high into the air to crash down again on the defenseless crowd and the soldiery of Cera.

The Rosa Eldi sank to her knees and howled like a dog, but such elemental forces answered to no man, woman, or goddess. There was nothing she could do to reverse the devastation.

Messages

NEARLY seven hundred people—men and women of Istria; children, nomads, hill people, soldiers, and slaves—perished that day, either drowned by the raging floodwaters or dashed to death against the broken walls. Many of them died with the name of the Goddess on their lips or in their hearts; the Rose of the World felt each death as a wound.

She lay in a swoon on the great bed, entirely unaware that the Lord of Cantara had removed her robe and gazed like a famished man upon her naked flesh.

But no matter how he desired the woman who lay in a fever before him, Tycho Issian could not bring himself to mount her while she was unconscious. There might be pleasure in the act for its own sake, but not the quality of pleasure he desired, for the connection was what he craved: to gaze into those sea-green eyes even as he penetrated to the heart of her. Nothing else would suffice.

And so he sat and he watched as she writhed and wept, and sometimes he drank the best wine from the Duke of Cera's cellars as he watched, and sometimes he undressed himself and lay down beside her and ran his hands across her silken hips; and sometimes he moved her this way and that like a doll or a puppetmaster's mannequin, and gazed and gazed; and even when he touched her, she knew him not, for her mind was a wasteland, and nothing mattered beyond the catastrophe she had caused.

TWO days later, there came a great knocking at the door of the chamber.

"My lord, my lord!"

He was disinclined to answer such an urgent cry: it could only mean bad news. But the hammering and the shouting carried on, so he gave a weary sigh, slung a robe around his shoulders, and went to the door.

"What is it?" he demanded through the crack.

"The Eyrans are coming, lord. Their sails line the horizon!"

Tycho Issian swore violently. The northerners had evidently not had the sense to stay at home and lick their wounds after all. He should have known, he chided himself, as he clothed himself once more and looked regretfully upon the prone white body on the snowy bed. If the Rose of the World should afflict him so, who had done nothing but gaze upon her, how much more crazed with longing and vengeance must be the man who had taken her to wife?

DOWNSTAIRS in the staterooms, there was hubbub. Having ascertained that there was nothing to be seen from the castle—since the citadel was half a mile inland and a series of deeply incised hills lay between it and the coast—with ill-disguised bad grace the Lord of Cantara rode out with the Ceran Guard to survey the enemy.

THE sails of the Eyran fleet were dense against the lowering sky and the whole great expanse of sea was covered by their hulls. The sight of them sent a chill through the heart of every Istrian ranged along the low cliffs that day.

"By the Lady," one man murmured, "there must be a thousand ships coming against us."

It was an overestimate by a frightened man, but Tycho Issian turned to the captain of the guards and his expression was anguished. "Is Cera's castle the strongest fortification in the area?"

The captain looked back at him as if he was mad, but knowing the Cantaran lord's reputation, he decided to mince his words. "It was, your lord. Upon a time. Until the flood took the great wall down."

No one could fathom how the city walls could have succumbed so swiftly to the sudden access of water, nor whence the destroying force had come. There had been little rain; the rivers had been running low for some weeks: they had even had to irrigate the winter crops. The captain—a grizzled veteran of the last war who had languished cheerfully in the lower ranks of the local guard until his rapid promotion following the loss of his superior—had spent the last two days retrieving bodies from the water which surrounded the castle and giving them over to city officials for identification and burial. It had not been a pleasant task; made worse by the fact that several of his militiamen had lost friends and relatives in the flood. Finding your wife or mother bloated and swollen with river water, her head caved in by rocks, was enough to rob a man of his hope, his future, his wits. It was rumored that some soldiers had deserted, even gone to join the Footloose; though given the paucity of organization following the demise of the Duke of Cera, it had proved impossible to ascertain whether death or the urge for a new kind of life had overtaken those who were missing from their posts.

The rest of his men had been employed in engineering a new bridge to provide access and egress from the city. Trouble was, all the best carpenters were in Forent. The woodworkers of Cera specialized in pretty furniture and minor household repairs; all the larger trees had long ago been harvested, leaving the spindly behind, where the woods had not been entirely cleared for vines and other crops. Bridge building was not their strong point. As a result, the structure they had erected had the shoddy, makeshift look of a very temporary solution. As they had ridden over it this morning, it had shaken and rattled beneath the horses' hooves; if they were very unlucky, they'd be swimming home.

"Then we must return to the city and muster our men."

Instead of galloping straightway to do just this, the captain hesitated.

"Should we not station a company of men on the beach to drive back the invaders into the sea?" he suggested tentatively.

"Would you rather hang out flags along the shore to confirm our presence to them? With any luck they'll sail on to Hedera or Forent and seek the Rose there, giving us the time we need to make our preparation. Besides, we lost enough good men in the flood: I'll need every soldier we have left to us defending Cera's citadel."

The Lord of Cantara turned and caught his protesting horse and after two awkward efforts, managed to remount. Behind him, the captain caught his brother's sardonic eye and shrugged helplessly. This lord was not a man to take advice from anyone, let alone a lowly garrison man, not a man to admit his weaknesses to anyone.

He gave an ostentatious cough.

Tycho Issian fixed him with a gimlet stare. "What?"

"Well, sir, I was wondering whether you and the lady would stand a better chance riding inland, to Jetra." The Lord of Cantara regarded this new speaker closely, but the guard returned a guileless face to him. The man had a point, but it would never do to admit it. At last, having apparently pondered the suggestion for at least twenty seconds, he said, "If you do not wish to fight for the honor of your nation and preserve its people and its ways from the barbarian horde, then you may die swiftly here at the end of my sword."

And after that, no one made audible any word of dissent.

"You," Tycho Issian declared, jabbing a finger at a young man on a good horse. "You stay here and watch their movements. Report back as soon as you see whether they are going to land or sail on. Understand?"

The young man nodded quickly, though he knew well enough he was not going to be waiting around here for the barbarians to find him. He would be riding hell for leather for his sister's house at Calastrina just as soon as the southern lord had gone his way.

THE Duke of Cera had been a man with limited military experience and much vanity. As a result, the garrison at Cera were possessed of exquisite uniforms, precise parade formations, and precious little fighting skill. They were decent men, on the whole, but life had been too easy for too long in this prosperous city. Given five years of hard schooling under ruthless mercenary leaders, those men left standing after the flood would make a halfway decent castle guard, but as a force to hold back barbarian invaders, they were so much chaff in the wind.

As Tycho Issian inspected the motley force ranged up in the great courtyard, he regretted his decision to sail for the luxurious comforts of Cera rather than returning to Forent, where the libidinous lord had at least retained sufficient ambitious self-interest to maintain a tough fighting squad. And for the first time since Rui Finco's unfortunate demise, he regretted, too, the loss of a man who might have had enough strategic thinking to make some sense of the perilous situation which faced them now.

Sestria was the closest town, but it was barely more than a marketplace and a few weavers' sheds; beyond that lay Ixta, but given the dissolute character of that city's lord, a man who was clearly far more interested in parting perfumed harlots from their diaphanous clothing than in maintaining a well-drilled soldiery, he hardly dared hope for salvation from that quarter. Calastrina had never been fortified, and Alta was no more than a fishing port. It would take men from Forent several days, even if force-marched, to reach Cera; but given the loss of their lord, would they come? And could they hold out that long if the Eyrans did attack?

In truth, if he admitted it to himself, the south was not in a state of readiness for anything which approximated a full-scale war. Most of the Istrian aristocracy, after long years of affluent peace, had no experience of war, and no instinctive love of it either; their fathers having either perished in the last conflict with the old enemy or succumbed to the excesses which had created an empire founded on slavery and hedonism. But neither did they ennoble more deserving men or entrust them with positions suitable to their skills. As a result, the man to whom responsibility for recruiting, training, and maintaining the country's standing army had fallen following the sad deaths of Hesto and Greving Dystra had turned out to be a lily-skinned wastrel who had lined his own coffers handsomely from the army fund and failed to check on the rigor of his delegated officers who, in turn, knowing that their superior was not interested in their success or otherwise in turning out a well-schooled militia, had drunk most of the proceeds and done little to curb the excesses of the uniformed rabble which called itself the Istrian army. Half of them would have been criminals, had the law been properly applied; the rest had been rousted out of prisons, brothels, and drinking houses at the call to arms. He had known this, all of this, and turned a blind eye, or rather, blind faith, believing that passion like his own would carry the day.

In addition, building the invasion fleet had consumed a great sum of money and much of their manpower. He had won what he had gone for, but what good had it done him? He pictured the Rosa Eldi—still unconscious, her mind as closed to him as a locked vault, her apparently lifeless body spread-eagled as he had left her—and knew with a sudden biting insight that she would never succumb to him as she had to Ravn Asharson, knew that her unconsciousness was her last form of defense against him, the ultimate retreat.

This knowledge came to him with the force of an epiphany.

A lesser man might have cut his losses and made for the safety of his southern home with all speed, but Tycho Issian's obsession was a grand and towering force. Disappointment and obdurate pride made him all the more determined to hold on to his prize.

He would make a stand at Cera, send out messenger birds for reinforcements and see Ravn Asharson truly dead, this time.

Anger burned in him, a grim and steadfast flame.

First, he had the pigeonmaster summoned from his tower. Then, he went in search of Virelai.

"ANY sign, lookout?"

"Nothing, sire."

"What say you, Stormway: if you had stolen a king's wife and had an entire fleet in pursuit of you, where would you head for?"

The old retainer stroked his beard, his forehead knotted. "Well, Cera is the closest and finest of the cities on this coast, as I recall, but Forent is better fortified, and Jetra safest of all. But if I were the abductor and you on my tail, I'd be heading as far and as fast inland as my horses could carry me."

Ravn Asharson frowned. If the southern lord had made for Jetra, it lengthened both the odds of their success and the time before he would see his wife and child again.

"Damn it. We'll have to send out scouts." He kicked the strakes viciously. "Another wasted day."

"More if we're unlucky."

Ravn fixed the Earl of Shepsey with a forbidding glare. "We won't be unlucky. We are in the right; the god will smile on us."

"Ah, gods . . ." The Master glided to a halt beside them. "You do not seem able to help yourself from invoking these arbitrary beings, my lord king." He smiled benignly. "Instead of following my advice and trusting to the services of those you can see and touch. Like myself."

Egg Forstson, who had taken a thorough and instinctive dislike to this old trickster, grimaced and looked away. His eyes sought out the Rockfaller, Aran Aranson, seated in the stern of the ship, idly turning a piece of frayed rope over and over in his fingers. He seemed distracted, out of sorts, not at all the same man with whom Egg had stood back to back in battle all those years ago. Skirting the rowers and their gear, the Earl of Shepsey made his way avast and touched Aran on the shoulder. The Rockfaller started, as if woken out of a dream. His hazel-gray eyes blinked, disoriented.

The king's adviser shook his head. "Aran, Aran . . . You look as if you are in another world."

The Rockfaller grunted, rubbed a hand across his face. "A world of grief, Egg, that I am."

"Grief?"

The piercing eyes searched his face. "Tell me, Egg, and tell me true. Have you heard word of the women of Rockfall and what befell them?"

The Earl of Shepsey shook his head, mystified. "What befell the women of Rockfall," he echoed. "No. Is it a riddle, my friend?"

"It is that," Aran said, hugging his knees. "A most terrible riddle. What happens when a wolf leaves his den to hunt, and his cubs are left defenseless?"

Egg shrugged and laughed uncomfortably. "Well, he must hope that no foe happens by . . ."

Aran Aranson nodded morosely. "I am that wolf, Egg. I left the women of Rockfall without a hope when I sailed thoughtlessly on my quest for gold."

Now Egg Forstson's eyes gleamed. "Gold?"

Aran waved his hand impatiently. "It's not the gold that's important in this story, Egg, it's the people. I've learned that lesson well, and too late."

"What has happened to your family, Aran?"

"Taken by raiders." Aran laughed bitterly. "While I was indulging an obsession." He tied another knot in the string, then gazed out at the sea, his eyes dull.

Egg Forstson tightened his grip on the Rockfaller's shoulder. "Well, you've come to the right place to search for them," he said gruffly. "We'll find them, Aran. We will."

"Like you found Brina?"

The Earl of Shepsey's hand came off the other man as if he were a hot kettle. "That's unkind, Aran. I looked for her, as well you know; and the babes. Illa and Kiri. We never had time to decide on a name for the unborn one. Sur knows what she called her."

"Her?"

"I always thought it would be a daughter. She'd be twenty summers old now; more. And Brina in the autumn of her years."

"If they're not dead." Aran stated it flatly, with a single-browed frown.

"They're not dead." The White Queen had touched him and told him Brina was alive; though he had been afraid at the time and thought it trickery, he had come to believe her all the same.

"Perhaps it might be better that she were. Bera, too. Katla, I am quite sure, would never submit to them."

Egg looked shocked. "You truly think it better they die than survive— what—rape? Humiliation? Surely our women are worth more than that? You speak as if they are market goods, which lose value if bruised or dirtied. If you weigh them so lightly, you might as well be Istrian yourself."

Aran bristled. "Careful now, old man. Your king is too enraptured by the beguiling words of the mage to pay much notice to the splash you'd make going over the side."

"Ah yes, the mage. Now how was it again that you came to be traveling with him?"

Aran sighed, looked skyward. He had no wish to rehearse that sorry tale again. Then his eyes narrowed. "What's that?"

Egg squinted. "My sight isn't what it was. Looks like a bird to me."

"It is."

"So? It is the air, birds fly in the air: show me a fish flying up there and I might be deflected from my question."

"It is a messenger pigeon, I would wager on it."

The Earl of Shepsey yelled up to the lookout, who twisted on his perch, followed the old man's pointing finger, then turned back gesticulating excitedly.

"Messenger pigeon!"

The cry went up. Archers scrambled for their bows, wrapped away against the warping power of salt waves in waxed cloth at the bottom of their sea chests. Furs and sleeping bags of sealskin were strewn across the deck, followed by tools and knives and whetstones, lamps and wicks and flints.

"Allow me, my lord."

Rahe stepped to the gunwale and with a hieratic gesture drew from the depths a glimmer of silver, silver which then shot out of the ocean and into the air as swift and straight as any arrow. A moment later the pigeon plummeted suddenly, spiraling wing over wing. A moment later, two creatures, unnaturally joined, hit the deck: a pretty Calastrian racing pigeon, heart-pierced by the bony proboscis of a gleaming, wet garfish.

Attached to its tail was a long white ribbon of silk. Ravn knelt and untied it, flattened it carefully across his knee. He frowned, turned it over, then back again.

He looked back at the mage questioningly.

"There's nothing on it," he said. "Nothing at all—not a word, not a knot."

Rahe raised his eyebrows. "May I?" he enquired, taking up the message-ribbon before Ravn had even had a chance to respond. He held the fluttering silk up in front of his face, shook it, sniffed it. "Ah," he said. "Ah, I see. How interesting." He smiled at the Eyran king. "Very crafty."

"How can you have found a message in this bit of rag?" Ravn asked, balling his fists. "It's unmarked, I swear it."

"To the untrained eye, perhaps," the mage said. "Ah, Virelai, Virelai . . ." He winked, then breathed upon the ribbon.

Letters flowered suddenly as if seeded in the silk. Those close enough to have witnessed both the fish arrow and this latest miracle made the sign of Sur's anchor and whispered to one another. *A seither*, the word went around, *the king has a seither at his beck*. That was good news, in their circumstances, surely? Some were less sure. *Remember the Nemesis,* said one; *magic can be a dangerous ally*.

"Read it, then, man!" Ravn demanded, his face flushed.

"Enemy ships in sight. Send Forent and Hedera men to Cera at once." Ravn took a deep breath, closed his eyes.

"Cera," he said softly. "Cera. Now I shall have you."

ONE third of Ravn's fleet was sent east under the command of the Earl of Ness to harry the coastal towns of Forent and Hedera, which would not be expecting attack. By nightfall, the rest of the Eyran force had been deployed and a stealthy invasion was well underway. Two dozen ships were left to blockade the river's mouth to prevent any sudden breakout from Cera. The crews of the *Forest Cat* and the *Eagle's Flight* hauled their ships up onto the strand where earlier that day Tycho Issian and his captains had watched their approach and made their way stealthily inland to observe the city and report movements back to their king. They took with them three ravens and the Filasen twins, known for their fleetness of foot and fell-running agility.

A force of vessels sailed south and west to secure the coastline from Ixta to Cera. Satisfied that he had blocked reinforcements from reaching the Lord of Cantara and would shortly have cut off all possible escape routes, Ravn led the rest of his navy up the wide river mouth. There was no wind in this sheltered valley, so they took down the sails and rowed silently, their faces and beards limned with silver, their eyes gleaming in the moonlight. Each man the king had chosen to accompany him harbored a loathing for the Southern Empire. Each man had lost a relative—a grandfather, a father, a wife, a daughter—and they were eager for retribution.

Aran Aranson rowed beside Odd Barnason, a man who had watched helplessly from another ship as his son burned to death during the battle for Halbo. Together they pulled their oar sleekly through the water, putting their backs into the movement, driving the ship determinedly forward. Thoughts of Bera and Katla accompanied the rhythm of each stroke, making his own expression grim. One glimpse showed that Odd was thinking the same. What he had said to Egg earlier that day had been no more than hollow, bitter words; he could not imagine an existence without his wife and his daughter, no matter what travails had come to them. They might even, it occurred to him, be here in this very city. And if they were alive, he swore he would rescue them. After that, they must decide for themselves whether they wished his company or not.

And if they were dead, he thought, his jaw firming against the pain of such a possibility, then he would avenge them, and lose his life in the process.

The lassitude which had afflicted him since his discovery of the disaster that had come to Rockfall began to slough away with each pull of the oar through these foreign waters. The very obstinacy which had brought him under the thrall of magic—to Virelai's map and the lure of gold, to Sanctuary and the wiles of the mage—now formed a hardpan of determination through which nothing else could permeate. Purpose put backbone into his stroke and iron into his soul.

As a cloaking mist gathered around them, it was a very different Aran Aranson who advanced into enemy territory than the broken man who had left the smoking ruins of his home.

JUST before first light, Tycho Issian rose from the bed beside the torpid body of the Rose of the World and joined his sentries on the battlements. There was little to be seen. An enveloping mist lay over the landscape below, blanketing the vista. Only the tops of the highest hills poked through the inversion layer, stark against the white as if all the color in the world had seeped away in the night.

A single shape moved above the mist, its wings' wide primary feathers spread like fingers. Sideways, it slipped on an unseen air current and vanished.

Tycho Issian turned to the captain of the sentry. "Do ravens make their home in these parts?"

The man he addressed was young and town bred. His eyes went wide at the enquiry. Impatiently, the Lord of Cantara repeated his question, addressing all the men lined along the crenellations.

They avoided his eye; all but one, an ancient soldier oiling the mechanism on his crossbow. "Not around here, no sir," he said softly. "Not since the forest was cut down."

He inserted a quarrel, lifted the weapon, and sighted down its length; but the raven was gone and nothing else stirred.

Tycho Issian felt a tremor in his stomach.

"Summon the archers," he told the captain. "Every man of them. Make sure they are well supplied with ammunition. When this mist clears, they may have many targets to test their skill."

Then he turned on his heel and fled down the stairs, his heart hammering in his chest.

THE raven brought curious news.

Ravn wound the knotted string thoughtfully around his hand and stashed it in his jerkin. Then he turned to Rahe. "Thank you for the mist, Master Sorcerer, but I think it is now time for us to survey our whereabouts and treat the enemy to a view they will never forget."

Rahe inclined his head. He muttered words into the ether, and waited. Nothing happened. He pursed his lips. It would hardly do for the northern king to realize this useful weather event had been little of his doing. The mist was a natural phenomenon, though he had gathered the threads of it and drawn it more closely over their fleet than might otherwise have been the case.

"Well?" said Ravn impatiently. "Come along, get rid of the stuff now that it has served its purpose."

"Patience, my lord, patience. There are a million million droplets of water suspended in the air above us. Do you wish them to turn to a torrent and overwhelm the ships?"

Ravn ground his teeth. He gave the signal for oars to be shipped and watched as the crew of *Sur's Raven* moved quickly and expertly to his will. The signal was passed from ship to ship; and from ship to ship a great hush spread as everyone waited further command. Ravn unsheathed his blade and touched its pommel to his forehead. The metal was cool against his hot skin; he could feel his blood boiling inside him, ready to fuel his muscles to action. All around him, men hunched over their weapons, testing the edges of their swords and spears, checking the fixings on their bowstrings, running their fingers down the fletchings of arrows. They were the things men always did in the unsettling lull before conflict, automatic actions designed to divert their minds from inevitable thoughts of pain and death.

At last, the sun began to do its work, the first rays lancing down through the cloud layer to touch the water with chilly light, and now Rahe made a great effort to help it on its way.

As the mist began to clear, they saw the city of Cera before them, its towers gleaming golden in the new light. All along the battlements of its walls, men in the bright armor and red tabards of the city stood ranged.

"It seems we are expected," Ravn said softly. "But no matter. They would have known of our presence soon enough."

He gave orders for the fleet to be beached where a great shallow curve in the river offered a long muddy strand, then *Sur's Raven* and two flanking ships sailed on, anchoring the vessels just out of arrowshot. Ravn vaulted over the gunwale, splashed through the shallow water, to stare up at the castle. It was, indeed, as the message had told: the city's ancient guard wall was gone. He could see the shattered remnants at the eastern end of the fosse. What lay within was an elegant castle and behind that an extensive and lovely town—but one which was no longer well fortified. A wide, rather muddy lake stretched out all around so that a second Cera shimmered in reflection of the original. The roofs of a number of buildings seemed to have been recently submerged beneath the waters of this lake, for they appeared to be in good repair: no slates or tiles missing, their chimneys pointed, one weathercock spinning forlornly in the gentle breeze.

Interesting.

A rickety-looking bridge had been erected from the great ironbound gate at the front of the castle to a patch of churned ground on the river side of the lake. This, too, looked new, for the wood was not yet silvered by the elements.

Beyond the muddy moat, smooth walls of dressed stone rose to turreted towers and a narrow battlement. Somewhere inside those walls his wife and child were captive. If the power of his gaze could have burned through rock, Cera's pretty castle would surely have been incinerated at that moment.

His men ranged up behind him, spear heads glittering. Behind them, the beached fleet made a forest of prows and masts as far as the eye could see. It was a sight to strike terror into the heart of any Istrian. Ravn gathered his breath to hail the inhabitants of the castle and challenge his enemy to emerge; when suddenly a door within the great gate opened and two splendidly-caparisoned horsemen issued out of it and trotted nervously out onto the bridge.

Ravn held up his hand before his bowmen shot them full of quills. "Let them come!" he cried.

The two young riders bore white pennants and looked fearful, despite their rich trappings.

Ravn turned to Stormway. "Have they come to surrender already, Bran?" he wondered aloud, but the old man laughed. "Not the Lord of Cantara," he said. "The man's a fanatic by all accounts. They probably come to offer *you* terms of surrender."

Ravn snorted, but Stormway was not short of the mark.

The riders dismounted and one of them approached. "Which of you is the leader of this force?" he enquired in heavily accented Old Tongue.

"I am."

The man looked Ravn up and down disbelievingly. He was more finely turned out by far than the dirty-looking barbarian who stood before him in his scuffed leather armor covered in rust-spotted iron disks, his patched leather breeches, salt-stained boots, and tangled black hair. But the piercing eyes which looked haughtily down at his were hard and unwavering. He decided not to query the speaker's claim.

"I bring a missive from the Lord of Cantara, commander of the City of Cera," he said.

Ravn put out his hand, but the messenger shook his head.

"My lord of Cantara says that you are to leave here at once, you and your army. You must set sail at once and be gone by noon."

"And if I do not?" Ravn was visibly amused by such effrontery.

"That is all I am to tell you." The first rider took a step back, but Ravn gripped him swiftly by the arm and gave him into the custody of the Earl of Stormway. "Not so fast, messenger. There is more, I know it."

The man bowed his head and shot a glance back at his companion. This young man was trembling visibly. He held onto his horse's reins so hard it seemed that he feared he might simply crumple to the ground if he let go. "Flavo, give the Eyran king the rest of the message."

Staring at the mud between his boots, the second rider mumbled something inaudible.

"Speak up, son!" Bran roared, and the boy jumped as if bee-stung.

"He says: your wife and child will remained unharmed as long as you leave here by noon and do not return."

Ravn took a step forward, but the boy's terror had taken hold of him. He tried to mount his horse, but the animal shied and stepped away, leaving him sprawling on the ground. River mud seeped into his silver-trimmed cloak and fine silk hose. Then he was on his feet again and running for his life back toward the citadel. One of the archers drew his bow, but Ravn knocked it down.

"No," he said curtly, his face suffused with blood. "Let him go. My message to the Istrian lord will make all the more impact if they see the state in which he returns."

At his elbow, Egg Forstson looked puzzled. "But your grace has not sent a message back to them."

"That may take a little time."

THE screams of the first messenger lasted for many spine-chilling minutes, then were abruptly cut off. In Cera's castle, men looked fearfully at one another and talked in low voices. Nothing happened for the best part of an hour, during which time Tycho Issian paced furiously up and down the battlements. Then a horse broke loose from the Eyran lines and hammered its way back over the bridge toward the city.

The Lord of Cantara took the stairs down to the courtyard at a run.

No one had yet dared to open the gate. He berated the guards roundly and slid the bolts back himself. Moments later, he wished he had not done so, for in through the stone arch came a monstrosity. The elegant bay and its richly-dressed rider which had left the castle a short time before now returned horribly changed. One guard promptly vomited onto the flagstones; another fainted clean away. Bucking and rolling its eyes, the animal took four men to control it; but not before it had dislodged the larger part of its obscene cargo. It stood, looking down at the thing it had borne, whickering in distress, its new, second, head hanging limply from the coarse stitches which held it to its neck.

At its feet lay the rest of what remained of the messenger: namely, his skin. It had been flayed, with supernatural exactitude, from his body, and stretched upon a framework of branches. A message had been carved into it; and judging by the amount of blood smeared across the letters, carved while the hide was still on the unfortunate messenger.

SEND OUT MY WIFE + BOY

OR WE TAKE DOWN YR CITY

STONE BY STONE

+ FLAY ALIVE ALL WITHIN

A MAGE RIDES WITH US: THIS IS HIS WORK

EXPECT NO REINFORCEMENTS

YR PIGEONS ARE DEAD

It was signed with a barely legible flourish: Ravn Asharson had never devoted a great deal of his time to learning the universal written code on parchment, let alone on skin.

White with rage, Tycho Issian dropped the foul thing onto the ground, then kicked it viciously around the courtyard till it was broken

and indecipherable, and he was sweating and bespattered. The onlookers watched, appalled. If this was the prepossession of the man in command, surely they were better off fleeing the city now and taking their
chances. Indeed, as soon as the lord went back into the castle, some did
just that, casting off their uniforms and running to fetch their wives and
children. No one stopped them.

On the stairs, the Lord of Cantara found Virelai cowering forlornly by
an arrow slit. He looked even paler than usual. Tears coursed down his
cheeks.

"A mage!" Tycho howled, hauling him upright. "They say they have a
mage with them. *I* have a sorcerer: how many of you damned magic
makers are there in this world?"

"It is Rahe," Virelai whispered. "He has come for me."

"Rahay? Who is this Rahay?"

"My master," the pale man murmured, wringing his hands. "I stole
his magic. I stole the Rose from him . . ."

Now Tycho looked thunderous. "The Rose? The woman I rescued
from the Eyran king? The Rosa Eldi? *My* Rose?"

Virelai nodded dumbly.

The Lord of Cantara regarded him through narrowed eyes. Then his
face went shuttered and still, a sign that he was calculating something.
"But if she was his, why has he allied himself to Ravn Asharson? Is it a
ruse? Does he use the barbarian as his stalking horse, I wonder? Perhaps
all is not lost." He caught Virelai by the shoulders, shook him roughly.
"Stop this. I need your arts. Pull yourself together, man!"

BY the time the lord holding Cera responded to the message, the sun
was climbing in the sky and Ravn Asharson was twitching with impatience. Tycho Issian appeared on the battlements in his finest garb. Beside him stood a tall figure in the flowing green silk of an Istrian
sabatka. In her arms, a baby was cradled.

Ravn caught his breath, felt a stabbing pain in his heart.

"It is her!" he cried.

Rahe frowned. "It is a veiled woman. It could be anyone."

"I would know my wife anywhere."

Rahe stared up at the battlements, his white beard bristling with distrust. Then he made an incantation and, shuddering, disappeared. In his place, a kestrel hovered. It perched for a second on the startled king's shoulder then, digging its talons sharply into the skin, it gathered itself and soared into the air. Straight as an arrow it flew for the castle, circled briefly over the heads of the Lord of Cantara and his entourage, then planed swiftly sideways and returned to the Eyran lines. It came to rest on the grassy sward by the river, where it stood, head down, tiny breast visibly palpating. Just as Ravn thought it was about to expire, its shape shimmered blearily, and in its place an old man lay prostrate on the ground, gasping for breath.

After what seemed an age, Rahe pushed himself clumsily to his feet and, swaying, lurched back to the king, who regarded him ruefully.

"If the small matter of shape-shifting can reduce you to near death, I am concerned that your powers may not be such as you vaunted, Master Magician."

Rahe drew himself up. "Shape-shifting is no 'small matter,' my boy. It is perhaps the greatest transformation a mage can perform, for it requires both a spell of making and unmaking, rather than a mere spell of seeming."

Ravn shifted from one foot to the other, possibly a displacement activity to stop him from kicking the mage. "What did you see?"

"It is the Rose," the mage pronounced mournfully. "Only her lips were visible, but ah, how well I remember those lips!"

Ravn crushed the question which begged to be aired. Then he asked, "And my son?"

Rahe shrugged. "There was a child in her arms. Ask me no details. Babies are babies. They all look the same."

Now a white pigeon came winging its way from the castle.

Ravn stared at it, one eyebrow raised. "A messenger bird, mage, or do they also have a shape-shifter?"

The old man looked away, irritated.

"Only one way to find out," muttered Ravn, taking up his bow.

Down came the bird, cleanly spitted. A dead bird, that was all. A warrior retrieved it for the king.

Ravn unwound the fabric from the bird's tail. *"The woman and child are my hostages,"* he read. *"Leave now, or we shall see whether your heir can fly."* He balled the silk up in his fist. "By the god, I shall rip his heart out!" He turned to Rahe. "Can you not turn yourself into a fire-drake and incinerate him where he stands?"

The mage spread his hands apologetically. "Unfortunately, my lord king, I can only transform myself into creatures which still exist in this world. The firedrake has been extinct for a great time now."

"Well, a lion, then; an eagle—tear his eyes out, then carry my queen and son back to me."

"A lion could never leap so high; and as an eagle, well . . . they would shoot me down before I ever got the chance to approach their lord, and then you would have squandered your most precious weapon."

Ravn looked him up and down distastefully. "You do not seem so precious to me at the moment. Indeed, word of your presence does not appear to have dismayed them much at all. Damnation. Bran, Egg!"

The two old advisers came quickly to his side.

"He threatens my boy if we do not withdraw."

The earls exchanged glances. They looked haggard. Neither wanted to speak first.

"What? Out with it!"

Egg looked at his feet. Stormway sighed. "He has nothing to lose by using one of them as a demonstration of his determination, while he still holds the other as a hostage against your conduct."

Ravn's eyes bulged. "He would hurt my son?" He paused, fury gathering. "He would hurt my *wife?*"

Egg shook his head quickly. "Not your wife, sire. I am sure he will do nothing to harm the lady. But the boy . . ."

Ravn gritted his teeth. "He would not dare." He turned to his men. "Do we bow to this threat?" he cried. "Do we crawl away from this place like beaten dogs, or do we show its lord what happens to those who steal our loved ones?"

The Eyrans roared and waved their swords, then beat them, booming, against their linden shields so that a great drumbeat rose up through the ranks.

Ravn touched his fist to his chest where the drumming reverberated through his breastbone like courage incarnate. "You see, Bran? Nothing will stop them. We shall take this castle and I shall tow its lord's carcass back to Halbo behind my ship!"

TYCHO Issian rubbed his hands together. "Well done, Virelai. Magnificent, in fact."

Virelai was still trembling uncontrollably. Partly it was that the proximity of the Master was hard to bear, partly that he now knew the identity of the White Queen beneath whose robe he now cowered, holding up the child, his arms shuddering with the effort of it. Why did she not strike him down, even now, in her semiconscious state? He had used her unforgivably as they traveled the world; he had shown her no respect, yet she had never once chided him for his lewd schemes, for the money he had taken from her despoliation. And now he had made her walk, to perform this despicable tableau. Was there no end to his ignominy?

"Now, give me the boy."

Virelai looked up through the slit in the robe. "The boy?"

"They have not yet withdrawn."

"It has been mere minutes, my lord. Aaah—!"

Smarting from the well-aimed kick, Virelai almost dropped the baby himself.

"Indeed, that drumming sound they are making sounds most warlike. Defiant; provocative. Well, I cannot have them doubting my word."

As if comprehending the threat to it, the child began to cry and twist in Virelai's hands. He held on grimly, but it struggled harder. Its wail rose in volume. The next thing he knew, he had lost his hold on it and the Lord of Cantara was dangling it over the parapet.

"My lord, you cannot—"

The baby's cry was suddenly distant and waning; then it ceased altogether.

RAVN Asharson sank to his knees in the mud.

"Ulf," he whispered. "My god, my son . . ."

He stared at the spot, several hundred yards away, where the tiny body had fallen.

Behind him, the drumming stuttered and died.

Deceptions

THE Eyran troops withdrew. They sailed around the bend in the river, drew up their ships, and pitched their tents on the bank, gathered what little brushwood they could find, set up cook fires, and dug latrines under the orders of those two old campaigners, the Earls of Stormway and Shepsey. That night the camp was muted. Men huddled together, talking quietly, remembering their families at home, or those taken by the Istrians. Others knotted memento-strings.

Bard Rolfson's string read thus:

The leader sailed his sea-cold ship
Into Cera's clean stream
Came before the castle calling
The strong, silver-giving king
For his queen, cruelly captured
By Istria's evil ill-doer
That lying lord hiding in his lair
Gave out grim threats:
Wulf flew, fairest of offspring
Brave walls will be broken down;
The fierce raven-feeder
Will vaunt his victory.

But the fierce raven-feeder sat apart from the rest of the men and said a word to no one. All night he honed his sword, and his thoughts were dark.

AT first light the next morning, a prisoner was brought into the camp, a slight figure wrapped in a cloak, seen slipping from the castle's postern gate by Jarn Filason and another of the scouts. It was a woman, carrying a swaddled bundle in her arms.

When her hood was drawn back, there was a gasp. "Leta! Leta Gullwing!"

"My lord!"

The girl stumbled, would have fallen had Jarn not caught her arm.

"I . . . I cannot believe you are alive! They said you were, but—oh, I saw you die."

Ravn frowned. "Not I."

"On the deck of my father's ship."

"As you can see, I am hale."

"How can it be?" Her soft dark eyes searched his face in wonder. "It is a marvel."

But Ravn's eyes had slipped to the object in her arms. He took in the shape and size of it, the way she cradled it, and his heart lurched. "Is it—?"

"It is Ulf, but he was not your son, my lord," she said softly. "Nor am I Leta Gullwing." And when he started to contradict her, she went on quickly, before she lost the courage to speak the truth to this man for whom she yearned, now miraculously restored to her, "My name is Selen Issian. I am the daughter of the man who stole your wife and who now commands Cera's castle. How I came to Halbo is too long a story to tell now, but you must take my word for it. The baby you believed to be your own was in fact mine, got upon me by a vile rape and taken from me by the woman known by some as Rose of the World, and by the seither at your court. By sorcery, they made it appear she bore your child, and I was rendered complicit in that deceit, for which I am now most ashamed." She raised her eyes to his for a brief moment, saw the hurt and puzzlement there, and returned her gaze to the muddy ground. "Ulf was killed yesterday: but not by being dropped from the castle wall. Instead, my . . ." she faltered, "my . . . father . . . killed him . . . declaring he wanted no . . . bastards dogging his steps . . . I came to bury him in a better place than Cera." And now she tenderly pushed back the swaddling around the baby's face, and all could see for themselves that the child they had known as the king's heir was truly dead.

"And the baby dropped from the walls?" Egg Forstson enquired, his voice steady, though tears stood in his eyes.

"The undercook's child," Selen sobbed. "Taken from her by force."

There was a long silence. Then: "Why have you come to me?" Ravn asked softly.

Selen Issian drew herself up. "I came to see if it was really you. And, if it was, to tell you the truth, so that you may leave with honor and nothing lost," she declared.

"But my wife—"

"The Rose of the World has shed not a single tear for you. She has not mourned your parting, has spoken not a word of sorrow; and since she was brought to Cera, she has spent her time cloistered, naked, and compliant, in my father's quarters. He says they will marry and she will bear him many sons. But he, too, will be deceived, for she has told me she is a barren creature who can bear no children."

Ravn Asharson stared at her in horror. At last, he said, "You are mad."

"Sire."

A tall, haggard-looking, dark-haired man had appeared at the king's shoulder. He looked vaguely familiar. Ravn waved at him impatiently. "What?"

"I have heard some of this woman's story before."

"How is that possible?"

"I am Aran Aranson. My daughter Katla was accused at the Allfair last year of being involved in some violent offense against this very woman. You, sire, stood by and watched her condemned to the pyres."

"I did?" Ravn seemed amazed. "Your daughter, you say?"

Aran nodded. "Katla Aransen of Rockfall. It did seem you were not in your right mind at the time—"

Now he had the king's attention. Ravn mulled this over.

"Rockfall. Ah, yes. I summoned you to the muster. You did not come, or send ships."

"I was . . . otherwise engaged. And when I returned to Rockfall, my home had been burned, my family taken by raiders."

Ravn smiled bleakly. "Well, on that score, at least, it seems we are quits, my friend."

Aran bowed his head.

"And what of this woman's story?" the king prompted.

"The name she has given to you is the name she gave to my daughter Katla and her cousin Erno Hamson when they found her bruised and bleeding, fleeing her attacker at the Allfair. Selen Issian. The daughter of the Lord of Cantara." He turned to the Istrian girl. "Katla would be happy, I am sure, to know that you have survived. Is Erno inside the castle?"

Selen shook her head. "I have not seen him for many months." She gave Aran Aranson an unsteady smile. "If it had not been for the actions of your brave daughter, sir, I am sure I would have died. But did she survive the pyres? Erno was sure she'd died."

"Yes," Aran said grimly. "Yes, she survived that ordeal. But where she is now, I have no idea."

During this conversation, Ravn Asharson's expression had taken on the lean, hard, calculating look of his father, the Gray Wolf.

"I cannot claim to understand this web of lies, but if one part of it is true, then it seems that fate may have delivered a most fortunate gift to us." He turned to Jarn Filason. "Bring one of the ravens," he ordered. "I think we need to let the Istrian lord know that we now hold his daughter captive as he holds my wife."

Selen Issian gasped in horror. "I came to you for sanctuary, not to be held as a hostage!" she cried. "And because I thought you cared for me, in some small way." She scanned his face, expectant of some response, but it remained hard, impassive. Now, with dawning realization, she felt herself a fool; worse, a heartsick fool. "I thought you would want to know the truth," she groaned. "But it seems you do not care for it at all, just as you do not care for me. I had expected better of you—and Eyra—but you are just like my father. You use women when it suits you, but we are no more to you than possessions to be treasured or traded, just pieces on a gameboard—"

Ravn shrugged, untouched by this accusation. "When I first knew you, I thought you a good companion to my wife, and a good nurse to my child; but it seems you are either mad or Istrian, and since my child is dead, I have no further use for you. Though my warriors may . . ." He gave her the wolfish grin which had always previously turned her knees to water but now chilled her to the bone; then he looked aside. "The raven, Jarn, hurry!"

"A BIRD has arrived, my lord."

"From Forent, or Ixta?"

"It is . . . a raven, my lord."

"A raven? Since when did Forent use ravens to carry their messages?"

"I believe it has come from the enemy force, my lord."

"But they have withdrawn." There was a pause as the Lord of Cantara crossed to the window and looked out. When he turned back, his expression was grim. "Give me the message."

The guard handed over the curl of parchment and stood well back.

"To the Lord of Cantara from Ravn Asharson, King of Eyra," he read aloud. He scanned the rest, then waved the guard away. When the door was safely closed, he continued: *"You have shown your mettle against babes in arms, now I challenge you to try your metal against me. Single combat, the hour after dawn tomorrow, on the sward outside your keep. If I win, you will cede me the castle and my wife. If you win, I will give you back your daughter, Selen, and my army will withdraw. Dawn tomorrow, wife-stealer, or we will take the city down stone by stone!"*

Virelai gazed at him with limpid eyes. "Will you do it?"

Tycho Issian laughed. "Hardly. The man's a warrior, trained in the arts of battle since he could walk. Whereas I—" he shrugged. "No, my dear Virelai: you will be going in my place."

"I?" The sorcerer was aghast. "I can barely lift a sword, let alone wield one. Besides, there is a geas upon me—"

"Geas? I don't give a whore's toss for your geas. What's the point of you if you cannot kill a man with magic?"

Virelai's eyes filled with bitter salt. "Can you not just send back a message refusing his challenge?"

"And be branded a coward?"

"But if I lose—"

"How can you lose? You are a sorcerer, while he—he is just a man."

"A very strong and angry man."

"But a man, nonetheless. I will find you something of mine to wear. Maybe the crimson, it cuts a dash. The semblance I know you can manage. He will only need to see your face once. Then you can don a helm and use all your skills to disable him."

Virelai turned away, his face drawn, his chin quivering.

"Oh, and Virelai?"

Keeping the tears barely in check, Virelai looked back. "My lord?"

"I want him dead. The barbarian king. Stone dead. Do you hear me? Merely wounded won't do. They're tough, these Eyrans. Amputated limbs, lost eyes, sword in the guts—somehow they manage to survive, and we can't have that. No: stone dead. Make it look good, and I will reward you well. Very well, indeed. Why—" his black eyes glittered with malice, "I think I may well give you my daughter Selen. Have you seen my daughter? Come, look there. See—standing by the barbarian standard-bearer? How they came to capture her, the Lady only knows. Still, there she is, and quite comely, though I say so myself. Ruined as she is, I can hardly marry her to another lord, so why not keep a sorcerer in the family? How would you like that, eh? It is very fitting, I think. Like a chevalier knight, you will save my daughter from the savage horde, and in exchange win her hand and a castle in the desert. Perfect. They would make songs of it—if they knew the truth!"

Virelai fled down the corridor. *If only*, he thought, *my magical skills were more advanced, I would turn myself into a bird as the Master did and flee this terrible place for ever.*

IT was a red sun which slipped over the hills the next morning, and many men on both sides of the keep's walls made superstitious signs, each taking it as a portent of ill omen. Ravn Asharson donned his armor with great care and deliberation, checking each strap, each buckle, testing the links in his mail. He whistled as he prepared, an old folk song: "The Maid of Kurnow." The older warriors looked from one to another: it had been one of Ashar Stenson's favorites, too.

"Blood will out," the Earl of Stormway observed to Egg Forstson, who merely shrugged and cracked his knuckles.

"I don't like this, Bran. Not at all."

"I don't trust them either, but other than station our archers among the trees, there is no more we can do to safeguard him."

"Impetuous whelp!"

"He's not the cub you think him anymore, Egg. Remember how he won the swordplay at the Allfair."

"Aye, sword*play*. And he nearly lost an eye then. This is to the death, and he's our king. Lose him and there will be mayhem back in Eyra. With Bardson gone, there's not even a clear successor."

Stormway hung his head. "You're right, of course. But what choice do we have?"

The Earl of Shepsey leaned in close. "Talk to the mage," he whispered dramatically. "See what he can do."

His companion looked appalled. "Egg! Where's your honor?"

"Honor stole from me long ago all I ever cared about."

"But Ravn would be furious."

"Furious, but still alive."

AS the sun rose, Cera's great ironbound gates swung open. Two heralds rode out onto the rickety bridge, their great banners all in scarlet and silver fluttering bravely on the breeze. Behind them, looking curiously unstable on a magnificent bay stallion, came the Lord of Cantara, his crimson cloak billowing. Behind him, a pair of pages carried a gleaming helm of silver and a greatsword sheathed in scarlet leather. Reaching the sward on the other side of the lake, he swung down from the horse, which bucked and danced away, its eyes rolling. When he took the sword from the page, he fumbled and almost dropped it on the ground as if he had misjudged the weight of it.

The Earls of Shepsey and Stormway exchanged bewildered glances.

"We may not need the sorcerer's aid after all," whispered Egg with a grin.

"Or he may be cleverer than he looks," Bran replied warningly.

"All style and no substance," averred one of the oarsmen behind them, and his colleagues muttered their approval of this judgment.

"Fancy gear doesn't make a warrior," jeered the navigator of the *Ax*.

"True, but the crimson may hide the blood our Stallion will shed!" returned the captain of the *She-Bear,* and the men all roared their laughter.

Tight-lipped and without a word, Tycho Issian saluted the Eyran king with a fist to the chest, and with hawk nose and jutting chin lifted proudly, donned the helmet. The sun's first rays struck the polished silver with such force, it hurt the eyes to look at him.

Ravn scowled. "I am little surprised you have no words for me, deceiver," he said. "You had better pray to your bitch-goddess that your sword will speak for you more eloquently!"

And then, hefting his great weapon, he charged the Istrian lord, who lifted his sword awkwardly and parried the first blow so that the blades rang in the still morning air and the sound reverberated off the city's walls like the clanging of a death knell.

Virelai trembled and shifted his grip on his sword. His arm was numbed and weak from that first blow, his fingers barely able to clutch the hilt, yet already the northern king was coming at him again, and there was no time for spellcraft. His mind felt blank. Even though he had abandoned the spell of seeming which had so occupied his efforts all this while, no useful stratagem came to mind. He concentrated on stepping out of Ravn's way, ducking inelegantly and swinging his sword around in some semblance of a stroke, but the onlooking Eyrans catcalled. So that had hardly looked convincing.

Sweat ran down inside the bright clothing. The straps on the metalled breastplate chafed his skin; the helmet pinched his ears, trapping him inside it. He was aware of even the tiniest discomfort—a ridiculous matter, since the next discomfort he was likely to know was that of an arm, a leg, or even his head being lopped off by Ravn Asharson's fearsome blade.

Again the northern king came at him, and again Virelai danced away.

"At least put up some sort of fight!" Ravn snarled. "Or next time I will not be playing with you, wife-stealer and child-killer. Next time I shall carve the flesh from your bones as neatly as from a roasted fowl. Aye, and draw your organs out through your back so men can see the lily of your liver."

The mouthguard of the helmet muffled Virelai's whimper. *Oh, Great Lady*, he prayed, *do not let me die like this. Please save me from this wild man who is your husband. Help me, please, my Goddess. I should have been stronger. I should have saved you in Halbo, but I did not know how, I was weak and afraid. But never as afraid as I am now!*

He realized suddenly that he was mouthing the words inanely, a pathetic mantra to a goddess who would—if she would deign to return her consciousness to the world—surely smile upon his much-deserved death, a death which would see her back in the arms of the man she had chosen. The prayer seemed hollow even to himself.

I deserve to die. I know it, he wailed silently. *But not like this, not as I have truly begun to live. Oh, my Lady, hear me!*

The next blow fell upon his hopelessly inadequate and largely ornamental shield, which promptly split in two and fell from his hand. He staggered backward, weeping, almost falling on his arse, and the Eyrans cheered.

But suddenly there were words on his lips, recalled out of thin air as it seemed, and then his sword arm came up as if of its own accord and swept Ravn Asharson's killing blow away as if it had been made with a willow stick. Ravn, wearing no helm, looked momentarily surprised at this abrupt change of competence in an opponent he had written off as a fool. He firmed his jaw.

The next encounter set the northern king off balance as his attack was parried with a fierceness which turned defense to offense. The blade in Virelai's hand shimmered with a sudden access of power and he knew that from somewhere deep in his unconscious mind he must have dredged up a suitable enchantment. He did not think it would kill the Eyran, but it might at least save his own skin while he tried to think of a more decisive strategy.

Up came his sword arm again. Light as air it felt, the muscles somehow imbued with golden fire instead of blood. Again, the blades rang and Ravn Asharson fell back, bemused.

In the Eyran ranks, one man stared hard, shaken out of the miasma of concentration in which he had been wrapped. *Magic!* he thought, suddenly furious at this intrusion on his own domain. *He's using the spell of ultimate defense!* For a second, maybe two, this realization permeated Rahe's aging brain; then he knew who the man in crimson truly was. "Virelai!"

"What?" The Earl of Stormway was immediately at his side, his regard disapproving beneath those great white straggling brows. "What did you say? Have you cast your protective net over our king yet? It certainly does not look that way . . ."

"Damned upstart! Little runt! How dare he steal from me and flaunt his theft thus! I'll show him why I am called the Master. Now he will meet his match, the worm, the insect, the . . . the . . . rat's turd!"

Bran frowned. He had little trust for sorcery and seers at the best of times, but this old man was clearly mad, and working himself up into a fine frenzy.

Seconds later, he felt dizzy, disoriented, as if the world had subtly shifted out of kilter. Then Egg Forstson was stumbling against him, and out of the corner of his eye he thought he glimpsed Aran Aranson, the Master of Rockfall, carrying an unconscious Ravn Asharson from the battlefield. But when he turned back to the sward, there was his king, as real as ever, battling fiercely against the Istrian. He blinked, shook his head, feeling slightly nauseous.

He cleared his throat, glanced at the Earl of Shepsey. "Are you all right, Egg?"

Egg Forstson looked at him curiously. "Funny you should ask," he said, screwing up his face. "For a moment there I felt distinctly odd. A bit woozy. Didn't sleep much last night, you know."

Bran turned and scanned the spot where he had been so sure he had seen his king. But there was no one there now, though the guards beside the royal tent looked strangely blank-faced.

"Oh!"

A great cry went up from the watching soldiers: for Ravn was now bearing down upon his foe with a real fury, his sword scything the air as if he would shortly harvest the Istrian's head. The Lord of Cantara reacted with extraordinary speed and skill and together the blades swung, ratcheting off one another with a sound which offended the ear. Then the two men spun away from each other, changing their stances, and circled like two wolves assessing each other's form.

Almost, the watching Eyrans forgot that the outcome of this contest brought with it either rousing victory or humiliating defeat, so swept up were they in the skillful play of feet and hands and brawn and iron. None had ever seen a battle like it. With bated breath they waited for the next charge, the next clash of blade on blade. Who would ever have thought the soft southerner who had practically fallen from the horse which had carried him out of the city gates might show his mettle in such a brave fashion?

"SO, Virelai, now we shall see what you have learned from your trove of stolen secrets!"

Inside the shimmer of the spellcraft which showed the likeness of Ravn Asharson to the onlookers, Virelai glimpsed the identity of his opponent. The shock was so great, he almost vomited.

"Master . . ." he gasped.

"Yes, you slug! The master whom you robbed and left to die, such was your gratitude for all the years I raised you as my own." Spittle sprayed out of the old man's mouth, showering Virelai with a slimy mist. "The master whose greatest possession you stole away, without the least understanding of what you did or had. The master whose store of knowledge you ravaged and destroyed!"

This last, at least, was grossly unfair, since it had been Rahe himself who, in the grip of a sustained despair, had set about dismantling his icy kingdom and the treasures within, but Virelai had neither the energy nor the will to deny him.

Nor had he time to utter a single word, for suddenly tentacles were wrapped around his neck, tentacles with suckers which leeched onto the skin and tightened like a noose.

"Aaaargh!" Repulsed and terrified, he tore at them, but they coiled harder, and then there were more of them—six, eight!—all snaking out from Rahe's torso to seek a hold on him. With a superhuman effort he lopped off three of the vile appendages and, squirming, shrank to half his size. The tentacles fell away from him, but now Rahe was towering over him with a snarl of triumph on his livid face. Perhaps the shrinking spell had not been a good idea. Virelai reversed it swiftly, and then it was he who loomed over the old man on legs which were abruptly ten feet long and—though the Lady knew how on Elda he had managed *this*—bent *backward* like a crane's.

"Very nice, Virelai. Quick thinking, if not entirely stylish. But can you counter this?"

A solid pack of muscle rammed his legs out from under him. He hit the ground with terrible impact and lay there, his heart thumping so loudly he could barely hear the curses of his opponent. He pushed himself up on elbows which would hardly take his own weight and stared in horrified fascination. The bull the Master had transformed himself into was mutating even as he watched, its neck elongating, its head changing shape. Teeth flowered briefly on its face and chest, then died back and were replaced by feathers. Spines shot out of its back. Its tail fell off and wriggled away across the ground.

Then the bull was back, pawing the ground, its vast horns lowered to gore. Virelai, himself again, leaped to his feet, his heart pumping with adrenaline. Shape-shifting at this level was beyond his powers. The smaller magics of seeming and unseeming might fool the eye of an ordinary beholder; but there was nothing he could do against a mage with the powers of making and unmaking.

Trembling, he faced the monster with sword outstretched, his arm shaking so much that the tip of the blade wavered blearily in the sharp morning light. A sound much like a laugh erupted from the creature. Then it charged. Pulverized earth shot up from its pounding hooves into clouds of dust.

Dust . . .

Muttering frantically, Virelai whipped the dust into a sandstorm that mazed the changing beast. Then, under the cover of its gritty blanket, he ran.

He did not get far. Something shot out and curled around his left ankle, yanking him off his feet. His sword flew out of his hand. He hit the ground facedown, unable even to see what horror it was that had floored him.

Perhaps it was just as well. While all the spectators could make out through the kicked-up earth and the blur of movement were two men engaged in a deadly combat Virelai, when he finally turned his head, found himself confronting an entity flung from out of the bowels of the earth. Fiery red it was, and all over scales. Men had made legends of it and called it "drake" and "dragon"; but this was no creature of myth, nor did it much look like the splendid but etiolated beasts the women of Eyra had stitched on their ancient tapestries, with their bat-stretched wings, their intelligent heads, and gripping claws; neither did it resemble the noble adversaries to the first gods which the poets Callisto and Flano had wreathed about in dramatic phrases and cadenced verses.

He cried out in despair.

Inside his splendid disguise, Rahe smiled. Let the boy whimper and imagine his cruel death; let him believe the transformation was one of fact, not seeming. He would die, one way or another; if not from wounds, then from fear.

Virelai knew the creature: from books, from tales; and from that last grim day in Sanctuary, as the Master conjured and destroyed the magics he had hoarded for millennia. Then, he had been terrified beyond his wits, even though it offered him no harm. It was a beast that was made to chew the bones of the earth and regurgitate them as streams of lava. No man, surely, could withstand it.

Its multifaceted eyes, as alien and unreadable as any blowfly's, watched him, unblinking. Then, with its tail wrapped around Virelai's foot, it inched forward across the sward, crushing the grass in its wake; but all the Istrians watching from the battlements could see was their lord lying prostrate and the Eyran king advancing on him with slow menace.

Virelai reached deep inside himself, and found . . . nothing. Not a word, not a spell, nothing but an eerie silence. Gone was the man who had garnered the courage to flee the icy fastness, to make a life out in the world; gone was the man who had lived off his wits and the Rosa Eldi's charms; gone was the man who had loved Alisha Skylark and seen her child struck down on a muddy riverbank by Jetran militiamen; gone, too, was the man who had been resurrected by the death-stone, and who had felt its power flow through him to restore the conjurer and Saro Vingo. Fear rippled through him, reducing him, mote by mote.

In place of the man was the frightened boy he had been in Sanctuary, bullied and mistreated by the man who had become as much a monster in his mind as the beast which now confronted him.

He had often heard men say that imminent death brought memories of one's life flitting through the mind like moths to a fire, to offer their color and vitality, and then burn to ashes, one by one by one, and so he found it now, images tumbling chaotically and at random. Quite abruptly, and with a sudden clarity, he remembered the scrap of paper he had found discarded beneath the charred table, the last remnant of the *Book of Making and Unmaking.*

The words swam before his eyes; a partial magic, but had he learned enough since then to complete and adapt it?

He closed his eyes and found it helped not to see the terrifying thing that advanced upon him.

And then, forehead to the chilly grass, he repeated those words he could recall and added a name he had found in the Master's grimoire. Then he risked a look behind him.

For a moment the chimera froze to the ground, one massive forefoot poised in midstep; then it began to dwindle. First, it shrank in size, though still maintaining the form in which it had appeared; then its outline blurred and shifted, took on mannish characteristics, and became smaller still. Scales gave way to skin, claws to fingers; the tail shriveled completely away. A moment later, there was the mage, an old man, naked on the grass, loose skin hanging in swags from his belly and arms where the beast's wings had been; then he, too, was shrinking. A young man stood before him for a brief while, handsome and arrogant, his long hair and beard a brilliant red in the sun; then he was no more than a boy; a toddling child; a baby; a fetus. . . .

Virelai stared in amazement. He had done, this. He, Virelai, hopeless apprentice and skivvy; thief and procurer; coward and mountebank. He had cast a spell upon the most powerful sorcerer ever to have walked Elda's hills, and reduced him to—what? He pushed himself cautiously to his feet and gazed at the place where the mage had stood. An egg? A seed? He could not even see what was left of the Master at all.

Pride swelled in his chest; pride, followed by a sudden, unexpected sorrow. He turned his face up to the battlements to see what had been made there of his strange victory, but the spectators gazed back, bemused, a little dissatisfied. Then someone shouted, but he could not catch the words. He screwed his face up and they shouted again. It seemed a warning, or an admonition. He turned and was shocked to see the Master resurrecting himself, clothing, sword, and all, rising up from the muddy grass to advance upon him with an expression of murderous loathing.

From the castle walls, men began to shout and women wailed. Where moments before it had seemed to them that Ravn Asharson had fallen and—well, vanished into the ground—now the northern king was on his feet, sword poised for a killing thrust; and their lord was weaponless, and seemingly unmanned.

Virelai knew then that he was going to die and that all the magic in the world could not save him.

"YOU cannot kill me, Virelai. Haven't I told you that a thousand times and more? Though I am most impressed by the increase in your skills since you left my tutelage. Where is the cat, I wonder? Did you rip the magic out of poor Bëte, and leave the poor beast gutted for the crows?"

When there was no response, the mage took another step toward Virelai, till the pale sorcerer could feel the old man's breath upon him.

"And I wonder," said the Master, his eyes the cold blue of deep ice, "whether *I* can kill *you*. Is it, indeed, possible to kill a thing which never lived? Now there's a question for the philosophers." He watched Virelai's face with delicious curiosity, but saw only puzzlement there. Excellent— the boy had not the least idea of what he was talking about.

"Did I ever tell you how I came upon you, Virelai?"

"As a baby. In the southern hills," the sorcerer quavered. "Left out to die. You took me to your stronghold to raise me as your own . . ."

"My own. Ah yes, I *made* you my own." He scanned Virelai's face. "Made you, you hear me, boy?"

Virelai felt something inside him break. "What do you mean?"

The Master narrowed his eyes. "You look different, Virelai." He squinted, came closer. "You are different. Not so fishlike and wan. Quite hale, in fact. And that's surely against nature. Away from the source you should have crumbled away to nothing by now."

"Crumbled?" Horrible suspicions began to itch at his skull. He remembered how his skin had begun to dry and flake, how he had sought Alisha Skylark's aid, how her unguents had held back the process. And he remembered how she had touched him with the death-stone . . . "What source?" he asked sharply.

"Why, me, you fool! And Sanctuary: the source of magic."

A chill ran through Virelai then.

"I am a thing of magic?"

"Oh, yes: did I never tell you?"

Virelai stared down at his own hand, flexing impotently at his side. It looked real enough: pale of skin, slightly freckled by the southern sun, the knuckles swollen, the blond hairs sprouting at the wristbone. Then he looked back at the mage.

"I don't believe you," he said softly. "I'm as real as any man."

"I ripped you from her belly. You were half-formed, a fishy thing, all bulbous eyes and limbs like fins. I would have left you there to expire, on the desert ground; but she implored me. I did it for her, to begin with," he mused. "Strange really, how even as she lay there, bleeding into the sand, she had a mother's instinct. You wouldn't expect that from a goddess. But when I took her magic from her, she forgot about you. She forgot about everything. Even herself.

"It's a disgusting tale, really. You were the spawn of incest—her brother's brat. They have no morality, these deities, none at all. They count themselves apart from the rest of us, you see: different, better. I proved her wrong. You should thank me, really, for I made sure you would never repeat the brother's transgression, nor be as a man with her. And then, since you were worse than nothing, I took you for myself. I filled you with my magic: I gave you life. You were my greatest experiment, Virelai, but see how you repaid me!

"Now here we stand, father and son, as it were; battling it out for supremacy. The way of the world, over and over, human nature will always revert to type. Not that either of us are very human!" He barked a vicious laugh.

"No fight left in you, boy? Ah, you lost your sword? That is a shame. Still, you fought bravely while you were able. Well, the best man has won!"

"Mother, save me—" Virelai whispered. He stood there, swaying, his vision filling with a swarm of black flecks. Then he felt his knees begin to buckle.

FROM her tower room window, the Rose of the World looked down upon the battlefield far below, drawn from her bed by the pull of sorcery. She saw the contest play itself out in two planes of existence: the apparent and the magical. She saw how Virelai was sent out to face the man she had known as her husband, and how he defended himself as well as he could with the small spellcraft he could muster; then she saw the mage who had imprisoned her in his ice world stride onto the field. That was what had fully woken her, in the end. There was a rage inside her when she saw him at last, that wicked old man, stumbling out across the field, draped in the guise of the handsome northern king, for all the world like some legendary hero. She saw how with a swiftly spoken spell of seeming the Master confused the onlookers so that they missed the clumsy transition as he took Ravn Asharson's place. But no detail did she miss: how the mage placed his hand on the Eyran's breastplate and with a sleep spell quelled his fighting spirit, just enough to render him unconscious and transfer him into the arms of a tall Eyran with hollow eyes and a ravaged face, who dragged her husband from the sward. She saw how Rahe had to touch the greatsword with a spell of lightness in order to heft it at all; saw the veins bulge blue and knotted in his weedy old arms; saw his eyes alight with killing fervor as he bore down upon his erstwhile apprentice.

The chimeras bothered her not at all; though they clearly terrified poor Virelai. Could he not see they were only illusions, that the old man was not strong enough in his powers to become the beasts he presented so ferociously? Apparently not. She watched as the old man hooked Virelai's ankle out from under him; she watched as Virelai fought back with magic; as the mage flowed back through his own self and out the other side.

And she saw—for seconds only, but seconds which burned themselves on her retinas and her memory—the man the mage had once been, long centuries ago—tall and red-haired, hawknosed and arrogant: a king among men. That was how he had looked the day he had entrapped her brother, cast him down in a sorcerous stupor, and imprisoned him deep in the volcano. The day he had caught her and bound her, all unknowing as she was of the ways of trickery, with a clever net of spellcraft; the day he had torn her clothes from her and raped her on the sand. Before he had stared at her belly and—

Words drifted up to her. Strange words. Sad words.

Mother, save me . . .

She gazed down at the combatants, watched as Virelai crumpled to the ground in a dead faint. The Master advanced upon him, grinning. He grabbed up a handful of the sorcerer's long white hair, knotted his fist in it, brought Virelai's chin off the ground . . .

ONE cut was all it would take to destroy forever the thing he had made. It was a fitting end, and probably the only effective one. The northerners had many superstitions about afterwalkers, the dead which rose and carried on an existence against all odds, against nature. Just as he had allowed Virelai to do. It had been curious to fill the aborted fetus with his sorcery, to bring it swiftly through its growth, to set it to running and talking, fetching and carrying. It had become a walking testament to his remarkable powers. Every day, it reminded him of his prowess. He had even become quite fond of it, in his own way. Until it had tried to kill him, and had stolen the Beast and the Woman. Two of the world's three most powerful entities, did he but know it.

The Master could not help but smile. Such a fool, such a waste.

"I must take your head, Virelai, my boy," he cooed over the unconscious figure. "That's what you have to do with the reanimated, you know. Sever the head from the body and keep them apart from one another. The Eyrans bury the head on an island, if they can. They believe that a circle of salt and water will hold a restless spirit at bay. Or sometimes they burn it all to ashes. But I'll need your head for just a little while, my boy I must have a token to show the Istrians the victory is mine, and claim my prize."

He stopped for a moment, as if listening to a voice inaudible to all others. "And Tycho Issian, whose guise you still carry, thanks to my skill? Ah, well he shall perish swiftly, before he can raise any alarm."

There came a powerful rumble which shook the ground, filled the air.

The Master frowned. It was unusual, but not unheard of, for there to be earthquakes this far north in the Istrian continent. He steadied his hold on the hilt and the hair. "I'm sorry, Virelai: but you had a good long run—"

He swung the blade.

It hit something solid; but it was not Virelai's neck.

FROM the battlements people cried out in wonder and awe.

From the Eyran lines, men did the same, shielding their vision against a sudden white light which flashed briefly, leaving a jagged afterimage on the eyeball. And when the light faded, there it was: the world's most massive tree—an ash, by the look of it, with its deeply incised bark, its vast crown of leaves—quite unseasonal even in the milder southern continent—its wide, gnarly roots. Its trunk displaced both lake and bridge and stretched from foot to battlement of Cera's tall castle; and in its topmost branches, apparently lifeless, lay a single figure, garbed in crimson and silver.

King Ravn's men clutched their talismans and made the sign of Sur's anchor to ward off this evil sorcery; and in Cera's castle, Tycho Issian felt a searing pain in his head and fell to his knees. Others prostrated themselves, begging the Goddess to protect them. Did they but know it, she was standing close by them, in the tower room to the west of the battlements, gazing out over what she had brought forth from the earth, her eyes like lamps.

RAVN Asharson shook his head. He felt odd, dislocated from himself. But there was no pain, nor any blood that he could see, no lost limb nor obvious wound. He had little recollection of the fight, and none at all of this tree which had sprung out of nowhere, churning up the ground, displacing the muddy water of the moat, crashing up through the makeshift drawbridge, showering debris in its wake.

At his elbow, Rahe had appeared as if by magic. The old man stared upward till his neck muscles stood out like corded rope. He was red in the face, his eyes bloodshot, and he was breathing too heavily for his exertions to have been caused by a simple walk across the sward. He looked, if anything, afraid.

"By the seven hells," he muttered. "She's come back to herself. And she knows, she knows . . ."

"Knows what?"

The Master started, forgetting he had spoken aloud. A crafty expression came over his face. "She . . . ah . . . knows you have come for her, my lord."

Given the presence of the Eyran army, that was indisputable.

"Where did the tree come from?"

Rahe fixed him with a beady eye. "Your queen," he said maliciously. "Seems to have taken something of a fancy to this Tycho Issian." Then, before the northern king could ask him anything else, he turned on his heel and limped back to the Eyran lines.

Ravn frowned. Nothing was making sense.

"HOW can this be?"

The Rosa Eldi waited for the topmost branch to bring her its freight, then helped the pale man in through the window. Safe at last on the bed, he stirred briefly, his eyelids fluttering, then was lost to her again. She ran a cool hand across his cheek, feeling the life in him: her life, the life of Elda. It ran strong in his veins, though it had not always been the way of it. She felt the traces of the Master's old magic on him, and she would soon scour that out.

"Virelai," she breathed. "Open your eyes. Virelai . . . my son . . ."

BY nightfall, by which time it was abundantly clear that the Istrians had no intention of parting with his wife, nor of ceding the castle to him, Ravn was in a towering fury.

"We shall besiege them," he insisted.

"But, Ravn—"

The eyes he turned on the Earl of Stormway were as black as ink. The reflection of the sconce flickered deep inside that grim regard, a small light in a very dark place.

"I will not leave this place without her. No matter how long it takes and even if I have to keep the promise I sent Cantara's lord." He turned to the guard captain. "Send men into the forest to find whatever timber they can. Send another contingent to unearth and drag back the biggest rocks they can find. Dismantle that farm over there—" he indicated a stone house and outbuildings on the far side of the river valley. A curl of smoke wafted foolishly from its chimney.

The guard captain hesitated. "It's full dark, sire—"

Ravn waved the man away impatiently. "What do I care for that? I will not have my wife spend an hour longer than necessary in the company of this Istrian trickster. Bran?"

"Sire?" Stormway's disbelief made the single syllable two.

"Send me the engineer."

"Karl Hammerhand?"

"At once. And rope, we'll need rope." He paused, thinking. "Strip the ships, the rigging, the hawsers, everything."

"Sire!"

The fire in Ravn Asharson's eyes seemed more now than a mere reflection of candlelight: they shone with the incandescence of madness.

"We will not be leaving here without her; without her, we will have no need of ships."

38

The Bone Quarter

FOLLOWING Persoa's trail proved to be impossible. It was not only that the hillman had carefully disguised his tracks, but because of the very nature of the ground. South of Cantara, where the farmers had given up trying to tame the soil, they encountered a region of dense scrub full of prickly plants and straw-dry grasses. Beyond that, the land gave itself up to full desert, to endless vistas of dunes and bare rock battened below a bowl of hot blue sky. In this ever-shifting, ever-mutable place, nothing held its shape for long. The dunes were always on the move, grain by grain by grain, in a ponderous, inexorable ebb and flow, and then the wind intervened with all the arbitrary playfulness of a bored child, rearranging the topography to its own satisfaction, then demolishing what it had made to start over again.

Katla shielded her eyes against the glare of reflected sun. Her first reaction to the sight of the desertlands had been one of wonder and delight. The dunes stretched away from her to the dusky smudges of the mountains on the far horizon in serried ranks, their replications made elegant by the sharp contrast of sun and shadow. There was a stark simplicity in the stripped-down vista, a harsh beauty which reminded her of deep ocean, or the uplands of Rockfall in winter, when the land lay cloaked in snow and ice, its features rendered mysterious and deceptively lovely. A foot wrong there could reward you with a twisted ankle, a broken leg, a plunge down a crevasse; here, the dangers were more insidious. In the highlands of home, Katla knew every cave and overhang, every rocky lee. Exposed to the teeth of Eyra's treacherous winter storms she could, if worse came to worst, dig herself a snowhole and suck ice for moisture and wait for the weather to blow over. But here, there was no shelter, no sustenance, and although to one raised in the cold, wet north, it was hard to see sunshine as anything other than a blessing, the desert sun was mercilessly hot. It beat down on her head like a hammer, stole the strength and vitality from her muscles, parched her inside and out.

If she stopped to think about the prospect of this journey for more than a few seconds, she would have had to admit to the fear that they would die in this place, worn out and burned up. But her comrades seemed determined. She glanced sideways at Saro Vingo, riding to her left, and thought, unwillingly but for the hundredth time, how exotic he looked, swathed in the style of the desert tribesmen, only his flashing dark eyes visible between the folds of white cotton Flavia Issian had made them all wear.

He caught her looking and bobbed his head away awkwardly. Then he moved forward to join the mercenary leader. Mam's wide hips moved with the sway of her horse, and her chin thrust resolutely south. She had barely said a word since they'd started out, and every so often Katla saw a tremor in her thigh as if she had to resist spurring her mount to a gallop, the quicker to catch up with Persoa.

On the first night, they hobbled the horses and set up a light circular tent on a frame of flexible willow which the nomads had brought to them, along with a dozen skins of fresh water, a sack of flatbreads and nutritious pastes made from olives and tomatoes, apricots and berries from Cantara's storerooms, as well as muslin-wrapped sausages and jerked meat. There was also a pot of foul-smelling white grease from one of the old women. "Even though it may offend your nose, it will also save it!" the crone had told Mam, and advised that they smear it on their hands and lips, too.

As the sun fell below the hazy horizon, the temperature dipped and continued to fall. Katla awoke in the small hours of that night with her teeth chattering. She sat up and rubbed her face and hands, then wrapped her clothes around her so that the air could not get in. Then she lay awake for an age, listening to the regular rise and fall of Saro's breathing, amid the stertorous snores of the mercenary leader. When she was still awake to see the first light prick the tent flap in the morning, she was not a happy woman.

"You snore like a bullfrog!" she chided Mam as they broke their fast.

The mercenary shrugged. "No one's ever complained before."

"Who would dare?"

The sharpened teeth glinted in a half-smile.

THEY crossed the unforgiving desert terrain for another two days without incident; on the third came a change in the weather.

It was Saro who spotted the telltale signs: sand smoking off the tops of the high dunes like spindrift off a mountain. He pointed it out to Mam, who grumbled something about not having the time or inclination to indulge herself with poetic observations of the scenery. Forced instead to address Katla, he said, "We should take shelter. I've heard about the sandstorms out here. There's an ancient legend about an entire army vanishing in the Bone Quarter—a thousand men, and all their horses and yeka, too. They left Tagur amid cheering crowds who strewed rose petals under their feet; they were expected to reach Gibeon four days later. The story goes that a great mage sent a sandstorm which swallowed them up. They were never seen again."

Katla quirked an eyebrow. Then she frowned. Shading her eyes, she stared into the distance. "Can you see the mountains?" she said suddenly.

Saro looked. Where before the peaks of the Dragon's Backbone had shown as a hazy indigo outline against the fierce blue of the sky, now he could see no delineation at all between earth and air.

Soon after, the first of the winds began to buffet them. Sand stung their faces in the gap in the headpieces till they were forced to relinquish clear sight and pull the fabric higher. Bitten in a thousand places by the stinging grains, the horses skittered nervously. Saro urged his mount forward and gestured to Mam, who gave a reluctant nod. In the lee of one of the great barchans they crouched anxiously, with the horses pulled down beside them, hoping that the vast arc of sand above them would not abruptly plummet down upon their heads. This was worse than an avalanche, Katla thought, scanning the darkening air full of whirling devils and columns; this was worse than a white-out blizzard.

It seemed to go on forever, the storm, and was accompanied by an unearthly howling as if a thousand ghosts had risen and were dancing with glee. She could not help but think of that lost army, its armor rattling against its bones, a thousand voices raised in fury at their senseless deaths out here in this pitiless place, where neither goddess nor blind chance could save them. At some point, though it was impossible to tell when, day passed into night and then into day again. The wind changed direction, bringing the sand driving into the flank of the dune. They moved around its base on hands and knees, one hand clamping their linen masks tight to their faces, the other dragging the reins of their mounts.

The animals were plains-bred, sturdy beasts with great endurance and a strong desire for survival; even so, Mam's horse could take the howling sand in its nostrils and ears no more. Eyes rolling, plaintive whinnies splitting the air, it hurled itself upright and away from the group, dragging the reins out of the mercenary leader's grasp. For a moment it bucked and shied as if it, too, were dancing, then it galloped into the storm. After that, there was nothing any of them could do but watch as its darker shape melded with the airborne sand and disappeared into the gloom.

Nobody said a word: there was nothing to say. And no one wanted a mouthful of desert.

After an unknowable amount of time, the raging noise died away and light returned to the world. The landscape into which they emerged had been repatterned by the storm, the dunes oriented in a new direction, vast striations radiating out of the south. But in the clearer air the spiny peaks of the Dragon's Backbone stood out more clearly against the pale horizon and they took heart from that and carried on; first one walking while two rode, then changing places.

There was no sign of the lost horse, not even its hoofprints impressed into the new surface of the desert; but as the sun began its diurnal fall, its red rays limning their right sides like fire, they spotted something on the ground a few hundred yards ahead, something in this monochromatic world which broke the eternal symmetry of the desert.

As they came closer, the shape resolved itself into something smaller than a horse.

A man.

"Persoa!"

Mam fell from her horse and ran stumbling toward the figure with no care for anything, leaving Katla to grab the reins before they lost a second mount.

It was not the hillman. They found Mam staring puzzledly down at the thing on the sand, one hand up to her mouth. Even facedown, it was clear that in life he had been a much bigger man than the eldianna, great of girth, tall of stature. He had been dead for some time. Through the ripped fabric of his clothing, it could be seen that the skin was parched and dried to leather. His outthrown hand had split apart. It was vast: a giant's hand.

The body was hard to turn over, but at last the dead man fell back with a whoomph, sending out a billow of dust that had them all coughing.

Katla wailed. Mam stared. "I'm sure I've seen him somewhere before," she mused, entirely unaffected by the ghastly sight the corpse presented, now that it was obviously not Persoa.

"It's Urse," Katla whispered. "Urse One Ear."

And indeed the dead man had only a single ear; as well as a disfiguring rift which all but bisected his face, a mangled throat, and a torso striped with wounds.

Katla turned a shocked face to Mam. "But why is he here? The last I saw of him, he was taking ship with my father on the expedition to Sanctuary."

Saro knelt and pulled aside the torn clothing. "Bëte," he said softly. He bent his head.

"Bet?" Katla frowned.

"Bëte. A great cat. One of the Three. I think she must have done this, for I never saw a cat as large as her, and these clawmarks are huge. Was this man a friend of yours?"

The tears in Katla's eyes spoke for themselves. She nodded dumbly, wondering what could possibly have taken Urse so far from the arctic seas into which the *Long Serpent* had sailed, what had become of the rest of the expedition, to her father and her brother.

There was nothing to be done: no ritual or rite that would suffice, and burial was pointless in a region in which the sands shifted day by day. In the end they arranged Urse in a more dignified position, laid stones upon his eyes, and Katla called upon Sur to accept his wandering spirit into his halls, even though the big man had not died at sea or in war.

The last thing she expected was an answering voice.

I will take him, Katla Aransen; but I need you and the sword you bear. Hurry to me! Hurry south!

Katla looked around, bewildered. "Did you say something, Saro?" she said suspiciously.

Saro gazed back at her, curious. "No."

He had clearly heard nothing either.

Katla closed her eyes. The voice thrummed through her still, vibrating in the bones of her legs, in her rib cage, and skull. She remembered that sensation. She shuddered. Perhaps she was losing her mind; perhaps she had lost it long ago.

Striding over to the bay she had been riding, she laid her hand on the fox-headed pommel of the great blade which was slung across the beast's flank. The metal was strangely hot to the touch, not sun-warmed, but fiery. She mounted up thoughtfully. Even after she had relinquished her hold on it, her fingers were still tingling; soon she found herself unconsciously cradling the arm which the seither had healed. It had begun to pulse and to burn like a reminder of the pyres. The sensation filled her with dread.

Ahead of her, the Red Peak showed on the horizon as a smoke-shrouded spike.

URSE'S was not the only corpse they found that day; but the next one was odder by far.

This time, Mam would not go near it. Despite all her apparent pragmatism, she was still superstitious at heart, and one gift of luck—which she counted as her reprieve that the first man had not been Persoa—must surely be paid for.

And Katla could not help but dread that where Urse had been there might next be her father or Fent.

So it was left to Saro to approach the hunched figure. He did so cautiously, for it was sitting in a slump, head lowered to its chest, looking as if it was taking a rest from a long and weary walk. Whatever it was, it was not Persoa, not unless the desert had a very strange way with the dead. The man—for such Saro judged it to be, though merely as a result of the remnants of its breeches—had expired long before Urse One Ear, for the ivory of bone shone through tatters of skin gone black with rot and weathering. It had no eyes left to it, and no nose or lips either, and its hands were skeletal, clasped in its threadbare lap. The boots it wore had been of fine quality once and were still in good condition, but of a fashion so long out of date that Saro had seen a pair only in the library where his father had kept his curios. That pair had belonged to a distant ancestor. They were almost three hundred years old. He frowned and sat back on his haunches.

As he did so, the thing moved, though it might just have been the breeze, or its old bones shifting.

Unnerved, Saro scrabbled backward as fast as he possibly could, never taking his eyes off the corpse.

"What?" demanded Katla. "What is it?"

"Who is it?" cried Mam. There was an uncharacteristic quaver in her voice.

"I don't know." Saro hauled himself upright, "except that it's no man who has lived these past three hundred years." Pale skin showed around his eyes where it had been a dark golden tan before.

Katla made a face. "That's just fanciful," she declared grimly. She trudged over to the figure and stared down at it. But Saro was right. It looked ancient, maybe even one of the lost army of which he had spoken, except that it carried no weapon. She hunkered down beside it, relieved that it could not possibly be anyone she knew. Its wind-dried, eyeless face gazed back at her, grinning. She noticed that there was a patch of skin in the center of its forehead which was a different color than the rest—a wan pink, where all around was blackish gray, as if that had been the last part of it to die. Most strange.

Curiosity satisfied, she levered herself to her feet and turned to walk back to her companions. Something snagged at her. She reached around behind and her questing fingers met something hard and cool and jointed. Turning in slow horror, she found the thing had hold of her tunic.

"Aargh!" she dragged herself free and stared at the corpse.

It stared back. Though it had no extant features, she could have sworn it looked disappointed. Then it raised the withered forearm which had grabbed at her and pointed out into the desert, south, toward the Red Peak. It tried to get up, the bones in its legs and hips grinding against one another as it struggled for purchase, then gave up, exhausted.

"No." Katla shook her head. "No, that can't be." She backed away, making the sign of Sur's anchor. "Did you see that? Did you?" she demanded of Mam and Saro.

Saro nodded mutely; Mam just stared, mouth open.

"I saw it," Saro confided, still white around the gills. "Katla, I think I know what it is."

She glared at him. "It's obvious what it is. A dead man, an afterwalker."

"Reanimated," he said softly. "It's a dead man which has been brought back to some semblance of life. By the death-stone. By Alisha."

Katla shuddered, remembering Erno Hamson's words to the Lord of Cantara about a stone which could heal the sick and raise the dead. There was no reason for her to be here, she thought suddenly. She could take one of the horses and return to the north, row back to Rockfall if she had to, away from all this. But that would leave Mam and Saro in this gods-forsaken place, with only a single mount. She knew she could not do it.

As for Saro, he felt his doom approaching.

He braced his shoulders and tried very hard not to think about the vision which had plagued him since the Lord of Cantara had embraced him in Jetra's Star Chamber.

Then he approached the dead man. "Were you raised by the Wanderer, Alisha Skylark?" he asked it solemnly and waited for a response, although to do so felt absurd—surreal. "With the eldistan—the death-stone?"

The thing shifted slightly, cocking its head as if to listen with non-existent ears. Saro repeated his question in the tongue of the hill people. Now the dead man moved its bony fingers to the pink spot on its head and touched it thoughtfully. Then it nodded once, almost imperceptibly, then with greater emphasis, its jaws clacking, confirming Saro's worst fears. Again, it tried to rise, as if the very mention of the eldistan had galvanized it.

Saro stepped quickly away. The company in which he traveled was already peculiar enough, without adding this bizarre newcomer to the band.

They made a broad circle around the straggler from Alisha Skylark's dead army, and continued south.

39

The Red Peak

IT took another day to reach the foothills of the Dragon's Backbone;
but still there was no sign of Persoa or his mount. They did, however,
pass three more revived corpses in various states of decomposition and
animation, and each time they gave them a very wide berth.

At a small, almost-dried oasis, they tethered the horses to a pair of
palm trees within reach of the muddy pool, stashed the packs, and carried on afoot, for ahead the ground rose steeply into ashy screes and
rocky channels which promised to be both unstable and inhumane. It
hardly seemed fair to expect the animals to climb the side of a volcano
which they would themselves have problems ascending.

The going was hard even from the start. The air was thick with sulfur, so that the lungs burned with every breath, and although the alti-
tude and the mountains afforded more shade, still it was every bit as hot
as the desert, for the volcano was alive with fumes. Sweating out moisture she couldn't afford to lose, Mam scrambled up the choked defile as
if every second lost would result in tragedy.

Katla glanced at Saro and grimaced. The Istrian looked as exhausted
as she felt, his eyes red-rimmed through lack of sleep and the constant
grit which showered from the sky here. A shadow fell across her and she
looked up. Above them, high up, black birds hovered warily, wings outstretched, primary feathers spread like fingers.

"Lammergeyers," Saro said, following her gaze. "Carrion birds."

Katla knew what that meant. She bit her lip. Eschewing the rubble-filled path up which the mercenary leader was battling, she opted instead for a slab of smoother rock, sole and palms flat against its surface for the best possible friction. At once, a great jolt of energy flowed through her, inflaming her muscles, filling her head with pounding blood. Voices boomed and jostled for attention, echoing around her skull like bats in a dark cave. She moved up the rock, trying to ignore these sensations, but the voices got louder and more insistent. One of them broke through her concentration altogether.

"Katla!"

Saro's warning cry dragged her back to herself, though she could not make out what he was saying.

Disoriented, Katla pushed down on the lip of rock on which she had set her left foot and levered herself into a standing position. She rubbed her hands across her sticky face, breaking the contact with the rock and at once the voices fled away. It was hot, so hot. She was burning up. *I must have become remarkably unfit,* she thought.

"The sword!" Saro cried again.

Too late, she understood. By then it was afire. She felt her hair catch in its flame, felt the blade ignite down its length so that her shoulders, her back, her buttocks and thighs felt its dangerous heat. Turning, she wrestled it off with swift instinct and cast it aside.

"The flaming sword!"

Above her, Mam had stopped in mid-stride and was gazing down at her in awe. "It's the tattoo Persoa has on his back."

Katla stared at the blade. It was aflame from hilt to point, shooting out its fire in a great swirl of color. She could feel the heat it gave off from where she stood, a killing heat, like a bone-fire. She reached around and gingerly explored her hair and shoulders, those parts she could reach, fully expecting to find skin and hair and clothing sloughing away beneath her fingers. But she could find no damage. None at all.

She presented her back to Saro. "Am I all right?" she asked nervously. "Has it burned me?"

Saro shook his head mutely.

Frowning, Katla approached the sword. The flames guttered as she neared it, clearing from the hilt as if in invitation. The fox in the pommel seemed to grin at her. Her hand wanted to take up the weapon. Her right palm itched for it, as if part of itself were missing. She gritted her teeth and darted a finger to the hilt. It was warm, but not hot; it welcomed her touch. She curled her grasp around it, hefted it suddenly. Virid green flames gouted among the red and orange. Then a great force drew her arm out in front of her and drew her body after it, as if she were a lodestone and the mouth of the Red Peak was the Navigator's Star.

Mam stood aside to let her pass and for the first time, Katla saw fear on the mercenary's face.

"The sword knows," Katla said. "It heeds the call of its maker."

How she knew this, she had no idea, but it came to her with all the clarity and compulsion of a fact.

Mam and Saro exchanged harrowed glances, then followed after the flame-haired girl with the flaming sword.

SOME hundreds of feet above the desert plateau there came a commotion from above, then a rain of debris. Rocks skittered past the climbers, narrowly missing them. Mam flattened herself against the side of the defile, panting, and scanned above for what had dislodged the detritus. Above, the shape of Katla was suddenly eclipsed by a larger shape entirely, and out of nowhere a huge black horse came plummeting toward them.

Saro stared.

It was Night's Harbinger.

He called the stallion's name, watched its ears flick—once, twice, as if in recognition of his voice; then it was past him in a thunder of hooves, its fiery eyes rolling. He watched it disappear into the gloom below, puzzling over the glimpse of red muscle and white bone exposed in haunches which bunched and flowed with a power and grace he remembered well.

A few minutes later, they came upon its erstwhile rider, seated below the mouth of a cave, the roof of which appeared to glow with a fierce red light.

With a start, the figure looked up.

Bony hands cradled a bony chin, but this was no afterwalker, no re-animated corpse.

"Alisha!"

Saro remembered the nomad woman on the journey he had taken with her caravan, south from Jetra. Then, he had thought her wonderfully attractive, with her springy masses of auburn curls, her warm olive skin, unusual pale eyes, and luscious body. Now, only the striking pallor of those eyes remained, points of light in a stripped and sun-blackened face which had sunken in on itself, adding decades to her thirty-odd years. The simple human consequences of grief and starvation had taken their toll; but how much of this ravened, feral appearance had been caused by her use of the death-stone?

Beside her, a small figure lay curled in on itself, as if asleep. Saro felt his heart thud disturbingly against his ribs, an instinctive reflex, as if his body was preparing to run even before his mind had reached such a decision.

"Falo?" He could not keep the quiver out of his voice.

As if stirred by the sound of its name, the thing shifted its position, coming up on one elbow to look at him. Saro wished it had not. Falo it undoubtedly was—or whatever was left of him, once the carrion creatures, natural entropy, and the privations of the desert had taken their toll. Apart from the arm the boy had lost to the militiamen, the reanimated child had also lost its eyes, and misshapen lumps and cavities now covered by some sort of gray skin suggested that wild dogs had worried and feasted on its corpse.

Alisha Skylark put an arm around the boy and drew him close.

"He's not well," she rasped, her voice hoarse from the heat and lack of water. "He must rest. The others are inside the mountain, helping the Man. But he and I can do no more." She looked mournful. "And even our horse has deserted us."

"Night's Harbinger?"

Alisha cocked her head. "The same. He fell when they ambushed us, but the stone brought him back to me." Her hand went instinctively to her breastbone, patted and rubbed: a strange, placatory gesture.

"And Falo?" Saro could not take his eyes from the macabre sight of the boy, lolling his skull against his mother's arm.

Alisha blinked. "The stone won't work on Falo anymore. But he looks much better than he was," she added brightly and smiled at Saro, her teeth a startling flash of white. "Don't you think?"

"Give me the stone, Alisha," Saro said sternly, coming up the slopes to stand over the pair.

She looked mulish. "It might work again, away from here."

"It might. But you must give it to me. You know it is my burden to bear, not yours."

She stared at him and he thought for a terrible moment that he would have to overpower her and her dead boy and forcibly take the stone from her; then she reached inside her robes and held out her hand to him. On the flat of her outstretched palm lay the eldistan which Hiron the moodstone-seller had given him at the Allfair, the stone which might be the most dangerous object in all the world, pale and innocuous now, a cloudy yellow in color, as if it, like the woman, lacked focus and energy.

As simply as that, it was done, and Saro had what he had come here to fetch. Even so, it was with considerable reluctance that he closed his hand around the death-stone. As he did so, it glowed briefly with a bright white light as if recognizing its true owner, then subsided abruptly.

His heart raced.

"Ah," Alisha sighed morosely. "That was the end of it. One little spark of life, and now it's gone again. You wasted it," she accused.

Grimly, Saro turned to his companions. Mam's face was twisted into a grimace of disgust, but Katla remained impassive, her face lit by the unearthly fires of the sword. Then, without a word, she walked past him, drawn by the flaming blade, scrambled over a boulder in the path and disappeared into the mouth of the cave, the sword illuminating it with weird new light.

Saro watched her go, watched till the illumination flickered and vanished with her. He stood there irresolute. With the stone restored to him, his task here was accomplished. He could turn and leave, make his way back across the desert and go north to find the Goddess. His companions were on their own quests now. If Persoa were still alive, he felt sure he and Mam would find one another. And Katla, too, was powerful, self-sufficient, even when not possessed by the sword. She didn't need him, didn't love him, barely seemed even to like him. There was nothing keeping him here.

But all the logic in the world had no bearing on his heart.

Tucking the stone into the empty pouch he wore around his neck, he strode after the Eyran girl, quickening his stride till he was almost at a run, scrambling over rocks and scree with the reckless determination of a man about to lose the one thing in his life that truly mattered.

MAM watched Saro run after Katla Aransen with an unreadable expression which fell somewhere between admiration and sorrow, had there been anyone there to interpret it. But there was no one left in this grim place but a mad woman and a dead boy. Even so, she could not pass them without asking the question that burned inside her.

"Have you seen a man come this way," she asked Alisha Skylark. "A hillman, from Farem?"

The nomad looked blank.

"A handsome man, with the tattoos of his tribe on his face?"

A twitch—of recognition, or irritation?

"An eldianna," she persisted.

At this, Alisha looked up. "Eldianna," she repeated softly. *"Eldianna ferinni monta fuegi."*

"What?" Mam took a hasty step forward, lowering her face to the woman's.

Alisha cringed away, a protective arm shielding Falo from this terrifying looking creature with the wild white-blonde braids and glinting saw-tooth maw.

Mam straightened up, hands spread. "Persoa," she said. "His name is Persoa. Please tell me if you've seen him. I must find him. I must—"

Tears sprang to her eyes. No one on Elda had ever seen Finna the Teeth weep before, and if anything it was even more alarming than her habitual grimace. But the nomad woman reached out and caught Mam by the hand. "You love him, yes? The eldianna?"

Now the tears fell. Mam wiped them away with her free hand, snorted horribly, and hawked over her shoulder. "I do," she mumbled. "Yes, I do." She fixed the nomad woman with a fierce stare. "If you have seen him, you must tell me, please."

"Yesterday, I think it was. He came yesterday. He tried to take the stone from me, but I wouldn't let him have it. He was angry, he shouted at me. Then he saw Falo here, and he cried and went away."

"Where, where did he go?"

Alisha gestured vaguely behind her. "Into the mountain," she said. "He went into the mountain of fire. To help."

"Help who?"

The nomad woman turned a smile of utmost gentleness upon the mercenary, transforming her ravaged features to a sudden beauty.

"Sirio," she said simply. "They are freeing Sirio. The Three will be One again, and then we shall all be released from this wheel of fire and torment." She cradled her son tight, rocking him to and fro. "We shall all be free, Falo, I promise."

Mam left the mad woman crooning to her long-dead son, and took the path into the volcano with her jaw thrust out like the prow of a warship breasting a stormwave.

"KATLA! Katla, stop! Wait!"

Brought up short by the sound of her name, she turned and stared back over her shoulder. Fiery lights shone in her eyes. She looked like the spirit of the volcano, Saro thought with a shiver, an avenging spirit with an avenging sword. He remember now how frightened he had been by her when he had taken up the blade in the corridors of Jetra's castle and he had thought she might strike him down for his temerity. He had seen her wield it with such determined violence he had thought her possessed by it; he remembered how alien she had seemed to him then, how remote and inaccessible. But through it all, he loved her still, for all his denials and evasions. Guaya's touch had released him not only from the gift of empathy, it seemed. It had also confirmed the depths of his passion and released him from his fear.

"Katla," he called, and his voice was low and steady. "Katla, wherever you are going, I'm coming with you. If you walk into the depths of Falla's fire, I will walk with you; if you enter the kingdom of the dead, I will be there at your side. If you fight, I will fight with you; I will guard your back like the warriors of old, against all comers, be they man, beast, or afterwalker."

Those shining, inimical eyes swept over him, and he felt himself both assessed and judged in a few long seconds. Then she bent down, picked something up out of the darkness, and threw it toward him.

"If you are going to fight with me, you will need a blade."

He saw the blur of its long shape catch the light as it fell end over end, and knew that he must show his mettle now or never. Rather than stepping away to allow the weapon to fall harmlessly at his feet, he took a pace forward and readied himself to catch it, knowing that if he misjudged the take, he might lose his hand, or worse.

The pommel end came toward him out of the gloom and he caught it neatly, turning with the blade's momentum, dancing in a tight circle.

When he came around to face Katla Aransen again, she was gone. Only her voice echoed behind her. "It's been a dead man's sword once. Take care it is not such again."

Grinning, Saro ran to catch up with her.

The farther they penetrated into the cave system the brighter came the light from below and a great clamor began to reverberate off the cavern's walls: shouts and screams, roars and howls, groans and wails, and the clash of metal on metal. And when the path they trod began to angle downward, with every step it became hotter and hotter.

Saro wiped his hand across his face and wondered what scene might be revealed to them when they reached the source of these hellish sounds. However hard he tried, he could not escape the comparisons his mind threw at him to the noise that Tanto's victims had made as they died by their hundreds in the torments of his pyres. Almost, he expected his brother to leer up out of the darkness at them, vaster than ever and gruesome with death.

But the sight that met them when they finally came down into the pit of the mountain was stranger and more terrible by far.

Driven thus far by the death-stone, drawing their vitality from the very land they traversed, now the dead appeared to be compelled by another cause entirely. From his vantage point above them, Saro could see that Alisha Skylark's reanimated army was fighting and dying anew. But such was the chaos and the crush of figures, it was hard to tell just what they might be battling, other than the mountain itself, for great gouts of fire and smoke and hurled rock obscured the scene.

He stared in horror as a blackened figure shot backward out of the fury of it all, followed shortly after by one of its discorporated limbs, ribbons of fabric or flesh trailing after it. Then, from the center of the hubbub, something gave a full-throated roar that made the hair stand up on his neck.

"Bëte," he whispered. How could a cat, no matter how great, survive in a place like this? How could anyone? The sulfurous fumes belching up from the fiery depths singed the cavity of his chest every time he took a breath: he found himself breathing as shallowly as was possible to maintain consciousness and life.

But nothing was slowing down Katla Aransen. On she strode, the flaming sword at one with its new surroundings, leading her down and down. Saro tried not to imagine what horrors they were about to be engulfed by, what death might await him there—tried not to think at all. Head down, sweat pouring in rivulets inside his clothing, he followed Katla down into the pit of the world and the death-stone pulsed against his ribs like a second heart.

The dead were everywhere. Or rather, the second-time dead were everywhere, strewn around in grotesque postures like dolls torn apart by a vicious child. Some of the corpses smoked with heat, bones newly exposed, white against blackened skin. Some lay as if asleep, but did not stir even when fire licked their faces. Others appeared to be hard at work, engaged in some kind of excavation, for boulders had been piled high to one side of the cavern, while half-molten rock came flying up out of the ground on the other as if propelled from somewhere out of sight. Beyond this, a battle was in full fray, and this—of course—was where Katla was headed.

There, three figures—two men and a vast black creature—battled against a single foe. It was no bigger than the two men it fought, and considerably smaller than the great cat; yet it fought with such agility and ferocity that it was able to keep them at bay with one hand while picking off recruits from the dead army with the other and hurling them with unimaginable strength against the walls of the cavern, or back down into the molten lava below.

Saro gasped. He thought that he recognized two of the combatants. But Katla, though she had not yet realized it, knew more.

"Persoa!" he cried out; and, "Bëte!"

Katla's response was quieter; but even in the ruddy light he could tell that all her natural color had drained from her face.

"Tam," she breathed. "By all that is holy . . . Tam Fox . . ."

Then, unwillingly, she turned her eyes on their opponent, standing there with his feet in the magma, shrouded by drapes of hot yellow smoke.

The Master of Sanctuary had lavished all his most potent skills on the one who battled his son, the eldianna, and the Beast. The transformation which had overtaken him had been thorough, but was not so complete that Katla Aransen did not recognize her own brother. He did not much resemble her twin any longer, though his hair flamed as red as hers, and his eyes shone a cold and piercing blue. From head to foot his skin was as black as charcoal and shone with a dull metallic sheen. One limb shone brightest of all, as if all human trace of it—all the muscle and sinew and tendon and bone, the flesh and blood of it—had been removed and replaced by the cartiliginous matter of some vast insect, for it appeared to be an arm no more, but a great, hooked scythe, like the killing claw of a gigantic crab or mantis.

"Fent!"

Slowly, the creature's head swiveled to search her out, the eyes fixed themselves upon her. Then a curtain of smoke came down again, obscuring one from the other. Even so, Katla felt her heart flip, felt a seed of doubt take root in her stomach and send its shoots flowing up through her breast and down into her knees, making her tremble. What appalling fate had overtaken her brother since last she had seen him, tricking her into the knot game on the top of the Hound's Tooth, jeering at her as he and his treacherous friend had bound and gagged her and then left her tied to a chair, before running down the cliff path to take her place in her father's ship? And whatever must have become of the rest of her father's expedition? How on Elda could two of its members have turned up on the opposite side of the world from the arctic seas around Sanctuary, one dead in the desert, the other—her own twin brother—made a monster and now fighting her friends amid the dead in the bowels of a volcano? Abruptly, she felt herself out of her depth, displaced; afraid.

Katla . . . Katla . . . You have come . . . I feel you near me. Take strength from the sword. Soon I shall be free . . .

The sword heard the voice of its master, even if Katla was too disoriented to heed it. It swung toward the thing which had been Fent as if of its own accord and suddenly she found that she was running, her feet dragged forward, unwilling, to confront her brother. Up went the sword, then down in a great shearing blow. The monstrous arm rose to fend off the falling blade and a terrible screech ripped through the air as the blade ground and scraped on the adamantine substance of that limb. Katla staggered back, feeling her own arm go numb to the elbow, and watched in amazement as the flames that ran the length of the sword turned purple, then green, then all manner of other unnatural hues.

Fent laughed and, turning, found that his other three opponents had had the nerve to creep closer while he dealt with his sister. Lunging out, he sent the hillman flying backward with a single murderous swipe. Then he turned his attention back to Katla, who was still fighting to keep control of the sword as it whirled wildly through the air.

"Ha, sister!" the monster cried, and even the timber of Fent's voice was changed, for it was low and booming where before it had been light and nasal, and where before it had owned an edge of sharp malice, now that edge had been honed to a steely nonchalance. "Now it is truly just like one of the old hero tales, as twin fights twin, one light, one dark, for the fate of the world!"

Then he came at her with a single bounding leap, the curved blade of his new hand leveled at her head. Katla ducked and spun, bringing the greatsword up in a scything stroke of her own. Again, claw met blade and sparks flew like hot iron off a whetstone. Breathing hard, Katla fell back, considering her next move.

"Tired already, sister? Surely not—we've only just begun!"

"Fent—Fent—what has happened to you?" she panted. "What have you become?"

"What—you mean this?" He wielded the limb at her, grinning madly.

"I don't remember you complaining when the seither gave you back your arm! Rahe has made me what I should always have been. You, you have a sword and I—"

The arm came crashing down and the sword swung up desperately and spun off it with a screech. Katla danced backward, trying to keep her balance. If she fell, he would not spare her, she knew it with a terrible, deep certainty. There was no feeling left in him at all. Nevertheless, she had to try to engage him somehow.

"Rahe—who is Rahe? Did you reach Sanctuary? Did the expedition succeed? Where is Da?"

"So many questions, little sister! Still the yapping little fox-haired bitch, I see."

Again, the claw came down at her in a blur of darkness, and again Katla slipped away and let the sword take its swing. This time, the blade ricocheted off the strange limb, catching Fent on the shoulder, and he hissed in what might have been pain.

"That was not friendly, Katla. Not friendly at all."

Now he leaped high, right over her head, so that she was forced to fall to her knees to avoid him, but as if attached to the monstrous boy by an invisible thread, the sword followed him, dragging her arms around in an uncomfortable arc, this time nicking at his legs.

Fent let fly a howl of fury and he turned and thrashed the inviolate limb down on the blade so that it rang and chimed. Black smoke billowed off it, but when the smoke cleared, the fire which encompassed it burned brighter than ever.

SARO watched this unnerving bout feeling as if he were in a dream and sunk to the waist in rising sand. He could barely make out what was happening down below him, for there was a frantic bustle of activity everywhere he looked, all obscured by belching smoke and vapors. In the spaces where the smoke cleared, he thought he glimpsed the dead in the heart of the volcano, where no live thing could ever exist, dislodging rock after rock as if digging for treasure. Meanwhile, the three figures on the other side of the chamber dodged in and out of view, striking and falling back. Then he saw Persoa hurled against the wall as if by a giant's hand, saw the hillman strike the rock with a crash and slide to the ground, and lie there dazed—or dead.

With his heart in his mouth, he searched for Katla, only to see her on her knees, the greatsword held unsteadily overhead. He looked down at the weapon he held in his own hand with misgiving. What could he could do to help Katla with this small, notched weapon he bore? Especially against a warrior who moved so fast it was impossible to follow his movements. But he had vowed to fight with her, to guard her back against all comers, and no matter how short the odds of survival, he knew he must keep his word. With a yell, he shook off his torpor and charged down into the hellish arena, sword raised like an ax.

More by luck than by judgment he managed not to fall into the bubbling pit of fire, though smoke drifted everywhere as thick as cloth. He waved his arm frantically about, and as the vapor cleared before him, he saw the thing Katla had called Fent barely two yards away, bearing down upon her with a feral grin.

Yelping, Saro ran at him, keeping low. He had meant to take him in the stomach with the ball of his skull, but the monster was too quick for him. Sidestepping, it caught him a glancing blow with its more ordinary hand, sending him sprawling. But Saro was not to be dismissed so lightly, and shoving himself upright again with a speed born of sheer desperation, he flicked out with the dead man's sword and managed to stick the point of the blade into the crook of Fent's knee as he charged again at Katla.

Fent stumbled, then snarled with rage and whipped around, and now Saro truly knew the meaning of fear as he got his first good look at Katla's opponent. For here in front of him was a perverse reflection of his beloved. The figure was small and wiry, with whipcord muscles and pointed features just like Katla's, except where her skin was a pale golden, this creature's was black as if charred, yet smooth and unblemished, unmarked by battle or fire. Its hair, standing out in a wild red halo, was the exact same hue as Katla's, and the mad blue eyes which crackled fiercely out of its fine-boned face reminded him uncomfortably of Katla's eyes when she took back the greatsword from him in Jetra Castle and he had thought himself about to die.

And when the thing raised its arm, he saw with horror and disgust that this was where any resemblance to Katla Aransen ended, for the appendage was far removed from the likeness of any human limb, being hard and massive and shaped like the claw of a Galian lobster, with two great cutting blades which clacked one against the other, the edges serrated, slightly overlapping, razor-sharp.

He brought his sword up in a despairing gesture and waited for the killing blow to fall. For a moment, he even closed his eyes. At least he had won Katla a few seconds, he thought. She might have had time to scramble away. Then something jostled his elbow, something warm and silky-hard, and when he looked down, there was Bëte at his side, shoulders bunched, muzzle wrinkled in fear and anger, black gums curled back to expose her great fangs, her amber eyes fixed on the advancing figure. The roar she gave throat to hummed and buzzed in his breastbone, giving him both heart and strength. He remembered the fighting spirit of the little cat he had rescued at his villa, a tiny thing against what must have seemed to it overwhelming odds; and felt the despair slough away from him.

"For Katla!" he cried, and ran full tilt at the monster.

Man and Beast struck Fent together, and their joined momentum bowled him over. Suddenly, Saro found himself on the lip of the pit, teetering dangerously, then sharp teeth sank themselves into belt and cloth and skin and dragged him back. But in that moment, he glimpsed a bizarre sight down there. The army of dead men—or the few of them who were left—were unearthing a figure from the depths of the heart of the mountain, a figure which had been weighted down with massive boulders and pillows of cooled lava. It was a man; beyond that, the figure defied description. It had the semblance of flesh, the shape of flesh, but he swore that through that flesh he could make out the molten rock beneath it, as if it were ghostly, the shade of what had once been a man and now was but a vision.

"What is that?" he cried wildly.

It seemed the world had changed shape again, become surreal, more dreamlike than before, for now there was a voice in his head and he knew it to belong to the great cat, knew it with the core of him which knew truth from seeming.

The God lies below you, and he is being raised.

Three shall become One again, and Rahe shall be cast down! But first we must deal with this creature he has sent against us, for it is indefatigable and filled with stolen magic!

There was a shriek from behind them and Saro turned again, with dread, to find Katla fallen and the black figure pinning her to the ground with its massive claw. The greatsword lay at some distance away, its flames all but extinguished.

"Bëte!" he cried. "Save her!"

But another got there first.

The red-bearded man flung himself across the smoking ground and thrust himself between Fent, kicking the great claw away from the girl. He towered over the black figure; but for all that, he had no weapon; nor any clothes either, save a twist of filthy cloth around his hips. Even so, he bared his teeth at Fent as if willing him to do his worst. Incongruously, Saro felt a great wave of jealously crash over him, seeing the man guarding Katla like a wolf standing over his fallen mate.

Then a cloud of smoke billowed up out of the pit and swarmed over everything and Saro could see no more.

When it cleared, an even more alarming sight met his eyes. The red-bearded man lay collapsed across Katla's body. There was blood everywhere, over the man, over the ground, over Katla. It was impossible to tell whose blood it was, both lay motionless. Saro felt his heart stop, and knew then that if she died, he did not want it to start again. He felt a great howl welling up inside him, but before he could give voice to it, the pit erupted.

The dead came swarming up into the chamber, their hair and skin on fire, and the black figure—having dealt with the irritating creatures which had stood in the way of its true goal—scythed them down one by one as if they were no more than nettles in a field. Then it reached down into the molten rock and with superhuman strength hauled out the essence of the incorporeal god which had lain buried there these long centuries.

It was Bëte who gave voice to the howl Saro had felt building inside him. She ran to the edge of the pit and stared in as the black figure closed its terrible pincers over her fellow deity, her claws digging into the rock as if she might leap into the fires to save Sirio from Rahe's monster. But even from where he stood, Saro could see how the intense heat of the mountain's heart seared her eyes and burned her fur, the awful acrid scent of it filled his nostrils. If she jumped into that cauldron of fire, she would die within seconds; and none would benefit from such a sacrifice.

Weak from his three-hundred year imprisonment, Sirio squirmed in Fent's grasp. At last, he gave a mighty cry. The four he had summoned from the corners of Elda had failed him at the last; and now all would be lost.

Saro felt the death-stone burning his skin.

"No," he whispered. "No. I cannot use it again. Not even for this."

And if Katla is dying, would you use it then?

Saro clenched his fist around the stone, tears burning his eyes. Would he? He did not know, though he thought he might, despite the worst consequences. Turning away from the struggle that was playing itself out in the pit, Saro stumbled across the smoking ground to where Katla and the red-haired man lay fatally entwined and cast himself to his knees beside them.

Neither figure moved. Blood had run across Katla's face, pooling at her nose and mouth, giving her a mask of gore and streaks of darker red among the flame of her hair. Tam Fox lay face-up across her, a great rent in the flesh of his shoulder and chest. *Let it be his wound which covers Katla in blood,* Saro prayed guiltily. *Let her be all right. Anything, I will give anything if she is all right.*

The moodstone pulsed and shone.

With trembling fingers, he tied his tunic tight shut over the stone and tried to ignore its insistent presence. Would he turn her into one of these gray-skinned afterwalkers? Could he condemn her to the sort of shambling life-in-death he had seen of Alisha's army? He knew he could not. "Katla," he said softly. "Katla, don't be dead."

There was no response. Gingerly, he touched her face. Her skin felt cool and unresponsive beneath his fingers, and slightly damp, like trodden mud. He laid his cheek to her nose and mouth, but could feel no breath. Nor, when he pressed the vein in her neck could he feel the slightest beat of blood there.

Silently, Saro wept.

And now a new voice rose in a wail. Saro's head snapped up. He twisted around to locate the source of the sound, and there was Mam, cradling the body of the hillman who lay crumpled on the ground below the rock against which he had been flung.

Such a waste of life and love and effort; and all for what?

Misery melded with anger, a white heat of fury and despair. Saro flung himself to his feet, the tears running freely down his face now. The greatsword lay glowing just a few feet away. Without a single coherent thought in his head he strode over to it, wrapped his fingers around the fox-headed pommel, and heaved it up. It felt massive, lumpen, awkward in his fist: a stupid piece of beaten metal made for destroying lives. Even its flames had gone out, and deep inside himself he felt the confirmation of the extinction of Katla's flame, too, for it had been her touch which ignited it, her life which gave it spark. He was sure of that now.

No matter. Nothing mattered.

He would kill the thing in the pit, and he would die; and then it would all be over. Wearily, he swung the sword onto his shoulder and trudged the twenty paces to the edge of the hole in the mountain and stared down. The god, it seemed, was proving hard to kill. Fent's claw slipped over and through the shadowy figure trying to find better purchase. And now Katla's twin was losing his temper. He stamped his feet in frustration and lava splashed up and fell back with a sizzle. He tried to dash Sirio's head against the rocky walls of the chasm; but the deity's form passed into the rock and then reappeared, apparently undamaged, though he hung limp and useless in the deformed creature's grip.

Infuriated now, Fent caught Sirio by what appeared to be his feet and whirled him around and around his head, like the men Saro had seen at the Allfair games with a boulder in a sling, competing for the longest throw. When he finally let go, the god flew overhead like a great, translucent arrow. He hit the side of the chamber without a sound, and vanished.

Fent stormed out of the pit. "Call yourself a deity?" he cried. "You're nothing but a sad excuse for a god! I have defeated you: I, Fent Aranson, of Rockfall . . ." he paused, thought for a moment. "And of Sanctuary," he amended. "If anyone is a god here, it is me!"

Bëte launched herself at him with a roar.

The attack was unexpected. Fent went down with a clatter like the sound of a hundred cooking pots tumbled over a cliff. Before he could recover himself, the great cat landed on his back, driving him into the ash. But even with Bëte's claws lacerating the strange black skin the mage had given him, Rahe's creature laughed.

"And they say you are a deity, too! But in the end you're just an over-grown farm cat, and I've killed a few of those in my time." He braced himself and made a bridge of his body so that Bëte could no longer reach the ground with all her paws. Slowly, he began to get to his feet while she growled and bit and grappled for a foothold. "Go play with little mice!" he jeered. "It's all you're fit for!"

Saro hefted the sword. Then he ran at the black figure with a mighty yell. At the last moment, Bëte leaped away. Flames blossomed suddenly down the length of the great blade—flames of crimson and scarlet, or-ange and gold and cleansing green—and crackled with life, and sud-denly it seemed that a hand closed over Saro's and took the sword away and a face gazed down into his own. It was Persoa, but he was much changed.

As the god inhabited his body, the hillman's inked patterns began to flow and change. The tribal tattoos uncoiled themselves from his face, ran down his neck and across his shoulders, met the blaze of colors upon his back and smoothed the strange designs away until there was nothing left but fair, luminous, unblemished skin, skin that was lighter in hue than the hillman's had ever been; and then his hair was evolving, too, turning from black to flaxen-gold; and his eyes changed suddenly from black to piercing blue.

The god, Sirio, touched the hilt of the sword briefly to his lips, and all the flames turned palest green like new ears of corn. Then, in a blur of motion he turned upon the creature which had once between Katla's twin and took his head off with a single clean stroke.

The head bounced once as it struck the floor of the chamber, red hair whipping over and over, then rolled into the pit and sank into the boil-ing magma. The body stayed where it stood, swaying gently, then at last crumpled to the ground with a crash. Sirio regarded its demise with minimal interest, then, as if cleaning away something unpleasant, he stooped, took hold of the terrible mutated limb, dragged the headless corpse to the pit, and pushed it over the edge with his foot. Down it went with barely a sound. He stood there watching, but no bubbles marked its progress; nothing stirred.

He turned to face his rescuers.

His eyes went first to Mam, on her knees still where the hillman's body had lain until so rudely purloined, her eyes round with grief and horror, and he smiled, a smile which might have been one of infinite compassion, or of faint amusement. It can be hard to read a god's expression.

"He says he is sorry for leaving you. He asks that you do not begrudge me his body and the strength I have taken from him. He says," Sirio cocked his head minutely as if trying to catch a distant sound. "He says, 'Good-bye, Finna, and go with love.' "

But if this was meant to comfort and placate the mercenary leader, it did not have the desired effect. Mam rose to her feet, eyes blazing, fists knotted. Then she ran at the god like a whirlwind. Blows rained upon his chest, his face, his arms. "I don't want you in the world, I want Persoa! Give him back to me, you thief! Get out of his body: give it back!"

Sirio allowed her to hit him again and again and gave no sign of feeling the blows as they fell, safe now in his new body. Then at last, as the fury ebbed out of her, he caught her to him and held her to him, his hand cradling her head as a mother might cradle a child. "His body was his gift to me, as he had always known it would be," he said. "He has been connected to the Three since the day he was born, through the rock, through the bones of Elda. We have known each other always. An eldianna is marked as the gods' own, did you not know?" And when Mam turned puzzled, reddened eyes to him, he placed his palm on her forehead. "Here, feel him. He is still here, within me, as all are who die in our name."

Slowly, a tremulous smile touched the mercenary's lips, then her face collapsed into anguish once more and she sank to the ground and wept softly with her arms over her head.

Now the god turned to Saro, regarded him for a solemn moment. "You bear something of my sister's," he said wonderingly.

Saro, drained by misery and despair, raised hollow eyes to the god and his hand went instinctively to the place on his chest where the death-stone hung beneath his clothing.

The god crossed the ground between them. "May I?" he asked.

Trembling, Saro untied the laces on his tunic and brought the eldistan into view.

Sirio's eyes fixed on it; then he took a step back and averted his gaze. "Feya's Tear—an accursed thing! So, she cried for me, then. What must he have done to her, that she could not come to my rescue? I have wondered that for three hundred years. Nothing could keep us apart. Nothing! She is mine and I am hers: we are part of each other. I thought he must have destroyed her, but recently I have sensed her in the world. I have sensed her here—" He clenched his fist against his chest. "She has returned to Elda, I know it," he said fiercely. "She has returned and I must find her." Something butted against his leg and he looked down. There was Bëte, as vast as any jungle feline, rubbing her cheek against his thigh with all the fervid adoration of a domestic cat. "No, I have not forgotten you. You have returned, too. Yes, yes, I know." Absently, Sirio lowered a hand to scratch behind her ear and the great cat's purr rumbled up through the chamber like the presage of an earthquake. "So, where is she, our lady?" he said softly, to no one in particular.

"They say she is on the coast of Istria," Saro replied. "Brought across the Northern Ocean by the Lord of Cantara. But, my lord, I must ask—"

"Cantara? Not Rahe?"

"Tycho Issian is the Lord of Cantara. My lord, I have a question—"

"A man, not a mage?"

Saro shook his head impatiently. "A terrible man, but no mage, my lord."

"The north coast, you say?"

Saro nodded. "Yes, lord, but—"

"And she is alive, and well?"

"I have seen her only once, lord, when she touched this stone and made it deadly. Men have died . . . others been resurrected . . . Katla Aran—"

"She cannot have been in her right mind. We do not willingly bring death to our people." But even as he said this, his fingers tightened around the hilt of the greatsword.

Saro stared at him. "But can you bring life?" The blue eyes pinned him to the spot, making him quail, but still he persisted. "Katla Aransen lies there, dead. She gave her life for you, though it would not have been a willing gift, for Katla was a fighter to the last. She said to me once that her god required no sacrifices in his name. But she has died for you, my lord—"

"I accept her gift, willingly offered or not. Do not ask for miracles, boy," Sirio said sternly. "Each life has its own length, and giving to one means taking from another."

"Do you have no gratitude in you, no grace? Is this what it is to be a god? To see the world as an endless round of living and dying, no one meaning more than any other, except as a way of keeping you alive?"

The mask of serene indifference was creeping back over Sirio's face.

Suddenly furious, Saro shouted: "As you feel for the Rosa Eldi, so I feel for Katla Aransen! Do you understand that?"

The suggestion of a frown marred the god's white forehead. "You are a mortal boy, and I—well, the gulf is vast. If she has died in my name, then she lives within me and shall abide there forever."

Saro's expression shattered into one of rage. "That's just a smug excuse! What good is it to me if she exists as some sort of spirit within you? I don't want her there, I want her here, with me, living and breathing, walking and climbing and running and loving. Here, in Elda. Here, in my arms!" He tugged at the god's arm, not caring now whether he might strike him down, not caring for anything.

Sirio regarded the strange scene contemplatively—a dead man lying almost naked across a dead woman—an unreadable expression on his pale face.

Saro, meanwhile, threw himself down beside Katla. He pulled her limp hand out from beneath her, chafed it, held it to his lips. It was barely warm, cooling fast despite the sulfurous heat of the cavern. He rubbed it harder, and harder still.

Sirio bent and touched the top of Tam Fox's fiery head. "I remember you," he said curiously. "I know who you are." He withdrew his hand. "I brought him here," he said happily to Saro as if delighted by his own prowess. "I sent a monster to upset his ship and I brought him here just as he was drowning, to save me." Then he transferred his touch to Katla

Aransen. "Ah," he breathed. "I know you, too, sword maker." He straightened up. "I have helped each of them back to Elda once before," he declared. "Which is quite sufficient a disruption in the balance of the world. I do not care to intervene a second time." He regarded Saro's stricken face and smiled, but his smile was not kind. "Besides, one of them still lives."

Saro's eyes became huge. "Which one?"

He was answered by a groan. Then Tam Fox blinked and groaned again. Stiffly, he brought his hand up to his face, regarded the drying gore on it distastefully, wincing as the pain from his great wound hit him. His eyes came to rest on the body of the woman beneath him.

"Katla!" Pushing himself upright, he looked down. "Ah . . . Katla, no . . ."

Saro stared in horror. He had thought the red-bearded man's wound terrible enough, but Katla's was worse. Her tunic had been sheared through below the ribs and he could see things shining in the gap, terrible, interior things that should never see the light. He closed his eyes. When he opened them again, the death-stone was in his hand. It burned a sickly yellow. Tears were streaming down his face. He stared at it, loathing it. He did not know what to do.

Then he turned to the god, thrusting the eldistan at him. "Take the stone, and return it to your sister. Then take me," he said urgently. "Take my life for Katla's. You said if you gave to one, you had to take from another: well, take my life from me and give it to her. She doesn't deserve to die, she's too full of life—" Sobs overwhelmed him.

Tam Fox shook his wild braids so that the bones and stones in them rattled and danced. He looked long upon the dead girl, and the planes of his rough-hewn face seemed to soften as he did so. "Ah, Katla," he said softly. "I had hoped to save you from such a fate." Then he transferred his attention to the sobbing Istrian. At last he sighed. He turned his lazy tawny gaze upon the god. "So there you are, Sirio, Lord of Men. This boy—who looks as if he has suffered enough, though he is barely old enough to know the meaning of the word—offers you the essence of his life if you will restore Katla Aransen. What has your world come to if such sacrifices are required of such tender lads?" He heaved himself onto one elbow and looked sorrowfully down at his ribboned chest. "But I've had a good long run, and by the looks of this, I'm not going to be doing a lot of acrobatics from now on." He made a grimace which turned into a wry smile. "My troupe is dead, my best friend lost to your Beast, and I have nowhere left to lodge my heart. If we're talking bargains here, then I offer you a better one than the boy can ever make you, as well you know, given my parentage."

Sirio glared at him. "Sons born of mages and seithers live long indeed; but it was your father's action which caused my world to come to this pass," he declared. Then, quick as a snake, he wrapped one hand in Tam Fox's braids and the other in Katla Aransen's flame-colored, bloody hair. "So I have few qualms at accepting this gift from *you*."

Tam Fox, his head wrenched sideways, looked up at the god steadily, golden lights shining in his tawny eyes. "Take it, then, quickly," he said through gritted teeth. "For her sake—take it now, before I change my mind."

There was a brief shudder, a trembling, in earth and air, as if time was shifting or energies were flowing; then the mummer chief's eyes rolled up in his head and Katla Aransen writhed sideways, coughing.

The movement made her wound gape ever wider, so that a loop of intestine spilled, gleaming, out into the furnace-light of the volcano.

Saro stared at this abomination, then up at the god, disbelieving. "I thought you were going to save her!" he cried in accusation.

Sirio frowned. "She is alive."

"But her wound is not healed—"

"Healing of wounds is not my province." He turned to the great cat at his feet. "We have a long journey ahead of us, you and I," he told it. "If we are to be reunited with our Rose. Are you ready?"

Bëte opened her mouth in a vast red arc which might have been a yawn or a gesture of assent. Then she rubbed her cheek against his leg and lumbered to her feet.

"You can't leave us! If you leave her like this, she'll die. No one can live a day with a wound like that."

Sirio looked minutely irritated. "Your lives are so short. What difference does it make if she lives one day or another ten years? All you people do is to inflict harm on one another and seek power. And when you gain power, all you do is seek more. Rahe had an entire kingdom in his thrall. Why did he have to rape my sister and steal her magic? Just to live longer and take more power. And now I must find him and redress *that* balance."

The Beast moved between them. It gazed down at Katla Aransen thoughtfully and for a long and terrible moment Saro feared that the scent of her warm blood had piqued its appetite, particularly when it bent its head and began to nose at the wound, making Katla cry out in agony.

Saro threw himself at the cat's neck, tried to haul it away. It shook him off as if he were a gnat and went back to its task, immune to his pummelling and threats.

At last it said quite clearly into his mind: *I have licked her wound closed for now, but you must take her to the Rosa Eldi if she is to be fully healed.*

Saro gazed down at Katla Aransen. Through the hole in her tunic, the edges of her wound had begun to knit, a translucent skin forming over the ropes of gut and he felt a sudden dart of hope spear his heart.

It will not last, the cat warned. *My skill is with creatures, not humans: you do not have our resilience.* It cocked its head. *Yes, yes, we will go now: do not fret. I know you hunger for her: I miss her, too.*

"Can't you take us with you?" Saro pleaded.

Bëte regarded him with her amber eyes. *Where we are going, you cannot follow. Be careful with her, and bring the eldistan.*

The War of the Rose

ALL along the Istrian coast the Eyran fleet harried and pillaged. They fired the town of Hedera for the eighth time in its long history and stole away treasures and women. Others sailed south and stormed Ixta, and the population fled inland, leaving their city unguarded, the gates wide open to the enemy. Merchants' warehouses along the quays were stuffed with booty—the lords of Ixta and Cera craved only the best and had sown a taste for luxury and competition in the region. What the Eyrans could fit onto their ships without sinking them, they stole; the rest they burned. Convinced that they had done the job bidden of them by their king, and satisfied with their spoils, some captains gave the order to turn back, their ships packed to the gunwales with stuffed antelopes and gilded pots, with the skins of spotted cats and jars of Jetran wine; but more ships arrived out of the mists of the Northern Ocean every day. These freebooters stormed the coastal towns and settlements, releasing hundreds of slaves and sending them into the hinterland with weapons and promises of reward for havoc wreaked. Farmers, field-workers, even livestock were savaged and slain, the slaves' fury was so great for the years of cruelty and disdain they had endured; buildings were destroyed, barns torn down, crops trampled and burned.

Sestria initially put up more of a fight, but by dawn of the third morning the militia had lost heart and fled, leaving the townspeople to the mercy of the barbarian horde, but little mercy was showed. When the seneschal and his officers tried to make an official surrender, they were cut down where they stood and their heads stuck on pikes at the city's gates. Women were raped, children slaughtered. Blood lust drove the northern host.

By the time the eastern fleet reached Forent, terror had spread far and wide. Families packed up what little they could travel with and headed south for the safer inland towns. On their way they met Istrian soldiers coming north, but even that did not deter them from their flight.

With an eye to the main chance, the leaders of the Istrian militia had perceived that with the flower of their nobility decimated—either in the assault on the Eyran capital, or in the rather more mysterious circumstances leading up to the war, the way was open for men of courage and foresight to make their mark. The empire had not had an emperor for many an age; now it largely lacked an aristocracy. There were riches and castles for the taking, once the foreign invaders were repelled.

The men who answered the muster harbored ambitions of their own. They, too, knew an opportunity when it presented itself. And the sight of the refugees—rather than transfixing them with fear—merely spurred them on: clearly so many had abandoned their homes that there were sure to be fine pickings for the sharp-eyed and light-fingered. More and more men gathered to the standard raised by the new generals and came north to battle with the old enemy.

And so the tide of battle turned at Forent as the Istrian militia captured escaping slaves and pressed them into service, sending them out ahead of the troops to a certain death at the end of an Eyran blade. And while the northerners dealt with this rabble, Istrians rowed out into the harbor and fired the Eyran ships, then rounded on their enemy from behind. Drunk on their spoils and disdainful of the resistance they had so far encountered, the Earl of Blackwater and his men were entirely taken by surprise by this maneuver. They fought ferociously; but they were outnumbered: something else they had not expected. Two thousand Eyrans lost their lives in the battle for Forent, as well as an unknowable number of slaves. The sea ran red for miles around with the blood they sluiced out of the streets.

The army at Forent, thinking their job done, took occupation of the fine castle, made free with what pleasures they could come by in Rui Finco's city and drank his cellars dry.

Until the day a bird arrived, bearing news of the siege of Cera.

Leaving a garrison of trusted men under Bandino's command to keep Forent in some order, Manso Aglio, one-time captain of Jetra's militia and guard of the Miseria, ordered the rest of his force west. It would take some days to reach Cera, even at a forced march; but perhaps that was for the best. Let the raiders have their way with Cera's pathetic excuse for a militia; let them string up the unpleasant Lord of Cantara, whom he would happily see swing on the arm of a gibbet with the rooks pecking out his eyes; then they would make a heroic appearance to save the day. By which time the Eyrans would be soused with wine and sex, too stuporous to put up much resistance. He'd always fancied being master of Cera's fine castle. Nice parklands it had, he remembered from the days when he had been stationed there.

FROM an Eyran perspective, the siege of Cera had not been progressing well, for the castle had been built in ancient times when men knew the trick of raising massive walls which would withstand even the most savage assault, and although the stonework bore witness to the accuracy of the ballistas the northern army had constructed, they had not yet managed to breach its defenses in any significant way.

King Ravn Asharson sat now in the red light of yet another chilly dawn, and scowled at the grim prospect before him. The previous day the Eyrans had made their first attempt to scale the walls using a pair of siege towers. Every tree within a mile radius, the rigging of five of his ships, the flayed hides of a large herd of cattle, and a fortnight's trial and error had gone into the making of the towers, one of which now lay in ruins at the base of the walls like so much firewood, still smoking faintly from the boiling oil and burning pitch the defenders had loosed upon them. Worse, beside the burned and splintered remnants lay the corpses of a dozen of his men, also burned and splintered from the pitch and a long fall; neither of which had managed to kill them swiftly. The archers had done their best to speed the fallen men's demise; but the screams of the dying men haunted him still, and he knew that few of his comrades had enjoyed much sleep that night.

The second tower they had hauled out of range; but they would need a dozen or more to make an effective attack, and given the paucity of useful materials left to them, that would require the best part of his fleet. Personally, he had few qualms about such a sacrifice, but the earls were being difficult, and there were mutterings among the men, all of whom had expected to see a short, sharp action, swift victory, and a pile of Istrian silver to carry home. If they did not achieve a result soon, he knew there would be desertions, and no amount of threat or censure would turn *that* tide.

He ground his teeth in frustration. Some new stratagem was called for. Only sorcery was likely to break these walls, but the damned sorcerer had vanished, and none knew his whereabouts.

He sighed heavily. It was hard to believe that beyond this cheerless vista lay the most captivatingly beautiful woman in Elda, or that she should have been seen at the castle window helping the Lord of Cantara to safety from the branches of the vast ash tree which had sprung up so bizarrely. This latter detail had been supplied by Stormway. Ravn found he had no memory of the event at all. It was as if he had gone out to fight in his sleep and woken suddenly to find himself in another world entirely, one in which magic held sway. He still did not know whether he believed Bran's odd account, suspecting the old man of tampering with the facts to persuade him to leave the Rosa Eldi to the mercy of the Istrians; but the existence of the tree was undeniable.

He stared at it now, hating its knotted bark, its massive trunk and twisted limbs. They'd thought about hacking it down to provide the timber they needed for the siege towers; but as Egg had pointed out, it was so huge it would take a hundred of them to cut through it, and as soon as it had fallen, they'd be exposed to the Istrian bowmen from the castle walls.

"It is a mighty tree, is it not, my lord?"

He turned suddenly, and there was the mage.

"Where have you been? We could have used your efforts yesterday; but now a company of my best men lie dead—"

The Master waved a hand to cut off this tirade. "I have been inside the citadel," he said softly.

"Inside?" Ravn stared at him. "How?"

"Ask not how, my lord. Ask instead what I have discovered."

"Well?"

"Two birds on a single branch."

The king regarded him suspiciously. "Do not speak to me in riddles, old man, or I will have your head."

Rahe smiled, an expression which did not reach his pale and rheumy eyes. "Not here, my lord: the very air has ears."

BEING sequestered for the best part of a month in Cera's castle with screaming women and children, no fresh food, and all the wells full of mud and worse from the flood had been a far from pleasant experience for Tycho Issian. It was an experience he might have dealt with in better temper had the woman in the next chamber not locked and barricaded her door against him.

And to make matters worse, she had the sorcerer, Virelai, in there with her.

Day and night the Lord of Cantara had raged against her, but all he received by way of response was a taunting silence. He had sent guards to break down the door; but all they had succeeded in was splintering its veneer, beneath which gleamed an iron interior he could have sworn had never been there before. He ordered that no sustenance be delivered to the room and waited for her pleas; but none came. Then, driven to wild and jealous distraction, he had climbed into the garret above the tower room and bored a hole in the ceiling, tormented by visions in which the pale man straddled the pale woman and rode her relentlessly, or she sat astride his lap and held his head between her white breasts. He had bored one hole after another before she became aware of him and he was able to look down on her, seated in apparent chastity on the bed beside the sorcerer, his hands in hers, her lips moving in such quiet speech he could not hear what she said.

The last hole he had made was right above her: plaster trickled down from it like snow.

She had looked up then, and her green gaze pierced him.

"Go away," she had said with perfect clarity, and he had felt the words like icicles in his heart.

And curiously, he had done just as she requested. And he hadn't been back. He still wasn't sure why.

Since then he had sat and seethed. He had watched his archers try and fail to make their mark on the Eyrans. He had watched them send flight after flight of arrows out over the great tree; and he had watched most of them strike uselessly into the waterlogged ground fifty yards from the enemy lines, the sole casualty being one foolish Eyran, jeering at their efforts, who had strayed too far forward and been shot through the throat. This had raised a thin cheer from the soldiers on the battlements, but until the northerners had brought the siege towers within range every other arrow had been wasted. Military training had never been of high priority in this rich and complacent city.

And still there had been no sign of reinforcements, despite all the useless birds he had sent. A week ago he had sent out two boys by dead of night to carry word to Forent. Less than an hour after they had been thrust outside, screams had been heard in the hills beyond the town.

When the northerners had started to construct their engines of war, he had known himself doomed. Bringing down one of the towers had been a triumph, but he knew in his heart it would be a short-lived triumph. The Eyrans had all the time in the world, and access to every barn, every herd, every well in the environs of the city. It was a rich agricultural area; they could sit outside his walls for a year or more and experience no greater hardship than a slightly longer walk for provisions as the days spun by. In truth, they did not even need the siege engines. All they had to do was to sit outside his gates for another month, playing their barbarian games with sheeps' knuckles, braiding their hair, sharpening their swords, and the city and its starving populace would be theirs. And all for what? The sake of a strange and beautiful woman who filled men's minds with lust and withheld her bounties from them with a spiteful will. He could hardly think straight anymore, the blood beat so hard at his groin.

It was with dread that the Lord of Cantara rose from his sleepless bed that morning and peered through the window. Outside, dawn tinged the ground fog a cold and ominous red, but even though the chilly mist coated everything with clammy fingers, no sight could have been more delightful to his eyes.

The surviving siege tower lay abandoned, its war platform poking through the surf of fog like the wreck of some great ship. He scanned the horizon, but saw no masts. The cook fires were burned out and blackened; the cauldrons and tripods taken away, the tents dismantled. Even the stockade of cows looted from nearby farms lay unguarded. The cows lowed pitifully to be milked.

Where were the Eyrans?

There was not a single sign of them. They had given up: gone, sailed away. There could be no other explanation.

A huge and oppressive weight seemed to lift from his shoulders, to be replaced by swelling pride. Clearly his gamble with the boiling oil—every drop of cooking oil and lamp oil they had in the city used in a single grand gesture of defiance—had paid off and the enemy had lost heart. He laughed, suddenly joyful and filled with hope. He would surely be hailed as a hero for seeing off the barbarian horde.

This happy thought occupied him thereafter for the rest of the morning: then paranoia descended again. No man would willingly abandon the Rosa Eldi. He had with his own hands killed two guards who had tried to lay hands on her before the siege had begun. He knew her power. And so even as he sent men out to cull the cattle the northerners had left behind and called for a victory feast to be prepared three days hence, he set lookouts on the battlements and kept the soldiers at their positions for three nights to be quite sure that the Eyrans could play no trick upon him and take him by surprise.

On the fourth night, the city of Cera feasted.

And it was on the fourth night that Ravn Asharson made his move.

FESTIVITIES were at their height. The oxen had been roasted, every chicken in the city had been chased and cornered and roasted and stuffed with the last of the preserved figs. The men (no women were present except for three slavegirls who had had to be forcibly encased in their discarded sabatkas before being allowed in the presence of the Lord of Cantara) had drunk the cellars dry and now everyone was in fine voice, extolling the Duke of Cera's bard, who had just performed a fine, self-penned ballad entitled "The Heroic Stand of a Righteous Man" to honor Lord Tycho Issian's victory over the Eyran king. The less drunken among the gathering thought they detected some clever double meanings in the lyrics and were guffawing bawdily at the back of the hall, others were reminded of another song with a most similar tune and refrain, and were debating among themselves exactly what it was the bard had plagiarized, when the great doors opened and two figures stood framed beneath the ornate marble archway with its exquisite figurings of mosaic tile.

A hush fell across the hall. Even the most drunken fell silent and gazed in wonder.

Superficially at least, the two late entrants bore a striking resemblance to one another: both tall and slim and possessed of an almost luminous whiteness of skin. But where one had its long pale hair caught back in a tail, the other wore hers loose so that it cascaded like a waterfall in sunlight across her shoulders and breast. They looked like figures out of legend, out of a different age of Elda; and with good reason.

Together, they stepped over the threshold of the hall and walked with stately grace to the table where sat Lord Tycho Issian, his wine cup halfway to his lips, his eyes wide with surprise.

The Rose of the World came to a halt before the man who had stolen her from the northern king and inclined her head.

"My lord," she said in her soft, low voice, a voice which yet penetrated every corner of the room. "My son and I would speak with you."

Tycho Issian screwed up his eyes in consternation, and in an attempt to focus on the perfect face before him. Damn the wine—and damn the woman for choosing this moment to break her long, self-imposed isolation. Usually so abstemious in his drinking habits, he had allowed himself the luxury of celebration this night of all nights. The release of tension and the devotion of two attentive slave boys had assured his inebriation.

"Your what?"

He had not meant it to come out so belligerently. He watched her eyes fix upon him, glinting, and regretted his haste. Discomfited, he transferred his gaze to the sorcerer, and for the first time saw the likeness. He blinked, looked back at the Rosa Eldi. Truly, now that he saw it, it was uncanny. But the woman before him could be no more than— what?—twenty-three? twenty-four? Her face was unmarked by age; her body unmarked by childbirth. He frowned. It could not be possible.

A riot of thoughts assailed him, topmost of which was that his daughter—out of jealousy or spite—might have lied when she claimed the Rose of the World to be barren. And if she had, then he would have his own son from her after all. He would take her and—

"You are not listening to me."

His head snapped up. The pale woman had said something.

"I regret I did not catch what you said," he apologized carefully, each word an effort.

"I said," she enunciated again, "that your enemies are upon us."

There was a moment's shocked silence throughout the hall; then came a storm of voices.

Tycho Issian lumbered to his feet, the warmth of the wine draining abruptly away. "Here? Now, at this hour?" he slurred.

The Rosa Eldi beckoned him. "Come with me."

He put his hand out to take hers, but she withdrew it quickly. Up the main staircase she led him, till it spiraled around to the front of the castle. There, through the arrow slits she bade him look.

Outside, moonlight gleamed silver on the lake and the sward, lending a glamour to the wreckage of battle. Nothing stirred; or so it seemed. Then the Rose of the World spoke two words and a lucent glow illuminated the great tree. In the darkness, using their axes to make one step after another, a hundred men were scaling the ash's knotty trunk.

"GIVE up your castle to them," she said. "And let us go. It is the only way to avoid further bloodshed."

Tycho Issian staggered backward. "Give up? Let you go?" he echoed. He felt the compulsion she laid on the words nagging at his skull, and knew then that had he been sober, he would have been lost to whatever trickery this was. "Never!" he roared, wine and fury rising in a bloody haze to obliterate whatever cursed magic she was using on him. Before she could step away, he grabbed her by the arms, pulled her toward him and engulfed her lips with his own.

The Rose of the World gasped for breath, taken unawares by this vile assault. Death was upon her, rancid and rampant. She spat out his tongue, wrenched her head away from him, but he was too strong for her, and too drunk to care that he offended her sensibilities; too ignorant to know he held a goddess in his arms.

"You are mine," he told her thickly. "I shall never let you go."

He turned to find the sorcerer appear at the turn in the stairs, his pale face harrowed.

"We must go now," Virelai cried, quailing at the sight of his mother fainting in this monster's grasp. "At once, before he comes . . ."

"He?" An image of Ravn Asharson formed in the Lord of Cantara's mind: a young man, strong and virile and darkly handsome. What had she said of their union—*it was no invasion?* Women were sluts for a handsome face. They'd open their legs in an instant given half a chance. Which was why they must be robed and sequestered and kept well guarded, girded about by scripture and ritual. Well, he would not let this one out of his sight again.

"The Master," Virelai said hoarsely. "We must be away before the Master finds us."

The Lord of Cantara froze. Then, with the Goddess held hard against him with one arm, he struck out with his free hand and caught Virelai an eye-watering blow across the face.

"I am the only master here!" he hissed. Then: "Fetch three robes from the slaves' tiring room—" He indicated a doorway down the corridor.

The Rose of the World twisted out of the Istrian's grasp. She put out a hand to her son's face where the skin showed the livid mark of his assailant's fist. Coolness flowed from her fingertips: when she withdrew it, the cheek was smooth and white once more and there was no pain. "Do as he says," she said softly.

Moments later, three figures slipped out of the castle's postern gate, cloaked in black sabatkas, chill darkness, and the sorcerer's best attempt at a veiling spell.

Escape

"**Y**OU said they'd be here!"

Ravn Asharson turned on the mage with fury in his eyes.

Rahe glared around the deserted chamber, sniffing the air like a dog. "They were, I tell you; I saw them. I even stole up the tree again at sundown to make certain. The door was bound by spellcraft. They had imprisoned themselves against him. I can still smell the magic they used. They cannot have been gone for long."

Ravn sneered. "You lie, old man. You forget that I have just watched you scale this tree with utmost difficulty, and you're still wheezing like an old hound from the effort of it. My mother always said that a man who never takes another at his word is rarely surprised. Now I am beginning to wish I paid better attention to her bitter counsels. But I shall not be surprised again." He eased Trollbiter from its scabbard at his hip.

At this, Rahe put out his hand, and it seemed to all present that the sword in the King's hand became a supple, living thing. It writhed in his grip so that he let go of it in horror. None but Aran Aranson, who knew better by now than to fall for the old man's illusions, heard the clang as metal reverberated off flagstones.

"It pains me to waste my magic," Rahe snarled. He had exhausted himself by the transition from man to mouse and back again; so much so that he knew he could not risk it again for another ascent. His exhaustion made him furious. He made a fist, and the snake became a sword again. Without even a glance at Ravn Asharson, he marched to the door and ran his hands over it, muttering. A few seconds later he stood back, wiping his palms on his robe as if to rid them of another's dirty spellcraft. The door creaked open.

Outside, all was chaos. Word had spread quickly through the Istrian castle, and although none had yet seen hide nor hair of the enemy, panic was rife.

Men ran hither and thither, some armed, most not; many in their best robes, bleary-eyed and stumbling with drink. Women who had not even stopped to don their veils shepherded children bearing great bundles of household goods before them, though where they thought to find safe quarter in a besieged castle, who could say? Servants and slaves scurried among them, trying doors, fleeing down stairways. Some, though, sank down onto the ground and prayed to the Goddess, tripping up others who weren't looking where they were going. Of the soldiery there seemed little sign.

Aran Aranson followed his king down corridor after corridor, and wherever they ran, the inhabitants of Cera fled before them, terrified. At last, however, they came upon one unfortunate member of the city guard who had foolishly got turned around on himself in the maze of passageways and been separated from the rest of his troop. Ravn grabbed him and held him up against the wall by his throat.

"Where is she, my queen, the Rose of the World?" he rasped in Eyran, and the man's eyes went wide with fear. He gibbered something unintelligible, until Ravn repeated his question in the Old Tongue.

"She—she came into the gr–great h–hall," the man stammered. His legs were trembling so hard that if Ravn had let go, he would surely have crumpled. In moments he would wet himself. Aran had seen terror like this before. He looked away, embarrassed for the man.

"When?" Ravn let go the man's throat so he could at least speak.

"O–only minutes ag–go. It was the end of the f–feast. I was on the door, but B–Brina took p–pity on me and brought me some ale. Ev–everyone else was drunk," he added defensively.

"Brina?" Aran Aranson pushed forward. "Did you say Brina?"

Ravn turned on the Rockfaller furiously. "Do not interrupt your king! What care I about this Brina, when I'm looking for my wife?"

"She might be Egg's wife, sire, stolen away in the last war. It's an unusual name—"

Ravn barely paused. He shoved Aran away, then turned back to the guard, who had watched this interplay with apprehension. "And then?"

"Ah . . . and then . . . ah . . . she and the p–pale man, the s–sorcerer, came in and she said to the Lord of C–Cantara, the enemy are upon us, or s–suchlike, and though she said it only to him, we all h–heard, and after that it was m–mayhem."

"And where is she now?" Ravn's clipped tone suggested he was barely keeping violence in check.

"I . . . I d–don't know. She and the L–Lord Issian left the hall t–together."

"Damnation!" Ravn let the man go so suddenly that he lost his footing. Then he ran on down the corridor, shouting for his men to fan out, search all rooms, secure all exits.

Aran dawdled till the rest had gone. Too absorbed in getting to his feet and straightening his uniform, the guard was shocked to find the Rockfaller looming over him. He went paler still.

"Peace," said Aran. "This Brina, tell me, is she an Eyran woman?"

The guard—barely more than a boy, Aran realized belatedly—looked startled. "I . . . I couldn't s–say. She has an odd accent."

"And her age? Could she be fifty or so?"

The lad grimaced. He looked aside, concentrating. "That would be hard to say. Her hands are . . . veined and a little spotted. And her lips are thin, the skin around them pale and a bit puckered."

"You are very observant," Aran said approvingly.

The young man blushed. "I like to draw, sir. I'm not really a soldier. Well, no one is here, not really. We never drill or anything . . ." His hand shot to his mouth. "I also talk too much."

Aran's lips twitched as he fought down a smile. "Well, talk some more, then," he urged. "And then go cast off your uniform and make yourself scarce. Where might I find this Brina?"

The lad shrugged. "In this?" he waved his hand in a gesture which took in the whole castle and all the chaos it contained. "She could be anywhere. But you might try the kitchens, sir. That's where she works . . ."

Aran was not familiar with the layout of castles, but he followed his nose. The kitchens were deserted, which was not entirely surprising, but in the pantry beyond he heard voices. Half a dozen women were in there, all unveiled. One of them was a big woman with short red hair, bright blue eyes, and freckled arms: no Istrian, she. "Are you Brina, Egg Forstson's wife?" he hazarded in Eyran, and watched the woman's jaw drop.

"Egg? Did you say Egg . . . Forstson?"

Aran nodded.

She gaped. Then, "Who are you? Are you with King Ravn?"

Aran grinned. It seemed there were still miracles in the world. He answered all her questions, including the one which made her hands fly to her mouth and tears of joy prick her eyes. Then he asked, "Have you seen a woman called Bera Rolfsen? A beautiful woman, about forty years of age, with a proud face and long auburn hair, very fine skin, small hands, a fierce temper?" He realized by her gentle expression he was letting his tongue run away with him and reined himself in. "She was taken recently, only a few months ago, from the island of Rockfall. Or Katla Aransen, a girl with flame-red hair?"

Slowly, Brina shook her head.

"Did you say Katla Aran—sen?" This other voice was foreign, her Old Tongue sharply accented. Aran craned his neck to see beyond Brina a young woman with sallow skin and long dark hair coiled in braids around her ears. "I have met a Katla. In Forent, it was, at the seraglio there."

Aran felt his heart thump.

"And her mother, too," the woman went on, a crease appearing between her brows. "But she was not called Aransen, I think."

"In my country, we are named for our fathers," Aran said quickly. "Tell me, were they used as whores?"

The woman regarded him oddly. "Not houris, no. Katla she fight like a cat and the lord there like his women softer."

"And Bera? Where are they now?"

The woman spread her hands apologetically. "I do not know, I am sorry."

As abruptly as it had shone, hope died again. He bade Brina wait where she was, to bolt the door and open it only to him or Egg. It had been a long while since Ravn's army had been near women.

ON a hill to the south of Cera, the Lord of Cantara cast off his sabatka. "May the Goddess forgive me for impersonating a woman," he muttered. "It was for the best cause."

The Rosa Eldi inclined her head. "I forgive you," she said tonelessly.

He gave her an odd look. Then he glared at Virelai. "Well now, can you prove yourself truly useful and magic us up some horses?"

Virelai looked panicked. "No, my lord."

"Well, you can leave us, then, if this is the extent of your abilities."

"I think not." The Rose of the World placed a restraining hand on Virelai's arm. "He will stay with me."

"I do not want him here."

"Now that I have found my son, I will go nowhere without him."

Virelai felt a warm glow suffuse him. He did not know what it meant, only that he felt happier than he could ever remember feeling, other than those times in the back of Alisha Skylark's wagon.

Alisha: the death-stone. Panic reared up again, displacing the momentary sense of well-being. He must somehow tell the Goddess about her stone, about Saro Vingo and his quest to find it and save the world. But how could he do so in the presence of the very man he was most terrified of?

The Lord of Cantara was stomping about now, his face thunderous. "I have saved you from the barbarians," he stormed. "And for what? To play nursemaid to your whelp? I want my own son out of you; not one from whatever bizarre union spawned *him.*"

"He is my brother's son," she said softly. "My most beloved brother-husband." It was all coming back to her now, her memory. Over the past few days it had come flowing like a river in spate; it filled her head till she thought she would burst with sorrow.

Tycho Issian screwed his face up in disgust. "Your brother? What revolting perversion is this?" He stared from one to the other. "No wonder he emerged as this pale streak of life. He looks more like a fish than a man. Where I come from, they would have put such a freak of nature out on the hills and let the wolves take him."

The Rosa Eldi raised an eyebrow. "Ah, yes," she said softly. "You have been incarnated this time as a hillman. How interesting. You have hidden your origins well from the people around you, but you cannot hide your essence from me. I know one of my own, though it pains me to lay claim to you."

What had he said? Why had he told her something that might get him burned under the very laws he had himself instigated and enforced? And what did she mean by "this time" and "one of her own?" The woman was mad, her wits turned by her experiences among the barbarians; that would explain it all. But mad or no, he wanted her so badly that it hurt. The touch of her on the castle stairs inflamed him still.

"Claim me as your own, then," he said hoarsely. "Take me here, and now." He began to untie his breeches.

She turned her sea-green gaze upon him and his hand froze in its frenzied unbuttoning. "Falla's Rock," she said. "I shall claim you on Falla's Rock."

He regarded her in horror. "We are nowhere near the Moonfell Plain."

"It is my sacred place."

That stopped him. It was *a* sacred place, certainly, but women were forbidden it. Only the Goddess might set foot on such a holy site. It was the law, the law of sacrilege. However, he considered, laws were made by men, and men could revise them, particularly in such a special case. Perhaps her wits were not entirely fled if she wished to unburden herself of her sins by seeking absolution. As the current head of the Istrian state he could repeal the law, if he wished to—issue an exception for the Rosa Eldi alone. Besides, it would surely bless their union, wipe away all trace of taint from her congress with the northern king. He gritted his teeth. Could he wait that long? A sea passage was the fastest way to the Moonfell Plain from here, but the coast was held by Eyran raiders. By horse then. Across the Skarn Mountains? He shivered.

"We could, I am sure, find a temple near Ixta, and most villages keep their own shrine to the Lady," he offered hopefully.

"Falla's Rock," she repeated obstinately She had her own reasons.

He bowed his head. "How we will get there, I do not know. But if we make it to Falla's Rock, you promise you will take me there and then?"

She smiled. "Oh, yes," she said. "I swear on all that is holy that I shall take you then."

TERROR spread through Cera quicker than plague. With the lord holding a celebratory feast, the last thing anyone had expected was this sudden, violent incursion. Those who weren't too drunk to pick up their weapons in the first place took one look at the rampaging northerners and surrendered. The city fell to the Eyrans with barely a fight.

Once it became clear that the Rosa Eldi, the Lord of Cantara, and the sorcerer Virelai had somehow escaped, Ravn Asharson's temper was terrible to behold. Even the tender sight of Egg Forstson being reunited with the wife he had never thought to see again did nothing to mollify him. If anything, it enraged him further. He stormed around the corridors like a tornado—an arbitrary force of nature which might pass you by with barely a ruffling of the hair on your head, or strike out your life if you got in its way. Even his own men avoided him, crowding in behind him at a distance, scattering if he turned, running like rabbits to his every shouted command.

Aran Aranson took himself off quietly in the opposite direction, left the castle, and went out into the surrounding streets. No invaded town tended to offer pleasant sights, and Cera was no exception. For many, this was their first taste of war; it went to their heads faster than stallion's blood. Everywhere he looked, there was misrule: looting, rapine, fear. He dragged a pair of Fair Islanders off a girl barely old enough to have her courses and berated them soundly. They slunk off like beaten dogs, but he knew they would wait until he was gone and find another woman to hound. Around every corner, another atrocity, another crying child, another pleading man or woman. By the time he came to the streets near the market, he was sick of war, of being Eyran, and a man.

Here, the shutters were up and the place was deserted. But he could feel eyes upon him as he walked across the very square where less than a year before Tycho Issian had stood beside the pale man and his harnessed cat and whipped the crowd to a ferment and cries of holy war. It was a dangerous thing to do. In any town less cowed than this one, he might well feel the sudden impact of an arrow in his back. He walked with his hand on the hilt of his sword and his gaze darting everywhere at once, but no one showed himself. He was about to turn back and retrace his steps to the castle when he heard someone call his name.

His head shot up to meet the sound. The hairs rose down his spine.

It was a woman's voice, and for a second his heart rose into his mouth, thinking it might by some miracle be Bera or Katla, but when he turned to find the window whence it had issued, the face he glimpsed was at that moment unrecognizable to him. Without conscious thought, he found himself running, till the face resolved itself into one he knew well.

It was Kitten Soronsen.

The last time Aran had seen her, she had been parading about in the hall at Rockfall in a pair of exquisitely expensive but ridiculously impractical beaded slippers bought for her by some infatuated young man, her skirts held immodestly high and her laughter ringing off the rafters. She had been then a very pretty girl—Aran was not blind to her attractions, even if he thought her a silly, attention-seeking little minx, with her sharp tongue and her flirtatious glances—but the world had changed shape since then. Her opulent golden hair was lank and stringy, and her face was peaky, her chiseled features made bony by privation and suffering.

"Kitten!"

The warmth in his voice undid her. Tears sprang immediately from those red-rimmed eyes. When she came stumbling out of the door of the rude hovel she had been hiding in, the effects of her captivity became even more evident. She wore a robe of filthy homespun gone to rags at the hem, beneath which her feet were bare and callused. Arms like sticks clutched a swollen belly, and when she saw him looking at this new attribute in silent amazement, she wept even harder.

Then he was across the ground between them in three short strides and holding her close, the bones of her shoulder blades as spiky as chicken wings beneath his soothing hands.

"Oh, Kitten, what has happened to you?" Even as he asked this, he felt dread squeeze his ribs. If Kitten Soronsen, most beautiful of all Rockfall's girls, had been so ill-used, what chance was there for his older wife, or his feisty, intransigent daughter?

The tale she told him between her sobs was a strange one indeed, and though it was a somewhat different version to the story he might have heard from others' lips, still it was most painful and disturbing. Stolen by raiders and brought to the castle at Forent, where the lord was known to have an eye for the exotic, Kitten had for a brief while enjoyed special treatment at the hands of her new master on account of her beauty and spirit. But then he had gone away, and the rest of the stolen Eyran women had been taken out of the castle. She did not know what had become of Bera or Katla, except that they had been sent to the slave market. She had been kept on in the Forent seraglio, but the women there had been spiteful, jealous of her looks and the privileges that Rui Finco had conferred upon her. In addition, they had become uppity of late, and had started to question whether the Lord of Forent had a right to keep them locked away to use for his pleasure or that of his guests; for such was not the way with other women in the world. They had taken to removing their veils in private, and some bolder ones had even refused to wear the traditional sabatka at all, claiming the lovely silk robes were all of men's design, another way to imprison them and keep them in their bondage. Eventually, it seemed, there had been some kind of rebellion in the women's quarters at Forent, and one day they had simply walked out; for security had been lax since the lord had sailed away to war.

Kitten had stayed, not knowing where else to go or what else she might do other than please the noblemen she had been accustomed to serve. Except that they had all sailed away, too, and the only men left in the castle had been the castle staff, all of whom were too shocked by the disappearance of the women and consumed by fear for what their lord might do on his return to care about the fate of one enemy captive, no matter how pretty or well-versed in the arts of love.

For days she had sat in the women's quarters and waited for food and wine to be brought to her at the usual times, but of course, no one had come, and eventually she had been forced to venture out to seek whatever sustenance she could find. She had not made it far. The local militia had taken over the castle and were making the most of its cellars while its lord was absent. Drunken, rowdy soldiers were everywhere. When they had accosted her, she had been haughty with them. That had not sat well with their captain, who had been intensely irked to discover the famed seraglio missing. She would not tell Aran the details of that day, or the long night which had followed.

The next morning, bruised and light-headed with forced wine and sweetsmoke, she had run away, and passed out in the arms of a baker on his way to the market. She had woken in a filthy room, and there the baker's sons had all had their way with her. The baker had kept her tied to the bed for three days. On the fourth, his wife broke the door down, carried Kitten out to the yard, and put her on a nag.

And now . . .

And now, Kitten wept ever more plaintively and could not go on.

"We will get you home safely to Rockfall," Aran promised her kindly. "No one there will judge you for your condition." He did not add "for there is no one there left to judge you," but the words hung on the air between them even so, and Kitten just sobbed the louder.

BY the time Manso Aglio and his men breasted the ridge of the hills overlooking the small town of Vero, in the pretty wine-growing region bordering the White River twenty miles south of Cera, they had accumulated a very significant army. Refugees, starving slaves who reckoned joining up might at least get them fed, ragtag militia bands from the length and breadth of Istria's coastal area—all these had swelled the numbers to over six thousand. Much as Manso would have liked to kick his heels in Vero, which boasted a particularly robust red wine, he knew they would have to move on in a day or two at most, simply because they'd have eaten everything the townspeople had to offer, and all they had hoped to keep in safe storage, too.

On the other hand, the sharp edge of hunger often drove men to braver deeds and a faster result. Maybe it would do no great harm to make Vero a rest stop after their long march. This far inland, the settlements were unscathed by the war, though everyone had a story to tell about relatives on the coast, friends lost, property destroyed, atrocities committed. Manso had heard it all—and worse—before. It had taken him twenty-two years to make captain, and while he'd done his damnedest to avoid any dangerous action in the last war, he'd seen comrades spitted, burned, and hacked to death. Besides, after eight years in the Miseria, nothing surprised him any more about the violence man could do to man—or woman.

He shaded his eyes against the low sun. The town in the valley below looked as picturesque and prosperous as it always had. Smoke rose from chimneys and stretched vaguely out on the still air; rooks stood silent guard in the leafless trees; cows cropped pastures. Excellent, he thought. Roast beef tonight, with trenchers of bread and a thick wine gravy. His mouth started to water.

Something broke the cover of the trees down below, causing the rooks to fly up in a complaining cloud. Manso slipped down from his mount and waved his hand and the men behind him fell silently back below the ridgeline. He moved into the cover of a brake of bracken and watched, curious.

Three figures on horseback. He squinted. They came on up the hill, hugging the edge of the wood, where shadow obscured their identity. But moments later a fence forced them out into the sunlight. and Manso gasped. The first man he knew only too well; and as the riders approached, he soon realized he knew the third figure, too.

"By the Lady—"

He stood up out of the bracken, frowning.

The lead rider stopped dead, turned, and said something to his companions. Then he pressed his mount ahead of the others to greet the man on the horizon.

Tycho stared at the dark, fleshy man before him, searching his memory. He had seen this soldier before, he was sure of it. He smiled uncertainly. After a pause, the man smiled back. His silver-capped teeth gleamed in the sun. "Captain?"

"My lord." Beneath his breath, Manso Aglio swore vilely. Of all the men he had ever worked for, Tycho Issian was the most unpleasant. Apart, he thought unwillingly, from the Vingo boy. He shuddered: a fit ending that one had made. Already his mind was working at speed. If the Lord of Cantara had sent out the bird which had arrived in Forent a fortnight ago from the siege at Cera, then something dramatic must have occurred that he should be here, riding south with only two companions and no guards at all.

"My lord, your bird arrived only a few days ago. We have marched swiftly to relieve the city."

Tycho Issian waved a hand dismissively. "Cera is as good as fallen. You would be wasting your effort."

Manso's eyebrows shot up. "Fallen?" The unspoken question hung heavy on his lips: *Then how did you escape, my lord?*

"The Eyrans overran the city. I managed to rescue this lady and her son before the barbarians could take them."

The captain looked past the nobleman's shoulder to where these two sat their horses. The woman had pulled her veil aside and turned her face up to the sun. Her eyes were closed; she looked blissful. He felt a wave of sudden heat enfold him from the groin upward and could hardly drag his eyes away from her to glance at the man behind her. Now he breathed in sharply, for this one he knew as the sorcerer, Virelai—the man who had stolen his appearance in the attempt to free the other Vingo boy from the dungeons. He had never thought of him as a creature who had been birthed by any mortal means, let alone between the thighs of such a beauty. What misbegotten chance could have thrown such a strange trio together?

Manso beckoned the Lord of Cantara to join him on the ridge. He grinned, indicating the troops below. "As you can see, my lord, I think we should have little trouble taking back the city. We have already repelled the barbarian horde from Forent and its vicinity. Now we can drive the rest of the Eyran scum back into the sea where they belong."

Tycho regarded the vast army, scowling. "I think not."

"Not?"

"You will escort us to the Moonfell Plain."

"Moonfell? Why the Moonfell Plain? There is no need to defend the fairground—it's a wasteland—"

"That's an order, Captain."

Dark thoughts scudded through Manso's head. He could strike this nobleman's head off where he stood. Who would stop him? There was a new order in Istria now, and it had nothing to do with blood lineage and inherited wealth.

Tycho took a step backward, suddenly afraid. The dark thoughts had shown in those wide and brimming eyes, and he had not been mistaken, for now Manso Aglio's hand had traveled to the hilt of his sword. He opened his mouth to cry out, though the one who saved him came as a complete surprise.

The Rosa Eldi, appearing silently at the Lord of Cantara's side, covered the captain's sword hand with her cool fingers.

"You will ride with us to the Moonfell Plain, Manso Aglio. It is my will."

She removed her hand and watched with detached interest as the man's pupils flooded black and a ridiculous smile lit his face.

"I will ride with you through the very fires, my Lady."

"Indeed." She inclined her head, then rode back to where Virelai sat waiting, his face screwed up in concern and consternation.

"Why did you not let the man kill him?" he whispered to her. "Surely that would be for the best."

The Rose of the World smiled enigmatically. "There is a plan and a pattern for all things," she said serenely. "And even Tycho Issian is a part of that pattern."

HIS prize lost to him once again, and apparently gone of her own free will while naming him enemy, Ravn Asharson lost himself for a while in black moods. He allowed his men to rampage where they would; he turned blind eyes toward the violence and excess which surrounded him and drank himself into a stupor night after night. Sometimes he had women of the city brought to him; but they did not look like her, and more often than not, he sent them away. Those he kept expected brutality and rape; what they got was maudlin tears and impotence. Some light in this northern lord, once known as the Stallion of the North, had gone out. He was like a dead man walking.

Between the Living
and the Dead

KATLA Aransen could not even walk—or rather, Saro Vingo would
not let her. What the cat had told him echoed around his skull like a
mantra—*it will not last . . . you do not have our resilience . . . be careful with her*.

Katla had returned to consciousness with a vague sense of something being very wrong, a burning pain in her side, and the ability to
move barely a muscle. For a few terrible seconds she had thought herself paralyzed by whatever blow her demonic brother had dealt her,
though she could remember little of the battle, and nothing at all of
being wounded; then she looked down, and found herself bound hand
and foot. Around her, the red-lit interior of the Mountain of Fire bobbed
and swayed in a hallucinogenic manner. Perhaps she had not woken up
at all; she struggled to do so and the physical effort of it made her yelp
with pain.

Saro, walking ahead of her with her feet drawn up to his shoulder,
turned his head "Stop that!" he demanded, so sharply that she did.

The next voice came from behind her.

"It's for the best, Katla, so that you don't disturb your wounds."

The voice was Mam's, and that the mercenary leader should say such
a thing suggested she was in dire straits, for she knew Mam would sol-

dier on no matter how horrible her injuries, and would expect the same of anyone else.

She examined her circumstances more closely. It seemed they had bound her tight with strips of clothing, cords, anything that came to hand, and splinted the bundle with long swords still in their scabbards so that she could not bend and flop.

A chill spread through her limbs. Abruptly, she was cast back to the weeks following her own burning, when her wrecked hand, bound into a club of bandages, had caused her such agony in both flesh and mind. Then, she had thought herself crippled for life—and that had just been her hand. If her friends had bound her so to save her from these wounds, how much more dreadful must they be?

"Saro—" her voice trembled. She bit her lip to stop the trembling; then started again. "Saro, tell me truly, how bad is it?"

Saro Vingo turned slowly so that she saw his profile, limned scarlet by the volcano's weird light. At this awkward angle, his face appeared haggard and the one eye thus presented red-rimmed and distressed. He seemed unwilling to look at her, and it looked as if he had been crying. That scared her even more.

"Saro—"

"Katla. It's . . . not good. You have a wound in your side which mustn't be disturbed. If you walk, I fear you'll split it open. Bëte licked it till it healed over, but she said it wouldn't hold. We have to get you to the Rosa Eldi if you're to heal properly." Even as he said it, his words rang hollow. It sounded like something out of one of the more far-fetched fairy tales his mother had told him as a child.

This was all too much for Katla. She recalled the sight of the great cat, with its lolling red tongue and gleaming fangs. That . . . beast . . . had licked her wound closed? Now, she wished she *was* dreaming, but if that image was unsettling, the idea of being brought like a slain deer to the woman she had seen in the Halbo court was more disturbing yet. She shuddered.

"No."

"No?"

"I won't be trussed up like a sacrifice and presented to that witch!"

"She's not a witch. She's the Goddess."

"I don't believe in goddesses."

"Or gods? Or sorcery? Or the resurrection of the dead? Katla, you have surely seen too much by now to deny such things?"

She wouldn't answer, just glared at him pugnaciously. After a while she said simply: "Anyway, you don't even know where she is, except somewhere along the north coast. I could be like this for weeks—and what sort of state do you think I'd be in by then? Are you going to unwrap me every few hours so I can piss? Untie me at once. If I can't walk, I'll crawl!"

This volley of words struck him head on. Saro grimaced and glanced back at Mam. The mercenary leader flashed her teeth at him. Then she said, "Girlie, if that's what it takes, I'll do it myself. Saro's right. If you walk, you'll rip the wound open, and that'll be the end of you. I've lost enough of those I care about not to want to lose anyone else." Her regard was stony.

"What do you mean . . . ?" And suddenly Katla was visited by the image of Persoa being hurled against the rocks by the dreadful thing which had once been her brother, and how he had lain there, unmoving. "Ah . . . I'm sorry, Mam, so sorry."

There came a choking sound from behind her head which moments later turned into a sort of strangled cough. Katla felt tears prick her own eyes.

She lay there mute and motionless as they carried her out of the mountain, not daring to ask the questions that plagued her. *Is my brother dead? And Tam Fox, what about Tam Fox?* Had he been a dead man, revived? She had seen him drown, had seen him sink beneath churning waves with her own eyes. And yet he had looked whole and hale, his skin ruddy with the life of the living. She did not know how she felt about the idea of him, alive or dead, though; so she put that thought away. Instead, as though determined not to indulge her wish for avoidance, her mind presented her with the extraordinary sight of the dead down in the fiery pit, digging and unearthing, casting boulders up into the light, apparently excavating a god; and that did not reassure her of her understanding of the world at all. Everything felt like a dream, the worst kind of dream, which returned to haunt the waking hours with ever more graphic memory. But the crimson flare of pain in her side reminded her that consequences had come of this dream, consequences which would prove to be both real and lasting. Nothing would bring back the dead, and she might be joining their long ranks sooner than she had ever planned.

THE long climb left the bearers winded and panting, ready for a rest. But as soon as they emerged from the cave mouth, a woman's voice assailed them.

"Aiee! My son. Aiee!"

The next moment, Katla found herself laid on the ground beside another bundle, one of skin and bones. This bundle had no eyes and no lips. She looked away, repulsed.

"Alisha, Alisha," Saro soothed the woman. "Ah, Alisha. It had to happen. Let him go now."

But Alisha Skylark continued to rock and to keen, the tears running down her face. "He is gone, gone."

Despite the discomfort of lying on the rocky ground, Katla regarded the nomad curiously, having barely registered her presence on the way up the mountain. The skin-and-bone creature must be her son. Her long-dead son. Moved by the woman's distress, she reached out an instinctive hand and gripped her arm. For a moment she was disoriented by the sensation of buzzing, of a vital connection. "We have all lost someone," she said softly.

Alisha's head came up with a start and the tears stopped abruptly.

"What are you?" she cried, jerking her arm out of Katla's grasp. *"Tva sulinni es en serker inni . . . sarinni, dothinni."*

"She is Katla Aransen, my friend from the Northern Isles," Saro explained as gently as he could. It seemed the loss of Falo had finally turned her wits. "And she is badly hurt." He dropped to his knee beside the nomad woman. "Alisha, I know you to have great skill with herbs and plants—would you look at her wound?"

The nomad woman turned huge dark eyes upon him. "Will you use the eldistan for my son if I do?"

Saro shook his head. "No, Alisha," he said firmly. "You know I cannot."

She crossed her arms. "Then I cannot help you."

Saro sighed. He looked at Mam. The mercenary leader shrugged. "Every moment wasted is a moment wasted," she said enigmatically.

"Come with us, Alisha," Saro urged. "Come away from here. We are going back into the world now. If you stay here, you will die."

For a moment that sun-blackened face looked sly and thoughtful. Then, "I will follow you," she said simply. "Let me be with my son for a little while longer. I will follow you down."

THEY left the nomad woman and carried on down the rocky path, trying not to jounce Katla Aransen too brutally. It was hard going, for although gravity was with them, the light was not. By the time they made it into the steep defiles which gave out into the rambling, thorn-filled foothills of the Dragon's Backbone, they could hardly see anything. The night air wrapped around them, thick with sulfur and the trapped heat of the day.

Once, Saro lost his footing in the scree and Katla hit the ground with a jolt that made her cry out in pain. After that, he took it more slowly, sliding each foot in turn. Rocks skittered away down the slopes, smashing into each other, before fetching up at the bottom with a crash. Saro shuddered. If he weren't more careful, all three of them would go the same way.

On the ashy lower slopes the fumy air cleared, allowing the moonlight to show them easier paths, and after that they made better progress.

By the time they reached the parched little oasis where they had left the horses, all three felt dry as bone both inside and out. There, Saro and Mam released Katla from her bonds and laid her in the soft sand, then went to fill the waterskins with what little moisture remained in the tiny pool. The horses whickered at the sight of them, as if reassured to see normal human life after the bizarre comings and goings of the past few days. They made a sparse meal of bread that had gone so hard in the hot, dry air that it was impossible to chew unless mixed with the muddy water of the oasis, and a handful of dried fruit. Then Saro refastened

Katla's ties in case she thrashed while she slept, or—more likely—tried to get up and walk; and at last all three fell asleep, side by side in the maram grass.

THE next day, Katla was worse. She moaned in her sleep and would not wake properly. When Saro pressed his hand against her forehead, it felt hot and sticky to the touch. He said nothing to Mam, but she could tell by the tight line of his mouth just how worried he was by this. He scanned the rocky channels leading up the mountain for Alisha Skylark, for if anyone knew best how to tend a fever, it was a nomad healer; but there was no sign of her and eventually he gave up looking.

He spent a long hour trying to rig up some sort of frame whereby they might drag Katla across the desert behind the horses, but when he lay in it and had Mam draw him along to test it out, he felt every small unevenness the ground had to offer as a jolt in the spine which radiated out to jar every other bone in his body and knew that it would never do. Instead, he unwrapped Katla from her bindings, discarded the two swords and had Mam hand her feverish body up to him as he sat astride the nervous bay. Cradling Katla thus, with her head tucked beneath his chin and the feel of her silky hair against his skin, felt like an invasion of her private space, but he could see no alternative. Even so, when Mam offered to do the same after several hours of riding, Saro found himself shaking his head. "It's all right," he murmured. "I don't mind, though we should perhaps exchange mounts after our next stop to equal out the weight they bear."

Far from minding, he found it comforted him to have Katla so close that he could smell the muted spice of her sweat, feel the way her spine curved into his ribs with every breath she took. At least he knew she was still alive. Besides, if she woke up suddenly, disoriented, she was likely to struggle, and with Mam withdrawn into her grief he trusted only himself to maintain a sufficient vigil to save Katla from what might prove to be a fatal fall. Although, if she woke up with his arms around her, he suspected she might hurl herself from the horse out of sheer fury.

Into the oven of the desert they rode all day and on into the night, for the moon was waxing and shone brightly here where no clouds obscured its face, and it made sense to cover as much ground as they could while conditions were good. As they rode, Saro dreamed. His eyes were open and his body was aware of every tiny movement Katla made, but still he dreamed. He dreamed of a house made from boulders of granite, with walls so strong and thick that no one could shake or burn it down. Golden lichen grew on the slates of its roof where jackdaws chattered companionably; bright flowers for which he knew no name bloomed by its door. A rosy light lit the scene, as if the sun were westering, and when in his dream he turned, it was to find Katla Aransen walking up the hill toward him, her red hair falling loose to her waist, her wide mouth stretched in a delighted smile and her hands full of striped fish which she held out to him, as if offering him the bounty of the world. Behind her, small boats bobbed on a tranquil sea, and gulls cried overhead.

Tears began to stream down his face.

A little later, Katla moaned and twisted in his grasp, waking him fully, so that he clutched onto her with a reflex which made her cry out.

"Ssh, Katla, shh. It's all right. You're safe." As he said it, he wished it so with all his heart.

"Where are we?" She opened startled eyes and stared around, bewildered and afraid. "I dreamed I was being drawn down into the mountain's fires with a red sword by my side. I dreamed that the dead kept falling in on top of me, and that I was dead, too—"

"We are riding north through the Bone Quarter. No winds yet—we have been fortunate. We will keep riding while we are able. We need to get you to a place of safety."

Katla stopped her feeble struggling. "You've held me all this way?" she asked, turning so that she could look into his face.

Moonlight silvered Saro's eyes, moonlight or tears. He nodded mutely. That she had not immediately flown into a temper was proof enough if he needed it of the poor state she was in. "How are you feeling?" he asked gruffly when he had mastered himself sufficiently to speak.

Katla frowned. She closed her eyes. "I don't know. Something hurts, a dull throb like a fist clenching and unclenching deep inside me."

Saro freed one of his hands and brought it around to feel her forehead. It was burning more than ever, despite the chill of the desert night.

BEFORE noon the next day, having ridden as far as they could without rest, they drew the horses to a halt in the shade of a towering barchan dune. Here, they would be out of the sun till it swung around the shoulder of the dune, which might take some hours, long enough to feed and water the horses and to snatch some sleep.

The animals ate the parched grasses Mam had gathered at the oasis without complaint, though they shuffled their feet and threw their heads up when they were gone.

Having made Katla as comfortable as he could manage, Saro sat down beside her for a while and watched her as she slept. Beneath the thin, finely veined skin, her eyeballs darted back and forth in an agitated manner. Somewhere deep in that lovely skull she was dreaming again, and her dreams were disturbing. Sweat had burst out on her face once more; Saro felt the now-familiar dread grip his chest. Eventually, he could bear to watch over her torments no longer. Curling himself into a ball beside her, he closed his eyes.

The sound of a horse's neigh brought him to semiconsciousness. He lay in the shadow of the dune with his eyelids squeezed shut against the light and waited for the sound to repeat itself. When it didn't, he drifted back into a listless sleep in which it was impossible to stay comfortable for more than a few moments at a time and he dreamed that he could see the bones through Katla's skin and that the death-stone was glowing at his chest, urging him to use it.

Something touched him, tickling at his neck. He waved a hand at it distractedly and it went away. An insect, he thought sleepily, and turned onto his side.

A few minutes later it came again, brushing his collarbone, just inside the collar of his tunic. This time, more by instinct than judgment, his hand flew up to grasp whatever it was which disturbed his rest. His fingers closed on something hard and thin and determined. Someone yelped. Without letting go, he sat bolt upright.

"Alisha!"

The nomad woman bent over him, her eyes huge in the dying light of the day, but whether her expression was one of fear or fury at being thwarted in her quest, it was impossible to tell. How could one read an expression on a face worn almost to the bone by exhaustion, privation, and hurt, a face dried nearly to leather by the harsh air of desert and volcano? Whatever life was left in her seemed to be reserved deep inside, driven by the obsessive love she felt for her dead son. He pushed her away gently, relaced his tunic. The death-stone glowed against his skin, its wan light picking out the weave of the linen. So that part had been no dream.

"Please give it to me." Her voice was the fragile rasp of a moth's wing against a lamp. "I need it for Falo."

What could he say that he had not already said? She was beyond all reasoning. He looked over her shoulder, to find three horses tethered to the long knife Mam had driven deep into the sand where before there had been only two. One of them was bigger, darker, and more nobly proportioned than the others. He shivered. How the stallion had survived so long without contact with the stone, he could not imagine. He had been an iron-willed beast at the best of times, a born racer, a determined competitor. The fiery light of his will to survive against every odd glowed like an ember in the pit of the one eye he could see.

Across his back lay a carefully secured bundle. Saro sighed. When Alisha had not appeared while they were at the oasis, he had hoped she was making her final farewell to the boy, but that had clearly not been the way of it. He got up now, jaw set, and stalked over to Night's Harbinger. The other horses stood at the farthest extent of their tethers to the stallion, their eyes rolling. He did not blame them: such close proximity to the dead was enough to turn the gentlest creature wild.

With shaking fingers, he undid the straps which held Falo's corpse across the horse's withers, then he carried the pathetic bundle away into the desert. Alisha wailed and ran after him, only to be met by Mam, a solid wall of muscle. "Enough of this," said the mercenary leader. "We'll keep the horse till it drops; but the world has taken back your boy and you must let him go."

Saro buried the tiny body far out in the sands, as deep as he could manage with no better tool than a belt knife and dagger. He spent a long time gathering whatever rocks he could find and piling them on top of Falo's corpse. The grave might not withstand the worst sandstorm; but it should hold the boy till they were far enough away that Alisha could not scrabble him up again.

ALL night the nomad woman raved and wept, and there being no rest to be had while this was the case, they rode till dawn. As time passed she quieted, as if the distance spooling out between mother and son had a direct correlation on her state of mind. By afternoon she seemed withdrawn but less mad, and she slept when they made camp.

THE next day, when Saro held his waterskin to Katla's lips, she drank down three mouthfuls, then choked and coughed so violently that she spat up blood. She told him it hurt to breathe. He was aghast, but tried not to show it. He left her propped carefully against his pack and went to find Mam, who shook her head.

"That's a bad sign, lad," she said, shaking her head sadly. "It'll be an infection that's spread, or an internal injury making itself known. She'll not make it out of the desert. Better prepare yourself for that."

He went off and sat by himself in a steeply carved wadi where the shade was deep and cool and tried to think what to do. They were covering the ground as fast as they could, and still the desert stretched out around them, pitiless and unending, as far as the eye could see in all directions. But the Dragon's Backbone was sharply etched against the southern horizon and certainly seemed to be diminishing. Surely they would clear the sands in the next day. And if they didn't, and Katla continued her descent? He knew he could not simply let her die. He had seen Virelai cure with the stone, but could he harness its power to the good? He shut his eyes and tried to fend off the panic that came for him, knowing that he was not strong enough. "How I wish you were here, Virelai." It was no more than a murmur, but it did not go unheard.

"Virelai?"

Alisha Skylark stood at the top of the wadi, looking down. In the clear light her eyes were like cut turquoises, pale against the darkness of her face.

"Is he still alive?" She asked this with the inquisitiveness of the genuinely curious, her attention riveted on him.

"Yes," said Saro, remembering how close-lipped the sorcerer had been about the woman he had once loved and the circumstances in which they had parted. Now he knew more of that story, he could understand why Virelai had reacted so. "Yes, when I left him in Jetra, he was alive and well."

She sat down, her legs swinging over the edge of the channel's wall. "I loved him, you know."

"And he loved you. I am sure you will meet again."

She shook her head. "He hates me now." She paused. "And fears me, too. I used the death-stone on him, you know. Brought him back again."

"He was dead?" Saro was horrified.

She nodded, her gaze hooded. "His story was already strange beyond measure, but I could not bear to see him like that, with his beautiful eyes all filmed over and the blood caked in his hair. He did not thank me for raising him."

"When I last saw him, he healed me," Saro told her. "My hands and feet were mostly gone, I was dying of my own putrefaction and despair, and he healed me. A golden light came out of him. He looked as if he were brimming over with it."

She smiled, and the wizened face was suddenly transformed so that for a moment he could see a glimpse of her old beauty there. Perhaps sustenance and rest and distance from the madness behind them would restore it; perhaps it would restore them all. Except Katla.

As if she read his mind Alisha said suddenly, "The girl with the red hair, she is dying, is she not?"

Saro nodded miserably. "I don't seem to be able to do anything for her." He met her eyes. "And I will not use the stone."

She held his gaze steadily. "I know," she said softly. "It is a terrible object, and it turns a weak hand to terrible deeds. But I am ready now to do the thing you asked of me. On the mountain."

"You will look at her wound?"

She spread her hands. "I do not have much with me, except my knowledge and a few simples I rescued from . . ." She bit her lip.

With vivid clarity, Saro remembered the contents of the wagons strewn across the river plain, beside the torn and bleeding bodies left by the militia.

"I am not sure they will be enough."

But Saro was already on his feet.

UNWINDING the last bandage from Katla's abdomen, Alisha let out a great pent-up breath. The skin around the wound was livid and raised with heat. Closer in, it was yellow and sticky and blood had dried black beneath the strange film of skin which covered the worst area, where the exposed gut could be seen purple and convoluted beneath. It was beginning to stink.

She listened to Katla's heart and found a staccato beat. Her head came up from the girl's rib cage quickly and her expression was pained. "Not natural," she said softly. "Not natural at all." She didn't expand on this, and when Saro asked her what she meant she waved him away. "Boil me some water," she ordered. "Just a little. Boil it, then let it cool a while, and bring it to me then."

He did as he was told, glad to have a simple task to take his mind off what he wished he had not seen.

When he returned, she had taken a few things from her pack: a mortar and pestle, some packets of linen tied with grass stems, a long pewter spoon. She sorted through the parcels, sniffing each in turn till she found the one she wanted, and this she opened up with careful fingers. Inside lay a bundle of dead plants, gone desiccated so that they crumbled at her touch. They looked like mint, Saro thought, his hope failing suddenly.

"What is it?" he asked.

"Common prunella," she told him, which meant less than nothing. "The nomads call it self-heal. Canny soldiers carry it with them to war because it is well known for helping the body to heal inner wounds. If I give it to her as a syrup, it will cleanse the foulness out of her, and if I dress the surface with a paste of it, that will help, too. Once the infection's dealt with, her fever should break of its own accord. Then there's the goat's rue."

That sounded unpleasant. Saro watched her work, grinding the herb to a paste with a little of the water, then adding some berries from her pack. When the syrup was ready, she got him to sit Katla up, and while Mam held her head like a vice, spooned the liquid down, Saro held Katla's nose and mouth closed till it was gone and she could not cough it up. The rest was cooled and applied to the wound. Alisha got Mam to bandage the girl up, claiming her own weakness. "I'll never get them tight enough," she said. "And now I must address the lungs."

She smelled her way through her simples again, looking dissatisfied. She opened one bundle, only to discard it with a muttered "too dry" and took up another with a sigh. "Harshweed," she told a curious Saro. "It is not what I'd choose, but the mullein's gone to dust."

Inside this packet was a tangle of dark stems and a pile of purple flowerheads. Saro picked one up and sniffed it. "I know this one!" he said suddenly. "It grows on the hills near Altea."

"It'll grow in most hilly pastures so long as there's chalk underneath," she told him. "I got this in Faurea before—" she stopped.

Saro dropped his eyes.

She he boiled it up and strained it, boiled and strained again until it made a thick liquid of an indeterminate color he would not have expected at all from the hue of the flowers. It smelled horrible. She gave the resulting decoction over to him. "You'll have to sacrifice a waterskin to this," she said. "She'll need a good measure of it three times a day for several days if it's to make a difference. And that's your job," she added tartly.

Saro watched her as she packed her things away again. "You don't want to touch her, do you?" he accused.

All she gave him in reply to this was a hooded look.

WHATEVER Alisha Skylark had administered to Katla seemed to take effect a day later as they cleared the last dunes of the great desert and emerged into the wilderness of stone and scrub which bordered it. The patient was sleeping without taking the noisy, shallow breaths they had been accustomed to hear rasping through the night; and her temperature was lower. Mam, who had dressed a hundred battlefield wounds in her time, took to changing the dressings on Katla's, and proclaimed that the lividity was paling and the swelling was down. "She might yet live," she told Saro with her characteristic unsettling grin.

The nomad woman regarded the Eyran girl with her head on one side and a small smile. She had been riding up and looking at her so as much as seven or eight times a day, Saro noticed, and the smile seemed a sign of her professional pride in the results of her dosings. Working as a healer again seemed to have healed some hidden part of herself. She did not mention Falo again, though sometimes her eyes went cloudy and she allowed the stallion to fall back behind the others, lost in contemplation.

At night, the stars shone so brightly it was hard to look at them. Falla's Eye beamed down, a beacon for their journey. They had been lucky with the conditions in the desert, but life had taught Saro too many hard lessons for him to trust that all would be well.

The Call

AMID the atrocity of war, as many of Cera's inhabitants as could fled from the city, terrified for their lives, with no idea of where to go. Some wandered pathetically around the hinterland, sleeping in barns and out-buildings; some marched with hatred in their hearts and revenge fuel-ing their steps until they fell in with others of like mind, intent on a battle to drive the enemy from their shores for good and all.

But others heeded another call, a silent call which seemed to be borne on the air or in the stones of the ground; these folk would stop in the middle of whatever they were doing and find that their thoughts turned to that strange ashy wasteland which lay to the north and west of Cera as the crow flies, which they could not. Nothing tangible could be offered at the end of such a journey, for nothing lived there, nor was it habitable; yet those who opened their hearts were filled with certainty that hope awaited them in that place where their nobles and merchants met each year to trade and to gossip, to arrange marriages and settle lawsuits. The common ground: the Moonfell Plain.

Where, as one heresy had it, the goddess Falla and her cat would sit upon her rock and sing to the moon, whence the rock had fallen, to fetch them back; or, as another of the heresies told, where Falla and her husband-brother Sirio had come together in a mystical union with the great cat—Man, Woman, and Beast: the Three as One—to defeat Death himself and bring magic into the world. So many folk had burned for speaking of that old tale that few now recalled it. Sirio had long ago been written out of the old legends of the south, transformed from seed-giver to warrior to minor deity and at last to oblivion, as Falla had in the north, each culture embracing one aspect and one alone.

To reach their destination, these travelers were forced to head first south and then cut back sharply west and north around the deep incut where the Northern Ocean penetrated the Istrian mainland, for the Eyrans held the coastal sea, which offered the easiest route.

There they met other travelers, fleeing from Sestria and Ixta, from Hedera and Forent. Ahead of them lay the Skarn Mountains, at this season wild with blizzard and treacherous with avalanche. Yet none turned back.

From the Blue Woods they came, on horses, on mules, on yeka and wagons, on foot. Merchants and factors, peasants and townsfolk, carpenters and fishermen, artisans and slaves, nomads and magic makers, herbwives and healers. From Pex and Talsea and far Cantara; from Gila and Circesia; from Gibeon and Altea, Galia and the Eternal City of Jetra they came. They traversed the wide open spaces of the southern plains, they crossed deserts and scrublands, rocky hills and rolling fields. None made the journey in dread for their lives, though the hazards were clear and present. Some spoke of dreams or omens; others merely smiled to themselves, as if they had received a visitation and their fate was no longer their own.

They all had odd stories to tell: of birds flying north at the wrong time of year, of bears and horses traveling in concert with wolves and hares; of the dead walking; of a golden giant accompanied by a huge cat striding across the horizon.

Farther south, some weary travelers coming north out of the Bone Quarter had the luck to fall into company with a pious merchant and his family who owned a goods barge on the Golden River and were heading with all speed and no cargo for the northern coast. Two of the band were fit enough to lend a hand with the lock system and the steering. Out of sight, the wife made the sign against the evil eye when she saw the nomad woman, but when the healer cured her warts, she was all smiles. The fourth member of this group lay like one dead; secretly, the merchant expected to pitch her over the side by Talsea, or Pex at the latest.

The summons—if summons it was—traveled well beyond Istria. Far to the north, on the isles of the kingdom of Eyra, old men laid down the nets they were mending and listened intently, as if there was a voice on the wind, or in the mist roiling in off the sea. Children stopped playing and cupped their ears, or lay on the ground as if in a dream. Women hanging out the washing or breaking down grain with mortar and pestle closed their eyes, brows faintly wrinkled, as if they were concentrating.

A group of women from the villages between Ness and Blackwater set out to sea in the fishing vessels which had been beached while their husbands were at war. "We are promised a fair passage," Hesta Aralsen answered mysteriously when her cousin Merja queried the wisdom of traversing the Northern Ocean without a navigator or even a man aboard. "We will know the way."

Elderly merchants found themselves dreaming of the old crossing between Halbo and the Moonfell Plain, the pattern of stars clear in their heads, the urge to voyage still with them when they woke. Some acted on this urge; others did not. Families drew lots as to which members would sail and which would stay behind to care for the stock and the farms, the children, and the old. An extraordinary flotilla left Eyra's mainland: grand old trading barges and knarrs; fishing boats with worn, patched sails, ketches and skiffs. No craft seemed too mean or too small to join the call. Even some of the ships which had recently returned from the Southern Empire with their holds stuffed with goods unloaded at the docks, took on provisions, and turned south again.

Not everyone made their way to Moonfell buoyed up by anticipation and hope. For as many who heard and heeded the call in both Eyra and Istria, there were those who closed their hearts and clung to long-cherished beliefs and hatreds which made a sure and undeniable framework for the world, beyond which all was chaos and unreason. These girded on their swords, took up spear and shield, and mounted horses, or marched or sailed to confront the old enemy.

By the last days of Elda's winter, almost thirty thousand people were converging on the Moonfell Plain.

Moonfell

VIRELAI gazed at the serried ranks of peaks which stretched away from them, losing clarity in the distance to merge with the sky in a dreamlike haze. He felt much the same way himself, someone with a foot in two worlds, neither of which claimed him fully. He was a man, raised by a mage as a servant—but it also seemed he was a son to gods. What did that make him? He did not know, and found that the concept would not bear long or sane scrutiny.

Ahead, beyond the long column of army which marched in front of them, a distant col announced the start of the steep defile which would lead them down onto the Moonfell Plain.

The last time he had traveled this route across the Skarn Mountains, it had been in the joyous company of nomads on their way to the Allfair. With the Rosa Eldi and her cat—two of Elda's most powerful entities, had he but known it—stashed in the back of his wagon. Much of that leisurely time he had spent with Alisha and known the comfort of human warmth, of skin against skin, and had truly thought himself free of the destiny from which he had escaped. How different things were now.

They had stopped for no more than a few hours since they had set out on this journey. He ached from head to foot, but even his mount did not seem to wish for rest. Ears pricked, head constantly fighting his hand on the reins, it seemed eager for their destination. Or perhaps, Virelai considered, the horse felt the draw of the Rose of the World as did the men who rode beside him, their eyes fixed to the length of that slim back and the way her slight haunches sat the sturdy pony which bore her.

Every so often she would turn in the saddle and survey them and the army which straggled behind them with an unfathomable expression which lay, to Virelai's mind, somewhere closer to satisfaction than to any other emotion he could name. Her green eyes, so startling in that pale oval face, would skim over them and she would smile minutely before turning her face to the northern horizon once more, her silver-gold hair rippling like a waterfall down her back. And when Virelai glanced sideways, he would find Manso Aglio's ugly visage stretched in the most gormless grin, and Tycho Issian's straining with impatience.

But there came a time when she turned to them, her eyes shining with an excitement which seemed to crackle off her frame.

"He is coming!" she breathed. And she threw her head back and laughed, a sound which rang off the rocky peaks like an echoed shout of triumph.

Manso Aglio turned to the Lord of Cantara. "Who does she mean?" he whispered, not knowing why he lowered his voice so.

Tycho gritted his teeth. "Who do you think, you fool? Ravn Asharson, of course. The bloody Stallion of the North."

"WHY in the name of all that is holy would they be trekking an army through the Skarn Mountains?" Ravn Asharson rubbed a hand across wine-bleared eyes and stared at the man who had brought this news.

The Earl of Stormway shook his head. "I have no idea. But that is not all."

And then he told the King of Eyra how scouts had reported other movements, and not just troops either.

"The Moonfell Plain, Ravn. They're all heading for the Moonfell Plain."

The king frowned. It was where it had all begun, where he had first laid eyes of the woman whose loss haunted him by day and night; and where the war over her had truly started. So the Lord of Cantara thought to make the final battle a symbolic gesture, did he? He shoved himself to his feet, stood there swaying unsteadily, and the flask from which he had been swigging fell and spilled its contents. Blood-dark, the wine pooled out across the flagstones, a great liquid shadow to the man standing over it.

"Have the fleet made ready, Bran. We sail for the Moonfell Plain on the next tide!"

Stormway left the chamber with the sigh of a man saddled with a logistical nightmare.

LATER that morning they overtook the first caravan of travelers—a ragtag collection of folk: some nomads, some Istrian peasants, women without veils, men in homespun or rich robes, all weaponless.

The people they passed could not drag their eyes away from the woman who rode with this great army. They gazed in wonder at her, their expressions rapt. She, in turn, smiled upon them.

In contrast, Tycho Issian stared at them in disgust: the dregs of the earth, they were, the scum which had escaped his fires. Had he not been in such a hurry, he would have had them all scoured from the face of Elda. "Out of the way!" he yelled intemperately and lashed about him with his whip.

One thong caught a woman across her exposed face, as he had thought it might, cutting a deep scarlet line from cheek to jaw, and the creature fell to her knees with a shriek.

"Had you dressed with the modesty that befits a woman of my land, that would not have happened. Take it as a lesson!" he hissed, wiping clean the whip on his horse's mane.

But the Rose of the World slipped from her mount and crossed to the woman's side. "Take heart," she said softly, and cupped the welling cheek in the palm of her long hand. When she removed it, there was blood on her fingers, but none on the woman; even the line of the cut was fading. The Rosa Eldi laid her hand upon the white silk of her robe. Then she turned to Tycho Issian, her eyelids flat with loathing. Upon her belly the perfect imprint of a bloody hand was clearly marked for all to see.

"Harm my people, and you harm me," she told him with cold fury. She walked to her mount. The horse—a pied beast of blotched black and white, with an unruly eye and vile yellow teeth—whickered gently and nosed at her, unsettled by the sudden smell of gore. Then it sank down onto its hocks so that she might take her place in the saddle with grace and ease.

All around, the travelers murmured in awe; behind them, the soldiers craned their necks for a view of the pale woman. She was a rare one—you could hardly blame the Lord of Cantara for his interest.

Tycho Issian looked aside. He had seen the hatred in her eyes. A tiny spark of survival instinct suddenly nagged at him to abandon his course, to let her go where and with whom she would, while he was able, before it was too late, but his grand obsession stifled its cry at birth. On they rode, north, to the doom of the world.

ACROSS the wide mouth where the Golden River gave itself up to the mercies of the Northern Ocean, the shapes of many ships were silhouetted against the skyline. Katla Aransen struggled weakly up onto an elbow and stared at one in particular, taking in its brutish prow head, with its gaping mouth and serrated teeth, and the powerful lines of its hull.

"That's the *Troll of Narth*," she whispered. "I'd recognize it anywhere."

The merchant and his wife were hiding in the brig. The sight of an Eyran longship—no matter how legendary—did not fill *them* with delight. For his part, Saro Vingo gazed about in amazement. Elsewhere, all manner of other craft were converging upon the sea lanes heading west.

Mam, at the wheel, narrowed her eyes. "Something very strange is going on," she opined with less than remarkable insight.

"Strange indeed," said Katla, lying down again, every movement an effort, "for the *Troll* to have survived an ocean-crossing. They must be desperate for ships in Eyra if they're reduced to using the oldest vessel in the Isles."

Alisha smiled. "Moonfell," she said softly. "They are all heading for the Moonfell Plain."

Saro sighed. He had traveled this same route the previous year to his first Allfair. It felt an age ago, and he was far from the innocent, hopeful boy he had been then.

"I can feel it," Katla said suddenly. She closed her eyes. Sweat had beaded on her forehead. Her cheeks were sallow.

Saro experienced yet another stab of concern. "Your wound? It's hurting you?" He touched her shoulder, wishing for the first time that Guaya had not taken back her gift. He suspected Katla Aransen of dangerous stoicism where her injuries were concerned, for she rarely complained.

Katla's eyes snapped open. "The Rock, you idiot. I can feel the Rock."

And Saro was cast back to that first morning at the Fair, when he had stumbled out among the booths while the rest of his family were still snoring off the araque binge of the night before and been gifted with a vision: a girl whose skin shone gold in the sunlight, whose red hair made a nimbus around her head; a girl wearing, in Istrian terms, hardly anything at all, in that most sacred and forbidden of places on top of Falla's Rock. He smiled at her now, not even minding that she had called him "idiot." "I remember the Rock," he said quietly.

When she smiled back at him, he felt engulfed by flame, just as he had been that first time. "I shall climb it again," she declared; and abruptly his heart fell into a cold chasm, for he knew that her smile had been for the memory of the climb, and not for him at all. Knew, too, with a terrible leaden certainty, that she would never climb anything again. She was dying, though the fact of it went unsaid. He withdrew his hand.

"Not in your condition."

Katla made a face. He was right, she knew. She could feel the twist and pull of the wound, the wrongness of it. Once, when Mam's attention had been diverted by the overhead flight of geese heading north, she had steeled herself to look at the wound and had pulled the bandages away. That night, when the rest were asleep, she had wept until dawn.

"No," she whispered. "Not like this." And she turned her head away from him, her features pinched shut with misery.

"GOD'S prick, this armor chafes!"

"They don't cater for dwarves in the Istrian militia."

"Who are you calling dwarf, you overgrown bull's pizzle?"

Words could rarely make Joz Bearhand rise to the bait. He grinned. "It was your idea to join up with this lot," he reminded.

"Fat lot we've got to show for it." This last speaker was a tall, gaunt man with a skullcap and a lantern jaw. "We missed out at Forent, never got near Cera, and there's bloody scant pickings here." He cast his eyes mournfully over the landscape, kicked up a cloud of dust. "Unless you can find me a merchant with dung for brains and a fetish for ash."

"I thought there'd be whores."

"Dogo, you're an idiot. There's only whores here during the Allfair."

"How long do we have to wait for that, then?"

Doc rolled his eyes. "Somehow, I don't think there's going to be one here this year."

"Why are we here, anyhow?"

Joz shrugged. "To fight? It's generally what we do."

Dogo stared around. "Who shall we start with, then? That bunch of matrons over there?" He indicated a gaggle of women trying to drag their wagon out of the way before the track ran into a deep defile. Its back axle was broken, the wheels splayed apart. The column passed, stepping around it, no one stopping to help. "Or them?" A crowd of old men, some nomads and children, yeka, horses, dogs, and what looked a pair of wolves. *Surely not?* He shook his head and turned back. "Now this lot look more promising."

Doc shaded his eyes. "Isn't that—?"

Joz Bearhand swore horribly. "It's that bastard Tycho Issian," he pronounced.

"What, the one who's been burning Footloose the length and breadth of Istria?"

"The very same."

"Waste of good women."

"Women, men, children, Wandering folk, herbwives, hillmen, healers, heretics—anyone whose face didn't fit. An affront to human life, that one." Doc spat in the dust at his feet.

"Waste of good spit, that. My throat's so dry I'd roast a nomad myself if it'd earn me a decent ale . . . ow!"

Dogo's chinstrap broke under the impact of Joz's hand and the helmet went rolling off down the mountainside. The little man stepped to the edge of the trail to watch it bounce several times and come to a halt in the scrub grass at the bottom.

"Ah well, it's no great loss. Rubbish, these Istrian helmets are."

He turned back to his companions, just in time to see the arrow lodge in Doc's eye.

"TO me, to me!" The Lord of Cantara's voice shrieked over the whistle of arrow-flight, over the screams of injured horses and the cries of dying men falling around him. "Protect the lady!"

The Rosa Eldi stared around, eyes wide in bewilderment and horror. The ambush had been so swift— Her horse skittered suddenly as the man next to her howled in agony and fell sideways, half in and half out of his saddle.

"Virelai!" she cried.

But Virelai was gone, his mount taking flight in its terror, its rider flopping this way and that like a straw doll tossed into rapids. The Rose of the World kicked her own horse, and the black and white lifted its head and took off after the bay.

When Tycho looked back, she was gone, already fifty yards away, the piebald horse a moving patch of light and shadow amid the welter of bodies. Panic seized him. He drew his sword and flourished it wildly. "To me!" he cried again. "Follow her!"

Direct progress was difficult. Everywhere before them was chaos, as travelers and wagons, horses and dogs, wolves and goats and cats impeded both the Eyran attackers and the Istrian pursuers. Noncombatants scattered in all directions, screaming. Tycho hacked at them mercilessly. "Get out of the way!" His sword made brief, brutal contact and an arm flew overhead, spraying him with gore. The man to whom it had once belonged—an elderly nomad, separated from his small group—watched it in puzzlement, then crumpled to the ground.

BLOOD was in the air, in the ground: you could smell it, the iron-sweet tang of it. The lady was close, but there was a heaving melee all around her. Beyond, he could see the southern lord battling his way toward her like a man possessed, with half the Istrian army at his heels. Aran Aranson assessed the situation swiftly. It had started as a reconnaissance mission, an advance scouting party sent on to see what they could see, return silently, and report back, but when they had got to the top of the ridge, they had been amazed to find the enemy almost upon them. An ambush had seemed too good a chance to miss, the defile a perfect situation for a surprise attack. All they had to do was to create sufficient confusion, separate the Rose from the Istrians, carry her off back to Ravn, and make sail back to Eyra. Audacious and opportunistic, it might have made him the hero of the hour, but the situation was becoming more foolhardy by the second.

"Back, back to the plain!"

Aran gave the signal to disengage and those Eyrans within earshot or sightline took to their heels, dodging and weaving between the knots of traveling folk, the rocks, and the enemy. They were agile, sinewy men, born to rugged country and harsh conditions, and now they were running for their lives. Desperation provided fuel to their muscles. Unencumbered by armor or horses, they slipped back through the narrow defile from whence they had sprung and hurled themselves down the mountainside, surfing the screes, zigzagging between boulders, at a speed no Istrian could match. Even as targets for the archers, they proved too fleet and unpredictable, bobbing and jagging like hares; in moments they were gone.

Istrian militiamen poured through the gap after them, frustrated and furious to see them escape, oblivious to the shouted commands for order from behind them. Down the treacherous trackway they plunged, their horses sliding, loose rock skittering beneath their hooves. One horse lost its footing and plowed into two in front, which in turn slid sideways and tumbled, smashing unstoppably into a cadre of troops and spilling their shrieking riders down three hundred feet of broken ground.

Of the chaos ahead, Tycho Issian was unaware: all he knew was that the Rose was within sight and apparently unharmed, just passing through the defile on her runaway horse. Spurring on his mount, he trampled a dying soldier underfoot and raced after her. The piebald was a wily beast. It sensed clear air on the other side of the gap, a chance to escape the mayhem on this side. Head down, oblivious to the pursuit, and knowing only that its rider was anguished, it wove between knots of fighting men, terrified travelers, and loose animals straight for the gap.

Tycho swore foully. She was getting away. "Stop her!" he yelled, but no one heard him. He plowed through the middle of a wagon train, scattering children and dogs, rammed through a contingent of his own soldiery, and rode on, screaming imprecations.

An unhorsed Istrian tried to stop the piebald and was spun aside for his pains. Emerging through the gap in the defile, the Rosa Eldi's mount slid to a halt. The path below was jammed with fighting men and dying horses. When it turned to seek another way, the Lord of Cantara was upon it with a triumphant shout. He grabbed at its reins, drawing it alongside with such force he cut the piebald's mouth so that blood jetted from it, covering its rider's skirts. But the Rosa Eldi did not seem to be aware of anything: she had her hands clamped to her head and was screaming, a ululating wail of terror and despair.

Tycho grabbed her with more force than he'd been aware he owned and tried to haul her from her saddle into his. Her screaming stopped abruptly, but if he had expected thanks for his rescue, he was disappointed. She struggled out of his grasp, slipped to the ground, and stood there, her regard harrowed.

"Death! Death everywhere! Stop it, stop it! I have lost Virelai. Where is my son?"

"I have not seen him." This was a lie; he had seen the sorcerer's horse go down in the melee.

"Stop this bloodshed. Find my son!"

Tycho stared at her. "For Falla's sake, let me help you." He leaned down, reached out to catch her wrists, but she stepped away from him, wild-eyed, as she stumbled over a pair of twisted bodies.

She looked down and wailed again, muttering all the while, "Virelai, Virelai, where are you?" Blood had begun to soak into the hem of the white robe; already the ermine trim of the cloak was sodden with it.

"Are you mad? Do you want to die here?"

A soldier blundered up to her, stopped in his tracks at the sight of her, and stumbled like a dreaming man into the path of a runaway horse. She covered her face with her hands.

Manso Aglio dispatched the Eyran he had taken prisoner and looked to where his commander appeared to be in conversation with the White Woman in the midst of battle. He rolled his eyes, kneed his mount, and grabbed her up. "No indignity intended, lady," he apologized, tucking her over his cantle. "This way, my lord," he shouted to Tycho. "We've got them on the run!"

A RIDERLESS horse came thundering over him. He rolled into a ball, his arms wrapped around his head, and cowered into the neck of his own mount. Dying, the creature whinnied again and shifted its bulk minutely. He shoved at it, but to no avail; all it did was to settle itself even more firmly on his crushed leg. Panic and pain gripped him like a vise, putting all thoughts of magic to flight. He lay there, drifting in and out of consciousness, remembering the last time he had lain on a battlefield thus. Then, the number of men involved in the fray had been a fraction of those involved in this chaos, even without the innocents and animals which had been caught up in the battle. He sucked in a breath, expelled it slowly, tried to gather himself. From nowhere, a spell came to him and he clutched at it gratefully and muttered it over and over. The mantra took his mind off the pain in his leg, which was as well, for it was the worst he had ever experienced. After a while, the carcass of the beast had lightened so that he found he could move it just an inch, then two, until at last he was able to drag himself out from beneath its bulk and heaved himself up.

Of his mother and the Lord of Cantara there was no sign. The movement of the battle, if movement could be discerned amid the melee, was away from him, toward and beyond the gap in the cliffs ahead. True fear struck him now. What would happen if she were to be broken and battered down as he was, before she came into the full extent of her powers? What hope would there be for the world? What hope for him?

"Help me," he moaned and tried to make a shout of it. The sound vanished into the general noise without a trace.

He tried to stand, found his leg would not do anything he asked of it, and fell back down.

Suddenly, rough hands were upon him, lifting him up. He gazed around and found himself confronted by a giant of a man with an Eyran beard and steely eyes. He had no quarrel with the north; but how to convey that before the man slit his throat?

"You're the lord's sorcerer, aren't you?" the man said in the Old Tongue.

Virelai did not know whether to assent to this or not. He looked from the big Eyran to his companion, a small round man with a shock of black hair standing up in spikes sticky with sweat, or blood, or who knew what else.

"Got to be," opined the little man. "We'll get a reward for him."

"Aye, but from which side?"

"Does it matter?"

The big man raised his eyebrows. "I suppose not," he said, and threw Virelai over his shoulder.

"WE saw her, sire. We got as close as we could, but we could not capture her. She seemed unharmed, though distressed."

Ravn Asharson's face was alive with calculation. "How many of them?"

"Hard to say." Aran frowned. "Some thousands, though they are ill-disciplined and broke ranks at first blood. And there are a lot of ordinary folk—not soldiery—heading this way on foot, and in wagons. It's as if they've been drawn here, just like those in the boats." He gestured down at the strand where vessel after vessel was putting in.

"War is often a curiosity to those who have never fought," Ravn said dismissively. "Perhaps now they've seen some of its horror at first hand they'll turn back. Where's Stormway?"

"Overseeing the arrival of the rest of the fleet."

"Get down there, hurry them on. We'll carry the battle to them while they're in disarray. If we let them regroup down on the plain, their numbers will overwhelm us."

MANSO Aglio roared commands up and down the Istrian lines. He chivied, he swore, he whacked stragglers with the flat of his sword, he bullied them into some sort of order. Partway down the track to the wide plain, he drew them up behind a wall of rough lava which made a fine natural defense, the closest thing to a battlement he'd find in open ground. He was pleased with this strategic bent of mind he'd discovered in himself, pleased that he'd got it in him to command an army, pleased, too, in a way he didn't quite understand, that he'd saved the woman. It wasn't that he wanted her as a prize of war; no, it was something more . . . noble than that, though that seemed the least likely epithet he would ever apply to himself. She had seemed so vulnerable, so fragile, in the midst of the violence, so out of place, that he had been filled with what he could only think of as compassion. That had surprised him. He'd thought himself beyond finer feelings after serving in the Miseria all those years.

He looked for her now, safely back in the Lord of Cantara's custody, saw where the southern lord stood with his arms around her. It seemed, at first sight, as though they were locked in an embrace, but when he looked again it was clear that she was trying to pull away. For a moment, he felt compelled to help her; then he remembered who he was and laughed at this unwonted chivalry, then took himself off to do what he was good at: ordering soldiers around.

Tycho Issian wrestled the woman around so that she faced the plain. "Look, we can see the Rock from here. Will this not do?"

She turned to look at him in disbelief. "Of course not."

Desperate now, his erection so hot and hard he thought it might burn away the clothing that thwarted him, he pressed himself against her pelvis, felt the bones grind beneath him.

"It may be as close as we can get."

She pushed at him in disgust, thrust her head back, and looked him in the eye, her gaze like ice. "I shall claim you on the Rock, or nowhere."

The Voice of Command entered his soul, there was nothing he could do to prevent it. Turning to the gathered troops, he yelled, "Forward! To the Rock! To Falla's sacred Rock!"

Manso Aglio watched in dawning horror as his beautifully arrayed troops broke rank yet again and charged like the rabble they were down the slopes, screaming like souls in the torment of the Goddess's fires.

Mounting, Tycho Issian turned and grabbed up his prize. "Death or the Rock!" he cried again, "I will not be denied!" Forcing a kiss upon her, he saw in consternation that at his touch her eyes rolled up in her head.

THE press of vessels trying to put into the ashy strand was absurd, but the merchant had some little while ago transformed from the plumply ineffectual, nervous fellow whom his wife bullied mercilessly about what he should or should not say, eat, or do into an expert steersman with a glint in his eye. Smaller craft saw the barge coming and got out of the way.

Mam was up on the prow like the worst kind of figurehead, roaring at obstacles like a metal-toothed troll. That encouraged those competing for the same piece of beach to change their minds, too. She scanned the scene ahead and turned back to report, "If there's a goddess in among that lot, we'll have a job finding her."

Saro craned his neck. The sight which offered itself was alarming. He didn't know where to look first, for the entire vista was teeming with desperate groups of people. In the foreground, seasoned Eyran warriors shoved their way up from their beached vessels through a crowd of what appeared to be mere spectators, as if people had forgotten there was a war on and had turned up early to do business at an Allfair and were milling about in a purposeless way.

Farther up the strand, where only last year his family had pitched their booth, the melee deepened as a thick wave of fighters pressed its way up the slopes. Ahead of this, a line of Eyran spearmen held off the hapless cavalry of an enemy he could only suppose to be Istrian militia. It was a short defensive line, already dented in places, the Istrians flowing around the broken parts like surf around skerries.

Beyond the line of spears, more chaos.

Everywhere he looked, something odd snagged at his attention: a group of Eyran matrons in breeches made of sailcloth wading ashore from their anchored fishing smack; what appeared to be a herd of wild pigs dodging in and out of the crowd; Istrian women in robes without veils; mixed bands of nomads and townsfolk staring in bewilderment up the slopes as if they had expected something else here entirely. Among all this disorder, the great Rock rose like a castle, massive and four-square, its shoreward face rosy in the sunlight.

As if she sensed his attention, Katla Aransen turned her own face to the Rock, known for generations in her land as Sur's Castle, even if the southerners dedicated it to their goddess. Its proximity called to her above the cries and howls of the mass of humanity that washed around its foot as an ecstatic shudder in her bones, her skin; a shudder which flickered in her belly like the promise of life.

"Saro—" It was barely more than a whisper, but he turned at once, so attuned was he to her needs. "Saro, the Rock. You must take me to the Rock."

He gazed down at her in dismay, then back out into the melee.

She tugged at his sleeve. "Please, I know it's where I must be. I can feel it."

He shook his head. "We would never be able to get you there, and even if we did—"

Her eyes were febrile and bright. "You must. It's a place of power. Even if I die, I must die on the Rock."

The word caught at Saro's heart, gripped it painfully. He wrapped his fingers over hers. "All right," he said softly. "I promise, though I'm not sure how we'll manage it." He wondered why he made this promise as he disengaged himself gently and went to find Alisha Skylark.

The nomad woman was sitting down in the hold with her arms around her knees. She did not look up when he lowered himself down beside her.

"Will you look at Katla again, Alisha? She asks that we take her to the Rock, but I'm sure she's not strong enough to survive the attempt. Is there something you could give her, maybe even a draught that would put her to sleep while Mam and I carry her? I worry about the pain—it could be too much for her to bear."

Alisha shook her head. She was pale, he could see, paler than usual and her knuckles were white where she gripped her knees. "It is wrong," she said. "It is all wrong. Something terrible is here. I can feel it, but I do not understand it. It should be wonderful, but it is all wrong." She paused. Then: "Death is here," she whispered. "Death's shadow lies over everything."

Saro took a breath. "Alisha, we need your help. Katla may die otherwise."

She looked up then, and her eyes were sunken and hollow. "We are all going to die, Saro Vingo, every one of us."

And after that she would say no more.

When he went miserably back to the brig, he found Mam kneeling on the planking beside Katla. "It's not looking good," Mam said briskly. She beckoned to Saro. "Here, you feel. Her pulse is very fast."

Filled with dread, Saro flung himself down beside the Eyran girl and placed his fingers on the side of her neck. The pulse there was weak and fluttering, twice its normal speed. He made up his mind before he could allow panic to set in. "You and I must get her to Falla's Rock," he said to the mercenary leader. "Now."

The merchant and his wife were at the gunwale, surveying the scene nervously. "I didn't think it would be like this," the man said. "I thought it was a pilgrimage. I thought everyone would be on their knees, praying; that the Goddess would walk among us."

His wife smiled suddenly, her doughy face—pale from years of being hidden from the sun beneath a veiling sabatka—suddenly beatific. "She is among us. I can sense her presence. If you pray, you can feel her." She put her hand out to Saro. "Pray with us," she said.

Saro shook his head gently. "I'm sorry. I wish you well, and I thank you for our passage, but now we must leave you." He paused, remembering Alisha's words. "I hope you find the Goddess," he finished, and squeezed the matron's shoulder.

Somehow, they got Katla to the shore. She murmured at the jolt as Mam handed her down to Saro, but after that made no sound at all, nor did she open her eyes. The mercenary leader raked the way clear with the flat of her sword, growling at anyone who dared to impede her. Behind this great battering ram of a woman, Saro struggled along with

Katla in his arms. He could not see where he was going, could see hardly anything at all but the tangled white braids of the mercenary leader's head bobbing and weaving in front of him, that and the looming silhouette of the Rock an impossible distance away through all the conflict and confusion.

By now, the fighting had spilled down onto the plain itself. Black dust rose into the air, kicked up by the crazed passage of feet and hooves, by the charge of the living, and the fall of the dying. No way ahead seemed easier than any other; and Mam was soon forced to use both point and blade. A miasma of blood sprayed around Saro. He could feel it every time he breathed in; feel it, too, on his skin and in his hair. Katla moaned and twisted in his arms and opened her eyes.

KATLA Aransen had never been one to shrink from bloodshed, never one to shirk a fight. If she were truthful about it, she had felt most alive at those times when she had had a sword in her hand and an enemy at the other end of it. She had lost count of the number of men she had killed, and felt no shame about any part of that. She had fought because she must, to defend herself or her kin, she had fought when the cause was clear and needs must. But as she gazed upon the scene before her now, waking suddenly out of what seemed a dream of pain and torture into something far worse, she felt a powerful repulsion at what seemed a vista of random violence. It was as if the whole world had run mad. Everywhere she looked, something terrible was happening. It was not just that man fought man, or that Istrian fought Eyran; she took that much for granted. It was the extraordinary mixture of folk entangled in the conflict, for clearly not all of them were combatants. There were women, cowering out of the way of the men and their horses, women in traditional Istrian robes, nomad women, women in Eyran dress, women without veils. And children, too. Who in Sur's name would bring a child to this place of horror? she wondered, appalled.

Just as she was thinking this, a scrap of red, small, low down, caught her eye. It vanished between the feet of an Eyran spearman, then reappeared behind him in a yard of open space. She focused on it, frowning, then it was obscured again.

A fox. She had just seen a fox, in the middle of a battlefield.

Saro jumped suddenly sideways and came down with a thud that jolted her wound painfully. She closed her eyes. Perhaps she was already dying and her failing mind was offering her flickers of memory, interposed with the reality of the battle. That must be it. She dared another glimpse, but the fox was nowhere to be seen.

There was, however, a pair of wolves. Gray-coated, hoary around the muzzle, their golden eyes puzzled and yet determined, they threaded their way between the stamping feet. Overhead, a skein of swans flew, honking.

Exhausted, Katla closed her eyes again. *If you're going to torment me like this*, she told the god in her head, *then just get on with it and let me die. I'm in no mood for your games.*

THE Man and the Beast gazed down on the carnage below.

We are too late, it seems, the cat said.

If we had not meandered about collecting up your comrades, we would have been here long before her.

It is as much their right as any other living being's to witness what will come. They must remake the world, too. It is not just for your humans, you know.

Sirio pursed his mouth. *Even so, look at it down there. I should have kept the sword,* he conveyed with regret. *Where is our beloved? Something must be amiss: she would surely never allow such carnage unless she were out of her wits or—* He paused, suddenly afraid. *Your senses are finer than mine. Can you scry her out among all that chaos?*

The cat lifted its head and stared down at the heaving plain. It sniffed the air. Its ears twitched. Its whiskers bristled. Its tail flicked in an agitated manner, coiling and darting like a snake. At last it said, *I have called her, but she does not answer. Virelai hears me, though he cannot see her either, and his leg pains him too much to concentrate properly.*

It paused. *The other is down there, too, the Thief. I look forward to dealing with him.* And it showed the Man its fangs.

But the god had a faraway look on his face. *They are all praying,* he declared with satisfaction. *They call on me and my beloved. It is good to know we are not forgotten, even if they do invoke us mainly as they die.*

THERE was a lull in the battle as they neared the Rock, as if folk were afraid to fight in its shadow. Mam stared up. "It's damned tall," she judged. "And bloody steep, too." She glared at Saro. "Now what?"

"There are steps carved into it, around the other side," he wheezed.

Mam took in his gritted jaw, the strain in the corded muscles of his neck and shook her head. "You're about as strong as an Eyran chit," she said sadly, clicking her teeth. "Here, you take the sword and guard my back while I carry her up." She fixed him with a steely gaze. "If anything happens to me, it happens to Katla Aransen. Remember that."

They made the exchange gingerly, and in Saro's case with some regret. It was not just that he missed the touch of the girl against him—but that carrying her made him feel they were inextricably bound; that if one failed, so would the other, for he did not, he understood with sudden force, want to live without her. Neither did he much want to use the sword, even in their defense.

As Mam set her foot onto the first of the steps the ancient elders of the land had carved into the Rock, Katla revived a little from her daze. She reached out her hands. "Let me touch it," she begged.

Mam twisted a little sideways, but kept climbing. Katla trailed her palms over the rough surface, allowed the jangle of sensation it threw off to travel up her arms, into her skull, down through her spine.

"Ahhhh," she sighed.

Below her, climbing awkwardly with his back to the steps, Saro looked up and felt, out of nowhere, the sharp sting of jealousy.

WHEREVER the Rose of the World was, the fighting was fiercest, as if men were drawn to her presence.

Aran Aranson watched in sorrow as the Earl of Stormway fell to an Istrian spearman and suddenly found himself fighting at Ravn Asharson's back. They were deep inside the Istrian ranks now, surrounded on all sides, but nothing seemed to deter the Eyran king. His sword arced and thrust like the blade of an avenging god. "For Sur!" he yelled as he decapitated an opponent and spun to gut another. "For Sur and my love!" He sounded, Aran thought, as if he was thoroughly enjoying himself. He gritted his teeth and parried an inept blow from an Istrian lad young enough to be his son. He had some of Halli's dark look, too: an intense black regard from under the brim of his ill-fitting helmet. Yelling something unintelligible, he swiped at Aran again, but the Rockfaller found that when it came to it, he could not bring himself to kill the boy. Pulling back on his stroke, he spitted the lad neatly in the shoulder and passed on, hearing him howl. He'd recover—which was more than could be said for poor Halli.

The hot press of men stamped their way through the volcanic dust, sweating, hacking, groaning. They stumbled over the dead and the dying, never knowing whether it was a man they knew on whom they trampled, for to look down was to risk death oneself. Boys not yet able to grow even a stubble fought men with beards twisted into braids and threaded through with string and shells, ribbons off their wives' shifts, bits of bone and horn; lads coming to their first battle with an ache of suspense in the guts found themselves in deadly combat with grizzled veterans; new officers intent upon proving their worth battled anxiously against Eyran warriors who knew too many dirty tricks to let them fight the way they had learned in a practice square. Despite the disparity in numbers, the advantage was never held for more than a few minutes by either side.

On and on they fought, and above them the sun climbed past the zenith and began its slow downward descent. The battle wheeled around and soon, where they had been fighting uphill, Aran found himself moving downward with his king. Ahead of them, he thought he could for a moment glimpse the walnut-brown features of the Istrian lord whose theft of the Rose had caused this entire conflict; then he was gone away into the chaos and a dozen men had filled the gap between them.

Aran fought in a dream. He hacked and parried, hacked again, turned, found enemies all around. His arm ached; his body ached. In a brief moment of reflection, he found that his soul ached, too. Much as he had chafed at the boredom of the round of seasons at Rockfall rolling like a wheel on a flat road, each with its allotted tasks, the only unpredictability the weather; much as he had longed for adventure, for a chance to prove himself a man—a hero—this needless, brutish slaughter was not what he had sought; just as, in the end, he had not wanted the treasures of Sanctuary. He felt weary unto death. It would be so easy to let the next man take him down and stop the wheel entirely.

As he thought this, an image entered his mind: a vision of his wife, thinner than he remembered her, tougher-looking, in the company of other women he did not know. She stood on a knoll on the slopes above him, the peaks of the Skarn Mountains flaring away into the distance, their snow red with sunlight.

He blinked, brought back his focus just in time to see a man in a greasy goat-hide corslet coming at him with a short spear. Without conscious thought, he jabbed out hard and fast. In horrified fascination he watched the tip of his sword slipped neatly between the rusty iron plates stitched into the leather, watched the blade shear through the goat hide as if it were cloth and penetrate the man's chest without a sound. Blood welled through the hole, bubbled out over the tang of the blade, stuck in the goat hairs still visible on the leather, and trickled down the useless, ancient armor. The Istrian's knees buckled slowly; then he was down, his final scream echoing in Aran's head.

When he turned to look again, Bera was still where he had glimpsed her, gazing down into the melee. He knew she could not make him out among the chaos. Even so, he felt as if their eyes met across that killing ground, and he felt ashamed.

"HURRY—he's just ahead!"

"Where's he going?"

"Sur's Castle, by the look of it; and with the woman, too."

"He can't be meaning to go up the Rock, surely?"

Joz made a face. "Safest place, amid all this. And if you were commanding an army, where would you rather be—down here slipping around in the blood and guts, or up there with a clear view of the battlefield?"

"True."

"You've got to stop him—he's got my mother."

It was the first thing they'd heard the sorcerer say since Joz had picked him up.

"Your mother?" Joz was incredulous. "What, the White Lady?"

"The Rose of the World, the Goddess, yes."

"Goddess?" Even as they ran, Dogo snorted contemptuously. "She's a looker, right enough, but I wouldn't go that far—"

"If she's a goddess," Joz said evenly, "then how come she's let him sling her over his shoulder like a sack of turnips?"

"Yes," sniggered Dogo. "And if you're the son of a goddess, how come you're letting Joz do the same?"

"Why doesn't she just strike him dead and stop it all?"

"She can't. It's not in her nature, she makes things grow, she heals—"

Dogo howled. "What's the point of being a god if you can't kill people?"

So saying, he rammed his short sword through the back of the man in front of him, stepped aside to let him fall. Life was cheap, especially if you weren't getting paid for the job of taking it.

But by the time they reached Sur's Castle, the Lord of Cantara was halfway up the stairs. Arrows bounced harmlessly off the rock all around him. Two paces below, an ugly man in the boiled leather harness of a seasoned soldier followed, a limp figure in white draped over his shoulder.

Joz swore. "Now what?"

"Take him to the king?"

"If I know anything about Ravn Asharson, he'll be wherever the fighting is worst."

"To the ships, then," Dogo suggested, hamstringing a man who was showing too much interest in Joz's burden.

"Aye," said Joz. "Wait it out. Not our fight, after all."

Dogo grinned. "Could just nick the ship. Nice piece of work, *Sur's Raven*, as I recall."

Joz Bearhand gave no response to this thought. He was staring up at the Rock intently.

"By all the devils of the sea . . ."

Dogo followed the line of his gaze. There, on top of the Rock, was their erstwhile leader and the young man they knew as Saro Vingo, kneeling over someone who looked a lot like Katla Aransen.

"KATLA, Katla—"

"I don't think she can hear you, lad."

"But she said it was a place of power . . . I thought it would save her."

Mam placed a hand on his shoulder. There were tears in her eyes: she blinked them away quickly before Saro could look up and see them, the memory of Persoa's passing brought back to her sharply by the sight of Katla Aransen fading into unconsciousness.

Below the Rock, the fighting was more savage than ever. A desperate heave of men and weapons all were converging around its base, as if for some reason it had become the focal point of the battle. As she looked, a movement snagged her eye. Someone was coming up the carved stairs—

At once her sword was out and she was moving, calling back to Saro to beware, knowing even as she did so that he would not hear her, and that even if he did, he would not care.

A dark head appeared over the edge, but whoever it was, he was looking down below him, snarling at someone to hurry, hurry and did not see the danger about to befall him. Mam's eyes narrowed as she recognized the intruder. She balanced her blade and waited, her grin one of grim satisfaction. Here was the leader of the Istrian force at her mercy. She could have his head for nothing or present it to the Eyran king and earn herself a fortune. None of it made up for the tragedy of it all, but she knew a professional opportunity when it presented itself.

"Ha!" she yelled at him. "Come up quietly, my lord of Cantara, or go swiftly to your death."

Tycho's head snapped up. In the seconds in which he had to live, he gazed upon the mercenary, took in her fearsome aspect, the raised sword, the menace in her expression. His face contorted into a mask of repulsion.

"A woman!" he shrieked. "You're a woman! A woman—on Falla's Rock!"

Mam was taken aback. She laughed. "A woman, yes! A woman who's going to cleave your head from your shoulders!"

Fury and pent-up frustration lent him horrible speed. Faster than Mam could ever have expected, the southern lord had hoisted himself up and over the edge of the Rock and was on his feet, his sword waving wildly in front of him.

"Get your filthy carcass off this sacred place!" he howled.

Mam knocked his weapon away as if it had been a wet stick.

"The only carcass here will be yours," she growled, and brought her sword down in a vicious chop.

The blade described a mighty arc, bright silver like a leaping salmon flashing in the sunlight . . . and stopped dead, a hair's breadth from the skin of his exposed neck. Mam stared at her sword, nonplussed, tried a second stroke, which also failed to make contact.

A second figure appeared at the top of the steps, a second figure slipping from the hold of a third.

"You cannot kill him," said a voice distinctly, and suddenly there was a goddess standing in the light, a goddess with her hair in disarray and blood all over her robe, but a goddess nonetheless. She seemed to absorb all the available light, so that where before the day had seemed bright, now it seemed dull and lackluster. Mam could not take her eyes off her. She felt the marrow in her bones grow cold.

"Why not?" she croaked.

The Goddess smiled. "Because he is mine."

At this, Tycho Issian's expression became ravenous. "And you are mine, beloved."

Manso Aglio shook his head. He did not understand what was being played out here. It seemed despite all her protestations and histrionics, the pale woman would have the Lord of Cantara after all. He shook his head sadly. Women, he would never understand them.

The shadow of a slighter figure appeared behind that of the stout Istrian general. A tall, wiry man, his long black hair whipping in the wind, his fiercely handsome face as chiseled as a wood carving, a dagger gripped between his teeth.

Manso Aglio watched the Rosa Eldi's gaze slide past his master and
her eyes widen. When he turned, it was to see a bearded man, stealthy
as a cat, climbing up onto the Rock. Behind him came a clutch of northern warriors, their eyes alight with battle lust.

At this juncture, several things happened at once.

Behind Mam, there was a bubbling cough, followed by a low cry of
despair. Then Saro Vingo came running toward the Goddess, his fingers
scrabbling at the ties on his tunic. Light shone out of his hands, silver-
gold, the coldest light in the world.

"You must help Katla!" he cried, dragging the moodstone clear so
that she could see the thing she had made. "My lady, you must help her!
Use the stone—the death-stone: only you can save her—"

Tycho Issian stepped swiftly between the two of them and snatched
at the shining pendant. His hands closed over the stone and it reflected
in his eyes as if the light it emitted—and nothing else—was somehow
inside his skull, shining out.

A death-stone. He remembered with goddess-given clarity the words
of the northerner who had broken into his chambers at Jetra, the man
with the ill-dyed hair and rough accent: *a mighty weapon . . . a death-
stone . . . an artifact with the power over life and death.*

He gave a death's-head grin, his face made a diabolic mask by the
harsh play of light and shade.

"A death-stone," he mused. His grip on it tightened convulsively.

There was a cry behind him, and he turned just in time to see Manso
Aglio plummeting over the edge of the Rock with a dagger in his chest,
and five barbarians advancing upon him. In their forefront, his sword
red to the hilt, was King Ravn Asharson.

"Give me back my wife," he snarled.

Wild panic flickered briefly in the southern lord's eyes. Then he
swung the death-stone the his enemy, hauling Saro with it. "The lady is
not yours, barbarian!" he spat. "But I have a different gift for you."

On his knees, his neck dragged upward at an unnatural angle by the
pendant's sturdy thong, Saro saw a coruscating white light shatter the
air above his head. It broke through the cage of Tycho Issian's fingers in
a searing blast and tore toward Ravn Asharson.

The blast struck the King of Eyra square in the face, and his mouth opened in a silent scream. His sword spun away from him in what seemed a slow descent, till with a clatter it struck the rock at his feet and shattered into a dozen shards.

His eyes rolled up in his head.

Then, like an ax-toppled tree, he staggered backward and measured his full, dead length on the rock.

All across the vast battlefield, an unearthly cry rang out. It swept as a stormwind across the plain and out into the Skarn Mountains, skimming spindrift off the peaks to dance in the freezing air like a thousand dervishes. Down through the bones of the earth it ran, stopping streams in their tracks, bringing rockfalls and avalanches in its wake, causing herds of yeka in the Golden Hills to bolt for lower ground. In the far south of the Istrian continent, it brought lava flowing like blood.

Men fell to their knees, momentarily stunned. A pack of wolves, gathered now from their wide, rocky habitat, gave back the call so that it echoed like the wail of a thousand ghosts.

Up on Sur's Castle as she slid toward endless night, Katla Aransen felt the scream as a rumble beneath her torso, a thrumming which drummed in the skeleton for which she would soon no longer have need.

With a galvanic heave, the Rock broke itself in two. A great cloud of dust hurled itself into the air. When it settled, two new figures stood silhouetted against the skyline. One was a man, golden of hair, blue of eye, beatific of visage; the other a huge black cat.

"We answer your summons, sister-wife," said the man; and the cat roared its welcome.

RAHE, the world's greatest mage, watched these transformations with dawning terror. He had been keeping his distance from the violence of men, seeking an opportunity to take back his prize. *Let them all kill one another,* he had thought, with a certain satisfaction, *let them make their enemies' blood flow like rivers across this barren waste; let the fools wipe each other from the face of Elda.* Then, and only then, would he make his move. But the sight of Sirio, apparently unharmed, with the cat at its full and menacing size beside him, gave him horrible pause. He must escape! Since the Rose's return to herself, he had felt his powers dwindling day by day as the power he had stolen from her found its way back to the source: but the least use of magic in this place would draw her eye. Worse, it would draw the attention of the god and their beast. And that would be his death. He stared about in dismay. The sea was surely his best chance.

He threaded his way between discarded skiffs and dragged-up rowboats, between leaky coracles and beached hulls, looking for a vessel he could handle with his old-man strength and failing magic. It was then that he spied a familiar figure, pale as death, clutching what appeared to be a badly broken leg.

Rahe grinned from ear to ear. It seemed his store of luck had not entirely run dry.

ONE moment the world had been at his fingertips, his rival blasted to searing death before his very eyes; the next, the leather of the thong holding the pendant around the boy's neck had snapped, sending him to his knees, and Elda had erupted. Scrabbling to save himself from toppling off the Rock as it buckled and tore itself apart, Tycho Issian lost the stone, and then could not see it for the swirling dust.

When he finally raised his eyes, he stared about bewilderment. The world as he had known it was no more. Instead, a trio of figures bound by a shining golden light stood gazing down upon him. A man, a woman and a great cat, separate, yet joined. Names hovered on his lips, itched at his scalp. He did not know them—but he *knew* them.

Falla. Feya. Sirio. Sur. Bast. Beast. Bëte.

Come and join us, the woman said into his mind. And she smiled at him, a smile of infinite gentleness and humor, and extended a hand.

He stared. It was the Rosa Eldi, but she was much changed. Gone was her ethereal silvery pallor, her vulnerability, her fear. In their place was a woman all of gold, a woman who radiated confident, joyous life from every pore of her skin. Gone, too, was her robe. The Rosa Eldi had bloomed, had in an instant gone from perfect bud to perfect flower, wide open to the world. Her fragrance flooded out across the rock, musky and floral and hot. He caught his breath in bliss, and suddenly found himself on his feet, walking toward her like a man in a dream.

The tiniest voice at the back of his skull whispered warning, but he ignored it, pushed it down, intoxicated as he was by the sight of her lush curves, by the tumble of golden hair across those glorious round breasts, flushed with new blood, by the lift of her rosy nipples, by the curl of new golden hair at her pubis. Only the sea-green eyes had not changed, and they regarded him with the same chill they always had. Even so, he found himself taking her hand. The fingers closed on him, strong as iron; the green eyes bound him to her.

I know you now, she said into his mind, *though it has taken too long to recognize you. We are the Three: Man, Woman, and Beast; but you, you are Death: the Fourth. You have escaped us long enough, my friend. Look out across this battlefield, and see what you have made of our folk.*

And Death looked out across the plain and saw below how men fought each other with spear and ax, with sword and knife and crossbow. Ripping great red wounds in one another, they roared and hated and bled.

Now watch, urged the Rose of the World.

She closed her eyes and shaped a thought and in the wake of that thought an ineffable sensation trembled through the hands of every man holding a weapon on the Moonfell Plain that day.

When the sensation faded, each warrior looked down to find that the sword, the spear, or the bow they had a moment before been wielding had been transformed. Forged metal disintegrated, broke down to its component parts to flow as useless nuggets of ore to the ground; spearheads and arrowheads became first molten, then lumpen; carved staves and curved bone twisted in the grip and took back the form of tree and beast.

As the moment passed, they stared in puzzlement at these new tools—budding branches, ore-filled rock, and cattle horns; then started to beat one another, if rather less fatally, then with no lessening of violence, with these materials instead.

She shook her head sadly. Tears stood in the sea-green eyes. *You see how strong is your influence? Their hearts are so full of hatred they no longer see the truth of things.*

Sirio touched her shoulder. *Do not distress yourself, sister-wife. Perhaps it would be best to clean them all away, let life start anew.*

But look! Bëte nudged her leg. *Over there—something is happening.*

As one, the four deities gazed out across the plain.

A crowd of women had gathered on the slopes above the battlefield. At their head stood three women: an Eyran and two Istrians. The northern woman had hair of flame and salt, the other two, despite the wide disparity in their ages, were clearly related. Bera Rolfsen stood beside her new friend Flavia Issian and her granddaughter Selen, come it seemed, out of nowhere. Several hundred strong, and gaining numbers all the time as they made their way forward, the women pushed into the midst of the fighting men, and the warriors paused in their beatings, their new weapons hanging loosely by their sides and their faces full of confusion.

The older woman said something to her companion, and together they gripped the hems of their robes and hauled them up and over their heads to stand exposed and vulnerable in the middle of that arena of death. A moment later, the rest followed their example. Sabatkas, veils, tunics, jerkins, skirts, shifts, stockings—all were discarded. White flesh stood next to brown flesh, freckled skin to burnished skin; old next to young. The women of Elda stood forth in all their naked glory of sags and swags, curves and planes, bellies and breasts and hair of all shades of white to black and every variation in between. Some held hands and laughed, others looked somber; some blushed with embarrassment and gazed at their feet, while others looked the men around them brazenly in the eye.

For a moment, everything went quiet. Then, one by one, the men dropped their weapons.

The Four stared down at this bizarre spectacle, stunned to sudden silence. At last, the Rose of the World smiled. Then she threw back her head and laughed. *I do not think they need our help anymore. It seems they are ready to change their world without us. We have offered them the excuse for division and fanaticism long enough, do you not agree, brother?*

Sirio considered the women and his eyes were a little wistful. *Look at all this bounty to enjoy! I have been back in the world for such a short time, and now you are taking me from it.* He sighed.

Am I not enough for you?

Sirio drew his eyes back to his sister-wife and his smile was wry. *Feya, you are all that is or ever could be Woman.*

Neither do you need the bodies you have borrowed, she suggested softly.

True. Sirio shook his head, and the bones and shells in the braids clattered against the tattoos of his face.

Bëte yawned. *I have enjoyed my time here lately,* she declared. *But now I am ready to sleep.*

Feya released her grip on Tycho Issian. *I know you did not always know yourself and that you cannot help your nature,* she said sternly.

And, for a moment, some part of him flared with wild hope. It was soon to be quenched.

However, we cannot have you running rampant across our world any longer. Elda is out of balance. We must contain you. Every creature has the right to its own life, and you have taken too many, too soon. The death-stone became a vivid presence between them. Then it flared and burst into flame.

I welcome you to my fires, breathed the Goddess, and in an instant his clothes were gone from him and his erection was standing proud, wrapped about by a golden conflagration. She glanced down at it, amused. *Ah, Death,* she said into his mind, *always so virile, so determined to take as much of Life as you are able.*

She dropped her hand to cup his balls and delicious agony enveloped him. He felt his essence explode. He was at once vast and tiny, unbound yet contained. Light seared out across the world; then died abruptly.

Feya closed her hand over the death-stone. *Will you look after this precious object, or shall I?* she asked her brother-husband; but the Beast was quicker. Nudging her hand, the great cat knocked the stone into the air, caught it up between her glistening fangs, and swallowed it down, Death and all, then sat there between them, smiling as enigmatically as only a cat can.

The Rose of the World stroked its head. *It is as safe a place as any.*

Are you ready now, beloved?

Almost. There is one more thing to attend to. She gazed down into the milling crowd. *There they are, our faithful ones.*

A small group was moving up the strand. They stood taller than even the tallest of the warriors who surrounded them, and their limbs were long and lean. Some were male, some female. Most owned but a single eye, set square in the center of their foreheads. In their midst were three figures, one woman and two men. The woman looked fearful, as if she expected some new cruelty to be visited upon her. She carried the stub of a broken oar in one hand and with the other supported a hobbling man with long white hair which had come unbound out of its tail. He was pale and thin, and looked near to death. The third figure was an old man bound in a shining net of spellcraft. He sported a large purple bruise over one eye.

The group stopped in a space below the Rock and one figure stepped forward. It made an obeisance, then declared in a voice which carried far and wide: "We bring you Rahe the Mage, known by many as Rahay, King of the West. For all that he is our father, he has done wrong and must pay for his crimes against you and the world of Elda."

The Goddess gazed down. "Thank you, Festrin," she said, for all to hear. "We are grateful to you." She regarded the mage, and as she did so his shining bonds fell away to nothing. "Step forward, Rahe, Master of Nowhere."

Shuffling like the old man he was, the mage stepped clear of the group. When he tilted his head up at her, there was terror and loathing in his eyes. "Incinerate me, then!" he goaded. "Burn me in your fires as you have burned the southern lord. Do it, and have done."

Feya regarded him with her head on one side and said nothing, but Bëte snarled at the sight of him, and Sirio glared down. *He deserves burning, and worse. Why not hold him captive in the lavas of the Red Peak as he did to me all those centuries? Let him learn the true nature of the world's torment.*

The Goddess smiled. *He shall learn the true nature of the world,* she told him, *that I promise.* "Rahe Mage," she said aloud, "you have taken what was not yours and used it in the pursuit of vainglory and power, and in doing so you have warped all Elda, but now I take back what little you have left from your thievery."

With the tiniest movement of her hand it was done, the drawing back of her stolen magic. It shimmered in the air between the Three for the briefest of moments, then was gone. On the ground, the mage stared around, puzzled. He looked at his hands, touched himself through his clothes, frowned. "Alive," he muttered. "Still alive." He squinted up at the Goddess. "What trick is this?" he demanded. "Stop playing with me."

"No trick, old man. Go now, and make the most of what little time is left to you in reflection and peace."

And now Rahe began to feel the effect of the loss of the magic which had kept time at bay for so very long. His joints twinged and ached, his bones felt insubstantial, covered over by skin as frail as a whisper. When he breathed, he wheezed.

Tears of rage gathered, tears of self-pity.

"Ah, that's your game, is it?" he quavered. "I'd rather you burned me."

But they were not listening to him. Three had become One, an indeterminate form comprising all aspects of the deities it contained; this single figure now flowed from the top of the despoiled Rock to the ground below, coming to rest before Virelai and Alisha Skylark.

The nomad woman quailed away, trembling. "I was wrong to hit the old man," she cried. "I know. All violence is wrong and that is why the seithers have brought me before you. Punish me if you must." She lifted her eyes beseechingly, then looked away again, hazed by the brilliant sight. "But he was going to kill Virelai, and I could not let him do it."

"Peace, child," the One said. A glowing hand touched her face. "You did nothing wrong, and you acted out of love. We perceive that you have suffered greatly and we are sorry for your loss. We would like to give to you a gift—the gift of faith—Alisha Skylark: faith in the future."

Now the figure turned to the sorcerer.

Virelai gazed at the being in front of him, his face harrowed. If he had wished to be reunited with the mother he had but lately found, this was not she. Even so, "When Rahe ripped you from our belly before you had a chance to breathe, we begged him to save you," the One said. "But we never meant for him to make you his slave or to raise you in a wilderness, loveless and lawless. The stone has already reversed his deed, but now we heal the rest of you, and offer you a choice."

Virelai felt a wave of warmth envelope him, felt it knit up the bones of his leg, close the wounds, salve the flesh. He closed his eyes, unable to do anything but luxuriate in the sensation.

When he opened them again, the One was regarding him curiously.

He looks like you.

No, he looks like you.

A peal of laughter. *He looks like both of us.*

A rumble which lay somewhere between a growl and a purr. *At least he does not look much like me.*

"Here is your choice, Virelai. You may come with us, into the heart of the world and dwell with us there in magic."

"Or?"

"Or you may live here, in Elda. In love."

The world had been harsh to him. In it, he had been beaten and tortured, maligned and debased. He had witnessed atrocity and experienced more hurt than he knew could exist. He looked away from the shining being and found Alisha Skylark's eyes upon him, large with hopeless hope.

The choice tugged at him, unequal, unbearable.

"I cannot leave," he said softly.

"Oh, Virelai."

No one had ever spoken his name with such affection. He gazed into her eyes and saw himself reflected there, not as he thought of himself, but nobler and finer by far. He reached out a hand and cupped Alisha's ravaged face, watched in wonder as the area around his hand changed. The nomad woman's skin began to lose the appearance of sun-hardened leather, filled out, became as smooth and soft as he had remembered it.

He took his hand away, amazed.

A voice said: *Farewell then, Virelai. It is good that we leave someone behind us to help to heal the world.*

When he looked away from Alisha, it was to catch the spark of a bright light fading and the One was nowhere to be seen. He turned his face up to the sky, but all he found there were clouds. A gentle rain began to fall. It pattered onto his face like a blessing. Closing his eyes, he let it wash over him, felt it soaking his hair, his clothes, and when he looked down, it was to find green shoots sprouting in the black ash, tendrils and budded leaves. Daisies pushed their blind heads out into the light; clover and grasses came next, running like a vivid green fire out across the plain. A herd of wild horses followed the line of green, their hooves dashing up clouds of dust which fell back to earth as a rich loam.

Alisha Skylark gazed around in awe and delight. Overhead, a cloud of swallows soared and dived, their aerial turns as fast as a thought. Doves roosted now on the broken ledges of what had once been Falla's Rock. Vines crept up its southern slope.

While she watched, something on top of the Rock moved. She shaded her eyes.

She breathed a name, and Virelai turned to stare where she stared.

It was Saro Vingo.

Virelai watched as he stumbled to the edge of the shattered outcrop and stood there with his head in his hands, as if he were debating whether or not he would leap off. Something about the set of his shoulders told of absolute despair.

"Saro!" he called. He had never thought to see his friend again.

Dust covered Saro's face and hair, but tears had streaked his cheeks. His eyes were haunted. The gods were gone, and miracles were all about him; but the most important miracle of all had not occurred.

"Virelai . . ." It was barely a whisper, but the sorcerer heard it as clearly as if Saro was at his side. "Virelai, I have lost Katla."

KATLA Aransen drifted in the darkness. New pain revived her briefly, then retreated like a sea. The wound in her belly had opened; she could feel its wetness and the rawness of the interior exposed to air. She dragged in a breath and felt how it rasped and bubbled. Something was pressing down on her, crushing her chest and legs. She took another breath, shallower than the last, and it knifed through her. She coughed and twisted, and that racked her again.

Be strong, Katla.

There seemed to be a voice in the darkness with her, a voice that was so close it seemed almost inside her head, a voice she recognized but could put no name to. It comforted her to know she would not die alone in this darkness. Unless, she thought suddenly, she had merely dreamed the voice as a last comfort, and was talking to herself. Just like Old Ma Hallasen, cackling away to her goats and her cats on all matters of philosophy. Mad as a bat.

This is no dream, Katla. And I'd rather you didn't defame my old Ma.

Katla frowned. Everyone knew Old Ma had no children. Now she really was going mad. Deciding to test her theory, she asked aloud, "Where in Sur's name am I?"

Inside the Rock. It split apart when the gods erupted through it and you fell in.

Apart from the bit about the gods, she could have worked that out, if she could remember anything leading up to these latest events. The last thing she *could* remember was being at sea with everyone talking across her and the waves rocking the barge so gently that they took her away from all that disturbing chatter and rocked her to sleep. Weariness rolled over her now, promising to steal her away to a place where there was no pain, or anything else at all.

Stay awake, Katla. I can't afford to let you die.

Her eyes snapped open. "What?"

If you die, I die. So don't die.

That seemed fair enough, if she could only make sense of it. She tried to find a more comfortable position in which to have this strange discussion, but that just caused another wave of red agony to engulf her, so she stopped and lay there, panting. Now that her eyes were adjusting to the darkness, she could make out the rough shapes of boulders all around. Behind her, a splinter of light shone through the fractured rock, illuminating tiny details here and there. It seemed impossibly far away, no more than a tantalizing promise. She reached out with her right hand and felt about her. There were rocks jammed onto her chest and legs, but her head was in open space.

I wish I could lend you my strength, but another stole that from me, the voice told her. Which made no sense at all.

She managed to get a knee bent up so that her foot found some purchase and pushed feebly backward. A trickle of dust slithered down onto her face, making her cough, but she shoved herself an inch or two into the space behind her. It hurt, horribly, but she did it again, then again. The boulders shifted dangerously.

Be careful, Katla; be slow.

Being slow or careful had never come naturally to Katla Aransen, but she gritted her teeth and pushed again until her head touched solid rock. The jolt it gave her was shocking, disorienting. She reached up and felt it, allowing the natural energies it gave off to run down her arms, charging her muscles, filling her with heat.

Inside her, the voice sighed and fell abruptly silent.

Above her head she found a small ledge. It was sharp with rugosities, the best sort of hold. Her fingers curled over it and she pulled with what little strength she had left to her. For what seemed an age nothing happened, then she felt her hips slide against the ground. The crushing weight of the boulders above her shifted minutely. Again she heaved and they ground together with a rumble, raining dust down over her. A moment later there was a crash, and suddenly her legs were free. She drew them up in a galvanic heave and rolled sideways, feeling even as she did so how she tore herself. Noise and pain shattered her; she screamed out, and it seemed to her then that she screamed with two voices. Gasping and sweating she lay there as the world turned and changed and flowed, aware of nothing but the blood beating around her damaged body for long moments until silence fell.

SARO Vingo had never moved so fast in his life. When he heard the scream, he had swarmed down the broken planes of the Rock as if he had been climbing all his life. He swung down from the top on one hand, scrabbled his feet onto a ledge, braced himself against the widening crack, jammed his body sideways, and bridged down the chasm without a thought in his head except that the voice he had heard had been Katla Aransen's, and that meant she was still alive.

He transferred his weight and jumped down the last section, landing in a heap at the bottom. All around was a jumble of rock, and in the back of the cavern a splash of deep red picked out by a patch of sunlight.

"Katla!"

She blinked, tried to focus, and gave up.

I'm sorry, she said to the voice inside her, recognizing it now. *I'm sorry, I just don't think I can hold on any longer. I wish I could have saved you, but it seems I cannot even save myself.*

But there was no response, none at all. Exhausted, she closed her eyes.

"Katla!"

Nothing.

Something died in Saro, then. He felt his throat swell. A hand fell on his shoulder.

He turned. It was Virelai, and beside him was Alisha Skylark—not the haggard, demonic figure they had found crouching over the pitiful remains of her son, but Alisha Skylark as he remembered her as they rode with the nomad caravan beside a gentle river, who told him about the properties of plants and the patterns of the stars. She caught him in her arms now and held her face to his shoulder, rubbing his back as if he were a child.

"Hush now, Saro," she whispered. "Hush now."

The pale man knelt in the dust beside the dying girl. He straightened Katla Aransen's limbs, then bent and lifted her, grunting with the effort of it. Then out he walked, into the light, with her body in his arms.

Epilogue

"TELL me again about the Far West."

"I have only been there the once, and it was long ago. What I remember most particularly was the color of the place: golds and ochres, reds and a blue deeper even than Jetran pottery. They built tall there: towers and spires, minarets, and the like. It was a very pretty place. There were fountains in the squares, and tumbles of flowers from every sill. Doves roosted in the shadow of the eaves and cooed by day and night. I would fall asleep listening to them; except when the cats fought in the street outside."

"And the women. Tell me again about the women."

"You surprise me!"

"I am just curious: am I not allowed to be curious?"

"Ah, the women." A long sigh. "It really was a very great time ago." The speaker paused. You could sense the smile that spread across his face almost as a change in the air. "But they would be hard to forget. Some were dark-skinned with hair burnished to a sheen like polished bronze, while others had skin of ivory and hair the color of this snoring beauty here, as red as fire, down to their knees. There was one I knew would tie you up with it—"

"I don't snore!"

Tawny brows drew together in a frown, then one furious blue eye opened uncertainly, blinked, and stared.

"You!"

Katla Aransen heaved herself onto her elbows, and found that doing so didn't hurt as she had somehow expected. She stared around, trying not to look too nonplussed.

"Just how long have you been lying there listening to us?"

"Oh . . . forever. I heard the bit about the women. Well, several bits about women, actually." She fixed the speaker with an accusatory glare, then transferred her gaze to the other. "It seems you have enjoyed yourselves thoroughly, talking away about such things over my head."

"We have waited three days for you to wake up," said Saro Vingo defensively. "We had to amuse ourselves somehow."

Her eyebrows shot up. "Three days?" She trawled a surreptitious hand down her flank to her belly, felt around. Then she pulled open the shift she wore—an item of clothing which most definitely had *never* belonged to her—and stared down into its shadows at the place where the wound had been. All that marked it now appeared to be a pale pink scar. This, she pressed gingerly, and when that elicited no pain, harder and harder again.

"Virelai healed you," Saro said.

She took this in, chewing her lip.

"And how come you are here?" Katla demanded a few seconds later, glaring at visitor at the foot of the bed.

Tam Fox threw back his head, and the beads and bones rattled in his tawny braids. "Ah, Katla, I have much to thank you for." His vivid green eyes swept over her wickedly. "More than you could ever imagine." One heavy lid closed in a barely perceptible wink.

Saro laughed.

"What?" She stared from one to the other. "What are you laughing at?"

"We have all traveled a long, strange road, Katla. Sometimes it doesn't pay to examine closely every stone upon which we tread."

She rolled her eyes. "Whatever it is you're both trying to keep from me, I'll find it out. You know I will."

Voices sounded in the corridor outside and she stared at the ornate archway expectantly.

"Where am I, anyway?" she asked, to fill the moment before the door opened.

"Cera's fine castle, or what remains after your Eyran king had his way with it."

There were obviously far too many stories to be told. Even thinking about the implications of this was tiring. She sighed, and watched the door come open and a head peer around it.

"Mother!"

Bera Rolfsen grinned, and suddenly looked half her age.

"Katla, my love!" She flew across the room with her arms open, then at the last moment drew back.

Katla rolled her eyes. "I'm not made of twigs, you won't break me so easily."

It was the first embrace she could remember receiving from her somewhat austere mother; or maybe that was because she usually behaved so badly she rarely merited such treatment. Over Bera's shoulder, she watched the next visitor enter, and her jaw dropped.

"Father!"

Aran Aranson took in the tangle of limbs on the bed and his single-browed grimace lifted. He grinned, his dog-teeth white against the black of his beard. Despite the smile, he looked drawn and tired, a man who had too recently for comfort or reflection been through many hard experiences. He leaned against the doorjamb as if to join in the embrace would be to take too large a step from one world into another.

A shaft of sunlight speared the room, falling obliquely over Tam Fox. Like a great cat, he stretched and yawned. "Well, now, I must away," he said. "Now that the sleeper has awoken and all is well. I have promised to accompany Mam and Persoa to Jetra."

"Go?" she stopped herself before she said something she regretted, then added, "Persoa? But isn't he—?" Clearly the hillman had not died in the volcano, after all. She made a face. All this thinking hurt her head. It had been a lot easier being asleep all this time than having to deal with surprise after surprise.

Bera stood back off the bed and surveyed the tawny man. "So you're off are you, back to your wandering ways?" There was no disguising the chill in her voice. So one thing hadn't changed, then.

"Indeed." Tam Fox inclined his head. "I've been thinking of starting up another troupe. The little man, Dogo, has a remarkable aptitude for juggling; and Joz throws a mean knife."

"So, you're not going to make an honest woman of my daughter, then?" Bera enquired, hands on hips.

"Mother!" A shriek of outrage.

Saro went pale.

"Me?" The mummer's green eyes slid to Katla's astounded face, softened, darted away again. "I think not."

"Er, actually, I—" Saro started.

Tam Fox crossed the room swiftly and got him by the arm. "Come with me," he said, his fingers digging into Saro's bicep. "If you know what's good for you."

A family row was going on behind the door even by the time he closed it. "Saro, my lad, if you blunder in with a clumsy offer, you'll lose her forever. Is that what you want?"

Saro pulled himself free of Tam Fox's grasp. Gone from shock, to panic, to fury in such a brief space of time, now he was trembling.

"You'll have to give her a good long time to get used to the idea, and even then she may not have you. She's a wildcat, is Katla Aransen. She'll be hard to tame, maybe even impossible."

Saro's jaw firmed. "I don't want to tame her," he said angrily.

Tam Fox grinned. "Good lad." He sighed. "And good luck."

Then he turned on his heel.

"Will we see you again?" Saro called after him, not sure which of the likely answers he would prefer to hear.

At the end of the corridor, the mummer turned back. In the shadows his eyes glittered dangerously. "Oh, yes," he said softly. "I'm sure you will."